A NECESSARY END
&
PAST REASON HATED

The Inspector Banks series

GALLOWS VIEW

A DEDICATED MAN

THE HANGING VALLEY

WEDNESDAY'S CHILD

DRY BONES THAT DREAM

INNOCENT GRAVES

DEAD RIGHT

IN A DRY SEASON

COLD IS THE GRAVE

AFTERMATH

THE SUMMER THAT NEVER WAS

PLAYING WITH FIRE

Peter Robinson grew up in Yorkshire, but now lives in Toronto. His Inspector Banks series has won numerous awards in Britain, Europe, the United States and Canada. There are now fourteen novels in the series.

PETER
ROBINSON

A NECESSARY END
&
PAST REASON
HATED

INSPECTOR BANKS MYSTERIES

PAN BOOKS

A Necessary End first published 1989 in Viking by Penguin Books Canada. First published in Great Britain 1989 in Viking by Penguin Books. First published by Pan Books 2002. *Past Reason Hated* first published 1991 by Penguin Books Canada. First published by Pan Books 2002.

This omnibus edition published 2004 by Pan Books
an imprint of Pan Macmillan Ltd
Pan Macmillan, 20 New Wharf Road, London N1 9RR
Basingstoke and Oxford
Associated companies throughout the world
www.panmacmillan.com

ISBN 0 330 43255 9

1 3 5 7 9 8 6 4 2

A CIP catalogue record for this book is available from
the British Library.

Printed and bound in Great Britain by
Mackays of Chatham plc, Chatham, Kent

A NECESSARY END

For Martin, Chris, Steve and Paul – old friends
who all contributed

1

ONE

The demonstrators huddled in the March drizzle outside Eastvale Community Centre. Some of them held home-made placards aloft, but the anti-nuclear slogans had run in the rain like the red lettering at the beginning of horror movies. It was hard to make out exactly what they said any more. By eight thirty, everyone was thoroughly soaked and fed up. No television cameras recorded the scene, and not one reporter mingled with the crowd. Protests were passé, and the media were only interested in what was going on inside. Besides, it was cold, wet and dark out there.

Despite all the frustration, the demonstrators had been patient so far. Their wet hair lay plastered to their skulls and water dribbled down their necks, but still they had held up their illegible placards and shifted from foot to foot for over an hour. Now, however, many of them were beginning to feel claustrophobic. North Market Street was narrow and only dimly lit by old-fashioned gas lamps. The protestors were hemmed in on all sides by police, who had edged so close that there was nowhere left to spread out. An extra line of police stood guard at the top of the steps by the heavy oak doors, and opposite the hall more officers blocked the snickets that led to the winding back streets and the open fields beyond Cardigan Drive.

Finally, just to get breathing space, some people at the edges began pushing. The police shoved back hard. The agitation rippled its way to the solidly packed heart of the crowd, and suppressed tempers rose. When someone brought a placard down on a copper's head, the other demonstrators cheered. Someone else threw a bottle. It smashed harmlessly, high against the wall. Then a few people began to wave their fists in the air and the crowd started chanting, 'We want in! Let us in!' Isolated scuffles broke out. They were still struggling for more ground, and the police pushed back to contain them. It was like sitting on the lid of a boiling pot; something had to give.

Later, nobody could say exactly how it happened, or who started it, but most of the protestors questioned claimed that a policeman yelled, 'Let's clobber the buggers!' and that the line advanced down the steps, truncheons out. Then all hell broke loose.

TWO

It was too hot inside the Community Centre. Detective Chief Inspector Alan Banks fidgeted with his tie. He hated ties, and when he had to wear one he usually kept the top button of his shirt undone to alleviate the choking feeling. But this time he toyed with the loose knot out of boredom as well as discomfort. He wished he was at home with his arm around Sandra and a tumbler of good single malt Scotch in his hand.

But home had been a cold and lonely place these past two days because Sandra and the children were away. Her father had suffered a mild stroke, and she had gone down to Croydon to help her mother cope. Banks wished she were back. They had married young, and he found that the single life, after almost twenty years of (mostly) happy marriage, had little to recommend it.

But the main cause of Banks's ill humour droned on and on, bringing to the crowded Eastvale Community Centre a particularly nasal brand of Home Counties monetarism. It was the Honourable Honoria Winstanley, MP, come to pour oil on the troubled waters of North–South relations. Eastvale had been blessed with her presence because, though not large, it was the biggest and most important town in that part of the country between York and Darlington. It was also enjoying a period of unprecedented and inexplicable growth, thus marking itself out as a shining example of popular capitalism at work. Banks was present as a gesture of courtesy, sandwiched between two taciturn Special Branch men. Superintendent Gristhorpe had no doubt assigned him, Banks thought, because he had no desire to listen to the Hon. Honoria himself. If pushed, Banks described himself as a moderate socialist, but politics bored him and politicians usually made him angry.

Occasionally, he glanced left or right and noticed the restless eyes of the official bodyguards, who seemed to be expecting terrorist action at any moment. For want of their real names, he had christened them Chas and Dave. Chas was the bulky one with the rheumy eyes and bloated red nose, and Dave was blessed with the lean and hungry look of a Tory cabinet minister. If a member of the audience shifted in his or her seat, raised a fist to muffle a cough or reached for a handkerchief, either Chas or Dave would slip his hand under his jacket towards his shoulder holster.

It was all very silly, Banks thought. The only reason anyone might want to kill Honoria Winstanley would be for inflicting a dull speech on the audience. As motives for murder went, that came a long way down the list – though any sane judge would certainly pronounce it justifiable homicide.

Ms Winstanley paused and took a sip of water while the audience applauded. 'And I say to you all,' she continued in all-out rhetorical flight, 'that in the fullness of time, when the results of our policies have come to fruition and every vestige of socialism has been stamped out, all divisions will be healed, and the North, that revered cradle of the Industrial Revolution, will indeed prosper every bit as much as the rest of our glorious nation. Once again this will be a *united* kingdom, united under the banner of enterprise, incentive and hard work. You can already see it happening around you here in Eastvale.'

Banks covered his mouth with his hand and yawned. He looked to his left and noticed that Chas had become so enrapt by Honoria that he had momentarily forgotten to keep an eye open for the IRA, the PLO, the Baader-Meinhof group and the Red Brigade.

The speech was going down well, Banks thought, considering that members of the same government had recently told the North to stop whining about unemployment and had added that most of its problems were caused by poor taste in food. Still, with an audience made up almost entirely of members of the local Conservative Association – small businessmen, farmers and landowners, for the most part – such whole-hearted enthusiasm was only to be expected. The people in the hall had plenty of money, and no doubt they ate well, too.

It was getting even hotter and stuffier, but the Hon. Honoria showed no signs of flagging. Indeed, she was off on a laudatory digression about share-owning, making it sound as if every Englishman could become a millionaire overnight if the government continued to sell off national-ized industries and services to the private sector.

Banks needed a cigarette. He'd been trying to give up again lately, but without success. With so little happen-ing at the station and Sandra and the children away, he had actually increased his intake. The only progress he had made was in switching from Benson & Hedges Special Mild to Silk Cut. He'd heard somewhere that breaking brand loyalty was the first step towards stopping entirely. Unfortunately he was beginning to like the new brand more than the old.

He shifted in his seat when Honoria moved on to the necessity of maintaining, even expanding, the American military presence in Britain, and Chas gave him a chal-lenging glance. He began to wonder if perhaps this latest digression was a roundabout way of approaching the issue many people present wanted to hear about.

There had been rumours about a nuclear power station across the North York Moors on the coast, only about forty miles from Eastvale. With Sellafield to the west, that was one too many, even for some of the more right-wing locals. After all, radioactivity could be quite nasty when you depended on the land for your prosperity. They all remem-bered Chernobyl, and its tales of contaminated milk and meat.

And as if the peaceful use of nuclear power weren't bad enough, there was also talk of a new American air force base in the area. People were already fed up with low-flying jets breaking the sound barrier day in, day out. Even if the sheep did seem to have got used to them, they were bad for the tourist business. But it looked as if Honoria was going to skirt the issue in true politician's fashion and dazzle everyone with visions of a new golden age. Maybe the matter would come up in question time.

Honoria's speech ended after a soaring paean to education reform, law and order, the importance of military strength, and private ownership of council housing. She had made no reference at all to the nuclear power station or to the proposed air base. There was a five-second pause before the audience realized it was all over and began to clap. In that pause, Banks thought he heard signs of a commotion outside. Chase and Dave seemed to have the same notion too; their eyes darted to the doors and their hands slid towards their left armpits.

THREE

Outside, police and demonstrators punched and kicked each other wildly. Parts of the dense crowd had broken up into small skirmishes, but a heaving struggling central mass remained. Everyone seemed oblivious to all but his or her personal battle. There were no individuals, just fists, wooden sticks, boots and uniforms. Occasionally, when a truncheon connected, someone would scream in agony, fall to his knees and put his hands to the flow of blood in stunned disbelief. The police got as good as they gave, too; boots connected with groins, fists with heads. Helmets flew off and demonstrators picked them up to swing them by the straps and use as weapons. The fallen on both sides were trampled by the rest; there was no room to avoid them, no time for compassion.

One young constable, beset by two men and a woman, covered his face and flailed blindly with his truncheon; a girl, blood flowing down the side of her neck, kicked a policeman, who lay in the rain curled up in the foetal position. Four people, locked together, toppled over and crashed through the window of Winston's Tobacco Shop, scattering the fine display of Havana cigars, bowls of aromatic pipe tobacco and exotic Turkish and American cigarette packets onto the wet pavement.

Eastvale Regional Police Headquarters was only a hundred yards or so down the street, fronting the market square. When he heard the noise, Sergeant Rowe dashed outside and sized up the situation quickly. He then sent out two squad cars to block off the narrow street at both ends, and a Black Maria to put the prisoners in. He also phoned the hospital for ambulances.

When the demonstrators heard the sirens, most of them were aware enough to know they were trapped. Scuffles ceased and the scared protestors broke for freedom. Some managed to slip by before the car doors opened, and two people shoved aside the driver of one car and ran to freedom across the market square. A few others hurled themselves at the policemen who were still trying to block off the snickets, knocked them out of the way, and took off into the safety and obscurity of the back alleys. One muscular protestor forced his way up the steps towards the community centre doors with two policemen hanging on to the scruff of his neck trying to drag him back.

FOUR

Loud and prolonged applause drowned out all other sounds, and the Special Branch men relaxed their grips on their guns. The Hon. Honoria beamed at the audience and raised her clasped hands above her head in triumph.

7

Banks still felt uneasy. He was sure he'd heard sounds of an argument or a fight outside. He knew that a small demonstration had been planned, and wondered if it had turned violent. Still, there was nothing he could do. At all costs, the show must go on, and he didn't want to create a stir by getting up and leaving early.

At least the speech was over. If question time didn't go on too long he'd be able to get outside and smoke a cigarette in half an hour or so. An hour might see him at home with that Scotch and Sandra on the other end of the telephone line. He was hungry, too. In Sandra's absence, he had decided to have a go at haute cuisine, and though it hadn't worked out too well so far – the curry had lacked spiciness, and he'd overcooked the fish casserole – he was making progress. Surely a Spanish omelette could present no real problems?

The applause died down and the chairman announced question time. As the first person stood up and began to ask about the proposed site of the nuclear power station, the doors burst open and a hefty bedraggled young man lurched in with two policemen in tow. A truncheon cracked down, and the three fell on to the back row. The young man yelped in pain. Women screamed and reached for their fur coats as the flimsy chairs toppled and splintered under the weight of the three men.

Chas and Dave didn't waste a second. They rushed to Honoria, shielding her from the audience, and with Banks in front, they left through the back door. Beyond the cluttered storerooms, an exit opened on to a complex of back streets, and Banks led them down a narrow alley where the shops on York Road dumped their rubbish. In no time at all the four of them had crossed the road and entered the old Riverview Hotel, where the Hon. Honoria was booked to stay the night. For the first time that evening, she was quiet. Banks noticed in the muted light of the hotel lobby how pale she had turned.

Only when they got to the room, a suite with a superb view over the terraced river-gardens, did Chas and Dave relax. Honoria sighed and sank into the sofa, and Dave locked the door and put the chain on while Chas headed over to the cocktail cabinet.

'Pour me a gin and tonic, will you, dear?' said Honoria in shaky voice.

'What the hell was all that about?' Chas asked, also pouring out two stiff shots of Scotch.

'I don't know,' Banks said. 'There was a small demonstration outside. I suppose it could have—'

'Some bloody security you've got here,' said Dave, taking his drink and passing the gin and tonic to Honoria.

She gulped it down and put her hand to her brow. 'My God,' she said. 'I thought there was nobody but farmers and horse trainers living up here. Look at me, I'm shaking like a bloody leaf.'

'Look,' Banks said, hovering at the door, 'I'd better go and see what's happening.' It was obvious he wasn't going to get a drink, and he was damned if he was going to stand in as a whipping boy for the security organizers. 'Will you be all right?'

'A damn sight safer than we were back there,' Dave said. Then his tone softened a little and he came to the door with Banks. 'Yes, go on. It's your problem now, mate.' He smiled and lowered his voice, twitching his head in Honoria's direction. 'Ours is her.'

In the rush, Banks had left his raincoat in the community centre, and his cigarettes were in the right-hand pocket. He noticed Chas lighting up as he left, but hadn't the audacity to ask for one. Things were bad enough already. Flipping up his jacket collar against the rain, he ran down to the market square, turned right in front of the church and stopped dead.

The wounded lay groaning or unconscious in the drizzle, and police still scuffled with the ones they'd caught, trying to force them into the backs of the cars or into the Black Maria. Some demonstrators, held by their hair, wriggled and kicked as they went, receiving sharp blows from truncheons for their efforts. Others went peacefully. They were frightened and tired now; most of the fight had gone out of them.

Banks stood rooted to the spot and watched the scene. Radios crackled; blue lights spun; the injured cried in pain and shock while ambulance attendants rushed around with stretchers. It defied belief. A full-blown riot in East-vale, admittedly on a small scale, was near unthinkable. Banks had got used to the rising crime rate, which affected even places as small as Eastvale, with just over four-teen thousand people, but riots were surely reserved for Birmingham, Liverpool, Leeds, Manchester, Bristol or London. It couldn't happen here, he had always thought as he shook his head over news of Brixton, Toxteth and Tottenham. But now it had, and the moaning casualties, police and demonstrators alike, were witness to that hard truth.

The street was blocked off at the market square to the south and near the Town Hall, at the junction with Elmet Street, to the north. The gas lamps and illuminated window displays in the twee tourist shops full of Yorkshire woollen wear, walking gear and local produce shone on the chaotic scene. A boy, no more than fifteen or sixteen, cried out as two policemen dragged him by his hair along the glistening cobbles; a torn placard that had once defiantly read NO NUKES flapped in the March wind as the thin rain tapped a faint tattoo against it; one policeman, helmet gone and hair in disarray, bent to help up another, whose moustache was matted with blood and whose nose lay at an odd angle to his face.

In the revolving blue lights, the aftermath of the battle took on a slow-motion, surrealistic quality to Banks. Elongated shadows played across walls. In the street, odd objects caught the light for a second, then seemed to vanish: an upturned helmet, an empty beer bottle, a key ring, a half-eaten apple browning at the edges, a long white scarf twisted like a snake.

Several policemen had come out of the station to help, and Banks recognized Sergeant Rowe standing behind a squad car by the corner.

'What happened?' he asked.

Rowe shook his head. 'Demo turned nasty, sir. We don't know how or why yet.'

'How many were there?'

'About a hundred.' He waved his hand at the scene. 'But we didn't expect anything like this.'

'Got a cigarette, Sergeant?'

Rowe gave him a Senior Service. It tasted strong after Silk Cut, but he drew the smoke deep into his lungs nonetheless.

'How many hurt?'

'Don't know yet, sir.'

'Any of ours?'

'Aye, a few, I reckon. We had about thirty or so on crowd control duty, but most of them were drafted in from York and Scarborough on overtime. Craig was there, and young Tolliver. I haven't seen either of them yet. It'll be busy in the station tonight. Looks like we've nicked about half of them.'

Two ambulance attendants trotted by with a stretcher between them. On it lay a middle-aged woman, her left eye clouded with blood. She turned her head painfully and spat at Sergeant Rowe as they passed.

'Bloody hell!' Rowe said. 'That was Mrs Campbell. She takes Sunday school at Cardigan Drive Congregationalist.'

'War makes animals of us all, Sergeant,' Banks said, wishing he could remember where he'd heard that, and turned away. 'I'd better get to the station. Does the super know?'

'It's his day off, sir.' Rowe still seemed stunned.

'I'd better call him. Hatchley and Richmond, too.'

'DC Richmond's over there, sir.' Rowe pointed to a tall, slim man standing near the Black Maria.

Banks walked over and touched Richmond's arm.

The young detective constable flinched. 'Oh, it's you, sir. Sorry, this has got me all tense.'

'How long have you been here, Phil?'

'I came out when Sergeant Rowe told us what was happening.'

'You didn't see it start, then?'

'No, sir. It was all over in fifteen minutes.'

'Come on. We'd better get inside and help with the processing.'

Chaos reigned inside the station. Every square inch of available space was taken up by arrested demonstrators, some of them bleeding from minor cuts, and most of them complaining loudly about police brutality. As Banks and Richmond shouldered their way towards the stairs, a familiar voice called out after them.

'Craig!' Banks said, when the young constable caught

up with them. 'What happened?'

'Not much, sir,' PC Craig shouted over the noise. His right eye was dark and puffed up, and blood oozed from a split lip. 'I got off lucky.'

'You should be at the hospital.'

'It's nothing, sir, really. They took Susan Gay off in an ambulance.'

'What was she doing out there?'

'They needed help, sir. The men on crowd control. We just went out. We never knew it would be like this . . .'

'Is she hurt badly?'

'They think it's just concussion, sir. She got knocked down, and some bastard kicked her in the head. The hospital just phoned. A Dr Partridge wants to talk to you.'

A scuffle broke out behind them and someone went flying into the small of Richmond's back. He fell forward and knocked Banks and Craig against the wall.

Banks got up and regained his balance. 'Can't anyone keep these bloody people quiet!' he shouted to the station in general. Then he turned to Craig again. 'I'll talk to the doctor. But give the super a call, if you're up to it. Tell him what's happened and ask him to come in. Sergeant Hatchley, too. Then get to the hospital. You might as well have someone look at your eye while you pay a sick call on Susan.'

'Yes, sir.' Craig elbowed his way back through the crowd, and Banks and Richmond made their way upstairs to the CID offices.

First Banks reached into his desk drawer, where he kept a spare packet of cigarettes, then he dialled Eastvale General Infirmary.

Reception paged the doctor, who picked up the phone about a minute later.

'Are there any serious injuries?' Banks asked.

'Most of them are just cuts and bruises. A few minor head wounds. On the whole, I'd say it looks worse than it is. But that's not—'

'What about PC Gay?'

'Who?'

'Susan Gay. The policewoman.'

'Oh, yes. She's all right. She's got concussion. We'll keep her in overnight for observation, then after a few days' rest she'll be right as rain. Look, I understand your concern, Chief Inspector, but that's not what I wanted to talk to you about.'

'What is it, then?' For a moment, Banks felt an icy prickle of irrational fear. Sandra? The children? The results of his last chest X-ray?

'There's been a death.'

'At the demonstration?'

'Yes.'

'Go on.'

'Well, it's more of a murder, I suppose.'

'Suppose?'

'I mean that's what it looks like. I'm not a pathologist. I'm not qualified—'

'Who's the victim?'

'It's a policeman. PC Edwin Gill.'

Banks frowned. 'I've not heard the name. Where's he from?'

'One of the others said he was drafted in from Scarborough.'

'How did he die?'

'Well, that's the thing. You'd expect a fractured skull or some wound consistent with what went on.'

'But?'

'He was stabbed. He was still alive when he was brought in. I'm afraid we didn't . . . There was no obvious wound at first. We thought he'd just been knocked out like the others. He died before we could do anything. Internal bleeding.'

Banks put his hand over the receiver and turned his eyes up to the ceiling. 'Shit!'

'Hello, Chief Inspector? Are you still there?'

'Yes. Sorry, Doctor. Thanks for calling so quickly. I'll send down some more police guards. Nobody's to leave, no matter how minor their injuries. Is there anyone from Eastvale station there? Anyone conscious, that is.'

'Just a minute.'

Dr Partridge came back with PC Tolliver, who had accompanied Susan Gray in the ambulance.

'Listen carefully, lad,' Banks said. 'We've got a bloody crisis on our hands back here, so you'll have to handle the hospital end yourself.'

'Yes, sir.'

'There'll be more men down there as soon as I can round some up, but until then do the best you can. I don't want anyone from tonight's fracas to leave there, do you understand?'

'Yes, sir.'

'And that includes our men, too. I realize some of them might be anxious to get home after they've had their cuts dressed, but I need statements, and I need them while things are fresh in their minds. OK?'

'Yes, sir. There's two or three more blokes here without serious injuries. We'll see to it.'

'Good. You know about PC Gill?'

'Yes, sir. The doctor told me. I didn't know him.'

'You'd better get someone to identify the body formally. Did he have a family?'

'Don't know, sir.'

'Find out. If he did, you know what to do.'

'Yes, sir.'

'And get Dr Glendenning down there. We need him to examine the body. We've got to move quickly on this, before things get cold.'

'I understand, sir.'

'Good. Off you go.'

Banks hung up and turned to Richmond, who stood in the doorway nervously smoothing his moustache. 'Go downstairs, would you, Phil, and tell whoever's in charge to get things quietened down and make sure no one sneaks out. Then call York and ask if they can spare a few more men for the night. If they can't, try Darlington. And you'd better get someone to rope off the street from the market square to the Town Hall, too.'

'What's up?' Richmond asked.

Banks sighed and ran a hand through his close-cropped hair. 'It looks like we've got a murder on our hands and a hundred or more bloody suspects.'

2

ONE

The wind chimes tinkled and rain hissed on the rough moorland grass. Mara Delacey had jut put the children to bed and read them Beatrix Potter's *Tale of Squirrel Nutkin*. Now it was time for her to relax, to enjoy the stillness and isolation, the play of silence and natural sound. It reminded her of the old days when she used to meditate on her mantra.

As usual, it had been a tiring day; washing to do, meals to cook, children to take care of. But it had also been satisfying. She had managed to fit in a couple of hours throwing pots in the back of Elspeth's craft shop in Relton. If it was her lot in life to be an earth mother, she thought with a smile, better to be one here, away from the rigid rules and self-righteous spirituality of the ashram, where she hadn't even been able to sneak a cigarette after dinner. She was glad she'd left all that rubbish behind.

Now she could enjoy some time to herself without feeling she ought to be out chasing after converts or singing the praises of the guru – not that many did now he was serving his stretch in jail for fraud and tax evasion. The devotees had scattered: some, lost and lonely, had gone to look for new leaders; others, like Mara, had moved on to something else.

She had met Seth Cotton a year after he had bought the

place near Relton, which he had christened Maggie's Farm. As soon as he showed it to her, she knew it had to be her home. It was a typical eighteenth-century Dales farmhouse set in a couple of acres of land on the moors above the dale. The walls were built of limestone, with gritstone corners and a flagstone roof. Recessed windows looked north over the dale, and the heavy door head, supported on stacked quoins, bore the initials T.J.H. – standing for the original owner – and the date 1765. The only addition apart from Seth's workshop, a shed at the far end of the back garden, was a limestone porch with a slate roof. Beyond the back garden fence, about fifty yards east of the main house, stood an old barn, which Seth had been busy renovating when she met him. He had split it into an upper studio-apartment, where Rick Trelawney, an artist, lived with his son, and a one-bedroom flat on the ground floor, occupied by Zoe Hardacre and her daughter. Paul, their most recent tenant, had a room in the main house.

Although the barn was more modern inside, Mara preferred the farmhouse. Its front door led directly into the spacious living room, a clean and tidy place furnished with a collection of odds and sods: an imitation Persian carpet, a reupholstered 1950s sofa, and a large table and four chairs made of white pine by Seth himself. Large beanbag cushions lay scattered against the walls for comfort.

On the wall opposite the stone fireplace hung a huge tapestry of a Chinese scene. It showed enormous mountains, their snow-streaked peaks sharp as needles above the pine forests. In the middle distance, a straggling line of tiny human figures moved up a winding path. Mara looked at it a lot. There was no overhead light in the room. She kept the shaded lamps dim and supplemented them with fat red candles because she liked the shadows the flames cast on the tapestry and the whitewashed stone walls. Her favourite place to curl up was near the window in an old rocking chair Seth had restored. There she could hear the wind chimes clearly as she sipped wine and read.

In her early days, she had devoured Kerouac, Burroughs, Ginsberg, Carlos Castaneda and the rest, but at thirty-eight she found their works embarrassingly adolescent, and her tastes had reverted to the classics she remembered from her university days. There was something about those long Victorian novels that suited a place as isolated and slow-moving as Maggie's Farm.

Now she decided to settle down and lose herself in *The Mill on the Floss*. A hand-rolled Old Holborn and a glass of Barsac would also go down nicely. And maybe some music. She walked to the stereo, selected Holst's *The Planets*, the side with 'Saturn', 'Uranus' and 'Neptune', then nestled in the chair to read by candlelight. The others were all at the demo, and they'd be sure to stop off for a pint or two at the Black Sheep in Relton on the way back. The kids were sleeping in the spare room upstairs, so she wouldn't have to keep nipping out to the barn to check on them. It was half past nine now. She could probably count on at least a couple of hours to herself.

But she couldn't seem to concentrate. The hissing outside stopped. It was replaced by the steady dripping of rain from the eaves-troughs, the porch and the trees that protected Maggie's Farm from the harsh west winds. The chimes began to sound like warning bells. There was something in the air. If Zoe were home, she'd no doubt have plenty to say about psychic forces – probably the moon.

Shrugging off her feeling of unease, Mara returned to her reading: 'And this is Dorlcote Mill. I must stand a minute or two here on the bridge and look at it, though the clouds are threatening, and it is far on in the afternoon . . .' It was no good; she couldn't get into it. George Eliot's spell just wasn't working tonight. Mara put down the book and concentrated on the music.

As the ethereal choir entered the end of 'Neptune', the front door rattled open and Paul rushed in. His combat jacket was dark with rain and his tight jeans stuck to his stick-insect legs.

Mara frowned. 'You're back early,' she said. 'Where are the others?'

'I don't know.' Paul was out of breath and his voice sounded shaky. He took off his jacket and hung it on the hook at the back of the door. 'I ran back by myself over the moors.'

'But that's more than four miles. What's wrong, Paul? Why didn't you wait for Seth and the others? You could have come back in the van.'

'There was some trouble,' Paul said. 'Things got nasty.' He took a cigarette from his pack of Players and lit it, cupping it in his hands the way soldiers do in old war films. His hands were trembling. Mara noticed again how short and stubby his fingers were, nails bitten to the quick. She rolled another cigarette. Paul started to pace the room.

'What's that?' Mara asked, pointing in alarm to the fleshy spot at the base of his left thumb. 'It looks like blood. You've hurt yourself.'

'It's nothing.'

Mara reached out, but he pulled his hand away.

'At least let me put something on it.'

'I told you, it's nothing. I'll see to it later. Don't you want to hear what happened?'

Mara knew better than to persist. 'Sit down, then,' she

said. 'You're driving me crazy pacing around like that.'

Paul flopped on to the cushions by the wall, taking care to keep his bloodied hand out of sight.

'Well?' Mara said.

'The police set on us, that's what. Fucking bastards.'

'Why?'

'They just laid into us, that's all. Don't ask me why. I don't know how cops think. Can I have some wine?'

Mara poured him a glass of Barsac. He took a sip and pulled a face.

'Sorry,' she said. 'I forgot you don't like the sweet stuff. There's some beer in the fridge.'

'Great.' Paul hauled himself up and went through to the kitchen. When he came back he was carrying a can of Carlsberg lager and he'd stuck an Elastoplast on his hand.

'What happened to the others?' Mara asked.

'I don't know. A lot of people got arrested. The police just charged into the crowd and dragged them off left, right and centre. There'll be plenty in hospital, too.'

'Weren't you all together?'

'We were at first, right up at the front, but we got separated when the fighting broke out. I managed to sneak by some cops and slip down the alley, then I ran all the way through the back streets and over the moor. I'm bloody knackered.' His Liverpudlian accent grew thicker as he became more excited.

'So people did get away?'

'Some, yes. But I don't know how many. I didn't hang around to wait for the others. It was every man for himself, Mara. The last I saw of Rick he was trying to make his way to the market square. I couldn't see Zoe. You know how small she is. It was a bleeding massacre. They'd every-thing short of water cannons and rubber bullets. I've seen some bother in my time, but I never expected anything like this, not in Eastvale.'

'What about Seth?'

'Sorry, Mara. I've no idea what became of him. Don't worry, though; they'll be all right.'

'Yes.' Mara turned and looked out of the window. She could see her own reflection against the dark glass streaked with rain. It looked like a candle flame was burning from her right shoulder.

'Maybe they got away,' Paul added. 'They might be on their way back right now.'

Mara nodded. 'Maybe.'

But she knew there'd be trouble. The police would soon be round, bullying and searching, just like when Seth's old friend Liz Dale ran away from the nut house and hid out with them for a few days. They'd been looking for heroin then – Liz had a history of drug abuse – but as far as Mara remembered they'd just made a bloody mess of everything in the place. She resented that kind of intrusion into her world and didn't look forward to another one.

She reached for the wine bottle, but before she started pouring, the front door burst open again.

TWO

When Banks went downstairs, things were considerably quieter than they had been earlier. Richmond had helped the uniformed men to usher all the prisoners down to the cellar until they could be questioned, charged and released. Eastvale station didn't have many cells, but there was plenty of unused storage space down there.

Sergeant Hatchley had also arrived. Straw-haired, head

and shoulders above the others, he looked like a rugby prop forward gone to seed. He leaned on the reception desk looking bewildered and put out as Richmond explained what had happened.

Banks walked up to them. 'Super here yet?'

'On his way, sir,' Richmond answered.

'Can you get everyone together while we're waiting?' Banks asked. 'There's a few things I want to tell them right now.'

Richmond went into the open-plan office area, the domain of the uniformed police at Eastvale, and rounded up everyone he could. The men and women sat on desks or leaned against partitions and waited for instructions. Some of them still showed signs of the recent battle: a bruised cheekbone, torn uniform, black eye, cauliflower ear.

'Does anyone know exactly how many we've got in custody?' Banks asked first.

'Thirty-six, sir.' It was a constable with a split lip and the top button torn off his jacket who answered. 'And I've heard there's ten more at the hospital.'

'Any serious injuries?'

'No, sir. Except, well, Constable Gill.'

'Yes. So if there were about a hundred at the demo, there's almost a fifty-fifty chance we've already caught our killer. First, I want everyone searched, fingerprinted and examined for Gill's bloodstains. Constable Reynolds, will you act as liaison with the hospital?'

'Yes, sir.'

'The same procedure applies there. Ask the doctor to check the ten patients for blood. Next we've got to find the murder weapon. All we know so far is that PC Gill was stabbed. We don't know what kind of knife was used, so anything with a blade is suspicious, from a kitchen knife to a stiletto. There's some extra men on the way from York, but I want a couple of you to start searching the street thoroughly right away, and that includes having a good look down the grates, too. Clear so far?'

Some muttered, 'Yes, sir.' Others nodded.

'Right. Now we get to the hard work. We'll need a list of names: everyone we've got and anyone else we can get them to name. Remember, about sixty people got away, and we have to know who they were. If any of you recall seeing a familiar face we don't have here or at the hospital, make a note of it. I don't suppose the people we question will want to give their friends away, but lean on them a bit, do what you can. Be on the lookout for any slips. Use whatever cunning you have. We also want to know who the organizers were and what action groups were represented.

'I want statements from everyone, even if they've nothing to say. We're going to have to divide up the interrogations, so just do the best you can. Stick to the murder; ask about anyone with a knife. Find out if we've got any recorded troublemakers in the cells; look up their files and see what you come up with. If you think someone's lying or being evasive, push them as far as you can, then make a note of your reservations on the statement. I realize we're going to be swamped with paperwork, but there's no avoiding it. Any questions?'

Nobody said a word.

'Fine. One last thing: we want statements from all witnesses, too, not just the demonstrators. There must have been some people watching from those flats overlooking the street. Do the rounds. Find out if anyone saw anything. And rack your own brains. You know there'll be some kind of official inquiry into why all this happened in the first place, so all of you who were there might as well make a statement now, while the events are fresh in your minds. I want all statements typed and on Superintendent Gristhorpe's desk first thing in the morning.'

Banks looked at his watch. 'It's nine thirty now. We'd better get cracking. Anything I've overlooked?'

Several officers shook their heads; others stood silent. Finally a policewoman put her hand up. 'What are we to do with the prisoners, sir, after we've got all the statements?'

'Follow normal procedure,' Banks said. 'Just charge them and let them go unless you've got any reason to think they're involved in PC Gill's death. They'll appear before the magistrate as soon as possible. Is that all?' He paused, but nobody said anything. 'Right. Off you go then. I want to know about any leads as soon as they come up. With a bit of luck we could get this wrapped up by morning. And would someone take some of the prisoners upstairs? There'll be three of us interviewing up there when the super arrives.' He turned to Richmond. 'We'll want you on the computer, Phil. There'll be a lot of records to check.'

'The super's here now, sir.' PC Telford pointed to the door, which was out of Banks's line of vision.

Superintendent Gristhorpe, a bulky man in his late fifties with bushy grey hair and eyebrows, a red pock-marked face and a bristly moustache, walked over to where the three CID men were standing by the stairs. His eyes, usually as guileless as a baby's, were clouded with concern, but his presence still brought an aura of calm and unhurried common sense.

'You've heard?' Banks asked.

'Aye,' said Gristhorpe. 'Not all the details, but enough.

Let's go upstairs and you can tell me about it over a cup of coffee.' He put his hand on Banks's arm gently.

Banks turned to Sergeant Hatchley. 'You might as well get started on the interviews,' he said. 'We'll help you out in a minute when I've filled the super in.' Then the four CID men trudged upstairs and PC Telford ushered a brace of wet frightened demonstrators up after them.

THREE

'Zoe! Thank God you're all right!'

Paul and Mara stared at the slight figure in the glistening red anorak. Her ginger hair was stuck to her skull, and the dark roots showed. Rain dripped on to the straw mat just inside the doorway. She slipped off her jacket, hung it next to Paul's and walked over to hug them both.

'You've told her what happened?' she asked Paul.

'Yes.'

Zoe looked at Mara. 'How was Luna?'

'No trouble. She fell asleep when Squirrel Nutkin started tickling Mr Brown with a nettle.'

Zoe's face twitched in a brief smile. She went over to the bookcase. 'I threw an I Ching this morning,' she said, 'and it came up "Conflict". I should have known what would happen.' She opened the book and read from the text: '"Conflict. You are being sincere and are being obstructed. A cautious halt halfway brings good fortune. Going through to the end brings misfortune. It furthers one to see the great man. It does not further one to cross the great water."'

'You can't take it so literally,' Mara said. 'That's the problem. It didn't tell you what would happen, or how.'

Though she was certainly interested in the I Ching and tarot cards herself, Mara often thought that Zoe went too far.

'It's clear enough to me. I should have known something like this would happen: "Going through to the end brings misfortune." You can't get any more specific than that.'

'What if you *had* known?' Paul said. 'You couldn't call it off, could you? You'd still have gone. Things would still have worked out the same.'

'Yes,' Zoe muttered, 'but I should have been prepared.'

'How?' asked Mara. 'Do you mean you should have gone armed or something?'

Zoe sighed. 'I don't know. I just should have been prepared.'

'It's easy to say that now,' Paul said. 'The truth is nobody had the slightest idea the demo would turn nasty, and there wasn't a damn thing they could do about it when it did. There were a lot of people involved, Zoe, and if they'd've all done the I Ching this morning they'd've all got different answers. It's a load of cobblers, if you ask me.'

'Sit down,' said Mara. 'Have a glass of wine. Did you see what happened to the others?'

'I'm not sure.' Zoe sat cross-legged on the carpet and accepted Paul's glass. 'I think Rick got arrested. I saw him struggling with some police at the edge of the crowd.'

'And Seth?'

'I don't know. I couldn't see.' Zoe smiled sadly. 'Most people were bigger than me. All I could see was shoulders and necks. That's how I managed to get away, because I'm so little. That and the rain. One cop grabbed my anorak, but his hand slipped off because it was wet. I'm a Pisces, a slippery fish.' She paused to sip her Barsac. 'What'll happen to them, Mara, the ones who got caught?'

Mara shrugged. 'I should imagine they'll be charged and let go. That's what usually happens. Then the magistrate decides what to fine them or whether to send them to jail. Mostly they just get fined or let off with a caution.'

Mara wished she felt as confident as she sounded. Her uneasiness had nothing to do with the message Zoe had got from the I Ching, but the words of the oracle somehow emphasized it and gave her disquietude a deeper dimension of credibility: 'Going through to the end brings misfortune. It furthers one to see the great man.' Who was the great man?

'Shouldn't we do something?' Paul asked.

'Like what?'

'Go down there, down to the police station and find out what's happened. Try and get them out.'

Mara shook her head. 'If we do that, it's more likely they'll take us in for obstructing justice or something.'

'I just feel so bloody powerless, so useless, not being able to do a damn thing.' Paul's fists clenched, and Mara could read the words jaggedly tattooed just below his knuckles. Instead of the more common combination, LOVE on one hand and HATE on the other, his read HATE on both hands. Seeing the capitalized word so ineptly tattooed there reminded Mara how hard and violent Paul's past had been and how far he had come since they'd found him sleeping in the open early last winter on their way to a craft fair in Wensleydale.

'If we had a phone we could at least call the hospital,' Zoe said. 'Maybe one of us should walk down to Relton and do it anyway.'

'I'll go,' Mara said. 'You two have had enough for one

night. Besides, the exercise will do me good.'

She got to her feet before either of the others could offer to go instead. It was only a mile down to Relton, a village high on the southern slope of Swainsdale, and the walk should be a pleasant one. Mara looked out of the window. It was drizzling lightly again. She took her yellow cyclist's cape and matching rainhat out of the cupboard and opened the door. As she left, Paul was on his way to the fridge for another beer, and Zoe was reaching for her tarot cards.

Zoe worried Mara sometimes. Not that she wasn't a good mother, but she did seem too offhand. True, she had asked about Luna, but she hadn't wanted to go and look in on her. Instead she had turned immediately to her occult aids. Mara doted on both children: Luna, aged four, and Julian, five. Even Paul, just out of his teens, seemed more like a son than anything else at times. She knew she felt especially close to them because she had no children of her own. Many of her old schoolfriends would probably have kids Paul's age. What an irony, she thought, heading for the track – a barren earth mother!

The rain was hardly worth covering up for, but it gave an edge to the chill already present in the March air, and Mara was glad of the sweater she wore under her cape. The straight narrow track she followed was part of an old Roman road that ran diagonally across the moors above the dale right down to Fortford. Just wide enough for the van, it was drystone on both sides and covered with gravel and small chips of stone that crunched and crackled underfoot. Mara could see the lights of Relton at the bottom of the slope. Behind her the candle glowed in the window, and Maggie's Farm looked like an ark adrift on a dark sea.

She shoved her hands through the slits in her cape, deep into the pockets of her cords, and marched the way she imagined an ancient Roman would have done. Beyond the clouds, she could make out the pearly sheen of a half moon.

The great silence all around magnified the little sounds – the clatter of small stones, the rhythmic crunch of gravel, the swishing of her cords against the cape – and Mara felt the strain on her weak left knee that she always got going downhill. She raised her head and let the thin cool rain fall on her closed eyelids and breathed in the wet-dog smell of the air. When she opened her eyes, she saw the black bulk of distant fells against a dark grey sky.

At the end of the track, Mara walked into Relton. The change from gravel to the smooth tarmac of Mortsett Lane felt strange at first. The village shops were all closed. Television sets flickered behind drawn curtains.

Just to be sure, Mara first popped her head inside the Black Sheep, but neither Seth nor Rick was there. A log fire crackled in the corner of the cosy public bar, but the place was half empty. The landlord, Larry Grafton, smiled and said hello. Like many of the locals, he had come to accept the incomers from Maggie's Farm. At least, he had once told Mara, they weren't like those London yuppies who seemed to be buying up all the vacant property in the Dales these days.

'Can I get you anything?' Grafton called out.

'No. No, thanks,' Mara said. 'I was looking for Seth. You haven't seen him, have you?'

Two old men looked up from their game of dominoes, and a trio of young farm labourers paused in their argument over subsidies and glanced at Mara with faintly curious expressions on their faces.

'No, lass,' Grafton said. 'They've not been in since lunch time. Said they were off to that there demonstration in Eastvale.'

Mara nodded. 'That's right. There's been some trouble and they haven't come back yet. I was just wondering—'

'Is it right, then?' one of the farm labourers asked. 'Tommy Exton dropped in half an hour sin' and said there'd been some fighting in Market Street.'

Mara told him what little she knew, and he shook his head. 'It don't pay to get involved in things like that. Best left well alone,' he said, and returned to his pint.

Mara left the Black Sheep and headed for the public telephone box on Mortsett Lane. Why they didn't have a phone installed at the farm she didn't know. Seth had once said he wouldn't have one of the things in the house, but he never explained why. Every time he needed to make a few calls he went down to the village, and he never once complained. At least in the country you could usually be sure the telephones hadn't been vandalized.

The receptionist at Eastvale General Infirmary answered and asked her what she wanted. Mara explained that she was interested in news of a friend of hers who hadn't come home from the demonstration. The receptionist said, 'Just a minute,' and the phone hiccuped and burped a few times. Finally a man's voice came on.

'Can I help you, miss?'

'Yes. I'd like to know if you have a patient called Seth Cotton and one called Rick Trelawney.'

'Who is this calling?'

'I . . . I'd rather not say,' Mara answered, suddenly afraid that if she gave her name she would be inviting trouble.

'Are you a relation?'

'I'm a friend. A very close friend.'

'I see. Well, unless you identify yourself, miss, I'm afraid I can't give out any information.'

'Look,' Mara said, getting angry, 'this is ridiculous. It's not as if I'm asking you to break the Official Secrets Act or anything. I just want to know if my friends are there and, if so, how badly they're injured. Who are you, anyway?'

'Constable Parker, miss. If you've any complaints you'd better take them up with Chief Inspector Banks at Eastvale CID headquarters.'

'Chief Inspector Banks? CID?' Mara repeated slowly. She remembered the name. He was the one who had visited the farm before, when Liz was there. 'Why? I don't understand. What's going on? I only want to know if my friends are hurt.'

'Sorry, miss. Orders. Tell me your name and I'll see what I can do.'

Mara hung up. Something was very wrong. She'd done enough damage already by mentioning Seth and Rick. The police would surely take special note of their names and push them even harder than the rest. There was nothing to do but wait and worry. Frowning, she opened the door and walked back into the rain.

FOUR

'Fell like a broke-down engine, ain't got no drivin' wheel,' sang Blind Willie McTell.

'I know exactly what you mean, mate,' Banks mumbled to himself as he poured a Laphroaig single malt, an indulgence he could scarcely afford. It was almost two in the morning and the interrogations had produced no results so far. Tired, Banks had left the others to it and come home for a few hours' sleep. He felt he deserved it. *They* hadn't had to spend the morning in court, the afternoon on a wild-goose chase after a stolen tractor, and the evening listening to the Hon. Honoria, who would no doubt by now be sleeping the sleep of the truly virtuous before heading back, with great relief, down south in the morning.

Banks put his feet up, lit a cigarette and warmed the glass in his palm. Suddenly the doorbell rang. He jumped to his feet and cursed as he spilled a little valuable Scotch on his shirt front. Rubbing it with the heel of his hand, he walked into the hall and opened the door a few inches on the chain.

It was Jenny Fuller, the psychologist he had met and worked with on his first case in Eastvale. More than that, he had to admit; there had been a mutual attraction between them. Nothing had come of it, of course, and Jenny had even become good friends with Sandra. The three of them had often been out together. But the attraction remained, unresolved. Things like that didn't seem to go away as easily as they arrived.

'Jenny?' He slipped off the chain and opened the door wider.

'I know. It's two o'clock in the morning and you're wondering what I'm doing at your door.'

'Something like that. I assume it's not just my irresistible charm?'

Jenny smiled. The laugh lines around her green eyes crinkled. But the smile was forced and short-lived.

'What is it?' Banks asked.

'Dennis Osmond.'

'Who?'

'A friend. He's in trouble.'

'Boyfriend?'

'Yes, boyfriend.' Jenny blushed. 'Or would you prefer beau? Lover? Significant other? Look, can I come in? It's cold and raining out here.'

Banks moved aside. 'Yes, of course. I'm sorry. Have a drink?'

'I will, if you don't mind.' Jenny walked into the front room, took off her green silk scarf and shook her red hair. The muted trumpet wailed and Sara Martin sang 'Death Sting Me Blues'.

'What happened to opera?' Jenny asked.

Banks poured her a Laphroaig. 'There's a lot of music in the world,' he said. 'I want to listen to as much as I can before I shuffle off this mortal coil.'

'Does that include heavy metal and middle of the road?'

Banks scowled. 'Dennis Osmond. What about him?'

'Ooh, touchy, aren't we?' Jenny raised her eyes to the ceiling and lowered her voice. 'By the way, I hope I haven't disturbed Sandra or the children?'

Banks explained their absence. 'It was all a bit sudden,' he added, to fill the silence that followed, which seemed somehow more weighty than it should. Jenny expressed her sympathy and shifted in her seat. She took a deep breath. 'Dennis was arrested during that demonstration tonight. He managed to get in a phone call to me from the police station. He's not come back yet. I've just been there and the man on the desk told me you'd left. They wouldn't tell me anything about the prisoners at all. What's going on?'

'Where hasn't he come back to?'

'My place.'

'Do you live together?'

Jenny's eyes hardened and drilled into him like emerald

laser beams. 'That's none of your damn business.' She drank some more Scotch. 'As a matter of fact, no, we don't. He was going to come round and tell me about the demonstration. It should have been all over hours ago.'

'You weren't there yourself?'

'Are you interrogating me?'

'No. Just asking.'

'I believe in the cause – I mean I'm against nuclear power and American missile bases – but I don't see any point standing in the rain in front of Eastvale Community Centre.'

'I see.' Banks smiled. 'It *was* a nasty night, wasn't it?'

'And there's no need to be such a cynic. I had work to do.'

'It was a pretty bad night inside, too.'

Jenny raised her eyebrows. 'The Hon. Hon?'

'Indeed.'

'You were there?'

'I had that dubious honour, yes. Duty.'

'You poor man. It might have been worth a black eye to get out of that.'

'I take it you haven't heard the news, then?'

'What news?'

'A policeman was killed at that peaceful little demonstration tonight. Not a local chap, but one of us, nonetheless.'

'Is that why Dennis is still at the station?'

'We're questioning people, yes. It's serious, Jenny. I haven't seen Dennis Osmond, never even heard of him. But they won't let him go till they've got his statement, and we're not giving out any information to members of the public yet. It doesn't mean he's under suspicion or anything, just that he hasn't been questioned yet.'

'And then?'

'They'll let him go. If all's well you'll still have some of the night left together.'

Jenny lowered her head for a moment, then glared at him again. 'You're being a bastard, you know,' she said. 'I don't like being teased that way.'

'What do you want me to do?' Banks asked. 'Why did you come?'

'I . . . I just wanted to find out what happened.'

'Are you sure you're not trying to get him special treatment?'

Jenny sighed. 'Alan, we're friends, aren't we?'

Banks nodded.

'Well,' she went on, 'I know you can't help being a policeman, but if you don't know where your job ends and your friendships begin . . . Need I go on?'

Banks rubbed his bristly chin. 'No. I'm sorry. It's been a rough night. But you still haven't answered my question.'

'I'd just hoped to get some idea of what might have happened to him, that's all. I got the impression that if I'd lingered a moment longer down at the station they'd have had me in for questioning, too. I didn't know about the death. I suppose that changes things?'

'Of course it does. It means we've got a killer on the loose. I'm sure it's nothing to do with your Dennis, but he'll have to answer the same questions as the rest. I can't say exactly how long he'll be. At least you know he's not in hospital. Plenty of people are.'

'I can't believe it, Alan. I can understand tempers getting frayed, fists flying, but not a killing. What happened?'

'He was stabbed. It was deliberate; there's no getting around that.'

Jenny shook her head.

'Sorry I can't be any more help,' Banks said. 'What was Dennis's involvement with the demo?'

'He was one of the organizers, along with the students' union and those people from Maggie's Farm.'

'That place up near Relton?'

'That's it. The local women's group was involved, too.'

'WEEF? Dorothy Wycombe?'

Jenny nodded. Banks had come up against the Women of Eastvale for Emancipation and Freedom before – Dorothy Wycombe in particular – and it gave him a sinking feeling to realize that he might have to deal with them again.

'I still can't believe it,' Jenny went on. 'Dennis told me time and time again that the last thing they wanted was a violent confrontation.'

'I don't suppose anybody wanted it, but these things have a way of getting out of hand. Look, why don't you go home? I'm sure he'll be back soon. He won't be mistreated. We don't suddenly turn into vicious goons when things like this happen.'

'*You* might not,' said Jenny. 'But I've heard how you close ranks.'

'Don't worry.'

Jenny finished her drink. 'All right. I can see you're trying to get rid of me.'

'Not at all. Have another Scotch if you want.'

Jenny hesitated. 'No,' she said finally. 'I was only teasing. You're right. It's late. I'd better get back home.' She picked up her scarf. 'It was good, though. The Scotch. So rich you could chew it.'

Banks walked her to the door. 'If there are any problems,' he said, 'let me know. And I could do with your help, too. You seem to know a bit about what went on behind the scenes.'

Jenny nodded and fastened her scarf.

'Maybe you could come to dinner?' Banks suggested on impulse. 'Try my gourmet cooking?'

Jenny smiled and shook her head. 'I don't think so.'

'Why not? It's not that bad. At least—'

'It's just . . . it wouldn't seem right with Sandra away, that's all. The neighbours . . .'

'OK. We'll go out. How does the Royal Oak in Lyndgarth suit you?'

'It'll do fine,' Jenny said. 'Give me a call.'

'I will.'

She pecked him on the cheek and he watched her walk down the path and get into her Metro. They waved to each other as she set off, then he closed his door on the wet chilly night. He picked up the Scotch bottle and pulled the cork, thought for a moment, pushed it back and went upstairs to bed.

3

ONE

COP KILLED IN DALES DEATH DEMO, screamed the tabloid headlines the next morning. As he glanced at them over coffee and a cigarette in his office, Banks wondered why the reporter hadn't gone the whole hog and spelled cop with a k.

He put the paper aside and walked over to the window. The market square looked dreary and desolate in the grey March light, and Banks fancied he could detect a shell-shocked atmosphere hovering around the place. Shoppers shuffled along with their heads hung low and glanced covertly at the site of the demonstration as they passed, as if they expected to see armed guards wearing gas masks, and tear gas drifting in the air. North Market Street was still roped off. The four officers sent from York had arrived at about four in the morning to help the local men search the area, but they had found no murder weapon. Now they were trying again in what daylight there was.

Banks looked at the calendar on his wall. It was March 17, St Patrick's Day. The illustration showed the ruins of St Mary's Abbey in York. Judging by the sunshine and the happy tourists, it had probably been taken in July. On the real March 17, his small heater coughed and hiccuped as it struggled to take the chill out of the air.

He turned back to the newspapers. The accounts varied

a great deal. According to the left-wing press, the police had brutally attacked a peaceful crowd without provocation; the right-wing papers, however, maintained that a mob of unruly demonstrators had provoked the police into retaliation by throwing bottles and stones. In the more moderate newspapers, nobody seemed to know exactly what had happened, but the whole affair was said to be extremely unfortunate and regrettable.

At eight thirty, Superintendent Gristhorpe, who had been up most of the night interviewing demonstrators and supervising the search, called Banks in. Banks stubbed out his cigarette – the super didn't approve of smoking – and wandered into the book-lined office. The shaded table lamp on Gristhorpe's huge teak desk cast its warm glow on a foot-thick pile of statements.

'I've been talking to the assistant chief constable,' Gristhorpe said. 'He's been on the phone to London and they're sending a man up this morning. I'm to cover the preliminary inquiry into the demo for the Police Complaints Authority.' He rubbed his eyes. 'Of course, someone'll no doubt accuse me of being biased and scrap the whole thing, but they want to be seen to be acting quickly.'

'This man they're sending,' Banks asked, 'what's he going to do?'

'Handle the murder investigation. You'll be working with him, along with Hatchley and Richmond.'

'Do you know who he is?'

Gristhorpe searched for the scrap of paper on his desk. 'Yes . . . let me see . . . It's a Superintendent Burgess. He's attached to a squad dealing with politically sensitive crimes. Not exactly Special Branch, but not quite your regular CID, either. I'm not even sure we're allowed to know *what* he is. Some sort of political troubleshooter, I suppose.'

'Is that Superintendent Richard Burgess?' Banks asked.

'Yes. Why? Know him?'

'Bloody hell.'

'Alan, you've gone pale. What's up?'

'Yes, I know him,' Banks said. 'Not well, but I worked with him a couple of times in London. He's about my age, but he's always been a step ahead.'

'Ambitious?'

'Very. But it's not his ambition I mind so much,' Banks went on. 'He's slightly to the right of . . . Well, you name him and Burgess is to the right.'

'Is he good, though?'

'He gets results.'

'Isn't that what we need?'

'I suppose so. But he's a real bastard to work with.'

'How?'

'Oh, he plays his cards close to his chest. Doesn't let the right hand know what the left hand's doing. He takes short cuts. People get hurt.'

'You make him sound like he doesn't even have a left hand,' Gristhorpe said.

Banks smiled. 'We used to call him Dirty Dick Burgess.'

'Why?'

'You'll find out. It's nothing to do with his sexual activities, I can tell you that. Though he did have a reputation as a fairly active stud about town.'

'Anyway,' Gristhorpe said, 'he should be here around midday. He's taking the early Intercity to York. There's too long a wait between connections, so I'm sending Craig to meet him at the station there.'

'Lucky Craig.'

Gristhorpe frowned. Banks noticed the bags under his eyes. 'Yes, well, make the best of it, Alan. If Superintendent

Burgess steps out of line, I won't be far away. It's still our patch. By the way, Honoria Winstanley called before she left – at least one of her escorts did. Said all's well, apologized for his brusqueness last night and thanked you for handling things so smoothly.'

'Wonders never cease.'

'I've booked Burgess into the Castle Hotel on York Road. It's not quite as fancy or expensive as the Riverview, but then Burgess isn't an MP, is he?'

Banks nodded. 'What about office space?'

'We're putting him in an interview room for the time being. At least there's a desk and a chair.'

'He'll probably complain. People like Burgess get finicky about offices and titles.'

'Let him,' Gristhorpe said, gesturing around the room. 'He's not getting this place.'

'Any news from the hospital?'

'Nothing serious. Most of the injured have been sent home. Susan Gay's on sick leave for the rest of the week.'

'When you were going through the statements,' Banks asked, 'did you come across anything on a chap called Dennis Osmond?'

'The name rings a bell. Let me have a look.' Gristhorpe leafed through the pile. 'Yes, I thought so. Interviewed him myself. One of the last. Why?'

Banks explained about Jenny's visit.

'I took his statement and sent him home.' Gristhorpe read through the sheet. 'That's him. Belligerent young devil. Threatened to bring charges against the police, start an inquiry of his own. Hadn't seen anything, though. Or at least he didn't admit to it. According to records he's a CND member, active in the local anti-nuclear group. Amnesty International, too – and you know what Mrs Thatcher thinks of *them* these days. He's got connections with various other groups as well, including the International Socialists. I should imagine Superintendent Burgess will certainly want to talk to him.'

'Hmmm.' Banks wondered how Jenny would take that. Knowing both her and Burgess as he did, he could guarantee sparks would fly. 'Did anything turn up in the statements?'

'Nobody witnessed the stabbing. Three people said they thought they glimpsed a knife on the road during the scuffles. It must have got kicked about quite a bit. Nothing I've heard so far brings order out of chaos. The poor lighting didn't help either. You know how badly that street is lit. Dorothy Wycombe's been pestering us about it for weeks. I keep putting her on to the council, but to no avail. She says it's an invitation to rape, especially with all those unlit side alleys, but the council says the gas lamps are good for the tourist business. Anyway, PC Gill was found just at the bottom of the community centre steps, for what that's worth. Maybe if we can find out the names of the people on the front line we'll get somewhere.'

Banks went on to tell Gristhorpe what he'd discovered from Jenny about the other organizers.

'The Church for Peace group was involved, too,' Gristhorpe added. 'Did I hear you mention Maggie's Farm, that place near Relton?'

Banks nodded.

'Didn't we have some trouble with them a year or so ago?'

'Yes,' Banks said. 'But it was a storm in a teacup. They seemed a harmless enough bunch to me.'

'What was it? A drug raid?'

'That's right. Nothing turned up, though. They must

have had the foresight to hide it, if they had anything. We were acting on a tip from some hospital social workers. I think they were overreacting.'

'Anyway,' Gristhorpe said, 'that's about it. The rest of the people we picked up were just private citizens who were there because they feel strongly about nuclear power, or about government policy in general.'

'So what do we do now?'

'You'd better look over these statements,' Gristhorpe said, shoving the tower of paper towards Banks, 'and wait for the great man. Sergeant Hatchley's still questioning those people in the flats overlooking the street. Not that there's much of anything there. They can't have seen more than a sea of heads. If only the bloody TV cameras had been there we'd have had it on video. Those buggers in the media are never around when you need them.'

'Like policemen,' Banks said with a grin.

The phone rang. Gristhorpe picked it up, listened to the message and turned back to Banks. 'Sergeant Rowe says Dr Glendenning's on his way up. He's finished his preliminary examination. I think you'd better stay for this.'

Banks smiled. 'It's a rare honour indeed, the good doctor setting foot in here. I didn't know he paid house calls.'

'I heard that,' said a gruff voice with distinct Edinburgh accent behind him. 'I hope it wasn't meant to be sarcastic.'

The tall white-haired doctor looked down sternly at Banks, blue eyes twinkling. His moustache was stained yellow with nicotine, and a cigarette hung from the corner of his mouth. He was wheezing after climbing the stairs.

'There's no smoking in here,' Gristhorpe said. 'You ought to know better; you're a doctor.'

Glendenning grunted. 'Then I'll go elsewhere.'

'Come to my office,' Banks said. 'I could do with a fag myself.'

'Fine, laddie. Lead the way.'

'Bloody traitor.' Gristhorpe sighed and followed them.

After they'd got coffee and an extra chair, the doctor began. 'To put it in layman's terms,' he said, 'PC Gill was stabbed. The knife entered under the ribcage and did enough damage to cause death from internal bleeding. The blade was at least five inches long, and it looks like it went in to the hilt. It was a single-edged blade with a very sharp point. Judging by the wound, I'd say it was some kind of flick knife.'

'Flick knife?' echoed Banks.

'Aye, laddie. You know what a flick knife is, don't you? They come in all shapes and sizes. Illegal here, of course, but easy enough to pick up on the Continent. The cutting edge was extremely sharp, as was the point.'

'What about blood?' Gristhorpe asked. 'Nobody conveniently covered in Gill's type, I suppose?'

Dr Glendenning lit another Senior Service and shook his head. 'No. I checked the tests. And I'd have been very surprised if there had been,' he said. 'What most people don't realize is that unless you open a major vein or artery – the carotid or the jugular, for example – there's often very little external bleeding with knife wounds. I'd say in this case that there was hardly any, and what there was would've been mostly absorbed by the man's clothing. The slit closes behind the blade, you see – especially a thin one – and most of the bleeding is internal.'

'Can you tell if it was a professional job?' Gristhorpe asked.

'I wouldn't care to speculate. It could have been, but it

could just as easily have been a lucky strike. It was a right-handed up-thrust wound. With a blow like that on a dark night, I doubt that anybody would have noticed, unless they saw the blade flash, and there's not enough light for that on North Market Street. It would have looked more like a punch to the solar plexus than anything else, and from what I hear there was plenty of that going on. Now if he'd raised his hand above his head and thrust downwards . . .'

'People aren't usually so obliging,' Banks said.

'If we take into account the kind of knife used,' Gristhorpe speculated, 'it could easily have been a spontaneous act. Pros don't usually use flick knives – they're street weapons.'

'Aye, well,' said Gristhorpe, standing to leave, 'that's for you fellows to work out. I'll let you know if I find anything more at the post-mortem.'

'Who identified the body?' Banks asked him.

'Sister. Pretty upset about it, too. A couple of your lads did the paperwork. Luckily, Gill didn't have a wife and kids.' A quarter-inch of ash fell on to the linoleum. Glendenning shook his head slowly. 'Nasty business all round. Be seeing you.'

When the doctor had left, Gristhorpe stood up and flapped his hand theatrically in front of his face. 'Filthy bloody habit. I'm back to my office where the air's clean. Does this Burgess fellow smoke, too?'

Banks smiled. 'Cigars, if I remember right.'

Gristhorpe swore.

TWO

Over the valley from Maggie's Farm, mist clung to the hill-sides and limestone scars, draining them of all colour. Soon after breakfast, Seth disappeared into his workshop to finish restoring Jack Lippett's Welsh dresser; Rick did some shopping in Helmthorpe, then went to his studio in the converted barn to daub away at his latest painting; Zoe busied herself in her flat with Elsie Goodbody's natal chart; and Paul went for a long walk on the moors.

In the living room, Mara kept an eye on Luna and Julian while she mended the tears in Seth's jacket. The children were playing with Lego bricks and she often glanced over, awed by the look of pure concentration on their faces as they built. Occasionally an argument would break out, and Julian would complain that the slightly younger Luna wasn't doing things right. Then Luna would accuse him of being bossy. Mara would step in and give them her advice, healing the rift temporarily.

There was nothing to worry about really, Mara told herself as she sewed, but after what Seth and Rick had said about the dead policeman, she knew they could expect to come under close scrutiny. After all, they were different. While not political in the sense of belonging to any party, they certainly believed in protection of the environment. They had even allowed their house to be used as a base for planning the demo. It would only be a matter of time before the knock at the door. There was something else bothering Mara, too, hovering at the back of her mind, but she couldn't quite figure out what it was.

Seth and Rick had been tired and hungry when they got back just after two in the morning. Seth had been charged with threatening behaviour and Rick with obstructing a police officer. They hadn't much to add to what Mara had heard earlier except for the news of PC Gill's murder, which had soon spread around the police station.

In bed, Mara had tried to cheer Seth up, but he had been difficult to reach. Finally, he said he was tired and went to sleep. Mara had stayed awake listening to the rain for a long time and thinking just how often Seth seemed remote. She'd been living with him for two years now, but she hardly felt she knew him. She didn't even know if he really was asleep now or just pretending. He was a man of deep silences, as if he were carrying a great weight of sadness within him. Mara knew that his wife, Alison, had died tragically just before he bought the farm, but really she knew nothing else of his past.

How different from Rick he was, she thought. Rick had tragedy in his life, too – he was involved in a nasty custody suit with his ex-wife over Julian – but he was open and he let his feelings show, whereas Seth never said much. But Seth was strong, Mara thought – the kind of person every-one else looked up to as being really in command. And he loved her. She knew she had been foolish to feel such jealousy when Liz Dale had run away from the psychiatric hospital and come to stay. But Liz had been a close friend of Alison's and had known Seth for years; she was a part of his life that was shut off from Mara, and that hurt. Night after night Mara had lain awake listening to their muffled voices downstairs until the small hours, gripping the pillow tightly. It had been a difficult time, what with Liz, the plague of social workers and the police raid, but she could look back and laugh at the memory of her jealousy now.

As she sat and sewed, watching the children, Mara felt

lucky to be alive. Most of the time these days she was happy; she wouldn't change things for the world. It had been a good life so far, though a confusing one at times. After her student days, she had thrown herself into life – travel, communal living, love affairs, drugs – all without a care in the world.

Then she had spent four years with the Resplendent Light Organization, culminating in nine long months in one of their ashrams, where all earnings were turned over to the group and freedom was severely limited. There were no films, no evenings in the pub, no frivolous chatty gatherings around the fire; there was very little laughter. Mara had soon come to feel trapped, and the whole episode had left her with a bitter taste in her mouth. She felt she had been cheated into wasting her time. There had been no love there, no special person to share life with. But that was all over now. She had Seth – a solid dependable man, however distant he could be – Paul, Zoe, Rick and, most important of all, the children. After wandering and searching for so long, she seemed at last to have found the stability she needed. She had come home.

Sometimes, though, she wondered what things would be like if her life had been more normal. She'd heard of business executives dropping out in the 1960s; they took off their suits and ties, dropped acid and headed for Woodstock. But sometimes Mara dreamed of dropping in. She had a good brain; she had got a first in English Literature at the University of Essex. At times she could see herself all crisp and efficient in a business suit, perhaps working in advertising, or standing in front of a blackboard reading Keats or Coleridge to a class of spellbound children.

But the fantasies never lasted long. She was thirty-eight years old, and jobs were hard to come by even for the qualified and experienced. All those opportunities had passed her by. She knew also that she would no more be able to work in the everyday world, with its furious pace, its petty demands and its money-grubbing mentality, than she would be able to join the armed forces. Her years on the fringes of society had distanced her from life inside the system. She didn't even know what people talked about at work these days. The new BMW? Holidays in the Caribbean? All she knew was what she read in the papers, where it seemed that people no longer lived their lives but had 'lifestyles' instead.

The closest she came to a normal middle-class existence was working in Elspeth's craft shop in Relton three days a week in exchange for the use of the pottery wheel and kiln in the back. But Elspeth was hardly an ordinary person; she was a kindly old silver-haired lesbian who had been living in Relton with her companion, Dottie, for over thirty years. She affected the tweedy look of a country matron, but the twinkle in her eyes told a different story. Mara loved both of them very much, but Dottie was rarely to be seen these days. She was ill – dying of cancer, Mara suspected – and Elspeth bore the burden with her typical gruff stoicism.

At twelve o'clock, Rick knocked and came in through the back door, interrupting Mara's wandering thoughts. He looked every inch the artist: beard, paint-stained smock and jeans, beer belly. His whole appearance cried out that he believed in himself and didn't give a damn what other people thought about him.

'All quite on the western front?' he asked.

Mara nodded. She'd been half listening for the sound of a police car above the wind chimes. 'They'll be here, though.'

'It'll probably take them a while,' Rick said. 'There were a lot of others involved. We might not be as important as we think we are.'

He picked up Julian and whirled him around in the air. The child squealed with delight and wriggled as Rick rubbed his head against his face. Zoe tapped at the door and came in from the barn to join them.

'Stop it, Daddy!' Julian screamed. 'It tickles. Stop it!'

Rick put him down and tousled his hair. 'What are you two building?' he asked.

'A space station,' answered Luna seriously.

Mara looked at the jumble of Lego and smiled to herself. It didn't look like much of anything to her, but it was remarkable what children could do with their imaginations.

Rick laughed and turned to Zoe. 'All right, kiddo?' he asked, slipping his arm around her shoulder. 'What do the stars have to say today?'

Zoe smiled. She obviously adored Rick, Mara thought; otherwise she would never put up with being teased and treated like a youngster at the age of thirty-two. Could there be any chance of them getting together, she wondered. It would be good for the children.

'Elsie Goodbody's wasted as a housewife,' said Zoe. 'By the looks of her chart she should be in politics.'

'She's in domestic politics,' Rick said, 'and that's even worse. Anyone for the pub?'

They usually all walked down to the Black Sheep on Saturday and Sunday lunchtimes. The landlord was good about the children as long as they kept quiet, and Zoe took along colouring books to occupy them. Mara fetched Seth from his workshop, Julian got up on his father's shoulders, and Luna held Zoe's hand as they walked out to the track.

'Just a minute, I'll catch you up,' Mara said, dashing back into the house. She wanted to leave a note for Paul to tell him where they were; a formality really, an affectionate gesture. But as she wrote and her mind turned back to him, she suddenly realized what had been nagging her all morning.

Last night, Paul's hand had been bleeding and he had put an Elastoplast on it. This morning, when he came down, the plaster had slipped off, probably when he was washing, and the base of his thumb was as smooth as ever. There was no sign of a cut at all.

Mara's heart beat fast as she hurried to catch up with the others.

THREE

'Detective Superintendent Burgess, sir,' PC Craig said, then left.

The man who stood before them in Gristhorpe's office looked little different from the Burgess that Banks remembered. He wore a scuffed black leather sports jacket over an open-necked white shirt and close-fitting navy blue cords. The handsome face with its square determined jaw hadn't changed much, even if his slightly crooked teeth were a little more tobacco-stained. The pouches under his cynical grey eyes still suited him. His dark hair, short and combed back, was touched with grey at the temples, and by the look of it he still used Brylcreem. He was about six feet tall, well-built but filling out a bit, and looked as if he still played squash twice a week. The most striking thing about his appearance was his deep tan.

'Barbados,' he said, catching their surprise. 'I'd

recommend it highly, especially at this time of year. Just got back when this business came up.'

Gristhorpe introduced himself, then Burgess looked over at Banks and narrowed his eyes. 'Banks, isn't it? I heard you'd been transferred. Looking a bit pasty-faced, aren't you? Not feeding you well up here?'

Banks forced a smile. It was typical of Burgess to make the transfer sound like a punishment and a demotion. 'We don't get much sun,' he said.

Burgess looked towards the window. 'So I see. If it's any consolation, it was pissing down in London when I left.' He clapped his hands together sharply. 'Where's the boozer, then? I'm starving. Didn't dare risk British Rail food. I could do with a pint, as well.'

Gristhorpe excused himself, claiming a meeting with the assistant chief commissioner, and Banks led Burgess over to the Queen's Arms.

'Not a bad-looking place,' Burgess said, glancing around and taking in the spacious lounge with its dimpled copper-topped tables with black wrought-iron legs and deep armchairs by the blazing fire. Then his eyes rested on the barmaid. 'Yes. Not bad at all. Let's sit at the bar.'

Some of the locals paused in their conversations to stare at them. They knew Banks already, and Burgess's accent still bore traces of his East End background. As right-wing as he was, he didn't come from the privileged school of Tories, Banks remembered. His father had been a barrow boy, and Burgess had fought his way up from the bottom. Banks also knew that he felt little solidarity with those of his class who hadn't managed to do likewise. To the locals, he was obviously the London bigwig they'd been expecting after the previous night's events.

Banks and Burgess perched on the high stools. 'What'll

you have?' Burgess asked, taking a shiny black leather wallet from his inside pocket. 'I'm buying.'

'Thanks very much. I'll have a pint of Theakston's bitter.'

'Food?'

'The hotpot is usually good.'

'I think I'll stick to plaice and chips,' Burgess said. He ordered the food and drinks from the barmaid. 'And a pint of Double Diamond for me, please, love.' He lit a Tom Thumb cigar and poked it at Banks's glass. 'Can't stand that real ale stuff,' he said, rubbing his stomach and grimacing. 'Always gives me the runs. Ah, thank you, love. What's your name?'

'Glenys,' the barmaid said. She gave him a coy smile with his change and turned to serve another customer.

'Nice,' Burgess said. 'Not exactly your buxom barmaid type, but nice nonetheless. Lovely bum. A fiver says I'll bonk her before this business is over.'

Banks wished he would try. The muscular man drying glasses at the far end of the bar was Glenys's husband, Cyril. 'You're on,' he said, shaking hands. Though how Burgess would prove it if he won, Banks had no idea. Perhaps he'd persuade Glenys to part with a pair of panties as a trophy? The most likely outcome, though, would be a black eye for Burgess and a fiver in Banks's pocket.

'So, I hear you had a riot on your hands last night.'

'Not quite a riot,' Banks said, 'but bad enough.'

'It shouldn't have been allowed.'

'Sure. It's easy to say that from hindsight, but we'd no reason to expect trouble. A lot of people around here have sympathy with the cause and they don't usually kill policemen.'

Burgess's eyes narrowed. 'Including you? Sympathy with the cause?'

Banks shrugged. 'Nobody wants any more airbase activity in the Dales, and I'm no great fan of nuclear power.'

'A bloody bolshie on the force, eh? No wonder they sent you up here. Like getting sent to Siberia, I'll bet?' He chuckled at his own joke, then sank about half a pint in one gulp. 'What have you got so far, then?'

Banks told him about the statements they'd taken and the main groups involved in organizing the protest, including the people at Maggie's Farm. As he listened, Burgess sucked on his lower lip and tapped his cigar on the side of the blue ashtray. Every time Glenys walked by, his restless eyes followed her.

'Seventy-one names,' he commented when Banks had finished. 'And you think there were over a hundred there. That's not a lot, is it?'

'It is in a murder investigation.'

'Hmmm. Got anyone marked out for it?'

'Pardon?'

'Local troublemaker, shit-stirrer. Let's be honest about this, Banks. It doesn't look like we'll get any physical evidence unless someone finds the knife. The odds are that whoever did it was one of the ones who got away. You might not even have his name on your list. I was just wondering who's your most likely suspect.'

'We don't have any suspects yet.'

'Oh, come on! No one with a record of political violence?'

'Only the local Conservative member.'

'Very good,' Burgess said, grinning. 'Very good. It seems to me,' he went on, 'that there are two possibilities.

One: it happened in the heat of the moment; someone lost his temper and lashed out with a knife. Or two: it was a planned deliberate act to kill a copper, an act of terrorism calculated to cause chaos, to disrupt society.'

'What about the knife?' Banks said. 'The killer couldn't be sure of getting away, and we've found no traces of it in the area. I'd say that points more towards your first theory. Someone lost his temper and didn't stop to think of the consequences, then just got lucky.'

Burgess finished his pint. 'Not necessarily,' he said. 'They're kamikaze merchants, these bloody terrorists. They don't care if they get caught or not. Like you said, whoever it was just got lucky this time.'

'It's possible, I suppose.'

'But unlikely?'

'In Eastvale, yes. I told you, most of the people involved were fairly harmless; even the groups they belonged to have never been violent before.'

'But you don't have everyone's name.'

'No.'

'Then that's something to work on. Sweat the ones you've got and get a full list.'

'DC Richmond's working on it,' Banks said, though he could hardly see Philip Richmond sweating anyone.

'Good.' Burgess gestured to the barmaid. 'Another two pints, Gladys, love,' he called out.

'It's Glenys,' she said, then she blushed and lowered her head to keep an eye on the pint she was pulling.

'Sorry, love, I'm still train-lagged. Have one for yourself too, Glenys.'

'Thank you very much.' Glenys smiled shyly at him and took the money for a gin and tonic. 'I'll have it later when we're not so busy, if you don't mind.'

'As you will.' Burgess treated her to a broad smile and winked. 'Where were we?' he asked, returning to Banks.

'Names.'

'Yes. You must have a list of local reds and whatnot? You know the kind I mean – anarchists, skinheads, bum punchers, women's libbers, uppity niggers.'

'Of course. We keep it on the back of a postage stamp.'

'You mentioned three organizations earlier. What's WEEF?'

'Women of Eastvale for Emancipation and Freedom.'

'Oh, very impressive. Touch of the Greenham Common women, eh?'

'Not really. They mostly stick to local issues like poor streetlighting and sexual discrimination in jobs.'

'Still,' Burgess said, 'it's a start. Get your man – Richmond, is it? – to liaise with Special Branch on this. They've got extensive files on bolshies everywhere. He can do it through the computer, if you've got one up here.'

'We've got one.'

'Good. Tell him to see me about access.' Their food arrived, and Burgess poured salt and vinegar on his fish and chips. 'We can set them against each other, for openers,' he said. 'Simple divide and conquer tactics. We tell those WEEF people that the students' union has fingered them for the murder, and vice versa. That way if anyone does know anything they'll likely tell us out of anger at being dropped right in it. We need results, and we need them quick. This business can give us a chance to look good for once. We're always looking like the bad guys these days – especially since that bloody miners' strike. We need some good press for a change, and here's our chance. A copper's been killed – that gets us plenty of public sympathy for a start. If we can come up with some pinko terrorist we've got it made.'

'I don't think setting the groups against each other will get us anywhere,' Banks said. 'They're just not that aggressive.'

'Don't be so bloody negative, man. Remember, *somebody* knows who did it, even if it's only the killer. I'll get myself acclimatized this afternoon, and tomorrow' – Burgess clapped his hands and showered his plate with ash – 'we'll swoop into action.' He had a nasty habit of sitting or standing motionless for ages, then making a sudden jerky movement. Banks remembered how disconcerting it was from their previous meetings.

'Action?'

'Raids, visits, call them what you will. We're looking for documents, letters, anything that might give us a clue to what happened. Any trouble getting warrants up here?'

Banks shook his head.

Burgess speared a chip. 'Nothing like a Sunday morning for a nice little raid, I always say. People have funny ideas about Sundays, you know. Especially churchy types. They're all comfortable and complacent after a nice little natter with the Almighty, and then they get pissed off as hell if something interrupts their routine. Best day for raids and interrogations, believe me. Just wait till they get their feet up with the Sunday papers. You mentioned some dropouts at a farm earlier, didn't you?'

'They're not dropouts,' Banks said. 'They just try to be self-sufficient, keep to themselves. They call the place Maggie's Farm,' he added. 'It's the title of an old Bob Dylan song. I suppose it's a joke about Thatcher, too.'

Burgess grinned. 'At least they've got a sense of humour. They'll bloody need it before we're through.

We'll pay them a visit, keep them on their toes. Bound to be drugs around, if nothing else. How about dividing up the raids? Any suggestions?'

Banks had no desire to tangle with Dorothy Wycombe again, and sending Sergeant Hatchley to WEEF head-quarters would be like sending a bull into a china shop, as would sending Burgess up to Maggie's Farm. On the other hand, he thought, meeting Ms Wycombe might do Dirty Dick some good.

'I'll take the farm,' he said. 'Let Hatchley do the church group, Richmond the students, and you can handle WEEF. We can take a couple of uniformed men to do the searches while we ask the questions.'

Burgess's eyes narrowed suspiciously, then he smiled and said, 'Right, we're on.'

He knows I'm setting him up, Banks thought, but he's willing to go along anyway. Cocky bastard.

Burgess washed down the last of his plaice and chips. 'I'd like to stay for another,' he said, 'and feast my eyes more on the lovely Glenys, but duty calls. Let's hope we'll have plenty of reason to celebrate tomorrow lunch time. Why don't you catch up on a bit of paperwork this after-noon? There's not a lot we can do yet. And maybe this evening you can show me some of these quaint village pubs I've read about in the tourist brochures?'

The prospect of a pub crawl with Dirty Dick Burgess, following hot on the heels of an evening with the Hon. Honoria Winstanley, appealed to Banks about as much as a slap in the face with a wet fish, but he agreed politely. It was a job, after all, and Burgess was his senior officer. They'd be working together for a few days, probably, and it would do no harm to get on as good terms as possible. Make the best of it, Gristhorpe had said. And Banks did have a vague recollection that Burgess wasn't such bad company after a few jars.

Burgess slid off his chair and strode towards the door. 'Bye, Glenys, love,' he called out over his shoulder as he left. Banks noticed Cyril scowl and tighten his grip on the pump he was pulling.

Banks pushed his empty plate aside and lit a Silk Cut. He felt exhausted. Just listening to Burgess reminded him of everything he had hated about his days on the Met. But Burgess was right, of course; they were looking into a political murder, and the first logical step was to check out local activist groups.

It was the obvious relish with which the superintendent contemplated the task that irked Banks and reminded him so much of his London days. And he remembered Burgess's interrogation technique, probably learned from the Spanish Inquisition. There were hard times ahead for a few innocent people who simply happened to believe in nuclear disarmament and the future of the human race. Burgess was like a pit bull terrier; he wouldn't let go until he got what he wanted.

Oh, for a nice English village murder, Banks wished, just like the ones in books: a closed group of five or six suspects, a dodgy will, and no hurry to solve the puzzle. No such luck. He drained his pint, stubbed out the cigarette and went back across the street to read more statements.

FOUR

Mara sipped at her half of mild without really tasting it. She couldn't seem to relax and enjoy the company as usual. Seth sat at the bar chatting with Larry Grafton about some old furniture the landlord had inherited from his great-grandmother, and Rick and Zoe were arguing about astrology. By the window, the children sat colouring quietly.

What did it mean? Mara wondered. When she had tackled Paul about the blood on his hand the previous evening, he had gone into the kitchen and put on a plaster without showing her the cut. Now it turned out there was no cut. So whose blood had it been?

Of course, she told herself, anything could have happened. He could have accidentally brushed against somebody who had been hurt in the demo, or even tried to help someone. But he had clearly run all the way home; when he had arrived he had been upset and out of breath. And if the explanation was an innocent one, why had he lied? Because that's what it came down to in the end. Instead of telling the simple truth, he had let her go on believing he was hurt, albeit not badly, and she couldn't come up with a convincing reason why he had done that.

'You're quiet today,' Seth said, walking over with more drinks.

It's easy for you, she felt like saying. You can cover up your feelings and talk about hammers and planes and chisels and bevels and chamfering as if nothing has happened, but I don't have any small talk. Instead, she said, 'It's nothing. I'm just a bit tired after last night, I suppose.'

Seth took her hand. 'Didn't you sleep well?'

No, Mara almost said, No, I didn't bloody sleep well. I was waiting for you to share your feelings with me, but you never did. You never do. You can talk about work to any Tom, Dick and Harry, but not about anything else, not about anything important. But she didn't say any of that. She squeezed his hand, kissed him lightly and said she was all right. She knew she was just irritable, worried about Paul, and the mood would soon pass. No point starting a row.

Rick, his conversation with Zoe finished, turned to the others. Mara noticed streaks of orange and white paint in his beard. 'They were all talking about the Eastvale demo,' he said. 'Plenty of tongues started clucking in the grocer's when I walked in.'

'What did they think about it?' Mara asked.

Rick snorted. 'They don't think. They're just like the sheep they raise. They're too frightened to come out with an opinion about anything for fear it'll be the wrong one. Oh, they worry about nuclear fallout. Who doesn't? But that's about all they do, worry and whine. When push comes to shove they'll just put up with it like everything else and bury their heads in the ground. The wives are even worse. All they can do if anything upsets the nice, neat, comfortable little lives they've made for themselves is say tut-tut-tut, isn't it a shame.'

The door cracked open and Paul walked in.

Mara watched the emaciated figure, fists bunched in his pockets, walk over to them. With his hollow bony face, tattooed fingers and the scars, needle tracks and self-inflicted cigarette burns that Mara knew stretched all the way up his arms, Paul seemed a frightening figure. The only thing that softened his appearance was his hairstyle. His blond hair was short at the back and sides but long on top, and the fringe kept slipping down over his eyes. He'd brush it back impatiently and scowl but never mention having it cut.

Mara couldn't help thinking about his background. Right from childhood, Paul's life had been rough and hard. He never said much about his real parents, but he'd told

Mara about the emotionally cold foster home where he had been expected to show undying gratitude for every little thing they did for him. Finally, he had run away and lived a punk life on the streets, done whatever he'd had to to survive. It had been a life of hard drugs and violence and, eventually, jail. When they had met him, he had been lost and looking for some kind of anchor in life. She wondered just how much he really had changed since he'd been with them.

Remembering the blood on his hand, the way he had lied and the murdered policeman, she began to feel frightened. What would he do if she were to question him? Was she living with a killer? And if she was, what should she do about it?

As the conversation went on around her, Mara began to feel herself drifting off on a chaotic spate of her own thoughts. She could hear the sounds the others were making, but not the words, the meaning. She thought of confiding in Seth, but what if he took some kind of action? He might be hard on Paul, even drive him away. He could be very stern and inflexible at times. She didn't want her new family to split apart, imperfect as she knew it was. It was all she had in the world.

No, she decided, she wouldn't tell anyone. Not yet. She wouldn't make Paul feel as if they were ganging up on him. The whole thing was probably ridiculous anyway. She was imagining things, filling her head with stupid fears. Paul would never hurt her, she told herself, never in a million years.

4

ONE

Sunday morning dawned clear and cold. A brisk March wind blew, restoring the sun and the delicate colours of early spring to the lower hillsides. Women hung on to their hats and men clutched the lapels of their best suits as they struggled to church along Mortsett Lane in Relton. The police car, a white Fiesta Popular, with the official red and blue stripes on its sides, turned and made its way up the bumpy Roman road to Maggie's Farm. PC McDonald drove, with Craig silent beside him and Banks cramped in the back.

The view across the dale was superb. Banks could see Fortford on the valley bottom and Devraulx Abbey below Lyndgarth on the opposite slope. Behind them all the northern daleside rose, baring along its snowy heights scars of exposed limestone that looked like rows of teeth gleaming in the light.

Banks felt refreshed after an evening at home reading *Madame Bovary*, followed by a good night's sleep. Luckily, Dirty Dick had phoned to cancel their pub crawl, claiming tiredness. Banks suspected he had decided to drop in at the Queen's Arms – just around the corner from his hotel – to work on Glenys, but Burgess looked relatively unscathed the next morning. He seemed tired though, and his grey eyes were dull, like champagne that had lost its fizz. Banks wondered how he was getting on with Dorothy Wycombe.

As the car pulled on to the gravel outside the farmhouse, someone glanced through the window. When Banks got out, he could hear the wind chimes jingling like a piece of experimental music, harmonizing strangely with the wind that whistled around his ears. He had forgotten how high on the moorland Maggie's Farm was.

His knock was answered by a tall slender woman in her mid to late thirties wearing jeans and a rust-coloured jumper. Banks thought he remembered her from his previous visit. Her wavy chestnut hair tumbled over her shoulders, framing a pale heart-shaped face, free of make-up. Perhaps her chin was a little too pointed and her nose a bit too long, but the whole effect was pleasing. Her clear brown eyes looked both innocent and knowing at once.

Banks presented his warrant and the woman moved aside wearily. They knew we were coming sometime, he thought; they've just been waiting to get it over with.

'They'd better not damage anything,' she said, nodding towards McDonald and Craig.

'Don't worry, they won't. You won't even know they've been here.'

Mara sniffed. 'I'll get the others.'

The two uniformed men started their search, and Banks sat in the rocking chair by the window. Turning his head sideways, he scanned the titles in the pine bookcase beside him. They were mostly novels – Hardy, the Brontës, John Cowper Powys, Fay Weldon, Graham Greene – mixed in with a few more esoteric works, such as an introduction to Jung's psychology and a survey of the occult. On the lower shelves rested a number of older well-thumbed paperbacks – *The Teachings of Don Juan, Naked Lunch, The Lord of the*

Rings. In addition, there were the obligatory political texts: Marcuse, Fanon, Marx and Engels.

On the floor beside Banks lay a copy of George Eliot's *The Mill on the Floss.* He picked it up. The bookmark stood at the second page; that was about as far as he'd ever got with George Eliot himself.

Mara came back from the barn with the others, three of them vaguely familiar to Banks from eighteen months ago: Zoe Hardacre, a slight freckle-faced woman with frizzy ginger hair and dark roots; Rick Trelawney, a big bear of a man in a baggy paint-smeared T-shirt and torn jeans; and Seth Cotton, in from his workshop, wearing a sand-coloured lab coat, tall and thin with mournful brown eyes and neatly trimmed dark hair and beard framing a dark-complexioned face. Finally came a skinny, hostile-looking youth Banks hadn't seen before.

'Who are you?' he asked.

'Paul's not been here long,' Mara said quickly.

'What's your last name?'

Paul said nothing.

'He doesn't have to say,' Mara argued. 'He's done nothing.'

Seth shook his head. 'Might as well tell him,' he said to Paul. 'He'll find out anyway.'

'He's right, you know,' Banks said.

'It's Boyd, Paul Boyd.'

'Ever been in trouble, Paul?'

Paul smiled. It was either that or a scowl, Banks couldn't decide. 'So what if I have? I'm not on probation or parole. I don't have to register at the local nick everywhere I go, do I?' He fished for a cigarette in a grubby packet of Players. Banks noticed that his stubby fingers were trembling slightly.

'Just like to know who we've got living among us,' Banks said pleasantly. He didn't need to pursue the matter. If Boyd had a record, the Police National Computer would provide all the information he wanted.

'So what's all this in aid of?' Rick said, leaning against the mantelpiece. 'As if I need ask.'

'You know what happened on Friday night. You were arrested for obstructing a police officer.' Rick laughed. Banks ignored him and went on. 'You also know that a policeman was killed at that demonstration.'

'Are you saying you think one of us did it?'

Banks shook his head. 'Come on,' he said, 'you know the rules as well as I do. A situation like this comes up, we check out all political groups.'

'We're not political,' Mara said.

Banks looked around the room. 'Don't be so naive. Everything you have here, everything you say and do, makes a political statement. It doesn't matter whether or not any of you belongs to an official party. You know that as well as I do. Besides, we've got to act on tips we get.'

'What tip?' Rick asked. 'Who's been talking?'

'Never mind that. We just heard you were involved, that's all.' Burgess's trick seemed at least worth a try.

'So we were there,' Rick said. 'Seth and me. You already know that. We gave statements. We told you all we knew. Why come back pestering us now? What are you looking for?'

'Anything we can find.'

'Look,' Rick went on, 'I still don't see why you're persecuting us. I can't imagine who's been telling you things or what they've been saying, but you're misinformed. Just because we employed our right to demonstrate for a cause we happen to believe in, it doesn't give you the right to come around with these Gestapo tactics and harass us.'

'The Gestapo didn't need a search warrant.'

Rick sneered and scratched his straggly beard. 'With a JP like the one you've got in your pocket, I'd hardly consider that a valid argument.'

'Besides,' Banks went on, 'we're not persecuting you or harassing you. Believe me, if we were, you'd know it. Do any of you remember anything else about Friday night?'

Seth and Rick shook their heads. Banks looked around at the others. 'Come on, I'm assuming you were all there. Don't worry, I can't prove it. I'm not going to arrest you if you admit it. It's just one of you might have seen something important. This is a murder investigation.'

Still silence. Banks sighed. 'Fine. Don't blame me if things get rough. We've got a man up from London. A specialist. Dirty Dick, his friends call him. He's a hell of a lot nastier than I am.'

'Is that some kind of threat?' Mara asked.

Banks shook his head. 'I'm just letting you know your options, that's all.'

'How can we tell you we saw something if we didn't?' Paul said angrily. 'You say you know we were there. OK. Maybe we were. I'm not saying we were, but maybe. That doesn't mean we saw anything or did anything wrong. It's like Rick says, we had a right to be there. It's not a fucking police state yet.' He turned away sullenly and drew on his cigarette.

'Nobody's denying your right to be there,' Banks said. 'I just want to know if you saw anything that could help us solve this murder.'

Silence.

'Does anyone here own a flick knife?'

Rick said no and the others shook their heads.

'Ever seen one around? Know anyone who does have one?'

Again nothing. Banks thought he saw an expression of surprise flit across Mara's face, but it could have been a trick of the light.

In the following silence, Craig and McDonald came downstairs, shook their heads and went to search the outbuildings. Two small children walked in from the kitchen and hurried over to Mara, each taking a hand. Banks smiled at them, but they just stared at him, sucking their thumbs.

He tried to imagine Brian and Tracy, his own children, growing up under such conditions, isolated from other children. For one thing, there didn't seem to be a television in the place. Banks disapproved of TV in general, and he always tried to make sure that Brian and Tracy didn't watch too much, but if children saw none at all, they would have nothing to talk to their pals about. There had to be a compromise somewhere; you couldn't just ignore the blasted idiot box in this day and age, much as you might wish you could.

On the other hand, these children certainly showed no signs of neglect, and there was no reason to assume that Rick and the rest weren't good parents. Seth Cotton, Banks knew, had a reputation as a fine carpenter, and Mara's pottery sold well locally. Sandra even had a piece, a shapely vase glazed in a mixture of shades: green, ultramarine and the like. He didn't know much about Rick Trelawney's paintings, but if the local landscape propped up by the fireplace was his, then he was good, too. No, he had no call to impose his own limited perspective on them. If the children grew up into creative, free-thinking adults, their mind unpolluted by TV and mass culture, what could be so wrong about that?

Apart from the sounds of the wind chimes, they sat in silence until Rick finally spoke. 'Do you know,' he said to Banks, 'how many children come down with leukaemia and rare forms of cancer in areas around Sellafield and other nuclear power stations? Do you have any idea?'

'Look,' said Banks. 'I'm not here to attack your views. You're entitled to them. I might even agree. The thing is, what happened on Friday night goes beyond all that. I'm not here to argue politics or philosophy; I'm investigating a murder. Why can't you get that into your heads?'

'Maybe they can't be as neatly separated as you think,' Rick argued. 'Politics, philosophy, murder – they're all connected. Look at Latin America, Israel, Nicaragua, South Africa. Besides, the police started it. They kept us penned in like animals, then they charged with their truncheons out, just like some Chilean goon squad. If some of them got hurt too, they bloody well deserved it.'

'One of them got killed. Is that all right?'

Rick turned away in disgust. 'I never said I was a pacifist,' he muttered, looking at Seth. 'There'll be a local police inquiry,' he went on, 'and the whole thing'll be rigged. You can't expect us to believe there's going to be any objectivity about all this. When it comes to the crunch you bastards always stick together.'

'Believe what you like,' Banks said.

Craig and McDonald came back in through the kitchen. They'd found nothing. It was eleven o'clock. At twelve Banks was to meet Burgess, Hatchley and Richmond in the Queen's Arms to compare notes. There was nothing to be gained by staying to discuss nuclear ethics with Rick, so he stood up and walked over to the door.

As he held his jacket closed and pushed against the wind to the car, he felt someone staring at his back through the window. He knew he had sensed fear in the house. Not just fear of a police raid they'd been expecting, but something different. All was not as harmonious as it should have been. He filed away his uneasiness to be mulled over later along with the thousand other things – concrete or nebulous – that lodged themselves in his mind during an investigation.

TWO

'Nothing,' Burgess growled, grinding out his cigar viciously in the ashtray at the centre of the copper-topped table. 'Absolutely bugger all. And that woman's crazy. I'll swear I thought she was going to bite me.'

For the first time ever Banks felt a sudden rush of affection for Dorothy Wycombe.

All in all, though, the morning had been disappointing for everyone. Not surprisingly, the searches had produced no murder weapon or documents attesting to the terrorist plot that Burgess suspected; none of the witnesses had changed their statements and the reaction to Burgess's divide and conquer tactic had been negligible.

Sergeant Hatchley reported that the Church for Peace group seemed stunned by the murder and had even offered prayers for PC Gill in their service that morning. The students' union, according to DC Richmond, who had visited the leaders – Tim Fenton and Abha Sutton – at their flat, thought it typical of the others to blame them for what had happened, but insisted that assassination was not part of their programme for a peaceful revolution. While Burgess thought Dorothy Wycombe quite capable of murder – especially of a member of the male species – she had stuck to her guns and ridiculed any such suggestion.

'So it's back to square one,' Hatchley said. 'A hundred suspects and not one scrap of evidence.'

'I did find out from one of the lads on duty,' said Richmond, 'that Dorothy Wycombe, Dennis Osmond and some of the people from Maggie's Farm were close to the front at one time. But he said everything went haywire when the fighting started. He also said he noticed a punkish-looking kid with them.'

'That'd be Paul Boyd,' Banks said. 'He seems to live up at the farm, too. Run him through the computer, will you, Phil, and see what comes up. I wouldn't be surprised if he's done time. While you're at it, find out what you can about the lot of them up there. I've got a funny feeling that something's not quite right about that place.'

He glanced at Burgess, who seemed to be staring abstractedly over at Glenys. Her husband was nowhere in sight.

'Maybe we should have a look into Gill's background,' Banks suggested.

Burgess turned. 'Why?'

'Someone might have had a reason for wanting him dead. We'll get nowhere on means and opportunity unless the knife turns up, but if we could find a motive—'

Burgess shook his head. 'Not in a crime like this. Whether it was planned or spur of the moment, the victim was random. It could have happened to any of the coppers on duty that night. It was just poor Gill's bad luck, that's all.'

'But still,' Banks insisted, 'it's something we can do. Maybe the demo was just used as a cover.'

'No. It'll look bad, for a start. What if the papers find out we're investigating one of our own? We've got enough trouble already with an inquiry into the whole bloody mess. That'd give the press enough ammo to take a few cheap shots at us without making things easier for them. Jesus, there's enough weirdos and commies to investigate already without bringing a good copper into it. What about this Osmond character? Anyone talked to him yet?'

'No,' said Banks. 'Not since Friday night.'

'Right, this is what we'll do. Get another round in, Constable, would you?' Burgess handed Richmond a fiver.

Richmond nodded and went to the bar. Burgess had switched from Double Diamond to double Scotch, claiming it was easier on his stomach, but Banks thought he was just trying to impress Glenys with his largesse. And now he was showing her he was too important to leave the conference and that he had the power to order others to do things for him. Good tactics, but would they work on her?

'You and I, Banks,' he said, 'will pay this Osmond fellow a visit this afternoon. DC Richmond can check up on those dropouts you went to see and feed a few more names into the PNC. Sergeant Hatchley here can start making files on the leaders of the various groups involved. We want every statement cross-checked with the others for inaccuracies, and all further statements checked against the originals. Someone's going to slip up at some point, and we're going to catch the bugger at it. Bottoms up.' He drank his Scotch and turned to wink at Glenys. 'By the way,' he said to Banks, 'that bloody office you gave me isn't big enough to swing a dead cat in. Any chance of another?'

Banks shook his head. 'Sorry, we're pushed for space. It's either that or the cells.'

'What about yours?'

'Too small for two.'

'I was meaning for one. Me.'

'Forget it. I've got all my files and records in there. Besides, it's cold and the blind doesn't work.'

'Hmmm. Still . . .'

'You could do most of the paperwork in your hotel room,' Banks suggested. 'It's close enough, big enough and there's a phone.' And you'll be out of my way, too, he thought.

Burgess nodded slowly. 'All right. It'll do for now. Come on!' He jumped into action and clapped Banks on the back. 'Let's see if anything's turned up at the station first, then we'll set off and have a chat with Mr Dennis Osmond, CND.'

Nothing had turned up, and as soon as Richmond had located Paul Boyd's record and Banks had had a quick look at it, the pair set off for Osmond's flat in Banks's white Cortina.

'Tell me about this Boyd character,' Burgess asked as Banks drove.

'Nasty piece of work.' Banks slipped a Billie Holiday cassette in the stereo and turned the volume down low. 'He started as a juvenile – gang fights, assault, that kind of thing – skipping school and hanging around the streets with the rest of the deadbeats. He's been nicked four times, and he drew eighteen months on the last one. First it was drunk and disorderly, underage, then assaulting a police officer trying to disperse a bunch of punks frightening shoppers in Liverpool city centre. After that it was a drugs charge, possession of a small amount of amphetamines. Then he got nicked breaking into a chemist's to steal pills. He's been clean for just over a year now.'

Burgess rubbed his chin. 'Everything short of soccer

hooliganism, eh? Maybe he's not the sporting type. Assaulting a police officer, you say?'

'Yes. Him and a couple of others. They didn't do any real damage, so they got off lightly.'

'That's the bloody trouble,' Burgess said. 'Most of them do. Any political connections?'

'None that we know of so far. Richmond hasn't been on to the Branch yet, so we haven't been able to check on his friends and acquaintances.'

'Anything else?'

'Not really. Most of his probation officers and social workers seemed to give up on him.'

'My heart bleeds for the poor bastard. It looks like we've got a likely candidate. This Osmond is a social worker, isn't he?'

'Yes.'

'Maybe he'll know something about the kid. Let's remember to ask him. Where's Boyd from?'

'Liverpool.'

'Any IRA connections?'

'Not as far as we know.'

'Still . . .'

Dennis Osmond lived in a one-bedroom flat in north-east Eastvale. It had originally been council-owned, but the tenants had seized their chance and bought their units cheaply when the government started selling them off.

A shirtless Osmond answered the door and led Banks and Burgess inside. He was tall and slim with a hairy chest and a small tattoo of a butterfly on his upper right arm. He wore a gold crucifix on a chain around his neck. With his shaggy dark hair and Mediterranean good looks, he looked the kind of man who would be attractive to women. He moved slowly and calmly, and didn't seem at all surprised by their arrival.

The flat had a spacious living room with a large plate-glass window that overlooked the fertile plain to the east of Swainsdale: a chequerboard of ploughed fields, bordered by hedgerows, rich brown, ready for spring. The furniture was modern – tubes and cushions – and a large framed painting hung on the wall over the fake fireplace. Banks had to look very closely to make sure the canvas wasn't blank; it was scored with faint red and black lines.

'Who is it?' A woman's voice came from behind them. Banks turned and saw Jenny Fuller poking her head round a door. From what he could tell, she was wearing a loose dressing gown, and her hair was in disarray. His eyes caught hers and he felt his stomach tense up and his chest tighten. Meeting her in a situation like this was something he hadn't expected. He was surprised how hard it hit.

'Police,' Osmond said. But Jenny had already turned back and shut the door behind her.

Burgess, who had watched all this, made no comment. 'Can we sit down?' he asked.

'Go ahead.' Osmond gestured to the armchairs and pulled a black T-shirt over his head while they made themselves as comfortable as possible. The design on the front showed the CND symbol – a circle with a wide-spread inverted Y inside it, each branch touching the circumference – with NO NUKES written in a crescent under it.

Banks fumbled for a cigarette and looked around for an ashtray.

'I'd rather you didn't,' Osmond said. 'Second-hand smoke can kill, you know.' He paused and looked Banks over. 'So you're Chief Inspector Banks, are you? I've heard a lot about you.'

'Hope it was good,' Banks said, with more equilibrium than he felt. What had Jenny been telling him? 'It'll save us time getting acquainted, won't it?'

'And you're the whizz-kid they sent up from London,' Osmond said to Burgess.

'My, my, how word travels.' Dirty Dick smiled. He had the kind of smile that made most people feel nervous, but it seemed to have no effect on Osmond. As Banks settled into the chair, he could picture Jenny dressing in the other room. It was probably the bedroom, he thought gloomily, and the double bed would be rumpled and stained, the *Sunday Times* review section spread out over the creased sheets. He took out his notebook and settled down as best he could for the interrogation.

'What do you want?' Osmond asked, perching at the edge of the sofa and leaning forward.

'I hear you were one of the organizers of Friday's demonstration,' Burgess opened.

'So what if I was?'

'And you're a member of the Campaign for Nuclear Disarmament and the International Socialists, if I'm not mistaken.'

'I'm in Amnesty International as well, in case you don't have that in your file. And as far as I'm aware it's not a crime yet.'

'Don't be so touchy.'

'Look, can you get to the point? I haven't got all day.'

'Oh yes, you have,' Burgess said. 'And you've got all night, too, if I want it like that.'

'You've no right—'

'I've every right. One of your lot – maybe even you – killed a good honest copper on Friday night, and we don't like it at all. I'm sorry if we're keeping you from your fancy woman, but that's the way it is. Whose idea was it?'

Osmond frowned. 'Whose idea was what? And I don't like you calling Jenny names like that.'

'You don't?' Burgess narrowed his eyes. 'There'll be a lot worse names than that flying around, sonny, if you don't start to cooperate. Whose idea was the demonstration?'

'I don't know. It just sort of came together.'

Burgess sighed. '"It just sort of came together,"' he repeated mockingly, looking at Banks. 'Now what's that supposed to mean? Men and women come together, if they're lucky, but not political demonstrations – they're planned. What are you trying to tell me?'

'Exactly what I said. There are plenty of people around here opposed to nuclear arms, you know.'

'Are you telling me that you all just happened to meet outside the community centre that night? Is that what you're trying to say? "Hello, Fred, fancy meeting you here. Let's have a demo." Is that what you're saying?'

Osmond shrugged.

'Well, balls is what I say, Osmond. Balls to that. This was an organized demonstration, and that means somebody organized it. That somebody might have also arranged for a little killing to spice things up a bit. Now, so far the only somebody we know about for sure is you. Maybe you did it all by yourself, but I'm betting you had some help. Whose tune do you dance to, Mr Osmond? Moscow's? Peking's? Or is it Belfast?'

Osmond laughed. 'You've got your politics a bit mixed up, haven't you? A socialist is hardly the same as a Maoist. Besides, the Chairman's out of favour these days. And as for the IRA, you can't seriously believe—'

'I seriously believe a lot of things that might surprise

you,' Burgess cut in. 'And you can spare me the fucking lecture. Who gave you your orders?'

'You're wrong,' Osmond said. 'It wasn't like that at all. And even if there was somebody else involved, do you think I'm going to tell you who it was?'

'Yes, I do,' Burgess said. 'There's nothing more certain. The only question is when you're going to tell me, and where.'

'Look,' Banks said, 'we'll find out anyway. There's no need to take it on yourself to carry the burden and get done for withholding information in a murder investigation. If you didn't do it and you don't think your mates did either, then you've nothing to worry about, have you?' Banks found it easy to play the nice guy to Burgess's heavy, even though he felt a strong instinctive dislike for Osmond. When he questioned suspects with Sergeant Hatchley, the two of them switched roles. But Burgess only had one method of approach: head on.

'Listen to him,' Burgess said. 'He's right.'

'Why don't you find out from someone else then?' Osmond said to Banks. 'I'm damned if I'm telling you anything.'

'Do you own a flick knife?' Burgess asked.

'No.'

'Have you ever owned one?'

'No.'

'Know anybody who does?'

Osmond shook his head.

'Did you know PC Gill?' Banks asked. 'Had you any contact with him before last Friday?'

Osmond looked puzzled by the question, and when he finally answered no, it didn't ring true. Or maybe he was just thrown off balance. Burgess didn't seem to notice anything, but Banks made a mental note to check into the possibility that Osmond and Gill had somehow come into contact.

The bedroom door opened and Jenny walked out. She'd brushed her hair and put on a pair of jeans and an over-sized check shirt. Banks bet it belonged to Osmond and tried not to think about what had been going on earlier in the bedroom.

'Hello, love,' Burgess said, patting an empty chair beside him. 'Come to join us? What's your name?'

'In the first place,' Jenny said stiffly, 'I'm not "love", and in the second, I don't see as my name's any of your damn business. I wasn't even there on Friday.'

'As you like,' Burgess said. 'Just trying to be friendly.'

Jenny glanced at Banks as if to ask, 'Who is this bastard?' and Burgess caught the exchange.

'Do you two know each other?' he asked.

Banks cursed inwardly and felt himself turning red. There was no way out. 'This is Dr Fuller,' he said. 'She helped us on a case here a year or so back.'

Burgess beamed at Jenny. 'I see. Well, maybe you can help us again, Dr Fuller. Your boyfriend here doesn't want to talk to us, but if you've helped the police before—'

'Leave her alone,' Osmond said. 'She had nothing to do with it.' Banks had felt the same thing – he didn't want Burgess getting his claws into Jenny – and he resented Osmond for being able to defend her.

'Very prickly today, aren't we?' Burgess said. 'All right, sonny, we'll get back to you, if that's the way you want it.' But he kept looking at Jenny, and Banks knew he was filing her away for future use. Banks now found it hard to look her in the eye himself. He was only a chief inspector and Burgess was a superintendent. When things were going his way, Burgess wouldn't pull rank, but if Banks let any of his special feeling for Jenny show, or tried in any way to protect her, then Burgess would certainly want to humiliate him. Besides, she had her knight in shining armour in the form of Osmond. Let him take the flak.

'What were you charged with on Friday?' Burgess asked.

'You know damn well what I was charged with. It was a trumped-up charge.'

'But what was it? Tell me. Say it. Just to humour me.' Burgess reached into his pocket and took out his tin of Tom Thumbs. Holding Osmond's eyes with his own all the time, he slowly took out a cigar and lit it.

'I said I don't want you smoking in here,' Osmond protested on cue. 'It's my home and—'

'Shut up,' Burgess said, just loudly enough to stop him in his tracks. 'What was the charge?'

'Breach of the peace,' Osmond mumbled. 'But I told you, it was trumped up. If anyone broke the peace, it was the police.'

'Ever heard of a lad by the name of Paul Boyd?' Banks asked.

'No.' It was a foolish lie. Osmond had answered before he'd had time to register the question. Banks would have known he was lying even if he hadn't already learned, via Jenny, that Osmond was acquainted with the people at Maggie's Farm.

'Look,' Osmond went on, 'I'm starting an inquiry of my own into what happened on Friday. I'll be taking statements and, believe me, I'll make sure your behaviour here today goes into the final report.'

'Bully for you,' said Burgess. Then he shook his head slowly. 'You don't get it, do you, sonny? You might be able to pull those outraged-citizen tactics with the locals, but they won't wash with me. Do you know why not?'

Osmond scowled and kept silent.

'I said, do you know why not?'

'All right, no, I don't bloody well know why not!'

'Because I don't give a flying fuck for you or for others like you,' Burgess said, stabbing the air with his cigar. 'As far as I'm concerned, you're shit, and we'd all be a hell of a lot better off without you. And people I work with, they feel the same way. It doesn't matter if Chief Inspector Banks here has the hots for your Dr Fuller and wants to go easy on her. It doesn't matter that he's got a social conscience and respects people's rights, either. I don't, and my bosses don't. We don't piss around, we get things done; and you'd do well to remember that, both of you.'

Jenny was flushed and speechless with rage; Banks himself felt pale and impotent. He should have known that nothing would slip by Burgess.

'I can't tell you anything,' Osmond repeated wearily. 'Why can't you believe me? I don't know who killed that policeman. I didn't see it, I didn't do it, and I don't know who did.'

A long silence followed. At least it seemed long to Banks, who was aware only of the pounding of his heart. Finally Burgess stood up and walked over to the window, where he stubbed out his cigar on the white sill. Then he turned and smiled. Osmond gripped the tubular arms of his chair tightly.

'OK,' Burgess said, turning to Banks. 'We'll be off then, for the moment. Sorry to spoil your afternoon in bed. You can get back to it now, if you like.' He looked at Jenny and licked his lips. 'That's a fetching shirt you've got on, love,' he said to her. 'But you didn't need to leave it half unbuttoned just for me. I've got plenty of imagination.'

Back in the car, Banks was fuming. 'You were way out of line in there,' he said. 'There was no reason to insult Jenny, and there was especially no need to bring me into it the way you did. What the hell were you trying to achieve?'

'Just trying to stir them up a bit, that's all.'

'So how does making me out to be a bloody lecher stir them up?'

'You're not thinking clearly, Banks. We make Osmond jealous, maybe he lets his guard down.' Burgess grinned. 'Anyway, there's nothing in it, is there, you and her?'

'Of course there isn't.'

'Methinks this fellow doth protest too much.'

'Fuck off.'

'Oh, come on,' Burgess said calmly. 'Don't take it so seriously. You use what you need to get results. Christ, I don't blame you. I wouldn't mind tumbling her myself. Lovely pair of tits under that shirt. Did you see?'

Banks took a deep breath and reached for a cigarette. There was no point, he realized, in going on. Burgess was an unstoppable force. However angry and disorientated Banks felt, it would do no good to let more of it show. Instead, he put his emotions in check, something he knew he should have done right from the start. But the feelings still rankled as they knotted up below the surface. He was furious with Burgess, he was furious with Osmond, he was furious with Jenny, and he was furious with, most of all, himself.

Starting the car with a lurch, he shoved the cassette back in and turned up the volume. Billie Holiday sang 'God Bless the Child', and Burgess whistled blithely along as they sped through the bright blustery March day back to the market square.

THREE

They were all a bit drunk, and that was unusual at Maggie's Farm. Mara certainly hadn't been so tipsy for a long time. Rick was sketching them as they sat around the living room. Paul drank lager from the can, and even Zoe had turned giggly on white wine. But Seth was the worst. His speech was slurred, his eyes were watery, and his coordination was askew. He was also getting maudlin about the 1960s, something he never did when he was sober. Mara had seen him drunk only once before, the time he had let slip about the death of his wife. Mostly, he was well guarded and got on with life without moaning.

Things had begun well enough. After the police visit, they had all walked down to the Black Sheep for a drink. Perhaps the feeling of relief, of celebration, had encouraged them to drink more than usual, and they had splurged on a few cans of Carlsberg Special Brew, some white wine and a bottle of Scotch to take home. Most of the afternoon Seth and Mara had lounged about over the papers or dozed by the fire, while Paul messed about in the shed, Rick painted in his studio, and Zoe amused the children. Early in the evening they all got together, and the whisky and wine started making the rounds.

Seth stumbled over to the stereo and sought out a scratchy old Grateful Dead record from his collection. 'Those were the days,' he said. 'All gone now. All people care about today is money. Bloody yuppies.'

Rick looked up from his sketch pad and laughed. 'When was it ever any different?'

'Isle of Wight, Knebworth . . .' Seth went on, listing the rock festivals he'd been to. 'People really shared back then . . .'

Mara listened to him ramble. They had been under a lot of stress since the demo, she thought, and this was clearly Seth's way of getting it out of his system. It was easy to fall under the spell of nostalgia. She remembered the sixties, too – or more accurately the late sixties, when the hippie era had really got going in England. Things *had* seemed better back then. Simpler. More clear cut. There was us and them, and you knew *them* by the shortness of their hair.

'. . . Santana, Janis, Hendrix, the Doors. Jesus, even the Hare Krishnas were fun back then. Now they all wear bloody business suits and wigs. I remember one time—'

'It's all crap!' Paul shouted, banging his empty can on the floor. 'It was never like that. It's just a load of cobblers you're talking, Seth.'

'How would you know?' Seth sat up and balanced unsteadily on his elbow. 'You weren't there, were you? You were naught but a twinkle in your old man's eye.'

'My mum and dad were hippies,' Paul said scornfully. 'Fucking flower children. She OD'd, and he was too bloody stoned to take care of me, so he gave me away.'

Mara was stunned. Paul had never spoken about his true parents before, only about the way he had been badly treated in his foster home. If it was true, she thought, did he really see Seth and her in the same light? They were about the right age. Did he hate them too?

But she couldn't believe that. There was another side to the coin. Maybe Paul was looking for what he had lost, and he had found at least some of it at Maggie's Farm. They didn't take drugs and, while she and Seth might have grown up in the 1960s and tried to cling on to some of its ideals, they neither looked nor acted like hippies any longer.

'We're not like that,' she protested, looking over at Zoe for support. 'You know it, Paul. We care about you. We'd never desert you. It was fun back then for a lot of people. Seth's only reminiscing about his youth.'

'I know,' Paul said grudgingly. 'I can't say I had one worth reminiscing about, myself. Anyway, I'm only saying, Mara, that's all. It wasn't all peace and love like Seth tells it. He's full of shit.'

'You're right about that, mate,' Rick agreed, putting down his sketch pad and pouring another shot of Scotch. 'I never did have much time for hippies myself. Nothing but a moaning, whining bunch of little kids, if you ask me. Seth's just pissed, that's all. Look at him, anyway – he's a bloody landowner, a landlord even. Pretty soon it'll be baggy tweeds and out shooting pheasant every afternoon. Sir Seth Cotton, squire of Maggie's Farm.'

But Seth had slumped back against a beanbag and seemed to have lost all interest in the conversation. His eyes were closed, and Mara guessed that he was either asleep or absorbed in the soaring Jerry Garcia guitar solo.

'Where's your father now?' Mara asked Paul.

'I don't fucking know. Don't fucking care, either.' Paul ripped open another can of lager.

'But didn't he ever get in touch?'

'Why should he? I told you, he was too zonked out to notice me even when I was there.'

'It's still no reason to say everyone was like that,' Mara said. 'All Seth was saying was that the spirit of love was strong back then. All that talk about the Age of Aquarius meant something.'

'Yeah, and what's happened to it now? Two thousand years of this crap I can do without, thanks very much. Let's just forget the fucking past and get on with life.' With that, Paul got up and left the room.

Jerry Garcia played on. Seth stirred, opened one blood-shot eye, then closed it again.

Mara poured herself and Zoe some more white wine, then her mind wandered back to Paul. As if she weren't confused enough already, the hostility he'd shown tonight and the new information about his feelings for his parents muddied the waters even more. She was scared of approaching him about the blood on his hand, and she was beginning to feel frightened to go on living in the same house as someone she suspected of murder. But she hated herself for feeling that way about him, for not being able to trust him completely and believe in him.

What she needed was somebody to talk to, somebody she could trust from outside the house. She felt like a woman with a breast lump who was afraid to go to the doctor and find out if it really was cancer.

And what made it worse was that she'd noticed the knife was missing: the flick knife Seth said he had bought in France years ago. Everybody else must have noticed, too, but no one had mentioned it. The knife had been lying on the mantelpiece for anyone to use ever since she'd been at Maggie's Farm, and now it was gone.

FOUR

Banks ate the fish and chips he had bought on the way home, then went into the living room. Screw gourmet cooking, he thought. If that irritating neighbour, Selena Harcourt, didn't turn up with some sticky dessert to feed him up 'while the little woman's away', he'd have the evening to relax instead of mixing up sauces that never turned out anyway.

He had calmed down soon after leaving Burgess at the station. The bastard had been right. What had happened at Osmond's, he realized, had not been particularly serious, but his shock at finding Jenny there had made him exaggerate things. His reaction had been extreme, and for a few moments, he'd lost his detachment. That was all. It had happened before and it would happen again. Not the end of the world.

He poured a drink, put his feet up and turned on the television. There was a special about the Peak District on Yorkshire TV. Half watching, he flipped through Tracy's latest copy of *History Today* and read an interesting article on Sir Titus Salt, who had built a utopian community called Saltaire, near Bradford, for the workers in his textile mills. It would be a good place to visit with Sandra and the kids, he thought. Sandra could take photographs; Tracy would be fascinated; and surely even Brian would find something of interest. The problem was that Sir Titus had been a firm teetotaller. There were no pubs in Saltaire. Obviously one man's utopia is another man's hell.

The article made him think of Maggie's Farm. He liked the place and respected Seth and Mara. They had shown antagonism towards him, but that was only to be expected. In his job, he was used to much worse. He didn't take it personally. Being a policeman was like being a vicar in some ways; people could never be really comfortable with you even when you dropped into the local for a pint.

The TV programme finished, and he decided there was no point putting off the inevitable. Picking up the phone, he dialled Jenny's number. He was in luck; she answered on the third ring.

'Jenny? It's Alan.'

There was a pause at the other end. 'I'm not sure I want to talk to you,' she said finally.

'Could you be persuaded to?'

'Try.'

'I just wanted to apologize for this afternoon. I hadn't expected to see you there.'

Only the slight crackle of the line filled the silence. 'It surprised me, too,' Jenny said. 'You keep some pretty bad company.'

I could say the same for you, too, Banks thought. 'Yes,' he said. 'I know.'

'I do think you should keep him on a leash in future. You could maybe try a muzzle as well.' She was obviously warming to him again; he could tell.

'Love to. But he's the boss. How did Osmond take it?' The name almost stuck in his throat.

'He was pissed off, all right. But it didn't last. Dennis is resilient. He's used to police harassment.'

There was silence again, more awkward this time.

'Well,' Banks said, 'I just wanted to say I was sorry.'

'Yes. You've said that already. It wasn't your fault. I'm not used to seeing you in a supporting role. You're not at your best like that, you know.'

'What did you expect me to do? Jump up and hit him?'

'No, I didn't mean anything like that. But when he said what he did about us I could see you were ready to.'

'Was it so obvious?'

'It was to me.'

'I blew up at him in the car.'

'I thought you would. What did he say?'

'Just laughed it off.'

'Charming. I could have killed him when he said that about my shirt being undone.'

'It was though.'

'I dressed in a hurry. I wanted to know what was going on.'

'I know. I'm not trying to make out you did it on purpose or anything. It's just that, well, with a bloke like him around you've got to be extra careful.'

'Now I know. Though I hope I won't have the pleasure again.'

'He doesn't give up easily,' Banks said gloomily.

'Nor do I. Where are you? What are you doing?'

'At home. Relaxing.'

'Me too. Is Sandra back?'

'No.' The silence crackled again. Banks cleared his throat. 'Look,' he said, 'when I mentioned dinner the other day, before all this, I meant it. How about tomorrow?'

'Can't tomorrow. I've got an evening class to teach.'

'Tuesday?'

Jenny paused. 'I suppose I can break my date,' she said. 'It had better be worth it though.'

'The Royal Oak is always worth it. My treat. I need to talk to you.'

'Business?'

'I'm hoping you can help me get a handle on some of those Maggie's Farm people. Seth and Mara are about my age. It's funny how we all grew up in the sixties and turned out so different.'

'Not really. Everybody's different.'

'I liked the music. I just never felt I fitted in with the long-haired crowd. Mind you, I did try pot once or twice.'

'Alan! You didn't?'

'I did.'

'And here's me thinking you're so strait-laced. What happened?'

'Nothing, the first time.'

'And the second?'

'I fell asleep.'

Jenny laughed.

'Still,' Banks mused, 'Burgess is about my age, too.'

'He was probably sitting around in jackboots and a leather overcoat pulling the wings off flies.'

'Probably. Anyway, dinner. Eight o'clock all right?'

'Fine.'

'I'll pick you up.'

Jenny said goodnight and hung up. Still friends. Banks breathed a sigh of relief.

He went back to his armchair and his drink, but he suddenly felt the need to call Sandra.

'How's your father?' he asked.

Sandra laughed. 'Cantankerous as ever. But Mother's coping better than I'd hoped.' The line was poor and her voice sounded far away.

'How much longer will you be down there?'

'A few more days should do it. Why? Are you missing us?'

'More than you know.'

'Hang on a minute. We had a day in London yesterday and Tracy wants to tell you about it.'

Banks talked to his daughter for a while about St Paul's and the Tower of London, then Brian cut in and told him how great the record shops were down there. There was exactly the guitar he'd been looking for . . . Finally, Sandra came back on again.

'Anything happening up there?'

'You could say that.' Banks told her about the demo and the killing.

Sandra whistled. 'I'm glad I'm out of it. I can imagine how frantic things are.'

'Thanks for the support.'

'You know what I mean.'

'Remember Dick Burgess? Used to be a chief inspector at the Yard?'

'Was he the one who pawed the hostess and threw up in the geraniums at Lottie's party?'

'That's the one. He's up here, in charge.'

'God help you. Now I'm really glad I'm down here. He had his eyes on me too, you know, if not his hands.'

'I'd like to say it was good taste, but don't flatter yourself, love. He's like that with everyone in a skirt.'

Sandra laughed. 'Better go now. Brian and Tracy are at it again.'

'Give them my love. Take care. See you soon.'

After he'd hung up, Banks felt so depressed that he almost regretted phoning in the first place. Why, he wondered, does a phone call to a distant loved one only intensify the emptiness and loneliness you were feeling before you called?

At a loose end, he turned off the television in the middle of a pop music special that Brian would have loved and put on the blues tape an old colleague had sent him from London. The Reverend Robert Wilkins sang 'Prodigal Son' in his eerie voice, unusually thin and high-pitched for a bluesman. Banks slouched in the armchair by the gas fire and sipped his drink. He often did his best thinking while drinking Scotch and listening to music, and it was time to put some of his thoughts about Gill's murder in order.

A number of things bothered him. There were demonstrations all the time, much bigger than the one in Eastvale, and while opposing sides sometimes came to blows, policemen didn't usually get stabbed. Call it statistics, probability or just a hunch, but he didn't believe in Burgess's view of the affair.

And that was a problem, because it didn't leave much else to choose from. He still had uneasy feelings about some of the Maggie's Farm crowd. Paul Boyd was as dangerous character if ever he'd met one, and Mara had seemed extremely keen to come to his defence. Seth and Zoe had been especially quiet, but Rick Trelawney had expressed more violent views than Banks had expected. He didn't know what it added up to, but he felt that somebody knew something, or thought they did, and didn't want to communicate their suspicions to the police. It was a stupid way to behave, but people did it all the time. Banks just hoped that none of them got hurt.

As for Dennis Osmond, putting personal antipathy aside, Banks had caught him on two lies. Osmond had said he didn't know Paul Boyd when he clearly did, and Banks had also suspected him of lying when he denied knowing PC Gill. It was easy enough to see why he might have lied: nobody wants to admit a connection with a murdered man or a convicted criminal if he doesn't have to. But Banks had to determine if there was anything more sinister to it than that. How could Osmond have known PC Gill? Maybe they'd been to school together. Or perhaps Gill had had occasion to arrest Osmond at some previous anti-nuclear protest. If so, it should be on the files. Richmond would have the gen from Special Branch in the morning.

Nothing so far seemed much like a motive for murder though. If he was really cautious, he might be able to get something out of Jenny on Tuesday. She didn't usually resent his trying to question her, but she was bound to be especially sensitive where Osmond was concerned.

Perhaps he had reacted unprofessionally on finding

Jenny in Osmond's bedroom and to Burgess's approach to interrogation. But, he reminded himself, Dirty Dick had made him look a proper wally, and what was more he had insulted Jenny. Sometimes Banks thought that Burgess's technique was to badger everyone involved in a case until someone was driven to try to throttle him. At least then he could lay a charge of attempted murder.

Halfway through his third Laphroaig and the second side of the tape, Banks decided that there was only one way to get back at the bastard, and that was to solve the case himself, in his own way. Burgess wasn't the only one who could play his cards close to his chest. Let him concentrate on the reds under the bed. Banks would do a bit of discreet digging and see if he could come up with anyone who had a motive for wanting PC Edwin Gill, and not just any copper, dead.

But if Gill the person rather than Gill the policeman was the victim, it raised a number of problems. For a start, how could the killer know that Gill was going to be at the demo? Also, how could he be sure that things would turn violent enough to mask a kill? Most puzzling of all was how could he have been certain of an escape? But at least these were concrete questions, a starting point. The more Banks thought about it, the more the thick of a political demonstration seemed the ideal cover for murder.

5

ONE

The funeral procession wound its way from Gordon Street, where Edwin Gill had lived, along Manor Road to the cemetery. Somehow, Banks thought, the funeral of a fellow officer was always more solemn and grim than any other. Every policeman there knew it could just as easily have been him in the coffin; every copper's wife lived with the fear that her husband, too, might end up stabbed, beaten or, these days shot; and the public at large felt the tremor and momentary weakness in the order of things.

For the second time in less than a week, Banks found himself uncomfortable in a suit and tie. He listened to the vicar's eulogy, the obligatory verses from the *Book of Common Prayer*, and stared at the bristly necks in front of him. At the front, Gill's immediate family – mother, two sisters, uncles and aunts, nephews and nieces – snuffled and slipped each other wads of Kleenex.

When it was over, everyone filed out and waited for the cars to take them to the funeral lunch. The oaks and beeches lining the cemetery drive shook in the brisk wind. One moment the sun popped out from behind the clouds, and the next a five-minute shower took everyone by surprise. It was that kind of day: chameleon, unpredictable.

Banks stood with DC Richmond by the unmarked black police Rover – his own white Cortina was hardly the thing for a funeral – and waited for someone to lead the way. He wore a light grey raincoat over his navy blue suit, but his head was bare. With his close-cropped black hair, scar beside the right eye and lean angular features, he thought he must look a suspicious figure as he held his raincoat collar tight around his throat to keep out the cold wind. Richmond, rangy and athletic, wearing a camel hair overcoat and trilby, stood beside him.

It was early Tuesday afternoon. Banks had spent the morning reading over the records Richmond had managed to gather on Osmond and the Maggie's Farm crowd. There wasn't much. Seth Cotton had once been arrested for carrying an offensive weapon (a bicycle chain) at a mods and rockers debacle in Brighton in the early 1960s. After that, he had one marijuana bust to his credit – only a quid deal, nothing serious – for which he had been fined.

Rick Trelawney had been in trouble only once, in St Ives, Cornwall. A tourist had taken exception to his drunken pronouncements on the perfidy of collecting art, and a rowdy argument turned into a punch-up. It had taken three men to drag Rick off, and the tourist had ended up with a broken jaw and one permanently deaf ear.

The only other skeleton in Rick's cupboard was the wife from whom he had recently separated. She was an alcoholic, which made it easy enough for Rick to get custody of Julian. But she was now staying with her sister in London while undergoing treatment, and there was a legal battle brewing. Things had got so bad at one point that Rick had applied for a court order to prevent her from coming near their son.

There was nothing on Zoe, but Richmond had checked the birth registry and discovered that the father of her child, Luna, was one Lyle Greenberg, an American student who had since returned to his home in Eau Claire, Wisconsin.

On Mara there was even less. Immigration identified her as Moira Delacey, originally from Dublin. With her parents, she had come to England at the age of six, and they had settled in Manchester. No known Republican connections.

Most interesting and disturbing of all was Dennis Osmond's criminal record. In addition to arrests for his part in anti-government demonstrations – with charges ranging from breach of the peace to theft of a police officer's helmet – he had also been accused of assault by a live-in girlfriend called Ellen Ventner four years ago. At the woman's insistence, the charges had later been dropped, but Ventner's injuries – two broken ribs, a broken nose, three teeth knocked out and concussion – had been clearly documented by the hospital, and Osmond came out of the affair looking far from clean. Banks wasn't sure whether to bring up the subject when he met Jenny for dinner that evening. He wondered if she already knew. If she didn't she might not take kindly to his interference. Somehow, he doubted that Osmond had told her.

They were still waiting for the information from Special Branch, who had files on Osmond, Tim Fenton, the student leader, and five others known to have been at the demo. Apparently, the Branch needed Burgess's personal access code, password, voice-print and genetic fingerprint, or some equally ludicrous sequence of identification. Banks didn't expect much from them, anyway. In his own experience, Special Branch kept files on everyone who had ever brought a copy of *Socialist Weekly*.

Today, while Banks and Richmond were attending Gill's funeral, Burgess was taking Sergeant Hatchley to do the rounds again. They intended to revisit Osmond,

Dorothy Wycombe, Tim Fenton and Maggie's Farm. Banks wanted to talk to the students himself, so he decided to call on them when he got back that evening – if Burgess hadn't alienated them beyond all communication by then.

Burgess had been practically salivating at the prospect of more interrogations, and even Hatchley had seemed more excited about work than usual. Perhaps it was the chance to work with a superstar that thrilled him, Banks thought. The sergeant had always found *The Sweeney* much more interesting than the real thing. Or maybe he was going to suck up to Dirty Dick in the hope of being chosen for some special Scotland Yard squad. And the devil of it was, perhaps he would be, too.

Banks had mixed feelings about that possibility. He had got used to Sergeant Hatchley sooner than he'd expected to, and they had worked quite well together. But Banks had no real feeling for him. He couldn't even bring himself to call Hatchley by his first name, Jim.

In Banks's mind, Hatchley was a sergeant and always would be. He didn't have that extra edge needed to make inspector. Phil Richmond did, but unfortunately there wasn't anywhere for him to move up to locally unless Hatchley was promoted too. Superintendent Gristhorpe wouldn't have that, and Banks didn't blame him. If Burgess liked Hatchley enough to suggest a job in London, that would solve all their problems. Richmond had already passed his sergeant's exam – the first stage on the long road to promotion – and perhaps PC Susan Gay, who had shown remarkable aptitude for detective work, could be transferred in from the uniformed branch as a new detective constable. PC Craig would be opposed, of course. He still called policewomen 'wopsies', even though the gender-specific designation, WPC, had been dropped in favour of the neutral PC as far back as 1975. But that was Craig's problem; Hatchley was everyone's cross to bear.

Finally, the glossy black cars set off. Banks and Richmond followed them through the dull deserted streets of Scarborough to the reception. There was nowhere quite as gloomy as a coastal resort in the off-season. If it hadn't been for the vague whiff of sea and fish in the air, nobody would have guessed they were at the seaside.

'Fancy a walk on the prom after lunch?' Banks asked.

Richmond sniffed. 'Hardly the weather for that, is it?'

'Bracing, I'd say.'

'Maybe I'll wait for you in a nice cosy pub, if you don't mind, sir.'

Banks smiled. 'And put your notes in order?' He knew how fussy Richmond was about notes and reports.

'I'll have to, won't I? It'll not stick in my memory that long.'

On the way to Scarborough, Banks had put forward his theory about Gill's murder not being quite what it seemed. While Richmond had expressed reservations, he had agreed that it was at least worth pursuing. They had decided to chat up Gill's colleagues at the reception and see what they could pick up about the man. Burgess, of course, was to know nothing about this.

Richmond had argued that even if there was something odd about Gill, none of his mates would say so at his funeral. Banks disagreed. He thought funerals worked wonders on the conscience. The phony platitudes often stuck in people's craws and made them want to tell someone the truth. After all, it wasn't as if they were trying to prove corruption or anything like that against Gill; they just wanted to know what kind of man he was and whether he might have made enemies.

The procession pulled into the car park of the Crown
and Anchor, where a buffet had been arranged in the
banquet room, and the guests hurried through a heavy
shower to the front doors.

TWO

'Bloody hell! What stone did you crawl out from under?'
Burgess said when Paul Boyd walked into the front room
to see what was going on.

Paul scowled. 'Piss off.'

Burgess strode forward and clipped him around the
ear. Paul flinched and stumbled back. 'Less of your cheek,
sonny,' Burgess said. 'Show a bit of respect for your elders
and betters.'

'Why should I? You didn't show any fucking respect for
me, did you?'

'Respect? For you?' Burgess narrowed his eyes. 'What
makes you think you deserve any respect? You're an ugly
little pillock with a record as long as my arm. And that
includes assaulting a police officer. And while we're at it,
mind your tongue. There's ladies present. At least, I think
there are.'

Mara felt cold as Burgess ran his eyes up and down her
body.

Burgess turned back to Paul, who stood in the doorway
holding his hand to his ear. 'Come on, who put you up to
it?'

'Up to what?'

'Killing a police officer.'

'I never. I wasn't even there.'

'It's true, he wasn't,' Mara burst out. 'He was here with

me all evening. Somebody had to stay at home and look after the children.'

She had held her tongue so far, trying to figure Burgess out. He didn't seem as mild-mannered as Banks, and she was afraid of attracting his attention. Even as she spoke, her stomach muscles tensed.

Burgess looked at her again and shook his head. His eyes were as sharp as chipped slate. 'Very touching, love. Very touching. Didn't your mother and father teach you not to tell lies? He was spotted in the crowd. We know he was there.'

'You must have been mistaken.'

Burgess glanced at Paul, then looked at Mara again. 'Mistaken! How could anyone mistake this piece of garbage for someone else? You need your mouth washing out with soap and water, you do, love.'

'And don't call me love.'

Burgess threw up his arms in mock despair. 'What's wrong with you lot? I thought everyone called each other love up north. Anyway, I can't for the life of me see why you're defending him. He's got a limited vocabulary and, with a body like that, I doubt if he's much good in bed.'

'Bastard,' Mara said between clenched teeth. There was going to be no reasoning with this one, that was certain. Best just stick it out.

'That's right, love,' Burgess said. 'Get it off your chest. You'll feel all the better for it.' He eyed her chest, as if to prove his point, and turned to Paul again. 'What did you do with the knife?'

'What knife?'

'The one you used to stab PC Gill. The flick knife. Just your kind of weapon, I'd say.'

'I didn't stab anyone.'

'Oh, come on! What did you do with it?'

'I didn't have no fucking knife.'

Burgess wagged a finger at him. 'I warned you, watch your tongue. Are you getting all this, Sergeant Hatchley? The kid's denying everything.'

'Yes, sir.' Hatchley was sitting on the beanbag cushions, looking, Mara thought, rather like a beached whale.

'All we need is the knife,' Burgess said. 'Once we trace it back to you, you'll be in the nick before your feet can touch the ground. With your record, you won't have a chance. We've already placed you at the scene.'

'There were about a hundred other people there, too,' Paul said.

'Count them, did you? I thought you said you weren't there.'

'I wasn't.'

'Then how did you know?'

'Read it in the papers.'

'Read? You? I doubt you'd get past the comics.'

'Very funny,' Paul said. 'But you can't prove nothing.'

'You might just be right about that,' Burgess said. 'But remember, if I can't prove nothing, it means I *can* prove something. And when I do . . . when I do . . .' He left the threat hanging and turned to the room at large. They were all gathered in the house except Rick, who had taken the children to town for new clothes. 'The rest of you are just as guilty,' he went on. 'When we build a case against dickhead here, you'll all get done for withholding information and for being accessories. So if any of you know anything, you'd best tell us now. Think about it.'

'We don't know anything,' Seth said quietly.

'Well, there we are then.' Burgess sighed and ran his free hand through his hair. 'Stalemate.'

'And don't think we won't complain about the way you've treated us and how you hit Paul,' Mara said.

'Do it, love. See if I care. Want me to tell you what'll happen? If you're lucky, it'll get passed down the line back to my boss at the Yard. And do you know what? He's an even bigger bastard than I am. No, your best bet's to come clean, tell the truth.'

'I told you,' Paul said. 'I don't know anything about it.'

'All right.' Burgess dropped his cigar stub into a teacup balanced on the arm of a chair. The hot ash sizzled as it hit the dregs. 'But don't say I didn't warn you. Come on, Sergeant. We'll leave these people to think about it a bit more. Maybe one of them'll come to his senses and get in touch with us.'

Hatchley struggled to his feet and joined Burgess by the door. 'We'll be back, don't worry,' Burgess said. As they walked out of the small porch, he reached up, slapped the wind chimes and snarled, 'Bloody tuneless racket.'

THREE

Banks waited, glass of sherry in hand, until the crowd around the buffet had dwindled before he collected his own paper plateful of cold meat and salad.

'Ee, it's a bit of all right this, i'n't it,' a grey-haired woman in a powder-blue crêpe dress was saying to her friend.

'Aye,' the other said. 'Better'n old Ida Latham's do. Nobbut them little sarnies wi' t'crusts cuts off. No bigger'n a postage stamp they weren't. Cucumber, too. It allus gives me gas, cucumber does.'

'Chief Inspector Banks?'

The man who suddenly materialized beside Banks was about six foot two with a shiny bald head, fuzzy white hair above the ears and a grey RAF moustache. He wore a black armband over his dark grey suit and a black tie. Even the rims of his glasses were black. Banks nodded.

'Thought it must be you,' the man went on. 'You don't look like a relation, and I've never see you around here before. Superintendent Gristhorpe sent word you were coming.' He stretched out his hand. 'Detective Chief Inspector Blake, Scarborough CID.' Banks managed to balance his sherry glass on his plate and shake hands.

'Pleased to meet you,' he said. 'Shame it has to be at something like this.'

They walked over to a quieter and less crowded part of the hall. Banks put down his plate on a table – after all, he couldn't eat while talking – and took out a cigarette.

'How's the investigation going?' Blake asked.

'Nothing yet. Too many suspects. Anything could have happened in a situation like that.' He looked around the hall. 'Lot of people here. PC Gill must have been a popular bloke.

'Hmmm. Didn't know him well, myself. It's a big station.'

'Keen though,' Banks said. 'Volunteering for overtime on a Friday night. Most of our lads would've rather been at the pub.'

'It's more likely he needed the money. You know how half the bloody country lives on overtime. Has to, the wages we get paid.'

'True. Fond of money, was he?'

Chief Inspector Blake frowned. 'Are you digging?'

'We don't know anything about Gill,' Banks admitted.

'He wasn't one of ours. Every little bit helps. I'm sure you know that.'

'Yes. But this is hardly a normal case, is it?'

'Still . . .'

'As I said, I didn't really know him. I hear you've got a whizz-kid from the Yard in charge.'

Banks stubbed out his cigarette and picked up his plate. He knew he wasn't going to get anything out of Blake, so he ate his lunch while exchanging small talk. From the corner of his eye, he noticed Richmond talking to one of the uniformed pallbearers, probably one of the locals who had been bussed in with Gill to the demo. They had all given statements, of course, but none had seen Gill get stabbed. He hoped that Richmond was doing better than he was.

Chief Inspector Blake drifted away after about five minutes, and Banks took the opportunity to refill his sherry glass. At the bar, he found himself standing next to another pallbearer.

Banks introduced himself. 'Sad occasion,' he said.

'Aye,' PC Childers replied. He was young, perhaps in his early twenties. Banks felt irritated by his habit of looking in another direction while speaking.

'Popular bloke, PC Gill, by the look of it,' Banks said.

'Oh, aye. A right card, old Eddie was.'

'That right? Keen on his work?'

'You could say that. Certain parts of it, anyway.'

'I'll bet the overtime came in handy.'

'It's always good to have a bit extra,' Childers said slowly. Banks could tell he was holding back; whether out of friendship, a sense of occasion or out of simply duty, he couldn't be sure. But something was wrong. Childers was getting edgier, staring at the far wall. Finally, he excused himself abruptly and went to talk to his sergeant.

Banks was beginning to feel his mission had been wasted. He was also aware that very soon he would become an unwelcome guest if Childers and Blake mentioned his probings to others. Christ, he thought, they were a bloody sensitive lot here. It made him wonder if they'd got something to hide.

Back at the table for a helping of trifle, Banks manoeuvred himself next to a third pallbearer, a moon-faced lad with bright blue eyes and fine thinning hair the colour of wheat. Taking a deep breath, he smiled and introduced himself.

'I know who you are, sir,' the PC said. 'Ernie Childers told me. I'm PC Grant, Tony Grant. Ernie warned me. Said you were asking questions about Eddie Gill.'

'Just routine,' Banks said. 'Like we do in all murder investigations.'

Grant glanced over his shoulder. 'Look, sir,' he said, 'I can't talk to you here.'

'Where then?' Banks felt his heart speed up.

'Do you know the Angel's Trumpet?'

Banks shook his head. 'Don't know the place well. Only been here once before.'

'It'll take too long to explain,' Grant said. They finished helping themselves to dessert and turned around just in time to spot one of Grant's colleagues walking towards them.

'Marine Drive then, just round from the funfair,' Banks said quickly out of the corner of his mouth. It was the only place he could think of offhand. 'About an hour.'

'Fine,' Grant said as a uniformed sergeant joined them.

'Good of you to come, Chief Inspector,' the sergeant

said, holding out his hand. 'We appreciate it.'

Grant had merged back into the crowd, and as Banks exchanged trivialities with the sergeant, his mind was on the meeting ahead and the nervous covert way in which it had been arranged.

FOUR

'He made me feel dirty,' Mara said to Seth. 'The way he looked at me.'

'Don't let it get to you. That's just his technique. He's trying to goad you into saying something you'll regret.'

'But what about Paul? You saw the way he was picking on him. What can we do?'

Paul had taken off as soon as Burgess and Hatchley left. He had said he was feeling claustrophobic and needed a walk on the moors to calm down after the onslaught. He hadn't objected to Zoe's company, so Seth and Mara were left alone.

'What is there to do?' Seth said.

'But you saw the way that bastard went at him. I wouldn't put it past him to frame Paul if it came down to it. He *has* got a record.'

'They'd still need evidence.'

'He could plant it.'

'He couldn't just plant any old knife. It'd have to be the one that fitted the wound. They have scientists working for them. You can't put things across on that lot so easily, you know.'

'I suppose not.' Mara bit her lip and decided to take the plunge. 'Seth? Have you noticed that the knife's missing? That old flick knife from the mantelpiece.'

Seth looked at her in silence for a while. His brown eyes were sad, and the bags under them indicated lack of sleep. 'Yes,' he said, 'I have. But I didn't say anything. I didn't want to cause any alarm. It'll probably turn up.'

'But what if . . . what if that was the knife?'

'Oh come on, Mara. Surely you can't believe that. There are plenty of flick knives in the country. Why should it be that one? Somebody's probably borrowed it. It'll turn up.'

'Yes. But what if? I mean Paul could have taken it, couldn't he?'

Seth drummed his fingers on the chair arm. 'You know how many people were around on Friday afternoon,' he said. 'Any one of them could have taken it. When did you last notice it, for example?'

'I don't remember.'

'See? And it still doesn't mean it was the knife that was used. Someone might just have borrowed it and forgot to say anything.'

'I suppose so.' But Mara wasn't convinced. It seemed too much of a coincidence that a flick knife had been used to kill the policeman and the flick knife from the mantelpiece was missing. She thought Seth was grasping for straws in trying to explain it away as he was, but she wanted to believe him.

'There you are then,' he said. 'Why assume it's Paul just because he has a violent past? He's changed. You're thinking like the police.'

Mara wanted to, but she couldn't bring herself to tell Seth about the blood. Somehow, along with everything else, that information seemed so final, so damning.

She had decided to get in touch with that friend of Dennis Osmond's, Jenny. Mara liked her, though she wasn't too sure about Osmond himself. And Jenny was a professional psychologist. Mara could put her a theoretical case, using Paul's background, and ask if such a person was likely to be dangerous. She could say it was a part of some research she was doing for a story or something. Jenny would believe her.

'Maybe he should go away,' Seth said after a while.

'Paul? But why?'

'It might be best for him. For all of us. Till it's over. You can see how all this is getting to him.'

'It's getting to all of us,' Mara said. 'You, too.'

'Yes, but—'

'Where would he go? You know he hasn't got anybody else to turn to.' Despite her fears, Mara couldn't help but want to protect Paul. She didn't understand her feelings, but as much as she suspected him, she couldn't just give up and send him away.

Seth stared at the floor.

'It could look bad, too,' Mara argued. 'The police would think he was running away because he was guilty.'

'Let him stay, then. Just make up your mind.'

'Don't you care about him?'

'Of course I care about him. That's why I suggested he get away. Come on, Mara, which way do you want it? If I suggest he goes, I'm being cruel, and if he stays he might have to put up with a hell of a lot more from that fascist bastard we had round this afternoon. What do you want? Do you think he can take it? Look how he reacted to today's little chat. That was a picnic compared to what'll happen if they decide to take him in for questioning. And we can't protect him. Well? How much do you think he can take?'

'I don't know.' Things had suddenly got even more complicated for Mara. 'I want what's best for Paul.'

'Let's ask him, then. We can't make his decisions for him.'

'No! We've got to stand by him. If we approach him, he might think we believe he's guilty and want him out of the way.'

'But we'd have to approach him to ask if he'd like to go away for a while, until things settle down.'

'So we do nothing. If he wants to stay, he stays, and we stand by him, whatever. If he goes, then it's his decision. We don't force him out. He's not stupid, Seth. I'm sure he knows he's in for a lot of police harassment. The last thing he needs is to feel that we're against him, too.'

'OK.' Seth nodded and stood up. 'We'll leave it at that, I've got to go and do some work on that old sideboard now. I'm already late. You all right?'

Mara looked up at him and smiled. 'I'll manage.'

'Good.' He bent and kissed her, then went out to his workshop.

But Mara wasn't all right. Left to herself, she began to imagine all kinds of terrible things. The world of Maggie's Farm had seemed at first to offer the stability, love and freedom she had always been searching for, but now it had broken adrift. The feeling was like that she remembered having during a mild earthquake in California, when she'd travelled around the States with Matthew, aeons ago. Suddenly, the floor of the room, the house's foundations, the solid earth on which they were built, had seemed no more stable than water. A ripple had passed fleetingly under her, and what she had always thought durable turned out to be flimsy, untrustworthy and transient. The quake had only lasted for ten seconds and hadn't registered above five on the Richter scale, but the impression had remained with her ever since. Now it was coming back stronger than ever.

On the mantelpiece, among the clutter of seashells, pebbles, fossils and feathers, she could see the faint outline of dust around where the knife had been. As she wiped the surface clean, she thanked her lucky stars that the police had been looking for material things, not absences.

FIVE

Banks drove along Foreshore Road and Sandside by the Old Harbour. The amusement arcades and gift shops were all closed. In season, crowds of holidaymakers always gathered around the racks of cheeky postcards, teenagers queued for the ghost train, and children dragged their parents to the booths that sold candyfloss and Scarborough rock. But now the prom was deserted. Even on the seaward side, there were no stalls selling cockles, winkles and boiled shrimp. A thick high cloud cover had set in, and the sea sloshed at the barnacle-crusted harbour walls like molten metal. Fishing boats rocked at their moorings, and stacks of lobster pots teetered on the quayside. Towering over the scene, high on its promontory, the ruined castle looked like something out of a black and white horror film.

Banks dropped Richmond off at a pub near the West Pier and carried on along Marine Drive, parking just beyond the closed funfair. He buttoned up his raincoat tight and walked along the road that curved around the headland between the high cliff and the sea. Signs on the hillside warned of falling rocks. Waves hit the sea wall and threw up spray onto the road.

Tony Grant was already there, leaning on the railing

and staring out to the point where sea and sky merged in a uniform grey. He wore a navy duffel coat with the hood down, and his baby-fine hair fluttered in the wind. A solitary oil tanker was moving slowly across the horizon.

'I like it best like this,' he said as Banks joined him. 'If you don't mind getting a bit wet.'

They both looked out over the ruffled water. Salt spray filled the air and Banks felt the ozone freshen his lungs as he breathed deep. He shivered and asked, 'What is it you want to tell me?'

Grant hesitated. 'Look, sir,' he said after staring at the oil tanker for half a minute, 'I don't want you to get me wrong. I'm not a grass or anything. I've not been long on the force, and mostly I like it. I didn't think I would, not at first, but I do now. I want to make a career out of it.' He looked at Banks intensely. 'I'd like to join the CID. I'm not stupid; I've got brains. I've been to university, and I could maybe have got into teaching – that's what I thought I wanted to do – but, well, you know the job situation. Seems all that's going these days is the police force. So I joined. Anyway, as I said, I like it. It's challenging.'

Banks took out a cigarette and cupped his hand around his blue Bic lighter. It took him four attempts to get a flame going long enough. He wished Grant would get to the point, but he knew he had to be patient and listen. The kid was about to go against his peers and squeal on a colleague. Listening to the justification, as he had listened to so many before, was the price Banks had to pay.

'It's just that,' Grant went on, 'well . . . it's not as clean as I expected.'

Naive bugger, Banks thought. 'It's like anything else,' he said, encouraging the lad. 'There's a lot of bastards out there, whatever you do. Maybe our line of work attracts more than the usual quota of bullies, lazy sods, sadists and the like. But that doesn't mean we're all like that.' Banks sucked on his cigarette. It tasted different, mixed with the sea air. A wave broke below them and the spray wet their feet.

'I know what you're saying,' Grant said, 'and I think you're right. I just wanted you to know what side I'm on. I don't believe that the end justifies the means. With me they're innocent until proven guilty, as the saying goes. I treat people with respect, no matter what colour they are or how they dress or wear their hair. I'm not saying I approve of some of the types we get, but I'm not a thug.'

'And Gill was?'

'Yes.' A big wave started to peak as it approached the wall, and they both stepped back quickly to avoid the spray. Even so, they couldn't dodge a mild soaking, and Banks's cigarette got soggy. He threw it away.

'Was this common knowledge?'

'Oh, aye. He made no bones about it. See, with Gill it wasn't just the overtime, the money. He liked it well enough, but he liked the job more, if you see what I mean.'

'I think I do. Go on.'

'He was handy with his truncheon, Gill was. And he enjoyed it. Every time we got requests for manpower at demos, pickets and the like, he'd be first to sign up. Got a real taste for it during the miners' strike, when they bussed police in from all over the place. He was the kind of bloke who'd wave a roll of fivers at the striking miners to taunt them before he clobbered them. He trained with the Tactical Aid Group.'

The TAG, Banks knew, was a kind of force within a force. Its members trained together in a military fashion and learned how to use guns, rubber bullets and tear gas.

When their training was over, they went back to normal duties and remained on call for special situations like demos and picket lines. The official term for them had been changed to PSU – Police Support Unit – as the TAGs got a lot of bad publicity and sounded too obviously martial. But it was about as effective as changing the name of Windscale to Sellafield; a nuclear power station by another name . . .

'Is that how he behaved in Eastvale?' Banks asked.

'I wouldn't swear to it, but I'm pretty sure it was Gill who led the charge. See, things were getting a bit hairy. We were all hemmed in so tight. Gill was at the top of the steps with a few others, just looking down at people pushing and shoving – not that you could see much, it was so bloody dark with those old-fashioned street lamps. Anyway, one of the demonstrators chucked a bottle, and someone up there, behind me, yelled, "Let's clobber the bastards." I think I recognized Gill's voice. Then they charged down and . . . well, you know what happened. It needn't have – that's what I'm saying. Sure, there was a bit of aggro going on, but we could have sat on it if someone had given the order to loosen up a bit, give people room to breathe. Instead, Gill led a fucking truncheon charge. I know we coppers are all supposed to stick together, but . . .' Grant looked out to sea and shivered.

'There's a time to stick together,' Banks said, 'and this isn't it. Gill got himself killed, remember that.'

'But I couldn't swear to anything. I mean, officially . . .'

'Don't worry. This is off the record.' At least it is for now, he told himself. If anything came of their discussion, young Grant might find himself with a few serious decisions to make. 'How did the others feel about Gill?' he asked.

'Oh, most of them thought it was all a bit of a joke, a lark. I mean, there'd be Gill going on about clobbering queers and commies. I don't think they really took him seriously.'

'But it wasn't just talk? You say he liked smashing skulls.'

'Yes. He was a right bastard.'

'Surely they knew it?'

'Yes, but . . .'

'Did they approve?'

'Well, no, I wouldn't say that. Some, maybe . . . but I didn't, for one.'

'But nobody warned him, told him to knock it off?'

Grant pulled up his collar. 'No.'

'Were they scared of him?'

'Some of the lads were, yes. He was a bit of hard case.'

'What about you?'

'Me? Well, I wouldn't have taken him up on anything, that's for sure. I'm scarcely above regulation height myself, and Gill was a big bugger.'

A seagull screeched by them, a flash of white against the grey, and began circling over the water for fish. The tanker had moved far over to the right of the horizon. Banks felt the chill getting to him. He put his hands deep in his pockets and tensed up against the cold wet wind.

'Did any of the others actually like him?' he asked. 'Did he have any real mates at the station?'

'I wouldn't say so, no. He wasn't a very likeable bloke. Too big-headed, too full of himself. I mean, you couldn't have a conversation with him; you just had to listen. He had views on everything, but he was thick. I mean, he never really thought anything out. It was all down to Pakis and Rastas and students and skinheads and unemployed yobbos with him.'

'So he wasn't popular around the station?'

'Not really, no. But you know what it's like. A few of the lads get together in the squad room – especially if they've had TAG training – and you get all that macho tough-guy talk, just like American cop shows. He was good at that, Gill was, telling stories about fights and taking risks.'

'Are there any more like him in your station?'

'Not as bad, no. There's a few that don't mind a good punch-up now and then, and some blokes like to pull kids in on a sus just to liven up a boring night. But nobody went as far as Gill.'

'Did he have any friends outside the station?'

'I don't know who he went about with off duty.'

'Did he have a girlfriend?'

'I don't know. He never mentioned anyone.'

'So he didn't brag about having women like he did about thumping people?'

'No. I never heard him. Whenever he did talk about women it was always like they were whores and bitches. He was a foul-mouthed bastard. He'd hit them too, at demos. It was all the same to him.'

'Do you think he could have been the type to mess around with someone else's girlfriend or wife?'

Grant shook his head. 'Not that I know of.'

The seagull flew up towards the cliffs behind them, a fish flapping in its beak. The sea had settled to a rhythmic slapping against the stone wall, hardly sending up any spray at all. Banks risked another cigarette.

'Did Gill have any enemies that you know of?'

'He must have made plenty over the years, given his attitude towards the public,' Grant said. 'But I couldn't name any.'

'Anyone on the force?'

'Eh?'

'You said nobody at the station really liked him. Had anyone got a good reason to dislike him? Did he owe money, cheat people, gamble? Any financial problems?'

'I don't think so. He just got people's backs up, that's all. He talked about betting on the horses, yes, but I don't think he did it that much. It was just the macho sort of thing that went with his image. He never tried to borrow any money off me, if that's what you mean. And I don't think he was on the take. At least he was honest on that score.'

Banks turned his back to the choppy water and looked up towards the sombre bulk of the ruined castle. He couldn't see much from that angle; the steep cliff, where seabirds made their nests, was mottled with grass, moss and bare stone. 'Is there anything else you can tell me?' he asked.

'I don't think so. I just wanted you to know that all that crap at the funeral was exactly that. Crap. Gill was a vicious bastard. I'm not saying he deserved what happened to him, nobody deserves that, but those who live by the sword . . .'

'Did you have any particular reason to dislike Gill?'

Grant seemed startled by the question. 'Me? What do you mean?'

'What I say. Did he ever do you any harm personally?'

'No. Look, if you're questioning my motives, sir, believe me, it's exactly like I told you. I heard you were asking questions about Gill and I thought someone should tell you the truth, that's all. I'm not the kind to go around speaking ill of the dead just because they're not here to defend themselves.'

Banks smiled. 'Don't mind me, I'm just an old cynic. It's a long time since I've come across a young idealist like you on the force.' Banks thought of Superintendent Gristhorpe, who had managed to hang on to a certain amount of idealism over the years. But he was one of the old guard; it was a rare quality in youth these days, Banks had found, especially in those who joined the police. Even Richmond could hardly be called an idealist. Keen yes, but as practical as the day was long.

Grant managed a thin smile. 'It's nice of you to say that, but it's not exactly true. After all,' he said, 'I laid into them with the rest last Friday, didn't I? And do you know what?' His voice caught in his throat and he couldn't look Banks in the eye. 'After a while, I even started to enjoy myself.'

So, Banks thought, maybe Grant had told all because he felt ashamed of himself for acting like Gill and enjoying the battle. Getting caught up in the thrill of action was hardly unusual; the release of adrenalin often produced a sense of exhilaration in men who would normally run a mile from a violent confrontation. But it obviously bothered Grant. Perhaps this was his way of exorcizing what he saw as Gill's demon inside him. Whatever his reasons, he'd given Banks plenty to think about.

'It happens,' Banks said by way of comfort. 'Don't let it worry you. Look, would you do me a favour?' They turned and started walking back to their cars.

Grant shrugged. 'Depends.'

'I'd like to know a bit more about Gill's overtime activities – like where he's been and when. There should be a record. It'd also be useful if I could find out about any official complaints against him, and anything at all about his private life.'

Grant frowned and pushed at his left cheek with his

tongue as if he had a ulcer. 'I don't know,' he said finally, fiddling in his duffel coat pocket for his car keys. 'I wouldn't want to get caught. They'd make my life a bloody misery here if they knew I'd even talked to you like this. Can't you just request his record?'

Banks shook his head. 'My boss doesn't want us to be seen investigating Gill. He says it'll look bad. But if we're not seen . . . Send it to my home address, just to be on the safe side.' Banks scribbled his address on a card and handed it over.

Grant got into his car and opened the window. 'I can't promise anything,' he said slowly, 'but I'll have a go.' He licked his lips. 'If anything important comes out of all this . . .' He paused.

Banks bent down, his hand resting on the wet car roof.

'Well,' Grant went on, 'I don't want you to think I'm after anything, but you will remember I said I wanted to join the CID, won't you?' And he smiled a big broad innocent open smile.

Bloody hell, there were no flies on this kid. Banks couldn't make him out. At first he'd taken such a moral line that Banks suspected chapel had figured strongly somewhere in his background. But despite all his idealism and respect for the law, he might well be another Dirty Dick in the making. On the other hand, that damn smiling moon-face looked so bloody cherubic . . .

'Yes,' Banks said, smiling back. 'Don't worry, I won't forget you.'

6

ONE

In the cross-streets between York Road and Market Street, near where Banks lived, developers had converted terraces of tall Victorian family houses into student flats. In one of these, in a two-room attic unit, Tim Fenton and Abha Sutton lived.

If Tim and Abha made an unlikely-looking couple, they made an even more unlikely pair of revolutionaries. Tim had all the blond good looks of an American preppie, with dress sense to match. Abha, half-Indian, had golden skin, beetle-black hair and a pearl stud through her left nostril. She was studying graphic design; Tim was in the social sciences. They embraced Marxism as the solution to the world's inequalities, but were always quick to point out that they regarded Soviet Communism as an extreme perversion of the prophet's truth. Both were generally well mannered, and not at all the type to call police pigs.

They sat on a beat-up sofa under a Che Guevara poster while Banks made himself comfortable on a second-hand office swivel chair at the desk. The cursor blinked on the screen of an Amstrad PC, and stacks of paper and books overflowed from the table to the floor and on to any spare chairs.

After getting back from Scarborough, Banks had just had time to drop in at the station and see what Special

Branch had turned up. As usual, their files were as thin as Kojak's hair and gathered on premises as flimsy as a stripper's G-string. Tim Fenton was listed because he had attended a seminar in Slough sponsored by *Marxism Today*, and some of the speakers there were suspected of working for the Soviets. Dennis Osmond had attracted the Branch's attention by writing a series of violently anti-government articles for various socialist journals during the miners' strike, and by organizing a number of political demonstrations, especially against the American military presence in Europe. As Banks had suspected, their crimes against the realm hardly provided grounds for exile or execution.

Tim and Abha were predictably hostile and frightened after Burgess's visit. Banks had previously been on good terms with the two after successfully investigating a series of burglaries in student residences the previous November. Even Marxists, it appeared, valued their stereos and television sets. But now they were cautious and guarded. It took a lot of small talk to get them to relax and open up. When Banks finally got around to the subject of the demo, they seemed to have stopped confusing him with Burgess.

'Did you see anything?' Banks asked first.

'No, we couldn't,' Tim answered. 'We were right in the thick of the crowd. One of the cops shouted something and that was that. When things went haywire we were too busy trying to protect ourselves to see what was happening to anyone else.'

'You were involved in organizing the demo, right?'

'Yes. But that doesn't mean—'

Banks held up his hand. 'I know,' he said. 'And that's not what I'm implying. Did you get the impression that anyone involved – anyone at all – might have had more on his mind than just protesting Honoria Winstanley's visit?'

They both shook their heads. 'When we got together up at the farm,' Abha explained, 'everyone was just so excited that we could organize a demo in a place as conservative as Eastvale. I know there weren't many people there, but it seemed like a lot to us.'

'The farm?'

'Yes. Maggie's Farm. Do you know it?'

Banks nodded.

'They invited us up to make posters and stuff,' Tim said. 'Friday afternoon. They're really great up there; they've really got it together. I mean, Seth and Mara, they're like the old independent craftsmen, doing their own thing, making it outside the system. And Rick's a pretty sharp Marxist.'

'I thought he was an artist.'

'He is,' Tim said, looking offended. 'But he tries not to paint anything commercial. He's against art as a saleable commodity.'

So that pretty watercolour Banks had noticed propped by the fireplace at Maggie's Farm couldn't have been one of Rick's.

'What about Paul Boyd?'

'We don't know him well,' Abha said. 'And he didn't say much. One of the oppressed, I suppose.'

'You could say that. And Zoe?'

'Oh, she's all right,' Tim said. 'She goes in for all that bourgeois spiritual crap – bit of a navel-gazer – but she's OK underneath it all.'

'Do you know anything about their backgrounds, where they come from?'

They shook their heads. 'No,' Tim said finally. 'I mean

we just talk about the way things are now, how to change them, that kind of thing. And a bit of political theory. Rick's pissed off about his divorce and all that, but that's about as far as the personal stuff goes.'

'And you know nothing else about them?'

'No.'

'Who else was there?'

'Just us and Dennis.'

'Osmond?'

'That's right.'

'Do either of you recall seeing a flick knife that day, or hearing anyone mention one?'

'No. That's what the other bloke went on about,' Tim said, getting edgy. 'Bloody Burgess. He went on and on about a flick knife.'

'He almost came right out and accused us of killing that policeman, too,' Abha said.

'That's just his style. I wouldn't worry about it. Did anyone at the meeting mention PC Gill by name?'

'Not that I heard,' Tim said.

'Nor me,' said Abha.

'Have you ever heard anyone talk about him? Dennis Osmond, for example? Or Rick?'

'No. The only thing we knew about him,' Abha said, 'was that he'd trained with the TAG groups and he liked to work on crowd control. You know – demos, pickets and such.'

The chair creaked as Banks swivelled sharply. 'How did you know that?'

'Word gets around,' Abha said. 'We keep—'

Tim nudged her in the ribs and she shut up.

'What she means,' he said, 'is that if you're politically involved up here, you soon get to know the ones to watch

out for. You lot keep tabs on us, don't you? I'm pretty sure
Special Branch has a file on me, anyway.'

'Fair enough,' Banks said, smiling to himself at the
absurdity of it all. Games. Just little boys' games. 'Was this
fairly common knowledge? Could anyone have known to
expect Gill at the demo that night?'

'Anyone involved in organizing it, sure,' Tim said. 'And
anyone who'd been to demos in Yorkshire before. There
aren't many like him, thank God. He did have a bit of a
reputation.'

'Did you *know* he was going to be on duty?'

'Not for certain, no. I mean, he could have had flu or
broke his leg.'

'But short of that?'

'Short of that he was rarely known to miss. Look, I
don't know what all this is in aid of,' Tim said, 'but I think
you should know we're still going to do our own
investigation.'

'Into the murder?'

Tim gave him a puzzled glance. 'No. Into the police
brutality. We're all getting together again up at the farm in
a few days to compare notes.'

'Well, if you find anything out about PC Gill's death, let
me know.'

Banks looked at his watch and stood up. It was time he
went and got ready for his evening out with Jenny. After
he'd said goodbye and walked back down the gloomy
staircase to the street, he reflected how odd it was that
wherever he went all roads seemed to lead to Maggie's
Farm. More than that, almost anyone involved could have
known that Gill was likely to be there that night. If Gill
cracked heads in Yorkshire for a hobby, then the odds
were that one or two people might hold a strong grudge

against him. He wished Tony Grant would hurry up and send the information from Scarborough.

TWO

Mara put on her army surplus greatcoat and set off down the track for Relton. It was dark now and the stars were glittering flecks of ice in the clear sky. Distant hills and scars showed only as muted silhouettes, black against black. The crescent moon was up, hanging lopsided like a backdrop to a music-hall song. Mara almost expected a man with a top hat, cape and cane to start dancing across it way up in the sky. The gravel crackled under her feet, and the wind whistled through gaps in the lichen-covered drystone wall. In the distance, the lights of cottages and villages down in the dale twinkled like stars.

She would talk to Jenny, she decided, thrusting her hands deeper into her pockets and hunching up against the chill. Jenny knew Chief Inspector Banks, too. Though she distrusted all policemen, Mara had to admit that he was a hell of a lot better than Burgess. Perhaps she might also be able to find out what the police really thought, and if they were going to leave Paul alone from now on.

Mara's mind strayed back to the I Ching, which she had consulted before setting off. What the hell was it all about? It was supposed to be an oracle, to offer words of wisdom when you really needed them, but Mara wasn't convinced. One problem was that it always answered questions obliquely. You couldn't ask, 'Did Paul kill that policeman?' and get a simple yes or no. This time, the oracle had read: 'The woman holds the basket, but there are no fruits in it. The man stabs the sheep, but no blood flows. Nothing that acts to further.' Did that mean Paul hadn't killed anyone, that the blood on his hand had come from somewhere else? And what about the empty basket? Did that have something to do with Mara's barren womb? If there was any practical advice at all, it was to do nothing, yet here she was, walking down the track on her way to call Jenny. All the book had done was put her fears into words and images.

At the end of the track, Mara walked along Mortsett Lane, past the closed shops and the cottages with their television screens flickering behind curtains. In the dimly lit phone booth, she rang Jenny's number. She heard a click followed by a strange disembodied voice that she finally recognized as Jenny's. The voice explained that its owner was out, but that a message could be left after the tone. Mara, who had never dealt with an answering machine before, waited nervously, worried that she might miss her cue. But it soon came, the unmistakable high-pitched bleep. Mara spoke quickly and loudly, as people do to foreigners, feeling self-conscious about her voice: 'This is Mara, Jenny. I hope I've got this thing right. Please, will you meet me tomorrow lunch time in the Black Sheep in Relton? It's important. I'll be there at one. I hope you can come.' She paused for a moment and listened to the silence, feeling that she should add something, but she could think of nothing more to say.

Mara put the phone back gently. It had been rather like sending a telegram, something she had done once before. The feeling that every word cost money was very inhibiting, and so, in a different way, was the sense of a tape winding around the capstan past the recording head as she talked.

Anyway, it was done. Leaving the booth, she hurried

towards the Black Sheep, feeling lighter in spirit now that she had at least taken a practical step to deal with her fears.

THREE

Banks and Jenny sat in the bar over aperitifs while they studied the menu. The Royal Oak was a cosy place with muted lights, mullioned windows and gleaming copperware in little nooks and crannies. Fastened horizontally between the dark beams on the ceiling was a collection of walking sticks of all lengths and materials: knobbly ashplants, coshers, swordsticks and smooth canes, many with ornate brass handles. On a long shelf above the bar stood a row of toby jugs with such faces as Charles II, Shakespeare and Beethoven; some, however, depicted contemporaries like Margaret Thatcher and Paul McCartney.

Jenny sipped a vodka and tonic, Banks a dry sherry, as they tried to decide what to order. Finally, after much self-recrimination about the damage it would do to her figure, Jenny settled for steak *au poivre* with a wine and cream sauce. Banks chose roast leg of lamb. Much as he liked to watch the little blighters frolic around the dale every spring, he enjoyed eating them almost as much. They'd only grow up into sheep anyway, he reasoned.

They followed the waitress into the dining room, pleased to find only one other table occupied, and that by a subdued couple already on dessert. Mozart's Clarinet Quintet played quietly in the background. Banks watched Jenny walk ahead of him. She was wearing a loose top, cut square across the collarbone, which looked as if it had been tie-dyed in various shades of blue and red. Her pleated skirt was plain rust-red, the colour of her tumbling wavy hair, and came to midway down her calves. The tights she wore had some kind of pattern on them, which looked to Banks like a row of bruises up the sides of her legs. Being a gentleman, though, he had complimented her on her appearance.

The waitress lit the candle, took their orders and moved off soundlessly, leaving them with the wine list to study. Banks lit a cigarette and smiled at Jenny.

Despite the claims of *Playboy*, the Miss World contest and other promoters of the feminine image to men, Banks often found it was the most insignificant detail that made a woman physically attractive to him: a well-placed mole, a certain curve of the lips or turn of the ankle; or a mannerism, such as the way she picked up a glass, tilted her head before smiling or fiddled with a necklace while speaking.

In the case of Sandra, his wife, it was the dark eyebrows and the contrast they made with her naturally ash-blonde hair. With Jenny, it was her eyes, or rather the delta of lines that crinkled their outer edges, especially when she smiled. They were like a map whose contours revealed a sense of humour and a curious mixture of toughness and vulner-ability that Banks himself felt able to identify with. Her beautiful red hair and green eyes, her shapeliness, her long legs and full lips were all very well, but they were just icing on the cake. It was the lines around the eyes that did it.

'What are you thinking?' Jenny asked, looking up from the list.

Banks gave her the gist of it.

'Well,' she said, after a fit of laughter, 'I'll take that as a compliment, though there are many women who wouldn't. What shall we have?'

'They've got a nice Séguret 1980 here, if I remember rightly. And not too expensive, either. That's if you like Rhône.'

'Fine by me.'

When the waitress returned with their smoked salmon and melon first course, Banks ordered the wine.

'So what's all this decadence in aid of?' asked Jenny, her eyes twinkling in the candle flame. 'Are you planning to seduce me, or are you just softening me up for questioning?'

'What if I said I was planning to seduce you?'

'I'd say you were going about it the right way.' She smiled and looked around the room. 'Candlelight, romantic music, nice atmosphere, good food.'

The wine arrived, shortly followed by their main courses, and soon they were enjoying the meal to the accompaniment of the Flute Quartets.

Over dinner, Jenny complained about her day. There had been too many classes to teach, and she was tired of the undergraduates' simplistic assumptions about psychology. Sometimes, she confessed, she was even sick of psychology itself and wished she'd studied English literature or history instead.

Banks told her about the funeral, careful to leave out his meeting with Tony Grant. It would be useful to have something in reserve later, if he could steer her around to talking about Osmond. He also mentioned his visit to Tim and Abha and how Burgess's approach had soured the pitch.

'Your Dirty Dick is a real jerk,' Jenny said, employing an Americanism the man himself would have been proud of. 'Dare I ask about dessert?' she asked, pushing her empty plate aside.

'It's *your* figure.'

'In that case, I think I'll have chocolate mousse. Absolutely no calories at all. And coffee and cognac.'

When the waitress came, Banks ordered Jenny's dessert and brandy along with a wedge of Stilton and a glass of Sauternes for himself. 'You didn't really answer my question, you know,' he said.

'What question's that?'

'The one about seducing you.'

'Oh, yes. But I did. I said you were going about it the right way.'

'But you didn't say whether I'd get anywhere or not.'

Jenny's eyes crinkled. 'Alan! Are you feeling the itch because Sandra's away?'

Banks felt foolish for bringing the subject up in the first place. Flirting with Jenny might be fun, but it also had a serious edge that neither really wanted to get too close to. If it hadn't been for that damned incident at Osmond's flat, he thought, he'd never have been so silly as to start playing games like this. But when he had seen Jenny look round Osmond's bedroom door like that – the robe slipping off her shoulder, the tousled hair, the relaxed unfocused look that follows lovemaking – it hadn't only made him jealous, it had also inflamed old desires. He had felt that nobody else should enjoy what he couldn't enjoy himself. And he couldn't; of that there was no doubt. So he played his games and ended up embarrassing both of them.

He lit a cigarette to hide behind and poured the last of the Séguret. 'Change the subject?'

Jenny nodded. 'A good idea.'

The dessert arrived at the same time as a noisy party of businessmen. Fortunately, the waitress seated them at the far end of the room.

'This is delicious,' Jenny said, spooning up the chocolate mousse. 'I suppose you're going to question me now?
I've got a feeling that seduction would probably have been
a lot more fun.'

'Don't tempt me,' Banks said. 'But you're right. I would
like your help on a couple of things.'

'Here we go. Can I just finish my sweet first?'

'Of course.'

When the dishes were empty, Jenny sipped some
cognac. 'All right,' she said, saluting and sitting up to
attention. 'I'm all ears.'

'Were you there?' Banks asked.

'Where?'

'At the demo. You came to see me at two in the
morning. You said you'd been waiting at your house for
your boyfriend—'

'Dennis!'

'Yes, all right. Dennis.' Banks wondered why he hated
the sound of the name so much. 'But you could have been
at the demo, too.'

'You mean I could have been lying?'

'That's not what I'm getting at. You might have just
failed to mention it.'

'Surely you don't think I'm a suspect now? Being
seduced by Quasimodo would be more fun than this.'

Banks laughed. 'That's not my point. Think about it. If
you were there with Osmond right up until the time he got
arrested, then you'd be a witness that he didn't stab PC
Gill.'

'I see. So Dennis is a prime suspect as far as you're
concerned?'

'He is as far as Burgess is concerned. And that's what
counts.'

Banks wondered if he too wanted Osmond to be guilty. Part of him, he had to admit, did. He was also wondering whether or not to tell Jenny about the assault charges. It would be a mean thing to do right now, he decided, because he couldn't trust his motives. Would he be telling her for her own good, or out of the jealousy he felt, out of a desire to hurt her relationship with Osmond?

'I see what you mean,' Jenny said finally. 'No, I wasn't at the demo. I don't know what happened. Dennis has talked to me about it, of course, and, by the way, he's going ahead with his own inquiry into the thing, you know, along with Tim and Abha. And Burgess is going to come off pretty badly. Apparently he was around again today with Hatchley.'

Banks knew that. He also knew that the dirty duo had got no more out of anyone than they had the first time round. They'd probably be drowning their sorrows in the Queen's Arms by now, and with a bit of luck Dirty Dick would push it too far with Glenys and her Cyril would thump him.

'Back to the demo,' Banks said. 'What exactly has Dennis said?'

'He doesn't know what happened to that policeman. Do you think I'd be sitting here talking to you, answering your questions, if I wasn't trying to convince you that he had nothing to do with it?'

'So he saw nothing?'

'No. He said he heard somebody shout – he didn't catch the words – and after that it was chaos.'

That seemed to square with what Tony Grant and Tim and Abha had said about the riot's origin. Banks took a sip of Sauternes and watched it make legs down the inside of his glass.

'Did he ever mention PC Gill to you?'

Jenny shrugged. 'He may have done. I didn't have much to do with the demo, as I said.'

'Did you ever hear the name?'

'I don't know.' Jenny was getting prickly. 'I can't say I pay much attention to Dennis's political concerns. And if you're going to make a crack about that, forget it. Unless you want a lap full of hot coffee.'

Banks decided it was best to veer away from the subject of Osmond. 'You know the people at Maggie's Farm, don't you?' he asked.

'Yes. Dennis got friendly with Seth and Mara. We've been up a few times. I like them, especially Mara.'

'What's the set-up there?'

Jenny swirled the cognac and took another sip. 'Seth bought the place about three years ago,' she said. 'Apparently, it was in a bit of a state, which was why he got it quite cheaply. He fixed it up, renovated the old barn and rented it out. After Mara, Rick came next, I think, with Julian. He was having some problems with his wife.'

'Yes, I've heard about his wife,' Banks said. 'Do you know anything else about her?'

'No. Except according to Rick her name must be Bitch.'

'What about Zoe?'

'I'm not sure how she met up with them. She came later. As far as I know she's from the east coast. She seems like a bit of a space cadet, but I suspect she's quite shrewd, really. You'd be surprised how many people are into that New Age stuff these days. Looking for something, I suppose . . . Reassurance . . . I don't know. Anyway, she makes a good living from it. She does the weekly horoscope in the *Gazette* too, and takes a little booth on the coast on summer weekends for doing tarot readings and whatnot. You know, Madame Zoe, Gypsy Fortune Teller . . .'

'The east coast? Could it be Scarborough?'

Jenny shook her head. 'Whitby, I think.'

'Still,' Banks muttered, 'it's not far away.'

'What isn't?'

The waitress brought coffee, and Banks lit another cigarette, careful to keep the smoke away from Jenny.

'Tell me about Mara.'

'I like Mara a lot. She's bright, and she's had an interesting life. She was in some religious organization before she came to the farm, but she got disillusioned. She seems to want to settle down a bit now. For some reason, we get along quite well. Seth, as I say, I don't know much about. He grew up in the sixties and he hasn't sold out – I mean he hasn't become a stockbroker or an accountant, at least. His main interest is his carpentry. There's also something about a woman in his past.'

'What woman?'

'Oh, it was just something Mara said. Apparently Seth doesn't like to talk about it. He had a lover who died. Maybe they were even married, I don't know. That was just before he bought the farm.'

'What was her name?'

'Alison, I think.'

'How did she die?'

'Some kind of accident.'

'What kind?'

'That's all I know, really. I'm not being evasive. Mara said it's all she knows, too. Seth only told her because he got drunk once. Apparently he's not much of a drinker.'

'And that's all you know?'

'Yes. It was some kind of motor accident. She got knocked down or something.'

'Where was he living then?'

'Hebden Bridge, I think. Why does it matter?'

'It probably doesn't. I just like to know as much as I can about who I'm dealing with. They were involved in the demo, and every time I question someone, Maggie's Farm comes up.'

It would be easy enough to check the Hebden Bridge accident records, though where Gill might come into it, Banks had no idea. Perhaps he had been on traffic duty at the time? He would hardly have been involved in a religious organization either, unless he felt a close friend or relation had been brainwashed by such a group.

'What about Paul Boyd?' he asked.

Jenny paused. 'He's quite new up there. I can't say I know him well. To tell you the truth – and to speak quite unprofessionally – he gives me the creeps. But Mara's very attached to him, like he's a younger brother, or a son even. There's about seventeen years between them. He's another generation, really – punk, post sixties. Mara thinks he just needs tender loving care, something he's never had much of, apparently.'

'What do you think of Paul professionally?'

'It's hard to answer that. As I said, I haven't really talked to him that much. He seems angry, antisocial. Maybe life at the farm will give him some sense of belonging. If you think about it, what reason does he have to love the world? No adult has ever given him a break, nor has society. He feels worthless and rejected, so he makes himself look like a reject; he holds it to him and shouts it out, as people do. And that,' Jenny said with a mock bow, 'is Dr Fuller's humble opinion.'

Banks nodded. 'It makes sense.'

'But it doesn't make him a killer.'

'No.' He couldn't think of any more questions without returning to the dangerous territory of Dennis Osmond, and things had gone so well for the past half-hour or so that he didn't want to risk ending the evening on a sour note. Jenny was bound to be guarded if he really started pushing about Osmond again.

Banks picked up the bill, which Jenny insisted on sharing, and they left. The drive home went smoothly, but Banks felt guilty because he was sure he was a bit over the limit, and if anyone ought to know better about drunken driving, it was a policeman. Not that he felt drunk. After all, he hadn't had much to drink, really. He was perfectly in control. But that's what they all said when the crystals changed colour. Jenny told him not to be silly, he was quite all right. When he dropped her off, there was no invitation to come in for a coffee, and he was glad of that.

Luckily, he thought as he tried to fall asleep, Jenny hadn't pushed him about his own theories. If she had, he would have told her – and trusted her to make sure it got no further – about his little chat with Tony Grant on Marine Drive, the implications of which put a different light on things.

On the one hand, what Grant had told him made the possibility of a personal motive for killing Gill much more likely. He didn't know who might have had such a motive yet, but according to what Tim and Abha had said, almost any of the demonstrators – especially the organizers or people close to them – would have known to expect Gill at the demo. And if Gill was there, wasn't it a safe bet that violence would follow?

On the other hand, Banks found himself thinking that if

Gill had enemies within the force, perhaps a fellow policeman, not a demonstrator, might have taken the opportunity to get rid of him: someone whose wife or girlfriend
Gill had fooled around with, for example; or a partner in
crime, if he had been on the take. Tony Grant hadn't
thought so, but he was only a naive rookie, after all.

It wasn't an idea Banks would expect Burgess to
entertain for a moment; for one thing, it would blow all
political considerations off the scene. But another policeman would have expected Gill to cause trouble, could
have arranged to be on overtime with him and could have
been sure of getting away. None of which could be said for
any of the demonstrators. Nobody searched the police;
nobody checked their uniforms for Gill's blood.

Maybe it was the kind of far-fetched theory one usually
got on the edge of sleep and would seem utterly absurd in
the morning light. But Banks couldn't quite rule it out.
He'd known men on the Metropolitan force more than
capable of murdering fellow officers, and in many cases,
the loss would hardly have diminished the quality of the
human gene pool. The only way to find out about
the angle, though, was to press Tony Grant even further
into service. If there was anything in it, the fewer people
who knew about Banks's line of investigation, the better.
It could be dangerous.

And so, the Sauternes still warm in his veins and a
stretch of cold empty bed beside him, Banks fell asleep
thinking of the victim, convinced that someone not too far
away had had a very good reason for wanting PC Edwin
Gill dead.

7

ONE

Banks turned up the track to Gristhorpe's old farmhouse above Lyndgarth, wondering what the superintendent was doing at home on a Wednesday morning. The message, placed on his desk by Sergeant Rowe, had offered no explanation, just an invitation to visit.

Pulling up in front of the squat solid house, he stabbed out his cigarette and ejected the Lightning Hopkins cassette he'd been listening to. Breathing in the fresh cold air, he looked down over Swainsdale and was struck by the way Relton and Maggie's Farm, directly opposite on the south side of the dale, formed almost a mirror image of Lyndgarth and Gristhorpe's house. Like the latter, Maggie's Farm stood higher up the hillside than the village it was close to – so high it was on the verge of the moorland that spread for miles on the heights between dales.

Looking down the slope from the farmhouse, Banks could see the grey-brown ruins of Devraulx Abbey, just west of Lyndgarth. On the valley bottom, Fortford marked the western boundary of the river meadows. Swainsdale was at its broadest there, where the River Swain meandered through the flats until it veered south-east to Eastvale and finally joined the Ouse outside York.

In summer, the lush green meadows were speckled with golden buttercups. Bluebells, forget-me-nots and wild garlic grew by the riverside under the shade of ash and willow. The Leas, as they were called locally, were a favourite spot for family picnics. Artists set up their easels there too, and fishermen spent idle afternoons on the riverbank and waded in the shallows at dusk. Now, although the promise of spring showed in the grass and clung like a green haze around the branches of the trees, the meadows seemed a haunted and desolate spot. The snaking river sparkled between the trees, and a brisk wind chased clouds over from the west. Shadows flitted across the steep green slopes with a speed that was almost dizzying to watch.

Gristhorpe answered the door and led Banks into the living room, where a peat fire burned in the hearth, then disappeared into the kitchen. Banks took off his sheepskin-lined car coat and rubbed his hands by the flames. Outside the back window, a pile of stones stood by the unfinished drystone wall that the superintendent worked on in his spare time. It fenced in nothing and went nowhere, but Banks had enjoyed many hours placing stones there with Gristhorpe in companionable silence. Today, though, it was too cold for such outdoors activity.

Carrying a tray of tea and scones, Gristhorpe returned and sat down in his favourite armchair to pour. After small talk about the wall and the possibility of yet more snow, the superintendent told Banks his news: the inquiry into the demo had been suspended.

'I'm on ice, as our American cousins would put it,' he said. 'The assistant chief commissioner's been talking to the PCA about getting an outsider to finish the report. Maybe someone from Avon and Somerset division.'

'Because we're too biased?'

'Aye, partly. I expected it. They only set me on it in the

first place to make it look like we were acting quickly.'

'Did you find anything out?'

'It looks like some of our lads overreacted.'

Banks told him what he'd heard from Jenny and Tim and Abha.

Gristhorpe nodded. 'The ACC doesn't like it. If you ask me, I don't think there'll be an official inquiry. It'll be postponed till it's no longer an issue. What he's hoping is that Superintendent Burgess will come up with the killer fast. That'll satisfy everyone, and people will just forget about the rest.'

'Where does that leave you?'

'I'm taking a few days' leave, on the ACC's advice. Unless anything else comes up – something unconnected to Gill's death – then that's how I'll stay. He's right, of course. I'd only get in the way. Burgess is in charge of that investigation, and it wouldn't do to have the two of us treading on each other's toes. But don't let the bugger near my office with those foul cigars of his! How are you getting on with him?'

'All right, I suppose. He's got plenty of go, and he's certainly not stupid. Trouble is, he's got a bee in his bonnet about terrorists and lefties in general.'

'And you see things differently?'

'Yes.' Banks told him about the meeting with Tony Grant and the possibilities it had opened up for him. 'And,' he added, 'you'd think Special Branch would have known if there'd been some kind of terrorist action planned, wouldn't you?'

Gristhorpe digested the information and mulled it over for a few moments, then turned his light blue eyes on Banks and rubbed his chin. 'I'll not deny you might be right,' he said, 'but for Christ's sake keep your feet on the ground. Don't go off half-cocked on this or you could bring down a lot of trouble on yourself, and on me. I appreciate you want to follow your own nose – you'd be a poor copper if you didn't – and maybe you'd like to show Dirty Dick a thing or two. But be careful. Just because Gill turned out to be a bastard, it doesn't follow that's why he was killed. Burgess could be right.'

'I know that. It's just a theory. But thanks for the warning.'

Gristhorpe smiled. 'Think nothing of it. But keep it under your hat. If Burgess finds out you've been pursuing a private investigation, he'll have your guts for garters. And it won't be just him. The ACC'll have your balls for billiards.'

'I don't know as I've got enough body parts to go round,' Banks said, grinning.

'And this conversation hasn't taken place. I know nothing about what you're up to, agreed?'

'Agreed.'

'But keep me posted. God, how I hate bloody politics.'

Banks knew that the superintendent came from a background of Yorkshire radicals – Chartists, the anti-Corn Laws crowd – and there was even a Luddite lurking in the family tree. But Gristhorpe himself was conservative with a small c. He was, however, concerned with the preservation of human rights that had been fought for and won over the centuries. That was how he saw his job – as a defender of the people, not an attacker. Banks agreed, and that was one reason they got along so well.

Banks finished his tea and looked at his watch. 'Talking of Dirty Dick, I'd better be off. He's called a conference in the Queen's Arms for one o'clock.'

'Seems like he's taken up residence there.'

'You're not far wrong.' Banks explained about Glenys and put on his car coat. 'Besides that,' he added, 'he drinks like a bloody fish.'

'So it's not only Glenys and her charms?'

'No.'

'Ever seen him pissed?'

'Not yet.'

'Well, watch him. Drinking's an occupational hazard with us, but it can get beyond a joke. The last thing you need is a piss artist to rely on in a tight spot.'

'I don't think there's anything to worry about,' Banks said, walking to the car. 'He's always been a boozer. And he's usually sharp as a whippet. Anyway, what can I do if I think he is overdoing it? I can just see his face if I suggest a visit to AA.'

Gristhorpe stood by the car. Banks rolled the window down, slipped Lightning Hopkins back in the slot, and lit a cigarette.

The superintendent shook his head. 'It's about time you stopped that filthy habit, too,' he said. 'And as for that racket you call music . . .'

Banks smiled and turned the key in the ignition. 'Do you know something?' he said. 'I do believe you're becoming an insufferable old fogey. I know you're tone-deaf and wouldn't know Mozart from the Beatles, but don't forget, it wasn't that long ago you gave up smoking yourself. Have you no bad habits left?'

Gristhorpe laughed. 'I gave them all up years ago. Are you suggesting I should take some up again?'

'Wouldn't be a bad idea.'

'Where do you suggest I start?'

Banks rolled up the window before he said, 'Try sheep-shagging.' But judging by the raised eyebrows and the startled smile, Gristhorpe could obviously read lips. Grinning, Banks set off down the track, the still, deserted river meadows spread out below him, and headed for the Eastvale road.

TWO

Jenny was already five minutes late. Mara nursed her half of mild and rolled a cigarette. It was Wednesday lunch time, and the Black Sheep was almost empty. Apart from the landlord reading his *Sun*, and two old men playing dominoes, she was the only other customer in the cosy lounge.

Now that the time was close, she was beginning to feel nervous and foolish. After all, she didn't know Jenny *that* well, and her story did sound a bit thin. She couldn't put the real problem into words. How could she say that she suspected Paul had killed the policeman and that she was even beginning to be afraid living in the same house, but despite it all she wouldn't give him away and still wanted to keep him there? It sounded insane without the feelings that went with it. And to tell Jenny that she just wanted information for a story she was writing hardly ranked as the important reason for the meeting she had claimed on the telephone. Perhaps Jenny wasn't going to come. Maybe Mara hadn't responded to the answering machine properly and she hadn't even got the message.

All she could hear was the sound of asthmatic breathing from one of the old men, the occasional rustling of the newspaper, and the click of dominoes as they were laid on the hard surface. She swirled the beer in the bottom of her half-pint glass and peered at her watch again. Quarter past one.

'Another drink, love?' Larry Grafton called out.

Mara flashed a smile and shook her head. Why was it that she didn't mind being called love by the locals, but when Burgess had said it, her every nerve had bristled with resentment? It must be something in the tone, she decided. The old Yorkshiremen who used the word were probably as chauvinistic as the rest – in fact, sex roles in Dales family life were as traditional as anywhere in England – but when the men called women love it carried at least overtones of affection. With Burgess, though, the word was a weapon, a way of demeaning the woman, of dominating her.

Jenny arrived and interrupted her train of thought.

'Sorry I'm late,' she said breathlessly. 'Class went on longer than I expected.'

'It's all right,' Mara said. 'I haven't been here long. Drink?'

'Let me get them.'

Jenny went to the bar, and Mara watched her, a little intimidated, as usual, by her poise. Jenny always seemed to wear the right expensive-looking clothes. Today it was a waist-length fur jacket (fake, of course – Jenny wouldn't be caught dead wearing real animal fur), a green silk blouse, close-fitting rust cords and well polished knee-length boots. Not that Mara would want to dress like that – it wouldn't suit her personality – but she did feel shabby in her moth-eaten sweater and muddy wellingtons. Her jeans hadn't been artificially aged like the ones teenagers wore either; they had earned each stain and every faded patch.

'Quiet, isn't it?' Jenny said, setting the drinks down. 'You looked thoughtful when I came in. What was it?'

Mara told her her feelings about being called love.

'I know what you mean. I could have throttled Burgess when he did it to me.' She laughed. 'Dorothy Wycombe once chucked her drink at a stable lad for called her love.'

'Dorothy doesn't have much to do with us,' Mara said. 'I think we're too traditional for her tastes.'

Jenny laughed. 'You should count yourself lucky, then.' She took off her jacket and made herself comfortable. 'I heard she made mincemeat of Burgess. She gave Alan a hard time once, too. He gives her a wide berth now.'

'Alan? Is that the policeman you know? Chief Inspector Banks?'

Jenny nodded: 'He's all right. Why? Is that what you wanted to talk about?'

'What do you mean?'

'Don't be so cagey. I know you've come in for a lot of police attention since the demo. I just wondered if that was what was on your mind. Your message wasn't exactly specific, you know.'

Mara smiled. 'I'm not used to answering machines, that's all. Sorry.'

'No need. You just came across as frightfully worried and serious. Are you?'

A domino clicked loudly on the board, obviously a winning move. 'Not as much as I probably sounded, no,' Mara said. 'But it is about the demo. Partly, anyway.' She had decided that, as Jenny had mentioned Banks, she might as well begin by seeing if she could find anything out about the investigation, what the police were thinking.

'Go ahead, then.'

Mara took a deep breath and told Jenny about recent events at the farm, especially Burgess's visit.

'You ought to complain,' Jenny advised her.

Mara sniffed. 'Complain? Who to? He told us what

would happen if we did. Apparently his boss is a bigger bastard than he is.'

'Try complaining locally. Superintendent Gristhorpe isn't bad.'

Mara shook her head. 'You don't understand. The police would never listen to a complaint from people like us.'

'Don't be so sure about that, Mara. Alan wants to understand. It's only the truth he's after.'

'Yes, but . . . I can't really explain. What do they really think about us, Jenny? Do they believe that one of us killed that policeman?'

'I don't know. Really I don't. They're interested in you, yes. I'd be a liar if I denied that. But as far as actually suspecting anyone . . . I don't think so. Not yet.'

'Then why do they keep pestering us? When's it going to stop?'

'When they find out who the killer is. It's not just you, it's everyone involved. They've been at Dennis, too, and Dorothy Wycombe and the students. You'll just have to put up with it for the time being.'

'I suppose so.' The old men shuffled dominoes for another game, and a lump of coal shifted in the fire, sending out a shower of sparks and a puff of smoke. Flames rose up again, licking at the black chimney back. 'Look,' Mara went on, 'do you mind if I ask you a professional question, something about psychology? It's for a story I'm working on.'

'I didn't know you wrote.'

'Oh, it's just for my own pleasure really. I mean, I haven't tried to get anything published yet.' Even as she spoke, Mara knew that her excuse didn't ring true.

'OK,' Jenny said. 'Let me get another round in first.'

'Oh no, it's my turn.' Mara went to the bar and bought

another half for herself and a vodka and tonic for Jenny. If only she could get away with some of her fears about Paul allayed – without giving them away, of course – then she knew she would feel a lot better.

'What is it?' Jenny asked when they'd settled down with their drinks again.

'It's just something I'd like to know, a term I've heard that puzzles me. What's a sociopath?'

'A sociopath? Good Lord, this is like an exam question. Let me think for a bit. I'll have to give you a watered-down answer, I'm afraid. I don't have the textbook with me.'

'That's all right.'

'Well . . . I suppose basically it's someone who's constantly at war with society. A rebel without a cause, if you like.'

'Why, though? I mean, what makes people like that?'

'It's far from cut and dried,' Jenny said, 'but the thinking is that it has a lot to do with family background. Usually people we call sociopaths suffered abuse, cruelty and rejection from their parents, or at least from one parent, from an early age. They respond by rejecting society and becoming cruel themselves.'

'What are the signs?'

'Antisocial acts: stealing, doing reckless things, cruelty to animals. It's hard to say.'

'What kind of people are they?'

'They don't feel anything about what they do. They can always justify acts of cruelty – even murder – to themselves. They don't really see that they've done anything wrong.'

'Can anyone help them?'

'Sometimes. The trouble is, they're detached, cut off from the rest of us through what's happened to them.

They rarely have any friends and they don't feel any sense of loyalty.'

'Isn't it possible to help them, then?'

'They find it very hard to give love and to trust people, or to respond to such feelings in others. If you don't give your love, then you save yourself from feeling bad if it's rejected. That's the real problem: they need someone to trust them and have some feeling for them, but those are the things they find it hardest to accept.'

'So it's hopeless.'

'Often it's too late,' Jenny said. 'If they're treated early, they can be helped, but sometimes by the time they reach their teens the pattern is so deeply ingrained it's almost irreversible. But it's never hopeless.' She leaned forward and put her hand on Mara's. 'It's Paul you're asking about, isn't it?'

Mara withdrew sharply. 'What makes you say that?'

'Your expression, the tone of your voice. This isn't just for some story you're writing. It's for real, isn't it?'

'What if it is?'

'I can't tell you if Paul's a sociopath or not, Mara. I don't know enough about him. He seems to be responding to life at the farm.'

'Oh, he is,' Mara said. 'Responding, I mean. He's got a lot more outgoing and cheerful since he's been with us. Until these past few days.'

'Well, it's bound to get to him, all the police attention. But it doesn't mean anything. You don't think he might have killed the policeman, do you?'

'You mustn't tell anyone we've been talking like this,' Mara said quickly. 'Especially not Inspector Banks. All they need is an excuse to bring Paul in, then I'm sure that Burgess could force him to confess.'

'They won't do that,' Jenny said. 'You don't have any concrete reason for thinking Paul might be guilty, do you?'

'No.' Mara wasn't sure she sounded convincing. Things had gone too far for her, but it seemed impossible to steer back to neutral ground. 'I'm just worried about him, that's all,' she went on. 'He's had a hard life. His parents rejected him and his foster parents were cold towards him.'

'Well, that doesn't mean a lot,' Jenny said. 'If that's all you're worried about, I shouldn't bother yourself. Plenty of people come from broken homes and survive. It takes very special circumstances to create a sociopath. Not every ache and pain means you've got cancer, you know.'

Mara nodded. 'I'm sorry I tried to con you,' she said. 'It wasn't fair of me. But I feel better now. Let's just forget all about it, shall we?'

'OK, if you want. But be careful, Mara. I'm not saying Paul isn't dangerous, just that I don't know. If you do have any real suspicions . . .'

But Mara didn't hear any more. The door opened and a strange-looking man walked in. It wasn't his odd appearance that bothered her, though; it was the knife that he carried carefully in his hand. Pale and trembling, she got to her feet.

'I've got to go now,' she said. 'Something's come up . . . I'm sorry.' And she was off like a shot, leaving Jenny to sit and gape behind her.

THREE

'Bollocks!' said Burgess. 'They're shit-disturbers. You ought to know that by now. Why do you think they're interested in a nuclear-free Britain? Because they love peace? Dream on, Constable.'

'I don't know,' Richmond said, stroking his moustache. 'They're just students, they don't know—'

'Just students, my arse! Who is it tries to bring down governments in places like Korea and South Africa? Bloody students, that's who. Just students! Grow up. Look at the chaos students created in America over the Vietnam war – they almost won it for the commies single-handed.'

'What I was saying, sir,' Richmond went on, 'is that none of them are known to be militant. They just sit around and talk politics, that's all.'

'But Special Branch has a file on Tim Fenton.'

'I know, sir. But he's not actually *done* anything.'

'Not until now, perhaps.'

'But what could he gain from killing PC Gill, sir?'

'Anarchy, that's what.'

'With all due respect,' Banks cut in, 'that's hardly consistent. The students support disarmament, yes, but Marxists aren't anarchists. They believe in the class—'

'I know what bloody Marxists believe in,' Burgess said. 'They believe in anything if it furthers their cause.'

Banks gave up. 'Better have another try, Phil,' he said. 'See if you can tie any of them into more extreme groups, or to any previous acts of political violence. I doubt you'll come up with anything Special Branch doesn't know about already, but give it a try.'

'Yes, sir.'

'I need another drink,' Burgess said.

Sergeant Hatchley volunteered to go for a round. The Queen's Arms was busy. Wednesday was farmers' market day in Eastvale, and the whole town bustled with buyers and sellers. Glenys was too busy to exchange glances with Burgess even if she wanted to.

Burgess turned to Banks. 'And I'm still not happy about Osmond. He's on file, too, and I got the distinct impression he's been lying every time I've talked to him.'

Banks agreed.

'We'll have another go at him,' said Burgess. 'You can come with me again. Who knows, that bird of his might be there. If I put a bit of pressure on her, he might appeal to you for help and let something slip.'

Banks reached for a cigarette to mask his anger. The last thing he felt like was facing Osmond and Jenny together again. But in a way Burgess was right. They were looking for a killer, and they needed results. As each day went by, the media outcry became more strident.

When PC Craig came in and walked over to their table, he seemed unsure whom to address. After looking first to Banks and then to Burgess, like a spectator following the ball at Wimbledon, he settled on Banks.

'We've just had a call, sir, from Relton. There's a bloke in the pub there says he's found a knife. I just thought . . . you know . . . it might be the one we're looking for.'

'What are we waiting for?' Burgess jumped to his feet so quickly he knocked the table and spilt the rest of his beer. He pointed at Hatchley and Richmond. 'You two get back to the station and wait till you hear from us.'

They picked up Banks's white Cortina from behind the police station. Market Street and the square were so busy that Banks took the back streets to the main Swainsdale road.

Automatically, he reached forward and slipped a cassette into the player. 'Do you mind?' he asked Burgess, turning the volume down. 'Hello Central' came on.

'No. That's Lightning Hopkins, isn't it? I quite like blues myself. I enjoyed that Billie Holiday the other day, too.' He leaned back in the seat and lit a cigar from the dashboard lighter. 'My father bunked with a squadron of Yanks in the last war. Got quite interested in jazz and blues. Of course, you couldn't get much of the real stuff over here at that time, but after the war he kept in touch and the Yanks used to send him seventy-eights. I grew up on that kind of music and it just seemed to stick.'

Banks drove fast but kept an eye open for walkers on the verges. Even in March, the backpack brigade often took to the hills. As they approached Fortford, Burgess looked out at the river meadows. 'Very nice,' he said. 'Wouldn't be a bad place to retire to if it wasn't for the bloody weather.'

They turned sharp left in Fortford, followed the unfenced minor road up the daleside to Relton and parked outside the pub. Banks had been to the Black Sheep before; it was famous in the dale because the landlord brewed his own beer on the premises and you couldn't get it anywhere else. Black Sheep bitter had won prizes in national competitions.

If beer wasn't the first thing on Banks's mind when they entered, he certainly couldn't refuse the landlord's offer of a pint. Burgess declined the local brew and asked for a pint of Watney's.

Banks knew there were shepherds in the area, but they were an elusive breed and he'd never seen one before. Farmers who tended their own sheep were common enough, but on the south Swainsdale commons they banded together to hire three shepherds. Most of the sheep were heughed; they grew up on the farms and never strayed far. But not all of them; winter was a hard time, and many animals got buried under drifts. The shepherds know the moots, every gully and sinkhole, better than anyone else, and to them sheep are as different from one another as people.

Jack Crocker's face had as many lines as a tough teacher gives out in a week, and its texture looked as hard as tanned leather. He had a misshapen blob of a nose, and his eyes were so deeply hooded they looked as if they had been perpetually screwed up against the wind. His cloth cap and old flapping greatcoat set the final touches. His crook, a long hazel shaft with a metal hook, leaned against the wall.

'Christ,' Banks heard Burgess mutter behind him. 'A bloody shepherd!'

'I don't mind if I do,' Crocker said, accepting a drink. 'I were just fetching some ewes in for lambing, like, and I kicked that there knife.' He placed the knife on the table. It was a flick knife with a five-inch blade and a worn bone handle. 'I didn't touch it, tha knows,' he went on, putting a surprisingly smooth and slender forefinger to the side of his nose. 'I've seen telly.'

'How did you pick it up?' Burgess asked. Banks noticed that his tone was respectful, not hectoring as usual. Maybe he had a soft spot for shepherds.

'Like this.' Crocker held the ends of the handle between thumb and second finger. He really did have beautiful hands, Banks noticed, the kind you'd picture on a concert pianist.

Burgess nodded and took a sip of his Watney's. 'Good. You did the right thing, Mr Crocker.' Banks took an envelope from his pocket, dropped the knife in, and sealed it.

'Is it t' right one, then? T' one as killed that bobby?'

'We can't say yet,' Banks told him. 'We'll have to get some tests done. But if it is, you've done us a great service.'

'It weren't owt. It's not as if I were looking fer it.' Crocker looked away, embarrassed, and raised his pint to his lips. Banks offered him a cigarette.

'Nay, lad,' he said. 'In my job you need all t' breath you can muster.'

'Where did you find the knife?' Burgess asked.

'Up on t' moor, Eastvale way.'

'Can you show us?'

'Aye.' Crocker's face creased into a sly smile. 'It's a bit of a hike, though. And tha can't take thy car.'

Burgess looked at Banks. 'Well,' he said, 'it's your part of the country. You're the nature boy. Why don't you go up the moor with Mr Cocker here, and I'll phone the station to send a car for me?'

Yes, Banks thought, and you'll have another pint of Watney's while you're warming your hands in front of the fire.

Banks nodded. 'I'd get that knife straight to the lab if I were you,' he said. 'If you send it through normal channels they'll take days to get the tests done. Ask for Vic Manson. If he's got a spare moment he'll dust it for prints and persuade one of the lads to try for blood-typing. It's been exposed to the elements a bit, but we might still get something from it.'

'Sounds good,' Burgess said. 'Where is this lab?'

'Just outside Wetherby. You can ask the driver to take you straight there.'

Burgess went over to the phone while Banks and Crocker drank off their pints of Black Sheep bitter and set off.

They climbed a stile at the eastern end of Mortsett Lane and set off over open moorland. The tussocks of moor grass, interspersed with patches of heather and sphagnum, made walking difficult for Banks. Crocker, always ahead, seemed to float over the top of it like a hovercraft. The higher they climbed, the harsher and stronger the wind became.

Banks wasn't dressed for the moors either, and his shoes were soon mud-caked and worse. Though the slope wasn't steep, it was unrelenting, and he soon got out of breath. Despite the cold wind against his face, he was sweating.

At last the ground flattened out into high moorland. Crocker stopped and waited with a smile for Banks to catch up.

'By heck, lad, what'd tha do if tha 'ad to chase after a villain?'

'Luckily, it doesn't happen often,' Banks wheezed.

'Aye. Well, this is where I found it. Just down there in t' grass.' He pointed with his crook. Banks bent and poked around among the sods. There was nothing to indicate the knife had been there.

'It looks like someone just threw it there,' he said.

Crocker nodded. 'It would've been easy enough to hide,' he said. 'Plenty of rocks to stuff it under. He could've even buried it if he'd wanted.'

'But he didn't. So whoever it was must have panicked, perhaps, and just tossed it away.'

'Tha should know.'

Banks looked around. The spot was about two miles from Eastvale; the jagged castle battlements were just visible in the distance, down in the hollow where the town lay. In the opposite direction, also about two miles away, he could see the house and outbuildings of Maggie's Farm.

It looked like the knife had been thrown away on the wild moorland about halfway or more on a direct line between Eastvale and the farm. If someone from the farm had escaped arrest or injury at the demo, it would have been a natural direction in which to run home. That meant Paul or Zoe, as Rick and Seth had been arrested and searched. It could even have been the woman, Mara, who might have been lying about staying at home all evening.

On the other hand, anyone could have come up there in the past few days and thrown the knife away. That seemed much less likely though, as it was a poor method of disposal, more spontaneous than planned. Certainly it seemed to make mincemeat of one of Banks's theories – that a fellow policeman might have committed the murder. Again, the finger seemed to be pointing at Maggie's Farm.

Banks pulled the sheepskin collar tight around his neck and screwed up his eyes to keep the tears from forming. No wonder Crocker's eyes were hooded almost shut. There was nothing more to be done up here, he decided, but he would have to mark the spot in some way.

'Could you find this place again?' he asked.

'Course,' the shepherd answered.

Banks couldn't see how; there was nothing to distinguish it from any other spot of moorland. Still, it was Crocker's job to be familiar with every square inch of his territory.

He nodded. 'Right. We may have to get a few men up here to make a more thorough search. Where can I get in touch with you?'

'I live in Mortsett.' Crocker gave him the address.

'Are you coming back down?'

'Nay. More ewes to fetch in. It's lambing season, tha knows.'

'Yes, well, thanks again for your time.'

Crocker nodded curtly and set off further up the slope, walking just as quickly and effortlessly as if he were on the flat. At least, Banks thought, turning round, it would be easier going down. But before he had even completed the thought, he caught his foot in a patch of heather and fell face forward. He cursed, brushed himself off and carried on. Fortunately, Crocker had been going the other way and hadn't seen his little accident, otherwise it would have been the talk of the dale by evening.

He got back over the stile without further incident and nipped into the Black Sheep for another quick pint and a warm-up. There was nothing he could do now but wait for Burgess to finish at the lab. Even then, there might be no results. But a nice set of sweaty fingerprints on a smooth surface could survive the most terrible weather conditions, and Banks thought he had glimpsed flecks of dried blood in the joint between blade and handle.

8

ONE

A sudden heavy shower drove the shoppers from the market square. It was almost time to pack up and leave anyway; market days in winter and early spring were often cold and miserable affairs. But the rain stopped as quickly as it started, and in no time the sun was out again. Wet cobblestones reflected the muted bronze light, which slid into the small puddles and danced as the wind ruffled them.

The gold hands on the blue face of the church clock stood at four twenty. Burgess hadn't returned from the lab yet. Banks sat waiting by the window, the awkward venetian blind drawn up, and looked down on the scene as he smoked and drank black coffee. People crossed the square and splashed through the puddles that had gathered where cobbles had been worn or broken away. Everyone wore grey plastic macs or brightly coloured anoraks, as if they didn't trust the sun to stay out, and many carried umbrellas. It would soon be dark. Already the sun cast the long shadow of the Tudor-fronted police headquarters over the square.

At a quarter to five, Banks heard a flurry of activity outside his office, and Burgess bounded in carrying a buff folder.

'They came through,' he said. 'Took them long enough,

but they did it – a clear set of prints and a match with Gill's blood type. No doubt about it, that was the knife. I've already got DC Richmond running a check on the prints. If they're on record we're in business.'

He lit a Tom Thumb and smoked, tapping it frequently on the edge of the ashtray whether or not a column of ash had built up. Banks went back to the window. The shadow had lengthened; across the square, secretaries and clerks on their way home dropped in at Joplin's newsagent's for their evening papers, and young couples walked hand in hand into the El Toro coffee bar to tell one another about the ups and downs of their day at the office.

When Richmond knocked and entered, Burgess jumped to his feet. 'Well?'

Richmond stroked his moustache. He could barely keep the grin of triumph from his face. 'It's Boyd,' he said, holding out the charts. 'Paul Boyd. Eighteen points of comparison. Enough to stand up in court.'

Burgess clapped his hands. 'Right! Just as I thought. Let's go. You might as well come along, Constable. Where's Sergeant Hatchley?'

'I don't know, sir. I think he's still checking some of the witness reports.'

'Never mind. Three's enough. Let's bring Boyd in for a chat.'

They piled into Banks's Cortina and headed for Maggie's Farm. Banks played no music this time; the three of them sat in tense silence as the river meadows rolled by, eerie in the misty twilight. Gravel popped under the wheels as they approached the farm, and the front curtain twitched when they drew up outside the building.

Mara Delacey opened the door before Burgess had finished knocking. 'What do you want this time?' she asked angrily, but stood aside to let them in. They followed her through to the kitchen, where the others sat at the table eating dinner. Mara went back to her half-finished meal. Julian and Luna shifted closer to her.

'How convenient,' Burgess said, leaning against the humming refrigerator. 'You're all here together, except one. We're looking for Paul Boyd. Is he around?'

Seth shook his head. 'No. I've no idea where he is.'

'When did you last see him?'

'Last night, I suppose. I've been out most of the day. He wasn't here when I came back.'

Burgess looked at Mara. Nobody said anything, 'One of you must know where he is. What's it to be, now or down at the station?'

Still silence.

Burgess walked forward to pat Julian on the head, but the boy pulled a face and buried his head in Rick's side. 'It'd be a shame,' Burgess said, 'if things got so that you couldn't look after the kids here and they had to be taken away.'

'You'd never dare!' Mara said, her face flushed. 'Even you can't be as much of a bastard as that.'

Burgess raised his left eyebrow. 'Can't I, love? Are you sure you want to find out? Where's Boyd?'

Rick got to his feet. He was as tall as Burgess and a good thirty pounds heavier. 'Pick on someone your own size,' he said. 'If you start messing with my kid's life, you'll bloody well have me to answer to.'

Burgess sneered and turned away. 'I'm quaking in my boots. Where's Boyd?'

'We don't know,' Seth said quietly. 'He wasn't a prisoner here, you know. He pays his board, he's free to do what he wants and to come and go as he pleases.'

'Not any more he isn't,' Burgess said. 'Maybe you'd better get Gypsy Rose Lee here to ask the stars where he is, because if we don't find him it's soon going to be very hard on you lot.' He turned to Banks and Richmond. 'Let's have a look round. Where's his room?'

'First on the left at the top of the stairs,' Seth said. 'But you're wasting your time. He's not there.'

The three policemen climbed the narrow staircase. Richmond checked the other rooms while Banks and Burgess went into Paul's. There was only room for a single mattress on the floor and a small dresser at the far end, where a narrow window looked towards Eastvale. Sheets and blankets lay rumpled and creased on the unmade bed; dirty socks and underwear had been left in a pile on the floor. A stale smell of dead skin and unwashed clothes hung in the air. A couple of jackets, including a parka, hung in the tiny cupboard, and a pair of scuffed shoes lay on the floor. There was nothing much in the dresser drawers besides some clean underwear, T-shirts and a couple of moth-eaten pullovers. A grubby paperback copy of H.P. Lovecraft's *The Shadow over Innsmouth* lay open, face down on the pillow. On the cover was a picture of a semi-transparent frog-faced monster dressed in what looked like an evening suit. Out of habit, Banks picked the book up and flipped through the pages to see if Boyd had written anything interesting in the margins or on the blank pages at the back. He found nothing. Richmond came in and joined them.

'There's nothing here,' Burgess said. 'It doesn't look like he's scarpered though, unless he had a lot more clothes than this. I'd have taken a parka and a couple of sweaters if I'd been him. What was the weather like on the night Gill was stabbed?'

'Cool and wet,' Banks answered.

'Parka weather?'

'I'd say so, yes.'

Burgess took the coat from the cupboard and examined it. He pulled the inside of each pocket out in turn, and when he got to the right one, he pointed out a faint discoloured patch to Banks. 'Your men must have missed this the other day. Could be blood. He must have put the knife back in his pocket after he killed Gill. Hang on to this, Richmond. We'll get it to the lab. Why don't you two go and have a look in the outbuildings? You never know, he might be hiding in the wood pile. I'll poke around a bit more up here.'

Downstairs, Banks and Richmond went back into the kitchen and got Mara to accompany them with the keys. They left by the back door and found themselves in a large rectangular garden with a low fence. Most of the place was given over to rows of vegetables – dark empty furrows at that time of year – but there was also a small square sand-box, on which a plastic lorry with big red wheels and a yellow bucket and spade lay abandoned. At the far end of the garden stood a brick building with an asphalt roof, just a little larger than a garage, and to their left was a gate that led to the barn.

'We'll have a look over there first,' Banks said to Mara, who fiddled with the key ring as she followed them to the converted barn. It wasn't a big place, nowhere the size of many that had been converted into bunk barns for tourists, but it followed the traditional Dales design, on the outside at least, in that it was built of stone.

Mara opened the door to the downstairs unit first, Zoe's flat. Banks was surprised at the transformation from humble barn into comfortable living quarters; Seth had done a really good job. The woodwork was mostly unpainted, and if it looked a little makeshift, it was certainly sturdy and attractive in its simplicity. Not only, he gathered, did each unit have its own entrance, but there were cooking and bathing facilities too, as well as a large sparsely furnished living room, one master bedroom and a smaller one for Luna. But there was no sign of Paul Boyd.

The places were perfectly self-contained, Banks noticed, and if Rick and Zoe hadn't become friendly with Seth and Mara, they could easily have led quite separate lives there. Noting Mara's reaction to Burgess's threat and remembering what Jenny had said at dinner, Banks guessed that Mara's fondness for the children was one unifying factor – anyone would be glad of a built-in baby-sitter – and perhaps another was their shared politics.

Upstairs, the layout was different. Both bedrooms were quite small, and most of the space was taken up by Rick's studio, which was much less tidy than Zoe's large work table downstairs, with books and charts spread out on its surface. Seth had added three skylights along the length of the roof to provide plenty of light, and canvases, palettes and odd tubes of paint littered the place. From what Banks could see, Rick Trelawney's paintings were, as Tim Fenton had said, unmarketable, being mostly haphazard splashes of colour or collages of found objects. Sandra knew quite a bit about art, and Banks had learned from her that many paintings he wouldn't even store in the attic were regarded by experts as works of genius. But these were different, even he could tell; they made Jackson Pollock's angry explosions look as comprehensible as Constable's landscapes.

As he poked around among the stuff though, Banks discovered a stack of small watercolour landscapes

covered with an old sack. They resembled the one he'd
noticed in the front room on his last visit, and he realized
that they were, after all, Rick's work. So that was how he
made his money! Selling pretty local scenes to tourists and
little old ladies to support his revolutionary art.

Mara, who all the time had remained quiet, watching
them with her arms folded, locked up as they left and led
the way back to the house.

'You two go ahead,' Banks said when he had closed the
gate behind them. 'I'm off to take a peek in the shed. It's
not locked, is it?'

Mara shook her head and went back into the house
with Richmond.

Banks opened the door. The shed was dark inside and
smelled of wood shavings, sawdust, oiled metal, linseed
oil and varnish. He tugged the chain dangling in front of
him, and a naked bulb lit up, revealing Seth's workshop.
Planks, boards and pieces of furniture at various stages of
incompletion leaned against the walls. Spider webs hung
in the dark corners. Seth had a lathe and a full set of well
kept tools – planes, saws, hammers, bevels – and boxes of
nails and screws rested on makeshift wooden shelves
around the walls. There was no room for anyone to hide.

At the far end of the workshop, an old Remington office
typewriter sat on a desk beside an open filing cabinet.
Inside, Banks found only correspondence connected with
Seth's carpentry business: estimates, invoices, receipts,
orders. Close by was a small bookcase. Most of the books
were about antique furniture and cabinet-making techniques, but there were a couple of old paperback novels
and two books on the human brain, one of which was
called *The Tip of the Iceberg*. Maybe, Banks thought, Seth
harboured a secret ambition to become a brain surgeon.

Already a carpenter, he probably had a better start than most.

He walked back to the door and was about to turn off the light when he noticed a tattered notebook on a ledge by the door. It was full of measurements, addresses and phone numbers – obviously Seth's workbook. When he flipped through it, he noticed that one leaf had been torn out roughly. The following page still showed the faint impression of heavily scored numbers. Banks took a sheet from his own notebook, placed it on top and rubbed over it with a pencil. He could just make out the number in relief: 1139. It was hard to tell if it was in the same handwriting as the rest because the numbers were so much larger and more exaggerated.

Picking up the workbook, he turned to leave and almost bumped into Seth standing in the doorway.

'What are you doing?'

'This book,' Banks said. 'What do you use it for?'

'Work notes. When I need to order new materials, make measurements, note customers' addresses. That kind of thing.'

'There's a page missing.' Banks showed him. 'What does that mean – 1139?'

'Surely you can't expect me to remember that,' Seth said. 'It must have been a long time ago. It was probably some measurement or other.'

'Why did you tear it out?'

Seth looked at him, deep-set brown eyes wary and resentful. 'I don't know. Maybe it wasn't important. Maybe I'd written something on the back that I had to take with me somewhere. It's just an old notebook.'

'But there's only one page missing. Doesn't that strike you as odd?'

'I've already said it doesn't.'

'Did you tear out the page to give to Paul Boyd? Is it a number for him to call? Part of an address?'

'No. I've told you, I don't remember why I tore it out. It obviously wasn't very important.'

'I'll have to take this notebook away with me.'

'Why?'

'There are names and addresses in it. We'll have to check and see if Boyd's gone to any of them. As I understand it, he did spend quite a bit of time working with you in here.'

'But it's *my* notebook. Why would he be at any of those places? They're just people who live in the dale, people I've done work for. I don't want the police bothering them. It could lose me business.'

'We still have to check.'

Seth swore under his breath. 'Please yourself. You'd better give me a receipt, though.'

Banks wrote him one, then pulled the chain to turn off the light. They walked back to the house in silence.

Seth sat down again to finish his meal and Mara followed Banks towards the front of the room. They could hear Burgess and Richmond still poking about upstairs.

'Mr Banks?' Mara said quietly, standing close to him near the window.

Banks lit a cigarette. 'Yes?'

'What he said about the children . . . It's not true, is it? Surely he can't . . .?'

Banks sat in the rocking chair and Mara pulled up a small three-legged stool opposite him. One of Zoe's tarot decks, open at the Moon, lay on the table beside him. The moon seemed to be shedding drips of blood on to a path that led off into the distance between two towers. In the foreground, a crab was crawling up onto land from a pool, and a dog and a wolf stood howling at the moon. It was a disturbing and hypnotic design. Banks shivered, as if someone had just walked over his grave, and turned his attention to Mara.

'They're not your children, are they?' he said.

'You know they're not. But I love them as if they were. Jenny Fuller told me she knows you. She said you're not as bad as the rest. Tell me they can't make us give the children up.'

Banks smiled to himself. Not as bad as the rest, eh? He'd have to remember to tease Jenny about that back-handed compliment.

He turned to face Mara. 'Superintendent Burgess will do whatever he has to to get to the bottom of things. I don't think it'll come to taking the children away, but bear in mind that he doesn't make idle threats. If you know anything, you should tell us.'

Mara sucked on her bottom lip. She looked close to tears. 'I don't know where Paul is,' she said finally. 'You can't really think he did it?'

'We've got some evidence that points that way. Have you ever seen him with a flick knife?'

'No.'

Banks thought she was lying, but he knew it was no good pushing her. She might offer him a titbit of information in the hope that it would ease the pressure, but she wasn't going to tell the full truth.

'He's gone,' she said finally. 'I know that. But I don't know where.'

'How do you know he's gone?'

Mara hesitated, and her voice sounded too casual to be telling the truth. It made her face look thinner and more haggard. 'He's been upset these past few days, especially after your Superintendent Burgess came and bullied him. He thought you'd end up framing him because he's been in jail and because he . . . he looks different. He didn't want to bring trouble down on the rest of us, so he left.'

Banks turned over the next tarot card: the Star. A beautiful naked woman was pouring water from two vases into a pool on the ground. Behind her, trees and shrubs were blossoming, and in the sky one large bright central star was surrounded by seven smaller ones. For some reason, the woman reminded him of Sandra, which was odd because there was no strong physical resemblance.

'How do you know why he went?' Banks asked. 'Did he leave a note?'

'No, he just told me. He said last night he was thinking of leaving. He didn't say when.'

'Or where?'

'No.'

'Did he say anything about PC Gill's murder?'

'No, nothing. He didn't say he was running away because he was guilty, if that's what you mean.'

'And you didn't think to let us know he was running off, even though there's a chance he might be a killer?'

'He's no killer.' Mara spoke too quickly. 'I'd no reason to think so, anyway. If he wanted to go he was quite free as far as we were concerned.'

'What did he take with him?'

'What do you mean?'

Banks glanced towards the window. 'It's brass monkey weather out there; rains a lot, too. What was he wearing? Was he carrying a suitcase or a rucksack?'

Mara shook her head. 'I don't know. I didn't see him go.'

'Did you see him this morning?'

'Yes.'

'What time?'

'About eleven or half past. He always sleeps late.'

'What time did he leave? Approximately.'

'I don't know. I was out at lunch time. I left at twenty to one and got back at about two. He'd gone by then.'

'Was anyone else in the house during that time?'

'No. Seth was out in the van. He took Zoe with him because she had to deliver some charts. And Rick took the children into Eastvale.'

'And you don't know what Boyd was wearing or what he took with him?'

'No. I told you, I didn't see him go.'

'Come upstairs.'

'What?'

Banks headed towards the staircase. 'Come upstairs with me. Now.'

Mara followed him up to Paul's room. Banks opened the cupboard and the dresser drawers. 'What's missing?'

Mara put her hand to her forehead. Burgess and Richmond looked in at the doorway and carried on downstairs.

'I . . . I don't know,' Mara said. 'I don't know what clothes he had.'

'Who does the washing round here?'

'Well, I do. Mostly. Zoe does some, too.'

'So you must know what clothes Boyd had. What's missing?'

'He didn't have much.'

'He must have had another overcoat. He's left his parka.'

'No, he didn't. He had an anorak, though. A blue anorak.'

Banks wrote it down. 'What else?'

'Jeans, I suppose. He never wore much else.'

'Footwear.'

Mara looked in the cupboard and saw the scuffed shoes. 'Just a pair of old slip-ons. Hush Puppies, I think.'

'Colour?'

'Black.'

'And that's it?'

'As far as I know.'

Banks closed his notebook and smiled at Mara. 'Look, try not to worry about the children too much. As soon as Superintendent Burgess catches Paul Boyd, he'll forget all about the threats he made. If we catch him soon, that is.'

'I really *don't* know where he's gone.'

'OK. But if you come up with any ideas . . . Think about it.'

'People like Burgess shouldn't be allowed to run free,' Mara said. She folded her arms tightly and stared at the floor.

'Oh? What do you suggest we should do with him? Lock him up?'

She looked at Banks. Her jaw was clenched tight and her eyes burned with tears.

'Or should we have him put down?'

Mara brushed past him and hurried down the stairs. Banks followed slowly. Burgess and Richmond stood in the front room ready to leave.

'Come on, let's go,' Burgess said. 'There's nothing more here.' Then he turned to Seth, who stood in the kitchen doorway. 'If I find out you've been helping Boyd in any way, believe me, I'll be back. And you lot'll be in more trouble than you ever dared imagine. Give my love to the kids.'

TWO

Mara watched the car disappear down the track. She felt reassured by Banks, but wondered just how much he could do if Burgess had made his mind up about something. If the children were taken away, she thought, she could well be driven to murder the superintendent with her bare hands.

She became aware of the others behind her in the room. She hadn't told them anything about what had happened with Paul, and none of them knew yet that he had run off for good. For one thing, she'd hardly had time to say anything. They had all drifted back close to meal time anyway, when she was busy in the kitchen; then the police had arrived.

'What's going on, Mara?' Seth asked, coming up to her and resting his hand on her shoulder. 'Do you know?'

Mara nodded. She was trying to keep the tears from her eyes.

'Come on.' Seth took her hand and led her to a chair. 'Tell us.'

Seeing them all watching her, expectant, Mara regained her control. She reached for her tin of Old Holborn and rolled a cigarette.

'He's gone, that's all there is to it,' she said, and told them about seeing old Crocker carrying the knife into the Black Sheep. 'I ran back here to warn him. I didn't want the police to get him, and I thought if they'd got the knife they might find his fingerprints or something. He's been in jail, so they must be on record.'

'But what made you think of Paul?' Zoe asked. 'That knife was just lying around on the mantelpiece as usual, I suppose. Nobody ever paid it any mind. Any of the people here on Friday afternoon could have taken it.'

Mara drew on her cigarette and finally told them about the blood she'd seen on Paul's hand when he got back from the demo. The hand that turned out to be unmarked the following morning.

'Why didn't you tell us?' Seth asked. 'I don't suppose you approached Paul about it, either. There might have been a simple explanation.'

'I know that,' Mara said. 'Don't you think I've been over it time and again in my mind? I was frightened of him. I mean, if he had done it . . . But I wanted to stand by him. If I'd told you all, you might have asked him to leave or something.'

'How did he react when you came and told him the knife had been found?' Rick asked.

'He went pale. He couldn't look me in the eye. He looked like a frightened animal.'

'So you gave him money and clothes?'

'Yes. I gave him your red anorak, Zoe. I'm sorry.'

'It's all right,' Zoe said. 'I'd have done the same.'

'And I told the police he was probably wearing a blue one. He took his blue one with him, but he wasn't wearing it.'

'Where's he heading?' asked Rick.

'I don't know. I didn't want him to tell me. He's a survivor; he can live out on the streets. I gave him some money, some I'd saved from working at the shop and selling my pottery. He'll have enough to get wherever he wants.'

Later that evening, when the others had drifted off back to the barn and Seth had settled down with a book, Mara began to think about the few months that Paul had been around, and how alive he had made her feel. At first, he had been sullen and unresponsive, and there had come a point when Seth had considered asking him to leave. But Paul hadn't been long out of jail then; he wasn't used to dealing with people. Time and care had worked wonders. Soon he was taking long walks alone on the moors, and the claustrophobia that had so often made his nights unbearable in jail became easier to control. Nobody forced him to, but he really took to working with Seth.

When she thought about his progress and what it had all come to, Mara couldn't help but feel sad. It would all be for nothing if he got caught and sent to prison again. When she pictured him cold and alone in the strange and frightening world beyond Swainsdale, it made her want to cry. But she told herself again that he was strong, resourceful, a survivor. It wouldn't feel the same to him as it would to her. Besides, imagined horrors were always far worse than the reality.

'I hope Paul makes it far away,' Seth said in the silence that followed their lovemaking that night. 'I hope they never catch him.'

'How will we know where he is, what's happening to him?' Mara asked.

'He'll let us know one way or another. Don't you worry about it.' He put his arm around her and she rested her head against his chest. 'You did the right thing.'

But she couldn't help but worry. She didn't think they'd hear from Paul again, not after all that had happened. She didn't know what else she could have done, but she wasn't sure she had done the right thing. As she tried to sleep, she remembered the expression on his face just before he left. There had been gratitude, yes, for the warning, the money and the clothes, but there had also been resentment and disappointment. He'd looked as if he was being sent into exile. She didn't know if he'd expected her to ask him to stay no matter what – she certainly hadn't told him he *had* to go away – but there had been a hint of accusation in his actions, as if to say, 'You think I did it, don't you? You don't want me here causing trouble. You didn't trust me in the first place. I'm an outcast, and I always will be.' She hadn't told Seth and the others about that.

THREE

Banks waited his turn at the busy bar of the Queen's Arms while Burgess sat at a round table by the Market Street entrance. It was eight thirty. Hatchley had just left to keep a date with Carol Ellis, and Richmond had gone to a do at the rugby club.

Dirty Dick was clearly pleased with himself. He leaned back in his chair and positively beamed goodwill at everyone who looked his way. Nobody gave him much more than a scowl in return, though.

'Ey, Mr Banks,' said Cyril. 'A minute, if you've got one.'

'Course. For you, Cyril, anything. And you might as well pull me a pint of bitter and a pint of Double Diamond while you're talking.'

'It's about that there mate of yours.' Cyril nodded his head aggressively in the direction of Burgess.

'He's not really a mate,' Banks said. 'More like a boss.'

'Aye. Well, anyways, tell him to stop pestering my Glenys. She's got too much work to do without passing the time of day with the likes of him.' Cyril leaned forward and lowered his voice. The muscles bulged above his rolled-up shirt sleeves. 'And you can tell him I don't care if he is a copper – no disrespect, Mr Banks – if he doesn't keep out of my way I'll give him a bloody knuckle sandwich, so help me I will.'

Glenys, who seemed to have grasped the tenor of the conversation, blushed and busied herself pulling a pint at the other end of the bar.

'I'd be delighted to pass on your message,' Banks said, paying for the drinks.

'Don't forget his lordship's Double Diamond,' Cyril said, his voice edged with contempt.

'You can wipe that bloody grin off your face,' Burgess said after Banks had passed on Cyril's warning. 'You're a long way from collecting that fiver yet. She fancies me, does young Glenys, there's no doubt about it. And there's nothing like a bit of danger, a touch of risk, to get the old hormones flowing. Look at her.' True enough, Glenys was flashing Burgess a flush-cheeked smile while Cyril was looking the other way. 'If we could only get that oaf out of the way . . . Anyway, it's her night off next Monday. She usually goes to the pictures with her mates.'

'I'd be careful if I were you,' Banks said.

'Yes, but you're not me, are you?' He gulped down about half of his pint. 'Ah, that's good. So, we've got the bastard. Or will have soon.'

Banks nodded. That, he assumed, was why they were celebrating. Burgess was on his fourth pint already and Banks on his third.

They had done everything they could. Boyd had certainly done a bunk, though Banks had no idea how he knew about the discovery of the knife. It was likely he had headed for Eastvale and taken a bus. The number 43 ran along Cardigan Drive, on the town's western edge. He would simply have had to walk across the moors and up Gallows View to get there. Also, buses to York and Ripon passed along the same road. Somebody must have seen him. Banks had circulated his description to the bus companies and sent out his mugshot to police around the country, paying particular attention to Leeds, Liverpool and London. As Burgess said, it was simply a matter of time before he was caught.

'Where did you get that bloody scar?' Burgess asked.

'This?' Banks fingered the white crescent by his right eye. 'Got it in Heidelberg. It's a duelling scar.'

'Ha bloody ha! You're a funny man, aren't you? Have you heard the one about the—' Burgess stopped and looked up at the person standing over them. 'Well, well,' he said, scraping his chair aside to make room. 'If it isn't—'

'Dr Fuller,' Jenny said. She glanced at Banks and pulled up a chair next to his.

'Of course. How could I forget? Drink, love?'

Jenny smiled sweetly. 'Yes, please. I'll have a half of lager.'

'Oh come on, have a pint,' Burgess insisted.

'All right. A pint.'

'Good.' Burgess rubbed his hands together and set off for the bar. His thigh caught the edge of the table as he stood up. Beer rippled in the glasses but didn't spill.

Jenny pulled a face at Banks. 'What's with him?'

Banks grinned. 'Celebrating.'

'So I see.' She leaned closer. 'Look, I've got something to ask you—'

Banks put a finger to his lips. 'Not now,' he said. 'He's getting served. He'll be back soon.' True enough, in no time Burgess was on his way back, trying to carry three pints in his hands and slopping beer over the rims on to his shoes.

'What are you celebrating, anyway?' Jenny asked after Burgess had managed to set the drinks on the table without spilling much.

Banks told her about Paul Boyd.

'That's a shame.'

'A shame! You said he gave you the creeps.'

'He does. I'm just thinking of the others, that's all. It'll be a hell of a blow for Seth and Mara. They've done so much for him. Especially Mara.' Jenny seemed unusually distracted at the thought of Mara Delacey, and Banks wondered why.

'You know,' Burgess said, 'I'm a bit sorry it turned out to be Boyd, myself.'

Jenny looked surprised: 'You are? Why?'

'Well. . .' He moved closer. 'I was hoping it might be that boyfriend of yours. Then we could get him locked up for a good long while, and you and me could . . . you know.'

To Banks's surprise, Jenny laughed. 'You've got some imagination, I'll say that for you, Superintendent Burgess.'

'Call me Dick. Most of my friends do.'

Jenny stifled a laugh. 'I really don't think I could do that. Honest.'

'Aren't you relieved it's all over?' Banks asked her. 'I'll bet Osmond is.'

'Of course. Especially if it means we won't have to put up with any more visits from him.' She nodded at Burgess.

'I could still visit,' Dirty Dick said, and winked.

'Oh, put another record on. So where do you think Paul is?' she asked Banks.

'We've no idea. He took off early this afternoon, before we got a positive identification. Could be anywhere.'

'But you're confident you'll get him?'

'I think so.'

Jenny turned to Burgess. 'So your job's over, then? I don't suppose you'll want to stick around this godforsaken place much longer, will you?'

'Oh, I don't know.' Burgess lit a cigar and leered at her. 'It has its compensations.'

Jenny coughed and waved the smoke away.

'Seriously,' he went on, 'I'll stay around till he's brought in. There's a lot I want to ask him.'

'But that could take days, weeks.'

Burgess shrugged. 'It's the taxpayers' money, love. Your round again, Banks.'

'Nothing for me this time,' Jenny said. 'I'll have to be off soon.' She still had over half her drink left.

Feeling a little light-headed, Banks went to the bar.

''Ave you told him?' Cyril asked.

'Yes.'

'Good. I just hope he knows what's best for him. Look at the bugger, he can't keep his hands off them.'

Banks looked round. Dirty Dick seemed to have edged closer to Jenny, and his elbow rested on the back of her chair. She was behaving very calmly, Banks thought. It wasn't like her to take such sexist patronizing so well. Maybe she fancies him, he thought suddenly. If Glenys does, then maybe Jenny does, too. Perhaps he really does have the magic touch with women. At least he's available. And he's handsome enough, too. That casual look – the worn leather jacket, open-neck shirt – it suits him, as do the touches of grey hair at his temples.

Banks brushed the idea aside. It was ridiculous. Jenny was an intelligent tasteful woman. A woman like her could never fall for Dirty Dick's brazen charm. But women were a mysterious lot, Banks thought glumly, carrying the drinks back. They were always falling for worthless men. He clearly recalled the beautiful Anita Howarth, object of his adolescent lust back in the third form. She had been quite oblivious to Banks's lean good looks and taken up with that spotty good-for-nothing Steve Naylor. And Naylor hadn't seemed to give a damn about her. He gave the impression he would rather be playing cricket or rugby than go anywhere with Anita. But that just made her more crazy about him. And Banks had had to spend all his time fending off unwelcome advances from Cheryl Wagstaff, the one with the yellow buck teeth.

'I was just offering to show this lovely young lady the sights of London,' Burgess said.

'I'm sure she's seen them before,' Banks replied stiffly.

'Not the way I'd show her.' Burgess moved his arm so that his hand rested on Jenny's shoulder.

Banks was wondering if he should act gallantly this time and defend Jenny's honour. After all, they were sort of off duty. But he remembered she was quite good at taking care of herself. Her face took on an ominously sweet expression.

'Please take your hand off my shoulder, Superintendent,' she said.

'Oh, come on, love,' Burgess said. 'Don't be so shy. And call me Dick.'

'Please?'

'Give me a chance. We've hardly even got—'

Burgess stopped abruptly when Jenny calmly and slowly picked up her glass and poured the rest of her chilled lager on his lap.

'I told you I only wanted a half,' she said, then picked up her coat and left.

Burgess rushed for the gents. Luckily, Jenny had acted so naturally and everyone around them had been so engrossed in conversation, that the event had gone largely unnoticed. Cyril had seen it though, and his face was red with laughter.

Banks caught up with Jenny outside. She was leaning against the ancient pitted market cross in the centre of the square with her hand over her mouth. 'My God,' she said, letting the laughter out and patting her chest, 'I haven't had as much fun in years. That man's a positive throw-back. I'm surprised you seem to be enjoying his company so much.'

'He's not so bad,' Banks said. 'Especially after a few jars.'

'Yes, you'd need to be at least half pissed. And you'd need to be a man, too. You're all adolescents when it comes down to it.'

'He's got quite a reputation as a womanizer.'

'They must be desperate down south, then.'

Banks's faith in women was partially restored.

It was cold outside in the deserted square. The cobbles, still wet with rain, glistened in the dim gaslight. The church bells rang half past nine. Banks turned up his jacket collar and held the lapels close together. 'What was it you wanted to ask me?'

'It's nothing. It doesn't matter now.'

'Come on, Jenny, you're hiding something. You're not good at it. Is it to do with Paul Boyd?'

'Indirectly. But I told you, it doesn't matter.'

'Do you know why he ran away?'

'Of course not.'

'Look, I know you're a friend of Mara's. Is this to do with her? It could be important.'

'All right,' Jenny said, holding up her hand. 'Give it a rest. I'll tell you everything you want to know. You're getting almost as bad as your mate in there. Mara just wondered how the investigation was going, that's all. They're all a bit tense up at the farm, and they wanted to know if they could expect any more visits from God's gift to women. Will you believe me now that it doesn't matter?'

'When did you talk to her?'

'This lunch time in the Black Sheep.'

'She must have seen the knife,' Banks said, almost to himself.

'What?'

'The shepherd, Jack Crocker. He found the knife. She must have seen it, recognized it as Boyd's and dashed off to warn him. That's why he left just in time.'

'Oh, Alan, surely not?'

'I thought she was lying when I talked to her earlier. Didn't you notice any of this?'

'She did leave in rather a hurry, but I'd no idea why. I went just after. You're not going to arrest her, are you?'

Banks shook his head. 'It makes her an accessory,' he said, 'but I doubt we'd be able to prove it. And when Burgess gets Boyd, I don't think he'll spare another thought for Mara and the rest. It was just a bloody stupid thing to do.'

'Was it? Would you split on a friend, just like that? What would you do if someone accused Richmond of murder, or me?'

'That's not the point. Of course I'd do what I could to clear you. But she should have let us know. Boyd could be dangerous.'

'She cares about Paul. She's hardly likely to hand him over to you just like that.'

'I wonder if she's told him where to run and hide as well.'

Jenny shivered. 'It's cold standing about here,' she said. 'I should go before Dirty Dick comes out and beats me up. That's just about his level. And you'd better get back or he'll think you've deserted him. Give him my love.' She kissed Banks quickly on the cheek and hurried to her car. He stood in the cold for a moment thinking about Mara and what Jenny had said, then rushed back into the Queen's Arms to see what had become of the soused superintendent.

'She's certainly got spirit, I'll say that,' Burgess said, not at all upset by the incident. 'Another pint?'

'I shouldn't really.'

'Oh, come on, Banks. Don't be a party pooper.' Without waiting for a reply, Burgess went to the bar.

Banks felt that he'd had enough already, and soon he would be past the point of no return. Still, he thought, after a couple more pints he wouldn't give a damn anyway. He sensed that Burgess was lonely and in need of company in his moment of triumph, and he didn't feel he could simply desert the bastard. Besides, he had only an empty house to go home to. He could leave the Cortina in the police car park and walk home later, no matter how much he'd drunk. It was only a mile and a bit.

And so they drank on, and on. Burgess was easy enough to talk to, Banks found, once you got used to his cocky manner and stayed off politics and police work. He had a broad repertoire of jokes, an extensive knowledge of jazz and a store of tales about cock-ups on the job. On the Met, as Banks remembered, there were so many different departments and squads running their own operations that it wasn't unusual for the Sweeney to charge in and spoil a fraud squad stake-out.

An hour and two pints later, as Burgess reached the end of a tale about a hapless drug squad DC shooting himself in the foot, Banks suggested it was time to go.

'I suppose so,' Burgess said regretfully, finishing his drink and getting to his feet.

He certainly didn't seem drunk. His speech was normal and his eyes looked clear. But when they got outside, he had difficulty walking on the pavement. To keep himself steady, he put his arm around Banks's shoulder and the two of them weaved across the market square. Thank God the hotel's just around the corner, Banks thought.

'That's my only trouble, you know,' Burgess said. 'Mind clear as a bell, memory intact, but every time I go over the limit my motor control goes haywire. Know what my mates call me down at the Yard?'

'No.'

'Bambi.' He laughed. 'Bloody Bambi. You know, that little whatsit in the cartoon – the way the damn thing walks. It's not my sweet and gentle nature they're referring to.' He put his hand to his groin. 'Bloody hell, I still feel like I've pissed myself. That damn woman!' And he laughed.

Banks declined an invitation to go up to Burgess's room and split a bottle of Scotch. No matter how sorry he felt for the lonely bugger, he wasn't that much of a masochist. Grudgingly, Burgess let him go. 'I'll drink it myself, then,' were his final words, delivered at full volume in front of an embarrassed desk clerk in the hotel lobby.

As he set off home, Banks wished he'd brought his Walkman. He could be listening to Blind Willie McTell or

Bukka White as he walked. He was steady on his feet though, and arrived at the front door of the empty house in about twenty minutes. He was tired and he certainly didn't want another drink, so he decided to go straight to bed. As usual though, when things were bothering him he couldn't get to sleep immediately. And there were plenty of things about the Gill case that still puzzled him.

Motive was a problem, unless Burgess was right and Boyd had simply lashed out indiscriminately. In this case, it seemed that knowing *who* didn't explain *why*. Boyd wasn't political as far as anyone knew, and even street punks like him weren't in the habit of stabbing policemen at anti-nuclear demos. If someone had a private reason for wanting to do away with Gill, then there was plenty to consider in the personal lives of the other suspects: Osmond's assault charges, Trelawney's custody battle, Seth's wife's accident, Mara's religious organization, and even Zoe's seaside fortune-telling. It was hard to imagine a connection at this point, but stranger things had happened. Tony Grant's report might prove useful, if it ever arrived.

Banks was also curious about the prints on the knife. Usually when a knife is thrust into a body, the fingers holding the handle slip and any impression is blurred. Boyd's prints had been perfectly clear, just as if he had carefully applied each one. It could have happened if he'd folded up the knife and carried it in his hand before throwing it away, or if he'd picked it up after someone else had used it. There were other prints under his, but they were too blurred to read. They could be his too, of course, but there was no way of knowing.

Boyd had certainly carried the knife in his pocket. The stains inside the parka matched PC Gill's blood type. But if he had used it, why had he been foolish enough to pick it up after dropping it? He must have let it fall at some point, because several people had seen it being kicked around by the crowd. And if he had just left it there, it was very unlikely that it could have been traced to the farm.

But if Boyd hadn't done it, why had he picked up a knife that wasn't his? To protect someone? And who would he be more likely to protect than the people at Maggie's Farm? Or had there been someone else he knew and cared about who had access to the knife? There were a lot more questions to be asked yet, Banks thought, and Burgess was being very premature in celebrating his victory tonight.

Then there was the matter of the number torn out of Seth Cotton's notebook. Banks didn't know what it meant, but there was something familiar about it, something damn familiar. Boyd was close to Seth and spent plenty of time helping him in the workshop. Could the number be something to do with him? Could it help tell them where he'd gone?

It could be a phone number, of course. There were still plenty of four-digit numbers in the Swainsdale area. On impulse, Banks got out of bed and went downstairs. It was after eleven, but he decided to try anyway. He dialled 1139 and heard a phone ring at the other end. It went on for a long time. He was just about to give up when a woman answered, 'Hello. Rossghyll Guest House, bed and breakfast.' The voice was polite but strained.

Banks introduced himself and some of the woman's politeness faded when it became clear that he wasn't a potential customer. 'Do you know what time it is?' she said. 'Couldn't this have waited till morning? Do you know what time I have to get up?'

'It's important.' Banks gave a description of Paul Boyd and asked if she'd seen him.

'I wouldn't have that kind of person staying here,' the woman answered angrily. 'What kind of place do you think this is? This is a decent house.' And with that she hung up on him.

Banks trudged back up to bed. He'd have to send a man over, of course, just to be sure, but it didn't seem a likely bet. And if it was a phone number outside the local area, it could be almost anywhere. With the dialling code missing, there was no way of telling.

Banks lay awake a while longer, then he finally drifted off to sleep and dreamed of Burgess humble in defeat.

9

ONE

The overcast sky seemed to press on Banks's nagging headache when he set off for Maggie's Farm at eleven thirty the next morning. Burgess had called in earlier to say he was going over some paperwork in his hotel room and didn't want to be disturbed unless Paul Boyd turned up. That suited Banks fine; he wanted a word with Mara Delacey, and the less Dirty Dick knew about it the better.

He pulled up outside the farmhouse and knocked. He wasn't surprised when Mara opened the door and moaned, 'Not again!'

Reluctantly she let him in. There was no one else in the place. The others were probably working.

Banks wanted to get Mara away from the house, on neutral ground. Perhaps then, he thought, he could get her to open up a bit more.

'I'd just like to talk to you, that's all,' he said. 'It's not an interrogation, nothing official.'

She looked puzzled. 'Go on.'

Banks tapped his watch. 'It's nearly lunch time and I haven't eaten yet,' he said casually. 'Do you fancy a trip down to the Black Sheep?'

'What for? Is this some subtle way of getting me to accompany you to the station?'

'No tricks. Honest. What I've got to say might even be of advantage to you.'

She still regarded him suspiciously, but the bait was too good to refuse. 'All right.' She reached for an anorak to put over her sweater and jeans. 'I'm going into the shop this afternoon anyway.' She pulled back her thick chestnut hair and tied it in a ponytail.

In the car, Mara leaned forward to examine the tapes Banks kept in the storage rack Brian had bought him for his birthday the previous May – his thirty-eighth. There, mixed in with Zemlinsky's *Birthday of the Infanta*, Mozart's *Magic Flute*, Dowland's *Lachrymae* and Purcell's airs, were Lightning Hopkins, Billie Holiday, Muddy Waters, Robert Wilkins and a number of blues anthology tapes.

Picking up the Billie Holiday, Mara managed a thin smile. 'A policeman who likes blues can't be all bad,' she said.

Banks laughed. 'I like most music,' he said, 'except for country and western and middle-of-the-road crooning – you know, Frank Sinatra, Engelbert Humperdinck and that lot.'

'Even rock?'

'Even rock. Some, anyway. I must admit I'm still stuck in the sixties as far as that's concerned. I lost interest after the Beatles split up. I even know where the name of your house comes from.'

Banks was pleased to be chatting so easily with Mara. It was the first time his interest in music had helped create the kind of rapport he wanted with a witness. So often people regarded it as an eccentricity, but now it was actually helping with an important investigation. A common interest in jazz and blues had also helped him to relax with Burgess a little. Still, he thought, Mara probably wouldn't stay so convivial when she followed the drift of the questions he had to ask her.

They found a quiet corner in the pub by the tiled fireplace. In a glass case on the wall beside them was a collection of butterflies pinned to a board. Banks bought Mara a half of mild and got a pint of Black Sheep bitter for himself. Maybe the hair of the dog would do the trick and get rid of his headache. He ordered a ploughman's lunch; Mara asked for lasagne.

'Ploughman's lunches were invented for tourists in the seventies,' Mara said.

'Not authentic?'

'Not a bit.'

'Oh well, I can think of worse inventions.'

'I suppose you want to get down to business, don't you?' Mara said. 'Did Jenny Fuller tell you about our meeting?'

'No, but I figured it out. I think she's worried about you.'

'She needn't be. I'm all right.'

'Are you? I thought you'd be worried sick about Paul Boyd.'

'What if I am?'

'Do you think he's guilty?'

Mara paused and sipped some beer. She swept a stray wisp of hair from her cheek before answering. 'Maybe I did at first,' she said. 'At least, I was worried. I mean, we don't know a lot about him. I suppose I looked at him differently. But not now, no. And I don't care what evidence you've got against him.'

'What made you change your mind?'

'A feeling, that's all. Nothing concrete, nothing you'd understand.'

Banks leaned forward. 'Believe it or not, Mara, police-men have feelings like that, too. We call them hunches, or we put them down to our nose, our instinct for truth. You may be right about Boyd. I'm not saying you are, but there's a chance. Things aren't quite as cut and dried as they appear. In some ways Paul is too obvious.'

'Isn't that what appeals to you? How easy it is to blame him?'

'Not to me, no.'

'But . . . I mean . . . I thought you were sure, that you had evidence?'

'The knife?'

'Yes.'

'You recognized it, didn't you, when Jack Crocker brought it in here yesterday lunch time?'

Mara said nothing. Before Banks could speak again, the food arrived and they both tucked in.

'Look,' said Banks, after polishing off the best part of a chunk of Wensleydale and a pickled onion, 'let's assume that Boyd's innocent, just for the sake of argument.' Mara looked at him, but her expression was hard to fathom. Suspicion? Hope? Either reaction would be perfectly natural. 'If he is,' Banks went on, 'then it raises more questions than it answers. It's easier for everyone if Boyd turns out to be guilty – everyone but him, that is – but the easiest way isn't necessarily the true one. Do you know what I mean?'

Mara nodded and her lips curved just a little at the edges. 'Sounds like the Eightfold Path,' she said.

'The what?'

'The Eightfold Path. It's the Buddhist way to enlighten-ment.'

Banks speared another pickled onion. 'Well, I don't

know much about enlightenment,' he said, 'but we could do with a bit more light on the case.' He went on to tell her about the blood and prints on the knife. 'That much we know,' he said. 'That's the evidence, the facts, if you like. Boyd was there, and we can prove that he handled the murder weapon. Superintendent Burgess thinks it's enough to convict him, but I'm not sure myself. Given the political aspect though, he might just be right. Finding Boyd guilty will make us look good and it'll discredit everyone who seems a bit different.'

'Isn't that what you want?'

'I wish you'd stop making assumptions like that. You sound like a stoned hippie at a rock festival. Maybe you'd like to call me a pig too, and get it over with? Either that or grow up.'

Mara said nothing, but Banks saw the faint flush suffuse her face.

'I want the truth,' Banks went on. 'I'm not out to get any group or person, just a killer. If we assume that Boyd didn't do it, then why are his prints on the knife, and why was it found on the moors about halfway between Eastvale and Maggie's Farm?'

Mara pushed her half-eaten lasagne aside and rolled a cigarette. 'I'm no detective,' she said, 'but maybe he picked it up and threw it away on his way home, when he realized what it was.'

'But why? Would you have done something as stupid as that? Bent down at a demonstration to pick up a blood-stained knife? Think about it. Boyd had no guarantee of getting away. What if he'd been caught on the spot with the knife on him?'

'He'd probably have had time to drop it if he saw the cops closing in on him.'

'Yes, but it would still have his prints on it. I doubt if he'd have been calm enough to wipe it before they grabbed him. Even if he had, there would probably have been some of Gill's blood on him.'

'This is all very well,' Mara said, 'but I don't know what you're getting at.'

'I'll tell you in a moment.' Banks went to the bar and bought two more drinks. The place had filled up a bit since they'd come in, and there were even two well-wrapped hikers resting their feet by the fire.

Banks sat down and drank some beer. The hair of the dog was working nicely. 'It all comes back to the knife,' he said. 'You recognized it; Paul Boyd must have done, too. It comes from the farm, doesn't it?'

Mara turned aside and studied the butterflies.

'You're not helping anyone by holding back, you know. I only want you to confirm what we already know.'

Mara stubbed out her cigarette. 'All right, so it comes from the house. What of it? If you know already, why bother to ask?'

'Because Paul might have been protecting someone, mightn't he? If he found the knife and took it away, he must have thought it was evidence pointing to someone he knew, someone at the farm. Unless you think he's just plain stupid.'

'You mean one of us?'

'Yes. Who would he be most likely to protect?'

'I don't know. There were a few people up at the farm that afternoon.'

'Yes, I know who was there. Could anyone have taken the knife?'

Mara shrugged. 'It was on the mantelpiece, in plain view of everyone.'

'Whose knife is it?'

'I don't know. It's always been there.'

'Never mind, then. Let's just call it a communal flick knife. Do you think Paul would have picked it up to protect Dennis Osmond? Or Tim and Abha?'

Mara twirled a loose strand of hair. 'I don't know,' she said. 'He didn't know them very well.'

'What part did he play that afternoon? Was he around?'

'Most of the time, yes, but he didn't say much. Paul has an inferiority complex when it comes to students and political talk. He doesn't know about Karl Marx and the rest, and he doesn't have enough confidence in his own ideas to feel he can contribute.'

'So he was there but he wasn't very involved?'

'That's right. He agreed with everything in principle. I mean, he wasn't at the demo just to . . . just to . . .'

'Cause trouble?'

'No. He was there to demonstrate. He's never had a job, you know. He's got nothing to thank Thatcher's government for.'

'You say the knife was usually kept on the mantelpiece. Did you see anyone pick it up that afternoon, just to fidget with, perhaps?'

'No.'

'When did you notice it was missing?'

'What?'

'You must have noticed it was gone. Was it before you saw Jack Crocker walk in here with it yesterday?'

'I . . . I . . .'

Banks waved his hand. 'Forget it. I think I get the gist. You had noticed it was missing, and for some reason you thought Paul might have taken it with him last Friday.'

'No!'

'Then why did you run off and warn him?'

'Because I thought you'd pick on him if the knife had been found here. Jack Crocker works these moors. I knew when I saw him he couldn't have found it far away.'

'Plausible,' Banks said. 'But I'm not convinced. You weren't at the demo, were you?'

'No. It's not that I don't believe in the cause, but somebody had to stay home and look after the children.'

'You didn't put them to bed early and sneak out?'

'Are you accusing me?'

'I'm asking you.'

'Well, I don't know how you'd expect me to do that. The others had taken the van and it's a good four miles' walk across the moor to Eastvale.'

'So that leaves Paul, Zoe, Seth and Rick. Seth and Rick were arrested, but if Paul had picked up the knife at the demo, either one of them could have stabbed Gill, too.'

'I don't believe it.'

'Did Osmond or any of the others dislike you enough to want to put the blame on one of you?'

'I don't think so. Nobody had reason to hate us that much.'

'If you really hadn't noticed the knife for some time, someone else could have taken it earlier, couldn't they? Did you have any visitors during the week?'

'I . . . I don't remember.'

'Do you keep the place securely locked up?'

'You must be joking. We've nothing worth stealing.'

'Think about it. You see my problem, don't you? How it becomes more complicated if we leave Boyd out of it. And if someone did take the knife, there's premeditation involved. Do you know of anyone with a reason to murder PC Gill?'

'No.'

'Was he mentioned that afternoon up at the farm?'

'Not that I heard. But I was in and out. You know, making tea, clearing up.'

Banks drank some more Black Sheep bitter. 'Does the number 1139 mean anything to you?'

Mara frowned. The lines curved down from each side of her forehead and converged at the bridge of her nose. 'No,' she said. 'At least I don't think so. Why? Where did you find it?'

'It's not part of an address or a telephone number, for example?'

'I've told you, no. Not that I know of. It sounds vaguely familiar, but I can't place it.'

'Have you ever heard of the Rossghyll Guest House?'

'Yes, it's up the dale. Why?'

Banks watched her expression closely and saw no sign that the place meant anything to her. 'Never mind. Let me know if anything comes to you. It might be important.'

Mara finished her drink and shifted in her chair. 'Is there anything else?'

'Just one thing. It looks bad for Paul, running off like this. I know I can't ask you to turn him in, even if you do know where he is. But it really would be best for him if he gave himself up. Is there any chance of that?'

'It's unlikely. He's scared of the police, especially that bastard of a superintendent you've got.' She shook her head. 'I don't think he'll turn himself in.'

'If you hear from him, tell him what I said. Tell him I promise he'll get a fair deal.'

Mara nodded slowly. 'I don't believe it'll do much good though,' she said. 'He won't believe me. He doesn't trust us now any more than he trusts you.'

'Why not?'

'He knows I suspected him, just for a while. Paul's had so little love in his life he finds it hard enough to trust people in the first place. If they let him down, even in the slightest, then that's it.'

'Still,' Banks said, 'if you get the chance, put in a word.'

'I'll tell him. But I don't think any of us is likely to hear from Paul again. Can I go now?'

'Wait a moment and I'll give you a lift.' Banks still had half a pint left and made to finish it off.

Mara stood up. 'No, I'll walk. The shop's not far, and I could do with some fresh air.'

'Are you sure?'

'Yes.'

After she'd gone, Banks relaxed and savoured the rest of his beer. The meeting had gone better than he'd expected, and he had actually learned something about the knife. Mara had been evasive, mostly to avoid incriminating herself, but that was only to be expected. He didn't blame her for it.

Banks decided to keep his knowledge from Burgess for a while. He didn't want Dirty Dick to go charging in like a bloody elephant and frighten everyone into their corners as usual. Banks had managed to overcome some of Mara's general resentment towards the police – whether through Jenny's influence, his taste in music or sheer charm, he wasn't sure – but if Burgess turned up again, Mara's hatred for him would surely rub off on Banks as well.

By the time he set off back to Eastvale, his head had stopped aching and he felt able to tolerate some music. But he couldn't shake off the feeling that he was missing something obvious. He had the strange sensation that two insignificant things either he or Mara had said should be joined into one truth. If they made contact, a little bulb would light up and he would be that much closer to solving the case. Billie Holiday sang on regardless:

> *Sad am I, glad am I*
> *For today I'm dreaming of*
> *Yesterdays.*

TWO

Mara walked along the street, head down, thinking about her talk with Banks. Like all policemen, he asked nothing but bloody awkward questions. And Mara was sick of awkward questions. Why couldn't things just get back to normal so she could get on with her life?

'Hello, love,' Elspeth greeted her as she walked into the shop.

'Hello. How's Dottie?'

'She won't eat. How she can expect to get better when she refuses to eat, I just don't know.'

They both knew that Dottie wasn't going to get better, but nobody said so.

'What's wrong with you?' Elspeth asked. 'You've got a face as long as next week.'

Mara told her about Paul.

'I don't want to say I told you so,' Elspeth said, smoothing her dark tweed skirt, 'but I thought that lad was trouble from the start. You're best rid of him, all of you.'

'I suppose you're right.' Mara didn't agree, but there was no point arguing Paul's case against Elspeth. She hadn't expected any sympathy.

'Go in the back and get the wheel spinning, love,' Elspeth said. 'It'll do you a power of good.'

The front part of the shop was cluttered with goods for tourists. There were locally knitted sweaters on shelves on the walls, tables of pottery – some of which Mara had made – and trays of trinkets such as key rings bearing the Dales National Park emblem, the black face of a Swaledale sheep. As if that weren't enough, the rest of the space was taken up by fancy notepaper, glass paperweights, fluffy animals and fridge door magnets shaped like strawberries or Humpty Dumpty.

In the back though, the set-up was very different. First, there was a small pottery workshop, complete with wheel and dishes of brown and black metallic oxide glaze, and beyond that a drying room and a small electric kiln. The workshop was dusty and messy, crusted with bits of old clay, and it suited a part of Mara's personality. Mostly she preferred cleanliness and tidiness, but there was something special, she found, about creating beautiful objects in a chaotic environment.

She put on her apron, took a lump of clay from the bin and weighed off enough for a small vase. The clay was too wet, so she wedged it on a flat concrete tray, which absorbed the excess moisture. As she wedged – pushing hard with the heels of her hands, then pulling the clay forward with her fingers to get all the air out – she couldn't seem to lose herself in the task as usual but kept on thinking about her conversation with Banks.

Frowning, she cut the lump in half with a cheese wire to check for air bubbles, then slammed the pieces together much harder than usual. A fleck of clay spun off and hit her forehead, just above her right eye. She put the clay down and took a few deep breaths, trying to bring her mind to bear only on what she was doing.

No good. It was Banks's fault, of course. He had introduced her to speculations that caused nothing but distress. True, she didn't want Paul to be guilty, but if, as Banks had said, that meant someone else she knew had killed the policeman, that only made things worse.

Sighing, she started the wheel with the foot pedal and slammed the clay as close to the centre as she could. Then she drenched both it and her hands with water from a bowl by her side. As the wheel spun, clayey water flew off and splashed her apron.

She couldn't believe that any of her friends had stabbed Gill. Much better if Osmond or one of the students had done it for political reasons. Tim and Abha seemed nice enough, if a bit naive and gushing, but Mara had never trusted Osmond; he had always seemed somehow too oily and opinionated for her taste.

But what about Rick? He had strong political views, more so than Seth or Zoe. He'd often said someone should assassinate Margaret Thatcher, and Seth had argued that someone just as bad would take her place. But it was only a policeman who'd been killed, not a politician. Despite what Rick said about the police being mere instruments of the state, paid enforcers, she couldn't believe that would make him actually kill one of them.

She leaned forward, elbows in, and pushed hard to centre the clay. At last she managed it and, allowing herself a smile of satisfaction, stuck her thumb in the top and pushed down about an inch. She then filled the hole with water and began to drive deeper to where she wanted the bottom of the vase to be.

Holding the inside with one finger, she slowed the wheel and began to make a ridge from the outside bottom, raising the clay to the height she wanted. It took several times to get there, pulling just a little further each time, watching the groove flow up the outside of the clay and disappear.

She was determined not to let Banks get to her. There was no way she was going to start suspecting Rick the way she had Paul. She had good reason for worrying about him, she told herself: his violent past; the blood he had lied about. And the knife had his fingerprints on it. She had no reason at all for suspecting anyone else. If only Paul could get far away and never be seen again. That would be best – if the police continued to believe he had done it but were never able to find him.

She could hear Elspeth out front trying to sell a sweater to a customer. 'Traditional Dales pattern . . . local wool, of course . . . hand-knitted, naturally . . .'

Almost there. But her hands weren't steady, and when she'd lost her concentration she had increased the pressure with her right foot, speeding up the wheel. Suddenly the clay began to spin wildly off centre – insane shapes, like Salvador Dali paintings or plastic melting in a fire – and then it collapsed in on itself on the wheel-head. And that was that. Mara took the cheese wire and sliced off the mess. There was enough left for an egg cup maybe, but she couldn't face starting again. That damn Banks had ruined her day.

In disgust, she tore off her wet apron and cleaned the rest of the clay from the wheel. Putting on her anorak again, she walked through to the front.

'Sorry, Elspeth,' she said. 'I just can't seem to concentrate today. Maybe I'll go for a walk.'

Elspeth frowned. 'Are you sure you're all right?'

'Yes. Don't worry, I'll be fine. Give my love to Dottie.'

'Will do.'

As she left the shop, the bell clanged loudly behind her.

Instead of heading back home, she climbed the stile at the end of Mortsett Lane and struck out for the moors. As she walked, she ran over the events of last Friday afternoon up at the farm.

Most of the time she'd been in the kitchen preparing a stew for dinner – something to fortify them all against the cold and rain – and making pots of tea. The children had been a nuisance, too, she remembered. Overexcited because there were so many adults around, they'd kept coming in and tugging at her apron strings, pestering her. She hadn't been paying much attention to what the others were saying or doing in the front room even when she was there, and she hadn't noticed anybody pick up anything from the mantelpiece.

The only thing that struck a chord was that number Banks had mentioned: 1139, was it? She thought that she had heard it mentioned recently. Half heard it, really, because she had been thinking about something else at the time. The ashram, that was it. She had been remembering how, after the evening meal of brown rice and vegetables (every day!), they had all sat cross-legged in the meditation room, with its shrine to the guru and the smell of sandalwood incense heavy in the air. They had talked about how their lives had been empty until they had found the True Path. How they had been searching in all the wrong places for all the wrong things. And they had sung songs together, holding hands. 'Amazing Grace' had been a particular favourite. Somehow, the gathering at the farm that afternoon had made her think of those days, though it was different in almost every way.

That was what she had been thinking about when the

number had been mentioned. And she had been in the kitchen, too, because she clearly recalled the earthy feel of the potatoes she'd been peeling. Wasn't it odd how the mind worked? All the components of the experience were there, clear as day, but she couldn't remember who had mentioned the number, or in what context. And people had been in and out of the kitchen all afternoon.

Worrying about Paul again, wondering where he was, she lowered her head against the wind and marched on through the rough grass and heather.

THREE

There was little else to do but wait for Boyd to turn up. Whatever his suspicions, Banks had nothing concrete to go on, and he wasn't likely to have until he'd questioned Boyd. Dirty Dick was still sleeping last night's beer and Scotch off in his hotel room and Richmond was running around putting together as much information as he could get on the suspects. Criminal records weren't enough; they tended to leave out the all-too-important human factor, the snippet that gives a clue to motivation and makes the pattern clear.

Mostly Banks smoked too much and stared gloomily out of his window on to the grey market square. At four o'clock, he heard a knock on his door and called, 'Come in.'

PC Craig stood there looking as pleased as Punch. 'We've got a line on Boyd, sir,' he said, ushering in a stout middle-aged woman with curlers on her hair.

Banks pulled out a chair for her.

'This is Mrs Evans,' Craig said. 'I went knocking on doors on Cardigan Road to find out if anyone had seen

Boyd, and Mrs Evans here said she had. She kindly offered to come in with me and talk to you, sir.'

'Good work,' Banks said. Craig smiled and left.

Banks asked Mrs Evans what she'd seen.

'It was about three o'clock yesterday afternoon,' she began. 'I know the time because I'd just got back from Tesco's with the shopping and I were struggling to get off t' bus.'

'Which bus was that?'

'A forty-four. Two forty-six from t' bus station.'

Banks knew the route. The bus took the long way round Cardigan Road for the benefit of local passengers, then carried on to York.

'And you saw Paul Boyd?'

'I saw a lad what looked like that photo.' PC Craig had taken a prison photograph of Boyd to show from door to door. 'His hair's different now, but I know it was him. I've seen him before.'

'Where?'

'Around town. More often than not coming out of t' dole office. I always hold my handbag tighter when I see him. I know it's not fair to judge a book by its covers, but he looks like a bad sort to me.'

'Where did you see him this time?'

'He was running up Gallows View from t' fields.'

'From Relton way?'

'Aye, as t' crow flies.'

'And where did he go?'

'Go? He didn't go anywhere. He were running for t' bus. Just caught it an' all. Nearly knocked me over, and me carrying two heavy shopping bags.'

'What was he wearing? Do you remember?'

'Aye, that I do. A red anorak. I noticed because it

looked too small for him. A bit short in t' sleeves and tight around t' armpits.'

Why, Banks asked himself, wasn't he surprised that Mara had lied about Boyd's clothes?

'Was he carrying anything?'

'One of those airline bags – British Airways, I think.'

'Do you remember anything else?'

'Just that he seemed in such a hurry and looked worried. I mean, as a rule, like I said, it'd be me who'd be frightened of him, but this time he looked like he were scared out of his wits.'

Banks went over to the door and called Craig back. 'Thanks, Mrs Evans,' he said. 'We appreciate your coming in like this. PC Craig here will drive you home.' Mrs Evans nodded gravely and Craig escorted her out.

As soon as he was alone, Banks checked the bus time-table and found that the 2.46 from Eastvale was indeed the milk run to York; it didn't get there until 4.09. Next he phoned the York railway station and, after speaking to a succession of surly clerks, finally got put through to a pleasant woman in charge of information. From her, he discovered that Boyd could have taken a train almost anywhere between 4.15 and five o'clock: Leeds, London, Newcastle, Liverpool, Edinburgh, plus points in between and anywhere else that connections might take him. It didn't seem much of a help, but he called Sergeant Hatchley in and put him on tracking down the train catering crews and ticket collectors. It would mean a trip to York and it might take a long time, but at least it was action. Of course, Hatchley pulled a long face – it seemed he had plans for the evening – but Banks ignored him. It wasn't as if Hatchley had any other work to do. Why wag your own tail when you've got a dog?

At home that evening, Banks ate a tin of Irish stew and pottered restlessly about the house waiting to hear from Hatchley. At nine o'clock, unable to concentrate on reading and almost wishing he'd gone to York himself, he turned on the TV and watched a beautiful blonde policewoman and her loud-mouthed American partner dash around spraying London with lead. It was background noise, something to fill the emptiness of the house. Finally, he could stand his own company no longer and phoned Sandra.

This time he felt even more lonely after he hung up, but the feeling didn't last as long. Twenty minutes later Hatchley phoned from York. He had managed to get the addresses of most of the ticket collectors and catering staff on the trains out of York, but none of them lived locally. All in all, the first lead seemed to be petering out. That happened sometimes. Banks told Hatchley to go over to York CID headquarters and phone as many of the crew members as he could get through to, and to call back if he came up with anything. He didn't. At 11.30 Banks went to bed. Maybe tomorrow morning, after Boyd's photograph appeared in all the national dailies, they would get the break they needed.

10

ONE

The big break came early Friday morning. The Rossghyll Guest House proved to be a dead end, and all the train crews out of York had been too busy to remember anyone, but an Edinburgh barber phoned to say he recognized Paul Boyd's photograph in the morning paper. Though Banks found the man's accent difficult to understand, he managed to learn what Paul's new haircut looked like. Even more important, he discovered that Paul had ditched his red anorak for a new grey duffel coat.

As soon as he hung up, Banks checked the map. Paul had headed north rather than to London or Liverpool. That had been a clever move; it had gained him time. But now that his photograph was on the front page of all the tabloid dailies, his time was running out. In addition to getting the photo in the papers as soon as possible, Banks and his men had also circulated Boyd's description to police in all major cities, ports and airports. It was routine, the best they could do with limited knowledge, but now there was somewhere concrete to start.

Assuming that Paul would ultimately want to leave the country, Banks took out his AA road map and ran his finger up the outline of the Scottish coast looking for ways out. He could find only two ferry routes north of Edinburgh on the east coast. The first, from Aberdeen to

Lerwick, on the Shetlands, could take Boyd eventually to Bergen and Torsken, in Norway, or to Seydhisfjördhur, in Iceland. But looking at the fine print, Banks saw that those ferries ran only in summer and, as the grey sky and drizzle outside testified, it certainly wasn't summer.

Another ferry ran from Scrabster, further north, to Stromness on mainland Orkney, but that hardly seemed like a place to run and hide. Boyd would stand out there like an Eskimo in the tropics.

Turning to the west coast, Banks saw dozens of broken red lines leading to such places as Brodick on the Isle of Arran; Port Ellen on Islay; and Stornoway on Lewis in the Outer Hebrides. The whole map was a maze of small islands and ferry routes. But, Banks reasoned, none of those isolated places would suit Boyd. He would be trapped, as well as conspicuous, on any of Scotland's islands, especially at this time of year.

The only trip that made any sense in the area was Stranraer to Larne. Then Boyd would be in Northern Ireland. From there, he didn't need a passport to cross the border to the Republic. Boyd was from Liverpool, Banks remembered, and probably had Irish friends.

So the first call he made, after giving Richmond and Hatchley the task of informing the other Scottish ferry ports just in case, was to the police at Stranraer. He was told that there had been no sailings the previous day because of a bad storm at sea, but this morning was calm. There were sailings at 11.30, 15.30, 19.00 and 03.00, all with easy connections from Edinburgh or Glasgow. Banks gave Boyd's description and asked that the men there keep a special watch for him, especially at ferry boardings. Next he issued the new description to police in Edinburgh, Glasgow, Inverness, Aberdeen and Dundee, and passed a list of smaller places to PCs Craig and Tolliver downstairs. Then he phoned Burgess, who had been keeping a low profile in his hotel room since their drunken night, and gave him the news.

Banks knew from experience that leads like this could bring results in a matter of minutes or days. He was impatient to have Boyd in and get the truth out of him, as much to test his own theories as anything else, but he'd get nowhere pacing the room. Instead, he sent for some coffee and went over the files Richmond had put together.

Information is a policeman's lifeblood. It comes in from many sources: interviews, gossip, criminal records, informers, employers, newspaper reporters and registries of births, marriages and deaths. It has to be collated, filed and cross-referenced in the hope that one day it will prove useful. DC Richmond was the best ferret they had at Eastvale, in addition to being practically invisible on surveillance and handy in a chase. Sergeant Hatchley, though tough, tenacious and good at interrogation, was too lazy and desultory to tie everything together. He overlooked minor details and took the easy way out. Put more simply, Richmond enjoyed gathering and collating data whereas Hatchley didn't. It made all the difference.

Banks spread out the sheets in front of him. He already knew a bit about Seth Cotton, but he had to be thorough in his revision. In the end, though, the only extra knowledge he gleaned was that Cotton had been born in Dewsbury and that in the mid 1970s he had settled in Hebden Bridge and led a quiet life, as far as the local police were concerned. Richmond had picked up the accident report on Alison Cotton, which didn't say very much. Banks made a note to look into it further.

There was nothing new on Rick Trelawney either, apart

from the name and address of his wife's sister in London. It might be worth a call to get more details on the divorce.

Zoe Hardacre was a local girl. Or near enough. As Jenny had said, she hailed from Whitby on the east coast, not far from Gill's home town, Scarborough. After school she had tried secretarial work but drifted away. Employers had complained that she couldn't seem to keep her mind on the important tasks they gave her, and that she always seemed to be in another world. That other world was the one of the occult: astrology, palmistry and tarot card readings. She had studied the subjects thoroughly enough to be regarded as something of an expert by those who knew about such things. Now that the occult seemed to have come into fashion among the New Age yuppie crowd, she made a living of sorts producing detailed natal charts and giving tarot readings. Everyone seemed to agree that Zoe was harmless, a true flower child, though too young to have been part of the halcyon days of the 1960s. She seemed about as political as a flower, too: she supported human rights and she wanted the bomb banned, but that was as far as it went.

As far as Banks could make out, she had never come into contact with PC Gill. Banks imagined him bursting into her booth at Whitby, truncheon raised, and arresting her for charlatanism; or perhaps she had read his palm and told him he was a repressed homosexual. The absurdity of Banks's theories served only as a measure of his frustration over motive. The connection between one of the suspects and Gill's murder was there somewhere, but Banks didn't have enough data yet to see it. He felt as if he were trying to do a join-the-dots drawing with too few dots.

While Banks was almost convinced that Mara Delacey

had been at the farm looking after the children at the time PC Gill was stabbed, he glanced over her file anyway. She had started out as a bright girl, a promising student, gaining a good degree in English, but she had fallen in with the hippie crowd when LSD, acid rock, bandannas and bright kaftans were all the rage. The police knew she took drugs, but never suspected her of dealing in them. Despite one of two raids on places where she happened to be living, they had never even been able to find her in possession.

Like Zoe, Mara had done occasional stints of secretarial work, most often as a temp, and she had never really put her university education to practical use. She'd spent some time in the USA in the late 1970s, mostly in California. Back in England, she had drifted for a while, then become involved with a guru and ended up living in one of his ashrams in Muswell Hill for a couple of years. After that, the farm. There was nothing to tie Mara to PC Gill, unless he had crossed her path during the two years she had been in Swainsdale.

Banks walked over to the window to rest his eyes and lit a cigarette. Outside, two elderly tourists, guidebooks in hand, paused to admire the Norman tower, then walked into the church.

Nothing in what Banks had read seemed to get him any further. If Gill did have a connection with someone at the farm, it was well buried and he'd have to dig deep for it. Sighing, he sat down again and flipped open the next folder.

Tim Fenton had been born in Ripon and was now in his second year at Eastvale College of Further Education. With Abha Sutton, he ran the students' union there. It was a small one, and usually stuck to in-college issues, but students were upset about government health and education policies – especially as far as they were likely to affect grants – and took every opportunity to demonstrate their displeasure. Tim, whose father was an accountant, was only nineteen and had no blots on his copybook except for attending the seminar that had got him into Special Branch's files.

Abha Sutton was born in Bradford of an Indian mother and a Yorkshire father. Again, her upbringing had been solidly middle class, and like Tim, as Richmond had tried to tell Burgess, she had no history of violence or involvement in extremist politics. She had been living with Tim for six months now, and together they had started the college Marxist society. It had very few members though; many of the college students were local farmers' sons studying agriculture. Still, the Social Sciences department and the Arts faculty were expanding, and they had managed to recruit a few new members among the literary crowd.

Banks read even more closely when he got to Dennis Osmond's file. Osmond was thirty-five, born in Newcastle-upon-Tyne. His father had worked in the shipyards there, but unemployment had forced the family to move when Osmond was ten. Mr Osmond had found a job at the chocolate factory, where he'd been known as a strong union man, and he had been involved in the acrimonious and sometimes violent negotiations that marked its last days. Osmond himself, though given at first to more intellectual pursuits, had followed his father politically.

A radical throughout university, he had dropped out in his third year, claiming that the education he was being given was no more than an indoctrination in bourgeois values, and had taken up social work in Eastvale, where he'd been working now for twelve years. During that period, he had become one of the town's chief spokesmen, along with Dorothy Wycombe, for the oppressed, neglected and unjustly treated. He had also beaten up Ellen Ventner, a woman he had lived with. Some of his cronies were the kind of people that Burgess would want shot on sight – shop stewards, feminists, poets, anarchists and intellectuals.

Whatever good Osmond had done around the place, Banks still couldn't help disliking the man and seeing him, somehow, as a sham. He couldn't understand Jenny's attraction to him, unless it was purely physical. And Jenny, of course, still didn't know that Osmond had once assaulted a woman.

It was after one o'clock, time for a pie and a pint in the Queen's Arms. But no sooner had Banks settled down in his favourite armchair by the fire to read the *Guardian* than PC Craig came rushing into the pub.

'They've got him, sir,' he said breathlessly. 'Boyd. Caught him trying to get on the half past eleven ferry to Larne.'

Banks looked at his watch. 'It's taken them long enough to get on to us. Are they holding him?'

'No, sir. They're bringing him down. Said they should be here late this afternoon.'

'No hurry then, is there?' Banks lit a cigarette and rustled his paper. 'Looks like it's all over.'

But it didn't feel as if it was all over; it felt more like it was just beginning.

TWO

Burgess paced the office like an expectant father, puffing on his cigar and glancing at his watch every ten seconds.

'Where the bloody hell are they?' he asked for what seemed to Banks like the hundredth time that afternoon.

'They'll be here soon. It's a long drive and the roads can be nasty in this weather.'

'They ought to be here by now.'

The two of them were in Banks's office waiting for Paul Boyd. Scenting the kill, Burgess didn't seem able to relax but Banks felt unusually calm. Along Market Street the shopkeepers were shutting up for the day, and it was already growing dark. In the office, the heater coughed and the fluorescent light hummed.

Banks stubbed out his cigarette and said, 'I'm off for some coffee. Want some?'

'I'm jittery enough as it is. Oh, what the hell. Why not? Black, three sugars.'

In the corridor, Banks bumped into Sergeant Hatchley on his way downstairs. 'Anything?' he asked.

'No,' said Hatchley. 'Still waiting to hear. I'm on my way to check with Sergeant Rowe if there's been any messages.'

Banks took the two mugs of coffee back to his office and smiled when Burgess jumped at the sound of the door opening. 'It's all right,' he said. 'Don't get excited. It's only me.'

'Do you think the silly buggers have got lost?' Burgess asked, scowling. 'Or broken down?'

'I'm sure they know their way around just as well as anyone else.'

'You can never be sure with bloody Jocks,' Burgess complained. Eastvale was the furthest north he had ever been, and he had already made it quite clear that he didn't care to venture any further. 'If they've let that bastard escape—'

But he was interrupted by the phone. It was Sergeant Rowe. Boyd had arrived.

'Tell them to bring him up here.' Burgess took out another Tom Thumb. He lit it, brushed some ash off his shirt and picked up his coffee.

A few moments later there was a knock at the door, and two uniformed men entered with Paul Boyd between them. He looked pale and distant – as well he might, Banks thought.

'Sorry, sir,' said the driver. 'We had a delay setting off. Had to wait till the doc had finished.'

'Doctor?' Burgess said. 'Why, what's wrong? Young dickhead here didn't hurt anyone, did he?'

'Him? No.' The constable gave Paul a contemptuous glance. 'Fainted when they caught him, that's all, then came round screaming about walls closing in. Had to get the doc to give him a sedative.'

'Walls closing in, eh?' Burgess said. 'Interesting. Sounds like a touch of claustrophobia to me. Never mind. Sit him down, and you two can bugger off now.'

'See the desk sergeant about expenses and accommodation,' Banks said to the two Scotsmen. 'I don't suppose you'll be wanting to set off back tonight?'

The driver smiled. 'No, sir. Thanks very much, sir.'

'Thank *you*,' Banks said. 'There's a good pub across the road. The Queen's Arms. You can't miss it.'

'Yes, sir.'

Burgess could hardly wait to close the door behind

them. Paul sat facing Banks in a tubular metal chair with a wooden seat and back. Burgess, preferring a free rein and the advantage of height, chose to lean against the wall or stride around as he talked.

'Get the sergeant in, will you?' he asked Banks. 'With his notebook.'

Banks sent for Hatchley, who arrived red-faced and out of breath a minute later. 'Those bloody stairs again,' he grumbled. 'They'll be the death of me.'

Burgess pointed to a chair in the corner and Hatchley sat down obediently. He found a clean page in his note-book and took out his pencil.

'Right,' said Burgess, clapping his hands. 'Let's get cracking.'

Paul looked over at him, hatred and fear burning in his eyes.

If Burgess had one professional fault, Banks thought, it was as an interrogator. He couldn't seem to take any part but that of his own pushy aggressive self. It wouldn't prove half as effective with Boyd as the routine Banks and Hatchley had worked out, but it would have to do. Banks knew he would be forced into the role of the nice guy, the father confessor, for the duration.

'Why don't you tell us about it?' Burgess began. 'That way we won't have to resort to the Chinese water torture, will we?'

'There's nothing to tell.' Boyd glanced nervously at the window. The slats of the venetian blind were up, letting in grey light from the street below.

'Why did you kill him?'

'I didn't kill anyone.'

'Did you just lose your temper, is that it? Or did someone pay you? Come on, we know you did it.'

'I told you, I didn't kill anyone.'

'Then how come that knife with PC Gill's blood on it also happens to have your dabs all over it too? Are you trying to tell me you never touched it?'

'I didn't say that.'

'What are you trying to say?'

Paul licked his lips. 'Can I have a cigarette?'

'No, you bloody can't,' Burgess growled. 'Not until you've told us what happened.'

'I didn't do anything, honestly. I've never killed anyone.'

'So why did you run?'

'I was frightened.'

'What of?'

'Frightened you'd fit me up for it anyway. You know I've done time.'

'Is that how you think we operate, Paul?' Banks asked gently. 'Is that really what you think? You're wrong, you know. If you just tell us the truth you've nothing to fear.'

Burgess ignored him. 'How did your prints get on the knife?'

'I must have handled it, I suppose.'

'That's better. Now when did you handle it, and why?'

Paul shrugged. 'Could've been any time.'

'Any time?' Burgess shook his head with exaggerated slowness. 'No, it couldn't, sonny. No, it couldn't. Want to know why? Your prints were right on top, numero uno, clear as day. You were the last person to handle that knife before we found it. How do you explain that?'

'All right, so I handled it after it'd been used. That still doesn't mean I killed anyone.'

'It does unless you've got a better explanation. And I haven't heard one yet.'

'How did you know we'd found the knife?' Banks asked.

'I saw that shepherd find it on the moor, so I took off.'

He was lying, Banks thought. Mara had told him. But he let it go for the moment.

Paul fell silent. The floor creaked as Burgess paced the office. Banks lit a Silk Cut, his last, and leaned back in his chair. 'Look, Paul,' he said, 'consider the facts. One: we found PC Gill's blood on the knife, and the doc tells us the blade fits the wound. Two: we found your prints on the handle. Three: we know you were at the demo – you were seen. Four: as soon as things start adding up, you bugger off to Scotland. Now you tell me what to make of it all. What would you think if you were me?'

Paul still said nothing.

'I'm getting fed up of this,' Burgess snarled. 'Let's just lock the bastard up now. He's in on a warrant. We've got enough evidence. We don't need a confession. Hell, we don't even need a motive.'

'No!' Paul yelled.

'No what? You don't want us to lock you up? Dark down there, isn't it? Even a normal person feels the walls closing in on him down there in the dark.'

Paul was pale and sweating now, and his mouth was clamped so tight that the muscles in his jaw quivered.

'Come on,' Banks said. 'Why don't you just tell us. Save us all a lot of trouble. You say you've done nothing. If that's so, you've nothing to be worried about. Why hold back?'

'Stop mollycoddling him,' Burgess said. 'He's not going to talk, you know that as well as I do. He's guilty as sin, and he knows it.' He turned to Hatchley. 'Sergeant, send for a couple of men to take dickhead here down to the cells.'

'No!' Paul leaned forward and gripped the edge of the desk until his knuckles turned white.

Burgess gestured to Hatchley to sit down again. The command was a bit premature, as the sergeant moved slowly and hadn't even got as far as putting his notebook away.

'Let me make it easy for you, Paul,' Banks said. 'I'll tell you what I think happened and you tell me if it's true. All right?'

Paul took a deep breath and nodded.

'You took the knife from the farm. It was usually just lying around the place. It didn't belong to anyone in particular. Mara used it occasionally to cut twine and wool; maybe Seth used it sometimes to whittle a piece of wood. But that day you picked it up, carried it to the demo with you, and killed PC Gill. Then you folded the blade over again, made your way to the edge of the crowd, and escaped down an alley. You ran to the edge of town, then across the moors back to the farm – almost four miles. About halfway there, you realized what you'd done, panicked and chucked the knife away. Am I right, Paul?'

'I didn't kill anyone,' Paul repeated.

'But am I right about the rest?'

Silence.

'It's beginning to look like the thumbscrews for you, sonny.' Burgess leaned forward, his face only inches from Paul's. 'I'm getting bored. I'm sick of the bloody North and this miserable bloody weather. I want to get back home to London, the civilized world. Understand? And you're standing in my way. I don't like people who stand in my way, and if they do it for long enough, they get knocked down. Savvy?'

Paul turned to Banks. 'You're right about everything

else,' he said. 'But I didn't take the knife. I didn't kill the copper.'

'Police officer to you, dickhead,' Burgess snapped.

'How did you end up with it?' Banks asked.

'I got knocked down,' Paul said. 'At the demo. And I curled up, like, with my hands behind my neck and my knees up in my chest, in the . . . the . . . what do you call it?'

'Foetal position?'

'Yes, the foetal position. There were people all around me, it was bloody awful. I kept getting booted. Then this knife got kicked towards me. I picked it up, like you said, and made off. But I didn't know it had killed anyone. I just thought it was a good knife, too good to waste, so I took it with me. Then, on the moors, I saw there was blood on it so I flung it away. That's how it happened.'

'You're a bloody liar,' Burgess said. 'Do you think I'm an idiot? Is that what you take me for? I might be a city boy, but even I know there aren't any lights on the fucking moors. And even you're not stupid enough to lie there in the street, boots flying all around you, police everywhere, and think, "Oh, what a pretty bloodstained knife. I must take it home with me." You've been talking cobblers.' He turned to Banks. 'That's what you get for being soft with them, see. Spin you a yarn a bloody mile long.'

Swiftly, he grasped the back of Paul's neck and squeezed hard. Paul hung on to the edge of the desk and struggled, almost upsetting his flimsy chair. Then, just as abruptly, Burgess let go and leaned casually against the wall.

'Try again,' he said.

Paul massaged his neck and looked pleadingly at Banks, who remained impassive.

'It's true, I tell you,' Paul said. 'I swear it. I never killed him. I just picked up the knife.'

'Let's assume we believe you,' Banks said. 'That still leaves us with a problem, doesn't it? And that problem is: why? Why did you pick up the murder weapon and sneak it away from the scene of the crime? See what I mean? It doesn't add up.'

Paul shifted in his seat, casting nervous glances at Burgess, who stood just within his peripheral vision. 'I didn't even know there was a crime,' he said.

'Who are you protecting, Paul?' Banks asked.

'Nobody.' But Paul had answered so quickly and loudly that even the most gullible person in the world would have known he was lying. Recognizing his slip, he turned red and stared down at his knees.

'The people at Maggie's Farm took you in and cared for you, didn't they?' Banks said. 'They were probably the first people who ever did. You were lost, just out of jail, no job, nowhere to go, at the end of your tether, and then you met them. It's not surprising you'd want to protect them, Paul, but can't you see how transparent you're being? Who do you suspect?'

'I don't know. Nobody.'

'Osmond, Tim Fenton, Abha Sutton? Would you go out of your way to protect them?'

Paul said nothing.

Burgess slapped the metal table. 'Tell him!'

Paul jumped, startled by the sound. 'I might,' he said, glaring at Burgess. 'I might protect anyone who killed a pig.'

Burgess backhanded him across the face. Paul went with the blow and almost fell out of his chair.

'Try again, dickhead.'

Banks grabbed Burgess by the elbow and led him over

to the window. 'Don't you think,' he said between gritted teeth, 'that you'd do better using your brains instead of your bloody fists?'

'What's wrong with you, Banks? Gone soft? Is that why they sent you up here?'

Banks jerked his head towards Paul. 'He's used to hard knocks. They don't mean anything to him, and you bloody well ought to know that. You're satisfying your sadistic urges, that's all.'

Burgess sniffed and turned back to Paul, who sat wiping the blood from his mouth with the back of his hand, sneering at both of them. He had overheard, Banks realized, and he probably thought the whole scene was staged just to throw him off balance. 'You admit that when you found the knife on the ground you recognized it, right?' Banks asked.

'Yes.'

'And you didn't want any of your friends at the farm to get into trouble.'

'That's right.'

'So you took it and threw it away.'

'Yes. I went back on the moors to look for it a few times. I knew it was stupid just to throw it away without wiping it or anything, but I panicked. I should've taken it back to the farm and cleaned it up again, just like new. I know that now. I walked miles and miles looking for the bloody thing. Couldn't find it anywhere. And then that shepherd bloke turned up with it.'

'So who did you think you were protecting?'

'I don't know.' Paul took out a crumbled Kleenex and dabbed at the thin trickle of blood at the corner of his mouth. 'I've already told you, I didn't see who took the knife and I didn't see who used it.'

'We'll leave it for now, then.' Banks turned to Burgess. 'What do you think?'

'I still think he's lying. Maybe he's not as thick as he looks. He's trying to put the blame on his mates, subtle like.'

'I'm not too sure,' Banks said. 'He could be telling the truth. Problem is he's got no proof, has he? I mean, he could tell us anything.'

'And expect us to believe it. Let's lock him up for a while, anyway. Let him cool his heels. We'll question him again later and see if everything tallies.'

Paul, who had been glancing from one to the other with his mouth open, let out a cry. 'No! I've told you; it's the truth. What more do you want me to do?'

Burgess shrugged and leaned back against the wall. Banks reached for a cigarette; his packet was empty. 'Well, I'm inclined to believe him,' he said. 'At least for the time being. Are you sure you didn't see who took the knife, Paul?'

'No. It could've been anyone.'

'That gives us seven suspects, am I right?' Banks counted them off on his fingers. 'Seth, Rick, Zoe, Mara, Osmond, Tim and Abha. Was anyone else up there during the week before the demo? Anyone we don't know about?'

'No. And Mara wasn't there.'

'But the others all were? Zoe was?'

He nodded.

'Did any of them have a reason for killing PC Gill?' Banks asked. 'Anyone know him? Had a run-in with him before?'

Paul shook his head. 'Maybe the students. I don't know.'

'But I don't think you'd go out of your way to protect

them, Paul, I really don't. Was Gill mentioned that afternoon?'

'Not that I heard.'

'You see, it still doesn't ring true,' Banks said. 'Someone picking the knife up on purpose like that and taking it along, as if whoever did it knew he was going to do it. Premeditated, that is.'

'I don't know what you mean.'

'Oh, I think you do.' Banks smiled and stood up. 'I'm just off for some cigarettes,' he said to Burgess. 'I doubt that we'll get much more out of him.'

'Maybe not.' Burgess agreed. 'Pick me up a tin of Thumbs, will you?'

'Sure.'

'And give my love to Glenys.'

Banks was grateful for the cool fresh air outside the station. He stood for a moment, breathing in and out deeply, then crossed Market Street to the Queen's Arms.

'Twenty Silk Cut and a tin of Tom Thumbs, please, Cyril,' he said.

'These for that mate of yours?' Cyril asked, slapping the cigars on the counter.

'I wish you'd stop calling him my mate. You'll be getting me a bad name.'

'Well, my Glenys has been acting a bit funny lately. She's an impressionable lass, if you know what I mean, and headstrong. Gets it from that bloody mother of hers. It's just little things, things only a husband notices, but if I find that your mate's behind it, I'll . . . Well, I needn't spell it out for you, need I, Mr Banks?'

'Not to me, Cyril, no. Better not. I'll inform him of your concern.'

'If you would.'

Back outside, Banks noticed that the light had gone out in his office window. No doubt they'd sent Boyd down to the cells and gone for coffee. As he crossed the street, he heard a scream. It came from above, he was certain of that, but he couldn't pinpoint it exactly. Apprehensive, he hurried back upstairs and opened the door. The office was dark, but it wasn't empty.

When he flicked on the fluorescent light, Banks saw that Sergeant Hatchley had been sent away and only Boyd and Burgess remained. The slats on the venetian blind had been completely closed, shutting out all the light from the street, a feat Banks himself had never been able to manage in all the time he'd been in Eastvale.

Boyd was whimpering in the chair, sweating and gasping for breath. 'He turned the lights off,' he said, struggling to get the words out, 'and closed the blinds, the bastard.'

Banks glared at Burgess, who simply flashed him a 'Who, me?' look and said, 'I think he was telling the truth. At least, if he wasn't, he's just given the most convincing performance of his life.'

'Under duress.' Banks tossed him the cigars. Burgess caught the tin deftly, unwrapped it and offered Banks one. 'Celebrate with me?'

'I prefer these.' Banks lit a Silk Cut.

'You can have a smoke now if you want, kid,' Burgess said to Paul. 'Though with a breathing problem like yours, I'd watch it.'

Paul lit up and coughed till he was red in the face. Burgess laughed.

'So, what now?' Banks asked.

'We lock him up and go home.' Burgess looked at Paul. 'You're going to have plenty of time for long chats with the prison shrink about that claustrophobia of yours,' he said. 'In fact, you could say we're doing you a favour. Don't they say the best way to deal with a phobia is to confront it? And the treatment's free. What more could you ask for? You'd have to wait years on the National Health for that kind of service.'

Paul's jaw slackened. 'But I didn't do it. You said you believed me.'

'It takes a lot more than that to convince me. Besides, there's tampering with evidence, accessory after the fact of murder, wasting police time, resisting arrest. You've got a lot of charges to face.'

Burgess called downstairs and two constables came to escort Paul to the cells. He didn't struggle this time; he seemed to know there was no point.

When they were alone in the office, Banks turned to Burgess. 'If you pull a stunt like that on my patch again,' he said, 'I'll kick your balls into the middle of next week, superintendent or no fucking superintendent.'

Burgess held his gaze, but Banks felt that he took the threat more seriously than he had Rick Trelawney's.

After the staring match, Burgess smiled and said, 'Good, I'm glad we've got that out of the way. Come on, I could murder a pint.'

And he put his arm around Banks's shoulder and steered him towards the door.

11

ONE

The rattle of the letter box and the sound of mail slapping against the hall mat woke Banks early on Saturday morning. His mouth tasted like the bottom of a bird cage, and his tongue felt dry and furry from too many cigarettes and too much ale. He and Burgess had murdered more than one pint after Boyd's interrogation. It was getting to be a habit.

Banks still wasn't used to waking up alone in the big bed. He missed Sandra's warm body stirring beside him, and he missed the grumbles and complaints of Brian and Tracy getting ready for school or for Saturday morning shopping expeditions. But they'd all be back in a few days. With a bit of luck, the Gill case would be over by then and he would be able to spend some time with them.

Over coffee and burnt toast – why the toaster only burnt toast when *he* made it, Banks had no idea – he examined the mail: two bills, a letter and a new blues anthology tape from Barney Merritt, an old friend on the Met and, finally, just what he'd been waiting for – the package from Tony Grant.

The information, which Grant had copied in longhand from PC Gill's files, made interesting reading. Ever since picket control duty at the Orgreave coking plant during the miners' strike in 1984, Gill had volunteered for overtime at just about every demonstration that had come up in Yorkshire: protests outside US missile bases, marches against South Africa, National Front meetings, anything that had seemed likely to turn into a free-for-all. Gill certainly wasn't the only one, but he seemed to have been the kind of person who graduated from school bully to legalized goon. Banks wouldn't have been surprised if he had carved notches in his truncheon.

There were complaints against him too, generally for excessive use of force in subduing demonstrators. However, there were surprisingly few of these and no action had been taken on them, except perhaps a slap on the wrist now and then. The most interesting complaint came from Dennis Osmond, charging Gill with using unnecessary violence during a local demonstration in support of the Greenham Common women about two years ago. Another familiar name on the list was Elizabeth Dale, who had accused Gill of lashing out indiscriminately against her and her friends during a peaceful anti-nuclear march in Leeds. Banks couldn't immediately place her, as she didn't seem to belong to the pattern that included Paul Boyd and Dennis Osmond, but he knew her name. He made a note to check it in his files, then read carefully through the rest of the material. No other names stood out.

But the most important piece of information Banks gleaned from the files had nothing to do with Gill's behaviour; in fact, it was so damn simple he cursed himself out loud for not seeing it sooner. He always thought of his colleagues by name, even the uniformed men. Most policemen did – especially plain-clothes detectives. But it was a different matter for others. How could a member of the public name a particular police officer in a complaint, or even in a letter of commendation? He couldn't. That's why the numbers were so important. Called collar-numbers because they originally appeared on the small stand-up collars of the old police uniform, the metal numbers are now fixed to the officer's epaulettes and there was Gill's number staring him right in the face: PC 1139.

He remembered driving back from the Black Sheep after his lunch-time chat with Mara. He had been listening to Billie Holiday and wondering what it was he'd said that should have meant more than it did. Now he knew. He had mentioned Gill's name and, in his next question, the number. They had almost leaped together to complete the circuit, but not quite.

Banks put the papers away, grabbed his coat and hurried out to the car. It was a beautiful morning. The wind still blew cool but the sun shone in a cloudless sky. After the miserable late winter weather they'd been having recently, the smell of spring in the air – that strong mixture of wet grass and last autumn's decay – was almost over-whelming. As the pipes on Keats's Grecian urn appealed not to the 'sensual ear' but played 'spirit ditties of no tone', so this smell didn't so much titillate the sensual nose as it exhaled a scent of promise, a special feeling of anticipation and a definite quickening of the life force. It made him want to slip the Deller Consort recording of Shakespeare's songs into his Walkman and step lightly to work. But he would need the car for the visit he had to make later in the day. Still, he thought, no reason why he shouldn't follow the musical impulse where it led him, especially on a day like this, so he made a special trip back inside and found the cassette to play in the car.

It was after nine when he got to the office. Richmond was playing with the computer and Sergeant Hatchley was struggling over the Daily Mirror crossword. There was no sign of Dirty Dick. He sent for coffee and went to peer out of the window. The good weather had certainly enticed people outdoors. Tourists drifted in and out of the church, and some, wearing anoraks over warm sweaters, actually sat on the worn plinth of the market cross eating KitKats and drinking tea from Thermos flasks.

Banks spent an hour or more staring out on the busy square trying to puzzle out why PC Gill's number had turned up in Seth Cotton's old notebook. Had it even been Cotton's handwriting? He examined the book again. It was hard to tell, because only the faint imprint remained. The numbers were exaggeratedly large, too, unlike the smaller scrawl of most of the measurements. Carefully, he rubbed a soft pencil over the page again, but he couldn't get a better impression.

He remembered Mara Delacey telling him that Paul spent a lot of time working with Seth in the shed, so the number could just as likely have been written down by him. If so, that implied premeditation. Boyd's name hadn't appeared on Grant's list of complainants, but that didn't mean they hadn't come into conflict before. A kid with a record, like Paul, would hardly walk into the nearest police station and lodge a complaint.

The only thing of which Banks could be sure, after two cups of coffee and three cigarettes, was that somebody at Maggie's Farm knew of PC Gill before the demonstration and expected him to be there. The number had been written down hard enough to press through, and that indicated some degree of passion or excitement. Who had a grudge against Gill? And who had access to Seth Cotton's notebook? Anybody, really, as he never locked the shed. Boyd was the best candidate, given the evidence against him, but Banks had a nagging suspicion that he'd been telling the truth, especially when he stuck to his story after Burgess had put the lights out on him. But if Boyd was telling the truth, who was he more likely to be protecting than Seth, Mara, Rick or Zoe?

And where, Banks asked himself, did that leave Osmond, Tim and Abha?

Tim and Abha had so far been the only ones to admit to knowing of PC Gill's existence, which probably indicated that they had nothing to hide. Banks doubted, in fact, that they had anything to do with the murder. For a start, they had no real connection with the farm people other than a mutual interest in wanting to save the human race from total obliteration.

Osmond, however, was a friend of Rick, Seth and the rest. He had been up to the farm often, and he knew Gill's number all right, because he had used it on his complaint. Perhaps he had written it in the notebook himself, or had seen it there and recognized it. Paul Boyd may have been telling the truth about not killing PC Gill, but had he been an accomplice? Had there been two people involved?

Like so many of Banks's thinking sessions, this one was raising far more questions than it answered. Sometimes he thought he could solve cases only after formulating a surfeit of questions; he reached saturation point, and the overflow produced the answers.

Before he did anything else though, he needed something to stop the growling in his stomach. Burnt toast wasn't sufficient fuel for a detective.

On his way to the Golden Grill for elevenses, he bumped into Mara Delacey entering the station.

'I want to see Paul,' she said, brandishing the morning paper. 'It says here you've caught him. Is it true?'

'Yes.'

'Where is he?'

'Downstairs.'

'Is he all right?'

'Of course he is. What do you think we are, the Spanish Inquisition?'

'I wouldn't put anything past Burgess. Can I see Paul?'

Banks thought for a moment. It would be unusual to grant such permission, and Burgess wouldn't like it if he found out, but there was no reason Mara shouldn't see Boyd. Besides, it would give Banks the opportunity to ask him a couple of questions in Mara's presence. Through body language and facial expressions, people often gave more away than they intended when friends or enemies were nearby.

'All right,' he said, leading the way down. 'But I'll have to be there.'

'As you can see, I've not brought him a birthday cake with a file in it.'

Banks smiled. 'Wouldn't do him much good anyway. There aren't any bars on the window. He could only escape to the staircase and walk right up here.'

'But his claustrophobia,' Mara said, alarmed. 'It'll be unbearable for him.'

'We got a doctor.' Banks relished his small victory over Burgess's callousness. 'He's been given tranquillizers, and they seemed to help.'

The four cells were the most modern part of the building. Recently overcrowded with demonstrators, they were now empty except for Paul Boyd. Mara seemed surprised to find clean white tiles and bright light instead of dark dank stone walls. The only window, high and deep-set in the wall, was about a foot square and almost as thick. The cells always made Banks think of hospitals, so much so that he fancied he could smell Dettol or carbolic every time he went down there.

Boyd sat on his bunk and stared out through the bars at his visitors.

'Hello,' Mara said. 'I'm sorry, Paul.'

Boyd nodded.

Banks could sense tension between them. It was due in part to his being there, he knew, but it seemed to go deeper than that, as if they were unsure what to say to each other.

'Are you all right?' she asked.

'I'm OK.'

'Will you be coming back?'

Paul glared at Banks. 'I don't know. They're determined to charge me with something.'

Banks explained the procedure.

'So he might still be arrested for murder?' Mara asked.

'Yes.'

There were tears in her eyes. Paul stared at her suspiciously, as if he wasn't sure whether she was acting or not.

Banks broke the tense silence. 'Does the number 1139 mean anything to you?' he asked Boyd.

Paul seemed to consider the question, and his answer was an unequivocal no. Banks thought he was telling the truth.

'What do you know about the old notebook Seth kept in his workshop?'

Paul shrugged. 'Nothing. It was just for addresses, measurements and stuff.'

'Did you ever use it?'

'No. I was just an assistant, a dogsbody.'

'It wasn't like that, Paul,' Mara said. 'And you know it.'

'It doesn't matter now, does it? Except maybe it'll get me a job in the prison workshop.'

'Did anybody else ever use it, other than Seth?' asked Banks.

'Why should they?' Paul was obviously puzzled by the line of questioning. 'It wasn't important.'

'Do you know who took the knife?'

Paul looked at Mara as he answered. 'I've already told you I don't, haven't I?'

'I'm giving you another chance. If you really aren't responsible for PC Gill's death, any help you give us will count for you.'

'Oh, sure!' Paul got to his feet and started pacing the narrow cell. 'Why don't you just bugger off and leave me alone? I've nothing more to tell you. And tell the quack to bring me another pill.'

'Is there anything we can do, Paul?' Mara asked.

'You can leave me alone, too. I curse the day I met you and the rest of them. You and your bloody protests and demonstrations. Look where you've got me.'

Mara swallowed, then spoke softly. 'We're still on your side, you know. It wasn't anything to do with me, with any of us, that you got caught. You can come back to the farm whenever you want.'

Paul glared at her, and Banks could sense the questions each wanted to ask and the answers they hoped for. But they couldn't talk because he was there. Mara would implicate herself if she assured Paul she hadn't tipped the police off about the warning, the money and the clothes she'd given him. Paul would incriminate her if he thanked her or questioned her about these things.

'Come on.' Banks took Mara's arm gently. She shook

his hand off but walked beside him back upstairs. 'You've seen that he's all right. No bruises.'

'None that show, no.'

'How did you get here?' Banks asked as they walked out of the station into the glorious day.

'I walked over the moors.'

'I'll give you a lift back.'

'No. I'm happy walking, thanks.'

'No strings. I'm going up there anyway.'

'Why?'

'Just a few questions for Seth.'

'Questions, bloody questions.'

'Come on.'

Mara got into the Cortina beside him. She sat in silence with her hands on her lap as Banks pulled out of the car park and set off up North Market Street for the Swainsdale road. They passed the community centre steps, where Gill had been stabbed. The spot looked as innocent as everywhere else that day; no signs of violence and bloodshed lingered in the grey stone. Banks pushed the tape in and the Deller Consort sang 'It Was a Lover and His Lass'. Mara managed a weak smile at the hey nonny nos, peering curiously at Banks as if she found it hard to connect him with the music he played.

A couple of fishermen sat under the trees in the river meadows, and there were more walkers on the road than Banks had seen since the previous October. Even the wind chimes up at Maggie's Farm seemed to be playing a happier tune despite the misfortune that had befallen the place. But nature is rarely in harmony with human affairs, Banks thought. It follows its predetermined natural cycles, while we fall victim to random irrational forces, thoughts and deeds. It's natural to identify with the rain and clouds when we feel depressed, but if the sun shines brightly and we still feel depressed, we don't bother bringing the weather into it at all.

Banks found Seth in his workshop. Wearing his overalls, he was bent over the bench, planing a long piece of wood. Shavings curled and fell to the floor, releasing the clean scent of pine. Noticing his guest, he paused and put down his plane. Banks leaned against the wall near the dusty bookcase.

'What is it now?' Seth asked. 'I thought you'd got your man.'

'It does look like it. But I'm the kind who likes to tie up loose ends.'

'Unlike your friend.'

'Superintendent Burgess doesn't concern himself overmuch with little details,' Banks said. 'But he doesn't have to live up here.'

'How is Paul?'

Banks told him.

'So, what are your loose ends?'

'It's that number in your book.' Banks frowned and scratched the scar by his right eye. 'I've found out what it means.'

'Oh?'

'It was PC Gill's number. PC 1139.'

Seth picked up his plane and began to work slowly at the pine again.

'Why was it written in your notebook?'

'It's quite a coincidence, I'll admit that,' Seth said without looking up. 'But I told you, I haven't got the faintest idea what it meant.'

'Did you write it down?'

'I don't remember doing so. But pick any page of the

book and the odds are I'd hardly have it ingrained deeply in my memory.'

'Did you know PC Gill?'

'I never had the pleasure.'

'Could anyone else have scribbled it down?'

'Of course. I don't lock the place up. But why should they?'

Banks had no idea. 'Why did you tear the page out?'

'I don't know that I did. I don't recall doing so. Look, Chief Inspector—' Seth put his plane aside again and leaned against the bench, facing Banks – 'you're chasing phantoms. Anybody could have jotted that number down, and it could mean anything.'

'Like what?'

'A phone number. They still have four digits around here, you know. Or it could be part of a measurement, a sum of money, almost anything.'

'It's not a phone number,' Banks said. 'Do you think I haven't checked? It is PC Gill's number, though.'

'Coincidence.'

'Possibly. But I'm not convinced.'

'That's your problem.' Seth picked up the plane again and began working more vigorously.

'It could be your problem too, Seth.'

'Is that a threat?'

'No. I leave those to Superintendent Burgess. What I mean is, it would be very convenient if someone else had killed Gill -- you, say – and Paul Boyd took the blame. He really doesn't have a leg to stand on, you know.'

'What do you mean?' Seth paused again.

'I mean the odds are that he'll go down for it.'

'Are you saying he's confessed?'

'I'm not free to talk about things like that. I'm just

saying it looks bad, and if you know of anything that might help him you'd better tell me pretty damn quick. Unless it's to your advantage that Boyd gets charged with murder.'

'I don't know anything.' Seth bent over the length of pine and caressed the surface. His voice was tight, and he kept his face averted.

'I can understand it if you're protecting someone,' Banks went on. 'Like Mara tried to protect Paul. But think about what you're doing. By covering for someone else, you almost certainly condemn Paul. Does he mean so little to you?'

Seth slammed down the plane. He turned to face Banks, his face red and eyes bright. The vein by his temple throbbed. 'How can you talk like that?' he said in a shaky voice. 'Of course Paul means a lot to us. He's not been tried yet, you know. It's only you bastards who've convicted him so far. If he didn't do it, then he'll get off, won't he?'

Banks lit a Silk Cut. 'I'm surprised you've got such faith in justice, Seth. I'm afraid I haven't. The way things are these days, he may well be made an example of.'

Seth snorted. 'What would you do? Fix the jury?'

'We wouldn't need to. The jury's made up of ordinary men and women – law-abiding, middle-class citizens for the most part. They'll take one look at Boyd and want to lock him up and throw away the key.'

'He'll manage. And we'll stick by him. We won't let him down.'

'Admirable sentiments. But it might not be enough. Where did you live before you bought this place?'

Surprised, Seth had to think for a moment. 'Hebden Bridge. Why?'

'Where did you get the money from, for the farm?'

'If it's any of your business, I saved some and inherited a little from a dotty aunt. We . . . I also had a small business there, which I sold – a second-hand bookshop.'

'What kind of work did you do?'

'This kind.' Seth gestured around the workshop. 'I was a jack of all trades, showed the true Thatcherite entre-preneurial spirit. I made good money for good work. I still do.'

'Who ran the bookshop then?'

'My wife.' Seth spoke between his teeth and turned back to his wood.

'There was some kind of accident, wasn't there?' Banks said. 'Your wife?' He knew some of the details but wanted to see how Seth reacted.

Seth took a deep breath. 'Yes, there was. But it's still none of your business.'

'What happened?'

'Like you said. I had a wife. There was an accident.'

'What kind?'

'She was hit by a car.'

'I'm sorry.'

Seth turned on him. 'Why? Why the bloody hell should you be sorry? You didn't even know Alison. Just get the fuck out and let me get on with my work. I've nothing more to say to you.'

Banks lingered at the doorway. 'One more thing: Elizabeth Dale. Is that name familiar to you?'

'I know someone called Liz Dale, yes.'

'She's the woman who ran off from the mental hospital and ended up here, isn't she?'

'Why ask if you know already?'

'I wasn't sure, but I thought so. Do you know anything about a complaint she made against PC Gill?'

'No. Why should I?'

'She used his number: 1139.'

'So?'

'Bit of a coincidence, that's all: her complaint, his number in your notebook. Could she have written it?'

'I suppose so. But so could anyone else. I really don't know anything about it.' Seth sounded tired.

'Have you seen her recently? Has she been up here in the past few weeks?'

'No.'

'Do you know where she is?'

'We've lost touch. It happens.'

Seth bent over the pine again and Banks left, avoiding the house by using the side gate. In the car, he contemplated going to the barn to talk to Rick and Zoe. But they could wait. He'd had enough of Maggie's Farm for one day.

TWO

Burgess winked at Glenys, who smiled and blushed. Banks was the only one to notice Cyril's expression darken. They carried their drinks and ploughman's lunches back to the table.

'How's Boyd?' Burgess asked.

'He's all right. I didn't know you cared.'

Burgess spat the remains of a pickled onion into his napkin: 'Bloody awful stuff. Gives me heartburn.'

'I wouldn't be surprised if you're developing an ulcer,' Banks said, 'the way you go at life.'

Burgess grinned. 'You only live once.'

'Are you going to stick around and see what happens?'

'I'll stay a few more days, yes.' He eyed Glenys again. 'I'm not quite finished up here yet.'

'Don't tell me you're getting to like the North?'

'At least the bloody weather's improved, even if the people haven't.'

'Friendliest lot in the country, when you get to know them.'

'Tell me about it.' Burgess shoved in a chunk of Wensleydale and washed it down with Double Diamond.

Banks grimaced. 'No wonder you get heartburn.'

Burgess pushed his plate aside and lit a cigar. 'Tell me honestly, Banks. What do you make of Boyd? Guilty or not?'

'He's obviously involved. Deeply involved. But if you're asking do I think he killed Gill, the answer's no, I don't.'

'You could be right. He certainly stuck to his guns under pressure, and I don't think he's that tough.' Burgess prodded the air with his cigar. 'Personally, I don't give a damn what happens to Boyd. I'd rather see him go down for it than no one at all. But give me some credit. I'm not a bloody idiot, and if I'm not satisfied everything's wrapped up I like to know why. I get nagging feelings like every copper.'

'And you have one about Boyd?'

'A little one.'

'So what are you going to do?'

'Consider the alternatives. You heard what he said last night, about the others going up to the farm on Friday afternoon. That covers just about everyone we've had our eye on since this business started. Who do you reckon?'

Banks sipped some beer to wash down his lunch. 'It depends,' he said. 'Any of the people Boyd mentioned could have got access to the knife, and so could anyone else who went up there a few days before the demo. Nobody had noticed whether it was missing or not – at least nobody admits to noticing. If you're convinced it was a terrorist act, then obviously you're best starting with the most politically active of them: Osmond, Trelawney and the students. On the other hand, if you accept that there could have been some other motive, then you have to rethink the whole thing in more human terms: revenge, hatred, that kind of thing. Or maybe someone was trying to put the blame on the farm people, someone who had a reason to hate them or want them off their land.'

Burgess sighed. 'You make it sound so bloody complicated. Do you really think that's where the answer lies?'

'It's possible, yes.' Banks took a deep breath. 'Gill was a bastard,' he said. 'He liked thumping people, bashing heads. He's volunteered for more crowd control duties than I've had hot dinners. And another thing: Osmond made an official complaint about him for using undue force in another demo a couple of years back. So did a woman called Elizabeth Dale, in a separate incident. And she's got some connection with the farm crowd.'

Burgess drank some more beer and sucked his lips. 'How do you know?' he asked quietly.

Banks had been expecting this. He remembered Burgess's order not to look into Gill's record. 'Anonymous tip,' he said.

Burgess narrowed his eyes and stared as Banks took out a cigarette and lit it.

'I don't know if I believe you,' he said finally.

'It doesn't bloody matter, does it? It's what I'm telling you that counts. Do you want to get to the bottom of this or don't you?'

'Go on.'

'I'm saying we've got two options: terrorism or personal motive. Maybe they're both mixed up as well, I don't know.'

'And where does Boyd come in?'

'Either he did exactly as he told us, or he was an accomplice. So we dig deeper into his political background. Richmond's doing all he can at the computer, checking people Boyd knew in jail and any others he hung about with when the local police were keeping an eye on him. He spent some time in Ireland, which is where he was heading when we caught him, and some of the people he knew had connections with the IRA. We can't prove it, but we're pretty damn sure. We also have to consider the personal motive. Gill was the kind of person to make enemies, and it looks like Osmond was one of them.'

'In the meantime,' Burgess said, 'we hang on to Boyd.'

Banks shook his head. 'I don't think so.'

'Let him go?'

'Yes. Why not?'

'He scarpered last time. What's to stop him doing it again?'

'I think he found out that he'd nowhere to go. If you let him out, he'll go back to the farm and stay there.'

'But why let him out at all?'

'Because it might stir something up. If he's not guilty, there's still a chance he might know who is. He might slip up, set something moving.'

Burgess swirled the beer in his glass. 'So we charge him with tampering with evidence, wasting police time, and let him out. Is that what you're suggesting?'

'For the time being, yes. Have you got a better idea?'

'I'm not convinced,' Burgess said slowly, 'but I'll go

along with it. And,' he added, poking his cigar in Banks's direction, 'on your head be it, mate. If he buggers off again, you'll answer for it.'

'All right.'

'And we'll keep him in another night, just so he gets the message. I'll have another little chat with him, too.'

It was a compromise. Burgess was not the kind of man to give way completely to someone else's idea. It was the best deal he would get, so Banks agreed.

Burgess smiled over at Glenys. Down at the far end of the bar, a glass broke. 'I'll go get us a couple more, shall I?'

'Let me.' Banks stood up quickly. 'It's my round.' It wasn't, but the last thing they needed was a lunch-time punch-up between the landlord of the Queen's Arms and a detective superintendent from Scotland Yard.

'I'll take Osmond again, too,' Burgess said, when Banks got back. 'I don't trust you when that bird of his is around. You go all gooey-eyed.'

Banks ignored him.

'Can I take DC Richmond with me?' Burgess asked.

'What's wrong with Sergeant Hatchley?'

'He's a lazy sod,' Burgess said. 'How he ever made sergeant I don't bloody know. Every time he's been with me he's just sat there like a stuffed elephant.'

'He has his good points,' Banks said, surprised to find himself defending Hatchley. He wondered if the sergeant really had been nurturing a dream of Burgess's inviting him to join some elite Yard squad just because they both believed in the privatization of everything and in an England positively bristling with nuclear missiles. If he had, tough titty.

The difference between them, Banks thought, was that Hatchley just assumed attitudes or inherited them from his parents; he never thought them out. Burgess, on the other hand, really believed that the police existed to hold back the red tide and keep immigrants in their place so that the government could get on with the job of putting the Great back in Britain. He also believed that people like Paul Boyd should be kept off the streets so that decent citizens could rest easy in their beds at night. It never occurred to him for a moment that he might not pass for decent himself.

Banks followed Burgess back to the station and went up to his office. He had a phone call to make.

ONE

South of Skipton, the landscape changes dramatically. The limestone dales give way to millstone grit country, rough moorland for the most part, bleaker and wilder than anything in Swainsdale. Even the drystone walls are made of the dark purplish gritstone. The landscape is like the people it breeds: stubborn, guarded, long of memory.

Banks drove through Keighley and Haworth into open country, with Haworth Moor on his right and Oxenhope Moor on his left. Even in the bright sun of that spring-like day, the landscape looked sinister and brooding. Sandra hated it; it was too spooky and barren for her. But Banks found something magical about the area, with its legends of witches, mad Methodist preachers and the tales the Brontë sisters had spun.

Banks slipped a cassette in the stereo and Robert Johnson sang 'Hellbound on My Trail'. West Yorkshire was a long way from the Mississippi delta, but the dark jagged edges of Johnson's guitar seemed to limn the landscape, and his haunted, doom-laden lyrics captured its mood.

Dominated by mill towns at the valley bottoms and weaving communities on the heights, the place is a product of the Industrial Revolution. Majestic old mills with their tall chimneys of dark grainy millstone grit still remain. Many have now been scoured of two hundred years' soot and set up as craft and antiques markets.

Hebden Bridge is a mill town turned tourist trap, full of bookshops and antique shops. Not so long ago, it was a centre of trouser and corduroy manufacturing, but since the 1970s, when the hippies from Leeds and Manchester invaded, it has been more of a place for arts festivals, poetry readings in pubs and other cultural activities.

Banks drove down the steep hill from the moors into the town itself. Rows of tall terraced houses run at angles diagonally along the hillside and overlook the mills at the valley bottom. They look like four-storey houses, but are actually rows of two-storey houses built one on top of the other. You enter the lower house from a street or ginnel at one level, and the upper from a higher one at the back. All of which made it very difficult for Banks to find Reginald Lee's house.

Lee, Banks had discovered from his phone call to PC Brooks of the Hebden Bridge police, was a retired shop owner living in one of the town's two-tiered buildings. Just over three years ago he had been involved in an accident on the town's busy main street – a direct artery along the Calder valley from east to west – which had resulted in the death of Alison, Seth Cotton's wife.

Banks had also discovered from the police that there had been nothing suspicious about her death, and that Mr Lee had not been at fault. But he wanted to know more about Seth Cotton's background, and it seemed that the death of his wife was a good place to start. He was still convinced that the number written so boldly in the old notebook was PC Gill's and not just part of a coincidentally similar calculation. Whether Seth himself had written it down was another matter.

Lee, a small man in a baggy threadbare pullover, answered the door and frowned at Banks. He clearly didn't get many visitors. His thinning grey hair was uncombed, sticking up on end in places as if he'd had an electric shock, and the room he finally showed Banks into was untidy but clean. It was also chilly. Banks kept his jacket on.

'Sorry about the mess,' Lee said in a high-pitched whining voice. 'Wife died two years back and I just can't seem to get the hang of housework.'

'I know what you mean.' Banks moved some news-papers from a hard-backed chair. 'My wife's been away at her mother's for two weeks now and the house feels like it's falling apart. Mind if I smoke?'

'Not at all.' Lee shuffled to the sideboard and brought an ashtray. 'What can I help you with?'

'I'm sorry to bring all this up again,' Banks said. 'I know it must be painful for you, but it's about that accident you were involved in about three years ago.'

Lee's eyes seemed to glaze over at the mention. 'Ah, yes,' he said. 'I blame that for Elsie's death too, you know. She was with me at the time, and she never got over it. I retired early myself. Couldn't seem to . . .' He lost his train of thought and stared at the empty fireplace.

'Mr Lee?'

'What? Oh, sorry, Inspector. It is Inspector, isn't it?'

'It'll do,' Banks said. 'The accident.'

'Ah, yes. What is it you want to know?'

'Just what happened, in as much detail as you can remember.'

'Oh, I can remember it all.' He tapped his forehead. 'It's all engraved there in slow motion. Just let me get my pipe. It seems to help me concentrate. I have a bit of trouble keeping my mind on track these days.' He fetched a briar from a rack by the fireplace, filled it with rubbed twist and put a match to it. The tobacco flamed up and blue smoke curled from the bowl. A child's skipping rhyme drifted in from the street:

> *Georgie Porgie, pudding and pie,*
> *Kiss the girls and make them cry.*

'Where was I?'

'The accident.'

'Ah, yes. Well, it happened on a lovely summer's day. The sixteenth of July. One of those days when you can smell the moorland heather and the wild flowers even here in town. Not a cloud in the sky and everyone in that relaxed dozy mood you get in summer. Elsie and I were going for a ride to Hardcastle Crags. We used to do a lot of our courting up there when we were youngsters, like. So whenever the weather was good, off we went. I wasn't doing more than thirty – and I hadn't a drop of drink in me, never touch the stuff – when I came upon this lass riding along on her bicycle on my inside.' He faltered, sucked at his pipe as if it were an oxygen mask, and carried on. 'She was a bit wobbly, but then a lot of cyclists are. I always took special care when there were cyclists around. Then it happened. My front wheels were a foot or two away from her back. She was over by the kerb, like, not directly in front of me, and she just keeled over.'

'Just like that?'

'Aye.' He seemed amazed, even though he must have told the story dozens of times to the police. 'As if she'd hit a jutting stone. But there wasn't one. She might have bounced off the kerb or something. And she fell right in front of the car. I'd no time to stop. Even if I'd only been going five miles an hour I wouldn't have had time. She went right under the wheels. Keeled over, just like that.'

Banks let the silence stretch. Tobacco crackled in the pipe bowl and the repetitive chant continued outside. 'You said she was wobbling a bit,' he asked finally. 'Did she seem drunk or anything?'

'Not especially. Just like she was a learner, maybe.'

'Have you ever come across a policeman by the name of Edwin Gill. PC 1139?'

'Eh? Pardon me. No, the name and number aren't familiar. It was PC Brooks I dealt with at first. Then Inspector Cummings. I don't remember any Gill. Is he from around here?'

'Did you ever meet Seth Cotton?'

'Yes,' Lee said, relighting his pipe. 'I plucked up the courage to go and see him in hospital. He knew all the details and said he didn't blame me. He was very forgiving. Of course he was in a shocking state, still beside himself with grief and anger. But not at me. I only went the once.'

'In hospital? What was he doing there?'

Lee looked surprised. 'I thought you'd have known. He tried to kill himself a couple of days after the hospital phoned him about the accident. Slit his ankles. And they say he smashed the phone to bits. But someone found him before it was too late. Have you seen the lad lately?'

'Yes.'

'And how is he?'

'He seems to be doing all right.' Banks told him about the farm and the carpentry.

'Aye,' Lee said. 'He mentioned he were a carpenter.' He shook his head slowly. 'Terrible state he were in. Bad enough losing the lass, but the baby as well . . .'

'Baby?'

'Aye. Didn't you know? She were pregnant. Five months. The police said she might have fainted like, had a turn because of her condition . . .'

Lee seemed to drift off again, letting his pipe go out. Banks couldn't think of any more questions, so he stood up to leave. Lee noticed and snapped out of his daze.

'Off, are you?' he said. 'Sure you won't stay for a cup of tea?'

'No, thank you, Mr Lee. You've been very helpful. I'm sorry I had to put you through it all again.'

'There's hardly a day goes by when I don't think on it,' Lee said.

'You shouldn't keep torturing yourself that way,' Banks told him. 'Whichever way you look at it, no blame can possibly attach itself to you.'

'Aye, no blame,' Lee repeated. And his piercing inward gaze put Banks in mind of the actor Trevor Howard at his conscience-stricken best. There was nothing more to say. Feeling depressed, Banks walked back out to the street in the chilly spring sunshine. The children paused and stared as he passed by.

It was after five o'clock and the people down in the town were hurrying home from work. All Banks had to look forward to was a tin of ravioli on toast – which he would no doubt burn – and another evening alone.

Looking up the hillside to the west, he thought of Heptonstall, a village at the summit. He'd heard that the pub there served Timothy Taylor's beer, something he'd never tried. It had been a wasted and depressing afternoon as far as information was concerned, so he might as well salvage it somehow.

Alison Cotton's death had obviously been a tragic

accident, and that was all there was to it. She had either rubbed against the kerb and lost her balance, or she had fainted, perhaps due to the effects of her pregnancy. Banks could hardly blame Seth for not wanting to talk about it.

He got in his car and drove up the steep hill to Heptonstall. It was a quiet village at that time of day: narrow winding terraces of small dark cottages, many with the telltale rows of upper windows where weavers had once worked.

He lingered over his food and beer in the window seat of the Cross Inn, planning what to do next. The Timothy Taylor's bitter was good, smooth as liquid gold. Shadows lengthened and the fronts of the gritstone houses over the narrow street turned even darker.

It was late when he got home – almost ten – and he'd hardly had time to put his slippers on and sit down before the phone rang.

'Alan, thank God you're back. I've been trying to call you all evening.' It was Jenny.

'Why? What's wrong?'

'It's Dennis. His flat has been broken into.'

'Has he reported it?'

'No. He wants to see you.'

'He should report it.'

'I know, but he won't. Will you go and see him? Please?'

'Was he hurt?'

'No, he was out when it happened. It must have been sometime earlier this evening.'

'Was anything taken?'

'He's not clear about that. Nothing important, I don't think. Will you see him? Please?'

Banks could hardly refuse. In the first place, Jenny was clearly distraught on Osmond's behalf, and in the second, it might have a bearing on the case. If Osmond refused to come to him, then he would have to go to Osmond. Sighing, he said, 'Tell him I'll be right over.'

TWO

'You don't like me very much, do you, Chief Inspector?' said Osmond as soon as Banks had made himself comfortable.

'I'm not bowled over, no.'

Osmond leaned back in his armchair and smiled. 'You're not jealous, are you? Jenny told me how close you two got during that peeping Tom business.'

She did, did she, Banks thought angrily. Just how much had she told him? 'Could you just get on with it, please?' he said. 'I'm here, at Jenny's request, to investigate a break-in you haven't reported officially. The least you can do is stop trying to be so fucking clever.'

The smile disappeared. 'Yes, all right. For what good it'll do me.'

'First off, why didn't you report it?'

'I don't trust the police, certainly not the way I've been treated since the demonstration. Burgess was around here again this afternoon tossing insults and accusations about. And I don't want my apartment done over by a bunch of coppers, either.'

'Why not? What have you got to hide?'

'Nothing to hide, not in the way you mean it. But I value my privacy.'

'So why am I here?'

Osmond crossed his legs and paused before answering. 'Jenny persuaded me.'

'But you don't really want to talk about it?'

'What's the point? What can you do?'

'We could do our job if you'd let us. Check for finger-prints, interview neighbours, try to get a description. Was anything stolen?'

'A book.'

'What?'

'A book. Most of my books were pulled off the shelves, scattered on the floor, and I noticed when I put them back that one was missing.'

'Just one?'

'That's right. Marcuse's *One Dimensional Man*. Do you know it?'

'No.'

Osmond smiled smugly. 'I didn't think you would. It doesn't matter. Anyway, that's all.'

'That's all that was taken?'

'Yes.'

'How did they get in? The lock doesn't seem broken.'

'It's easy enough to open. They probably used a credit card or something. I've had to do that myself more than once.'

'And it works?'

'Yes. Unless the catch is on from the inside. Obviously, as I was out at the time, it wasn't.'

'Then I'd suggest the first thing you do is get a new lock. Preferably a deadlock.'

'I've already called the locksmith. He's coming on Monday.'

'Did you get the impression that they were looking for something? Or was it just vandalism?' Banks had his cigarette packet in his hand without thinking before he realized Osmond was a rabid non-smoker.

'Oh, go on, Chief Inspector.' Osmond allowed himself another superior smile. 'Pollute the atmosphere if you must. You're doing me a favour; it's the least I can do in return.'

'Thanks, I will.' Banks lit up. 'What might they have been looking for? Money?'

'I don't think so. There was a little cash in the dresser drawer, but they left it. There was also some quite valuable jewellery – it used to be my mother's – and they left that too. The only things disturbed were the books and some papers – nothing important – but there was no damage. I don't think it was vandalism.'

'But it was clear they'd seen the money and jewellery?'

'Oh, yes. The drawer was open and the contents of the jewellery box were spilled on the bed.'

'What do you think they were looking for?'

Osmond scratched his cheek and frowned. Noticing Banks's half inch of ash, he fetched an ashtray from the kitchen. 'In case of emergencies,' he said. 'Stolen property, I'm afraid. Courtesy of the Bridge, Helmthorpe.'

Banks smiled. Having got over his initial nervousness that, as with so many people, manifested itself in the form of rudeness, Osmond was making an attempt at least to smoothe the waters. He still wasn't comfortable around the police, but he was trying.

'Would you like a drink?'

'Scotch, if you've got it.' Osmond was prevaricating, making time to think. That meant his answer would be at best a blend of truth and falsehood, and it would be damn difficult for Banks to sort out which was which. But there was no point pushing him. Osmond liked being in control, and any challenge at this point would just make him clam up. Best wait for a gap in his defences and leap right through. Let him take his own sweet time.

Finally, drink in hand, Banks repeated his question.

'I don't want to appear unduly paranoid, Chief Inspector,' Osmond began slowly, 'but I've been involved with the CND and a number of other organizations for some years now, so I think I can speak from experience. I take it you know, of course, that I once made a complaint against the policeman who was killed?'

Banks nodded. 'You'd have saved us a lot of trouble if you hadn't lied in the first place.'

'That's easy for you to say. Anyway, your charming superintendent knew. He wouldn't let it drop. So I assume you know about it, too. Anyway, we come to expect that kind of thing. The CND doesn't take sides, Chief Inspector. Believe it or not, all we want is a nuclear-free world. But some members bring along strong political beliefs too, I won't deny it. I'm a socialist, yes, but that doesn't have anything to do with the CND or its aims.'

He paused and fingered his small gold crucifix. As Banks looked at him slouching on the sofa with his long legs crossed and his arms spread out along the back, the word languid came to mind.

'Have you noticed how things seem to come in packages?' Osmond went on. 'If you're anti-nuclear, people also expect you to be pro-choice, pro-union, pro-gays, anti-American, anti-apartheid and generally left wing. Most people don't realize that it's perfectly possible to be, say anti-nuclear and anti-apartheid without being pro-gay and pro-choice – especially if you're a Catholic. Oh, the permutations might differ a bit – some packages are more extreme and dangerous than others, for example – but you can pretty well predict the kind of things our members value. The point is that what we stand for is politically hot, and that draws attention to us from all sides. The government thinks we're in league with the Russians, so they raid our offices periodically and go over our files. The communists think we're allies in overthrowing a decadent capitalist government, so they woo us and infiltrate us with their own. It's a bloody mess, but we manage, through it all, to stick to our aims.'

'Are you saying you think the break-in was politically motivated?'

'That's about it.' Osmond lifted the Scotch bottle and raised his eyebrows. Banks held out his glass. 'And the theft of the book was a sort of calling card, or warning. So do you see what I mean about not expecting much help from the police? If Special Branch or MI5 or whoever are involved, you'd get your wrists slapped, and if it's the other side, you'd never catch them anyway.'

'But what were they looking for?'

'I don't know. Anyway, I don't keep my files here. Most of the important ones are at the CND office, and some of the stuff is at work.'

'The Social Services Centre?'

'Yes. I've got an office there. It's convenient.'

'So they didn't find what they were looking for because they didn't look in the right place.'

'I suppose so. The only current thing is the inquiry I'm making into the demo. I've already told you about that – and Superintendent Burgess, too. I've talked to quite a lot of people involved, trying to establish exactly what happened and how it could have been avoided. Tim and Abha are helping, too. They've got most of the info at their place. We're having a meeting up at the farm tomorrow to decide what to do about it all. Ever since your boss was taken off the job, we've been carrying on for him, and our results will be a hell of a lot less biased.'

'You're wrong,' Banks said, lighting another cigarette. 'The trouble with people like you, despite all your talk about packages, is that you tar everyone with the same brush. To you, all police are pigs. Superintendent Gristhorpe would have done a good job. He wouldn't have swept it all under the carpet.'

'Maybe that's why he was taken off,' Osmond said. 'I read in the paper that they were going to appoint an impartial investigating commission which, I suppose, means a bunch of high-ranking policemen from somewhere other than Eastvale, but most of us think they're just going to forget about the whole embarrassing affair. Once the killer is convicted – and it looks like you're well on your way to doing that – the anti-nuke lefties will be shown up for exactly what you all think we are – a gang of murderous anarchists – and the police will gain a lot of very useful public sympathy.'

Banks put his empty glass down and walked over to the window. 'Tell me about Ellen Ventner.'

Osmond paled. 'You certainly do your homework, don't you?'

'Ellen Ventner.'

'If you think I'm going to admit to those ludicrous charges against me, you must be crazy.'

'Much as it saddens me to say so, I'm not here to investigate those old charges. So you like to beat up women. That's your privilege.'

'You bastard. Are you going to tell Jenny?'

'I honestly don't know. Ellen Ventner didn't pursue the charges. God knows why, but a lot of women don't. Maybe she thought you were still a really sweet fellow underneath it all. But that doesn't alter what happened. You might think you're a very important man in the political scheme of things, but personally I doubt it. On the other hand, a woman you once assaulted might bear a grudge.'

'After four years?'

'It's possible.'

'Forget it. She wouldn't. Besides, she emigrated not long after we split up.'

'I can understand why she might have wanted to get as far away from you as possible. Just checking all the angles.'

Osmond glared, then looked into his glass and started to fiddle with his crucifix again. 'Look, it was only the once . . . She . . . I was drunk. I didn't mean to . . .'

Banks sat down opposite him again and leaned forward. 'When you made your complaint about PC Gill,' he asked, 'how did you do it?'

Osmond floundered. It was so easy, Banks thought. Stir up a man's emotions, then change the subject and you're in control again. He'd had enough of Osmond's lectures and his arrogance.

'What do you mean, how did I do it? I wrote a letter.'

'How did you refer to him?'

'By his number. How else?'

'1139?'

'Yes, that's it.'

'You still remember it?'

'Obviously.'

'So how did you know his name?'

'Look, I don't—'

'When I first asked you if you knew Gill, you said no. I didn't use his number, I used his name, and you recognized it when you lied to me.'

'He told me,' Osmond said. 'When I tried to stop him from hitting a woman at a demo once, he pulled me aside and told me to keep out of it. I told him I'd report him, and he said go ahead. When I looked at his number, he told me his name as well. Spelled it out in fact. The bastard was proud of what he was doing.'

So Osmond defended women in public and only hit them in private. Nice guy, Banks thought, but he kept his questions factual and direct. 'When you were up at Maggie's Farm on the afternoon of the demonstration, did you mention that number to anyone?'

'I don't know. I can't remember.'

'Think. Did you write it in a notebook, or see it written in a notebook?'

'No, I'd remember something like that. But I might have mentioned it. Really, I can't say.'

'How might you have mentioned it? Just give me a sense of context.'

'I might have said, "I wonder if that bastard PC 1139 will be out tonight." I suppose I'd have warned people about him. Christ, you can't be involved in demos around this part of the world and not know about PC bloody 1139.'

'So I gather.' Banks remembered what Tim and Abha had told him.

There was nothing more to ask. Banks said goodnight and Osmond slammed the door behind him. In the corridor, he decided to try the flats on that floor to see if anyone had noticed the housebreaker. There were only ten – five on each side.

At the third door, a man who had been nipping out to the off-licence at about a quarter to eight said he'd seen two men walking along the corridor on his way back. They had seen him too, but had made no move to run off or turn away. The description was average – most people are about as observant as a brick wall, Banks had discovered over the years – but it helped.

They were both tall and burly, and they both wore dark blue trousers, a bit shiny, probably the bottom part of a suit; one had on a black overcoat, fake leather, while the other wore a light trench coat; one had black hair, the other none at all and neither wore a hat or glasses. About facial features, the man remembered nothing except that both men had two eyes, a nose, a mouth, and two ears. They had walked confidently and purposefully, as if they knew where they were going and what they were about, not furtively, as he imagined criminals would have done. So, no, he hadn't seen any need to call the police. He was sorry now, of course. His speech was slurred, as if he'd already drunk most of what he'd bought at the off-licence. Banks thanked him and left.

Over the next four doors, Banks found himself told to piss off by a writer whose concentration he had disturbed and asked in for a cup of tea by a lonely military type who wanted to show off his medals. As yet, there had been no temptress in a negligee.

It wasn't until the ninth door that he found anyone else who knew anything. Beth Cameron wore tight checked slacks, which hardly flattered her plump hips and thighs, and a maroon cardigan over a shiny white blouse. Her curly brown hair showed traces of a recent perm, and she had the most animated face that Banks had ever seen. Every comment, every word, was accompanied by a curled lip, a raised eyebrow, a wrinkled nose, a deep frown or a mock pout. She was like one of those sponge hand-puppets he remembered from his childhood. When you put your hand inside it, you could wrench the face into the most remarkable contortions.

'Did you see anyone coming in or out of Mr Osmond's flat this evening?' Banks asked.

'No, no, I can't say I did. Wait a minute though, I did notice *something* odd. Not up here but down in the garage. It struck me as bit strange at the time, you know, but I just brushed it off. You do, don't you?'

'What did you see?'

'A blue Escort. And it was parked in Mr Handley's spot. He's often out during the evening – he's the entertainment reporter for the Eastvale *Gazette* – but still, I thought, that's no reason to steal the man's parking spot, is it? See, there's places for visitors outside. We don't encourage non-residents to park underground. It could lead to all sorts of trouble, couldn't it?'

'What time was this?' Banks asked.

'Oh, about eight o'clock. I was just bringing Lesley – that's my daughter – back from her piano lesson.'

'Did you see if there was anyone in the car?'

'Two men, I think. Sitting in the front.'

'Did you get a good look at them?'

'No, I'm sorry. They looked big, but I mean you just don't look at people, do you? Especially not in places like that. It doesn't do to make eye contact with strangers in an underground garage, does it?'

'No,' Banks said, 'I don't suppose it does. You didn't recognize either of the men, then?'

'No. Whatever happened, anyway?' Mrs Cameron suddenly frowned. 'There wasn't nobody assaulted, was there? I've been saying all along that place is too dark. Just asking for trouble it is.'

'Nobody was hurt,' Banks assured her. 'I'm just interested in that Escort. Have you noticed it before?'

'No, never. I did think of calling the police, you know. It did cross my mind they might be up to no good. But you don't want to cause a fuss, do you? It might all be perfectly innocent and there you'd be with egg on your face looking a proper fool. But I'd never forgive myself if someone got hurt.'

'Don't worry, it's nothing like that. You didn't get the number, by any chance?'

'No.' She laughed, then put her hand to her mouth. Her fingernails were painted pale green. 'I'm sorry, Mr Banks, but I always think it's so funny when the police go asking people that on telly. I mean, you don't go around collecting car numbers, do you? I don't think I even know my own.'

'Is there anything else you can think of?' Banks asked, without much hope.

Beth Cameron chewed her lower lip and frowned for a moment, then shook her head. 'No. Not a sausage. I didn't pay it much mind, really. They weren't doing nothing. Just sitting there like they were waiting to leave . . . Wait a minute!' Her eyebrows shot up almost to her hairline. 'I think one of them was bald. There was a light on the pillar by the car, you see. Dim as can be, but I could swear I saw a bald head reflecting the light.' Then her lips curved down at the edges. 'I don't suppose that's much help, though, is it?'

'Everything helps.' Banks closed his notebook and put it back into his inside pocket. At least he was certain now that the two men in the blue Escort were the same two who had been seen in the corridor near Osmond's flat. 'If you see the car again,' he said, handing her a card, 'would you please let me know?'

'Yes, of course I will, Mr Banks,' she said. 'Glad to be of use. Goodnight.'

At the last door Banks turned up nothing new. It had been a long time since he'd made door-to-door inquiries himself, and he had enjoyed it, but now it was going on for half past eleven and he was tired. Outside, the crisp cold air woke him up a bit. He stood by his car for a few moments and smoked a cigarette, thinking over what had happened that evening.

However much he had ridiculed the man's pretensions, he had to admit that Osmond was the type who made waves politically. Banks had a lot of sympathy for the CND and its goals, but he knew that, like so many peace-loving, well-meaning groups, it sometimes acted as a magnet for dangerous opportunists. Where there was organization there was politics, and where there was politics there was the aphrodisiac of power. Maybe Osmond *had* been involved in a plot to do with the demonstration. Perhaps his masters didn't trust him to keep his trap shut, and what had happened this evening had been intended as a kind of warning.

Banks found it hard to swallow all the cloak-and-dagger stuff, but the mere possibility of it was enough to send a shiver of apprehension up his spine. If there really was anything in the conspiracy theory, then it looked like these people – Russian spies, agents provocateurs, or whoever they were – meant business.

If that was true, Osmond might get hurt. That didn't concern Banks very much, but it did cause him to worry about Jenny. It was bad enough her being involved with a man who had beaten up a previous girlfriend, but much worse now there was a strong possibility that some very dangerous and cold-blooded people were after him too. None of it concerned Jenny directly, of course; she was merely an innocent bystander. But since when did governments or terrorists ever give a damn about innocent bystanders?

13

ONE

Maybe it was the spring weather, but the toasted teacakes in the Golden Grill tasted exceptionally good to Banks on Sunday morning. Burgess chose a doughnut filled with raspberry jam and dusted with icing sugar, which he dipped into his coffee. 'A taste I developed in America,' he explained, as Banks watched, horrified. 'They've got a place there called Dunkin' Donuts. Great.'

'What's happening with Boyd?' Banks asked.

'I had another chat with him. Got nowhere. Like you said, I let him go this morning, so we'll see what turns up now.'

'What did you do? Torture him again?'

'Well, there's not many can keep on lying when faced with their greatest fear. The way things stand now, I think we could get a conviction on Boyd, no problem, but we'd probably get chucked out of court if we tried to fit one of the others up – Osmond, for example. I say if we turn up nothing more in a couple of days, let's just charge Boyd with murder and I'll bugger off back to the Smoke a happy man.'

'What about the truth?'

Burgess treated Banks to a slit-eyed glance. 'We don't know Boyd didn't do it, do we? The Burgess Test not-withstanding. It's not infallible, you know. Anyway, I'm getting a bit sick of your moralizing about the truth all the bloody time. The truth's relative. It depends on your perspective. Remember, we're not judge and jury. It's up to them to decide who's guilty and who's not. We just present the evidence.'

'Fair enough, but it's up to us to make a charge that sticks, if only to stop us looking like prize berks in court.'

'I think we're solid on Boyd if we need to be. Like I say, give it a couple of days. Find anything interesting on the funny-farm lot?'

'No.'

'Those students puzzled me. They're only bloody kids – cheeky bastards, mind you – but their little minds are crammed full of Marx, Trotsky, Marcuse and the rest. They even have a poster of Che Guevara on the wall. I ask you – Che fucking Guevara, a vicious, murdering, mercenary thug got up to look like Jesus Christ. I can't understand what they're on about half the time, honest I can't. And I don't think they've got a clue, either. Pretty gutless pair, though. I can't see either of them having the bottle to stick a knife between Gill's ribs. Still, the girl's not bad. Bit chubby around the waist but a lovely set of knockers.'

'Osmond's place was broken into yesterday evening,' Banks said.

'Oh?'

'He didn't report it officially.'

'He should have done. You talked to him?'

'Yes.'

'Then you should have made a report. You know the rules.' He grinned. 'Unless, of course, you think rules are only for people like me to follow and for Jack the Lads like you to ignore?'

'Listen,' Banks said, leaning forward. 'I don't like your methods. I don't like violence. I'll use it if I have to, but there are plenty more subtle and effective ways of getting answers from people.' He sat back and reached for a cigarette. 'That aside, I never said I was any less ruthless than you are.'

Burgess laughed and spluttered over a mouthful of recently dunked doughnut.

'Anyway,' Banks went on, 'Osmond didn't seem to give a damn. Well, maybe that's too strong. At least, he didn't think we would do anything about it.'

'He's probably right. What *did* you do?'

'Told him to change his lock. Nothing was stolen.'

'Nothing.'

'Only a book. They'd searched the place, but apparently they didn't find what they were looking for.'

'What was that?'

'Osmond thinks they might have been after some papers, files to do with his CND stuff. He's got a touch of the cloak-and-dagger about him. Anyway, he keeps most of his files at the local office, and Tim and Abha have all the stuff on the demo. It seems they're having a meeting up at the farm this afternoon to plan their complaint strategy. It looks like the thieves wasted their time, whoever they were.'

'Who does he think it was? KGB? MI5? CIA?'

Banks laughed. 'Something along those lines, yes. Thinks he's a very important fellow does Mr Osmond.'

'He's a pain in the ass,' Burgess said, getting up. 'But I'll trip the bastard up before I'm done. Right now I'm off to catch up on some paperwork. They want everything in bloody quadruplicate down at the Yard.'

Banks sat over the rest of his coffee wondering why so

many people came back from America, where Burgess had been to a conference a few years ago, full of strange eating habits and odd turns of phrase – 'pain in the ass' indeed!

Outside on Market Street tourists browsed outside shop windows full of polished antiques and knitted woollen wear. The bell of the Golden Grill jangled as people dropped in for a quick cup of tea.

Banks had arranged to meet Jenny for lunch in the Queen's Arms at one o'clock, which left him well over an hour to kill. He finished his drink and nipped over to the station. First, he had to enlist Richmond's aid on a very delicate matter.

TWO

Mara was busy making scones for the afternoon meeting when Paul walked into the kitchen. Her hands were covered with flour and she waved them about to show she'd embrace him if she could. Seth immediately threw his arms around Paul and hugged him. Mara could see his face over Paul's shoulder and noticed tears in his eyes. Rick slapped Paul on the back and Zoe kissed his cheek. 'I did the cards,' she told him. 'I knew you were innocent and they'd have to let you go.' Even Julian and Luna, caught up in the adults' excitement, did a little dance around him and chanted his name.

'Sit down,' Seth said. 'Tell us about it.'

'Hey! Let me finish this first.' Mara gestured at the half made scones. 'It won't take a minute. And it was your idea in the first place.'

'I tell you what,' Paul said. 'I could do with a cup of tea. That prison stuff's piss-awful.'

'I'll make it.' Seth reached for the kettle. 'Then we'll go in the front room.'

Mara carried on with the scones, readying them for the oven, and Seth put the kettle on. The others all wandered into the front room except for Paul, who stood nervously behind Mara.

'I'm sorry,' he said. 'You know . . .'

She turned and smiled at him. 'Forget it. I'm just glad you're back. I should never had doubted you in the first place.'

'I was a bit . . . well, I did lie. Thanks for tipping me off, anyway. At least I had a chance.'

The kettle started boiling, and Seth hurried back in to make tea. Mara put the tray of scones in the oven and washed her hands.

'Right,' she said, drying them on her apron. 'I'm ready.'

They sat down in the living room and Seth poured tea.

'Come on then,' he urged Paul.

'Come on what?'

'Tell us what happened.'

'Where do you want me to start?'

'Where did you go?'

Paul lit a Players and spat a strand of loose tobacco from his upper lip. 'Edinburgh,' he said. 'Went to see an old mate, didn't I?'

'Did he help you?' Mara asked.

Paul snorted. 'Did he fuck. Bastard's changed a lot. I found the building easy enough. It used to be one of those grotty old tenements, but it's all be tarted up now. Potted plants in the stairwell and all that. Anyway, Ray answers the door and he doesn't recognize me at first – at least he pretends he doesn't. I hardly knew him, either. Wearing a bloody suit, he was. We say hello and then this bird comes out – hair piled up on top of her head and a black dress slit right down the front to her belly button. She's carrying one of those long-stemmed wineglasses full of white wine, just for the effect. "Who's this, Raymond?" she says, right la-di-da like, and I head for the stairs.'

'You didn't stay?' Mara said.

'Are you joking?'

'Do you mean your old friend wouldn't let you in?'

'Gone up in the world has old Raymond. Seems he was entertaining the boss and the wife – he's in computers – and he didn't want any reminders of his past. Used to be a real wild boy, but . . . Anyway, I left. Oh, I reckon he might have let me in if I'd pushed hard enough, stuck me in the cupboard or somewhere out of the way. But I wasn't having any.'

'So where did you go?' Seth asked.

'Just walked around for a while till I found a pub.'

'You didn't walk the streets all night, did you?' Mara asked.

'Like hell. It was colder than a witch's tit up there. This is bloody Scotland we're talking about. First thing the next morning I bought myself a duffel coat just to keep from freezing to death.'

'What did you do then, after you left the pub?'

'I met this bloke there,' Paul said, reddening. 'He said I could go back to his place with him. Look, I know what you're thinking. I'm not a fucking queer. But when you're on the streets, just trying to survive, you do what you have to, right? He was a nice enough bloke, anyway, and he didn't ask no awkward questions. Careful, he was, too, if you know what I mean.

'Next day I was going to head for Glasgow and look up another old mate, but I thought fuck that for a lark, best thing to do is get straight to Ireland. I've got mates there, and I don't think they've changed. If I'd got to Belfast *nobody* would have found me.'

'So what went wrong?' Seth asked.

Paul laughed harshly. 'Bloody ferry dock. I goes up to this shop bloke to buy some fags and when I walk away he shouts after me. I can't understand a bleeding word he's saying on account of the Jock accent like, but this copper sees us and gives me the look. I get nervous and take off and the bastards catch me.'

'Did the shopkeeper recognize you?' Mara asked. 'Your picture was in the papers, you know.'

'Nah. I'd just given him too much bloody money, that's all. He was shouting he wanted to give me my fucking change.' Paul laughed and the others laughed with him. 'It wasn't so funny at the time,' he added.

'What did the police do?' asked Rick.

'They've charged me with being an accessory. I'll have to go to court.'

'Then what?' Mara asked.

Paul shrugged. 'With my record I'll probably end up doing porridge again. That copper with the scar seems to think I might get off if they get a sympathetic jury. I mean, sometimes you respect people for standing by their mates, right? He says he might be able to get the charge reduced to giving false information and wasting police time. I'd only get six months max, then. But the other bloke tells me I'm looking at ten years. Who do you believe?'

'If you're lucky,' Mara said, 'Burgess might be gone by then and Banks'll take it easy on you.'

'What's wrong with him? He soft or something?'

Seth shook his head. 'Somehow I don't think so, no. He just has a different technique.'

'They're all bastards when you get right down to it,' Rick added.

Paul agreed. 'So what's been happening here?' he asked.

Seth filled him on the police visits. 'Apart from that, not much, really. We've all been worrying about you most of the time.' He ruffled Paul's hair. 'Glad you're back, kid. Nice new haircut, too.'

Paul blushed. 'Fuck off. Anyway, nothing's changed, has it?'

'What do you mean?' Mara asked.

'Well, they still don't have their killer and they're not going to stop till they do. And if they don't get someone else, I'm still their best bet. That Burgess bastard made that quite clear.'

'Don't worry about it,' Seth said. 'We won't let them blame it on you.'

Paul looked at his watch. 'Nearly opening time,' he said. 'I could do with a pint and some nosh.'

'We'll have to eat at the pub today, anyway,' Mara said. 'I've not made any dinner. What with that meeting and all . . .'

'What meeting?' Paul asked.

'We're getting together to talk about the demo this afternoon,' Rick said. 'Dennis is bringing Tim and Abha up about three. We want to look over statements and stuff to prove police brutality.'

'Well, you can count me out,' Paul said. 'I've had enough of that bleeding demo, and those fucking do-gooders. Sod 'em all.'

'You don't have to stick around,' Mara told him. 'Not if you don't want.'

'I think I'll go for a walk,' Paul said, calming down.

'Being cooped up in that cell hasn't done my head much good.'

'And I've got work to do,' Seth said. 'I've got to finish that bureau today. It's already overdue.'

'What's this?' Rick said. 'Is everybody copping out on us?'

'I'll put my twopenn'orth in first, don't worry,' Seth said. 'Then I'll get some work done. As for now, I think Paul's right. They do a nice Sunday lunch at the Black Sheep and I'm starving.'

Seth put his arm around Paul. The others stood up and went for their coats. In the fresh spring air, the seven of them walked down the track to Relton, happy together for the last time.

Except for Mara. The others might realize it too, she thought, but nobody's saying anything. If Paul isn't guilty, then someone else here is.

THREE

Jenny was already waiting when Banks came into the Queen's Arms at lunch time. Hungry, he arranged with Cyril for a few slices of roast leg of lamb. Glenys wasn't around, and Cyril, though he said nothing, seemed distracted.

'So,' Jenny said, resting her elbows on the table and cupping her chin in her hands, 'what's new? Dennis told me you dropped by. Thanks for going.'

'*He* didn't thank me.'

Jenny smiled. 'Well, he wouldn't, would he?'

'You didn't tell me it was you who persuaded him to talk to me in the first place.'

The lines around her eyes crinkled. 'Didn't I? Sorry. But did you find anything out?'

'Not really.'

'What does that mean?'

'It means no, I suppose. Have you ever noticed a blue Escort with two burly men in it hanging around Osmond's place?'

'No. Haven't you got *any* ideas, Alan?'

'Maybe one. It seems a bit far-fetched, but if I'm right . . .'

'Right about what?'

'Just an idea, that's all.'

'Can you tell me?'

'I'd rather not. Best wait and see. Richmond's working on it.'

'When will you know?'

'Tomorrow, I hope.'

The food arrived. 'I'm starving,' Jenny said, and the two ate in silence.

When he'd finished, Banks bought another round of drinks and lit a cigarette. Then he explained his doubts about Paul Boyd's guilt.

'Are you any closer to catching the real killer?' Jenny asked.

'It doesn't look like it. Boyd's still the closest we've got.'

'I can't believe that Dennis is a murderer, you know.'

'Are you speaking as a psychologist?'

'No. As a woman.'

'I think I'd trust that opinion more if it came from a professional.'

Jenny arched her eyebrows. 'What do you mean by that?'

'Don't bristle, it doesn't suit you. I mean that people – men and women – tend to be very protective about whoever they get involved with. It's only natural – you know that as well as I do. And not only that, but they deliberately blinker themselves sometimes, even lie. Look what Boyd did. If he really is innocent of murder, then he sure as hell risked a lot. And think about how Mara behaved. Whichever way you look at it now, it comes down to Seth, Rick or Zoe – with Mara, Tim and Abha, *and* your Dennis running close behind.'

'All right. As a professional, I don't think Dennis did it.'

'Just how much do you know about him?'

'What do you mean?'

'Never mind.'

'What? Come on. Out with it. If there's something I should know, tell me.'

Banks took a deep breath. 'Would you say Osmond is the kind of person to hit women?'

'What?'

Haltingly, Banks told her about Ellen Ventner. The more he said, the paler she became. Even as he told her, Banks wasn't sure of his motives. Was he doing it because he was worried about her association with Osmond, or was it out of pure vindictive jealousy?

'I don't believe it,' she whispered.

'Believe it. It's true.'

'Why are you telling me this?'

'I didn't want to tell you. You pushed me into it.'

'It was you who made me push you. You must have known how bloody humiliated it would make me feel.'

Banks shrugged. He could feel her starting to turn her anger against him. 'I'm sorry, that's not what I intended. He could be dangerous, Jenny. And I don't know about you, but I have problems understanding a person who rescues defenceless women from police brutality in public and beats them up in private.'

'You said it only happened once. There's no need to go making him into a monster. What do you expect me to do? Chuck him over just because he made a mistake?'

'I expect you to be careful, that's all. Osmond hit a woman once, put her in hospital, and he's also a suspect in a murder investigation. In addition, he seems to think the CIA, the KGB and MI5 are all after him. I'd say that merits a little caution, wouldn't you?'

Jenny's eyes glittered. 'You've never liked Dennis right from the start, have you? You've never even given him a chance. And now as soon as you find a bit of dirt on him, you sling it at me. Just what the bloody hell do you hope to achieve, Alan? You're not my keeper. I can take care of myself. I don't need a big brother to look out for me.'

She picked up her coat and swept out of the pub, knocking over her glass as she went. Faces turned to stare and Banks felt himself flush. Good one, Alan, he said to himself, you handled that really well.

He followed her outside, but she was nowhere in sight. Cursing, he went back to his office and tried to occupy his mind with work.

After a couple of false starts, he finally got through to Rick's wife's sister at her home in Camden Town. She sounded cagey and Banks first had to assure her that his call had nothing at all to do with the custody battle. Even then, she didn't sound as if she believed him.

'I just needed some information about Rick's wife, that's all,' he said. 'Were you always good friends?'

'Yes,' the sister answered. 'Our ages are close, so we always supported one another, even after she married

Rick. I don't want you to think I've anything against him, by the way. He's selfish and egotistical, but then most men are. Artists even more so. And I'm sure he's a good father. Pam certainly wasn't capable of taking care of Julian when they split up.'

'And now?'

'She's getting there. It's a long road though, alcoholism.'

'Did Pam ever have any connections up north?'

'Up north? Good Lord, no. I don't think she's ever been further north than Hendon.'

'Not even for a visit?'

'No. What's there to visit, anyway? It's all canals and slag heaps, isn't it?'

'So she's spent most of her life in either London or Cornwall?'

'Yes. They had a few months in France some years ago. Most painters seem to gravitate towards France at one time or another. But that's all.'

'Have you ever heard her mention a policeman called Gill – PC Edwin Gill, number 1139?'

'I've never heard her mention any policemen. No, I tell a lie. She said the local pub in Cornwall stayed open till all hours when the bobby was there. But I don't think that'd be your PC Gill.'

'No,' Banks said, 'it wouldn't. Did she ever attend political demonstrations – Greenham Common, the Aldermaston march, that kind of thing?'

'Pam's never been very political. Wisely so, if you ask me. What's the point? You can't trust one lot more than the other. Is that all, Chief Inspector?'

'Is she there? Can I talk to her?'

There was a short pause and Banks heard muffled sounds from the other end of the line. Finally, he could hear the phone changing hands and another voice came on, husky and weary as if doped or ill.

'Yes?'

Banks asked her the same questions he'd asked her sister, and the answers were the same. She spoke hesitantly, with long pauses between each sentence.

'Are the police involved in this custody battle?' Banks asked.

'Uh, no,' she answered. 'Just . . . you know . . . lawyers.'

Naturally, Banks thought. 'And you've never heard of PC Gill?'

'Never.'

'Has your sister visited Yorkshire recently?' Banks asked the question as soon as it came to him. After all, the sister might have got herself involved somehow.

'No. Here . . . looking after me. Can I go now? I've got to . . . I don't know anything.'

'Yes,' Banks said. 'That's all. Thanks for your time.'

He hung up and made notes on the conversation while it was fresh in his mind. The one thing that struck him as odd was that neither of the women had asked about Julian, about how he was. Why, he wondered, did Rick's wife want custody if she didn't even care that much about the child? Spite? Revenge? Julian would probably be better off where he was.

Next he called the Hebden Bridge police and asked for PC Brooks.

'Sorry to bother you again, Constable,' he said. 'I should probably have asked you all this before, but there's been rather too much going on here. Can you tell me anything about Alison Cotton, the woman who was killed in the car accident?'

'I remember her all right, sir,' Brooks said. 'It was my first accident and I . . . well . . . I er . . .'

'I know what you mean. It happens to us all. Did you know her before the accident?'

'Oh, aye. She'd been here a few years like, ever since the arty types discovered us, you might say.'

'And Alison was arty?'

'Aye. Helped organize the festival, poetry readings, that kind of thing. She ran the bookshop. I suppose you already know that.'

'What kind of a person was she?'

'She were a right spirited lass. Proper bonny, too. She wrote things. You know, poems, stories, stuff like that. I tried reading some in the local paper but I couldn't make head nor tail of it. Give me *Miami Vice* or *Dynasty* any day.'

'Was she ever involved in political matters – marches, demos, things like that?'

'Well,' PC Brooks said, 'we never had many things like that here. A few, but nowt much. Mostly "Save the Whales" and "Ban the Bomb". I don't know as she was involved though she did sometimes write bits for the paper about not killing animals for their fur and not making laboratory mice smoke five hundred fags a day. And about them women outside that missile base.'

'Greenham Common?'

'That's the one. When it comes down to it, I dare say she was like the rest, though. If some bandwagon came along, they jumped on it.'

'Ever heard of a PC Gill, 1139, from Scarborough?'

'Only what I've read in the papers, sir. I hope you catch the bastard who did it.'

'So do I. What about a friend of Cotton's called Elizabeth Dale? Heard of her?'

'Oh, aye. Liz Dale hung around with the Cotton crowd all right. Thick as thieves. I felt sorry for her, myself. I mean it's like a sickness, isn't it, when you get so you need something all the time.'

'Was she a registered addict?'

'Aye. She never really gave us any trouble. We just like to keep an eye on them, that's all, make sure they're not selling off half their prescriptions.'

'What kind of person is she?'

'Moody,' Brooks said. 'She got off drugs, but she were never really right afterwards. One day she'd be up, the next down. Right bloody yo-yo. But there was a lass with strong political opinions.'

'Liz Dale was political?'

'Aye. For a while, at least. Till she got it out of her system. Like I said, bandwagon.'

'But she was keener than the rest?'

'I'd say so, yes. Now Seth, he was never much more than partly interested. Rather be slicing up a piece of wood. And Alison, like I said, well, she had a lot of energy and she had to put it somewhere, but she was more your private artistic type. But Liz Dale, she was up to her neck in everything at one time.'

'Were Liz Dale and Alison Cotton especially close?'

'Like sisters.'

Banks thought of the complaint Dale had made against PC Gill. From that, he already knew she had attended at least one demonstration and come across him. Perhaps there had been others, too. Alison Cotton could have been with her. Perhaps this was the link he was looking for. But so what? Alison was dead; Reginald Lee had run her over by accident. It still didn't add up, unless everyone was lying and Liz Dale *had* been at Maggie's Farm and at the

Eastvale demonstration. Banks didn't know her, but if she did have a history of drug abuse, there was a chance she might be unbalanced.

'Thanks a lot,' Banks said. 'You've been a great help.'

'I have? Oh well—'

'Just one more thing. Do you know where Liz Dale lives?'

'Sorry, I can't help you there, sir. She's been away from here a few years now. I've no idea at all.'

'Never mind. Thanks anyway.'

Banks broke the connection and walked over to the window. At the far side of the square, just outside the National Westminster bank, a rusty blue Mini had slammed into the back of a BMW, and the two drivers were arguing. Automatically, Banks phoned downstairs and asked Sergeant Rowe to send someone over. Then he lit a cigarette and started thinking.

He certainly needed to know more about Liz Dale. If he could prove that she had been in the area at the time of the demo, then he had someone else with a motive for wanting to harm Gill. The Dale woman could easily have visited the farm one day earlier that week and taken the knife – Mara said that no one paid it any mind as a rule. If nobody had seen her, perhaps she had walked in and taken it while everyone was out. But was she at the demo? And why use Seth's knife? Did she have some reason other than revenge for wanting Gill dead? Obviously the best way to get the answer to that was to find Dale herself. Surely that couldn't prove too difficult.

As PC Craig approached the two drivers in the market square, Banks walked over to his filing cabinet.

FOUR

Mara stood inside the porch with Rick and Zoe and waved goodbye to Dennis Osmond and the others as they drove off. The sky was darkening in the west, and that early evening glow she loved so much held the dale in its spell, spreading a blanket of silence over the landscape. Flocks of birds crossed the sky and lights flicked on in cottages down in Relton and over the valley in Lyndgarth.

'What do you think?' she asked Rick, as they went back inside. The evening was cool. She hugged herself, then pulled on a sweater and sat in the rocking chair.

Rick's knees cracked as he knelt at the grate to start the fire. 'I think it'll work,' he said. 'We're bound to get the newspapers interested, maybe even TV. The police might try and discredit us, but people will get the message.'

Mara rolled a cigarette. 'I'll be glad when it's all over,' she said. 'The whole business seems to have brought us nothing but trouble.'

'Look on the bright side,' Rick said, turning to look at her. 'It's a blow against the police and their heavy-handed tactics. Even that woman from the Church for Peace group has started calling them pigs.'

'Still,' Mara said firmly, 'it would have been better for all of us if none of it had ever happened.'

'Everything's all right now,' Zoe said. 'Paul's back, we're all together again.'

'I know, but . . .'

Mara couldn't help feeling uneasy. True, Paul's return had cheered them up no end, especially Seth, who had been moping around with a long face the whole time he'd been away. But it wasn't the end. The police weren't going to rest until they'd arrested someone for the murder, and they had their eyes on the farm. Paul might still end up in jail as an accessory, a serious charge, Mara now realized. She wondered if Banks was going to charge her, too. He wasn't stupid; he must know she had warned Paul about Crocker finding the knife. Everything felt fragile. There was a chance she might lose it all, all the peace of mind and stability she had sought for so long. And the children, too. That didn't bear thinking about.

'Cheer up.' Rick crawled over and tilted her chin up. 'We'll have a party to celebrate Paul's release. Invite everyone we can think of and fill the place with music and laughter, eh?'

Mara smiled. 'I hope you're right.'

'Where is Paul, anyway?' Zoe asked.

'He went walking on the moors,' said Mara. 'I suppose he's just enjoying his freedom.' She almost added 'while it lasts' but decided that Rick was right; she at least ought to try to enjoy herself while things were going well.

'Seth didn't want much to do with us this afternoon, either,' Rick complained.

'Don't be like that, Rick,' Mara said. 'He's been getting behind in his work. This business with the police has been bothering him, too. Haven't you noticed how upset he's been? And you know what a perfectionist he is, what he's like about deadlines. Besides, I think he's just relieved Paul's back. He's as fed up with the aftermath of this bloody demonstration as I am.'

'We have to try and bring some good out of it,' Rick argued, placing the coal on top of the layered newspaper and wood chips. 'Don't you see that?'

'Yes, I do. I just think we all need a rest from it, that's all.'

'The struggle goes on. There is no rest.' Rick lit the fire in several places and stood the piece of plywood in front of the fireplace to make it draw. Behind the board the flames began to roar like a hurricane, and Mara could see red around the edges.

'Be careful,' she said. 'You know how wildly it burns with the wind up here.'

'Seriously,' Rick said, keeping an eye on the plywood shield, 'we can't stop now. I can understand your lack of enthusiasm, but you'll just have to shake yourself. Seth and Paul, too. You don't get anywhere against the oppressors by packing it in because you're fed up.'

'I sometimes wonder if you ever get anywhere,' Mara muttered.

She was aware that now she had found her home, Maggie's Farm, she was less concerned about the woes of the world. Not that she didn't care – she would be quite happy to write letters for Amnesty International and sign petitions – but she didn't want to make it her whole life, attending rallies, meetings and demonstrations. Compared to the farm, the children and her pottery, it all seemed so distant and pointless. People were going to go on being as cruel to one another as they always had been. But here was a place where she could make room for love. Why should it be contaminated by the sordid world of politics and violence?

'Penny for them?'

'What? Oh, sorry, Zoe. Just dreaming.'

'It's OK to dream.'

'As long as you don't expect them to come true without hard work,' Rick added.

'Oh, shut up!' Mara said. 'Just give it a rest, can't you, Rick? Let's pretend everything's all right for a few hours at least.'

Rick's jaw dropped, 'Isn't that what I said at first?' Then he shook his head and muttered something about women. Mara couldn't be bothered to take him to task for it.

Just then, the kitchen door flew open and Paul stood there, white and trembling. Mara jumped to her feet. 'Paul! What is it? What's wrong?'

At first he couldn't speak. He just leaned against the door jamb and tried to force the words out. Rick was beside him by then, and Zoe had reached for his hand.

'What is it, Paul?' she asked him softly. 'Take a deep breath. You must try to tell us.'

Paul followed her advice and went to slump down on the cushions. 'It's Seth,' he said finally, pointing towards the back garden. 'I think he's dead.'

14

ONE

Banks and Burgess rushed through the dark garden to Seth's workshop, where a bare bulb shone inside the half-open door. Normally, they would have been more careful on their approach to the scene, but the weather was dry and a stone path led between the vegetable beds to the shed, so there was no likelihood of footprints.

Burgess pushed the door open slowly and they walked in. Mixed with the scents of shaved wood and varnish was the sickly metallic smell of blood. Both men had come across it often enough before to recognize it immediately.

At first, they stood in the doorway to take in the whole scene. Seth was just in front of them, wearing his sand-coloured smock, slumped over his workbench. His head lay on the surface in a small pool of blood, and his arms dangled at his side. From where Banks was standing, it looked as if he had hit his head on the vice clamped to the bench slightly to his left. On the concrete floor over in the right-hand corner stood a small bureau in the Queen Anne style, its finish still wet, a rich glistening nut-brown. At the far end of the workshop, another bare light bulb shone over the area Seth used for office work.

It was only when Banks moved forward a pace that he noticed he had stepped in something sticky and slippery. The light wasn't very strong and most of the floor space around Seth was in semi darkness. Kneeling, Banks saw that what he had first taken for shadow was, in fact, more blood. Seth's feet stood at the centre of a large puddle of blood. It hadn't come from the head wound though, Banks realized, examining the bench again. There hadn't been much bleeding and none of the blood seemed to have dribbled off the edge. Bending again, he caught sight of a thin tubular object, a pen or a pencil perhaps, half-submerged in the pool. He decided to leave it for the forensic team to deal with. They were on their way from Wetherby and should arrive shortly after Dr Glendenning and Peter Darby, the young photographer, neither of whom had as far to travel.

Leaving the body, Banks walked cautiously to the back of the workshop where the old Remington stood on its desk beside the filing cabinet. There was a sheet of paper in the typewriter. Leaning forward, Banks was able to read the message: 'I did it. I killed the policeman Gill. It was wrong of me. I don't know what came over me. I'm sorry for all the trouble I caused. This is the best way. Seth.'

He called Burgess over and pointed out the note to him.

Burgess raised his eyebrows and whistled softly between his teeth. 'Suicide, then?'

'Looks like it. Glendenning should be able to give us a better idea.'

'Where the hell is this bloody doctor, anyway?' Burgess complained, looking at his watch. 'It can't take him that long to get here. Everywhere's within pissing distance in this part of the country.'

Burgess and Glendenning hadn't met yet, and Banks was looking forward to seeing Dirty Dick try out his aggressive arrogance on the doctor. 'Come on,' he said. 'There's nothing more to do in here till the others arrive.

We'll only mess up the scene. Let's go outside for a smoke.'

The two of them left the workshop and stood in the cool evening air. Glendenning, Banks knew, would smoke wherever he wanted and nobody had ever dared say a word to him, but then he was one of the top pathologists in the country, not a lowly chief inspector or superintendent.

From the doorway of the shed, they could see the kitchen light in the house. Someone – Zoe, it looked like – was filling a kettle. Mara had taken the news very badly, and Rick had called the local doctor for her. He had also phoned the Eastvale station, which surprised Banks, given Rick's usual hostility. Still, Seth Cotton was dead, there was no doubting that, and Rick probably knew there would be no way of avoiding an investigation. It made more sense to start out on the right foot rather than have to explain omissions or evasions later. Banks wondered whether to go inside and have a chat with them, but decided to give them a bit longer. They would have probably got over the immediate shock by the time Glendenning and the scene-of-crime team had finished.

At last, the back door opened and the tall white-haired doctor crossed the garden, a half-smoked cigarette hanging from the corner of his mouth. He was closely followed by a fresh-faced lad with a camera bag slung over his shoulder.

'About bloody time,' Burgess said.

Glendenning gave him a dismissive glance and stood in the doorway while Darby did his work. Banks and Burgess went back into the workshop to make sure he photographed everything, included the blood on the floor, the pen or pencil, the Queen Anne bureau and the type-writer. When Darby had finished, Glendenning went in.

He was so tall he had to duck to get through the door.

'Watch out for the blood,' Banks warned him.

'And there's no smoking at the scene,' Burgess added. He got no answer.

Banks smiled to himself. 'Ease up,' he said. 'The doc's a law unto himself.'

Burgess grunted but kept quiet while Glendenning felt for a pulse and busied himself with his stethoscope and thermometer.

About fifteen minutes later, while Glendenning was still making calculations in his little red notebook, the forensic team arrived, headed by Vic Manson, the fingerprints man. Manson was a slight academic-looking man in his early forties. Almost bald, he plastered the few remaining hairs over the dome of his skull, creating an effect of bars shadowed on an egg. He greeted the two detectives and went inside with the team. As soon as he saw the workshop, he turned to Banks. 'Bloody awful place to look for prints,' he said. 'Too many rough surfaces. And tools. Have you any idea how hard it is to get prints from well-used tools?'

'I know you'll do your best, Vic,' Banks said. He guessed that Manson was annoyed at being disturbed on a Sunday evening.

Manson snarled and got to work alongside the others, there to take blood samples and anything else they could find.

Banks and Burgess went back outside and lit up again. A few minutes later, Glendenning joined them.

'What's the news, Doc?' Burgess asked.

Glendenning ignored him and spoke directly to Banks. 'He's dead, and that's about the only fact I can give you so far.'

'Come on, Doc!' said Burgess. 'Surely you can tell us more than that.'

'Can you ask your pushy friend here to shut up, just for a wee while?' Glendenning said to Banks in a quiet nicotine-ravaged voice redolent of Edinburgh. 'And tell him not to call me Doc.'

'For Christ's sake.' Burgess flicked the stub of his cigar into the vegetable patch and stuck his hands deep in his pockets. He was wearing his leather jacket over an open-necked shirt, as usual. The only concession he had made to the cold was a V-necked sweater. Now that darkness had come, their breath plumed in the air, lit by the eerie glow of the bare bulb inside the workshop.

Glendenning lit another cigarette and turned back to Banks, who knew better than to rush him. 'It doesn't look to me,' the doctor said slowly, 'as if that head wound was serious enough to cause death. Don't quote me on it, but I don't think it fractured the skull.'

Banks nodded. 'What do you think was the cause?' he asked.

'Loss of blood. And he lost it from his ankles.'

'His ankles?'

'Aye,' Glendenning went on. 'The veins on the insides of each ankle were cut. I found a blade – most likely from a plane – lying in the blood, and it looks like it might have been used for the job. I'll have to make sure, of course.'

'So was it suicide?' Burgess asked.

Glendenning ignored him and went on speaking to Banks. 'Most suicides with a penchant for gory death,' he said, 'slit their wrists. The ankles are just as effective though, if not more so. But whether he inflicted the wounds himself or not, I canna say.'

'He's tried that way before,' Banks said. 'And there was a note.'

'Aye, well, that's your department, isn't it?'

'Which came first,' Banks asked, 'the head wound or the cut ankles?'

'That I can't say, either. He could have hit his head as he lost consciousness, or someone could have hit it for him and slit his ankles. If the two things happened closely in succession, it won't be possible to tell which came first, either. It looks like the head wound was caused by the vice. There's blood on it. But of course it'll have to be matched and the vice compared with the shape of the wound.'

'How long has he been dead?' Banks asked. 'At a guess.'

Glendenning smiled. 'Aye, you're learning, laddie,' he said. 'It's always a guess.' He consulted his notebook. 'Well, rigor's not much further than the neck, and the body temperature's down 2.5 degrees. I'd say he's not been dead more than two or three hours.'

Banks looked at his watch. It was six o'clock. So Cotton had probably died between three and four in the afternoon.

'The ambulance should be here soon,' Glendenning said. 'I called them before I set off. I'd better just bag the head and feet before they get here. We don't want some gormless young ambulance driver spoiling the evidence, do we?'

'Can you do the post-mortem tonight?' Banks asked.

'Sorry, laddie. We've the daughter and son-in-law down for the weekend. First thing in the morning?'

Banks nodded. He knew they'd been spoiled in the past by Glendenning's eagerness to get down to the autopsy immediately. It was more usual to be asked to wait until the next day. And to Glendenning, first thing in the morning was probably very early indeed.

The doctor went back inside, where Manson and his team were finishing up. A short while later the ambulance arrived, and two white-coated men bearing a stretcher crossed to the workshop. Seth looked oddly comical now, with his head in a plastic bag. Like some creature out of a 1950s horror film, Banks thought. The ambulance men tagged him, zipped him into a body bag and laid him on the stretcher.

'Can you leave by the side exit?' Banks asked, pointing to the large gate in the garden wall. 'They're shook up enough in the house without having to see this.'

The ambulance men nodded and left.

Manson came out five minutes later. 'Lots of prints,' he grumbled, 'but most of them a mess, just as I thought. At first glance though, I'd say they belong to only two or three people, not dozens.'

'You'll get Seth's, of course,' Banks said, 'and probably Boyd's and some of the others. Could you get anything from the blade?'

Manson shook his head. 'Sorry. It was completely covered in blood. And the blood had mixed to a paste with the sawdust on the floor. Very sticky. You'd have to wipe it all off to get anywhere, and if you do that . . .' He shrugged. 'Anyway, the doctor's taken it with him to match to the wounds.'

'What about the typewriter?'

'Pretty smudged, but we might get something. The paper, too. We can treat it with graphite.'

'Look, there's a handwriting expert down at the lab, isn't there?'

'Yes. Geoff Tingley. He's good.'

'And he knows about typewriting, too?'

'Of course.'

Banks led Manson back into the workshop and over to the old Remington. The suicide note was now lying beside it. Also on the desk was a business letter Seth had recently written and not posted. 'Dear Mr Spelling,' it read, 'I am most grateful for your compliments on the quality of my work, and would certainly have no objection to your spreading the word in the Wharfedale area. Whilst I always endeavour to meet both deadlines and quality standards, I am sure you realize that, this being a one-man operation, I must therefore limit the amount of work I take on.' It went on to imply that Mr Spelling should seek out only the best jobs for Seth and not bother him with stacks of minor repairs and commissions for matchbox-holders or lamp stands.

'Can you get Tingley to compare these two and let us know if they were typed by the same person?'

'OK.' Manson looked at the letters side by side. 'At a pinch I'd say they weren't. Those old manual typewriters have all kinds of eccentricities, it's true, but so do typists. Look at those "e"s, for a start.'

Banks looked. The 'e's' in Seth's business letter had imprinted more heavily than those in his suicide note.

'Still,' Manson went on, 'better get an expert opinion. I don't suppose his state of mind could be called normal, if he killed himself.' He placed each sheet of paper in an envelope. 'I'll see Geoff gets these first thing in the morning.'

'Thanks, Vic.' Banks led the way outside again.

Burgess stood with his hands still in his pockets in the doorway beside Peter Darby, who was showing him the

Polaroids he'd taken before getting down to the real work. He raised his eyebrows as Banks and Manson joined him. 'Finished?'

'Just about,' Banks said.

'Time for a chat with the inmates, then.' Burgess nodded towards the house.

'Let's take it easy with them,' Banks said. 'They've had a hell of a shock.'

'One of them might not have had, if Cotton was murdered. But don't worry, I won't eat them.'

In the front room, Zoe, Rick, Paul and the children sat drinking tea with the doctor, a young female GP from Relton. A fire blazed in the hearth and candles threw shadows on the whitewashed walls. Music played quietly in the background. Banks thought he recognized Bach's Third 'Brandenburg' Concerto.

'Mara's under sedation,' Rick said. 'You can't talk to her.'

'That's right,' the doctor agreed, picking up her bag and reaching for her coat. 'I just thought I'd wait and let you know. She took it very badly, so I've give her a sedative and put her to bed. I'll be back in the morning to check.'

Banks nodded, and the doctor left.

'How about some tea?' Burgess said, clapping his hands together and rubbing them. 'It's real brass monkey weather out there.'

Rick scowled at him, but Zoe brought two cups and poured the steaming liquid.

Burgess smiled down at her. 'Three lumps and a splash of milk, love, please.'

'What happened?' Zoe asked, stirring in the sugar. Her eyes were red and puffy from crying.

'That's for you to tell us, isn't it?' Burgess said. He

really was being quite polite, Banks noticed. 'All we know is that Seth Cotton is dead and it looks like suicide. Has he been depressed lately?' He took a sip of tea and spluttered. 'What the fuck is this?'

'It's Red Zinger,' Zoe said. 'No caffeine. You shouldn't really have milk and sugar with it.'

'You're telling me.' Burgess pushed the tea aside. 'Well, was he?'

'He was upset when Paul was in jail,' Zoe answered. 'But he cheered up this morning. He seemed so happy today.'

'And he never said anything about ending it all?'

'Never.' Zoe shook her head.

'I gather you had some kind of meeting this afternoon,' Banks said. 'Who was here?'

Rick eyed him suspiciously but said nothing.

'Just Dennis Osmond, Tim and Abha, that's all,' Zoe answered.

'What time were they here?'

'They arrived about half two and left around five.'

'Were you all present?'

Zoe shook her head. 'Seth stayed for a few minutes then went to . . . to work.'

'And I went for a walk,' Paul said defiantly. 'I needed some fresh air after being cooped up in your bloody jail for so long.'

'Not half as long as you will be if you don't knock off the cheek, sonny,' said Burgess.

'Was it you who found the body?' Banks asked.

'Yes.'

'Don't be shy. Tell us about it,' Burgess prompted him.

'Nothing to tell, really. I just got back from my walk and decided to look in on Seth and see how he was doing. I helped him, you know. I was sort of an apprentice. When I opened the door—'

'The door was closed?' Burgess asked.

'Yes. But it wasn't locked. Seth never locked it.'

'And what did you see?'

'You know what I saw. He was sprawled out on the bench, dead.'

'How did you know he was dead? Did you feel his heart?'

'No, of course I didn't. I saw the blood. I called his name and he didn't answer. I just knew.'

'Did you touch anything?' Banks asked.

'No. I ran in here and told the others.'

'Did you go near the typewriter?'

'Why should I? I didn't even notice the bloody thing. All I saw was Seth, dead.'

It was hard to know whether or not he was telling the truth. The shock of what he'd seen made his responses vague and defensive.

'So you left everything just as you found it?' Banks said.

'Yes.'

'This afternoon, during the meeting,' Burgess asked, 'did anyone leave the room for any length of time?'

'We all left at one time or another,' said Zoe. 'You know, to go to the toilet, stretch our legs, whatever.'

'Was anyone gone for a long time?'

'I don't know. We were talking. I don't remember.'

'So someone could have been away for, say, ten minutes?'

'I suppose so.'

'I know you were all busy playing at being concerned citizens,' Burgess said, 'but surely one of you must have noticed if anyone was gone too long?'

'Look,' Rick cut in, 'I thought you said it was suicide. What are you asking these questions for?'

'I said it *looked* like suicide,' Burgess answered coldly. 'And I'll ask whatever bloody questions I think necessary, without any comments from you, Leonardo, thank you very much.'

'Did any of you hear the typewriter at any time this afternoon?' Banks asked.

'No,' Zoe answered. 'But we wouldn't anyway. The walls are thick and the workshop's right at the far end of the garden. Well . . . you've seen where it is. We were all here in the front room. We could never even hear Seth sawing or using his drill from here.'

Banks glanced at Burgess. 'Anything else?'

'Not that I can think of right now,' the superintendent said, subdued again after his exchange with Rick. 'I don't want any of you buggering off anywhere, hear me?' he added, wagging his finger and giving Paul a particularly menacing look. 'There'll be more questions when we've got the results of the post-mortem tomorrow, so be available, all of you.'

Banks and Burgess left them to their grief. Down the valley side, the lights of Relton looked inviting in the chilly darkness.

'Pint?' Burgess suggested.

'Just what I had in mind,' said Banks. They got into the Cortina and bumped away down the track towards the Black Sheep.

TWO

The pillow felt like a cloud, the bed like cotton wool. Mara lay on her back, drifting, but not quite asleep. When she had first heard the news, she had lost control completely. The tears seemed to spurt from her eyes, her heart began to beat wildly, and the breath clogged in her throat. But the doctor's injection had taken care of all that, trading spasms and panic for clouds and cotton wool.

She could hear the muffled voices downstairs, as if from a great distance, and they made her think of those times when Seth and Liz Dale had stayed up late talking. How jealous she had been then, how insecure. But Liz was long gone, and Seth, they told her, was dead.

Dead. The thought didn't register fully through the layers of sedative. She thought she should still be crying and gasping for breath, but instead her body felt as heavy as iron and she could hardly move. Her mind seemed to have a life of its own, wandering over events and picking them out like those miniature mechanical cranes that dipped into piles of cheap trinkets and sweets at seaside arcades. You put your money in and off the crane went, with its articulated grip, inside the glass case. You held down a button to make it swing over and pressed another to make it drop on to the heap of prizes. If you were lucky, you got a chocolate bar, a cigarette lighter or a cheap ring; if not, the metal claw came up empty and you'd wasted your money. Mara had never won anything. Just as well, her father had always said; chocolate is bad for teeth, you're too young to smoke and those rings will turn your finger green inside a week.

But her mind felt like one of those machines now, one

she could not control. It circled her life, then swooped and snatched up the memory of the first time she and Seth had met. Just out of the ashram and eager to escape London, Mara had taken on a friend's flat in Eastvale when the friend emigrated to Canada.

She needed a job and decided to seek craft work before falling back on her secretarial skills, which were pretty rusty by then. Luckily, she heard of Elspeth's shop in Relton and went out to see her. Dottie had just become too ill to work – the pottery workshop was hers – and Mara got the job of helping out in the shop and the use of the facilities. It didn't bring in much money, but it was enough, along with the commission on the pottery. Her rent wasn't very high and she lived cheaply. But she was lonely.

Then, one day after work, she had dropped in at the Black Sheep. It was pay day and she had decided to treat herself to a glass of lager and a cheese and onion sandwich. No sooner had she started to eat than Seth walked in. He stood at the bar, tall and slim, his neatly trimmed dark hair and beard frosted with grey at the edges. And when he turned round, she noticed how deep and sad his eyes were, how serious he looked. Something passed between them – Seth admitted later that he'd noticed it too – and Mara felt shy like a teenager again. He smiled at her and she remembered blushing. But when he came over to say hello, there was no phoney coyness on her part; there were never any silly games between them.

He was the first person she'd met in the area with a background similar to her own. They shared tastes in music and ideas about self-sufficiency and the way the world should be run; they had been to the same rock festivals years ago and had read the same books. She went back with him to the farm that night – he was the only one living there at that time – and she never really left, except to give notice to her landlord and move her meagre belongings.

It was a blissful time, a homecoming of the spirit for Mara, and she thought she had made Seth happy too, though she was always aware that there was a part of him she could never touch.

And now he was dead. She didn't know how, or what had killed him, just that his body had ceased to exist. Her spiritual beliefs, which she still held to some extent, told her that death was merely a beginning. There would be other worlds, other lives perhaps for Seth's spirit, which was immortal. But they would never again drink wine together in bed after making love, he would never kiss her forehead the way he did before going to the workshop, or hold her hand like a boy on his first date on the way down to the Black Sheep. And that was what hurt: the absence of living flesh. The spirit was all very well, but it was far too nebulous an idea to bring Mara much comfort. The miniature crane withdrew from the heap of prizes and held nothing in its metal claw.

Downstairs, the voices droned on, more like music, a raga, than words with meaning. Mara felt as if her blood had thickened to treacle and darkened to the colour of ink. Her body was getting heavier and the lights in the glass case were going out; it was half in shadows now, the prizes indistinguishable from one another. And what happens when the lights go out in the funfair? Mara began to dream.

She was alone on the moors. A huge full moon shone high up, but the landscape was still, dark and bleak. She stumbled over heather and tussocks of grass, looking for something.

At last she came to a village and went into the pub. It

was the Black Sheep but the place was all modern, with video games, carpets and bare concrete walls. A jukebox was playing some music she didn't understand. She asked for the farm, but everyone turned and laughed at her, so she ran out.

This time it was daylight outside, and she was no longer in Swainsdale. The landscape was unfamiliar, softer and more green, and she could smell a whiff of the sea nearby.

In a hollow, she saw an old farmer holding wind chimes out in front of him. They made the same music as the jukebox and it frightened her this time. She found her voice and asked him where Maggie's Farm was. 'Are you the marrying maiden?' he asked her, smiling toothlessly. 'The basket is empty,' he went on, shaking the wind chimes. 'The man stabs the sheep. No blood flows. Misfortune.'

Terrified, Mara ran off and found herself in an urban landscape at night. Some of the buildings had burned out and fires raged in the gutted shells; flames licked around broken windows and flared up high through fallen roofs. Small creatures scuttled in dark corners. And she was being followed, she knew it. She hadn't been able to see anyone, just sensed darting movements and heard rustling sounds behind her. For some reason she was sure it was a woman, someone she should know but didn't.

Before the dream possessed her completely and turned her into one of the scavengers among the ruins, before the shadow behind tapped her on the shoulder, she struggled to wake up, to scream.

When she opened her eyes, she became conscious of someone sitting on the bedside pressing a damp cloth to her forehead. She thought it must be Seth, but when she turned and looked closely it was Zoe.

'Is it morning?' she asked in a weak voice.

'No,' said Zoe, 'it's only half past nine.'

'He really is dead, isn't he, Zoe?'

Zoe nodded. 'You were having a nightmare. Go to sleep now.' Mara closed her eyes again. The cool cloth smoothed her brow, and she began to drift. This time there was only darkness ahead, and the last thing she felt before she fell asleep was Zoe's hand gripping her tightly.

THREE

'Anything wrong?' Larry Grafton asked, pulling Banks a pint of Black Sheep bitter.

Banks glanced at Burgess, who nodded.

'Seth Cotton's dead,' he answered, and felt ears prick up behind him in the public bar, where most of the tables were occupied.

Grafton turned pale. 'Oh no, not Seth,' he said. 'He was only in here this lunch time. Not Seth?'

'How did he seem?' Banks asked.

'He was happy as a pig in clover,' Grafton said. 'That young lad was back and they all seemed to be celebrating. You're not telling me he killed himself, are you?'

'We don't know yet,' Burgess said, picking up his pint of Watney's. 'Anywhere quiet the chief inspector and I can have a little chat? Police business.'

'Aye, you can use the snug. There's no one in there.'

The snug was aptly named. Hidden away behind a partition of smoked glass and dark wood, there was room for about four people, and even that would be a tight squeeze.

Banks and Burgess made themselves comfortable, both

of them practically draining their drinks before even reaching for smokes.

'Have a cigar,' Burgess said, offering his tin.

'Thanks.' Banks took one. He didn't enjoy cigars as a rule, but thought that if he tried them often enough he might eventually come to like them.

'And I think I'd better get a couple more drinks in before we start,' Burgess said. 'Thirsty work, this.'

He was back in a moment carrying another pint of bitter for Banks and, this time, a pint of draught Guinness for himself.

'Right,' he said, 'I can tell you're not happy about this. Don't clam up on me, Banks. What's bothering you?'

'Let's take it at face value, for a start,' Banks suggested. 'Then maybe we can see what's wrong.'

'Suicide?'

'Yes.'

'But you don't think so?'

'No. But I'd like to play it through and see if I can pin down my ideas.'

'All right. Cotton murdered Gill, then he was overcome with remorse and slit his ankles. Case closed. Can I go back to London now?'

Banks smiled. 'But it's not as simple as that, is it? Why would Cotton murder PC Gill?'

Burgess ran a hand through his greying Brylcreemed hair. 'Bloody hell, I thought we'd been through all this before. We're talking about a political crime; call it an act of terrorism. Motive as such doesn't apply.'

'But Seth Cotton was perhaps the least political of the lot of them,' Banks argued. 'Except maybe for Mara, or Zoe Hardacre. Sure, he was anti-nuclear, and he no doubt believed in social equality and the evils of apartheid. But so do I.'

Burgess sniffed. 'You might be the murder expert around here, but I know about terrorism. Believe me, anyone can get involved. Terrorists play on people's ideals and warp them to their own ends. It's like the brain-washing religious cults do.'

'Do you think Gill's death was calmly planned and executed, or was it a crime of passion?' Banks asked.

'A bit of both. Things aren't so clear-cut in this kind of crime. Terrorists are very emotional about their beliefs, but they're cold and deadly when it comes to action.'

'The only thing Seth Cotton cared passionately about was his carpentry, and perhaps Mara. If he did commit suicide, I doubt it was anything to do with politics.'

'We have his note, don't forget. It's a confession.'

'Let's leave that for later. Why did he kill himself? If he's the kind of person you're trying to make out he is, why would he feel remorse after succeeding in his aim? Why would he kill himself?'

Burgess doodled in the foam of his Guinness. 'You expect too many answers, Banks. As often as not, there just aren't any. Can't you leave it at that?'

Banks shook his head and stubbed out the cigar. It tasted like last week's tea leaves. He swigged some more Black Sheep bitter to get rid of the taste and lit a Silk Cut. 'It's because there's too many questions,' he said. 'We still don't know much about Cotton's political background before he came to the farm, though if there'd been any subversive activity I'm sure Special Branch would have a record of it. And what about his behaviour over the last few days? How do you read that?'

'They said he seemed happy when Boyd was released. Is that what you mean?'

'Partly.'

'Well, of course he'd be happy,' Burgess said. 'If he knew the kid wasn't guilty.'

'Why should he care? It'd be better for a cold-blooded terrorist to let someone else go down for what he'd done. So why kill himself?'

Burgess shrugged. 'Because he knew we'd get to him soon.'

'So why didn't he just disappear? Surely his masters would have taken care of him in Moscow or Prague or wherever.'

'More likely Belfast. But I don't know. It's not unusual for suicides to appear happy once they've decided to end it all.'

'I know that. I'm just not sure that he was happy because he'd decided to kill himself.'

Burgess grunted. 'What's your theory, then?'

'That he was killed, and it was made to look like a suicide.'

'Killed by who?'

Banks ignored the question. 'We won't know anything for certain until the doctor does his post-mortem,' he said, 'but there's a few things that bother me about the note.'

'Go on.'

'It doesn't ring true. The damn thing's neither here nor there, is it? Cotton confesses to killing Gill, but doesn't say why. All he says is, "I don't know what came over me." It doesn't square with what we know of him.'

'Which is?'

'Precious little, I admit. He was a closed book. But I'd

say he was the kind who'd either not bother with a note at all, or he'd explain everything fully. He wouldn't come out with such a wishy-washy effort as the one we saw. I think he'd have used Gill's number too, not his name. And I don't know if you had a good look, but it seemed very different from that business letter on the desk. The pressure on the characters was different, for a start.'

'Yes,' Burgess said, 'but don't forget the state of mind he must have been in when he typed it.'

'I'll grant you that. Still . . . and the style. Whoever wrote that suicide note had only very basic writing skills. But the business letter was more than competent and grammatically correct.'

Burgess slapped the table. 'Oh come on, Banks! What's the problem? Is it too easy for you? Business letters are always written in a different style; they're always a bit stuffy and wordy. You wouldn't write to a friend the same way you would in a business letter, would you, let alone a suicide note. A man writing his last words doesn't worry about grammar or how much pressure he puts on each letter.'

'But that's just it. Those things are unconscious. Someone used to writing well doesn't immediately become sloppy just because he's under pressure. If anything, I'd have expected a more carefully composed message. And you don't think about how each finger hits the keys when you're typing. It's something you just do, and it doesn't vary much. Why leave it in the typewriter, too? Why didn't he put it on the bench in front of him?'

'And what I'm saying,' Burgess argued, 'is that his state of mind could account for all your objections. He must have been disturbed. Contemplation of suicide has an odd effect on a man's character. You can't expect everything to be the same as usual when a bloke's on the verge of slitting his bloody ankles. And remember, you said he'd tried that before.'

'That is a problem,' Banks agreed. 'Whoever did it must have known about the previous attempt and copied it to make it look more like a genuine suicide.'

'That's assuming somebody else did it. I'm not sure I agree.'

Banks shrugged. 'We'll see what forensic says about the note. But I'm not happy with it at all.'

'What about the bureau?'

'What about it?'

'He'd obviously just finished it, hadn't he? The coat of varnish was still fresh. And he'd moved it to the corner of the workshop. Doesn't that imply anything?'

'That he was tidying things up behind him, you mean? Tying up loose ends?'

'Exactly. Just like a man on the point of suicide. He finished his last piece of work, put it carefully aside so he wouldn't get blood all over it, then he slit his fucking ankles. When he got weak and passed out, he hit his head on the vice, accounting for the head wound.'

Banks stared into the bottom of his glass. 'It could have happened that way,' he said slowly. 'But I don't think so.'

'Which brings us back to the big question again,' Burgess said. 'If we're to follow your line of reasoning, if you *are* right, then who killed him?'

'It could have been any of them, couldn't it? Zoe said as much.'

'Yes, but she might have said that to get herself and her mates off the hook. I'm thinking of one of them in particular.'

'Who?'

'Boyd.'

Banks sighed. 'I was afraid you'd say that.'

'I'll bet you bloody were.' Burgess leaned forward so suddenly that the glasses rattled on the table. Banks could smell the Guinness and cigar smoke on his breath. 'If we play it your way, there's no getting round the facts. Boyd was missing all afternoon, unaccounted for. We only have his word that he was walking on the moors. I shouldn't think anybody saw him. It would have been easy for him to get in by the side gate and visit Seth while everyone in the house was wrapped up in their own little games. Nothing odd about that. He helped Seth a lot, and the shed would be full of his fingerprints anyway. They talk, and he kills Seth – pushes his head forward to knock him out on the vice, then slits his ankles.' Burgess leaned back again, satisfied, and folded his arms.

'All right,' Banks said. 'I agree. It fits. But why? Why would Boyd kill Seth Cotton?'

Burgess shrugged. 'Because he knew something to link Boyd to Gill's murder. It makes sense, Banks, you know it does. Why you're defending that obnoxious little prick is beyond me.'

'Why was Cotton so miserable when Boyd was in jail,' Banks asked, 'and so happy when he came out?'

Burgess lit another Tom Thumb. 'Loyalty, perhaps? He knew something and was worried he might be called on to give evidence. He wasn't sure he could carry on with his lies and evasions under pressure. Boyd gets out, so Cotton feels immediate elation. They talk. Cotton tells Boyd what he knows and how glad he is he won't have to testify under oath, so Boyd gets worried and kills him. Remember, Boyd knew he wasn't quite off the hook, whatever Cotton might have made of his release. And you know how terrified the kid is of enclosed spaces. He'd do anything to avoid a life sentence.'

'And the note?'

'Let's say you're right about that. Boyd typed it to clear himself, put the blame on someone who isn't able to defend himself. It's a cowardly kind of act typical of someone like him. That explains the pressure on the keys and the literacy level. Boyd isn't very well educated. He was spending most of his time on the streets by the time he was thirteen. And he couldn't explain anything about Cotton's motives because he killed Gill himself. So,' Burgess went on, 'even if we see it your way, I still come out right. Personally, I don't give a damn whether it was Boyd or Cotton. Either way, we've cracked it. Which way do you want to go? Toss a coin.'

'I'm still not convinced.'

'That's because you don't want to be.'

'What do you mean by that?'

'You know damn well what I mean. You've argued yourself into a corner. It was your idea to let Boyd out and see what happened. Well, now you've seen what's happened. No sooner is he out than there's another death. That makes you responsible.'

Banks took a deep breath. There was too much truth for comfort in what Burgess was saying. He shook his head. 'Somebody killed Seth,' he said, 'but I don't think it was Boyd. For all the kid's problems, I believe he genuinely cared. The people at Maggie's Farm are the only ones who have ever done anything for him, gone out on a limb.'

'Come off it! That sentimental bullshit doesn't work on me. The kid's a survivor, an opportunist. He's nothing more than a street punk.'

'And Cotton?'

Burgess sat back and reached for his glass. The chair creaked. 'Good actor, accomplice, innocent bystander, conscience-stricken idealist? I don't bloody know. But it doesn't matter now, does it? He's dead. It's all over.'

But Banks felt that it did matter. Somehow, after what had happened that afternoon, it seemed to matter more now than it ever had before.

'Is it?' he said. Then he stubbed out his cigarette and drained his glass. 'Come on, let's go.'

15

ONE

Eastvale General Infirmary stood on King Street, about half a mile west of the police station, not far from the comprehensive school. Because the day was warming up nicely, Banks decided to walk. As he left the station, he turned on his Walkman and listened to Muddy Waters sing 'Louisiana Blues' as he made his way through the warren of narrow streets with their cracked stone walls, gift shops and overpriced pubs.

The hospital itself was an austere Victorian brick building. About its high draughty corridors hung an air of fatalistic gloom. Not quite the hospital I'd choose if I were ill, Banks thought, fiddling with the Walkman's off switch in his overcoat pocket.

The mortuary was in the basement, which, like the police station's cell area, was the most modern part of the building. The autopsy room had white-tiled walls and a central metal table with guttering around its edges to channel off the blood. A long lab bench, complete with Bunsen burners and microscopes, stretched along one wall, with shelving above it for jars or organs, tissue samples and prepared chemical solutions.

Fortunately, the table was empty when Banks entered. A lab assistant was in the process of scrubbing it down, while Glendenning stood at the bench, a cigarette dangling from his mouth. Everyone smoked in the mortuary; they did it to keep the stench of death at bay.

The lab assistant dropped a surgical instrument into a metal kidney bowl. Banks winced at the sound.

'Let's go into the office,' Glendenning said. 'I can see you're a bit pink around the gills.'

Glendenning's office was small and cluttered, hardly befitting a man of his stature and status, Banks thought. But this wasn't America; healthcare was hardly big business, despite private insurance plans. Glendenning took his white lab coat off, smoothed his shirt and sat down. Banks shifted some old medical journals from the only remaining chair and placed himself opposite the doctor.

'Coffee?'

Banks nodded. 'Yes, please.'

Glendenning picked up his phone and pressed a button. 'Molly, dear, do you think you could scrape up two cups of coffee?' He covered the mouthpiece and asked Banks how he liked his. 'One black no sugar, and the usual for me. Yes, three sugars, that's right. What diet? And don't bring that vile muck they drink at reception. What? Yes. I know you'd run out yesterday, but that's no excuse. I haven't paid my coffee money for three weeks? What is this, woman, the bloody Inquisition?' He hung up roughly, ran a hand through his white hair and sighed. 'Good staff are hard to find these days. Now, Mr Banks, let's see what we have here.' He riffled through the stack of papers on his desk.

He probably knew it all off by heart, Banks thought, but needed the security of his files and sheets of paper in front of him just as Richmond always liked to read from his notebook what he knew perfectly well in the first place.

'Seth Cotton, aye, poor chappie.' Glendenning took a pair of half-moon reading glasses from his top pocket and held the report at arm's length as he peered down his nose at it. Having done with that, he put it aside, took off his glasses and sat back in his chair with his large but delicate hands folded on his lap. The coffee arrived, and Molly, giving her boss a disapproving glance on the way, departed.

'Last meal about three hours before death,' Glendenning said. 'And a good one too, if I may say so. Roast beef, Yorkshire pudding. What better meal could a condemned man wish for?'

'Haggis?'

Glendenning wagged his finger. 'Dinna extract the urine, Mr Banks.'

Banks sipped some coffee. It was piping hot and tasted good. Clearly it wasn't the 'vile muck' from reception.

'No evidence of poisoning, or indeed of any other wounds bar the external. Mr Cotton was in perfectly good health until the blood drained out of his body.'

'Was that the cause of death?'

'Aye. Loss of about five pints of blood usually does cause death.'

'What about the blow to the head? Was it delivered before or after the cuts to the ankles?'

Glendenning scratched his head. 'That I can't tell you. The vital reaction was quite consistent with a wound caused before death. As you saw for yourself, there was plenty of blood. And the leucocyte count was high – that's white blood cells to you, the body's little repairmen. Had the blow to the head occurred some time after death, then of course there would have been clear evidence to that effect, but the two wounds happened so closely together that it's impossible to say which came first. Cotton was certainly alive when he hit his head – or when someone hit it for him. But how long he survived after the blow, I can't tell. Of course, the head wound may have caused loss of consciousness, and it's very difficult to slash your ankles when you're unconscious, as I'm sure you're aware.'

'Could he have hit his head while bending down to make the cuts?'

Glendenning pursed his lips. 'I wouldn't say so, no. You saw the blood on the bench. None of it had trickled on to the floor. I'd say by the angle of the wound and the sharp edges of the vice that his head was resting exactly where it landed after the blow.'

'Could someone have come up behind him and pushed his head down on to the vice?'

'Now you're asking me to speculate, Mr Banks. All I can tell you is that I found no signs of scratching or bruising at the back of the neck or the head.'

'Does that mean no?'

'Not necessarily. If you come up behind someone and give his head a quick push before he has time to react, then I doubt it would show.'

'So that means it must have been someone he knew. He'd have noticed anyone else creeping up on him. Whoever did it must have been in the workshop already, someone he didn't mind having around while he carried on working.'

'Theories, theories,' Glendenning said. 'I don't know why you're not satisfied with suicide. There's absolutely no evidence to the contrary.'

'No medical evidence, perhaps.'

'I'm sorry,' said Glendenning. 'I'd like to be able to help

you more, but those are the facts. While the blow to the head may well have caused complications had Mr Cotton lived, it was in no way responsible for his death.'

'Complications? What complications?'

Glendenning frowned and reached for another cigarette from the box on his desk. It looked antique, and Banks noticed some words engraved in ornate italics on the top. 'To Dr C.W.S. Glendenning, on Successful Completion of . . .' He couldn't read the rest. He assumed it was some kind of graduation present.

'All kinds,' Glendenning answered. 'We don't know a great deal about the human brain, Mr Banks. A lot more than we used to, of course, but still not enough. Certain head wounds can result in effects far beyond the power of the blow and the extent of the apparent damage. Bone chips can lodge in the tissue, and even bruising can cause problems.'

'What problems?'

'Almost anything. Memory loss – temporary or permanent – hearing and vision problems, vertigo, personality change, temporary lapses of consciousness. Need I go on?'

Banks shook his head.

'But in the case of Mr Cotton, of course, that's something we'll never know.'

'No.' Banks got to his feet. 'Anyway, thank you very much, Doctor.'

Glendenning inclined his head regally.

On the way back to the station, Banks hardly heard Muddy Waters. According to Glendenning, Cotton could have been murdered, and that was enough for Banks. Of course the doctor wouldn't commit himself – he never did – but even an admission of the possibility was a long way for him to go. If Burgess was right, there was a good chance Boyd had done it, and that left Banks with Seth's blood on his hands.

As if that weren't enough, something else nagged at him: one of those frustrating little feelings you can't quite define, like having a name on the tip of your tongue, or an itch you can't scratch. He didn't want to be premature, but it felt like the familiar glimmer of an idea. Disparate facts were coming together, and with a lot of hard thinking, a bit of help from the subconscious and a touch of luck, they might actually lead to the answer. He was still a long way from that as yet, and when Muddy Waters started singing 'Still a Fool' Banks believed him.

It was eleven o'clock, according to the church clock, and Burgess would be out questioning Osmond and the students. In his office, Banks called the forensic lab and asked for Vic Manson. He had to wait a few minutes, and finally Vic came on the line.

'The prints?' Banks asked.

'Yes. Four sets. At least four identifiable sets. One belongs to the deceased, of course, another to that Boyd character – the same as the ones we found on the knife – and two more.'

'They'll probably be Mara's and one of the others',' Banks said. 'Look, thanks a lot, Vic. I'll try and arrange to get the others fingerprinted for comparison. Is Geoff Tingley around?'

'Yep. Just a sec, I'll get him for you.'

Banks could hear distant voices at the end of the line, then someone picked up the receiver and spoke. 'Tingley here. Is it about those letters?'

'Yes.'

'Well, I'm almost positive they weren't typed by the same person. You can make a few allowances for changes in pressure, but these were so wildly different I'd say that's almost conclusive. I could do with a few more samples of at least one of the writers, though. It'll give me more variables and a broader scope for comparison.'

'I'll see what I can do,' Banks said. There were probably other examples of Seth's typing in the filing cabinet. 'Would it do any good if we got a suspect to type us a sample?' he asked.

'Hmmm. It might do. Problem is, if he knew what we were after it wouldn't be too difficult to fake it. I'd say this chap's a plodder, though. You can tell it's been pecked out by the overall high pressure, each letter very deliberately sought and pounced on, so to speak. Hunt-and-peck, as I believe they call the technique. The other chap was a better typist; still two fingers, I'd say, but fairly quick and accurate. Probably had a lot more practice. And there's another thing, too. Did you notice the writing styles of the letters were—'

'Yes,' Banks said. 'We spotted that. Good of you to point it out, though.'

Tingley sounded disappointed. 'Oh, it's nothing.'

'Thanks very much. I'll be in touch about the samples and testing. Could you put Vic on again? I've just remembered something.'

'Will do.'

'Are you still there?' Manson asked a few seconds later.

'Yes. Look, Vic, there's a couple more points. The type-writer for a start.'

'Nothing clear on that, just a lot of blurs.'

'Was it wiped?'

'Could have been.'

'There was a cloth on that table, wasn't there? One of those yellow dusters.'

'Yes, there was,' said Manson. 'Do you want me to check for fibres?'

'If you would. And the paper?'

'Same, nothing readable.'

'What about that pen, or whatever it was we found on the floor. Have you had time to get round to that yet?'

'Yes. It's just an ordinary ballpoint, a Bic. No prints of course, just a sweaty blur.'

'Hmmm.'

The pen had been found in the puddle of blood, just below Seth's dangling right arm. If he was right-handed, as Banks thought he was, he could have used the pen to write a note before he died. It could have just fallen there earlier of course, but Seth had been very tidy, especially in his final moments. Perhaps he had written his own note, and whoever killed him took it and replaced it with the second version. Why? Because Seth hadn't murdered Gill and had said so clearly in his note? That meant he had committed suicide for some other reason entirely. Had he even named the killer, or was it an identity he had died trying to protect?

Too many questions again. Maybe Burgess and Glendenning were right and he was a fool not to accept the easy solutions. After all, he had a choice: either Seth Cotton was guilty as the note indicated and had really killed himself, or Paul Boyd, fearing discovery, had killed him and faked the note. Banks leaned closer towards the second of these, but for some reason he still couldn't convince himself that Boyd had done it – and not only because he took the responsibility for letting the kid out of jail. Boyd certainly had a record, and he had taken off when the knife was discovered. He could be a lot tougher and more clever than anyone realized. If he was faking his claustrophobia, for example, so that even Burgess was more inclined to believe him because of his fear of incarceration, then anything was possible. But so far they had nothing but circumstantial evidence, and Banks still felt that the picture was incomplete. He lit a cigarette and walked over to look down on the market square. It brought no inspiration today.

Finally, he decided it was time to tidy his desk before lunch. Almost every available square inch was littered with little yellow Post-it notes, most of which he had acted on ages ago. He screwed them all up and dropped them in the bin. Next came the files, statements and records he'd read to refresh his memory of the people involved. Most information was stored in the records department, but Banks had developed the habit of keeping brief files on all the cases he had a hand in. At the top was his file on Elizabeth Dale. Picking it up again, he remembered that he had just pulled it out of the cabinet, after some difficulty in locating it, when Sergeant Rowe had called with the news of Seth Cotton's death.

He opened the folder and brought back to mind the facts of the case – not even a case, really, just a minor incident that had occurred some eighteen months ago.

Elizabeth Dale had checked herself into a psychiatric hospital on the outskirts of Huddersfield, complaining of depression, apathy and general inability to cope with the outside world. After a couple of days' observation and treatment, she had decided she didn't like the service and ran off to Maggie's Farm, where she knew that Seth Cotton, an old friend from Hebden Bridge, was living. The hospital authorities informed Eastvale that she had spoken about her friend with the house near Relton, and they asked the local social services to please check up and see if she was there.

She was. Dennis Osmond had been sent to the farm to try to convince her to return to the hospital for her own good, but Ms Dale remained adamant: she was staying at the farm. Osmond also had the nerve to agree that the place would probably do her good. In anger and desperation, the hospital sent out two men of its own, who persuaded Elizabeth to return with them. They had browbeaten her and threatened her with committal, or so Seth Cotton and Osmond had complained at the time.

Because Elizabeth Dale also had a history of drug addiction, the police were called out when the hospital employees said they suspected the people at the farm were using drugs. Banks had gone out there with Sergeant Hatchley and a uniformed constable but they had found nothing. Ms Dale went back to the hospital, and as far as Banks knew, everything returned to normal.

In the light of recent events though, it became a more intriguing tale. For one thing, both Elizabeth Dale and Dennis Osmond were connected with PC Gill via the complaints they had made independently. And now it appeared there was yet another link between Osmond and Dale.

Where was Elizabeth Dale now? He would have to go to Huddersfield and find her himself. He'd learned from experience that it was no use at all dealing with doctors over the phone. But that would have to wait until tomorrow. First, he wanted to talk to Mara again, if she was well enough. Before setting off, he considered phoning Jenny to try to make up the row they'd had on Sunday lunch time.

Just as he was about to call her, the phone rang.

'Chief Inspector Banks?'

'Speaking.'

'My name is Lawrence Courtney, of Courtney, Courtney and Courtney, Solicitors.'

'Yes, I've heard of the firm. What can I do for you?'

'It's what I might be able to do for you,' Courtney said. 'I read in this morning's newspaper that a certain Seth Cotton has died. Is that correct?'

'That's right, yes.'

'Well, it might interest you to know, Chief Inspector, that we are the holders of Mr Cotton's will.'

'Will?'

'Yes, will.' He sounded faintly irritated. 'Are you interested?'

'Indeed I am.'

'Would it be convenient for you to call at our office after lunch?'

'Yes, certainly. But look, can't you tell me—'

'Good. I'll see you then. About two thirty, shall we say? Goodbye, Chief Inspector.'

Banks slammed the phone down. Bloody pompous solicitor. He cursed and reached for a cigarette. But a will? That was unexpected. Banks wouldn't have thought such a nonconformist as Seth would have bothered making a will. Still, he did own property and a business. But how could he have had any idea that he was going to die in the near future?

Banks jotted down the solicitor's name and the time of the meeting and stuck the note to his desk. Then he took a deep breath, phoned Jenny at her university office in York and plunged right in. 'I'm sorry about yesterday. I know what it must have sounded like, but I couldn't think of a better way of telling you.'

'I overreacted.' Jenny said. 'I feel like an idiot. I suppose you were only doing your job.'

'I wasn't going to tell you, not until I realized that being around Osmond really might be dangerous.'

'And I shouldn't have mistaken your warning for interference. It's just that I get so bloody frustrated. Damn men! Why do I never seem able to choose the right one?'

'Does it matter to you, what he did?'

'Of course it matters.'

'Are you going to go on seeing him?'

'I don't know.' She affected a bored tone. 'I was getting rather tired of him, anyway. Have there been any developments?'

'What in? The break-in or the Gill murder?'

'Well, both, seeing as you ask. What's wrong? You sound a bit tense.'

'Oh, nothing. It's been a busy morning, that's all. And I was nervous about calling you. Have you read about Seth Cotton?'

'No. I didn't have time to look at the paper this morning. Why, what's happened?'

Banks told her.

'Oh God. Poor Mara. Do you think there's anything I can do?'

'I don't know. I've no idea what state she's in. I'm calling in on her later this afternoon. I'll mention your name if you like.'

'Please do. Tell her how sorry I am. And if she needs to talk . . . What do you think happened, or can't you say?'

'I wish I could.' Banks summed up his thoughts for her.

'And I suppose you're feeling responsible? Is that why you don't really want to consider that Boyd did it?'

'You're right about the guilt. Burgess would never have let him go if I hadn't pressed him.'

'Burgess hardly seems like the kind of man to bow to pressure. I can't see him consenting to do anything he didn't want to.'

'Perhaps you're right. Still . . . it's not just that. At least, I don't think so. There's something much more complex behind all this. And don't accuse me of over-complicating matters – I've had enough of that already.'

'Oh, we are touchy today, aren't we? I had no such thing in mind.'

'Sorry. I suppose it's getting to me. About the break-in. I've got something in the works and we'll probably know by tonight, tomorrow morning at the latest.'

'What's it all about?'

'I'd rather not say yet. But don't worry, I don't think Osmond's in any kind of danger.'

'Are you sure?'

'Absolutely.'

'If you're right?'

'Am I ever wrong? Look, before you choke, I've got to go now. I'll be in touch later.'

Though where he had to go he wasn't quite certain. There was the solicitor, but that wasn't until two thirty. Feeling vaguely depressed, he lit another cigarette and went over to the window. The Queen's Arms, that was it. A pie and a pint would soon cheer him up. And Burgess had made a tentative arrangement to meet there around one thirty and compare notes.

TWO

Banks found the offices of Courtney, Courtney and Courtney on Market Street, quite close to the police station. Too close, in fact, to make it worthwhile turning on the Walkman for the journey.

The firm of solicitors was situated in what had once been a tea shop, and the new name curved in a semicircle of gold lettering on the plate glass window. Banks asked the young receptionist for Mr Lawrence Courtney, and after a brief exchange on the intercom, was shown through to a large office stacked with legal papers.

Lawrence Courtney himself, wedged behind a large executive desk, was not the prim figure Banks had expected from their phone conversation – three-piece suit, gold watch chain, pince-nez, nose raised as if perpetually exposed to a bad smell – instead he was a relaxed plump man of about fifty with over-long fair hair, a broad ruddy face and a fairly pleasant expression. His jacket hung behind the door. He wore a white shirt, a red and green striped tie and plain black braces. Banks noticed that the top button of the shirt was undone and the tie had been loosened, just like his own.

'Seth Cotton's will,' Banks said, sitting down after a brisk damp handshake.

'Yes. I thought you'd be interested,' said Courtney. A faint smile tugged at the corners of his pink rubbery lips.

'When did he make it?'

'Let me see . . . About a year ago, I think.' Courtney found the document and read off the date.

'Why did he come to you? I'm not sure how well you knew him, but he didn't seem to me the kind of person to deal with a solicitor.'

'We handled the house purchase,' Courtney said, 'and when the conveyance was completed we suggested a will. We often do. It's not so much a matter of touting for business as making things easier. So many people die intestate, and you've no idea what complications that leads to if there is no immediate family. The house itself, for example. As far as I know, Mr Cotton wasn't married, even under common law.'

'What was his reaction to your suggestion?'

'He said he'd think about it.'

'And he thought about it for two years?'

'It would appear so, yes. If you don't mind my asking, Chief Inspector, why all this interest in his reason for making a will? People do, you know.'

'It's the timing, that's all. I was just wondering why then rather than any other time.'

'Hmmm. I imagine that's the kind of thing you people have to think about. Are you interested in the contents at all?'

'Of course.'

Courtney unfolded the paper fully, peered at it, then put it aside again and hooked his thumbs in his braces. 'Not much to it, really,' he said. 'He left the house and what little money he had – somewhere in the region of two thousand pounds, I believe, though you'll have to check with the bank – to one Mara Delacey.'

'Mara? And that's it?'

'Not quite. Oddly enough he added a codicil just a few months ago. Shortly before Christmas, in fact. It doesn't affect the original bequest, but merely specifies that all materials, monies and goodwill relating to his carpentry business be left to Paul Boyd, in the hope that he uses them wisely.'

'Bloody hell!'

'Is something wrong?'

'It's nothing. Sorry. Mind if I smoke?'

'If you must.' Courtney took a clean ashtray from his

drawer and pushed it disapprovingly towards Banks. Undeterred, Banks lit up.

'The way I see things, then,' Banks said, 'is that he left the house and money to Mara after he'd only known her for a year or so, and the carpentry business to Paul after the kid had only been at the farm for a couple of months.'

'If you say so, Chief Inspector. It would indicate that Mr Cotton was quick to trust people.'

'It would indeed. Or that there was nobody else he could even consider. I doubt that he'd have wanted his goods and chattels to go to the state. But who knows where Boyd might have got to by the time Cotton died of natural causes? Or Mara. Could he have had some idea that he was in danger?'

'I'm afraid I can't answer that,' Courtney said. 'Our business ends with the legal formalities, and Mr Cotton certainly made no mention of an imminent demise. If there's anything else I can help you with, of course, I'd be more than willing.'

'Thank you,' said Banks. 'I think that's all. Will you be informing Mara Delacey?'

'We will take steps to get in touch with beneficiaries in due course, yes.'

'Is it all right if I tell her this afternoon?'

'I can't see any objection. And you might ask her – both of them, if possible – to drop by. I'll be happy to explain the procedure to them. If you have any trouble with the bank, Chief Inspector, please refer them to me. It's the National Westminster – or NatWest, as I believe they call themselves these days – the branch in the market square. The manager is a most valued client.'

'I know the place.' Know it, Banks thought, I practically stare at it for hours on end every day.

'Then goodbye, Chief Inspector. It's been a pleasure.'

Banks walked out into the street more confused than ever. Before he got back to the station, however, he'd managed to put some check on his wild imaginings. The will probably didn't come into the case at all. Seth Cotton had simply had more foresight than many would have credited him with. What was wrong with that? And it was perfectly natural that, with his parents both dead and no close family, he would leave the house to Mara. And Paul Boyd was, after all, his apprentice. It was a gesture of faith and confidence on Seth's part.

Even if Mara and Paul had known what they had coming to them, neither, Banks was positive, would have murdered Seth to get it. Life for Mara was clearly better with Seth than without him, and whatever ugliness might be lurking in Boyd's character, he was neither stupid nor petty enough to kill for a set of carpenter's tools. So forget the will, Banks told himself. Nice gesture though it was, it is irrelevant. Except perhaps for the date. Why wait till two years after Courtney had suggested it before actually getting the business done? Procrastination?

It also raised a more serious question: had Seth felt that his life was in danger a year ago? If so, why had it taken so long for the danger to manifest itself? And had that fear somehow also renewed itself around Christmas time?

Before returning to his office, he nipped into the National Westminster and had no problem in getting details of Seth's financial affairs, such as they were: he had a savings account at £2343.64, and a current account which stood at £421.33.

It was after three thirty when he got back to the station, and there was a message from Vic Manson to the effect that, yes, fibres matching those from the duster had been found on the typewriter keys. But, Manson had added with typical forensic caution, there was no way of proving whether the machine had been wiped before or after the message had been typed. The pressure of fingers on the keys often blurs prints.

Banks's brief chat with Burgess over lunch had revealed nothing new, either. Dirty Dick had seen Osmond and got nowhere with him. Early in the afternoon he was off to see Tim and Abha, and he was quite happy to leave Mara Delacey to Banks. As far as Burgess was concerned, it was all over bar the shouting, but he wanted more evidence to implicate Boyd or Cotton with extremist politics. Most of the time he'd had his eye on Glenys, and he'd kept reminding Banks that it was her night off that night. Cyril, fortunately, had been nowhere in sight.

Banks left a message for Burgess at the front desk summarizing what Lawrence Courtney had said about Seth's will. Then he called Sergeant Hatchley, as Richmond was busy on another matter, to accompany him and to bring along the fingerprinting kit. He slipped the Muddy Waters cassette from his Walkman and hurried out to the car with it, a huffing and puffing Hatchley in tow. It was time to see if Mara Delacey was ready to talk.

'What do you think of Superintendent Burgess?' Banks asked Hatchley on the way. They hadn't really had a chance to talk much over the past few days.

'Off the record?'

'Yes.'

'Well . . .' Hatchley rubbed his face with a ham-like hand. 'He seemed all right at first. Bit of zip about him. You know, get up and go. But I'd have thought a whizz-kid like him would have got a bit further by now.'

'None of us have got any further,' Banks said. 'What do you mean? The man's only flesh and blood after all.'

'I suppose that's it. He dazzles you a bit at first, then . . .'

'Don't underestimate him,' Banks said. 'He's out of his element up here. He's getting frustrated because we don't have raving anarchists crawling out of every nook and cranny in the town.'

'Aye,' said Hatchley. 'And you thought I was right wing.'

'You are.'

Hatchley grunted.

'When we get to the farm, I want you to have a look at Seth's filing cabinet in the workshop,' Banks went on, pulling on to the Roman road, 'and see if you can find more samples of his typing. And I'd like you to fingerprint everyone. Ask for their consent, and tell them we can get a magistrate's order if they refuse. Also make sure you tell them that the prints will be destroyed if no charges are brought.' Banks paused and scratched the edge of his scar. 'I'd like to have them all type a few lines on Seth's typewriter, too, but we'll have to wait till it comes back from forensic. All clear?'

'Fine,' Hatchley said.

Zoe answered the door, looking tired and drawn.

'Mara's not here,' she said in response to Banks's question, opening the door only an inch or two.

'I thought she was under sedation.'

'That was last night. She had a good long sleep. She said she felt like going to the shop to work on some pots, and the doctor agreed it might be good therapy. Elspeth's there in case . . . just in case.'

'I'll go down to the village, then,' Banks said to

Hatchley. 'You'll have to manage up here. Will you let sergeant in, Zoe?'

Zoe sighed and opened the door.

'Are you coming back up?' Hatchley asked.

Banks looked at his watch. 'Why not meet in the Black Sheep?'

Hatchley smiled at the prospect of a pint of Black Sheep bitter, then his face fell. 'How do I get there?'

'Walk.'

'Walk?'

'Yes. It's just a mile down the track. Do you good. Give you a thirst.'

Hatchley wasn't convinced – he had never had any problems working up a thirst without exercise before – but Banks left him to his fate and drove down to Relton.

Mara was in the back bent over her wheel, gently turning the lip of a vase. Elspeth led him through, muttered, 'A policeman to see you,' with barely controlled distaste, then went back into the shop itself.

Mara glanced up. 'Let me finish,' she said. 'If I stop now, I'll ruin it.' Banks leaned against the doorway and kept quiet. The room smelled of wet clay. It was also hot. The kiln in the back generated a lot of heat. Mara's long brown hair was tied back, accentuating the sharpness of her nose and chin as she concentrated. Her white smock was stained with splashed clay.

Finally, she drenched the wheel-head with water, sliced off the vase with a length of cheese wire, then slid it carefully on to her hand before transferring it to a board.

'What now?' Banks asked.

'It has to dry.' She put it away in a large cupboard at the back of the room. 'Then it goes in the kiln.'

'I thought the kiln dried it.'

'No. That bakes it. First it has to be dried to the consistency of old cheddar.'

'These are good,' Banks said, pointing to some finished mugs glazed in shades of orange and brown.

'Thanks.' Mara's eyes were puffy and slightly unfocused, her movements slow and zombie-like. Even her voice, Banks noticed, was flatter than usual, drained of emotion and vitality.

'I have to ask you some questions,' he said.

'I suppose you do.'

'Do you mind?'

Mara shook her head. 'Let's get it over with.'

She perched on the edge of her stool and Banks sat on a packing crate just inside the doorway. He could hear Elspeth humming as she busied herself checking on stock in the shop.

'Did you notice anyone gone for an unusually long time during the meeting yesterday afternoon?' Banks asked.

'Was it only yesterday? Lord, it seems like months. No, I didn't notice. People came and went, but I don't think anyone was gone for long. I'm not sure I would have noticed, though.'

'Did Seth ever say anything to you about suicide? Did he ever mention the subject?'

Mara's lips tightened and the blood seemed to drain from them. 'No. Never.'

'He'd tried once before, you know.'

Mara raised her thin eyebrows. 'It seems you knew him better than I did.'

'Nobody knew him, as far as I can tell. There was a will, Mara.'

'I know.'

'Do you remember when he made it?'

'Yes. He joked about it. Said it made him feel like an old man.'

'Is that all?'

'That's all I remember.'

'Did he say why he was making it at that time?'

'No. He just told me that the solicitor who handled the house, Courtney, said he should, and he'd been thinking about it for a long time.'

'Do you know what was in the will?'

'Yes. He said he was leaving me the house. Does that make me a suspect?'

'Did you know about the codicil?'

'Codicil? No.'

'He left his tools and things to Paul.'

'Well, he would, wouldn't he? Paul was keen, and I've got no use for them.'

'Did Paul know?'

'I've no idea.'

'This would be around last Christmas.'

'Maybe it was his idea of a present.'

'But what made him think he was going to die? Seth was what age – forty? By rights he could expect to live to seventy or so. Was he worried about anything?'

'Seth always seemed . . . well, not worried, but pre-occupied. He'd got even more morbid of late. It was just his way.'

'But there was nothing in particular?'

Mara shook her head. 'I don't believe he killed himself, Mr Banks. He had lots to live for. He wouldn't just leave us like that. Everyone depended on Seth. We looked up to him. And he cared about me, about us. I think somebody must have killed him.'

'Who?'

'I don't know.'

Banks shifted position on the packing crate. Its surface was hard and he felt a nail dig into the back of his right thigh. 'Do you remember Elizabeth Dale?'

'Liz. Yes, of course. Funny, I was just thinking about her last night.'

'What about her?'

'Oh, nothing really. How jealous I was, I suppose, when she came to the farm that time. I'd only known Seth six months then. We were happy but, I don't know, I guess I was insecure. Am.'

'Why did you feel jealous?'

'Maybe that's not the right word. I just felt cut out, that's all. Seth and Liz had known each other for a long time, and I didn't share their memories. They used to sit up late talking after I went to bed.'

'Did you hear what they were talking about?'

'No. It was muffled. Do smoke if you want.'

'Thanks.' She must have noticed him fidgeting and looking around for an ashtray. He took out his packet and offered one to Mara.

'I think I will,' she said. 'I can't be bothered to roll my own today.'

'What did you think about Liz Dale?'

Mara lit the cigarette and inhaled deeply. 'I didn't like her, really. I don't know why, just a feeling. She was messed up of course, but even so, she seemed like someone who used people, leaned on them too much, maybe a manipulator.' She shrugged wearily and blew smoke out through her nose. 'She was Seth's friend, though. I wasn't going to say anything.'

'So you put up with her?'

'It was easy enough. She was only with us three days before those SS men from the hospital took her back.'

'Dennis Osmond came up first, didn't he?'

'Yes. But he was too soft, they said. He didn't see why she shouldn't stay where she was, especially as she hadn't been committed or anything, just checked herself in. He argued with the hospital people, but it was no good.'

'How did Osmond and Liz get along?'

'I don't know really. I mean, he stuck up for her, that's all.'

'There wasn't anything between them?'

'What do you mean? Sexual?'

'Anything.'

'I doubt it. They only met twice, and I wouldn't say she was his type.'

'And that was the first time Seth met Osmond?'

'As far as I know.'

'Did you get the impression that Osmond had known Liz before?'

'No, I didn't. But impressions can be wrong. What are you getting at?'

'I'm not sure myself. Just following my nose.'

'Mr Banks,' Mara whispered suddenly, 'do you think Dennis Osmond killed Seth? Is that it? I know Seth couldn't have done it himself, and I . . . I can't seem to think straight.'

'Steady on.' Banks caught her in his arms as she slid forward from the stool. Her hair smelled of apples. He sat her on a stiff-backed chair in the corner, and her eyes filled with tears. 'All right?'

'Yes. I'm sorry. That sedative takes most of the feeling out of me, but . . .'

'It's still there?'

'Yes. Just below the surface.'

'We can continue this later if you like. I'll drive you home.' He thought how pleased Hatchley would be to see the Cortina turning up again.

Mara shook her head. 'No, it's all right. I can handle it. I'm just confused. Maybe some water.'

Banks brought her a glass from the tap at the stained porcelain sink in the corner.

'So are we,' he said. 'Confused. It looked like a suicide in some ways, but there were contradictions.'

'He wouldn't kill himself, I'm sure of it. Paul was back again. Seth was happy. He had the farm, friends, the children . . .'

Banks didn't know what to say to make her feel better.

'When he tried before,' she said, 'was it because of Alison?'

'Yes.'

'I can understand that. It makes sense. But not now. Someone must have killed him.' Mara sipped at her water. 'Anyone could have come in through the side gate and sneaked up on him.'

'It didn't happen like that, Mara. Take my word for it, he had to know the person. It was someone he felt comfortable with. Have you seen or heard anything from Liz Dale since she left?'

'I haven't, no. Seth went to visit her in hospital a couple of times, but then he lost touch.'

'Any letters?'

'Not that he told me about.'

'Christmas card?'

'No.'

'Do you know where she is now?'

'No. Is it important?'

'It could be. Do you know anything about her background?'

Mara frowned and rubbed her temple. 'As far as I know she's from down south somewhere. She used to be a nurse until . . . Well, she fell in with a bad crowd, got involved with drugs and lost her job. Since then she just sort of drifted.'

'And ended up in Hebden Bridge?'

'Yes.'

'Did you see her do any drugs at the farm?'

'No. And I'm not just saying that. She was off heroin. That was part of the problem, why she was unable to cope.'

'Was Seth ever an addict?'

'I don't think so. I think he'd have told me about that. We talked about drugs, how we felt about them and how they weren't really important, so I think he'd have told me.'

'And you've no idea where Liz is now?'

'None at all.'

'What about Alison?'

'What about her? She's dead.'

A hint of bitterness had crept into her tone, and Banks wondered why. Jealousy? It could happen. Plenty of people were jealous of previous lovers, even dead ones. Or was she angry at Seth for not making her fully a part of his life, for not sharing all his feelings? She unfastened her hair and shook her head, allowing the chestnut tresses to cascade over her shoulders.

'Can I have another cigarette?'

'Of course.' Banks gave her one. 'Surely Seth must have told you something,' he said. 'You don't live with someone for two years and find out nothing about their past.'

'Don't you? And how would you know?'

Banks didn't know. When he had met Sandra, they had been young and had little past to talk about, none of it very interesting. 'It doesn't make sense,' he said.

The shop bell clanged and broke the silence. They heard Elspeth welcoming a customer, an American by the sound of his drawl.

'What are you going to do now?' Banks asked.

Mara rubbed her eyes. 'I don't know. I'm too tired to throw another pot. I think I'll just go home and go to bed early.'

'Do you want a lift?'

'No. Really. A bit of fresh air and exercise will do me good.'

Banks smiled. 'I wish my sergeant felt the same way.'

'What?'

Banks explained and Mara managed a weak smile.

They walked out together, Banks collecting a sour look from Elspeth on the way. Outside the Black Sheep, Mara turned away.

'I am sorry, you know, about your loss,' Banks said awkwardly to her back.

Mara turned round and stared at him for a long time. He couldn't make out what she was thinking or feeling.

'I do believe you are,' she said finally.

'And Jenny sends her condolences. She says to give her a call if you ever need anything . . . a friend.'

Mara said nothing.

'She didn't betray your confidence, you know. She was worried about you. And you went to her because you were worried about Paul, didn't you?'

Mara nodded slowly.

'Well, give her a call. All right?'

'All right.' And tall though she was, Mara seemed a slight figure walking up the lane in the dark towards the Roman road. Banks stood and watched till she was out of sight.

Hatchley was already in the Black Sheep – halfway through his second pint, judging by the empty glass next to the half-full one in front of him. Banks went to the bar first, bought two more and sat down. As far as he was concerned, Hatchley could drink as much as he wanted. He was a lousy driver even when sober, and Banks had no intention of letting him anywhere near the Cortina's driving seat.

'Anything?' the sergeant asked.

'No, not really. You?'

'That big bloke with the shaggy beard put up a bit of an argument at first, but the little lass with the red hair told him it was best to cooperate.'

'Damn,' Banks said. 'I knew there was something I'd forgotten. Mara's prints. Never mind, I'll get them later.'

'Anyway,' Hatchley went on, 'most of the letters in the cabinet were carbons, but I managed to rescue a couple of drafts from the bin.'

'Good.'

'You don't sound so pleased,' Hatchley complained.

'What? Oh, sorry. Thinking of something else. Let's drink up and get your findings sent over to the lab.'

Hatchley drained his third pint with astonishing speed and looked at his watch. 'It's going on for six thirty,' he said. 'No point rushing now; they'll all have buggered off home for the night.' He glanced over at the bar. 'Might as well have another.'

Banks smiled. 'Unassailable logic, Sergeant. All right. Better make it a quick one though. And it's your round.'

THREE

At home, Banks managed to warm up a frozen dinner without ruining it. After washing the dishes – or rather rinsing his knife and fork and coffee cup and throwing the foil container into the rubbish bin – he called Sandra.

'So when do I get my wife back?' he asked.

'Wednesday morning. Early train,' Sandra said. 'We should be home around lunch time. Dad's a lot better now and Mum's coping better than I'd imagined.'

'Good. I'll try and be in,' Banks said. 'It depends.'

'How are things going?'

'They're getting more complicated.'

'You sound grouchy, too. It's a good sign. The more complicated things seem and the more bad-tempered you get, the closer the end is.'

'Is that right?'

'Of course it is. I haven't lived with you this long without learning to recognize the signs.'

'Sometimes I wonder what people do learn about one another.'

'What's this? Philosophy?'

'No. Just frustration. Brian and Tracy well?'

'Fine. Just restless. Brian especially. You know Tracy, she's happy enough with her head buried in a history book. But with him it's all sports and pop music now. American football is the latest craze, apparently.'

'Good God.'

Brian had changed a lot over the past year. He even seemed to have lost interest in the electric train that Banks had set up in the spare room. Banks played with it himself more than Brian did, but then, he had to admit, he always had done.

To keep the emptiness after the conversation at bay, he poured out a glass of Bell's and listened to Leroy Carr and Scrapper Blackwell while he tried to let the information that filled his mind drift and form itself into new patterns. Bizarre as it all seemed, a number of things began to come together. The problem was that one theory seemed to cancel out the other.

The doorbell woke him from a light nap just before ten o'clock. The tape had long since ended and the ice had melted in his second Scotch.

'Sorry I'm so late, sir,' Richmond said, 'but I've just finished.'

'Come in.' Banks rubbed his eyes. 'Sit down. A drink?'

'If you don't mind, sir. Though I suppose I am still on duty. Technically.'

'Scotch do? Or there's beer in the fridge.'

'Scotch will do fine, sir. No ice, if you don't mind.'

Banks grinned. 'I'm getting as bad as the Americans, aren't I, putting ice in good Scotch. Soon I'll be complaining my beer is too warm.'

Richmond fitted his long athletic body into an armchair and stroked his moustache.

'By the way you're playing with that bit of face fungus there,' Banks said, 'I gather you've succeeded.'

'What? Oh yes, sir. Didn't know I was so obvious.'

'Most of us are, it seems. You'd not make a good poker player and you'd better watch it in interrogations. Come on then, what did you find?'

'Well,' Richmond began, consulting his notebook, 'I did exactly as you said, sir. Hung around discreetly near Tim and Abha's place. They stayed in all afternoon.'

'Then what?'

'They went out about eight, to the pub I'd guess. And

about half an hour later that blue Escort pulled up and two men got out and disappeared into the building. They looked like the ones you described. They must have been waiting and watching somewhere nearby, because they seemed to know when to come, allowing a bit of a safety margin in case Tim and Abha had just gone to the shop or something.'

'You didn't try to stop them from getting in, did you?'

Richmond seemed shocked. 'I did exactly as you instructed me, sir, though it felt a bit odd to sit there and watch a crime taking place. The front door is usually left on the latch, so they just walked in. The individual flats are kept locked though, so they must have broken in. Anyway, they came out about fifteen minutes later carrying what looked like a number of buff folders.'

'And then what?'

'I followed them at a good distance, and they pulled into the car park of the Castle Hotel and went inside. I didn't follow, sir – they might have noticed me. And they didn't come out. After they'd been gone about ten minutes, I went in and asked the desk clerk about them and got him to show me the register. They'd booked in as James Smith and Thomas Brown.'

'How imaginative. Sorry, carry on.'

'Well, I rather thought that myself, sir, so I went back to the office and checked on the number of the car. It was rented by a firm in York to a Mr Cranby, Mr Keith J. Cranby, if that means anything to you. He had to show his licence of course, so that's likely to be his right name.'

'Cranby? No, it doesn't ring any bells. What happened next?'

'Nothing, sir. It was getting late by then so I thought I'd better come and report. By the way, I saw that barmaid

Glenys, going into the hotel while I was waiting outside. Looked a bit sheepish, she did too.'

'Was Cyril anywhere in sight?'

'No. I didn't see him.'

'You've done a fine job, Phil,' Banks said. 'I owe you for this one.'

'What's it all about?'

'I'd rather not say yet, in case I'm wrong. But you'll be the second to find out, I promise. Have you eaten at all?'

'I packed some sandwiches.' He looked at his watch. 'I could do with a pint, though.'

'There's still beer in the fridge.'

'I don't like bottled beer.' Richmond patted his flat stomach. 'Too gassy.'

'And too cold?'

Richmond nodded.

'Come on, then. We should make it in time for a jar or two before closing. My treat. Queen's Arms do you?'

'Fine, sir.'

The pub was busy and noisy with locals and farm lads in from the villages. Banks glanced at the bar staff and saw neither Glenys nor Cyril in evidence. Pushing his way to the bar, he asked one of the usual stand-in barmaids where the boss was.

'Took the evening off, Mr Banks. Just like that.' She snapped her fingers. 'Said there'd be three of us so we should be able to cope. Dead cagey, he was too. Still, he's the boss, isn't he? He can do what he likes.'

'True enough, Rosie,' Banks said. 'I'll have two pints of your best bitter, please.'

'Right you are, Mr Banks.'

They stood at the bar and chatted with the regulars, who knew better than to ask too many questions about their work. Banks was beginning to feel unusually pleased with himself, considering he still hadn't found the answer. Whether it was the chat with Sandra, the nap, Richmond's success or the drink, he didn't know. Perhaps it was a combination of all four. He was close to the end of the case though, he knew that. If he could solve the problem of two mutually exclusive explanations for Gill's and Seth's deaths, then he would be home and dry. Tomorrow should be an interesting day. First he would track down Liz Dale and discover what she knew; then there was the other business . . . Yes, tomorrow should be very interesting indeed. And the day after that, Sandra was due home.

'Last orders, please!' Rosie shouted.

'Shall we?' Richmond asked.

'Go on. Why not,' said Banks. He felt curiously like celebrating.

16

ONE

Dirty Dick was conspicuous by his absence the following morning. Banks took the opportunity to make a couple of important phone calls before getting an early start.

Just south of Bradford, it started to rain. Banks turned on the wipers and lit a cigarette from the dashboard lighter. On the car stereo, Walter Davis sang, 'You got bad blood, baby, I believe you need a shot.'

It was so easy to get lost in the conurbation of old West Yorkshire woollen towns. Built in valleys on the eastern edges of the Pennines, they seemed to overlap one another, and it was hard to tell exactly where you were. The huge old textile factories, where all the processes of clothes-making had been gathered together under one roof in the last century looked grim in the failing light. They were five or six storeys high, with flat roofs, rows of windows close together and tall chimneys you could see for miles.

Cleckheaton, Liversedge, Heckmondwike, Brighouse, Rastrick, Mirfield – the strange names Banks usually associated only with brass bands and rugby teams – flew by on road signs. As he drew nearer to Huddersfield, he slowed and peered out through his rain-splattered windscreen for the turn-off.

Luckily the psychiatric hospital was at the northern end

of town, so he didn't have to cross the centre. When he saw the signpost, he followed directions to the left, down a street between two derelict warehouses.

The greenery of the hospital grounds came as a shock after so many miles of bleak industrial wasteland. There was a high brick wall and a guard at the gate, but beyond that the drive wound its way by trees and a well-kept lawn to the modern L-shaped hospital complex. Banks parked in the visitors' area, then presented himself at reception.

'That'll be Dr Preston,' said the receptionist, looking up Elizabeth Dale in her roll file. 'But the doctor can't divulge any information about his patients, you know.'

Banks smiled. 'He will see me, won't he?'

'Oh, of course. He's with our bursar now, but if you'll wait he should be finished in ten minutes or so. You can wait over in the canteen if you like. The tea's not too bad.'

Banks thanked her and walked towards the cluster of bright orange plastic tables and chairs.

'Oh, Mr Banks?' she called after him.

He turned.

She put her hands to the sides of her mouth and spoke quietly and slowly, mouthing the words as if for a lip-reader. 'You won't wander off, will you?' She flicked her eyes right and left as if to indicate that beyond those points lay monsters.

Banks assured her that he wouldn't, bought a cup of tea and a Penguin biscuit from the pretty teenage girl at the counter and sat down.

There was only one other person in the canteen, a skinny man with a pronounced stoop and hair combed straight back from his creased brow. He was dressed as a vicar. Seeing Banks, he brought his cup over and sat down. He had a long thin nose and a small mouth. The shape of his head, Banks noticed, was distinctly odd; it was triangular, and the forehead sloped sharply backwards. With his hair brushed straight back, standing at forty-five degrees, he looked as if his entire face had been sculpted by a head-on wind.

'Mind if I join you?' he asked, smiling in a way that screwed up his features grotesquely.

'Not if you don't mind my smoking,' Banks replied.

'Go ahead, old chap; doesn't bother me at all.' His accent was educated and southern. 'Haven't seen you here before?'

It should have been a comment, but it sounded like a question.

'That's not surprising,' Banks said. 'I've never been here before. I'm a policeman.'

'Oh, jolly good!' the vicar exclaimed. 'Which one? Let me guess: Clouseau? Poirot? Holmes?'

Banks laughed. 'I'm not as clumsy as Clouseau,' he said. 'Nor, I'm afraid, am I as brilliant as Poirot and Holmes. My name's Banks. Chief Inspector Banks.'

The vicar frowned. 'Banks, eh? I haven't heard of him.'

'Well, you wouldn't have, would you?' Banks said, puzzled. 'It's me. I'm Banks. I'm here to see Dr Preston.'

The vicar's expression brightened. 'Dr Preston? Oh, I'm sure you'll like him. He's very good.'

'Is he helping you?'

'Helping me? Why, no. I help him, of course.'

'Of course,' Banks said slowly.

A nurse paused by the table and spoke his name. 'Dr Preston will see you now,' she said.

The vicar stuck out his hand. 'Well, good luck, old boy.'

Banks shook it and muttered his thanks.

'That man back there,' he said to the nurse as she

clicked beside him along the corridor, 'should he be wandering around freely? What's he in for?'

The nurse laughed. 'That's not a patient; that's the Reverend Clayton. He comes to visit two or three times a week. He must have thought *you* were a new patient.'

Bloody hell, Banks thought, you could go crazy hanging around a place like this.

Dr Preston's office lacked the sharp polished instruments, kidney bowls, hypodermics and mysterious odds and ends that Banks usually found so disconcerting in Glendenning's lair. This room was more like a comfortable study with a pleasant view of the landscaped grounds.

Preston stood up as Banks entered. His handshake was firm and brief. He looked younger than Banks had expected, with a thatch of thick shiny brown hair, a complexion as smooth as a baby's bottom, and cheeks just as chubby and rosy. His eyes, enlarged behind spectacles, were watchful and serious.

'What can I do for you, Chief Inspector?' he asked.

'I'm interested in an ex-patient of yours called Elizabeth Dale. At least, I think she's an ex-patient.'

'Oh, yes,' Preston said. 'Been gone ages now. What exactly is it you wish to know? I'm sure you realize that I'm not at liberty to—'

'Yes, Doctor, I understand that. I don't want the details of her illness. As I understand it, she was suffering from depression.'

'Well' – the doctor unbent a paper clip on his blotter – 'I suppose in layman's terms . . . But you said that's not what you came about?'

'That's right. I just want to know where she is. Nothing confidential about that, is there?'

'We don't usually give out personal information.'

'It's important. A murder inquiry. I could get a court order.'

'Oh, I don't think that will be necessary,' Preston said quickly. 'The problem is though, I'm afraid we don't know where Miss Dale is.'

'No idea?'

'No. You see, we don't keep tabs on ex-patients as a rule.'

'When did she leave here?'

Preston searched through his files. 'She stayed for two months.' He read off the dates.

'Is that usual? Two months?'

'Hard to say. It varies from patient to patient. Miss Dale was . . . Well, I don't think I'm giving too much away if I tell you she was difficult. She'd hardly been here a couple of days before she ran off.'

'Yes, I know.' Banks explained his involvement. 'As far as I understand though, she admitted herself in the first place, is that right?'

'Yes.'

'Yet you treated her as if she had escaped from a high-security prison.'

Preston leaned back in his chair and his jaw muscles twitched. 'You have to understand, Chief Inspector, that when anyone arrives here, they are given a whole range of tests and a complete physical examination. On the basis of these, we make a diagnosis and prescribe treatment. I had examined Miss Dale and decided she required treatment. When she disappeared we were naturally worried that she . . . Well, without the proper treatment, who knows what might have become of her? So we took steps to persuade her to come back.'

'Doctor knows best, eh?'

Preston glared at him.

'How was she when she'd completed her treatment?' Banks asked.

'Given your hostile attitude, I don't know that I care to answer that.'

Bank sighed and reached for a cigarette. 'Oh, come on, Doctor, don't sulk. Was she cured or wasn't she?'

Preston passed an ashtray as Banks lit up. 'That'll kill you, you know.' He seemed to take great pleasure in the observation.

'Not before I get an answer from you, I hope.'

Preston pursed his lips. 'I imagine you know about Elizabeth Dale's drug problem?'

'Yes.'

'That was part of the cause of her mental illness. When she came to us she'd been off heroin for about a month. Naturally, we're not equipped to deal with addicts here, and if Miss Dale had been still using drugs we would have had to send her elsewhere. However, she stayed, on medication I prescribed, and she made some progress. At the end of two months, I felt she was ready to leave.'

'What did *she* feel?'

Preston stared out of his window at the landscaped garden. A row of topiary shrubs stood close to the building, cut in the shapes of birds and animals.

'Miss Dale,' Preston started slowly, 'was afraid of life and afraid of her addiction. The one led to the other, an apparently endless circle.'

'What you're saying is that once she'd got used to the idea she'd have been happy to stay here for ever. Am I right?'

'Not just here. Any institution, anywhere she didn't have to make her own decisions and face the world.'

'And that's the kind of place I'm likely to find her in?'

'I'd say so, yes.'

'Can you be any more specific?'

'You might try a DDU.'

'DDU?'

'Yes. A drug dependency unit, for the treatment of addicts. Elizabeth had been in and out of one a couple of times before she came to us.'

'So she hadn't been cured?'

'How many are? Oh, some, I agree. But with Elizabeth it was on and off, on and off. The cure worked for a while – Methadone hydrochloride in gradually decreasing doses. It's rather like chewing nicotine gum when you're trying to stop smoking. Helps with some of the severe physical symptoms, but—'

'That's not enough?'

'Not really. Many addicts get hooked again as soon as the opportunity for a fix arises. Unfortunately, given the network of friends they have, that can be very soon.'

'So you think a DDU might have Liz as a patient, or might know where she is?'

'It's likely.'

'Where is the nearest one?' Banks slipped out his notebook.

'The only local one is just outside Halifax, not too far away.' Preston continued to give directions. 'I hope she's not in any trouble,' he said finally.

'I don't think so. Just need her to help us with our inquiry.'

Preston adjusted his glasses on the bridge of his nose. 'You do have a way with words, you policemen, don't you?'

'I'm glad we've got something in common with

doctors.' Banks smiled and stood up to leave. 'You've been a great help.'

'Have I?'

Banks beat a hasty retreat from the hospital back on to the rainswept roads and headed for Halifax. He soon found the DDU, using the Wainhouse Tower as a landmark as Dr Preston had suggested. Originally built as a factory chimney, the tall black tower was never used as one and now stands as a folly and a lookout point, its top ornamented in a very un-chimney-like pointed Gothic style.

Banks found the DDU up a steep side street. It was set back from the road at the top of a long sloping lawn and looked like a Victorian mansion. It also had an eerie quality to it, Banks felt. He shivered as he made his approach. Not the kind of place I'd want to find myself in after dark, he thought.

There were no walls or men at the gate here. Banks walked straight inside and found himself standing in a spacious common room with a high ceiling. On the walls hung a number of paintings, clearly the work of patients, dominated by an enormous canvas depicting an angel plummeting to earth, wings ablaze and neck contorted so that it looked straight at the viewer, eyes red and wild, raw muscles stretched like knotted ropes. It could have been Satan on his way to hell. Certainly the destination, impressionistically rendered in the lower half of the painting, was a dark and murky place. He shuddered and looked away.

'Can I help you?' A young woman came up to him. It wasn't clear from her appearance whether she was a member of staff or a patient. She was in her early thirties perhaps, and wore jeans and a dark brown jacket over a white blouse. Her long black hair was plaited and pinned back.

'Yes,' Banks said. 'I'm looking for Elizabeth Dale. Is she here, or do you know where I can find her?'

'Who are you?'

Banks showed her his identification.

The woman raised her eyebrows. 'Police? What do you want?'

'I want to talk to Elizabeth Dale,' he repeated. 'Is she here or isn't she?'

'What's it about?'

'I'm the one who asks the questions,' Banks said, irritated by her brusque haughty manner. Suddenly, he realized who she must be. 'Look, Doctor,' he went on, 'it's nothing to do with drugs. It's about an old friend of hers. I need some information to help solve a murder case, that's all.'

'Elizabeth's been here for the past month. She can't be involved.'

'I'm not saying she is. Will you just let me to talk to her?'

The doctor frowned. Banks could see her brain working fast behind her eyes. 'All right,' she said finally. 'But treat her gently. She's very fragile. And I insist on being present.'

'I'd rather talk to her alone.' The last thing Banks wanted was this woman watching over the conversation like a lawyer.

'I'm afraid that's not possible.'

'How about if you remained within calling distance? Say, the other end of this room?' The room was certainly large enough to accommodate more than one conversation.

The doctor smiled out of the side of her mouth. 'A

compromise? All right. Stay here while I fetch Elizabeth. Take a seat.'

But Banks felt restless after being in the car. Instead, he walked around the room looking at the paintings, almost all of which illustrated some intense level of terror: mad eyes staring through a letter box; a naked man being dragged away from a woman, his features creased in a desperate plea; a forest in which every carefully painted leaf looked like a needle of fire. They sent shivers up his spine. Noticing plenty of pedestal ashtrays around, he lit up. It was warm in the room, so he took off his car coat and laid it on a chair.

About five minutes later, the doctor returned with another woman. 'This is Elizabeth Dale,' she said, introducing them formally, then walked off to the far end of the room, where she sat facing Banks and pretended to read a magazine. Liz took a chair on his left, angled so they could face one another comfortably. The chairs were well padded, with strong armrests.

'I saw you looking at the paintings,' Elizabeth said. 'Quite something, aren't they?' She had a melodic hypnotic voice. Banks could easily imagine its persuasive powers. He had a feeling, however, that it would probably become tiresome after a while: whining and wheedling rather than beautiful and soft.

Elizabeth Dale smoothed her long powder-blue skirt over her knees. Her slight frame was lost inside a baggy mauve sweater with two broad white hoops around the middle. If she was Seth's contemporary that made her about forty, but her gaunt waxy face was lined like that of a much older woman and her black hair, hacked short rather than cut, was liberally streaked with grey. It was a face that screamed of suffering; eyes that had looked deep inside and seen the horror there. Yet her voice was beautiful. So gentle, so soothing, like a breeze through woods in spring.

'They're very powerful,' Banks said, feeling his words pathetically inadequate.

'People see those things here,' Elizabeth said. 'Do you know what this place used to be?'

'No.'

'It was a hospital, a fever hospital, during the typhoid epidemics in the last century. I can hear the patients screaming every night.'

'You mean the place is haunted?'

Elizabeth shrugged. 'Maybe it's me who's haunted. People go crazy here sometimes. Break windows and try to cut themselves with broken glass. I can hear the typhoid victims screaming every night as they're burning up and snapping bones in convulsions. I can hear the bones snap.' She clapped her hands. 'Crack. Just like that.'

Then she put her hand over her mouth and laughed. Banks noticed the first and second fingers of her right hand were stained yellow with nicotine. She rummaged inside her sweater and pulled out a packet of Embassy Regal and a tarnished silver lighter. Banks took out a cigarette of his own and she leaned forward to give him a light. The flame was high and he caught a whiff of petrol fumes as he inhaled.

'You know,' Elizabeth went on, 'for all that – the ghosts, the screaming, the cold – I'd rather be here than . . . than out there.' She nodded her head towards the door. 'That's where the real horror is, Mr Banks, out there.'

'I take it you don't keep up with the world then. No newspapers, no television?'

Elizabeth shook her head. 'No. There is a television

here, next door. But I don't watch it. I read books. Old books. Charles Dickens, that's who I'm reading now. There's opium-taking in *Edwin Drood*, did you know that?'

Banks nodded. He had been through a Dickens phase some years ago.

'Have you come about the complaint?' Elizabeth asked.

'What complaint?'

'It was years ago. I made a complaint about a policeman hitting people with his truncheon at a demonstration. I don't know what became of it. I never heard a thing. I was different then; things seemed more worthwhile fighting for. Now I just let them go their way. They'll blow it up, Mr Banks. Oh, there's no doubt about it, they'll blow us all up. Or is it drugs you want to talk about?'

'It's partly about the complaint, yes. I wanted to talk to you about Seth Cotton. Seth and Alison.'

'Good old Seth. Poor old Seth. I don't want to talk about Seth. I don't have to talk to you, do I?'

'Why don't you want to talk about him?'

'Because I don't. Seth's private. I won't tell you anything he wouldn't, so it's no good asking.'

Banks leaned forward. 'Elizabeth,' he said gently, 'Seth's dead. I'm sorry, but it's true.'

At first he thought she wasn't going to react at all. A little sigh escaped her, nothing more than a gust of wind against a dark window. 'Well, that's all right then, isn't it?' she said, her voice softer, weaker. 'Peace at last.' Then she closed her eyes and her face assumed such a distant holy expression that Banks didn't dare break the silence. It would have been blasphemy. When she opened her eyes again, they were clear. 'My little prayer,' she said.

'What did you mean, poor Seth?'

'He was such a serious man, and he had to suffer so

much pain. How did he die, Mr Banks? Was it peaceful?'

'Yes,' Banks lied.

Elizabeth nodded.

'The problem is,' Banks said, 'that nobody knew very much about him, about his feelings or his past. You were quite close to Seth and Alison, weren't you?'

'I was, yes.'

'Is there anything you can tell me about him, about his past, that might help me understand him better. I know he was upset about Alison's accident—'

'Accident?'

'Yes. You must know, surely? The car—'

'Alison's death wasn't an accident, Mr Banks. She was murdered.'

'Murdered?'

'Oh, yes. It was murder all right. I told Seth. I made him believe me.'

'When?'

'I figured it out. I used to be a nurse, you know.'

'I know. What did you figure out?'

'Are you sure Seth's dead?'

Banks nodded.

She eyed him suspiciously, then smiled. 'I suppose I can tell you then. Are you sitting comfortably? That's what they say before the story on *Children's Hour*, you know. I used to listen to that when I was young. It's funny how things stick in your memory, isn't it? But so much doesn't. Why is that, do you think? Isn't the mind peculiar? Do you remember Uncle Mac and *Children's Favourites*? *Sparky and the Magic Piano*? Petula Clark singing "Little Green Man"?'

'I'm sorry, I don't remember,' Banks said. 'But I'm sitting comfortably.'

Elizabeth smiled. 'Good. Then I'll begin.'

And she launched into one of the saddest and strangest stories that Banks had ever heard.

TWO

What Liz Dale told him confirmed what he had been beginning to suspect. His theories were no longer mutually exclusive, but he felt none of his usual elation on solving this case.

He drove back to Eastvale slowly, taking the longest, most meandering route west through the gritstone country away from the large towns and cities. There was no hurry. On the way, he listened to scratchy recordings of the old bluesmen: gamblers, murderers, ministers, alcoholics, drug addicts singing songs about poverty, sex, the devil and bad luck. And the signs flashed by: Mytholmroyd, Todmorden, Cornholme. In Lancashire now, he skirted the Burnley area on a series of minor roads that led by the Forest of Trawden, then he was soon back in Craven country around Skipton, where the grass was lush green with limestone-rich soils.

He stopped in Grassington and had a pub lunch, then cut across Greenhow Hill by Pateley Bridge and got back to Eastvale via Ripon.

Burgess was waiting in his office. 'You owe me a fiver,' he said. 'A couple of glasses of Mumm and she was all over me.'

'There's no accounting for taste,' Banks said.

'You'll have to take my word for it. I'm not crass; I don't go in for stealing knickers as a trophy.'

Banks nodded towards the superintendent's swollen

purplish cheek. 'I see you've got a trophy of a kind.'

'That bloody husband of hers. Mistrustful swine.' He fingered the bruise. 'But that was later. He's lucky I didn't pull him in for assaulting a police officer. Still, I suppose he deserved a swing at me, so I let him. All nice and quiet.'

'Very magnanimous of you.' Banks pulled a five-pound note from his wallet and dropped it on the desk.

'What's wrong with you today, Banks? Sore loser?' Burgess picked up the money and held it out. 'Fuck it, you don't have to pay if you're that hard up.'

Banks sat down and lit a cigarette. 'Ever heard of a fellow called Barney Merritt?' he asked.

'No. Should I?'

'He's an old friend of mine, still on the Met. He's heard of you. He's also heard of DC Cranby. Keith J. Cranby.'

'So?' The muscles around Burgess's jaw tightened and his eyes seemed to turn brighter and sharper.

Banks tapped a folder on his desk. 'Cranby and a mate of his – possible DC Stickley – rented a blue Escort in York a couple of days ago. They drove up to Eastvale and checked into the Castle Hotel, the same place as you. I'm surprised you didn't pass each other in the lobby, it's not that big a place.'

'Do you realize what you're saying? Maybe you should reconsider and stop while the going's good.'

Banks shook his head and went on.

'The other day they broke into Dennis Osmond's flat. They didn't find what they were looking for, but they took one of his political books to put the wind up him. He thought he had every security force in the world after him. Yesterday evening they broke into Tim and Abha's apartment and took away a number of folders. That was after I told you where the information they'd collected on the demo was kept.'

Burgess tapped a ruler on the desk. 'You have proof of all this, I suppose?'

'If I need it, yes.'

'What on earth made you think of such a thing?'

'I know your methods. And when I mentioned the Osmond break-in you didn't seem surprised. You didn't even seem to care very much. That was odd, because my first thought was that it might have had a bearing on the Gill case. But, of course, you already knew all about it.'

'And what are you going to do?'

'I just don't understand you,' Banks said. 'What the bloody hell did you hope to achieve? You used the same vigilante tactics they did in Manchester after the Leon Brittan demo.'

'They worked though, didn't they?'

'If you call hounding a couple of students out of the country and drawing national attention to the worst elements of policing good, then yes, they worked.'

'Don't be so bloody naive, Banks. These people are all connected.'

'You're paranoid, do you know that? What do you think they are? Terrorists?'

'They're connected. Union leaders, bolshie students, ban-the-bombers. They're all connected. You can call them misguided idealists if you want, but to me they're a bloody menace.'

'To who? To what?'

Burgess leaned forward and gripped the desk. 'To the peace and stability of the nation, that's what. Whose side are you on, anyway?'

'I'm not on anyone's side. I've been investigating a

murder, remember? A policeman was killed. He wasn't a very good one, but I don't think he deserved to end up dead in the street. And what do I find? You bring your personal bloody goon squad from London and they start breaking and entering.'

'There's no point arguing ethics with you, Banks—'

'I know, because you don't have a leg to stand on.'

'But let me remind you that I'm in charge of this case.'

'That still doesn't give you the right to do what you did. Can't you bloody understand? You with all your talk about police image. The vigilante stuff only makes us end up looking like the bad guys, and bloody stupid ones at that.'

Burgess sat back and lit a cigar. 'Only if people find out. Which brings us back to my question. What are you going to do?'

'Nothing. But you're going to make sure those files are returned and that the people involved are left alone from now on.'

'Am I? What makes you so sure?'

'Because if you don't, I'll pass on what I know to Superintendent Gristhorpe. The ACC respects his opinion.'

Burgess laughed. 'You're not very well connected, you know. I don't think that'll do much good.'

'There's always the press, too. They'd love a juicy story like this. Dennis Osmond has a right to know what was done to him, too. Whatever you think, I don't believe it would do your future promotion prospects much good.'

Burgess tapped his cigar on the rim of the ashtray. 'You're so bloody pure of heart, aren't you, Banks? A real crusader. Better than the rest of us.'

'You were out of line and you know it. You just thought you could get away with it.'

'I still can.'

Banks shook his head.

'You're forgetting that I'm your superior officer. I can order you to hand over whatever evidence you've got.'

'Balls,' said Banks. 'Why don't you send Cranby and Stickley in to steal it?'

'Look,' Burgess said, reddening with anger, 'you don't want to cross me. I can be a very nasty enemy. Do you really think anyone's going to take any notice of your accusations? What do you think they'll do? Kick me off the force? Dream on.'

'I don't really care what they do to you. All I know is that the press will have a field day with it.'

'You'd be sawing off the branch you're sitting on. Think about where your loyalty lies. We do a difficult enough job as it is without taking an opportunity to set everyone against us. Have you considered that? What effect it would have on you lot up here if it did get out? I don't have to live here, thank God, but you do.'

'Damn right I do,' said Banks. 'And that's the point. You can come here and make a bloody mess then bugger off back to London. I have to live and work with these people. And I like it. It took me long enough to get accepted as far as I have been, and you come along and set back relations by years. Take it or leave it. Give back the files, call off your goons and it's forgotten, another unsolved break-in.'

'Oh, what a bleeding hero we are! And what if I put on a bit more pressure, got a couple of higher-ups to order you to hand over your evidence? What then, big man?'

'I've already told you,' Banks said. 'It's not me you need to worry about; it's the press, Osmond and the students.'

'I can handle them.'

'It's up to you.'

'That's it?'

'That's it. Take your pick.'

'Who's going to believe a couple of loony lefties anyway? And everyone knows the press is biased.'

Banks shrugged. 'Maybe nobody. We'll see.'

Burgess jerked to his feet. 'I won't forget this, Banks,' he snarled. 'When I make my report on this investigation—'

'It's over,' Banks said wearily.

'What is?'

'The investigation.' Banks told him briefly about his conversation with Elizabeth Dale.

'So what happens now?'

'Nothing. Except maybe you piss off back home.'

'You're not going to go blabbing the whole bloody story to the press?'

'No point, no. But I think Mara and the others have a right to know.'

'Yes, you would.' Burgess strode over to the door. 'And don't think you've won, because you haven't. You won't get out of it as easily as all that.'

And he left, the threat hanging in the air.

Banks stretched out his hands in front of him and noticed they were shaking. Even though the office was cool, his neck felt sweaty under the collar. His legs were weak too, as he found out when he grabbed another cigarette and walked over to the window. It wasn't every day you got the chance to be high-handed with a senior officer, especially a whizz-kid like Dirty Dick Burgess. And it was the first time Banks had ever seen him ruffled.

Maybe he *had* made a dangerous enemy for life. Perhaps Burgess had even been right and he was overplaying the crusader role. After all, he played it a bit close to the edge himself sometimes. But to hell with it, he thought. It wasn't worth dwelling on. He picked up his coat, pocketed his cigarettes and set off for the car park.

THREE

The rain had stopped and the afternoon sun was charming wraiths of mist from the river meadows and valley sides. Banks's Cortina crackled up the track and pulled up outside the farmhouse.

Mara answered the door on his second knock and let him in.

'I suppose you want to sit down?' she asked.

'It might take a while.' Banks made himself comfortable in the rocking chair. The children sat at the table colouring, and Paul slouched on the beanbag cushions reading a science-fiction book.

'Where are Rick and Zoe?' Banks asked.

'Working.'

'Can you go and get them, please? I'd like to talk to all of you. And would it be too much to ask for some tea?'

Mara put the kettle on first, then went out to the barn to fetch the others. When she came back, she saw to the tea while Rick and Zoe sat down.

'What the bloody hell is this?' Rick demanded. 'Haven't we had enough? Where's your friend?'

'He's packing.'

'Packing?' Mara said, walking in slowly with the teapot and mugs on a tray. 'But—'

'It's all over, Mara. Almost over, anyway.'

Banks poured himself some tea, lit a cigarette and turned to Paul. 'You wrote that suicide note, didn't you?'

'I don't know what you're talking about.'

'Come off it, the time for messing around is over. The pressure on the keys was different from that on the letters Seth typed, and his style was a hell of a lot better than yours. Why did you do it?'

'I've told you, I didn't do anything.' They were all staring at him now and he began to turn red.

'Shall I tell you why you did it?' Banks went on. 'You did it to deflect the blame from yourself.'

'Wait a minute,' Mara said. 'Are you accusing Paul of killing Seth?'

'Nobody killed Seth,' Banks said quietly. 'He did it himself.'

'But you said—'

'I know. And that's what we thought. It was the note that confused me. Seth didn't write it; Paul did. But he didn't kill anyone. When Paul found him, Seth was already dead. Paul just took the opportunity to type out a note of confession, hoping it would get him off the hook. It didn't seem like such a bad thing to do, I'm sure. After all, Seth was dead. Nothing could affect him any more. Isn't that right, Paul?'

Paul said nothing.

'Paul?' Mara turned to face him sternly. 'Is it true?'

'So what if it is? Seth wouldn't have minded. He wouldn't have wanted us to go on being persecuted. He was dead, Mara. I swear it. All I did was type out a note.'

'Had he written anything himself?' Banks asked.

'Yes, but it said nothing.' He pulled a scrap of paper out of the back pocket of his jeans and passed it over. It read, 'Sorry, Mara.' Just that. Banks passed it to Mara, and tears filled her eyes. She wiped them away with the back of her hand. 'How could you, Paul?' she said.

Paul sat forward and hugged his knees. 'It was for all of us,' he said. 'Can't you see? To keep the police off our backs. It's what Seth would have done.'

'But he didn't,' Banks said. 'Seth had no idea that Paul would forge a note. As far as he was concerned, his suicide would be accepted for what it was. He never imagined that we'd see it as murder. If his death led us to the truth, so be it, but he wasn't going to explain. He never did while he was alive, so why should he when he was about to die?'

'The truth?' Mara said. 'Is that what you're going to tell us now?'

'Yes. If you want me to.'

Mara nodded.

'You might not like it.'

'After all we've been through,' she said, 'I think you owe it to us.'

'Very well. I think Seth killed himself out of shame, among other reasons. He felt he'd let everyone down, including himself.'

'What do you mean?'

'I mean that Seth stabbed PC Gill and he couldn't live with what he'd done. Paul had already suffered for it. Seth would never have let him take the blame. He'd have confessed himself rather than that. When Paul was released, he was happy for him. What it meant for Seth though, was that the police would get even closer to him now. It was just a matter of time. I'd already seen PC Gill's number in his notebook and those books in his workshop. I knew it was his knife, too. I'd asked him about Elizabeth Dale, and he knew how unstable she was. All I had to do was find her and get her to talk. Seth knew all this. He knew it would soon be all over for him.'

Mara was pale. Her hands trembled as she tried to roll a cigarette. Banks offered her a Silk Cut and she took it. Zoe went around and poured tea for everyone.

'I can't believe this, you know,' Mara said, shaking her head. 'Not Seth.'

'It's true. I'm not saying that he intended to kill PC Gill. He couldn't be sure that the demo would turn nasty, even though Gill was supposed to be there. But he went prepared. He knew very well the kind of things that were likely to happen if Gill was around. That's why I asked you if you'd heard anyone mention Gill's number that afternoon. Someone had it in for him and knew he'd be there.'

'I thought it sounded vaguely familiar,' Mara said, speaking quietly as if to herself. 'I was in the kitchen, I think, with Seth.'

'And Osmond mentioned the number.'

'I . . . It could have been like that. But why Seth? He wasn't like that. He was a gentle person.'

'I agree, on the whole,' Banks said. 'But the circumstances are very unusual. I had to find Liz Dale to put it all together. She told me a very curious thing, which was that Alison, Seth's wife, was murdered. Now that didn't make sense to me, because I'd spoken to the local police and to the man who ran her over. It was an accident. He hadn't killed her deliberately. It had ruined his life, too.

'Seth tried to commit suicide after Alison's death, but he failed. He got on with his life but he never got over his grief, and that's partly because he never expressed it. You know he didn't like to talk about the past; he kept it all bottled up inside, all those feelings of grief and guilt. We always blame ourselves when someone we love dies, because maybe, just in a fleeting moment, we've wished them dead, and we tell ourselves that if things had been just a little different – if Seth had ridden to the shops that day instead of Alison – then the tragedy would never have happened. Liz was the only one who really knew what went on, and that was only because she was a close friend of Alison's. According to the Hebden Bridge police, Alison was more outgoing, spirited and communicative than Seth. Because he was the "strong silent type", everyone thought he was really in control, calm and cool, but he was torturing himself inside.'

'I still don't see,' Mara said. 'What does all this have to do with that policeman who got killed?'

Banks blew gently on the surface and sipped some tea. It tasted of apple and cinnamon. 'Liz Dale filed a complaint about PC Gill's vicious behaviour during a demo she went to with Alison Cotton. Seth hadn't been there himself. During the demo, Liz told me, Alison was struck a glancing blow on her temple by Gill. It was just one of many such incidents that afternoon. Alison didn't want to make a fuss and attract police attention by making a complaint, but Liz was far more political in general. When nothing came of it, she didn't pursue it any further. She'd lost interest by then – heroin made her forget politics – and like you she assumed that the police wouldn't listen to someone like her.'

'Can you blame her?' Rick said. 'They obviously didn't, did they? It hardly seems that—'

'Shut up,' Banks said. He spoke quietly, but forcefully enough to silence Rick.

'Over the next few months,' he went on, 'Alison started to show some unusual symptoms. She complained of frequent headaches, she was becoming forgetful and she suffered from dizzy spells. Shortly afterwards she became pregnant, so she put her other troubles out of her mind for a while.

'One time though, she really scared Seth and Liz. She started speaking as if she were a fourteen-year-old girl. Her family had been on holiday in Cyprus then, staying with an army friend of her father's who was stationed there, and she started describing a warm evening walk by the Mediterranean in Famagusta in great detail. Apparently even her voice was like that of a fourteen-year-old. Finally she snapped out of it and recalled nothing. She just laughed when the others told her what she'd been talking about.

'But that did it as far as Seth was concerned. He was worried she might have a brain tumour or something, so he insisted she tell the doctor. According to Liz, the doctor had nothing much to say except that pregnancy can do strange things to a woman's mind as well as her body. Alison told him that the symptoms started *before* she got pregnant but he just said something about people having funny spells, and that was that.

'A few weeks later, she went to the local shop one evening and got lost. It was about a two-minute walk away, and she couldn't find her way home. Seth and Liz found her wandering the streets an hour later. Anyway, things didn't get much better and she went to see the doctor again. At first he tried to blame the pregnancy again, but Alison stressed the terrible headaches, lapses of memory and slipping in and out of time. He said not to worry, but he arranged for a CAT scan, just to be on the safe side. Well, you know the National Health Service. By the time her appointment came around, she was already dead. And they couldn't do a proper autopsy later because of the accident – her head was crushed.

'Seth had his breakdown, attempted suicide, put himself back together and bought the farm, where he lived in isolation for a while until you came along, Mara. He proved himself capable of moving on, but he carried all the weight of the past with him. He was always a serious person, a man of strong feelings, but there was a new darker dimension to him after the shock of Alison's death.'

'It doesn't make sense,' Mara said. 'If all that's true, why did he wait so long before doing what you say he did?'

'Two reasons really. First, he wasn't convinced until about a year ago. That's around the time he made his will. According to Liz, about eighteen months ago he'd read an article in a magazine about a similar case. A woman showed symptoms like Alison's after receiving a relatively mild blow to the head, and she later crashed her car. Just after he'd read this and started thinking about the implications, Liz ran off from the hospital and came to stay. He talked to her about it, and she agreed it was a definite possibility. After all, Alison's attack only began to occur shortly after the demo. Liz hadn't been a very good nurse – not good enough to come up with a diagnosis at the time – but she knew something about the human body, and once Seth had put the idea into her head, she helped to convince him.

'That's when they were up talking all the time,' Mara said. 'Is that what they were talking about?'

'Mostly, yes. Next, Seth went on to study the subject himself. I even saw two books on the human brain in his workshop, though I'd no idea what significance they had. One was called *The Tip of the Iceberg*. Seth just left them there; he never really tried to cover his tracks at all. And then there was PC Gill's number in his notebook. Liz said she wrote it down for him the last time she was here. He must have torn it out in anger after he'd heard Gill would be at the demo.'

'You said there were two reasons he didn't act straight away,' Mara said. 'What's the other one?'

'Seth's character, really. You know he wasn't normally quick-tempered or impatient. Far from it, he needed lots of patience in his line of work. He wasn't the type to go out seeking immediate vengeance, either. And remember, he'd never really got over his grief and his guilt. I imagine he repressed his anger in the same way, and it all festered together, under the surface, and finally turned into hatred – hatred for the man who had robbed him of his wife and child. And it wasn't just a man; it was a policeman, an enemy of freedom.' He glanced at Rick, who was listening closely and sucking on a strand of his beard.

'But there was nothing he could do. It had happened so long ago and there was no evidence – even if he had believed that the police would listen to his story. I don't think he really considered revenge, but when Osmond mentioned the number that afternoon, something gave. The whole business had been eating away at him for so long, and he felt so impotent.

'He snatched up the knife, expecting trouble. I shouldn't imagine he really believed he would kill Gill, but he wanted to be prepared. When he dropped the knife later and it got kicked away, he must have been surprised to find no blood on him. Most of Gill's bleeding was internal. So he kept quiet. There were over a hundred people at that demo. As far as Seth was concerned, that seemed to mean we hadn't a snowball in hell's chance of finding the killer. Besides, we'd be after the politicos, and he wasn't especially active that way.' Banks paused and sipped some more tea. 'If Paul hadn't taken the knife and thrown it away, we might never have known where it came from. None of you would ever have told us it was missing, that's for certain. Liz had described Gill to him as well – a big man with his teeth too close to his gums – and he was easy to spot up there on the steps. That's where the most light was, above the doors. And Seth was near the front of the crowd. When they got close in the scuffles, Seth saw the number on Gill's epaulette and—'

'My God!' Zoe said. 'So that's it . . .'

'What?'

'When the police started to charge, I was next to Seth, right at the front, and the first thing that policeman did was lash out at a woman standing on my other side. She looked a bit like you, Mara.'

'What happened next?' Banks asked.

'I didn't really see, I was frightened. I got pushed away. But I looked up at Seth and I saw an expression on his face. It was . . . I can't really describe it, but he was pale and he looked so different . . . so full of hate.'

They all remained silent as they digested what Zoe had said. She couldn't have known at the time, but what Seth was seeing was a replay, an echo of what happened to Alison. Given that, Banks thought, what Seth had done was even more understandable. He had been pushed far beyond breaking point.

'Liz Dale told you all about his background?' said Mara finally.

'Yes. Everything else made sense then: Seth's behaviour, the knife, the number, the books.'

'If . . . if you'd found her earlier, talked to her, would that have saved Seth?'

'I don't think so. It's not as easy as that. It was actually carrying out the crime that finished him. He'd spent all his hate and anger, and he felt empty. He might have committed suicide sooner if he hadn't been lucky and got away from the demo clean. I imagine he thought he could live with what he'd done at first, but as the investigation went on he realized he couldn't. I don't think he could have faced prison either, and he knew that we'd find him. All that talking to Liz Dale has done is put things in perspective and made the motive clear.

'And Liz is a difficult person. Her grasp on reality is pretty tenuous, for a start. She knew nothing of the demo or of Gill's murder. And I honestly don't think she'd have told me about Seth unless I'd told her he was dead. I probably wouldn't even have known the right questions to ask. I'm not making excuses, Mara. We make mistakes in this job, and usually someone suffers for them. But the rest of you lie, evade and treat us with hostility. There's good and bad on both sides. You can't look back and say how things might have been. That's no good.'

Mara nodded slowly. 'Do you think Seth was right?'

'Right about what?'

'About Gill being responsible for Alison's death.'

'I think there's a good chance, yes. I've spoken to the police doctor about it too, and he agrees. But we'll never know for sure. Liz Dale was wrong, though – Alison wasn't murdered. Gill might not have been a good policeman, but he didn't *intend* to kill her.

'But look at it from Seth's point of view. He'd lost everything he valued – in the most horrible way – and he'd lost it all to a man who abused the power the state gave him. Seth came of age in the late sixties and early seventies. He was anti-authoritarian, and he lost his wife and unborn child to a representative of what he saw as oppressive authority. It's no wonder he had to hit back eventually, especially considering what Zoe just told us, or go mad. That's why he made the will when he did, I think, because knowing what had happened to Alison – knowing the real cause of her death – changed things, and he wasn't sure he could be responsible for his actions any more. He wanted to make certain you got the house.'

Mara covered her face with both hands and started to cry. Zoe went over to comfort her and the children looked on, horror-stricken. Paul and Rick seemed rooted where they sat. Banks rose from the chair. He'd done his job, solved the crime, but it didn't end there for Mara. For her, this was only the beginning of the real pain.

'But why couldn't he be happy here?' she cried from behind her hands. 'With me?'

Banks had no answer to that.

He opened the door and late afternoon sunshine flooded in. At the car, he turned and saw Mara standing in the doorway watching him, arms folded tightly across her chest, head tilted to one side. The sunlight caught the tears in her eyes and made them sparkle like jewels as they trickled down her cheeks.

All the way home through the wraiths of mist, Banks could hear the damn wind chimes ringing in his ears.

PAST REASON HATED

This one is for the Usual Suspects

1

ONE

Snow fell on Swainsdale for the first time that year a few days before Christmas. Out in the dale, among the more remote farms and hamlets, the locals would be cursing. A heavy snowfall could mean lost sheep and blocked roads. In past years, some places had been cut off for as long as five weeks. But in Eastvale, most of those crossing the market square on the evening of 22 December felt a surge of joy as the fat flakes drifted down, glistening in the gaslight as they fell, to form a lumpy white carpet over the cobblestones.

Detective Constable Susan Gay paused on her way back to the station from Joplin's newsagents. Outside the Norman church stood a tall Christmas tree, a gift from the Norwegian town with which Eastvale was twinned. The lights winked on and off, and its tapered branches bent under the weight of half an inch of snow. In front of the tree, a group of children in red choirgowns stood singing 'Once in Royal David's City'. Their alto voices, fragile but clear, seemed especially fitting on such a beautiful winter's evening.

Susan tilted her head back and let the snowflakes melt on her eyelids. Two weeks ago she would not have allowed herself to do something so spontaneous and frivolous. But now that she was *Detective* Constable Gay, she could afford to relax a little. She had finished with courses and exams, at least until she tried for sergeant. Now there would be no more arguing with David Craig over who made the coffee. There would be no more walking the beat, either, and no more traffic duty on market day.

The music followed her as she headed back to the station:

And He leads His children on
To the place where He is gone.

Directly in front of her, the new blue lamp hung like a shopsign over the doorway of the Tudor-fronted police station. In an attempt to change the public image of the force, tarnished by race riots, sex scandals and accusations of high-level corruption, the government had looked to the past: more specifically, to the fifties. The lamp was straight out of *Dixon of Dock Green*. Susan had never actually seen the programme, but she understood the basic idea. The image of the kindly old copper on the beat had caused many a laugh around Eastvale Regional Headquarters. Would that life were simple, they all said.

Her second day on the job and all was well. She pushed open the door and headed for the stairs. Upstairs! The inner sanctum of the CID. She had envied them all for so long – Gristhorpe, Banks, Richmond, even Hatchley – when she had brought messages, or stood by taking notes while they interrogated female suspects. No longer. She was one of them now, and she was about to show them that a woman could do the job every bit as well as a man, if not better.

She didn't have her own office; only Banks and Gristhorpe were allowed such luxuries. The hutch she shared with Richmond would have to do. It looked over the carpark out the back, not the market square, but at least she had a desk, rickety though it was, and a filing cabinet of her own. She had inherited them from Sergeant Hatchley, now exiled to the coast, and the first thing she had had to do was rip down the nude pin-ups from the cork bulletin board above his desk. How anybody could work with those bloated mammaries hanging over them was beyond her.

About forty minutes later, after she had poured herself a cup of coffee to keep her awake while she studied the latest regional crime reports, the phone rang. It was Sergeant Rowe calling from the front desk.

'Someone just phoned in to report a murder,' he said.

Susan felt the adrenalin flow. She grasped the receiver tighter. 'Where?'

'Oakwood Mews. You know, those tarted-up bijou terraces at the back of King Street.'

'I know them. Any details?'

'Not much. It was a neighbour who called. Said the woman next door went rushing into the street screaming. She took her in, but couldn't get much sense out of her except that her friend had been murdered.'

'Did the neighbour take a look for herself?'

'No. She said she thought she'd better call us right away.'

'Can you send PC Tolliver down there?' Susan asked. 'Tell him to check out the scene without touching any-thing. And tell him to stay by the door and not let anyone in till we get there.'

'Aye,' said Rowe, 'but shouldn't—'

'What's the number?'

'Eleven.'

'Right.'

Susan hung up. Her heart beat fast. Nothing had happened in Eastvale for months – and now, on only her second day on the new job, a murder. And she was the only member of the CID on duty that evening. Calm down, she told herself, follow procedure, do it right. She reached for her coat, still damp with snow, then hurried out the back way to the car park. Shivering, she swept the snow off the windscreen of her red Golf and drove off as fast as the bad weather allowed.

TWO

> *Four and twenty virgins*
> *Came down from Inverness,*
> *And when the ball was over*
> *There were four and twenty less.*

'I think Jim's a bit pissed,' Detective Chief Inspector Alan Banks leaned over and said to his wife, Sandra.

Sandra nodded. In a corner of the Eastvale Rugby Club banquet room, by the Christmas tree, Detective Sergeant Jim Hatchley stood with a group of cronies, all as big and brawny as himself. They looked like a parody of a group of carol singers, Banks thought, each with a foaming pint in his hand. As they sang, they swayed. The other guests stood by the bar or sat at tables chatting over the noise. Carol Hatchley – née Ellis – the sergeant's blushing bride, sat beside her mother and fumed. The couple had just changed out of their wedding clothes into less formal attire in readiness for their honeymoon, but Hatchley, true to form, had insisted on just one more pint before they left. That one had quickly turned into two, then three . . .

> *The village butcher, he was there,*
> *Chopper in his hand.*
> *Every time they played a waltz,*
> *He circumcised the band.*

It didn't make sense, Banks thought. How many times could you circumcise one band? Carol managed a weak smile, then turned and said something to her mother, who shrugged. Banks, leaning against the long bar with Sandra, Superintendent Gristhorpe and Philip Richmond, ordered another round of drinks.

As he waited, he looked around the room. It was done up for the festive season, no doubt about that. Red and green concertina trimmings hung across the ceiling, bedecked with tinsel, holly and the occasional sprig of mistletoe. The club tree, a good seven feet tall, sparkled in all its glory.

It was twenty past eight, and the real party was just beginning. The wedding had taken place at Eastvale Congregational Church late in the afternoon, and it had been followed by a slap-up meal at the rugby club at six. Now the speeches had been made, the plates cleared away and the tables moved for a good Yorkshire knees-up. Hatchley had hired a DJ for the music, but the poor lad was still waiting patiently for a signal to begin.

> *Singing 'Balls to your father,*
> *Arse against the wall.*
> *If you've never been shagged on a Saturday night.*
> *You've never been shagged at all.'*

'Four and Twenty Virgins' was coming to a close. Banks could tell. There would be a verse about the village schoolmistress (who had unusually large breasts) and one about the village cripple (who did unspeakable things with his crutch), then a rousing finale. With a bit of luck, that would be the end of the rugby songs. They had already performed 'Dinah, Dinah, Show Us Yer Leg (A Yard Above Your Knees)', 'The Engineer's Song' and a lengthy, improvized version of 'Mademoiselle from Armentieres'. The sulky DJ, who had been pretending to set up his equipment for the past hour, would soon get his chance to shine.

Banks passed the drinks along to the others and reached for a cigarette. Gristhorpe frowned at him, but Banks was used to that. Phil Richmond was also smoking one of his occasional panatellas, so the superintendent was having a particularly hard time of it. Sandra had stopped smoking completely, and Banks had agreed not to smoke in the house. Luckily, although most of the police station had been declared a non-smoking area, he was still permitted to light up in his own office. Things had got so bad, though, that even alleged criminals brought in for interrogation could legally object to any police officer smoking in the interview rooms. It was a sorry state of affairs, Banks mused: you could beat them to your heart's content, as long as the bruises didn't show, but you couldn't smoke in their presence and get away with it.

Sandra raised her dark eyebrows and breathed a sigh of relief when 'Four and Twenty Virgins' came to an end. But her joy was short lived. The choir of rugby forwards refused to leave the stage without giving their rendition of 'Good King Wenceslas'. Despite groans from the captive audience, a dirty look from the DJ and a positive flash of fury from Carol's eyes, Sergeant Hatchley led them off:

> Good King Wenceslas looked out
> Of his bedroom window.
> Silly bugger, he fell out . . .

Gristhorpe looked at his watch. 'I think I'll be off after this one. I just overheard someone say it's snowing pretty heavily out there now.'

'Is it?' Sandra said. Banks knew she loved snow. They walked over to the window at the far end of the room and glanced out. Clearly satisfied with what she saw, Sandra pulled the long curtains open. It had been snowing only lightly when they had arrived for pre-dinner drinks at about five, but now the high window framed a thick swirl of white flakes falling on the rugby field. Others turned to look, oohing and aahing, touching their neighbours on the arm to tell them what was happening. As they walked back, Banks took Sandra in his arms and kissed her.

'Got you,' he said, then he looked up and Sandra followed his gaze to the mistletoe hanging above them.

Sandra took his arm and walked beside him back to the bar. 'I don't mean to be rude or anything,' she said, 'but when's this racket going to end? Don't you think some-one should have a word with Jim? After all, it *is* Carol's wedding day . . .'

Banks looked at Hatchley. Judging by his flushed face and the way he swayed, there wouldn't be much of a wedding night for the bride.

> *Brightly shone his arse that night,*
> *Though the frost was cruel . . .*

Banks was just about to walk across and say something – only concerned that he might sound too much like the boss when he was just a wedding guest – when he was saved by the DJ. A long and loud blast of feedback issued from the speakers and stopped Hatchley and his mates in their tracks. Before they could regather their wits for a further onslaught, several quick-thinking members of the party applauded. At once, the singers took this as their cue for a bow and the DJ as his opportunity to begin the real music. He adjusted a couple of dials, skipped the patter, and before Hatchley and his mob even knew what had hit them the hall was filled with the sound of Martha and the Vandellas singing 'Dancing in the Street'.

Sandra smiled. 'That's more like it.'

Banks glanced over at Richmond, who looked very pleased with himself. And well he might. There had just been a big change-around at Eastvale Regional Police Headquarters. Sergeant Hatchley had been a problem for some time. Not suitable material for promotion, he had stood in Richmond's way, even though Richmond had passed his sergeant's examination with flying colours and shown remarkable aptitude on the job. The trouble was, there just wasn't room for two detective sergeants in the small station.

Finally, after months of trying to find a way out of the dilemma, Superintendent Gristhorpe had seized the first opportunity that came his way. Official borders had been redrawn and the region had expanded eastwards to take in a section of the North York Moors and a small stretch of coastline between Scarborough and Whitby. It seemed a good idea to place a small CID outpost on the coast to deal with the day-to-day matters that might arise there, and Hatchley came to mind as the man to head it. He was competent enough, just lazy and inattentive to detail. Surely, Gristhorpe had reasoned to Banks, he couldn't do much damage in a sleepy fishing village like Saltby Bay?

Hatchley had been asked if he fancied living by the seaside and he had said yes. After all, it was still in Yorkshire. As the time of the move coincided with his impending marriage, it had seemed sensible to combine

the two celebrations. Though Hatchley remained a sergeant, Gristhorpe had managed to wangle him a small pay
increase, and – more important – he would be in charge.
He was to take David Craig, now a detective constable,
with him. Craig, soaking up the ale at the other end of the
bar, didn't look too pleased about it.

Hatchley and his wife were off to Saltby Bay that night
– or, the way things were going, the next morning – where
he was to take two weeks' leave to set up their cottage by
the sea. His only complaint was that it wouldn't be
summer for a long time. Apart from that, Hatchley seemed
happy enough with the state of affairs.

In Eastvale, Richmond had got his promotion to
detective sergeant at last, and Susan Gay had been brought
upstairs as their new detective constable. It was too early
to know whether the arrangement would work, but Banks
had every confidence in both Richmond and Gay. Still, he
felt sad. He had been in Eastvale almost three years, and
during that time he had grown to like and depend on
Sergeant Hatchley, despite the man's obvious faults. It had
taken Banks until last summer to call the sergeant by his
first name, but he felt that Hatchley, with Superintendent
Gristhorpe, had been responsible for helping him adapt to
Yorkshire ways after his move from London.

The music slowed down. Percy Sledge started singing
'When a Man Loves a Woman'. Sandra touched Banks's
arm. 'Dance?'

Banks took her hand and they walked towards the
dance floor. Before they got there, someone tapped him
gently on the shoulder. He turned and saw DC Susan Gay,
snowflakes still melting on the shoulders of her navy coat
and in her short, curly blonde hair.

'What is it?' Banks asked.

'Can I have a word, sir? Somewhere quiet.'

The only quiet place was the toilets, and they could hardly go charging off into the gents' or ladies'. The alternative was the corner opposite the DJ, which seemed to be deserted. Banks asked Sandra if she minded missing this one. She shrugged, being used to such privations, and went back to the bar. Gristhorpe, Banks noticed, gallantly offered her his arm, and they went onto the dance floor.

'It's a murder, at least a possible murder,' DC Gay said, as soon as they had found a quieter spot. 'I didn't see the superintendent when I came in, so I went straight to you.'

'Any details?'

'Sketchy.'

'How long ago was this?'

'About ten minutes. I sent PC Tolliver to the house and drove straight over here. I'm sorry to spoil the celebrations, but I couldn't see what else—'

'It's all right,' Banks said, 'you did fine.' She hadn't, but that was hardly her fault. She was new to the job and a murder report had cropped up. What should she have done? Well, she could have gone to check out the scene herself, and she might have found, as nine times out of ten one did, that there had been some mistake, or a prank. Or she might have waited for the PC to call in and let her know the situation before running off and dragging her chief inspector away from his ex-sergeant's wedding celebration. But Banks didn't blame her. She was young yet, she would learn, and if they really were dealing with a murder, the time saved by Susan's direct action could prove invaluable.

'I've got the address, sir.' She stood there looking at him, keen, expectant. 'It's on Oakwood Mews. Number eleven.'

Banks sighed. 'We'd better go then. Just give me a minute.'

He went back to the bar and explained the situation to Richmond. The music speeded up again, into the Supremes' 'Baby Love', and Gristhorpe led Sandra back from the dance floor. When he heard the news, he insisted on accompanying Banks to the scene, even though it was by no means certain they would find a murder victim there. Richmond wanted to come along, too.

'No, lad,' said Gristhorpe, 'there's no point. If it's serious, Alan can fill you in later. And don't tell Sergeant Hatchley. I don't want it spoiling his wedding day. Though judging by the look on young Carol's face he might have already done that himself.'

'Are you taking the car?' Sandra asked Banks.

'I'd better. Oakwood Mews is a fair distance from here. There's no telling how long we'll be. If there's time, I'll come back and pick you up. If not, don't worry, Phil will take good care of you.'

'Oh, I'm not worried.' She slipped her arm in Richmond's and the new detective sergeant blushed. 'Phil's a lovely mover.'

Banks kissed her quickly and set off with Gristhorpe.

Susan Gay stood waiting for them by the door. Before they got to her, one of Hatchley's rugby club cronies lurched over and tried to kiss her. From behind, Banks saw him put his arms around her, then double up and stagger back. Everyone else was too busy dancing or chatting to notice. Susan looked flushed when Banks and Gristhorpe got there. She put her hand to her mouth and muttered, 'I'm sorry,' while the rugby player pointed, with a hurt expression on his face, to the sprig of mistletoe over the door.

●

THREE

It was no false alarm; that much, at least, was clear from the expression on PC Tolliver's face when Banks and the others reached number eleven Oakwood Mews. After Gristhorpe had issued instructions to send for Dr Glendenning and the scene-of-crime team, the three detectives went inside.

The first thing Banks noticed when he entered the hall was the music. Muffled, coming from the front room, it sounded familiar: a Bach cantata, perhaps? Then he opened the living-room door and paused on the threshold. The scene possessed a picturesque quality, he felt, which even extended, at first, to masking the ugliness of the corpse on the sofa.

A log fire crackled in the hearth. Its flames tossed shadows on the sheepskin rug and over the stucco walls. The only other light came from two red candles on the polished oak table in the far corner, and from the Christmas tree lights in the window. Banks stepped into the room. The flames danced and the beautiful music played on. On the wall above the stereo was a print of one of Gauguin's Tahitian scenes: a coffee-skinned native woman, naked to the waist, carrying what looked like a bowl of red berries as she walked beside another woman.

As he approached the sofa, Banks noticed that the sheepskin rug was dotted with dark blotches, as if the fire had spat sparks, which had seared the wool. Then he became aware of that sickling, metallic smell he had come across so often before.

A log shifted on the fire; flames leapt in all directions and their light played over the naked body. The woman lay stretched out, head propped up on cushions in what would have been a very inviting pose had it not been for the blood that had flowed from the multiple stab wounds in her throat and chest and drenched the whole front of her body. It glistened like dark satin in the firelight. From what Banks could see, the victim was young and pretty, with smooth, olive skin and shoulder-length, jet-black hair. Bending over her, he noticed that her eyes were blue, the intense kind of blue that makes some dark-haired people all that much more attractive. Now their stare was cold and lifeless. In front of her, on the low coffee table, stood a half-empty teacup on a coaster and a chocolate layer cake with one slice missing. Banks covered one fingertip with his handkerchief and touched the cup. It was cold.

The spell broke. Banks became aware of Gristhorpe's voice in the background questioning PC Tolliver, and of Susan Gay standing silent beside him. It was her first corpse, he realized, and she was handling it well, better than he had. Not only was she not about to vomit or faint, but she, too, was glancing around the room, observing the details.

'Who found the body?' Gristhorpe asked PC Tolliver.

'Woman by the name of Veronica Shildon. She lives here.'

'Where is she now?' Banks asked.

Tolliver nodded towards the stairs. 'Up there with the neighbour. She didn't want to come back in here.'

'I don't blame her,' said Banks. 'Do you know who the victim is?'

'Her name's Caroline Hartley. Apparently, she lived here too.'

Gristhorpe raised his bushy eyebrows. 'Come on, Alan, let's go and hear what she has to say. Susan, will you stay down here till the scene-of-crime team arrives?'

Susan Gay nodded and stood aside.

There were only two rooms and a bathroom upstairs. One room had been converted into a sitting room, or a study, with bookcases covering one wall, a small roll-top desk under the window and a couple of wicker armchairs arranged below the track-lighting. The bedroom, Banks noticed from the landing, was done out in coral and sea-green, with Laura Ashley wallpaper. If two women lived in the house and there was only one bedroom, he reasoned, then they must share it. He took a deep breath and went into the study.

Veronica Shildon sat in one of her wicker chairs, head in hands. The neighbour, who introduced herself as Christine Cooper, sat beside her. The only other place to sit was the hard-backed chair in front of the desk. Gristhorpe took it and leaned forward, resting his chin on his fists. Banks stood by the door.

'She's had a terrible shock,' Christine Cooper said. 'I don't know if she'll be able to tell you much.'

'Don't worry, Mrs Cooper,' Gristhorpe said. 'The doctor will be here soon. He'll give her something. Is there anyone she can stay with?'

'She can stay with me if she wants. Next door. We've got a spare room. I'm sure my husband won't mind.'

'Fine.' Gristhorpe turned towards the crying woman and introduced himself. 'Can you tell me what happened?'

Veronica Shildon looked up. She was in her mid-thirties, Banks guessed, with a neat cap of dark-brown hair streaked with grey. Handsome rather than pretty, her thin face and lips, and everything in her bearing, spoke of dignity and refinement, perhaps even of severity. She held a crumpled tissue in her left hand and the fist of her right was clenched so tightly it was white. Even as he admired her appearance, Banks looked for any signs of blood on her hands or her clothing. He saw none. Her grey-green eyes, red around the rims, couldn't quite focus on Gristhorpe.

'I just got home,' she said. 'I thought she was waiting for me.'

'What time was this?' Gristhorpe asked.

'Eight. A few minutes after.' She didn't look at him when she answered.

'Where had you been?'

'I'd been shopping.' She looked up, but her eyes appeared to be staring right through the superintendent. 'That's just it, you see. I thought for a moment she was wearing the present I'd bought her, the scarlet camisole. But she couldn't have been, could she? I hadn't even given it to her. And she was dead.'

'What did you do when you found her?' Gristhorpe asked.

'I . . . I ran to Christine's. She took me in and called the police. I don't know . . . Is Caroline really dead?'

Gristhorpe nodded.

'Why? Who?'

Gristhorpe leaned forward and spoke softly. 'That's what we have to find out, love. Are you sure you didn't touch anything in the room?'

'Nothing.'

'Is there anything else you can tell us?'

Veronica Shildon shook her head. She was clearly too distraught to speak. They would have to leave their questions until tomorrow.

Christine Cooper accompanied Banks and Gristhorpe to the study door. 'I'll stay with her till the doctor comes, if you don't mind,' she said.

Gristhorpe nodded and they went downstairs.

'Organize a house-to-house, would you?' Gristhorpe asked PC Tolliver before they returned to the living room. 'You know the drill. Anyone seen entering or leaving the house.' The constable nodded and dashed off.

Back inside the front room, Banks noticed for the first time how warm it was and took off his raincoat. The music stopped, then the needle came off the record, returned to the edge of the turntable and promptly started on its way again.

'What *is* that music?' Susan Gay asked.

Banks listened. The piece – elegant, stately strings accompanying a soprano soloist singing in Latin – sounded vaguely familiar. It wasn't Bach at all, Italian in style rather than German.

'Sounds like Vivaldi,' he said, frowning. 'But it's not what it is bothers me so much, it's why it's playing, and especially why it's been set to repeat.'

He walked over to the turntable and knelt by the album cover lying face down on the speaker beside it. It was indeed Vivaldi: *Laudate pueri*, sung by Magda Kalmár. Banks had never heard of her, but she had a beautiful voice, more reedy, warm and less brittle than many sopranos he had heard. The cover looked new.

'Should I turn it off?' Susan Gay asked.

'No. Leave it. It could be important. Let the scene-of-crime boys have a look.'

At that moment the front door opened and everyone stood aghast at what walked in. To all intents and purposes, their visitor was Santa Claus himself, complete with beard and red hat. If it hadn't been for the height, the twinkling blue eyes, the brown bag and the cigarette dangling from the corner of his mouth, Banks himself wouldn't have known who it was.

'I apologize for my appearance,' said Dr Glendenning. 'Believe me, I have no wish to appear frivolous. But I was just about to set off for the children's ward to give out their Christmas presents when I got the call. I didn't want to waste any time.' And he didn't. 'Is this the alleged corpse?' He walked over to the sofa and bent over the body. Before he had done much more than look it over, Peter Darby, the photographer, arrived along with Vic Manson and his team.

The three CID officers stood in the background while the specialists went to work collecting hair and fabric samples with tiny vacuum cleaners, dusting for prints and photographing the scene from every conceivable angle. Susan Gay seemed enthralled. She must have read about all this in books, Banks thought, and even taken part in demonstration runs at the police college, but there was nothing like the real thing. He tapped her on the shoulder. It took her a few seconds to pull her eyes away and face him.

'I'm just nipping back upstairs,' Bank whispered. 'Won't be a minute.' Susan nodded and turned to watch Glendenning measure the throat wounds.

Upstairs, Banks knelt in front of the armchair. 'Veronica,' he said gently, 'that music, Vivaldi, was it playing when you got home?'

With difficulty, Veronica focused on him. 'Yes,' she said, with a puzzled look on her face. 'Yes. That was odd. I thought we had company.'

'Why?'

'Caroline . . . she doesn't like classical music. She says it makes her feel stupid.'

'So she wouldn't have put it on herself?'

Veronica shook her head. 'Never.'

'Whose record is it? Is it part of your collection?'

'No.'

'But you like classical music?'

She nodded.

'Do you know the piece?'

'I don't think so, but I recognize the voice.'

Banks stood up and rested his hand on her shoulder. 'The doctor will be up soon,' he said. 'He'll give you something to help you sleep.' He took Christine Cooper's arm and drew her on to the landing. 'How long have they been living here?'

'Nearly two years now.'

Banks nodded towards the bedroom. 'Together?'

'Yes. At least . . .' She folded her arms. 'It's not my place to judge.'

'Ever any trouble?'

'What do you mean?'

'Rows, threats, feuds, angry visitors, anything?'

Christine Cooper shook her head. 'Not a thing. You couldn't wish for quieter, more considerate neighbours. As I said, we didn't know each other very well, but we've passed the time of day together now and then. My husband . . .'

'Yes?'

'Well . . . he was very fond of Caroline. I think she reminded him of our Corinne. She died a few years ago. Leukaemia. She was about Caroline's age.'

Banks looked at Christine Cooper. She seemed to be somewhere in her mid-fifties, a small, puzzled-looking woman with grey hair and a wrinkled brow. That would make her husband about the same age, or a little older perhaps. A paternal attachment, most likely, but he made a mental note to follow it up.

'Did you notice anything earlier this evening?' he asked.

'Like what?'

'Any noise, or anyone calling at the house?'

'No. I can't really say I did. The houses are quite solid, you know. I had my curtains closed, and I had the television on until eight o'clock, when that silly game show came on.'

'You heard nothing at all?'

'I heard doors close once or twice, but I couldn't be sure whose doors.'

'Can you remember what time?'

'When I was watching television. Between seven and eight. I'm sorry I'm not more use to you. I just didn't pay attention. I didn't know it would be important.'

'Of course not. Just one more small point,' Banks said. 'What time did Mrs Shildon arrive at your house?'

'Ten past eight.'

'Are you sure?'

'Yes. I was in the kitchen then. I looked at the clock when I heard someone shouting and banging on my door. I hadn't heard any carol singers, and I wondered who could be calling at that time.'

'Did you hear her arrive home?'

'I heard her door open and close.'

'What time was that?'

'Just after eight – certainly not more than a minute or two after. I'd just switched the television off and gone to start on Charles's dinner. That's why I heard her. It was quiet then. I thought it was my door at first, so I glanced up at the clock. It's a habit I have when I'm in the kitchen. There's a nice wallclock, a present . . . but you don't want to know about that. Anyway, I wasn't expecting Charles back so early so I . . . Just a minute! What are you getting at? Surely you can't believe—'

'Thank you very much, Mrs Cooper, that'll be all for now.'

When Mrs Cooper had gone back into the study, Banks had a quick look through the bedroom for any signs of blood-stained clothing, but found nothing. The wardrobe was clearly divided into two halves: one for Veronica's more conservative clothes and the other for Caroline's, a little more modern in style. At the bottom sat a carrier bag full of what looked like unwrapped Christmas presents.

The whole house would have to be searched thoroughly before the night was over, but the scene-of-crime team could do that later. What bothered Banks for the moment was the gap of almost ten minutes between Veronica Shildon's arriving home and her knocking on her neighbour's door. A lot could be accomplished in ten minutes.

Back downstairs, Banks led Vic Manson over to the turntable.

'Can you get this record off and dust the whole area for prints? I want the cover and the inside sleeve bagged for examination, too.'

'No problem.' Manson set to it.

Everyone looked up when the music stopped. It had cast such a spell over the scene that Banks felt like a dancer cut off in the middle of a stately pavane. Now everyone seemed to notice for the first time exactly what the situation was. It was harsh and ugly, especially with all the lights on.

'Have they found anything interesting yet?' Banks asked Gristhorpe.

'The knife. It was on their draining-board in the

kitchen, all washed, but there are still traces of blood. It looks like one of their own, from a set. Did you notice that cake on the table in front of the sofa?'

Banks nodded.

'It's possible she'd used the knife to cut herself a slice earlier.'

'Which would make it the handiest weapon,' Banks said, 'if it was still on the table.'

'Yes. And there's this.' The superintendent held out a crumpled sheet of green Christmas wrapping paper with silver bells and red holly berries on it. 'It was over by the music centre.' He shrugged. 'It might mean something.'

'It could have come from the record,' Banks said, and told Gristhorpe what Veronica had said.

Dr Glendenning, who had taken off his beard and hat and unbuttoned the top half of his Father Christmas outfit, walked over to them and stuck another cigarette in his mouth.

'Dead three or four hours at the most,' he said. 'Bruise on the left cheek consistent with a hard punch or kick. It might easily have knocked her out. But cause of death was blood loss due to multiple stab wounds – at least seven, as far as I can count. Unless she was poisoned first.'

'Thanks,' Gristhorpe said. 'Any way of telling how it happened?'

'At this stage, no. Except for the obvious – it was a bloody vicious attack.'

'Aye,' said Gristhorpe. 'Was she interfered with sexually?'

'On a superficial examination, I'd say no. No signs of it at all. But I won't be able to tell you any more until after the post-mortem, which I'll conduct first thing tomorrow morning. You can have the lads cart her to the mortuary whenever they're ready. Can I be off now? I hate to keep those poor wee kiddies waiting.'

Banks asked him if he would drop in on Veronica Shildon first and give her a sedative. Glendenning sighed but agreed. The ambulance men, who had been waiting outside, came in to take away the body. Glendenning had covered the hands with plastic bags to preserve any skin caught under the fingernails. As the ambulance men lifted her on to the stretcher, the cuts around her throat gaped open like screaming mouths. One of the men had to put his hand under her head so that the flesh didn't rip back as far as the spine. That was the only time Banks saw Susan Gay visibly pale and look away.

With Caroline Hartley's body gone, apart from the blood that had sprayed on to the sheepskin and the sofa cushions, there was very little left to indicate what horror had occurred in the cosy room that night. The forensic team bundled up the rug and cushions to take with them for further examination, and then there was nothing left to show at all.

It was after ten thirty. PC Tolliver and another two uniformed constables were still conducting house-to-house enquiries in the area, but there was little else the CID could do until morning. They needed to know Caroline Hartley's movements that evening: where she had been, who she had seen and who might have had a reason to want her dead. Veronica Shildon could probably tell them, but she was in no state to answer questions.

Gristhorpe and Susan Gay left first. Then, after leaving instructions for the scene-of-crime team to search the house thoroughly for any signs of blood-stained clothing, Banks returned to the rugby club to see if Sandra was still there. Snow swirled in front of his headlights and the road was slippery.

When Banks pulled up outside the rugby club in the northern part of Eastvale it was almost eleven o'clock. The lights were still on. In the foyer, he kicked the clinging snow off his shoes, brushed it from his hair and the shoulders of his camel-hair overcoat, which he hung up on the rack provided, and went inside.

He stood in the doorway and looked around the softly lit banquet hall. Hatchley and Carol had finally left, but plenty of others remained, still holding drinks. The DJ had taken a break and someone sat at the piano playing Christmas carols. Banks saw Sandra and Richmond sitting on their stools at the bar. He stood and watched them sing for a few moments. It was a curiously intimate feeling, like watching someone sleep. And like sleepers, their faces wore innocent, tranquil expressions as their lips mouthed the familiar words:

> *Silent night, holy night*
> *All is calm, all is bright*

2

ONE

'What have we got so far?' Gristhorpe asked at eight o'clock the following morning. As Banks knew from experience, the superintendent liked to call regular conferences in the early stages of an investigation. Although he had been at the scene the previous evening, he would now leave the fieldwork to his team and concentrate on co-ordinating their tasks and dealing with the press. Gristhorpe, unlike some supers Banks had worked with, believed in letting his men get on with the job while he handled matters of politics and policy.

In the conference room, the four of them – Gristhorpe, Banks, Richmond and Susan Gay – reviewed the events of the previous evening. Nothing had come in yet from forensics or from Dr Glendenning who was just about to start the post-mortem. The only new information they had obtained had resulted from the house-to-house enquiry. Three people had been visiting number eleven Oakwood Mews separately that evening. Nobody could describe them clearly – after all, it had been dark and snowing, and the street was not well lit – but two independent witnesses seemed to agree that one man and two women had called there.

The man had called first, around seven o'clock, and Caroline had admitted him to the house. Nobody had seen him leave. Not very long after, a woman had arrived, talked briefly to Caroline on the doorstep, then left without entering the house. One witness said she thought it might have been someone collecting for charity, what with it being Christmas and all, but then a collector wouldn't have missed the opportunity of knocking on everyone else's door as well, would she? And no, there had been no obvious signs of a quarrel.

The final visitor – according to the sightings – called shortly after the other woman left and went inside the house. Nobody had noticed her leave. That, as far as they could pin down, was the last time Caroline Hartley had been seen alive by anyone but her killer. Other visitors may have called between about half past seven and eight, but nobody had seen them. Everybody had been watching *Coronation Street*.

'Any ideas about the record?' Gristhorpe asked.

'I think it might be important,' Banks said, 'but I don't know why. According to Veronica Shildon, it wasn't hers, and the Hartley girl didn't like classical music.'

'So where did it come from?' Susan Gay asked.

'Tolliver said that one of the witnesses thought the man who called was carrying a shopping bag of some sort. It could have been in there – a present, say. That would explain the wrapping paper we found.'

'But why would anyone bring a woman a present of something she didn't like?'

Banks shrugged. 'Could be any number of reasons. Maybe it was someone who didn't know her tastes well. Or it might have been intended for Veronica Shildon. All I'm saying is that it's odd and I think we ought to check it out. It's also strange that someone should put it on the turntable and deliberately leave it to repeat *ad infinitum*.

We can be reasonably certain that Caroline wouldn't have played it, so who did, and why? We might even be dealing with a psycho. The music could be his calling card.'

'All right,' Gristhorpe said after a short silence. 'Susan, why don't you get down to Pristine Records and see if they know anything about it.'

Susan made a note in her book and nodded.

'Alan, you and Detective Sergeant Richmond here can see what you can get out of Veronica Shildon.' He paused. 'What do you make of their relationship?'

Banks scratched the little scar by the side of his right eye. 'They were living together. And sleeping together, as far as I could tell. Nobody's spelled it out yet, but I'd say it's pretty obvious. Christine Cooper implied much the same.'

'Could that give us an angle?' Gristhorpe suggested. 'I don't know much about lesbian relationships, but anything off the beaten track could be worth looking into.'

'A jealous lover, something like that?' Banks said.

Gristhorpe shrugged. 'You tell me. I just think it's worth a bit of scrutiny.'

The meeting broke up and they went their separate ways, but not before Sergeant Rowe came up to them in the corridor with a form in his hand.

'There's been a break-in at the community centre,' he said, waving the sheet. 'Any takers?'

'Not another!' Banks groaned. It was the third in two months. Vandalism was becoming as much of a problem in Eastvale as it seemed to be everywhere else in the country.

'Aye,' said Rowe. 'Dustbin men noticed the back door broken open when they picked up the rubbish half an hour ago. I've already notified the people involved with that amateur dramatic society. They're the only ones using the place at the moment – except for your wife, sir.'

Rowe was referring to Sandra's new part-time job managing Eastvale's new gallery, where she arranged exhibitions of local art, sculpture and photography. The Eastvale Arts Committee had applied as usual for its grant, fully expecting significant cuts, if not an outright refusal. But that year, whether due to some bureaucratic blunder or a generous fiscal whim, they had been given twice what they had asked for and found themselves looking for ways to spend the money before someone asked for it back. The cheque didn't bounce; months passed and they received no letter beginning, 'Due to a clerical oversight, we are afraid . . .' So the large upstairs room in the community centre was set aside and redecorated for gallery space.

'Any damage upstairs?' Banks asked.

'We don't know yet, sir.'

'Where's the caretaker?'

'On holiday, sir. Gone to the in-laws in Oldham for Christmas.'

'All right, we'll take care of it. Susan, drop by there before you go to the record shop and see what's going on. It shouldn't take too long.'

Susan Gay nodded and set off.

Banks and Richmond turned down by the side of the police station towards King Street. The snow had stopped early in the morning, leaving a covering about six inches thick, but the sky was still overcast, heavy with more. The air was chill and damp. On the main streets cars and pedestrians had already churned the snow into brownish-grey slush, but in those narrow, winding alleys between Market Street and King Street it remained almost untouched except for the odd set of footprints and the patches that shopkeepers had shovelled away from the pavement in front of their doors.

This was the real tourist Eastvale. Here, the antique dealers hung up their signs and antiquarian booksellers advertised their wares alongside numismatists and bespoke tailors. These weren't like the cheap souvenir shops on York Road; they were specialty shops with creaking floors and thick, mullioned windows, where unctuous, immaculately dressed shopkeepers called you 'sir' or 'madam'.

Oakwood Mews was a short cul-de-sac, a renovated terrace with only ten houses on each side. Black-leaded iron railings separated each small garden from the pavement. In summer, the street blossomed in a profusion of colours, with many houses sporting bright hanging and window boxes. It had even won a 'prettiest street in Yorkshire' prize several years ago, and the plaque to prove it was affixed to the wall of the first house. Now, as Banks and Richmond approached number nine, the street looked positively Victorian. Banks almost expected Tiny Tim to come running up to them and throw his crutches away.

Banks knocked on the Coopers' door. It was made of light, panelled wood, and the shiny knocker was a highly polished brass lion's head. A wealthy little street this, obviously, Banks thought, even if it was only a terrace block of small houses. They were brick built, pre-war, and had recently been restored to perfection.

Christine Cooper answered the door in her dressing gown and invited them in. Unlike the more cosy, feminine elegance of number eleven, the Cooper place was almost entirely modern in decor: assemble-it-yourself Scandinavian furniture and off-white walls. The kitchen, into which she led them, boasted plenty of shelf- and surface-space and every gadget under the sun, from microwave to electric tin opener.

'Coffee?'

Banks and Richmond both nodded and sat down at the large pine breakfast table. It had been set close to a corner to save space, and someone had fixed bench seating to the two adjacent walls. Both Banks and Richmond sat on the bench with their backs to the wall. Banks had no trouble fitting himself in, as he was only a little taller than regulation 172 centimetres; but Richmond had to shift about to accommodate his long legs.

Mrs Cooper faced them from a matching chair across the table. The electric coffee-maker was already gurgling away, and they had to wait only a few moments for their drinks.

'I'm afraid Veronica isn't up, yet,' Mrs Cooper said. 'Your doctor gave her a sleeping pill and she was out like a light as soon as we got her into bed. I explained everything to Charles. He's been very understanding.'

'Where is your husband?' Banks asked.

'At work.'

'What time did he get home last night?'

'It must have been after eleven. We sat up and talked about . . . you know . . . for a while, then we went to bed about midnight.'

'He certainly works long hours.'

Mrs Cooper sighed. 'Yes, especially at this time of year. You see, he runs a chain of children's shops in North Yorkshire, and he's constantly being called from one crisis to another. One place runs out of whatever new doll all the kids want this year and another out of jigsaw puzzles. I'm sure you can imagine the problems.'

'Where was he yesterday evening?'

Mrs Cooper seemed surprised at the question, but she answered after only a slight hesitation. 'Barnard Castle. Apparently the manager of the shop there reported some stock discrepancies.'

There was probably nothing in it, Banks thought, but Charles Cooper's alibi should be easy enough to check.

'Maybe you can give us a bit more background on Caroline Hartley while we're waiting for Mrs Shildon,' he said.

Richmond took out his notebook and settled back in the corner seat.

Mrs Cooper rubbed her chin. 'I don't know if I can tell you much about Caroline, really. I knew her, but I didn't feel I *really* knew her, if you know what I mean. It was all on the surface. She was a real sparkler, I'll say that for her. Always full of beans. Always a smile and a hello for everyone. Talented, too, from what I could gather.'

'Talented? How?'

'She was an actress. Oh, just amateur like, but if you ask me, she'd got what it takes. She could take anybody off. You should have seen her impression of Maggie Thatcher. Talk about laugh!'

'Was this theatrical work local?'

'Oh, yes. Only the Eastvale Amateur Dramatic Society.'

'Was this her first experience with theatre?'

'I wouldn't know that. It was only a small part, but she was excited about it.'

'Where does she come from?'

'Do you know, I can't say. I know nothing about her past. She could be from Timbuktu for all I know. As I said before, we weren't *really* close.'

'Do you know if she had any enemies? Did she ever tell you about any quarrels she might have had?'

Mrs Cooper shook her head, then blushed.

'What is it?' Banks asked.

'Well,' Mrs Cooper began, 'it's nothing really, I don't suppose, and I don't want to go getting anybody into trouble, but when two women live together like . . . like they did, then somebody somewhere's got to be unhappy, haven't they?'

'What do you mean?'

'Veronica's ex-husband. She was a married woman before she came here. I shouldn't think he'd be very happy about things, would he? And I'll bet there was someone in Caroline's life, too – a woman or a man. She didn't seem the kind to be on her own for too long, if you know what I mean.'

'Do you know anything about Veronica Shildon's ex-husband?'

'Only that they sold the big house they used to have outside town and split the money. She bought this place and he moved off somewhere. The coast, I think. The whole thing seemed very hush-hush to me. She's never even told me his name.'

'The Yorkshire coast?'

'Yes, I think so. But Veronica can tell you all about him.'

'You didn't see him in the neighbourhood yesterday evening, did you?'

Mrs Cooper pulled her robe together at the front, looking down and making a double chin as she did so. 'No. I told you all I saw or heard last night. Besides, I wouldn't recognize him from Adam. I've never seen him.'

Banks heard stairs creak and looked around to see Veronica Shildon standing in the doorway. She was dressed as she had been the previous evening – tight jeans, which flattered her slim, curved hips, trim waist and flat stomach, and a high-necked, chunky-knit green sweater, which brought out the colour in her eyes. She was tall, about five foot ten, and poised. Banks thought there was something odd about seeing her in such casual wear; she looked as if she belonged in a pearl silk blouse and a navy business suit. She had taken the time to brush her short hair and put a little make-up on, but her face still looked drawn underneath it all, and her eyes, disarmingly honest and naked, were still red from crying.

Banks tried to stand up, but he was too closely wedged in by the table.

'I'm sorry to bother you so soon,' he said, 'but the quicker we get moving the more chance we have.'

'I understand,' she said. 'Please don't worry about me. I'll be all right.'

She swayed a little as she walked towards the table. Mrs Cooper took her elbow and guided her to a chair, then brought her some coffee and disappeared, muttering something about things to attend to.

'In cases like this,' Banks began, 'it helps if we know what the person was doing, where she was, previous to the incident.' He knew he sounded trite, but somehow he couldn't bring himself to say 'victim' and 'murder'.

Veronica nodded. 'Of course. As far as I know Caroline went to work, but you'll have to check that. She runs the Garden Café on Castle Hill Road.'

'I know it,' Banks said. It was an elegant little place, very up-market, with a stunning view of the formal gardens and the river.

'She usually finishes at three on a weekday, after the lunchtime crowd. They don't open for tea off-season. On a normal day she'd come home, do some shopping, or perhaps drop by at the shop for a while to help out.'

'Shop?'

'I own a flower shop – or rather my partner and I do. It's mostly a matter of his money and my management. It's just round the corner from here, down King Street.'

'You said on a "normal" day. Was yesterday not normal?'

She looked straight at him and her eyes let him know that his choice of words had been inappropriate. Yesterday, indeed, had not been normal. But she simply said, 'No. Yesterday after work they had a rehearsal. They're doing *Twelfth Night* at the community centre. It's quite a heavy rehearsal schedule as the director's set on actually opening on twelfth night.'

'What time did rehearsals run?'

'Usually between four and six, so she would have been home at about quarter past six, if she'd come home immediately.'

'And was she likely to?'

'They often went for a drink after, but yesterday she came straight home.'

'How do you know?'

'I phoned to see if she was there and to tell her I'd be a bit late because I was doing some shopping.'

'What time?'

'About seven.'

'How did she sound?'

'Fine . . . she sounded fine.'

'Was there any special reason for her not going for a drink with the others yesterday?'

'No. She just said she was tired after rehearsal and she . . .'

'Yes?'

'We've both been so busy lately. She wanted to spend some time with me . . . a quiet evening at home.'

'Where had you been that evening?'

Veronica didn't show a flicker of resentment at being asked for an alibi. 'I closed the shop at five thirty, then I went for my six o'clock appointment with Dr Ursula Kelly, my therapist. She's Caroline's too. Her office is on Kilnsey Street, just off Castle Hill. I walked. We do have a car but we don't use it much in town, mostly just for trips away.' She blew on her coffee and took a sip. 'The session lasted an hour. After that, I went to the shopping centre to buy a few things. Christmas presents mostly.' She faltered a little. 'Then I walked home. I . . . I got here about eight o'clock.'

No doubt it would be possible to check her alibi in the shopping centre, Banks thought. Some shopkeepers might remember her. But it was a busy time of year for them, and he doubted that any would be able to recollect what day and what time they had last seen her. He could examine the receipts, too. Sometimes the modern electronic cash registers gave the time of purchase as well as the date.

'Can you tell me exactly what happened, what you did, from the moment you left the shops and walked home last night?'

Veronica took a deep breath and closed her eyes. 'I walked home,' she began, 'in the snow. It was a beautiful evening. I stopped and listened to the carol singers in the market square for a while. They were singing "O, Little Town of Bethlehem". It's always been one of my favourites. When I got home I . . . I called out hello to Caroline, but she didn't answer. I thought nothing of it. She could have been in the kitchen. And then there was the music . . . well, that was odd. So I took the opportunity and crept upstairs to hide the presents in the wardrobe. Some were for her, you see, the . . .' She paused, and Banks noticed her eyes fill with tears. 'It seemed so important just to put them out of sight,' she went on. 'I knew there would be plenty of opportunity to wrap them later. While I was up there, I washed and changed and went back downstairs.

'The music was still playing. I opened the door to the living room and . . . I . . . at first I thought she was wearing the new scarlet camisole. She looked so serene and so beautiful lying there like that. But it couldn't be. I told you last night, I hadn't give it to her then. I'd just bought her the camisole for Christmas and I'd put it in the bottom of the wardrobe with everything else. Then I went closer and . . . the smell . . . her eyes . . . Veronica put her mug down and held her head in her hands.

Banks let the silence stretch for a good minute or two. All they could hear was the soft ticking of Mrs Cooper's kitchen wall clock and a dog barking in the distance.

'I understand you were married,' Banks said, when Veronica had wiped her eyes and reached out for her coffee again.

'I still am, officially. We're only separated, not divorced. He didn't want our personal life splashed all over the newspapers. As you may have gathered, Caroline and I lived together.'

Banks nodded. 'Why should the newspapers have been interested? People get divorced all the time for all kinds of reasons.'

Veronica hesitated and turned her mug slowly in a circle on the table. She wouldn't meet his eyes.

'Look,' Banks said, 'I hardly need remind you what's

happened, how serious this is. We'll find out anyway. You can save us a lot of time and trouble.'

Veronica looked up at him. 'You're right, of course,' she said. 'Though I don't see how it can have anything to do with all this. My husband was – is, Claude Ivers. He's not exactly a household name, but enough people have heard of him.'

Banks certainly had. Ivers had once been a brilliant concert pianist, but several years ago he had given up performance for composition. He had received important commissions from the BBC, and a number of his pieces had been recorded. Banks even had a tape of his, two wind quintets; they possessed a kind of eerie, natural beauty – not structured, but wandering, like the breeze in a deep forest at night. Veronica Shildon was right. If the press had got hold of the story she would have had no peace for weeks. *News of the World* reporters would have been climbing the drainpipes and spying in bedroom windows, talking to spiteful neighbours and slighted lovers. He could just see the headlines: HIGHBROW MUSICIAN'S WIFE IN LESBIAN LOVENEST.

'Where is your husband now?' Banks asked.

'He lives in Redburn, out on the coast. He said the seclusion and the sea would be good for his work. He always did care about his work.'

Banks noticed the bitterness in her tone. 'Do you ever see one another?'

'Yes,' she said. A smile touched her thin lips. 'It was an acrimonious parting in many ways, but there *is* some affection left. We don't seem able to stamp that out, whatever we do.'

'When did you last see him?'

'About a month ago. We occasionally have dinner if

he's in town. I rarely visit the coast, but he comes here from time to time.'

'To the house?'

'He's been here, yes, though he's always worried someone will see him and know who he is. I try to tell him that people don't actually recognize composers in the street any more than they do writers, that it's only television and film stars have to put up with that, but . . .' She shrugged.

'Did he know Caroline?'

'He could hardly *help* knowing her, could he? They'd met a few times.'

'How did they get on?'

Veronica shrugged. 'They never seemed to have much to say to one another. They were different as chalk and cheese. He thought she was a scheming slut and she thought he was a selfish, pompous ass. They had nothing in common but affection for me.'

'Was there any open antagonism?'

'Open? Good Lord no. That isn't Claude's way. He sniped from time to time, made sarcastic comments, cruel remarks, that kind of thing.'

'Directed towards Caroline?'

'Directed towards both of us. But I'm sure he blamed Caroline for leading me astray. That's how he saw it.'

'Was it that way?'

Veronica shook her head.

'Was Caroline ever married?'

'Not that I know of.'

'Was she living with anyone before she met you?'

Veronica paused and gripped her coffee mug in both hands as if to warm them. Her fingers were long and tapered and she had freckles on the backs of her hands. She wore a silver ring on the middle finger of her right hand. As she spoke, she looked down at the table. 'She was living with a woman called Nancy Wood. They'd been together about eight months. The relationship was going very badly.'

'Where does Nancy Wood live?'

'In Eastvale. Not too far from here. At least, she did the last I heard.'

'Did Caroline ever see her after they split up?'

'Only by accident once or twice in the street.'

'So they parted on bad terms?'

'Doesn't everyone? Much as I admire Shakespeare, I've often wondered where the sweetness is in the sorrow.'

'And before Nancy Wood?'

'She spent some time in London. I don't know how long or who with. A few years, at least.'

'What about her family?'

'Her mother's dead. Her father lives in Harrogate. He's an invalid – been one for years. Her brother Gary looks after him. I told one of your uniformed men last night. Will someone have called?'

Banks nodded. 'Don't worry, the Harrogate police will have taken care of it. Is there anything else you can tell me about Caroline's friends or enemies?'

Veronica sighed and shook her head. She looked exhausted. 'No,' she said. 'We didn't have a lot of close friends. I suppose we tried to be too much to one another. At least that's how it feels now she's gone. You could try the people at the theatre. They were her acquaintances, at least. But we didn't socialize very much together. I don't think any of them even knew about her living with me.'

'We're still puzzled about the record,' Banks said. 'Are you sure it isn't yours?'

'I've told you, no.'

'But you recognized the singer?'

'Magda Kalmár, yes. Claude and I once saw her in *Lucia di Lammermoor* at the Budapest Opera. I was very impressed.'

'Could the record have been intended as a Christmas present from your husband?'

'Well, I suppose it could . . . but that means . . . no, I haven't seen him in a month.'

'He could have called last night, while you were out.'

She shook her head. 'No. I don't believe it. Not Claude.'

Banks looked over at Richmond and nodded. Richmond closed his notebook. 'That's all for now,' Banks said.

'Can I go home?' she asked him.

'If you want.' Banks hadn't imagined she would want to return to the house so soon, but there was no official objection. Forensics had finished with the place.

'Just one thing, though,' he said. 'We'll need to have another good look through Caroline's belongings. Perhaps Detective Sergeant Richmond can accompany you back and look over them now?'

She looked apprehensive at first, then nodded. 'All right.'

They stood up to leave. Christine Cooper was nowhere in sight, so they walked out into the damp, overcast day and shut the door behind them without saying goodbye.

Veronica opened her front door and went in. Banks lingered at the black iron gate with Richmond. 'I'm going to the community centre,' he said. 'There should be someone from the theatre group there since they've been notified of the break-in. How about we meet up at the Queen's Arms, say twelve or twelve-thirty?' And he went on to ask Richmond to check Veronica Shildon's purchases and look closely at the receipts for corroboration of her alibi. 'And check on Charles Cooper's movements yesterday,' he added. 'It might mean a trip to Barnard Castle, but see if you can come up with anything by phone first.'

Richmond went into the house and Banks set off up the steep part of King Street with his collar turned up against the cold. The community centre wasn't very far; the walk would be good exercise. As he trudged through the snow, he thought about Veronica Shildon. She presented an odd mixture of reserve and frankness, stoical acceptance and bitterness. He was sure she was holding something back, but he didn't know what it was. There was something askew about her. Even her clothes didn't seem to go with the rather repressed and inhibited essence that she projected. 'Prim and proper' was the term that sprang to mind. Yet she had left her husband, had gone and set up house with a woman.

All in all, she was an enigma. If anything, Banks thought, she seemed like a woman in the process of great change. Her reference to the analyst indicated that she was at least concerned with self-examination.

It seemed to Banks as if her entire personality had been dismantled and the various bits and pieces didn't quite fit together; some were new, or newly discovered, and others were old, rusted, decrepit, and she wasn't sure whether she wanted to discard them or not. Banks had an inkling of what the process felt like from his own readjustment after the move from London. But Veronica's changes, he suspected, went far deeper. He wondered what she had been like as a wife, and what she would become in the future now that Caroline Hartley had been so viciously excised from her life. For the younger woman had had a great influence on Veronica's life; Banks was certain of that. Was Veronica a killer? He didn't think so, but who could say anything so definite about a personality in such turmoil and transition?

TWO

On her way to the community centre, DC Susan Gay thought over her behaviour of the previous day and found it distinctly lacking. She had felt even more miserable than usual when she went home from Oakwood Mews that night. Her small flat off York Road always depressed her. It was so barren, like a hotel room, so devoid of any real stamp of her presence, and she knew that was because she hardly spent any time there. Mostly she had been working or off on a course somewhere. For years she had paid no attention to her surroundings or to her personal life. The flat was for eating in, sleeping in and, occasionally, for watching half an hour of television.

It seemed like a lifetime since she'd last had a boy-friend, or anyone more than a casual date, anyone who *meant* something to her. She accepted that she wasn't especially attractive, but she was no ugly sister, either. People had asked her out; the problem was that she always had something more important to do, something related to her career. She was beginning to wonder if the normal sexual impulse had somehow drained away over the years of toil. That incident with the rugby player last night, for example. She knew she shouldn't have responded with such obvious revulsion. He was only being friendly, even if he was a bit rough about it. And wasn't that what mistletoe was for? But she had to overreact.

Banks and Gristhorpe had both noticed, she was certain. She wondered what they must think of her.

Damn! The front doors of the community centre, a Victorian sandstone building on North Market Street, were still locked. That meant Susan would have to double back to the narrow street behind the church. Shivering, she hunched up against the cold and turned around.

It seemed now that the whole of yesterday evening had been a nightmare. First she had run off half-cocked out of the station at the first sign of trouble, without even bothering to check if the call was genuine or not. Then she had gone straight to Banks. She had seen Gristhorpe by the bar, of course, but she hadn't approached him because she was terrified of him. She knew he was said to be a softie, really, but she couldn't help herself. He seemed so self-contained, so sure of himself, so *solid*, just like her father.

The only thing she was proud of was her reaction at the scene. She hadn't fainted, even though it was her first corpse, and a messy one at that. She had managed to maintain a detached, clinical view of the whole affair, watching the experts at work, getting the feel of the scene. There had been only one awkward moment, as the body was being carried away, but anyone could be forgiven for paling a bit at that. No, her behaviour at the scene had been exemplary. She hoped Banks and Gristhorpe had noticed that, and not only her faults.

And now she was on her way to investigate a case of vandalism while the others got to work on the murder. It wasn't fair. She realized she was the new member of the team, but that didn't mean she always had to be the one to handle the petty crimes. How could she get ahead if she didn't get to work on important cases? She had already sacrificed so much for her career that she couldn't bear to contemplate failure.

Finally, she got to the back entrance, down an alley off the northern part of York Road. The back door had obviously been jemmied open. Its meagre lock was bent and the wood around the jamb had cracked. Susan walked down the long corridor, lit only by a couple of bare sixty-watt bulbs, to where she could hear voices. They came from a room off to her right, a high-ceilinged place with exposed pipes, bare brick walls pied with saltpetre, and more dim lighting. The room smelled of dust and moth-balls. There she found a man and a woman bent over a large trunk. They stood up as she walked in.

'Police?' the man asked.

Susan nodded and showed her new CID identification card.

'I must admit, I didn't expect a woman,' he said.

Susan prepared to say something withering, but he held up a hand. 'Don't get me wrong, I'm not complaining. I'm not a sexist pig. It's just a surprise.' He peered at her in the poor light. 'Wait a minute, aren't you . . . ?'

'Susan Gay,' she said, recognizing him now that her eyes had adjusted to the light. 'And you're Mr Conran.' She blushed. 'I'm surprised you remember me. I was hardly one of your best students.'

Mr Conran hadn't changed much in the ten years since he had taught the sixteen-year-old Susan drama at Eastvale Comprehensive. About ten years older than her, he was still handsome in an artsy kind of way, in baggy black cords and a dark polo-neck sweater with the stitching coming away at the shoulder seam. He still had that vulnerable, skinny, half-starved look that Susan remembered so well, but despite it he looked healthy enough. His short fair hair was combed forward, flat against his skull; beneath it, intelligent and ironic grey eyes looked out from a pale, hollow-cheeked face. Susan had hated drama, but she had had a crush on Mr Conran. The other girls said he was a queer, but they said that about everyone in the literature and arts departments. Susan hadn't believed them.

'James,' he said, stretching his hand out to shake hers. 'I think we can dispense with the teacher-pupil formalities by now, don't you? I'm directing the play. And this is Marcia Cunningham. Marcia takes care of props and costumes. It's she you should talk to, really.'

As if to emphasise the point, Conran turned away and began examining the rest of the storage room.

Susan took her notebook out. 'What's the damage?' she asked Marcia, a plump, round-faced woman in grey stretch slacks and a threadbare alpaca jacket that looked at least one size too large for her.

Marcia Cunningham sniffed and pointed to the wall. 'There's that, for a start.' Crudely spray-painted across the bricks were the words FUCKING WANKERS. 'But that'll wash off easy enough,' she went on. 'This is the worst. They've shredded our costumes. I'm not sure if I can salvage any of them or not.'

Susan looked into the trunk. She agreed. It looked like someone had been to work on them with a large pair of scissors, snipping the different dresses, suits and shirts into pieces and mixing them all together.

'Why should anyone do that?' Marcia asked.

Susan shook her head.

'At least they left the shoes and wigs alone,' she said, gesturing towards the other two boxes of costumes.

'Has anyone checked upstairs?' Susan asked.

Marcia looked surprised. 'The gallery? No.'

Susan made her way down the corridor to the stairs,

cold stone with metal railings. There were several rooms upstairs, some of them used for various groups such as the Philately Society or the Chess Club, others for local committee meetings. All of them were locked. The glass doors to the new gallery were locked too; no damage had been done there. She went back down to the props room and watched Marcia picking up strands of slashed material and moaning.

'All that work, all those people who gave us stuff. Why do they do this?' Marcia asked again. 'What bloody point is there?'

Susan knew numerous theories of hooliganism, from poor potty training to the heartlessness of modern England, but all she said was, 'I don't know.' People don't want to hear theories when something they value has been destroyed. 'And short of catching them red-handed, we can't promise much, either.'

'But this is the *third* time!' Marcia said. 'Surely by now you must have some kind of lead?'

'There are a few people we're keeping our eye on,' Susan told her, 'but it's not as if they've stolen anything.'

'Even that would be more understandable.'

'What I mean is, we'd find no evidence even if we suspected someone. There's no stolen property to trace them. Have you thought of employing a night watchman?'

Marcia snorted. 'A night watchman? How do you think we can afford that? I know we got a bonanza grant this year, but we didn't get that much. And most of it's gone already on costumes and stuff.'

'I'm sorry,' Susan said. She realized this was an inadequate response, but what else was there to say? A constable walked the beat, but he couldn't spend his whole night in the alley at the back of the community centre. There had been other break-ins, too, and other incidents of vandalism. 'I'll make out a report,' she said, 'and let you know if we come up with anything.'

'Thanks a lot.'

'Don't be so rude, Marcia.' James Conran reappeared and put his hand on Marcia's shoulder. 'She's only trying to help.' He smiled at Susan. 'Aren't you?'

Susan nodded. His smile was so infectious she could hardly keep from responding, and the effort to maintain a detached expression made her flush.

Marcia rubbed her face until her plump cheeks shone. 'I'm sorry, love,' she said. 'I know it's not your fault. It's just so bloody frustrating.'

'I know.' Susan put her notebook back in her handbag. 'I'll be in touch,' she said.

Before she could turn to leave, they heard footsteps coming along the corridor. Conran looked surprised. 'There's nobody else supposed to be coming here, is there?' he asked Marcia, who shook her head. Then the door creaked open and Susan saw a familiar face peep around. It was Chief Inspector Banks. At first she was relieved to see him. Then she thought, why the hell is he here? Checking up on me? Can't he trust me to do a simple job properly?

THREE

Detective Sergeant Philip Richmond was glad that Veronica Shildon had not wanted to stand over him as he searched the two upper rooms. He never could tolerate the feel of someone looking over his shoulder. Which was one of the reasons he liked working with Banks, who usually left him to get on with the job his own way.

The bedroom smelled of expensive cologne or talcum. As he looked at the large bed with its satiny coral spread, he thought of the two women in there together and the things they did to each other. The images embarrassed him and he got back to work.

Richmond took the bag of presents out of Veronica's half of the wardrobe and spread them on the bed: a Sheaffer fountain pen and pencil set, a green silk scarf, some Body Shop soaps and shampoos, a scarlet camisole, the latest Booker Prize winner . . . all pretty ordinary stuff. The receipts were dated but none of them gave the time the purchase had been made. Richmond made a list of items and shops so the staff could be questioned.

The dresser drawers contained mostly lingerie. Richmond picked his way through it methodically, but found nothing hidden away, nothing that shouldn't be there. He moved on to the study.

In addition to the books – none of them inscribed – there was also a roll-top desk in the corner under the window. There was nothing surprising in it: letters to Veronica Shildon, some from her husband, about practical and financial matters; a few bills; Veronica's address book, mostly empty; a house insurance policy; receipts and guarantees for the oven, the fridge and items of furniture, and that was about all. None of it any use to Richmond.

Just when he was beginning to wonder whether Caroline Hartley had had any possessions at all, he came across a manila envelope with 'Caroline' written on the front. Inside were a pressed flower, her birth certificate (which showed she had been born in Harrogate twenty-six years ago), an expired passport with no stamps or visas, and a black and white photograph of a woman he didn't recognize. She had piercing, intelligent eyes, and her head was slightly tilted to one side. Her medium-length hair was swept back, revealing a straight hairline and ears with tiny lobes. Her lips were pressed tight together, and there was something about the arrogant intensity of her presence that Richmond found disturbing. He wouldn't have described her as beautiful, but striking, certainly. Across the bottom were the words 'To Carrie, Love Ruth', written with a flourish.

Making sure he hadn't missed anything, Richmond went back downstairs, taking the envelope of Caroline's possessions with him. Veronica Shildon turned on the small electric fire in the front room when he entered.

'I'm sorry,' she said, 'I can't be bothered to light a real fire now. We use this most of the time anyway. It seems to be warm enough. Some tea?'

'Yes, please, if it's no trouble.'

'It's already made.'

Richmond sat down, avoiding the cushionless sofa in favour of an armchair. After Veronica had poured, he held out the photograph to her. 'Who's this woman?' he asked. 'Can you tell me anything about her?'

Veronica glanced at the photograph and shook her head. 'It's just someone Caroline used to know in London.'

'Surely she must have told you something about her.'

'Caroline didn't like to talk about her past very much.'

'Why not?'

'I don't know. Perhaps it was painful for her.'

'In what way?'

'I told you. I don't know. I've seen the picture before, yes, but I don't know who it is or where you can find her.'

'Is it an old girlfriend?' Richmond felt embarrassed as he asked the question.

'I should think so, wouldn't you?' Veronica said evenly.

'Mind if I take it with me?'

'Not at all.'

'Caroline didn't seem much of a one for possessions,' Richmond mused. 'There's hardly anything of hers but clothes. No letters, nothing.'

'She liked to travel light, and she had no sentimental regard for the past. Caroline always looked ahead.'

It was a simple statement, but Richmond heard the irony in Veronica Shildon's voice.

She shrugged. 'A few of the books are hers. Some of the jewellery. All the non-classical records. But she didn't go in much for keepsakes.'

Richmond tapped the photograph. 'Which makes it all the more odd she should have hung on to this. Thank you, Ms Shildon. I'd better be off now.'

'Aren't you going to finish your tea?'

'Best not,' he said. 'I'll have to get back to work or my boss'll skin me alive. Thanks very much anyway.' Richmond could sense her unease. She looked around the room before glancing at him again and nodding.

'All right, if you must.'

'Will you be all right?' he asked. 'You could always go back to Mrs Cooper's, if you feel—'

'I'll be all right,' she said. 'I'm still in a bit of a daze. I can't believe it's really happened.'

'Is there no one you can go to, until you're feeling better?'

'There's my therapist. She says I can call her any time, day or night. I might do that. We'll see. But do you know the oddest thing?'

Richmond shook his head.

She folded her arms and nodded towards the room in general. 'I can take all this. The room where it happened. I didn't think I'd be able to bear it after last night, but it doesn't bother me in the slightest to be here. It just feels empty. Isn't that strange? It's the loneliness, Caroline's absence, that hurts. I keep expecting her to walk in at any moment.'

Richmond, who could think of no reply, said goodbye and walked out into the snow. He still had about an hour before his lunchtime meeting with Banks in the Queen's Arms. He could use that time to check on Charles Cooper's movements the previous evening and perhaps see if he could find out anything about the mysterious Ruth.

3

ONE

The gears screeched as Susan Gay slowed to turn onto the Harrogate road. Luckily, the snow hadn't been so heavy south of Eastvale. It lay piled up against the hedgerows, but the roads had been cleared and the temperature hadn't dropped low enough to make the surface icy. She was out of the Dales now, in the gently rolling country south of Ripon. Nothing but the occasional stretch of stone wall, or a distant hamlet, showed through the thin white veil of snow.

She still felt angry at herself for being so damn jumpy. Banks had only dropped by the community centre to break the news of Caroline Hartley's death and to discover what time she had left the rehearsal the previous evening. But Susan hadn't known anything about Caroline's part in the play, so how could she help assuming that Banks was checking up on her? Anyway, she had kept quiet and matters had soon become clear to her.

When Banks had gone, she'd walked to Pristine Records in the shopping centre by the bus station. The girl with the white-face make-up and hair like pink champagne pointed out the small classical section and, when pushed, leafed idly through the stock cards. No, they hadn't sold a copy of *Lousy whatsit* lately; they hadn't even had a copy in. Ever. Using her own initiative, Susan also checked Boots and W. H. Smiths, both of which had small record departments, but she had no luck there either. The record was imported from Hungary, and whoever had bought it hadn't done so in Eastvale.

Over lunch at the Queen's Arms, information had been pooled and tasks assigned by Superintendent Gristhorpe. According to Banks, Caroline had left the Garden Café just after three o'clock, as usual, probably done a bit of shopping, then attended rehearsal at four. James Conran said they had finished at ten to six and everyone had left by five to. He himself had been the last to leave. He had gone out the back way, as usual, locked up and strolled over to the Crooked Billet on North York Road for a couple of drinks. In the caretaker's absence, he and Marcia Cunningham were the only ones in the drama group to have keys to the centre, although an extra set had been lodged at the police station in case of emergencies. Members of the other societies housed in the centre also had keys, including Sandra Banks.

Presumably, Caroline had gone straight home, because a neighbour across the street told one of the constables that she had seen Miss Hartley enter the house. It had happened at the same time the neighbour had gone over to her window to close a chink in the curtains during the commercial break in *Calendar*, which would have been about six fifteen.

Richmond had not been able to find out much about Charles Cooper's movements. The clerk who had been at the Barnard Castle shop on the evening in question had the day off today. He planned to visit Barnard Castle and ask around some more after he had talked to Veronica Shildon's therapist and made a start on tracking down Ruth. Banks was off to visit Claude Ivers, Veronica's estranged husband, and Susan herself had drawn the job of talking to Caroline's family in Harrogate. In addition to keeping tabs on the break-in, she was still on the murder team. Thank God the Harrogate police had at least broken the news of Caroline's death. That was one distasteful task she had been spared.

She drove up Ripon Road by the huge Victorian hotels – the Cairn, the Majestic, the St George – dark stone mansions set back behind vast walled lawns and croquet greens. As she kept an eye on the road, Susan found herself hoping that the Hartley case wouldn't be solved by Christmas. That way she could legitimately beg off visiting her parents in Sheffield. Home visits were always tense. Susan found herself regaled with stories about her brother the stockbroker and her sister the lawyer. Of course, neither of them could ever make it home for Christmas; her brother lived in London and her sister in Vancouver. But she had to hear all about them, nonetheless. And whatever Susan herself achieved was always belittled by her siblings' success stories, pieced together from occasional letters and the odd newspaper clipping, and by her parents' disapproval of the course she had chosen. She could make chief constable and they would still look down on her. With a bit of luck, Caroline Hartley's murder would keep her busy well into the new year. Susan had a feeling they might be dealing with a nutter – the violence of the wounds and the music left playing seemed to point that way – and nutters, she remembered from her training, were always difficult to catch.

The town of Harrogate soon banished thoughts of psychopaths. All formal gardens and elegant Victorian buildings, it was a spa town, like Bath, a place people retired to or visited to attend business conventions. Ripon

Road became Parliament as she drove past the Royal Baths and Betty's Tea Room, then its name changed again to West Park. She turned left onto York Place, the road that ran by the Stray, a broad expanse of parkland in the town centre renowned for its vibrant flower displays in spring. Now it looked cool and serene under its layer of snow.

The Hartleys lived in a large house off Wetherby Road on the southern outskirts of the town. From the outside, it looked like something out of Edgar Allan Poe: the House of Usher, Susan thought, the way it appeared in that Roger Corman film that used to scare her when she was a little girl. The black stone was rough and pitted like coke, and the upper oriels seemed to stare out like bulging eyes. When Susan rang the doorbell she half expected an enormous manservant with a green complexion to answer and say 'You rang?' in a deep voice. But the boy who came to the door was far from enormous. He was in his late teens, judging by the pale, spotty face, the spiky hair and the look of dazed contempt for the world on his face, and he was as skinny as a rake.

'What is it?' he asked in an edgy, high-pitched voice. 'We don't want anything. There's been a death in the family.'

'I know,' Susan said. 'That's why I'm here.' She showed her card and he stepped back to let her in. She followed him down the gloomy hallway to a room that must once have been a study or library. The ceiling was high, with curlicues at the corners and an ornate fixture at the centre from which the chandelier had once hung. Dark wainscotting came waist high.

But the room was a mess. Much of the fine oak panelling was scratched with graffiti and pitted where darts had been thrown at it. The huge windows, framed by heavy, moth-eaten drapes, were filmed with cobwebs and grime. Magazines and newspapers lay scattered all over the threadbare carpet. Beer cans and cigarette ends littered the hearth and the old stone fireplace, and the stuffing was coming out of the huge green velvet-upholstered settee. The room was an elegant Victorian sanctuary reduced to a teenager's private wasteland.

The boy didn't ask Susan to sit down, but she found a chair that looked in reasonable condition. Before she sat, she began to undo her coat, but as she did so she realized that it was freezing in the room, as it had been in the hall. There was no heat at all. The boy didn't seem to notice or care, even though he was only wearing jeans and a torn t-shirt. He lit a cigarette and slumped on the settee. More stuffing oozed out, like foam from a madman's mouth.

'So?' he said.

'I'd like to see your father.'

The boy laughed harshly. 'You must be the first person to say that in five years. People don't usually *like* to see my father. He's a very depressing man. He makes them think of death. The grim reaper.'

The boy's thin face, only a shade less white than the snow outside, certainly made Susan think of death. He looked in urgent need of a blood transfusion. Could he really be Caroline Hartley's brother? It was hard to see a resemblance between the boy and his sister. Caroline, when she was alive, must have been a beautiful woman. Even in death she had looked more alive than her brother.

'Can I see him?'

'Be my guest.' The boy pointed towards the ceiling and flicked his ash towards the littered fireplace.

Susan walked up the broad staircase. It must have been wonderful once, with thick pile carpeting and guests in evening dress standing around sipping cocktails. But now it was just bare, creaky wood, scuffed and splintered in places, and the banister looked like someone had been cutting notches in it. There were pale squares on the walls showing where paintings had been removed.

Without a guide or directions, it took Susan three tries before she opened the right door. Her first try had led her into a bathroom, which seemed clean and modern enough; the second revealed the boy's room, where the curtains were still closed and faint light outlined messy bedsheets and last week's underwear on the floor; and the third took her into a warm, stuffy room that smelled of cough lozenges, camphor and commodes. A one-element electric fire radiated its heat close to the bed, and there, in a genuine four-poster with the curtains open, a shadow of a man lay propped up on pillows. The bags under his eyes were so dark they looked like bruises, his complexion was like old paper, and the hands that grasped the bedclothes around his chest were more like talons. His skin looked as if it would crack like parchment if you touched it. As she approached, his watery eyes darted towards her.

'Who are you?' His voice was no more than a frightened whisper.

Susan introduced herself and he seemed to relax. 'About Caroline?' he said. A faraway look came into his ruined eyes, pale yokes floating in glutinous albumen.

'Yes,' Susan said. 'Can you tell me anything about her?'

'What do you want to know?'

Susan wasn't sure. She had taken statements as a uniformed constable and studied interview techniques at police college, but it had never seemed as haphazard as this. Superintendent Gristhorpe hadn't been much help either. 'Find out what you can,' he had told her. 'Follow your nose.' Clearly it was a matter of sink or swim in the CID. She took a deep breath and wished she hadn't; the warmed-up smell of terminal illness was overpowering.

'Anything that might help us find her killer,' she said. 'Did Caroline visit you recently?'

'Sometimes,' he muttered.

'Were you close?'

He shook his head slowly. 'She ran away, you know.'

'When did she run away?'

'She was only a child and she ran away.'

Susan repeated her question and the old man stared at her. 'Pardon? When did she go? When she was sixteen. Only a child.'

'Why?'

A look of great sadness came into his eyes. 'I don't know. Her mother died, you know. I tried the best I could, but she was so hard to manage.'

'Where did she go?'

'London.'

'What did she do there?'

He shook his head. 'Then she came back. That's when she came to see me.'

'And again since?'

'Yes.'

'How often?'

'When she could. When she could get away.'

'Did she ever tell you anything about her life down in London?'

'I was so happy to see her again.'

'Do you know where she lived, who her friends were?'

'She wasn't a bad girl, not really a *bad* girl.'

'Did she write from London?'

The old man shook his head slowly on the pillow.

'But you still loved her?'

'Yes.' He was crying now, and the tears embarrassed him. 'I'm sorry . . . could you please . . .?' He pointed to a box of tissues on the bedside table and Susan passed it to him.

'She wasn't *bad*,' he repeated when he'd settled down again. 'Restless, angry. But not *bad*. I always knew she'd come back. I never stopped loving her.'

'But she never talked about her life, either in London or in Eastvale?'

'No. Perhaps to Gary. . . . I'm tired. Not a *bad* girl,' he repeated softly.

He seemed to be falling asleep. Susan had got nowhere and could think of no more questions to ask. Clearly, the old man had not jumped out of bed, hurried over to Eastvale and murdered his daughter. Maybe she would get more out of the son. At least he seemed angry and bitter enough to give something away if she pushed him hard enough. She said goodbye, though she doubted that the old man heard, and made her way back downstairs. The boy was still sprawled on the sofa, a can of lager open beside him on the floor. Despite the cold, she could still smell, underlying the smoke, a faint hint of decay, as if pieces of meat lay rotting under the floorboards.

'When did you last see your sister?' she asked.

He shrugged. 'I don't know. A week, two weeks ago? She came when she felt like it. Time doesn't have much meaning around this place.'

'But she had visited you recently?'

Gary nodded.

'What did she talk about?'

He lit a cigarette and spoke out of the corner of his mouth. 'Nothing. Just the usual.'

'What's the usual?'

'You know . . . job, house . . . relationships . . . The usual crap.'

'What's wrong with your father?'

'Cancer. He's had a couple of operations, chemo-therapy, but . . . you know.'

'How long has he been like this?'

'Five years.'

'And you look after him?'

The boy tensed forward and points of fire appeared in his pale cheeks. 'Yes. Me. All the fucking time. It's bring me this, Gary, bring me that. Go get my prescription, Gary. Gary, I need a bath. I even sit him on the fucking toilet. Yes, I take care of him.'

'Does he never leave his room?'

He sighed and settled back on the sofa. 'I told you, only to go to the bathroom. He can't manage the stairs. Besides, he doesn't want to. He's given up.'

That explained the state of the place. Susan wondered if the father knew, suspected, or even cared that his son had taken over the huge cold house to live whatever life of his own he could scrounge from the responsibilities of the sickroom. She wanted to ask him how he put up with it, but she already knew the scornful answer she would get. 'Who else is there to do it?'

Instead she asked, 'How old were you when your sister ran away?'

He seemed surprised by the change in direction and had to think for a moment. 'Eight. There's eight years between us. She'd been a bitch for years, had Caroline. The atmosphere was always tense. People were always rowing or on the verge of rows. It was a relief when she went.'

'Why?'

He turned away so she couldn't see his eyes. 'Why? I don't know. She was just like that. Full of poison. Especially towards me. Right from the start she tormented me, when I was a baby. They found her trying to drown me in my bath once. Of course they said she didn't realize what she was doing, but she did.'

'Why should she want to kill you?'

He shrugged. 'She hated me.'

'Your father says he loved her.'

He cast a scornful glance towards the ceiling and said slowly, 'Oh yes, she always was the apple of his eye, even after she took off to London to become a tramp. Caroline could do no wrong. But who was the one left looking after him?'

'Why did you say tramp? How do you know?'

'What else would she do? She didn't have any job skills, but she was sixteen. She had two tits and a cunt like any other bird her age.'

If Susan was expected to be shocked by his crudity, she was determined not to show it. 'Did you ever see her during that period?'

'Me? You must be joking. It was all right for a while till mum got sick and died. It didn't take her longer than a month or two, not five years like that miserable old bastard upstairs. I was thirteen then, when he started. Took to his bed like a fish to water and it's been the same ever since.'

'What about school?'

'I went sometimes. He sleeps most of the time, so I'm okay unless he has one of his awkward phases. I left last year. No jobs anyway.'

'But what about the health service? Don't they help?'

'They send a nurse to look in every once in a while. And

if you're going to mention a home, don't bother. I'd have him in one before you could say Jack Robinson if I could, but there's no room available unless you can pay.' He gestured around the crumbling house. 'As you can see, we can't. We've got his pension and a bit in the bank and that's it. I've even sold the bloody paintings, not that they were worth much. Thank God the bloody house is paid for. It must be worth a fortune now. I'd sell it and move somewhere cheaper if I could but the old bastard won't hear of it. Wants to die in his own bed. Sooner the better, I say.'

Susan realized that Gary was drunk. As he'd been talking he'd finished one can of lager and most of a second, and he had obviously drunk a few before she arrived.

'Did you know anything at all about Caroline's life?' she asked.

His bright eyes narrowed. 'I knew she was a fucking dyke, if that's what you mean.'

'How did you know that?'

'She told me. One of her visits.'

'But your father doesn't know?'

'No. It wouldn't make a scrap of difference if he did, though. It wouldn't change his opinion. As far as he's concerned the sun shone out of her arse and that's all there is to it.' He tossed the empty can aside and picked up another from the low, cigarette-scarred table.

'How do you feel about her death?'

Gary was silent for a moment, then he looked directly at Susan. 'I can't say I feel much at all. If you'd asked me a few years ago, I'd have said I felt glad. But now, nothing at all. I don't really care. She made my life a misery, then she left and lumbered me with the old man. I never had a chance to get out like her. And before that, she made everyone's life miserable at home. Especially mum's. Drove her to an early grave.'

'Did you talk to her much when she visited?'

'Not by choice,' he said, reaching for another cigarette. 'But sometimes she wanted to talk to me, explain things, like she was taking me into her confidence. As if I cared. It was funny, almost like she was apologizing for everything without ever quite getting round to it. Do you know what I mean? "I want you to know, Gary," she says, "how much I appreciate what you're doing for Dad. The sacrifices you're making. I'd help if I could, you know I would . . ." and all that fucking rubbish.' He imitated her voice again: ' "I want you to know, Gary, that I'm living with a woman in Eastvale and I'm happy for the first time in my life. I've really found myself at last. I know we've had problems in the past . . ." Always that "I want you to know, Gary . . ." as if I fucking cared what she did, the slut. So she's dead. I can't say I care one way or another.'

Susan didn't know whether to believe him. There was more pent-up passion and rage in his tone than she could handle, and she wasn't sure where it was coming from. All she knew was that she had to get out of this oppressive house, with its vast cold and crumbling spaces. She was beginning to feel dizzy and nauseated listening to Gary Hartley's high-pitched vitriol, which, she suspected, had as much to do with self-pity at his own weakness as anything else. Quickly, she muttered her farewell and headed for the door. As she walked down the hallway she heard an empty lager can crash against the wainscotting, followed by the screech of the top being ripped off another.

Outside, she breathed in the cold damp air and leaned

against the roof of her car. Her gaze fixed on the melting snow that dripped from the branches of a tall tree. Her hands were shaking, but not from the cold.

Before she had driven far, she realized that she needed a drink. She pulled into the car park of the first decent-looking pub she saw outside town. There, in a comfortable bar lit and warmed by a real coal fire, she sipped a small brandy and thought about the Hartleys. She felt that her visit had barely scraped the surface. There was so much bitterness, anger and pain festering underneath, so many conflicting passions, that it would take years of psycho-analysis to sort them out.

One thing was clear, though: whatever the reasons for the family's strife, and whatever Caroline's reasons for running away, Gary Hartley certainly had a very good motive for murder. His sister had ruined his life; he even seemed to blame her for his mother's death. Had he been a different kind of person, he would have handled the burden some other way, but because he was weak and felt put upon, blood had turned to vinegar in his veins. As Susan had just seen, it didn't take more than a few drinks to bring the acid to the surface.

It would be very interesting to know what Gary Hartley had been doing between seven and eight o'clock the previous evening. As he had told her, the old man slept most of the time, so it would have been easy for Gary to nip out for a while without being missed. She hadn't asked him for an alibi, and that was an oversight. But, she thought, taking another sip of brandy and warming her hands by the fire, before we start to get all paranoid again, Susan, let's just say this was only a preliminary interview. It would be a good idea to approach Gary Hartley again with someone else along. Someone like Banks.

As she tilted her head back and finished the rest of her drink, she noticed the bright Christmas decorations hung across the ceiling and the string of cards on the wall above the stone fireplace. That was another thing she remembered about the Hartley house. In addition to the cold and the overwhelming sense of decay, there had been nothing at all in the entire huge place to mark the season: not a Christmas tree, not a card, not a sprig of holly, not a cutout Father Christmas. In that, she realized bitterly, the place resembled her own flat all too closely. She shivered and walked out to the car.

TWO

Banks drove carefully down the hill into Redburn as his tape of Bartok's third string quartet neared its end. The gradient wasn't quite as steep as at Staithes, where you had to leave your car at the top and walk, but it was bad enough. Luckily, the snow had petered out somewhere over the heathered reaches of the North York Moors and spared the coast.

The narrow hill meandered alongside the beck down to the sea, and it wasn't until he turned the final corner that Banks saw the water, a heaving mass of grey sloshing against the sea wall and showering the narrow promenade with silver spray. Redburn was a small place: just the one main street leading down to the sea, with a few ginnels and snickets twisting off it where cottages were hidden away, half dug into the hillside itself, all sheltered in the crescent of the bay. In summer the jumble of pastel colours would make a picturesque scene, but in this weather they seemed out of place, as if a piece of the

Riviera had been dug up and transported to a harsher climate.

Banks turned left at the front, drove to the end of the road and parked outside the Lobster Inn. Where the road ended, a narrow path led up the hillside, providing the only access to the two or three isolated cottages that faced the sea about halfway up: ideal places for artists.

The cold whipped the breath out of him and the air seemed full of sharp needles of moisture, but Banks finally reached his goal, the white cottage with the red pantile roof. Like the rest of the village, it would look pretty in summer with its garden full of flowers, he thought, but in the dull grey air, with the wind curling smoke from the red chimney, it took on a desolate aspect. Banks knocked at the door. Somewhere the wind was whistling and banging a loose shutter. He thought of Jim Hatchley and wondered how much he was enjoying the seaside not many miles away.

The woman who answered his knock had the kind of puzzled expression on her face that he'd expected. There couldn't be many people dropping in on such a day in such an isolated place.

She raised her dark eyebrows. 'Yes?'

Banks introduced himself and showed his card. She stood aside to let him in. The room was a haven from the elements. A wood fire crackled in the hearth and the smell of fresh-baked bread filled the air. The wooden furniture looked primitive and well-used, but homely. The woman herself was in her mid-twenties, and the long skirt and blouse she wore outlined her slender figure. She had a strong jaw and full, red lips. Beneath her fringe of dark hair, two large brown eyes watched him go over and rub his hands in front of the fire.

Banks grinned at her. 'No gloves. Silly of me.'

She held out her hand. 'I'm Patsy Janowski. Pleased to meet you.' Her grip was firm and strong. Her accent was American.

'I'm here to see Mr Ivers,' he said. 'Is he at home?'

'Yes, but he's working. You can't see him now. He hates to be disturbed.'

'And I would hate to disturb him,' Banks said. 'But it's important.'

She gave him a thoughtful look, then smiled. It was a radiant smile, and she knew it. She looked at her watch. 'Why don't I make us some tea and you can try some of my bread. It's fresh from the oven. Claude will be down in twenty minutes or so for a short break.'

Banks considered the options. Either way he would have surprise on his side, and if he let Ivers finish his session, the man would probably be better disposed towards him. Was that what he wanted? At this stage, he decided, it would be helpful. He also felt a great sense of respect for the music the man created and would have been loath to interrupt the creative process. In addition, he had to admit that the prospect of tea and fresh bread was one that appealed very strongly.

He smiled back at Patsy Janowski. 'Sounds good to me. Mind if I smoke?'

'Go ahead. I don't myself, but Claude's a pipe man. I'm used to it. I won't be a minute.'

Banks sat in front of the fire and lit up. The chair was hard and creaked whenever he shifted position, but in an odd way it was comfortable. A few minutes later, Patsy came back in with a plate full of warm bread and a steaming teapot covered with a pink quilted cosy. She put them on the low table in front of the fire then fetched butter and strawberry jam. That done, she sat opposite Banks.

'Nice place,' he said, buttering the bread.

'Yes. Claude bought it after he split up with his wife. They had this enormous mansion near Eastvale, and you know what prices are like these days. This was comparatively cheap. Needed a bit of work. And he always wanted to live by the sea. He says it inspires his work. You know, the sea's rhythms, its music.'

As she spoke, Banks noticed, her lively eyes flitted from one thing to another: his wedding ring, the scar by his right eye, his left foot, the middle button on his shirt. It wasn't as if she were avoiding eye contact, more as if she were conducting an inventory.

Banks nodded at what she said. He had noticed musical imitations of the ebb and flow of waves in Ivers's previous work. Perhaps such effects would be even more prevalent in the future. Certainly between the hiss and crackle of the fire he could hear waves pounding the rough sea wall.

'What about you?' Banks asked.

'What about me?'

'What do you do? It's a bit out of the way here, isn't it?'

She shrugged. 'Why should you assume I'd prefer the city? Do you think I like cruising the bars, going to discos, taking my credit cards shopping?' She smiled before he could answer. 'I love it here. I can amuse myself. I read, I draw a little. I like to cook and go for long walks. And I'm working on my PhD dissertation. That keeps me busy.'

'Consider me suitably chastised,' Banks said.

'Thank you.' She treated him to the radiant smile again, then frowned. 'What is it you want with Claude?'

'It's a personal matter.'

'We do live together, you know. It's not as if I was just a neighbour dropping in for gossip.'

Banks smiled. She had at least answered a question before he'd had to ask it. 'Do you know his ex-wife, Veronica Shildon?'

'I've met her. Why, has anything—?'

Banks held up a hand. 'Don't worry, nothing's happened to her,' he said.

'And she's not really his ex-wife,' Patsy said. 'They're still married.' She sounded as if she didn't like that state of affairs. 'Wanted to avoid the scandal. More bread?'

'Mmm, I think I will.' Banks reached forward. 'A drop more tea as well, if there is any.'

'Sure.'

'How did you meet Claude Ivers?'

Patsy looked at the pen in Banks's top pocket. 'I was studying at York when he was teaching a music appreciation course. I took it and kind of . . . well, he noticed me. We've been living together here for a year now.'

'Happily?'

'Yes.'

'How often have you met Veronica?'

'Three or four times. They were very civilized about things. At least they were by the time I came on to the scene.'

'What about Caroline Hartley?'

Her jaw set. 'You'll have to ask Claude about her. I've met her once or twice, but I can't say I know her. Look, if it's—'

At that moment they heard a cracking on the stairs and both turned in unison to see Claude Ivers duck under the low lintel and walk into the room. He made an imposing figure – tall, gaunt, stooped – and there was no doubt about the power of his presence. He wore a jersey and baggy jeans, and his grey hair stuck up in places as if he had been running his hand through it. His skin was reddish and leathery, like that of a man who has spent a lot of time in the wind and sun, and a deep 'V' of concentration furrowed the bridge of his nose. He looked to be in his early fifties. An inquisitive glance passed between Ivers and Patsy before she introduced Banks. Ivers shook hands and sat down. Patsy went to see to his coffee.

'What do you want to see me about?' he asked.

Banks repressed a childish urge to tell him he liked his music. 'Bad news, I'm afraid,' he said. 'Caroline Hartley, your wife's companion. She's dead.'

Ivers lurched forward and gripped the sides of his chair. 'Good God! What? How?'

'She was murdered.'

'But that's absurd. Things like that don't happen in real life.'

'I'm sorry. It's true.'

He shook his head. 'Is Veronica all right?'

'She's very upset, obviously, but apart from that she's okay. I take it you still care?'

'Of course I do.'

Banks heard something crash down heavily in the kitchen.

'If you don't mind my saying so, Mr Ivers,' he went on, 'I find that very difficult to understand. If my wife—'

He waved Banks's comparison aside. 'Listen, I went through everything any normal man would go through. Everything. Not just anger and rage, but disbelief, disgust, loss of self-esteem, loss of self-confidence. I went through hell. Christ, it's bad enough when your wife runs away with another man, but another woman . . .'

'You forgave her?'

'If that's the right word. I could never entirely blame Veronica in the first place. Can you understand that? It was as if she'd been led astray, fallen under someone else's influence.'

'Caroline Hartley's?'

He nodded.

'Would you tell me what happened?'

For several moments there was silence but for the fire, the sea and muted sounds from the kitchen. Finally, Ivers stared at Banks, then cracked his fingers and stretched back in the chair.

'All right,' he said. 'You're a stranger. Somehow that makes it easier. And we don't get many people to talk to around here. Sometimes I get a bit stir-crazy, as Patsy puts it. There's not a lot to it, really. One day everything was fine. She was happy, we were happy. At least I thought so. Maybe she got a bit bored from time to time, got depressed now and then, but we had a good solid marriage, or so I thought. Then she started seeing a therapist, didn't tell me why. I don't think she knew herself, but I suspect it was a bit of a trend among bored, middle-class housewives. It didn't seem to be doing her much harm at first so I didn't object, but then, out of the blue, there's this new friend. It's all "Caroline says this" and "Caroline says that". My wife starts to change in front of my eyes. Can you believe that? She even started using this other girl's language, saying things she would never say herself. She started calling things she liked "neat". "Really neat", she'd say! That wasn't Veronica. And she started dressing differently. She'd always been a bit on the formal side, but now she'd wear jeans and a sweatshirt. And there was all that interminable talk about Jung and self-actualization. I think she once told me I was too much the thinking type, or some such rot. Said my music was too intellectual and not emotional enough. And she got interested in stuff she'd never cared about when I'd tried to interest her – theatre, cinema, literature. She was never in, always around at Caroline's. Then she even started suggesting that *I* should go to therapy too.'

'But you didn't?'

He stared into the fire and paused, as if he realized he had already given too much away, then he said quietly, 'I have my demons, Mr Banks, but they also fire me. I'm afraid that if I subjected them to therapy I'd have no more fuel, no more creativity. Whatever Veronica might say, my music's born from conflict and feeling, not just technical skill.' He tapped his head. 'I really hear those things. And I was afraid if I opened my head to some shrink all the music would escape and I would be condemned to silence. I couldn't live like that. No, I didn't go.'

Patsy returned with the coffee. Ivers took it, smiled at her, and she sat on the floor beside him with her legs curled under her and her hand resting on his thigh.

'Did you know at the start of the friendship that Caroline was a lesbian?' Banks asked.

'Yes. Veronica told me Caroline was living with a woman called Nancy Wood. Fair enough, I thought. Live and let live. I'm a musician, not the bohemian type, perhaps, but I've been around enough oddballs in my time not to worry about them too much. And I'm fairly broad-minded. So Caroline was a lesbian. I never for a moment thought that my wife . . .'

'So if you blamed anyone it was Caroline?'

'Yes.' He hesitated, realizing what he'd said. 'But I didn't kill her, if that's what you're getting at.'

'What did you do yesterday evening?'

He sipped his coffee and spoke, half into the mug. 'Stayed in. With Patsy. We don't go out all that much.'

Patsy looked at Banks and nodded in agreement. He saw shadows behind her eyes. He wasn't sure he believed her. 'Do you own a car?' he asked.

'We both do.'

'Where do you park?'

'We've got spots reserved in the village, behind the pub. Obviously there's no parking up here.'

'When did you last see your wife?'

He thought for a moment. 'About a month ago. I was in Eastvale on business and I dropped in to see how Veronica was doing. I called at the shop first. I usually do that to avoid meeting Caroline, but sometimes if it's evening I just have to face it out.'

'How did Caroline react to these visits?'

'She'd leave the room.'

'So you never spoke to her?'

'Not much, no. And Veronica would be tense. I'd never end up staying long if Caroline was around.'

'Are you sure that was the last time you visited the house, a month ago?'

'Yes, of course I am.'

'You didn't go there yesterday evening?'

'I told you. We stayed in.'

'You're a musician,' Banks said. 'You must know Vivaldi's work.'

'I – of course I do.'

'Do you know the *Laudate pueri*?'

Ivers turned aside and reached for some bread and butter. 'Which one? He wrote four, you know.'

'Four what?'

'Four settings for the same liturgical piece. I think it's Psalm 112, but I can't be sure. Why do you ask?'

'Have you heard of a singer called Magda Kalmár?'

'Yes. But I—'

'Did you usually buy your wife a Christmas present?'

'I did last year.'

'And this year?'

He buttered his bread as he spoke. 'I was going to. Am. I just haven't got round to it yet.'

'Better hurry up, then,' Banks said with a smile. 'Only one more shopping day to Christmas.' He put his cup down on the hearth and stood up to leave. 'Thank you very much for the tea and bread,' he said to Patsy, 'and it was an honour to meet you Mr Ivers. I've enjoyed your music for a long time.'

Ivers raised an eyebrow. Banks was thankful he just nodded and didn't say anything about being surprised that policemen listened to music.

Banks walked over to the door and Ivers followed him. 'About Veronica,' he said. 'She must be in a terrible state. Do you think she needs me?'

'I don't know,' Banks said. He honestly didn't. Did a wife who lost her female lover turn back to her husband for comfort? 'Maybe you should ask her.'

Ivers nodded, and the last thing Banks noticed before the door closed was the darkening expression in Patsy Janowski's eyes, fixed on the pipe in Ivers's hand.

He made his way against the wind back to the car and drove up the hill again. The Ivers household had left him with a strange feeling. However rustic and cosy it was, he couldn't help but suspect that all was not well, and that nobody had told him the complete truth. He had little doubt that Ivers had bought the record for Veronica and had more than likely delivered it, too. But he couldn't prove it. As soon as he could, he would go back to visit Claude Ivers again.

THREE

The Queen's Arms was never very busy at five o'clock on a winter's afternoon. It was too late for the lunchtime drinkers and too early for the after-work crowd. The only other customers, apart from Banks, Richmond and Susan Gay, were three or four people with shopping bags full of Christmas presents.

The three of them sat in the deep armchairs around the fire. Banks and Richmond were drinking pints and Susan had accepted a brandy and soda. They had pooled their notes and still had nothing concrete to go on. Richmond had discovered that Nancy Wood had left Eastvale for an extended trip to Australia. A phone call to immigration had established that she was indeed there. Richmond followed with a call to the Sydney police, who got back to him a couple of hours later with positive confirmation. That was one serious suspect eliminated.

Richmond had so far got nowhere with the photograph of Ruth, the mysterious woman. The record, too, remained unexplained. They would have to start canvassing classical record shops all over England, and that would take time. Veronica Shildon's therapist had confirmed that Veronica had left her office at about seven o'clock the previous evening, as usual, and that she had mentioned going shopping.

'You said that Caroline ran off to London when she was sixteen?' Banks said to Susan.

'That's what her brother told me.'

'And she was down there for about six years before she came up to Eastvale. A lot can happen in that time. Any idea where she was?'

'Sorry, sir, they didn't seem to know anything. Either that or they weren't saying.'

'Was that the feeling you got?'

'There was certainly something weird about them.' Susan shuddered as she spoke.

'Never mind. We'll find out when we talk to them again. Maybe you can get a printout from the PNC, Phil? Caroline Hartley might have a record down there. Runaways often get in trouble with the law.'

Richmond nodded.

'Any other leads?' Banks asked.

They shook their heads. He smiled. 'Don't look so bloody despondent, Susan. At least it means you'll get Christmas Day at home.'

'Sir?'

'If we don't solve a murder in twenty-four hours, the odds are we'll be at it a long time. A day here or there isn't going to make a lot of difference unless we come up with a hot lead tomorrow. And it *is* Christmas. Things slow down. You know as well as I do it's impossible to get anything done for a couple of days. Nobody's around, for a start. All we can do is get the statements sorted out and see if we can build up a clear picture of the victim. You find often enough that the seeds of the death are in the life, so to speak, and given the life Caroline Hartley led that may have been more apt in her case. We'll do what we can with the photo, the record and the London connection, and in a day or two we'll visit her family again and push a bit harder. Maybe you and I could have a bit of a chat with the amateur dramatic society again, too, Susan. There might be some connections there – jealousy, rivalry, something like that.'

Susan nodded.

'And I don't think Veronica Shildon's coming clean with us, either,' Banks went on. 'But then she's not likely to. She'll be protecting Caroline's memory, especially if there's any shady business in the girl's past. Her alibi checks out, but there are ten minutes unaccounted for between her return home and going to Christine Cooper's. She could have nipped back earlier, too, say between seven and half past, if she'd wanted to, and only pretended to arrive later. Then there's Cooper himself, and his wife for that matter. If there was anything odd going on between those two households, who knows what kind of can of worms it might have opened. All I'm saying is that we should keep an open mind while we let them all stew for a while. Let them enjoy Christmas. Maybe we'll do the rounds again on Boxing Day when they're all full and comfy. An old sparring partner of mine from the Met, Dirty Dick Burgess, always used to prefer Sundays for surprise raids. Boxing Day's probably even better.'

Richmond raised his eyebrows at the mention of Burgess. Banks and Dirty Dick had locked horns over a politically sensitive case in Eastvale last spring, and they had hardly parted on the best of terms. Apart from Banks and Burgess, only Richmond knew the full story.

Banks looked at his watch and finished his pint. 'Right. I'd better be off now. I want to see if that post-mortem report's turned up yet.' It was already dark outside and the snow had just started falling again.

The report had indeed turned up. Banks skipped the technical details for the layman's synopsis that Dr Glendenning always courteously provided.

There was nothing new at first. She had been hit, probably punched, on the cheek, and the blow could have rendered her unconscious. After that, she had been viciously and repeatedly stabbed with her own kitchen knife. The only blood found at the scene was hers. Her dressing gown had no bloodstains on it, so it had been removed – or Caroline herself had removed it – before the stabbing. Glendenning had found no signs at all of sexual interference. He had, however, found crumbs of chocolate cake in several of the wounds, which led him to believe that the knife had been lying by the cake on the table. If so, Banks thought, they were probably dealing with a spur of the moment attack, a weapon at hand, grabbed and used in anger. There were no signs of skin or blood under her fingernails, which meant she hadn't had a chance to fight off her attacker.

And that was it, apart from the general information. Banks read idly through – health basically sound, appendix scar, gave birth to a child . . . He stopped and read that part over again. According to Glendenning, who had been as thorough as usual, the cervix showed a multiparous os, which meant the deceased had, at some point, had a baby.

That cast an interesting new light on things. Not only did it mean she had had at least one heterosexual relationship, it might also explain why she went to London, or what might have happened to her down there. All the more imperative, therefore, to find out exactly where she'd been and what she'd done. Banks felt that the photograph was a clue. Given that it was the only memento she'd kept, apart from a pressed flower, Ruth was obviously someone important from Caroline's past.

Banks walked over to the window and looked out on the market square. It looked like one of Brueghel's winter scenes. The tree was lit up and shoppers crossed the whitened cobbles to and fro with their packages. Banks was glad he'd done his Christmas shopping a week ago. The only thing that remained was the booze. He'd buy that tomorrow: a bottle of port, a nice dry sherry, perhaps some Ciardhu single malt, if he could afford it. Then his thoughts drifted back to Caroline Hartley. A baby. What a bloody turn up! And if there was a baby, somewhere there had to be a father. Maybe a father with a grudge.

Eager to find out if there had been any progress on the record and the scrap of wrapping paper, he phoned the forensic lab and asked for Vic Manson.

Manson was slightly breathless when he came on the line. 'What is it? I'd just this minute put my overcoat on. I was on my way out.'

Banks smiled to himself and lit a cigarette. Manson was always on his way somewhere. 'Sorry, Vic. I won't keep you long. Just wanted to know if you've got anything for us on the Hartley murder.'

Manson sighed. 'Not a lot. No dabs we can't account for. The knife was washed, but we found traces of blood and crumbs where the blade meets the handle.'

'What about the record?'

'Nothing. Besides, people usually hold records by the edge. No room for prints there. The cover and inside sleeve were clean, too.'

'Anything else?'

'It looked new, the record. As far as we can tell it was in mint condition, only been played a few times.'

'How many?'

'Can't tell for sure – two or three at the most – but take our word, it was new.'

'The paper?'

'Common or garden Christmas wrapping paper. Could have come from anywhere. It does look like it had been wrapped around the record, though. It fits to a tee. But there's no gift tag with the murderer's name on, unfortunately.'

'Well, at least we've got something. Thanks, Vic. Look, can you send the record over to me when you've done with it?'

'Of course. Tomorrow okay?'

'Fine. Don't let me keep you any longer. And have a good Christmas.'

'You too.'

Banks hung up, walked back to the window and lit a cigarette. What the hell was it about the music that bothered him? Why did it have to mean something? He would find out as much as he could about Vivaldi's *Laudate pueri*, all four versions. Claude Ivers admitted he knew them, but that didn't mean anything. He must have known that if he'd feigned ignorance, given his musical reputation, Banks would have immediately become even more suspicious. But Ivers knew more than he let on, that was for certain. And so did Patsy Janowski, she of the wandering eyes. Well, give them time, he thought, as he smoked and looked down on the Brueghel scene, they're not going anywhere. Let them think they're safe, then . . .

4

ONE

James Conran lived in a small terrace house on the north-west edge of town, where Cardigan Drive met North Market Street and turned into the main Swainsdale road. At the far end of his living room, a manual typewriter sat on a table by the window. The view to the west along snow-shrouded Swainsdale was superb. Bookcases flanked the table on both sides with books on all subjects. Banks took a quick glance: history, theatre, music, but hardly any fiction. A small sofa and two matching armchairs formed a semicircle around the hearth, where a coal fire smouldered. On the wall above the mantelpiece hung a poster advertising a performance of *The Duchess of Malfi* at Stratford. There was no television set, but a music centre with a compact-disc player stood opposite the fireplace. Banks ran his eyes over the records and discs, most of them the works of classical composers: Beethoven, Zelenka, Bax, Stanford, Mozart, Elgar. There was some Vivaldi, including the *Stabat Mater*, but not the *Laudate pueri*.

Conran, having explained to Banks how Susan had once been one of his pupils, was now fussing over her and offering to make tea. Both she and Banks accepted.

'Nice collection of discs,' Banks observed. 'Are you a musician?'

'Merely a dabbler,' Conran said. 'I sang with the church choir when I was a boy, then with an amateur outfit in York. I also directed the choir at Eastvale Comprehensive for a few years – mostly, I might add, because no one else would take on the job. But that's just about the limit of my musical abilities. I *am* a good listener, however.'

As Conran made tea in the kitchen, Banks continued reading book and record titles. It helped get a sense of people, he always thought, to discover their tastes in literature and music. Conran definitely read to learn, not for pleasure, which hinted at a certain amount of intellectual and artistic ambition. His record collection, while fairly eclectic, favoured choral works, perhaps an unconscious left-over from his choir days. The fact that he owned a compact-disc player showed he was serious about his listening. Though she said she liked classical music, Veronica Shildon only had an old stereo system, a turntable complete with arm and spindle for stacking records. No one who genuinely loved music would play it on such antiquated equipment, especially if they could afford better. No, Veronica Shildon's priorities lay elsewhere than music – in decor, perhaps, in creating the sense of a cosy and comfortable home. But Conran clearly valued his artistic pleasures over material ones.

Banks warmed his hands by the fire. 'I should imagine you got to know Caroline Hartley pretty well during rehearsals for *Twelfth Night*,' he said. 'Can you tell us anything about her?'

'Such as what?'

'Anything at all. Her habits, moods, your impression of her. Believe me, every little bit helps.'

'It's very difficult,' Conran said. 'I mean, I didn't know her that well. None of us did really.'

'What was your relationship with her?'

Conran frowned. 'Relationship? I'd hardly say we had a relationship. What are you implying?'

'You were directing her in a theatrical production, isn't that so?'

'Well, yes . . . but—'

'That's a relationship.'

'I see . . . I . . . I thought. Anyway, yes, I directed her on stage. It was a purely working relationship. You don't really find out much about people when you're busy telling them where to stand and how to speak, you know.'

'What did you think of her?'

'She was a very talented and attractive girl, a natural. It's a real tragedy. She'd have gone far had she lived.'

'Yet you only gave her a small part.'

'It was her first performance. She needed more experience. But she was quick. It wouldn't have taken her long to get to the top if she'd put her mind to it. *Mercurial*. I think that's the best word to describe her talent.'

'How did she get on with the rest of the cast?'

Conran shrugged. 'All right, I suppose.'

'Did she form any special relationships? Was she close to anyone in particular?'

'Not that I know of. We're all pretty chummy, really, when it comes down to it. After all, this isn't the West End. It's meant to be fun. That's the reason I'm involved.'

'She did join you for drinks after rehearsals sometimes, didn't she?'

'Yes, usually. But you can hardly get to know somebody in a group situation like that.'

'Who did she talk to?'

'Everyone, really.'

'How did she behave?'

'I don't understand.'

'Was she comfortable with the group?'

'As far as I could tell.'

'Did you know she was a lesbian?' Banks asked.

'Caroline?' He shook his head. 'I don't believe it.'

'Do you have evidence to the contrary?'

'Of course not,' Conran snapped. 'Stop twisting everything I say. What I mean is I'm surprised. She . . .'

'She what?'

'Well, you don't expect things like that, do you? She seemed quite normal to me.'

'Heterosexual?'

Conran looked at Susan as if pleading for support. 'You're doing it again. I've no knowledge of her sex life at all. All I'm saying is she *seemed* normal to me.'

'So she didn't tell you anything about her private life?'

'No. She kept herself to herself. I knew nothing at all about what she did when she left the hall or the pub.'

'Oh, come on! Surely some of the men in the cast must have tried it on with her. Maybe you even tried yourself. Who wouldn't? How did she respond?'

'I'm not sure what you mean.'

'It's obvious enough. Was she cold, polite, friendly, rude . . .?'

'Oh, I see. Well, no, she certainly wasn't cold. She'd joke and flirt like the rest, I suppose. It's not something I actually thought about. She was always friendly and cheerful, or so it seemed to me.'

'Terrible waste, don't you think? A beautiful woman like that, and no man stood a chance with her.'

Conran glanced down into his mug and muttered, 'It takes all sorts, Chief Inspector.'

'Who did she usually sit next to?'

'It varied.'

'Did you notice anything at all that hinted at a more than superficial relationship with anyone in the cast, male or female?'

'No.'

Banks sipped some tea and leaned back in his chair. 'In a close group like that, you must get all sorts of pressures. I've heard that actors sometimes have very fragile egos. Did you get many tantrums or rows? Any professional jealousies?'

'Only over petty matters,' Conran said, 'like you'd get in any team situation. As I said, we're in it for pleasure, not ambition or fame.'

' "Petty matters"? Can you be a bit more specific?'

'I honestly can't remember any examples.'

'Anything involving Caroline Hartley?'

He shook his head.

'Was there any special reason why Caroline didn't join you all for a drink after rehearsal on December twenty-second?'

'Nobody went to the pub that evening. We didn't always go, you know. It was a very casual thing.'

'But you went?'

'Yes. Alone. I wanted to mull over the rehearsal. I seem to be able to think better about things like that when there's a bit of noise and festive activity around me.'

'Drink much?'

'A bit. I wasn't drunk, if that's what you mean?'

'Had anything odd happened between four and six? Any fights, threats, arguments?'

'There was nothing unusual, no. Everybody was tired, that's all. Or they had shopping to do. Surely you can't think one of the cast—'

'Right now, I'm keeping an open mind.' Banks put down his mug. 'Why did you give up teaching, Mr Conran?'

If Conran was surprised by the abrupt change in questioning, he didn't show it. 'I'd always wanted to write. As soon as I had a little success I decided to burn my bridges. Much as I enjoyed it, teaching made too many demands on my time and energy.'

'How do you make your living now? Surely not from the Eastvale Amateur Dramatic Society?'

'Good Lord, no! That's just a hobby, really. I work as a freelance writer. I've also had a few plays produced on television, some radio work.'

Banks looked around the room again. 'Don't you even watch your own work?'

Conran laughed. 'I *do* have a television, as a matter of fact. I don't watch it very often so I keep it upstairs in the spare room. One of the advantages of being a bachelor. Plenty of space.'

'Are you working on anything right now?'

Conran beamed and sat forward, hands clasped in his lap. 'As a matter of fact, I am. I've just got this wonderful commission from the BBC to dramatize John Cowper Powys's novel, *Weymouth Sands*. It'll be a hard task, very hard, but it pays well, and it's an honour to be involved. I'm not the only writer in the project, of course, but still . . .'

'You're a long way from Weymouth,' Banks remarked. 'Come from down there?'

'Little Cheney, actually. You won't have heard of it. It's a small village in Dorset.'

'I thought I could spot a trace of that Hardy country burr. Well, Mr Conran, sorry to have bothered you on

Christmas Eve. Hope we haven't kept you from your family.'

'I have no family,' Conran said, 'and you haven't kept me from anything, no.' He stood up and shook hands, then helped Susan on with her coat.

Back outside at the car, Banks turned to Susan and said, 'Do you know, I think he fancies you.'

Susan blushed. 'He probably fancies anything in a skirt.'

'You could be right. He seemed a bit edgy, didn't he? I wonder if there's more to this dramatic society than meets the eye? You know the kind of thing, fiery passions lurking beneath the surface of dull suburban life.'

Susan laughed. 'Could be,' she said. 'Or perhaps he's just shaken up.'

'And did I miss something,' Banks said, 'or did he tell us nothing at all?'

'He told us nothing,' Susan agreed. 'But I certainly got the impression he knew much more than he let on.'

Banks opened the car door. 'Yes,' he said. 'Yes, I think he did, didn't he. That's the trouble with cases like this. Everybody's got something to hide.'

TWO

On Christmas Eve at four o'clock the Queen's Arms was packed. Businessmen, off work early for the holidays, loosened their ties, smoked cigars and laughed themselves red in the face at dirty jokes; friends met for a last few drinks before parting to spend the holidays with their families; groups of female office workers drank brightly coloured concoctions and laughed about the way the mailroom boy's hands had roamed during the office party. A large proportion of the Eastvale police force, denied their favourite spot by the fire, had pulled together two round tables with dimpled copper tops and cast-iron legs for their own party. It was a movable feast; men nipped over from the station for a quick one, then returned to cover for others. Even Fred Rowe managed to drop by for a couple of pints while young Tolliver took over the front desk. The only real continuity was provided by the CID – Gristhorpe, Banks, Richmond and Susan Gay – who had managed to hang on to their chairs amidst the chaos around them.

Everyone seemed to be having a good time. The atmosphere was cheery with its blazing fire and green and red decorations. The only thing Banks found objectionable, especially after a couple of pints, was the music that Cyril, the landlord, had piped in for the occasion. It sounded like airport-music versions of Christmas carols. Gristhorpe didn't seem to mind, but he was tone-deaf.

After the visit to Conran's, they had achieved very little that day, and nothing more would be achieved by working longer. By mid-afternoon it had been almost impossible to reach anyone on the phone. If you did happen to be lucky enough, all you got for your trouble was a drunken babble in the earpiece. Police work may never stop completely, but it does slow down at times. The only coppers working harder than ever now would be the road patrols chasing after drunken drivers.

Richmond had talked to Caroline's staff at the Garden Café, but found out nothing more about her. No, they had never suspected she might be a lesbian; she had kept her private life to herself, just as Conran had said. She was cheerful and friendly, yes, good with customers, but a closed book when it came to her personal life. She never talked about boyfriends or shared her problems, as some of the other women did.

Richmond had also dropped in on Christine Cooper and taken her through her story again. The details matched word for word. He had first taken the initiative of phoning his mother and asking her what had happened on the 22 December broadcasts of *Emmerdale Farm* and *Coronation Street*. Passing himself off as a fan who had missed his favourite programmes, he asked Christine Cooper to give him a blow by blow description of them, which she did. That accounted for her whereabouts between seven and eight o'clock. Caroline Hartley had last been seen alive around seven-twenty, answering the door to a female visitor. Unless Christine Cooper had nipped out during the commercials and stabbed her with the handy kitchen knife, or unless she was such a cunning killer she had videotaped the television programmes in case someone asked about them, then it looked as if she was out of the running. So far, Richmond had not been able to satisfy himself about her husband's alibi, but he planned to pay a visit to Barnard Castle after Christmas, when the shop reopened.

The only new fact he had discovered, via the PNC, was that Caroline Hartley had been arrested for soliciting in London five years ago. That seemed to back up what her brother, Gary, had said about her life there, but it still left a lot unsaid. Had Gary actually known what she was doing, or had he made an inspired guess? Both he and Caroline's father said that Caroline had never contacted them during her time in London. Were they lying? If so, why?

For the moment, though, the festive season chased away day to day concerns. Even Susan Gay was knocking back the Old Peculiar and chatting with the others more easily than she usually did.

'What are you doing over the holidays?' Banks asked her over the racket.

'Going home.'

'Because if you're stuck for somewhere,' he went on, 'you can always join us for Christmas dinner. I know you don't get enough time off to really go anywhere.'

'Thanks,' Susan said, 'but it's all right. Sheffield's not that far.'

Banks nodded. Richmond, he knew, would be spending the day with his family in town. Gristhorpe was coming to the Banks's this year. For their first two Christmases up north, Banks and his family had gone out to his farmhouse where Mrs Hawkins, the woman 'what did for him', had done them proud. This year, however, Mrs Hawkins and her husband had been invited to their daughter's in Cambridge. It would be the first Christmas away for them, but as the daughter had recently borne them a grandchild, they could hardly refuse. Gristhorpe had played hard to get at first, but had succumbed without too much of a fight at Banks's third invitation. Banks suspected that it was actually Sandra's telling Gristhorpe that the house was now a 'smoke-free environment' that had finally tipped the balance.

At five o'clock, Banks decided it was time to leave. He had had three pints of Theakston's bitter, just about the right amount to work up an appetite. Sandra would be expecting him for dinner. He was due to help with the big meal tomorrow – mostly the dull stuff, he imagined, chopping vegetables and setting the table, as his cooking skills were limited – but tonight was Sandra's treat.

He said his goodbyes and wandered out into the snow,

which had been falling on and off all day. Opposite, the blue lamp outside the police station shed its avuncular light. Banks didn't know why he hated it so much, but he did. It was phoney, a kind of cheap nostalgia for a time when things were simpler – or at least we fooled ourselves into believing they were simpler – when the goodies wore white and the baddies wore black. Maybe it really had been like that, but Banks doubted it. Certainly nothing could ever have been simple for the Caroline Hartleys and Veronica Shildons of this world.

Anyway, he told himself, no more gloomy thoughts. He stuck on his headphones and fiddled with the Walkman in his pocket. The music he'd chosen was his own tribute to the season: Benjamin Britten's *A Ceremony of Carols*. It was difficult, though, to put the case out of his mind: not the investigation, the details or the leads, but the sheer fact of Caroline Hartley's brutal murder. Even at the pub he had felt at times like a spectator, watching everyone celebrate, but was held back from joining in by what he had seen at number eleven Oakwood Mews. Still, it was Christmas Eve and he had to make an effort to be jolly for his family's sake.

The snow was crisp and squeaky. At last Eastvale had the white Christmas it had been screaming for during the past three or four rainy ones. Coloured lights winked on and off in windows, and Banks felt for a moment that fleeting sense of peace and relaxation in the air that seems to arise and flourish briefly when the commercial fervour of the season begins to abate.

He remembered his own childhood Christmases: the sleepless nights before the big day; the early mornings opening presents; the disappointment the year his parents hadn't been able to buy him the bicycle he wanted because his father was out of work; the joy two years later when he got an even better one than he had expected.

At home, the decorations were up, the lights were on and the children were brimming with excitement and curiosity about their presents. At least Tracy was. Brian, being seventeen, was much more cool about the whole thing.

'No, you can't open them tonight,' Banks told his daughter.

'But Laura Collins says they do at her house. Oh, go on, Dad. Please!'

'No!' Banks wasn't about to have a lifetime's tradition changed because of Laura Collins. Tracy pouted for a while, but she wasn't the kind to sulk for long.

Brian kept quiet, as though he didn't even care whether he got a present. All that interested him was pop music, and Banks had bought him a second-hand guitar he'd spotted in a shop window. Of course, it would mean a bit of noise to put up with. Banks didn't have much regard for his son's taste, but far be it from him to stand in the way of the lad's musical ambitions. Euterpe, like God, works in mysterious ways; raucous pop music might inspire someone to learn the guitar, but tastes change, and the talent might well end up in the service of jazz, blues or classical music.

Tracy had been a good deal less specific in her demands, but both Banks and Sandra had thought it a good idea to acknowledge that she was no longer a little girl. She was, after all, fifteen, and though her interest in history remained steady, and had even extended to take in literature, she had a new look in her eyes when the subject of boys came up. Banks had also noticed the odd pop star poster surreptitiously making its way onto her bedroom wall. So rather than books, they had bought her some fashionable new clothes and a make-up kit. When Banks looked at his children now, it was with a tinge of sadness in his heart. Next year he would be forty, and soon he would lose them to their own lives completely.

After a tasty beef stew with dumplings – a frugal dinner to counterbalance tomorrow's blow-out – came that time of evening when Banks could start to relax: the children out or occupied in their rooms, the television turned off, a tumbler of good Scotch, quiet music and Sandra beside him on the sofa. When he went for his refill, he remembered the photograph he had brought home in his briefcase along with the record Vic Manson had sent over that afternoon. He had hardly looked at it, but something about it rang a bell. Sandra, with her knowledge of photography, should be able to help him. He took the photograph out and handed it to her.

'What do you think of that?'

Sandra examined it close up, then held it at arm's length. 'Do you mean technically?'

'Any way you like.'

'Well, it's obviously good, a professional job. You can tell that by the lighting and the way he's made it seem like a relaxed pose. She looks very studious. A striking woman. Good quality paper, too.'

'Why would someone have a photograph like that taken?'

'Well, lots of people have portraits done . . . but I see what you mean.'

'There's something about it I can't put my finger on,' Banks said. 'Somehow, I think it's more than a portrait. I just wondered if you had any ideas.'

'Hmm. That look in her eyes. Very intelligent, a bit

haughty. I wonder if that was her or the photographer.'

'What do you mean?'

'Some photographers really capture a person's essence in their portraits, but some create an image – you know, for pop stars or advertising. I'm just not sure what this is.'

'That's it!' Banks slapped the chair arm. 'An image. A pose. Why would someone want a photographer to create an image?'

Sandra put the photograph carefully aside on the coffee table. 'For publicity, I suppose.'

'Right. That's what was bothering me. It must be a publicity picture of some kind. That gives us a chance of tracking her down.'

'You need to find this woman?'

'Yes.'

'You'll still have a hell of a job. It could be for anything – modelling, movies, theatre.'

Banks shook his head. 'Caroline had an interest in theatre, but I get the impression that's more of a recent passion. Still, she could be an actress. She's attractive, yes, but she's no model. You said it yourself – look at the intelligence, the arrogance in that tilt of the head and the eyes. And Veronica Shildon said the woman wrote poetry.'

'A book jacket?'

'Those are the lines I was thinking along. It could be a publicity still for an author's tour or something. That should narrow things down a bit. We can check with publishers and theatrical agents.' Banks paused for a moment, then went on. 'Speaking of Caroline Hartley, did you ever meet her?'

'I met her a couple of times with the group, when I went for a drink with Marcia after working late in the gallery. But I didn't know her. I never even spoke to her.'

'What was your impression?'

'I can only tell you how she acted as part of a group in a pub. She was very beautiful. You couldn't help but notice her smooth complexion and her eyes. Notice and envy.' Sandra put her hand to her own cheek which Banks had always thought of as soft and unblemished. 'In looks, she reminded me a bit of that actress who played Juliet in the old film. What's her name? . . . Olivia Hussey. And mostly she was vivacious, sparkling. Though she did seem to have her quiet periods, as if the energy was a bit of a hard act to keep up sometimes.'

'Quiet periods?'

'Yes. I just remember her staring into space sometimes, looking a bit lost. Never for long, because there was always somebody wanting to attract her attention, but it was noticeable.'

'Did she seem especially close to anyone else in the group?'

'I don't know. She chatted and laughed with them all, but only in a general, friendly way.'

'You never saw her arguing with anyone?'

'No.'

'Did you know she was a lesbian?'

'Not until you told me. But why would I?'

'I don't know. I just wondered if it was in any way obvious to you.'

'No – to both questions.'

'Did you ever notice anyone obviously chatting her up?'

Sandra laughed. 'Well, most of the men did, yes.'

'How did she react?'

'I'd say she played them along nicely. If anything, I'd have said she was a flirt, a bit of a tease, really. But now I know the truth . . .'

'Self-protection, I suppose. What about the women?'

Sandra shook her head. 'I didn't notice anything.'

'Did James Conran usually turn up for a drink? He's the only one I've met apart from Marcia, the costume manager.'

'Usually, yes. He seems like a pleasant fellow. A bit theatrical, highly strung. Drinks a fair bit. I mean, a lot of actors are really shy, aren't they? They have to get themselves tanked up and play parts to express themselves. And he's a bit of a practical joker. Nothing serious, he just likes arranging for someone's drink to be all tonic and no gin, for example, or having the barman tell someone there's none of their favourite pub grub left. I'd say he's a bit of a ladies' man, too. You know, that vulnerable look, the dedicated, suffering artist. He's pretty sure of himself really, I'll bet. He just finds the act useful. And I know for a fact he's been having it off with Olivia.'

'Olivia who?'

'I don't know her real name. The actress who's playing Olivia. They had a bit of a tiff in the pub one night, in the corridor that leads to the toilets, and I happened to overhear them arguing. She seemed to think now he'd got what he wanted he wasn't interested any more, and she told him that was fine with her, because she hadn't liked it much anyway.'

'When was this?'

'Quite early on in rehearsals. I can't remember exactly. Mid-November, maybe?'

'Did he ever make a pass at you?'

'No. He knew I was married to a tough detective who'd beat him to a pulp if he did.'

Banks laughed. 'What about Caroline?'

'You mean did he come on to her?'

'Yes.'

'Well, he contrived to sit next to her often enough and arrange for the occasional bit of accidental body contact. I'd say he was putting the moves on her, yes.'

No wonder Conran had been so tetchy when Banks had asked about his relationship with Caroline. People often denied their true relationships with victims, especially with murder victims.

'How did she react?' he asked.

'She pretended she didn't notice, but she was always polite and friendly towards him. After all, he *is* the director.'

'I should hardly think directors of local amateur dramatic societies have casting couches.'

'No, but they could make a person's life difficult if they wanted.'

'I suppose so. What about this Olivia? Might she have had good reason to resent Caroline's presence?'

'Not that I noticed. Look, Alan, do you think you could pack it in for a while? It's Christmas Eve. I'm not used to being interrogated in my own home. You know I'm glad to be of help whenever I can, but I didn't know Caroline Hartley was going to get herself murdered, so I didn't pay a lot of attention to who she did or didn't talk to.'

Banks scratched his head. 'Sorry love. I can't seem to let it drop, can I? Another drink?'

'Please. I don't mean to be—'

Banks held up his hand. 'It's okay. You're right. Not another word.'

He brought the drinks and turned out the main lights. All they had left was the light from the Christmas tree, from the fake log in the electric fire and a red candle he lit and placed on the low table. He could hear a monotonous pop song playing upstairs on Brian's portable cassette player.

When he sat down again, he put his arm around Sandra.

'That's more like it,' she said.

'Mmm. Tell me something. Do you think you could ever see yourself going to bed with another woman?'

'What do you have in mind? Inviting Jenny Fuller over for a threesome?'

'Unfortunately Jenny's away for Christmas.'

Sandra hit him gently on the chest. 'Beast.'

'No, seriously. Could you?'

Sandra was quiet for a moment. Her dark eyebrows knit together and tiny candle flames burned in her blue eyes. Banks sipped his drink and wished he could have a cigarette. Maybe later, while Sandra was getting ready for bed, he could nip outside in the cold and have a few quick drags. That should soon cure him of the habit.

'Well, hypothetically, the idea doesn't offend me,' Sandra said finally. 'I mean, it's nothing I think about much, but it doesn't disgust me. It's hard to explain. I've had crushes, what schoolgirl or schoolboy hasn't? But they never led to anything. I can't say I've thought about it a lot over the years, but there's something about the idea of being with another woman that's sort of comforting in a way. It doesn't feel threatening to me, when I think about it. I'm probably not making much sense, but I've had a few drinks, and you did ask.'

'I think I understand,' Banks said.

'Men always like the idea of two women together, don't they? It excites them.'

Banks had to admit that it did, but he didn't know why. So far, he hadn't allowed himself to picture the sexual side of Veronica's relationship with Caroline, though he guessed they had been a passionate couple. And where there's passion, he mused, snuggling closer to Sandra, there's often likely to be violence, even murder.

THREE

Susan left the pub shortly after Banks, and as soon as she got home to the bare, empty flat, she felt dizzy. First she drank a large glass of water, then she turned on the television and lay down on the sofa. The picture looked blurred. Suddenly she started to feel horribly depressed and nauseated. She remembered the lies she had told Banks about going home to Sheffield for Christmas. She had no intention of going. She would phone and tell her parents she couldn't make it because she was working on an important case. A murder. And she would spend the day in her flat doing a few domestic chores and reading that new American book on homicide investigation. She had enough food – a tin of spaghetti, a frozen chicken dinner – so she didn't need to go out and risk being seen by someone. Because she only lived half a mile or so from Banks, she would have to be careful.

She had bought and wrapped her presents days ago. She would try to pay a visit home next week or early in the new year. Somehow, it was easier on non-festive occasions. The forced enjoyment of the season only exacerbated her discomfort. For the same reason, she had always hated and avoided New Year's Eve parties.

The TV picture still looked blurred. When she closed her eyes, the world spun around and seemed to pull her into a swirling vortex that made her stomach heave. She opened her eyes again quickly. She felt sick but didn't want to get up. The third time she tried, her thoughts settled down and she fell into an uneasy sleep.

In her dream she moved into a room like the one Gary Hartley lived in, and she called it home. A high-ceilinged, dark, cold place crumbling around her as she stood there. And when she looked at the far wall it wasn't a wall at all but a mesh of cobwebs beyond which more ruined rooms with dusty floorboards and walls of flaking plaster stretched to infinity. When she went over to investigate, a huge fat spider dropped from the ceiling and hung inches from her nose. It seemed to be grinning at her.

Susan's own scream woke her. As soon as she came to consciousness she realized that she had been struggling for some time to get out of the nightmare. Her clothes were mussed up and a film of cold sweat covered her brow. Frantically, she looked around her at the room. It was the same, thank God. Dull, empty, characterless, but the same.

She staggered to the kitchen and splashed her face with cold water. Too much to drink. That Old Peculiar was powerful stuff. And Richmond had insisted on buying her a brandy and Babycham. No wonder she felt the way she did. She cursed herself for the fool she was and prayed to God she hadn't made an idiot of herself in front of the others.

She looked at her watch: seven o'clock. Her head felt a little clearer now, despite the dull ache behind her eyes.

She couldn't shake the dream, though, or the sense of panic it had caused in her. She made tea, paced about the room while the kettle boiled, switching TV channels; then, suddenly, she knew she had to do something about her bare, joyless flat. She couldn't go home, but neither could she spend Christmas Day in such a miserable place. The visit to Gary Hartley had shaken her up even more than she'd realized.

Panicking that it might be too late, she looked at her watch again. Twenty to eight. Surely some places in the shopping centre would be staying open extra hours tonight? Every year, Christmas seemed to get more and more commercial. They wouldn't miss a business opportunity like Christmas Eve, all those last-minute, desperate shoppers, guilty because they've forgotten someone. Susan hadn't forgotten anyone except herself. She grabbed her coat and dashed for the door. Still time. There had to be.

5

ONE

Christmas Day in the Banks household passed the way Christmas Days usually pass for small families: plenty of noisy excitement and too much to eat and drink. Downstairs at nine o'clock – a great improvement over the ridiculously early hours they had woken up on Christmas mornings past – Brian and Tracy opened their presents while Sandra and Banks sipped champagne and orange juice and opened theirs. Outside, framed in the bay window, fresh snow hung heavy on the roofs and eaves of the houses opposite and formed a thick, unmarked carpet across street and lawns alike.

Banks and Sandra were happy with their presents – mostly clothes, book or record tokens and the inevitable aftershave, perfume and chocolates. Brian quickly disappeared upstairs with his guitar, and Tracy spent an hour in the bathroom preparing herself for dinner.

Gristhorpe arrived about noon. They ate at one thirty, got the dishes out of the way as quickly as possible, then watched the Queen's Message, which Banks found as dull and pointless as ever. The rest of the afternoon the adults spent variously chatting, drinking and dozing. Around teatime, Banks and Sandra made a few phone calls to their parents and distant friends.

In deference to Gristhorpe's tin ear, Banks refrained

from playing music most of the time, but later in the evening, when Brian and Tracy had gone up to their rooms and the three adults sat enjoying the peace, he couldn't restrain himself. Off and on, he had been thinking about Caroline Hartley and was anxious to check out the music. He was sure that it had some connection with the murder. Now he could hold back no longer. He searched through his cassette collection for the Vivaldi he thought he had. There it was: the *Magnificat*, with *Laudate pueri* and *Beatus vir* on the same tape.

First he put on the record that Vic Manson had sent over from forensics. The familiar music, with its stately opening and pure, soaring vocal, disturbed him with the memory of what he had seen in Veronica Shildon's front room three days ago. He could picture again the macabre beauty of the scene: blazing fire, Christmas lights, candles, sheepskin rug, and Caroline Hartley draped on the sofa. The blood had run so thickly down her front that she had looked as if she were wearing a bib, or as if an undergarment had slipped up over her breasts. Carefully, he removed the needle.

'I was enjoying that,' Sandra said. 'Better than some of the rubbish you play.'

'Sorry,' Banks said. 'Try this.'

He put the cassette in the player and waited for the music to start. It was very different. The opening was far more sprightly, reminiscent of 'Spring' from *The Four Seasons*.

'What are you after?' Sandra asked.

Banks stopped the tape. 'They've got the same title, by the same composer, but they're different.'

'Any fool can hear that.'

'Even me,' Gristhorpe added.

'Claude Ivers was right then,' Banks muttered to himself. He could have sworn he had a piece by Vivaldi called *Laudate pueri*, but he hadn't recognized the music he heard at the scene.

The sleeve notes for the record told him very little. He turned to the cassette notes and read through the brief biographical sketch: Vivaldi – affectionately called '*il prete rosso*' because of his flaming red hair – had taken holy orders, but ill health prevented him from working actively as a priest. He had served at the *Pietà*, a kind of orphanage-cum-conservatory for girls in Venice, from 1703 to 1740 and would have been asked to compose sacred music when there was no choirmaster.

The blurb went on, outlining the composer's career and trying to pin down dates of composition. The *Laudate pueri* had probably been written for a funeral at the *Pietà*. One of its sections – the antiphon, '*Sit nomen Domini*' – revealed the liturgical context as a burial service for very young children. There was more about Vivaldi's setting being hardly solemn enough for a child's funeral, but Banks was no longer paying attention. He went back to the word sheet enclosed in the record sleeve and read through the translation: so few words so much music.

According to the translator, '*Sit nomen Domini benedictum ex hoc nunc et usque in saeculum*' meant, 'Blessed be the name of the Lord; from henceforth now and for ever'. What that had to do with funerals or children Banks had no idea. He realized he didn't know enough about the liturgy. He would have to talk to a churchman if he really wanted to discover the true relevance of the music.

The main point, however, was that what Banks now knew how the music tied in with the information he had got from Glendenning's post-mortem. Caroline Hartley had given birth to a child. According to Banks's theories so far, this had either been the reason for her flight to London or it had occurred while she had been there. Another chat with Veronica Shildon might clear that up.

Where was the child? What had happened to it? And who was the father? Perhaps if he could answer some of those questions he would know where to begin.

As far as musical knowledge went, Claude Ivers certainly seemed the most likely candidate to have brought the record. Already Banks was far from satisfied with his account of himself. Naturally, Ivers would deny having called at Veronica's house on the night of the murder; he was known to have a grudge against Caroline Hartley. But he must have realized he had left the record. Why take such a risk? Surely he must understand that the police would have ways of finding out who had bought the record, even if there was no gift tag on the wrapping? Or did he? Like many geniuses, his connection with the practical realities of life was probably tenuous. And Ivers couldn't have had anything to do with Caroline Hartley's baby unless they had known one another some time ago. Very unlikely.

'Put some carols on,' Sandra said, 'and stop sitting on the floor there staring into space.'

'What? Oh, sorry.' Banks snapped out of it and got up to freshen the drinks. He searched through the pile of records and tapes for something suitable. Kathleen Battle? Yes, that would do nicely. But even as 'O Little Town of Bethlehem' began, his mind was on Vivaldi's requiem for a dead child, Caroline Hartley's baby and the photograph of Ruth, the mystery woman. Christmas, or not, Veronica Shildon was going to get another visit very soon. He went into the hall, took his cigarettes and lighter from his jacket pocket and slipped quietly out into the backyard for a peaceful smoke.

TWO

'Veronica Shildon, this is Detective Constable Susan Gay.'

It was an embarrassing introduction, but it had to be made. Banks was well aware of the modern meaning of 'gay', but he was no more responsible for the word's diminishment than he was for Susan's surname.

Banks noticed the ironic smiled flit across Veronica's lips and saw Susan give a long-suffering smile in return – something she would never have done in other circumstances.

Veronica stretched out her hand. 'Good to meet you. Please sit down.' She sat opposite them, back straight, legs crossed, hands folded in her lap. The excessive formality of her body language seemed at odds with the casual slacks and grey sweatshirt she was wearing. She offered them some sherry, which they accepted, and when she went to fetch it she walked as if she'd put in a lot of time carrying library books on her head.

Finally, when they all had their glasses to hide behind, Veronica seemed ready for questions. Starting gently, Banks first asked her about the furniture, whether she wanted the sofa cushions and the rug back. She said no, she never wished to see them again. She was going to redecorate the room completely, and as soon as the holidays were over and the shops had reopened, she was going to buy a new suite and carpet.

'How are you managing with the flower shop?' he asked.

'I have a very trustworthy assistant, Patricia. She'll take care of things until I feel ready again.'

'Did Caroline ever have anything to do with your business? The shop, your partner . . .?'

Veronica shook her head. 'David, my partner, lives in Newcastle and rarely comes here. He was a friend of Claude's, one of the few that stuck with me when . . . Anyway, he regards the shop more as an investment than anything else.'

'And Patricia?'

'She's only eighteen. I assume she has her own circle of friends.'

Banks nodded and sipped some sherry, then he slipped the signed photograph from his briefcase.

'Are you sure you can't tell me any more about this woman?'

Veronica looked at the photograph again. 'It was something personal to Caroline,' she answered. 'I never pried. There were parts of her she kept hidden. I could accept that. All I know is that her name was Ruth and she wrote poetry.'

'Where does she live?'

'I've no idea, but Caroline lived in London for some years before she came up here.'

'And you've never met this Ruth, never seen her?'

'No.'

Banks bent to slip the photograph back into his briefcase and said casually, before he had even sat up to face her again, 'Did you know that Caroline had a conviction for soliciting?'

'Soliciting? I . . . I . . .' Veronica paled and looked away at the wall so they couldn't see her eyes. 'No,' she whispered.

'Is there anything at all you can tell us about Caroline's life in London?'

Veronica regained her composure. She sipped some sherry and faced them again. 'No.'

Banks ran his hand through his cropped hair. 'Come on, Ms Shildon,' he said. 'You lived with her for two years. She must have talked about her past. As I understand it, you were undergoing therapy. Caroline too. Do you seriously expect me to believe that two people digging into their psyches like that never spoke to one another about important things?'

Veronica sat up even straighter and gave Banks a look as cold and grey as the North Sea. 'Believe what you want, Chief Inspector. I've told you what I know. Caroline lived in London for a number of years. She didn't have a very happy time there. What she was working through in analysis was private.'

'How was she when you met her?'

'When I . . .?'

'When you first met.'

'I've told you. She was living with Nancy Wood. She seemed happy enough. It wasn't a . . . it was just a casual relationship. They shared a flat, I believe, but there was no deep commitment. What else can I say?'

'Was she more, or less, disturbed back then than she has been lately?'

'Oh, more. Definitely more. As I said, she seemed happy enough. At least on the surface. But she had some terrible problems to wrestle with.'

'What problems?'

'Personal ones. Psychological problems, like the ones we all have. Haven't you read the poem: "They fuck you up, your mum and dad. They don't mean to, but they do." ' She reddened when she'd finished, as if just realizing there had been a four-letter word in the literary quotation. 'Philip Larkin.'

Banks, who had heard from Susan all about the Hartley home, could certainly believe that. He knew something about Larkin's poetry, too, through Gristhorpe and a recent Channel Four special, and made a mental note to have another look at the poem later.

'But she was making progress?' he asked.

'Yes. Slowly, she was becoming whole. The scars don't go away, but you recognize them and learn to live with them. The better you understand why you are what you are, the more you're able to alter destructive patterns of behaviour.' She managed a wry smile at herself. 'I'm sorry if I sound like a commercial for my therapist, but you did ask.'

'Was anything bothering her lately? Was she especially upset about anything?'

Veronica thought for a moment and drank more sherry. Banks was coming to see this as a signal of a forthcoming lie or evasion.

'Quite the opposite,' Veronica said finally. 'As I told you, she was making great progress with regard to her personal problems. Our life together was very happy. And she was excited about the play. It was only a small part, but the director led her to believe there would be better ones to follow. I don't know if Mr Conran was leading her to expect too much, but from what she told me, he seemed convinced of her talent.'

'Did you ever meet James Conran?'

'No. Caroline told me all this.'

'Did she ever tell you that he fancied her?'

Veronica smiled. 'She said he chatted her up a lot. I

think she knew he found her attractive and felt she could use it.'

'That's a bit cold-blooded, isn't it?'

'Depends on your point of view.'

'How far was she willing to go?'

Veronica put her glass down. 'Look, Chief Inspector, I don't mind answering your questions when they're relevant, but I don't see how speaking or implying ill of the dead is going to help you at all.'

Banks leaned forward. 'Now you listen to me for a moment, Ms Shildon. We're looking for the person who killed your companion. At the moment we've no idea who this person might be. If Caroline did *anything* that might have led to her death, we need to know, whether it reflects well or badly on her. Now how far was she willing to go with James Conran?'

Veronica, pale and stiff, remained silent a while. When she spoke, it was in a quiet, tired voice. 'It was only an amateur dramatic society,' she said. 'The way you speak, anyone would think we were talking about a movie role. Caroline could flirt and flatter men's egos easily enough, but that's as far as she'd go. She wasn't mercenary or cold.'

'But she did lead men on?'

'It was part of her way of dealing with them. If they were willing to be led . . .'

'She didn't sleep with them?'

'No. And I would have known, believe me.'

'So everything seemed to be going well for Caroline. There was nothing to worry or upset her?'

Again, the hesitation, the lady-like sip of sherry. 'No.'

'It's best not to hold anything back,' he said. 'I've already told you, you can't have any idea what information might be valuable in an investigation like this. Leave decisions like that to us.'

Veronica looked directly at him. He could see courage, pain and stubborn evasion in her eyes. He let the silence stretch, then gave Susan, who had been busy taking notes, a discreet signal to go ahead.

'Veronica,' Susan asked softly, 'did you know about Caroline's baby?'

This time the reaction was unmistakably honest. She almost spilled her sherry and her eyes widened. 'What?'

Veronica Shildon certainly hadn't known about Caroline's baby, and the fact that she hadn't known surprised her. Which meant, Banks deduced, that she probably *did* know a lot more about Caroline than she was willing to let on.

'Caroline had a baby some years ago,' Susan went on. 'We can't say exactly when, but we were hoping you might be able to help.'

Veronica was able only to shake her head in disbelief.

'We're assuming she had it in London,' Banks said. 'That's why anything you can tell us about Caroline's life there would be a great help.'

'A baby,' Veronica echoed. 'Caroline? She never said a word . . .'

'It's true,' Susan said.

'But what happened to it? Where is it?'

'That's what we'd like to know,' Banks said. 'Did you know that music, the *Laudate pueri*, was used at burial services for children?'

Veronica looked at him as if she didn't understand. Her thin, straight lips pressed tight together and a frown spread over her brow from a deep V at the top of her nose. 'What does that have to do with it?' she asked.

'Maybe nothing. But someone put that record on and made sure it was going to stay on. You say it wasn't yours, so someone must have brought it. Perhaps the killer. You said you like classical music?'

'Of course. I could hardly have lived with Claude for ten years if I didn't, could I?'

Banks shrugged. 'I don't know. People make the strangest sacrifices for comfort and security.'

'I might have sacrificed my independence and my pride, Chief Inspector, but my love for music wasn't feigned, I assure you. I did then and still do enjoy all kinds of classical music.'

'But Caroline didn't.'

'What does it matter? I was quite happy to enjoy my records when she was out.'

Banks, who had often suffered Sandra's opposition to some of the music he liked, understood that well enough. 'Is it,' he asked, 'the kind of present your husband might have given you?'

'If you're expecting me to implicate Claude in this, I won't do it. We may have separated, but I wish him no harm. Are you trying to suggest that there is some obscure link between this music, the baby and Caroline's death?'

'The link seems obvious enough between the first two,' Banks said, 'but as for the rest, I don't know. If you'd never seen the record before, someone must have brought it over that evening. It would help a lot if we knew who the father of Caroline's child was.'

Veronica shook her head slowly. 'I didn't know. I really didn't know. About the baby, I mean.'

'Does it surprise you to discover that Caroline wasn't exclusively lesbian?'

'No, it's not that. After all, I've hardly been exclusively

so myself, have I? Most people aren't. Most people like us.'
She tilted her head back and fixed him with a cool, grey
look. 'It might interest you to know, Chief Inspector, just
for the record, that I'm not ashamed of what I am, and
neither was Caroline. But we weren't crusaders. We didn't
go around holding hands and mauling one another in
public. Nor did we proselytize on behalf of groups or
causes that seem to think sexual preference is an
important issue in everything from ordination as a Church
minister to what kind of breakfast cereal one buys. Like
most people's sex lives, ours was an intimate and private
matter. At least it was until the papers got hold of this
story. They soon discovered I was married to Claude, and
why we parted, and it hasn't taken them long to guess at
the nature of my relationship with Caroline.'

'I shouldn't worry too much,' Banks offered. 'People
pay much less attention to the gutter press during the
Christmas season. Do you know if Caroline had any affairs
while she was living with you? With men or women?'

Veronica fingered the neckline of her sweatshirt.
'You're very forthright, aren't you?'

'I sometimes have to be. Can you answer the question?'

Veronica paused, then said, 'As far as I know she didn't.
And I think I would have known. Of course, she was
attractive to men, and she knew it. She dealt with it as best
she could.'

'What were her feelings about men?'

'Fear, contempt.'

'Why?'

Veronica looked down into her glass and almost
whispered. 'Who can say where something like that starts?
I don't know.'

'What about you?'

'My feelings toward men?'

'Yes.'

'I can't see how that's relevant, Chief Inspector, but I certainly don't hate men. I suppose I fear them somewhat, like Caroline, but perhaps not as much. They threaten me, in a way, but I have no trouble dealing with them in the course of business. Mostly they confuse me. I certainly have no desire ever to live with one again.' She had finished her sherry and put the glass down on the low table as though announcing the end of the interview.

'Are you sure she wasn't involved with any members of the cast? Things like that do happen, you know, when people work together.'

Veronica shook her head. 'All I can say is that she never came home late or stayed out all night.'

'Did Caroline's brother ever visit you here?' Susan asked.

'Gary? He hardly left the house as far as I know.'

'You never met him?'

'No.'

'Did he know where the two of you lived?'

'Of course he did. Caroline told me she gave him the address in case of emergency. She'd drop by every once in a while to see how things were with her father.'

'You never went with her?'

'No. She didn't want me to.'

Banks could understand why. 'Did anyone know you were going shopping after your therapy session the other evening?' he asked.

'Nobody. At least, I . . . I mean, Caroline knew.'

'Apart from Caroline.'

'She might have told someone, though I can't think

why. I certainly don't announce such domestic trivia to the world at large.'

'Of course not. But you might have mentioned it to someone?'

'I might have. In passing.'

'But you can't remember to whom?'

'I can't even remember mentioning it to anyone other than Ursula, my therapist. Why is it important?'

'Did your husband know?'

She uncrossed her legs and shifted in her chair. 'Claude? Why would he?'

'I don't know. You tell me.'

Veronica shook her head. 'I told you, I've not seen him for a while. He phoned me yesterday to offer his condolences, but I don't think it would be a good time for us to meet again. Not for a while.'

'Tell me, is there any chance that your husband knew Caroline Hartley before you introduced them?'

'What a strange question. No, of course he didn't. How could he, without my knowing?'

Banks shook his head and gestured to Susan that they were about to leave. They stood up.

'Thanks for your time,' Banks said at the door. 'I hope it wasn't too painful for you.'

'Not too much, no. Incomprehensible, perhaps, but the pain was bearable.'

Banks smiled. 'I told you, it's best to leave the sorting out to us.'

She looked away. 'Yes.'

As he turned, she suddenly touched his arm and he swung around to face her again. 'Chief Inspector,' she said. 'This woman, Ruth. If you do find her, would you tell me? I know it's foolish, but I'd really like to meet her.

From what Caroline told me, Ruth had quite an influence on her, on the kind of life she'd begun to make for herself. I'm being honest with you. I know nothing more about her than that.'

Banks nodded. 'All right, I'll see what I can do. And if you remember anything else, please call me.'

She started to say something, but it turned into a quick 'Goodbye' and a hastily closed door.

The chill hit them as soon as they walked out into Oakwood Mews. Banks shivered and slipped on his black leather gloves, a Christmas present from Sandra. The sky looked like iron and the pavement was slick with ice.

'Well,' Susan said, as they walked carefully down the street, 'she didn't have much to tell us, did she?'

'She's holding back. I think she's telling the truth about not knowing the woman in the photograph, but she's holding back about almost everything else. Maybe you could pick up the key from the station and drop in at the community centre. Caroline may have left some of her things there, in a locker, maybe, or a dressing-table drawer.'

Susan nodded. 'Do you think we should bring her in to the station and press her a bit harder? I'm sure she knows something. Maybe if we kept her for a while, wore down her resistance . . .?'

Banks looked at Susan and saw a smart young woman with earnest blue eyes, tight blonde curls and a slightly snub nose gazing back at him. Good as she is, he thought, she's got a long way to go yet.

'No,' he said. 'It won't do any good. She's not holding back for reasons of guilt. It's a matter of pride and privacy with her. You might break her, given time, but you'd have to strip her of her dignity to do so, and she doesn't deserve that.'

Whether Susan understood or not, Banks didn't really know. She nodded slowly, a puzzled look clouded her eyes, then she shoved her hands deep in the pockets of her navy-blue coat and marched up King Street beside him. The crusted ice crackled and creaked under their winter boots.

THREE

There were certainly no dressing rooms at the community centre, not even for the lead players; nor were there any lockers. Susan wondered how they would manage when the play opened and they had to wear costumes and make-up. As she nosed around idly, she reflected on her Christmas.

On Christmas morning she had weakened and considered going to Sheffield, but in the end she had phoned and said she couldn't make it because of an important murder investigation. 'A murder?' her mother had echoed. 'How lurid. Well, dear, if you insist.' And that was that. She had spent the day studying and watching the old musicals on television. But at least, she remembered with a smile, she had been on time on Christmas Eve to buy a small tree and a few decorations. At least she had made the flat look a bit more like a home, even if there were still a few things missing.

There was not much else they could do about identifying the three visitors Caroline Hartley had received on the evening of her death until they had more information about the record and the woman in the photograph. They wouldn't get that until the shops and businesses were back into the swing of things again in a day or two. Banks had suggested a second visit to Harrogate for the following day, and though Susan was hardly looking forward to that, she was interested in what Banks would make of the set-up there.

Susan wasn't sure about Veronica Shildon at all, especially now that she had met her. The woman was too stiff and thin-lipped – the kind one could imagine teaching in an exclusive girls' school – and her posh accent and prissy mannerisms stuck in her craw. The idea of the two women in bed together made Susan's flesh crawl.

As she poked around, looking for anything that might have been connected with Caroline, she thought she heard a noise down the hallway. It could have come from anywhere. The backstage area, she had quickly discovered, was a warren of store rooms and cubby-holes. Slowly, she walked towards the stage entrance and peeked through a fire door. The lights were on in the auditorium, which seemed odd, but it was silent and she saw no one. Puzzled, she went to the props room.

Marcia had scrubbed the graffiti from the walls, Susan noticed, leaving only garish smears in places. The trunk of tattered costumes had gone. It was a shame about the vandals, she thought, but there was nothing, really, she could do. As she had told Conran and Marcia, the police had a good idea who the culprits were, but they didn't have the manpower to put a round the clock watch on them and could hardly arrest them with no evidence at all. PCs Tolliver and Bradley had had a word with the suspected ringleaders, but the kids were so cool and arrogant they had given nothing away.

Again, Susan thought she heard a noise like something being dragged across a wood floor. She stood still and listened. It stopped, and all she could hear was her own heart beating. Not even a mouse stirred. She shrugged and went on poking about the room. It was no use. She would pick up nothing about Caroline Hartley here by osmosis.

The door creaked open slowly behind her. She turned, ready to defend herself, and saw a uniformed policeman silhouetted in the doorway. What the hell? As far as she knew, they hadn't put a guard inside the place. She couldn't make out who it was; his helmet was too low over his brow and its strap covered his chin. The light behind her in the store room was too dim to be much help.

He stood with his hands clasped behind his back and bent his knees. 'Hello, hello, hello! What have we here?'

It was an assumed voice, she could tell that. Pretentiously deep and portentous. For a moment she didn't know what to do or say. Then he walked into the room and closed the door.

'I'm afraid,' he said, 'I shall have to ask you to accompany me to the Crooked Billet for a drink, and if you don't come clean there, we'll proceed to Mario's for dinner.'

Susan squinted in the poor light and saw that under the ridiculous helmet stood James Conran himself. Out of angry relief, she said, 'What the hell are you doing here?'

'I'm sorry,' he said, taking off the helmet. 'Couldn't resist playing a little joke. I saw you when you peeked into the auditorium. I'd just dropped by to check out some blocking angles from the floor.'

'But the uniform,' Susan said. 'I thought the costumes had all been destroyed.'

'This? I found it under the stage with a lot more old stuff. Been there for years. I suppose our previous incarnation must have left it all behind.'

Susan laughed. 'Do you always dress the part when you ask someone out to dinner?'

Conran smiled shyly. 'I'm not the most direct or confident person in the world,' he said, unbuttoning the high-collared police jacket. 'Especially when I'm talking to an ex-pupil. You may be grown-up now, but you weren't the last time I saw you. Maybe I need a mask to hide behind. But I did mean what I said. Would you consider at least having a drink with me?'

'I don't know.' Susan had nothing to do, nowhere to go but home, but she felt she couldn't just say yes. It was partly because he made her feel like that sixteen-year-old schoolgirl with a crush on the teacher again, and partly because he was connected, albeit peripherally, with a case she was working on.

'I think I should arrest you for impersonating a police officer,' she said.

He looked disappointed, and a faint flush touched his cheeks. 'At least grant the condemned man his last wish, then. Surely you can't be so cruel?'

Still Susan deliberated. She wanted to say yes, but she felt as if a great stone had lodged in her chest and wouldn't let out the air to form the words.

'Some other time, perhaps, then?' Conran said. 'When you're not so busy.'

'Oh, come on,' Susan said, laughing. 'I've got time for a quick one at the Crooked Billet at least.' To hell with it, she thought. Why not? It was about time she had some fun.

He brightened. 'Good. Just a minute then. Let me change back into my civvies.'

'One thing first,' Susan said. 'Did Caroline or any of the cast keep any of their private things here? I can't seem to find any lockers or changing areas.'

'We just have to make do with what we have,' Conran

said. 'It's all right at the moment, but at dress rehearsal and after . . . well, we'll see what we can do about some of those little cubby-holes off the main corridor.'

'So there's not likely to be anything?'

'Afraid not. If people brought their handbags or brief-cases to rehearsal, we just left them in here while we were on stage. The back door was locked, so nobody could sneak in and steal anything. Don't go away,' he said, and backed out of the room.

Susan put her hand over her mouth and laughed when he had gone. How shy and clumsy he seemed. But he did have charm and a sense of humour.

'Right,' he said, peeping around the door a couple of minutes later. 'Ready.'

They left the community centre by the back door, locked up and made their way down the alley to York Road. There, midway between the bus station and the pre-Roman site, stood the Crooked Billet. Luckily it wasn't too busy. They found a table by a whitewashed wall adorned with military emblems, and Conran went to fetch the drinks.

Susan watched him. His shirt hung out of the back of his trousers, under his sweater, he had rather round shoulders and his hair could have done with a trim at the back. Apart from that he was presentable enough. Slim, though more from lack of proper diet than exercise, she guessed; tall, and if not straight at least endearingly stooped. Very artistic, really. His eyes, she noticed as he came back, were two slightly different shades of blue-grey, one paler than the other. Funny, she had never noticed that at school.

'Here,' he said, putting a half of mild in front of her and holding out his pint. 'Cheers.' They clinked glasses.

'How's the investigation going?' he asked.

Susan told him there was nothing to report on the vandalism. 'I'm sorry about Caroline Hartley,' she went on. 'I noticed how upset you were when the Chief Inspector mentioned her death.'

Conran looked down and swirled the beer in his glass. 'Yes. As I told you on Christmas Eve, I can't say we were great friends. This was her first role with the company. I hadn't known her very long. Obviously, I didn't know her at all, really. But she was a joy to have around. Such child-like enthusiasm. And what talent! Untrained, but very talented. We've lost an important member of the cast. Not that that's why I was upset. A Maria can easily be replaced.'

'But not a Caroline Hartley?'

He shook his head. 'No.'

'Are you sure you weren't in love with her?'

Conran started as if he'd been stung. 'What? What on earth makes you ask that?'

'I don't know,' Susan said. And she didn't. The question had just risen, unbidden, to her lips. 'Just that everyone says she was so attractive. After all, you are a bachelor, aren't you?'

He smiled. 'Yes. I'm sorry. It's just that, well, here we are, having a drink together for the first time – our first date, so to speak – and you ask me if I was in love with another woman. Don't you think that's a bit odd?'

'Maybe. But were you?'

Conran smiled from the corner of his mouth and looked at her. 'You're very persistent. I'd guess that's something to do with your job. One day you must tell me all about it, all about your last ten years, why you joined the police.'

'And the answer to my question?'

He held his hands out, as if for handcuffs, and said in a Cockney voice, 'All right, all right, guv! Enough's enough! I'll come clean.'

The people at the next table looked over. Susan felt embarrassed, but she couldn't help smiling. She leaned forward and put her elbows on the table. 'Well?' she whispered.

'I suppose every man's a little bit in love with every beautiful woman,' Conran said quietly.

Susan blushed and reached for her drink. She didn't consider herself beautiful, but did he mean to imply that she was? 'That's a very evasive answer,' she said. 'And besides, it sounds like a quote.'

Conran grinned. 'But it's true, isn't it? Depending on one's sexual preference, I suppose.'

'I think it's disgusting, the way she lived,' Susan said. 'It's abnormal. Not that I mean to speak ill of the dead,' she blustered on, reddening, 'but the thought of it gives me the creeps.'

'Well, that was her business,' Conran said.

'But don't you think it's perverted?'

'I can think of worse things to be.'

'I suppose so,' Susan said, feeling she'd let too much out. What was wrong with her? She had been so hesitant about going out with him in the first place, and now here she was, exposing her fears. And to him, of all people. Surely, being in the arts, he must have come across all kinds of perverts. But she hadn't been able to help herself. The image of the two women in bed together still tormented her. And it was especially vivid as she had just come from talking to the cool, elegant Veronica Shildon. Slow down, Susan, she warned herself.

'Do you have any idea who the killer is?' Conran asked.

Susan shook her head.

'And what about your boss?'

'I'm never sure I know what he thinks,' Susan said. She laughed. 'He's an odd one is Chief Inspector Banks. I sometimes wonder how he gets the job done at all. He likes to take his time, and he seems so sensitive to other people and their feelings. Even criminals, I'll bet.' She finished her drink.

'You make him sound like a wimp,' Conran said, 'but I doubt very much that he is.'

'Oh no, he's not a wimp. He's . . .'

'Sympathetic?'

'More like empathetic, compassionate. It's hard to explain. It doesn't stop him from wanting to see criminals punished. He can be tough, even cruel, if he has to be. I just get the impression he'd rather do things in the gentlest way.'

'You're more of a pragmatist, are you?'

Susan wasn't sure if he was making fun of her or not. It was the same feeling she often had with Philip Richmond. Her eyes narrowed. 'I believe in getting the job done, yes. Emotions can get in the way if you let them.'

'And you wouldn't?'

'I'd try not to.'

'Another drink?' Conran asked.

'Go on, then,' she said. 'On two conditions.'

'What are they?'

'One, I'm buying. Two, no more shop talk. From either of us.'

Conran laughed. 'It's a deal.'

Susan picked up her handbag and went to the bar.

FOUR

'I've told you,' Detective Sergeant Jim Hatchley said to his new wife. 'It's not exactly *work*. You ought to know me better than that, lass. Look at it as a night out.'

'But what if I didn't want a night out?' Carol argued.

'I'm buying,' Hatchley announced, as if that was the end of it.

Carol sighed and opened the door. They were in the carpark at the back of the Lobster Inn, Redburn, about fifteen miles up the coast from their new home in Saltby Bay. The wind from the sea felt as icy as if it had come straight from the Arctic. The night was clear, the stars like bright chips of ice, and beyond the welcoming lights of the pub they could hear the wild crashing and rumbling of the sea. Carol shivered and pulled her scarf tight around her throat as they ran towards the back door.

Inside, the place was as cosy as could be. Christmas decorations hung from beams that looked like pieces of driftwood, smoothed and worn by years of exposure to the sea. The murmur of conversations and the hissing of pumps as pints were pulled were music to Hatchley's ears. Even Carol, he noticed, seemed to mellow a bit once they'd got a drink and a nice corner table.

She unfastened her coat and he couldn't help but look once again at the fine curve of her bosom, which stood out as she took off the coat. Her shoulder-length blonde hair was wavy now, after a perm, and Hatchley relished the memory of seeing it spread out on the pillow beside him that very morning. He couldn't get enough of the voluptuous woman he now called his wife, and she seemed to feel the same way. His misbehaviour at the reception had soon been forgiven.

Carol spotted the way he was looking at her. She blushed, smiled and slapped him on the thigh. 'Stop it, Jim.'

'I weren't doing anything.' His eyes twinkled.

'It's what you were thinking. Anyway, tell me, what did Chief Inspector Banks say?'

Hatchley reached for a cigarette. 'There's this bloke called Claude Ivers lives just up the road from here, some sort of highbrow musician, and he parks his car at the back of the pub. Banks wants to know if he took it out at all on the evening of December twenty-second.'

'Why can't he find out for himself?'

Hatchley drank some more beer before answering. 'He's got other things to do. And it'd be a long way for him to come, especially in nasty weather like this. Besides, he's the boss, he delegates.'

'But still, he needn't have asked *you*. He knows we're supposed to be on our honeymoon.'

'It's more in the way of a favour, love. I suppose I could've said no.'

'But you didn't. You never do say no to a night out in a pub. He knows that.'

Hatchley put a hand as big as a ham on her knee. 'I thought you'd be used to going with a copper by now, love.'

Carol pouted. 'I am. It's just . . . oh, drink your pint, you great lummox.' She slapped him on the thigh.

Hatchley obliged and they forgot work for the next hour, chatting instead about their plans for the cottage and its small garden. Finally, at about five to eleven, their glasses only half full, Carol said, 'There's not a lot of time left, Jim, if you've got that little job to do.'

Hatchley looked at his watch. 'Plenty of time. Relax, love.'

'But it's nearly eleven. You've not even gone up for a refill. That's not like you.'

'Trust me.'

'Well, you might not want another, though that's a new one on me, but *I* do.'

'Fine.' Hatchley muttered something about nagging wives and went to the bar. He came back with a pint for himself and a gin and tonic for Carol.

'I hope it's not all going to be like this,' she said when he sat down again.

'Like what?'

'Work. Our honeymoon.'

'It's one-off job, I've told you,' Hatchley replied. He drained about half his pint in one go. 'Hard work, but someone has to do it.' He belched and reached for another cigarette.

At about twenty past eleven Carol suggested that if he wasn't going to do anything they should go home. Hatchley told her to look around.

'What do you see?' he asked when she'd looked.

'A pub. What else?'

'Nay, lass, tha'll never make a detective. Look again.'

Carol looked again. There were still about a dozen people in the pub, most of them drinking and nobody showing any signs of hurrying.

'What time is it?' Hatchley asked her.

'Nearly half past eleven.'

'Any towels over the pumps?'

'What? Oh . . .' She looked. 'No. I see what you mean.'

'I had a word with young Barraclough, the local lad at Saltby Bay. He's heard about this place and he's told me all about the landlord. Trust me.' Hatchley put a sausage finger to the side of his nose and ambled over to the bar.

'Pint of bitter and a gin and tonic, please,' he said to the landlord, who refilled the glass without looking up and took Carol's tumbler over to the optic.

'Open late, I see,' Hatchley said.

'Aye.'

'I do so enjoy a pub with flexible opening hours. Village bobby here?'

The landlord scowled and twitched his head towards the table by the fire.

'That's him?' said Hatchley. 'Just the fellow I want to see.' He paid the landlord, then went and put the drinks down at their table. 'Won't be a minute, love,' he said to Carol, and walked over to the table by the fire.

Three men sat there playing cards, all of them in their late forties in varying degrees of obesity, baldness or greying hair.

'Police?' Hatchley asked.

One of the men, sturdy, with a broad, flat nose and glassy, fish-like eyes, looked up. 'Aye,' he said. 'What if I am?'

'A minute of your time?' Hatchley gestured to the table where Carol sat nursing her gin and tonic.

The man sighed and shook his head at his mates. 'A policeman's lot . . .' he said. They laughed.

'What is it?' he grunted when they'd sat down at Hatchley's table.

'I didn't want to talk in front of your mates,' Hatchley began. 'Might be a bit embarrassing. Anyways, I take it you're the local bobby?'

'That I am. Constable Kendal, at your service. If you get to the bloody point, that is.'

'Aye,' said Hatchley, tapping a cigarette on the side of his package. 'Well, that's just it. Ciggie?'

'Hmph. Don't mind if I do.'

Hatchley gave him a cigarette and lit it for him. 'Yon landlord seems a bit of a miserable bugger. I've heard he's a tight-lipped one, too.'

'Ollie?' Kendal laughed. 'Tight as a Scotsman's sphincter. Why? What's it to you?'

'I'd like to make a little bet with you.'

'A bet? I don't get it.'

'Let me explain. I'd like to bet you a round of drinks that you can get some information out of him.'

Kendal's brow furrowed and his watery eyes seemed to turn into mirrors. He chewed his rubbery lower lip. 'Information? What information? What the bloody hell are you talking about?'

Hatchley told him about Ivers and the car. Kendal listened, his expression becoming more and more puzzled. When Hatchley had finished, the constable simply stared at him open-mouthed.

'And by the way,' Hatchley added, reaching into his inside pocket for his card. 'My name's Hatchley, Detective Sergeant James Hatchley, CID. I've just been posted to your neck of the woods so we'll probably be seeing quite a bit of one another. You might mention to yon Ollie about his licence. Not that I have to remind you, I don't suppose, when it's an offence you've been abetting.'

Pale and resigned, Constable Kendal stood up and walked over to the bar. Hatchley sat back, sipped some more beer and grinned.

'What was all that about?' Carol asked.

'Just trying to find out how good the help is around here. Why do a job yourself if you can get someone else to do it for you? There's some blokes, and I've a good idea that landlord is one of them, who'll tell you it's pissing down when the sun's out, just to be contrary.'

'And you think he'll talk now?'

'Aye, he'll talk all right. No percentage in not doing, is there?' He ran a hand through his fine, straw-coloured hair. 'I've lived in Yorkshire all my life,' he said, 'and I've still never been able to figure it out. There's some places, some communities, as wide open as a nympho's legs. Friendly. Helpful. And there's others zipped up as tight as a virgin's – sorry, love – and I reckon this is one of them. God help us if anything nasty happens in Redburn.'

'Couldn't you just have asked the landlord yourself?'

Hatchley shook his head. 'It'll come better from the local bobby, believe me, love. He's got very powerful motivation for doing this. His job. And the landlord's got his licence to think about. Much easier this way. The more highly motivated the seeker, the better the outcome of the search. I read that in a textbook somewhere.'

About five minutes later, Kendal plodded back to the table and sat down.

'Well?' said Hatchley.

'He came in to open up at six – they don't go in for that all-day opening here except in season – and he says Ivers's car was gone.'

'At six?'

'Thereabouts, aye.'

'But he didn't see him go?'

'No. He did see that bird of his drive off, though.'

'Oh, aye?'

'Aye. American, she is. Young enough to be his daughter. Has her own car too. Flashy red sportscar. Well, you know these rich folk . . .'

'Tell me about her.'

'Ollie says she was getting in her car and driving off just as he came in.'

'Which way did she go?'

Kendal looked scornfully at Hatchley and pointed with a callused thumb. 'There's only one way out of here, up the bloody hill.'

Hatchley scratched his cheek. 'Aye, well . . . they haven't issued me my regulation ordnance survey map yet. So let's get this straight. At six o'clock, Ivers's car was already gone and his girlfriend was just getting into hers and driving off. Am I right?'

Kendal nodded.

'Owt else?'

'No.' Kendal stood up to leave.

'Just a minute, Constable,' Hatchley said. 'I won the bet. While you're on your feet I'll have a pint of bitter for myself and a gin and tonic for the missis, if it's no trouble.'

6

ONE

'What's Susan up to?' Richmond asked Banks on the way to Harrogate on the afternoon of December 27.

Driving conditions had improved considerably. Most of the main roads had been salted, and for the first time in weeks the sky glowed clear blue and the sun glinted on distant swaths and rolls of snow.

'I've got her chasing down the record,' Banks answered. 'Some shops might not even bother to reply unless we push them.'

'Do you think it'll lead anywhere?'

'It could, but I don't know where. It can't just have been on by accident. It was like some kind of macabre soundtrack. Call it a strong hunch if you like, but there was something bloody about it.'

'Claude Ivers?'

'Could be. At least we know now he lied to us about being out. We'll talk to him again later. What I want today is a fresh perspective on Caroline Hartley's family background. We've already got Susan's perceptions, now it's time for yours and mine. The old man couldn't have done it, so we'll concentrate on the brother. It sounds like he had plenty of motive, and nobody keeps tabs on his movements. It wouldn't have been hard for him to leave his father to sleep for a couple of hours and slip out.

From what Susan said, the old man probably wouldn't have noticed.'

'What about transport?'

'Bus. Or train. The services are frequent enough.'

They pulled up outside the huge, dark house.

'Bloody hell, it does look spooky, doesn't it?' Richmond said. 'He's even got the curtains closed.'

They walked up the path through the overgrown garden and knocked at the door. Nobody answered. Banks hammered again, harder. A few seconds later, the door opened slowly and a thin, pale-faced teenager with spiky black hair squinted out at the sharp, cold day. Banks showed his card.

'You can't see Father today,' Gary said. 'He's ill. The doctor was here.'

'It's you we want to talk to,' Banks said. 'If you don't mind.'

Gary Hartley turned his back on them and walked down the hall. He hadn't shut the door, so they exchanged puzzled glances and followed him, closing the door behind them. Not that it made much difference; the place was still freezing.

In the front room, Banks recognized the high ceiling, curlicued corners and old chandelier fixture that Susan had described. He could also see the evidence of what Gary Hartley had done to the place, its ruined grandeur: wainscotting pitted with dart holes, scratched with obscene graffiti.

Richmond looked stunned. He stood by the door with one hand in his overcoat pocket and the other touching the right side of his moustache, just staring around him. The room was dim, lit only by a standard lamp near the battered green-velvet sofa on which Gary Hartley lay smoking and studiously not looking at his visitors. A small colour television on a table in front of the curtained window was showing the news with the sound turned down. Empty lager cans and wine bottles stood along the front of the stone hearth like rows of soldiers. In places, the carpet had worn through so much that only the crossed threads remained to cover the bare floorboards. The room smelled of stale smoke, beer and unwashed socks.

It must have been beautiful once, Banks thought, but a beauty few could afford. Back in the last century, for every family enjoying the easy life in an elegant Yorkshire mansion like this, there were thousands paying for it, condemned to the misery of starving in cramped hovels packed close to the mills that accounted for their every waking hour.

Banks picked a scuffed, hard-backed chair to sit on and swept a pair of torn jeans to the floor. He managed to light a cigarette with his gloves on. 'What did your father do for a living?' he asked Gary.

'He owned a printing business.'

'So you're not short of a bob or two?'

Gary laughed and waved his arm in an all-encompassing arc. 'As you can see, the fortune dwindles, riches decay.'

Where did he get such language? Banks wondered. He had already taken in the remains of an old library in ceiling-high bookcases beside the empty fireplace: beautiful, tooled-leather bindings. Cervantes, Shakespeare, Tolstoy, Dickens. Now he saw a book lying open, face down, beside Gary's sofa. The gold embossed letters on the spine told him it was *Vanity Fair*, something he had always meant to read himself. What looked like a red-wine stain in the shape of South America had ruined the cover. So Gary Hartley drank, smoked, watched television and read the classics. Not much else for him to do, was there? Was he knowledgeable about music, too? Banks saw no signs of a stereo. It was eerie talking to this teenager. He couldn't have been more than a year or so older than Brian, but any other similarity between them ended with the spiky haircut.

'Surely there must be *some* money left?' Banks said.

'Oh, yes. It'll see him to his grave.'

'And you?'

He looked surprised. 'Me?'

'Yes. When he's gone. Will you have some money left to help you leave here, find a place of your own?'

Gary dropped his cigarette in a lager can. It sizzled. 'Never thought about it,' he said.

'Is there a will?'

'Not that he's shown me.'

'What'll happen to the house?'

'It was for Caroline.'

'What do you mean?'

'Dad was going to leave it for Caroline.'

Banks leaned forward. 'But she deserted him, she left you all. You've been taking care of him by yourself for all these years.' At least that was what Susan Gay had told him.

'So what?' Gary got up with curiously jerky movements and took a fresh pack of cigarettes from the mantelpiece. 'She was always his favourite, no matter what.'

'What now?'

'With her gone, I suppose I'll get it.' He looked around the cavernous room, as though the thought horrified him more than anything else, and flopped back down on the sofa.

'Where were you on the evening of December twenty-second?' Richmond asked. He had recovered enough to find himself a chair and take out his notebook.

Gary glanced over at him, a look of scorn on his face. 'Just like telly, eh? The old alibi.'

'Well?'

'I was here. I'm always here. Or almost always. Sometimes I used to go to school so they didn't get too ratty with me, but it was a waste of time. Since I left, I've got a better education reading those old books. I go to the shops sometimes, just for food and clothes. Then there's haircuts and the bank. That's about it. You'd be surprised how little you have to go out if you don't want to. I can do the whole lot in one morning a week if I'm organized right. Booze is the most important. Get that right and the rest just seems to fall into place.'

'What about your friends?' Banks asked. 'Don't you ever go out with them?'

'Friends? Those wallies from school? They used to come over sometimes.' He pointed to the wainscotting. 'As you can see. But they thought I was mad. They just wanted to drink and do damage and when they got bored they didn't come back. Nothing changes much here.'

'December twenty-second?' Richmond repeated.

'I told you,' Gary said, 'I was here.'

'Can you prove that?'

'How? You mean witnesses?'

'That would help.'

'I probably emptied out the old man's potty. Maybe even changed his sheets if he messed the bed. But he won't remember. He doesn't know one day from the next. I might even have dropped in at the off-licence for a few cans of lager and some fags, but I can't prove that either.'

Every time Gary talked about his father his tone hardened to hatred. Banks could understand that. The kid must be torn in half by his conflicts between duty and desire, responsibility and the need for freedom. He had given in and accepted the yoke, and he must both hate himself for his weakness and his father for making such a demand in the first place. And Caroline, of course. How he must have hated Caroline, though he didn't sound bitter when he spoke of her. Perhaps his hatred had been assuaged by her death and he had allowed himself to feel some simple pity.

'Did you go to Eastvale that evening?' Richmond went on. 'Did you call on your sister and lose your temper with her?'

Gary coughed. 'You really think I killed her, don't you? That's a laugh. If I was going to I'd have done it a few years ago, when I really found out what she'd lumbered me with, not now.'

Five or six years ago, Banks calculated, Gary would have been only twelve or thirteen, perhaps too young for a relatively normal child to commit sororicide – and surely he must have been living a more normal life back then. Also, as Banks had learned over the years, bitterness and resentment could take a long time to reach breaking point. People nursed grudges and deep-seated animosities for years sometimes before exploding into action. All they needed was the right trigger.

'Did you ever visit Caroline in Eastvale?' Banks asked.

'No. I told you, I hardly go out. Certainly not that far.'

'Have you ever met Veronica Shildon?'

'That the lezzie she was shacking up with?'

'Yes.'

'No, I haven't.'

'But Caroline visited you here?'

He paused. 'Sometimes. When she'd come back from London.'

'You told the detective constable who visited you a few days ago that you knew nothing of Caroline's life in London. Is that true?'

'Yes.'

'So for over five years, when she was between the ages of sixteen and twenty-one, you had no contact.'

'Right. Six years, really.'

'Did you know she had a baby?'

Gary sniffed. 'I knew she was a slut, but I didn't know she had a kid, no.'

'She did. Do you know what happened to it? Who the father was?'

'I told you, I didn't even know she'd had one.'

He seemed confused by the issue. Banks decided to take his word for the moment.

'Did she ever mention a woman called Ruth to you?'

Gary thought for a moment. 'Yeah, some woman who wrote poetry she knew in London.'

'Can you remember what she said about her?'

'No. Just that they were friends like, and this Ruth woman had helped her.'

'Is that all? Helped her with what?'

'I don't know. Just that she'd helped her.'

'What did you think she meant?'

He shrugged. 'Maybe took her in off the street or something, helped her with the baby. How should I know?'

'What was her last name?'

'She never mentioned it. Just Ruth.'

'Whereabouts in London did she live?'

'I've no idea.'

'You're sure there's nothing more you can tell us about her?'

Gary shook his head.

'Do you know anything about music?' Banks asked.

'Can't stand it.'

'I mean classical music.'

'Any music sounds awful to me.'

Another one with a tin ear, Banks thought, just like Superintendent Gristhorpe. But it didn't mean Gary knew nothing about the subject. He read a lot, and could easily have come across the necessary details concerning the Vivaldi piece, perhaps in a biography.

'The last time you saw Caroline,' he asked, 'did she tell you anything that gave you cause to worry about her, to think she might be in danger, frightened of something?'

Gary appeared to give the question some thought, then he shook his head. 'No.'

Again, Banks thought he was telling the truth. Just. But there was something on Gary's mind, below the surface, that made his answer seem evasive.

'Is there anything else you want to tell us?'

'Nope.'

'Right.' Banks nodded to Richmond and they headed for the door. 'Don't bother to see us out,' Banks said. 'We know the way.'

Gary didn't reply.

'Jesus Christ,' said Richmond when they'd got in the car and turned on the heater. 'What a bloody nutcase.' He rubbed his hands together.

'You wouldn't think, would you,' Banks said, looking at the tall, elegant stone houses, 'that behind such a genteel façade you'd find something so twisted.'

'Not unless you were a copper,' Richmond answered.

Banks laughed. 'Time for a pub lunch on the way back,' he said, 'then you can take a trip to Barnard Castle and I'll see about having a chat with the therapist.'

'Rather you than me,' Richmond said. 'If she's anything like she was when I saw her the other day she'll probably end up convincing you you need therapy yourself – after she's chewed your balls off.'

'Who knows, maybe I do need therapy,' Banks mused, then turned by the Stray, passed the Royal Baths and headed back towards Eastvale.

TWO

Ursula Kelly's office was on the second floor of an old building on Castle Hill Road. A back room, it was graced with a superb view over the formal gardens and the river to the eyesore of the East End Estate and the vale beyond. Not that you could see much today but a uniform shroud of white through which the occasional clump of trees, red-brick street or telegraph pole poked its head.

The waiting room was cramped and chilly, and none of the magazines were to Banks's taste. It wasn't an interview he was looking forward to. He had a great professional resistance to questioning doctors and psychiatrists during a case; much as they were obliged and bound by law, they had never, in his experience, proved useful sources of information. The only one he really trusted was Jenny Fuller, who had helped him out once or twice. As he looked out the window at the snow, he wondered what Jenny would make of Gary Hartley and the whole situation. Pity she was away.

After about ten minutes, Dr Ursula Kelly admitted him

to her inner sanctum. She was a severe-looking woman in her early fifties, with grey hair swept back tight and held firm in a bun. The lines of what might once have been a beautiful if harsh face were softened only by the plumpness of middle age. Her eyes, though guarded, couldn't help but twinkle with curiosity and irony. Apart from a few bookcases housing texts and journals, and the desk and couch in the corner, the consulting room was surprisingly bare. Ursula Kelly sat behind the desk with her back to the picture window, and Banks placed himself in front of her. She was wearing a fawn cardigan over her cream blouse, no white coat in evidence.

'What can I do for you, Chief Inspector?' she asked, tapping the eraser of a yellow HB pencil on a sheaf of papers in front of her. She spoke with a faint foreign accent. Austrian, German, Swiss? Banks couldn't quite place it.

'I'm sure you know why I'm here,' he said. 'My detective sergeant dropped by to see you the other day. Caroline Hartley.'

'What about her?'

Banks sighed. It was going to be just as hard as he had expected. Question – answer, question – answer.

'I just wondered if you might be able to tell me a little more than you told him. How long had she been a patient of yours?'

'I had been seeing Caroline for just over three years.'

'Is that a long time?'

Ursula Kelly pursed her lips before answering. 'It depends. Some people have been coming for ten years or more. I wouldn't call it long, no.'

'What was wrong with her?'

The doctor dropped the pencil and leaned back in her chair. She eyed Banks for a long time before answering.

'Let's get this clear,' she said finally. 'I'm not a medical doctor, I'm an analyst, primarily using Jungian methods, if that means anything to you.'

'I've heard of Jung.'

She raised her eyebrows. 'Good. Well, without going into all the ins and outs of it, people don't have to be ill to start seeing me. In the sense that you mean, there was nothing wrong with Caroline Hartley.'

'So why did she come? And pay? I'm assuming your services aren't free.'

Dr Kelly smiled. 'Are yours? She came because she was unhappy and she felt her unhappiness was preventing her from living fully. That is why people come to me.'

'And you make them happy?'

She laughed. 'Would that it were as easy as that. I do very little, actually, but listen. If the patient makes the connections, they cut so much deeper. The people who consult me generally feel that they are living empty lives, living illusions, if you like. They are aware of what potential they have; they know that life should mean more than it does to them; they know that they are capable of achieving, of feeling more. But they are emotionally numb. So they come for analysis. I'm not a psychiatrist. I don't prescribe drugs. I don't treat schizophrenics or psychotics. I treat people you would perceive as perfectly normal, on the outside.'

'And inside?'

'Ah! Aren't we all a mass of contradictions inside? Our parents, whether they mean to or not, bequeath us a lot we'd be better off without.'

Banks thought of Gary Hartley and the terrible struggles he had to live with. He also thought of the Philip Larkin poem that Veronica Shildon had quoted.

'Can you tell me anything at all about Caroline Hartley's problems?' he asked. 'Anything that might help solve her murder?'

'I understand your concern,' Ursula Kelly said, 'and believe me, I sympathize with your task, but there is nothing I can tell you.'

'Can't or won't?'

'Take it whichever way you wish. But don't think I'm trying to impede your investigation. The things Caroline and I worked on were childhood traumas, often nebulous in the extreme. They could have nothing to do with her death, I assure you. How could the way a child felt about . . . say . . . a lost doll result in her murder twenty years later?'

'Don't you think I'd be the best judge of that, as one professional to another?'

'There is nothing I can tell you. It was her feelings I dealt with. We tried to uncover why she felt the way she did about certain things, what the roots of her fears and insecurities were.'

'And what were they?'

She smiled. 'Even in ten years, Chief Inspector, we might not have uncovered them all. I can see by the way you're fidgeting you need a cigarette. Please smoke, if you wish. I don't, but it doesn't bother me. Many of my patients feel the need for infantile oral gratification.'

Banks ignored the barb and lit up. 'I don't suppose I need to remind you,' he said, 'that the rule of privilege doesn't apply to doctor-patient relationships as it does to those between lawyer and client?'

'It is not a matter of reminding me. I never even thought about it.'

'Well, it doesn't. You are, by law, obliged to disclose

any information you acquired while practising your profession. If necessary, I could get a court order to make you hand over your files.'

'Pah! Do it, then. There is nothing in my files that would interest you very much.' She tapped her head. 'It is all in here. Look, the women had problems. They came to me. Neither of them hurt anyone. They are not criminals, and they do not have any dangerous psychological disorders. Isn't that what you want to know?'

Banks sighed. 'Okay. Can you at least tell me what kind of progress Caroline was making? Was she happy lately? Was anything bothering her?'

'As far as I could tell, she seemed fine. Certainly she wasn't worried about anything. In fact, we'd come to . . .'

'Yes?'

'Let's just say that she'd recently worked through a particularly difficult trauma. They occur from time to time in analysis and they can be painful.'

'I don't suppose you'd care to tell me about it?'

'She had confronted one of her demons and won. And people are usually happy when they overcome a major stumbling block, at least for a while.'

'Did she ever talk about her brother, Gary?'

'It's not unusual for patients to talk about their families.'

'What did she have to say about him?'

'Nothing of interest to you.'

'She treated him very badly. Did she feel no guilt?'

'We all feel guilt, Chief Inspector. Do you not think so?'

'Perhaps *he* should have been your patient. He certainly seems to have his problems, thanks to his sister.'

'I don't choose my patients. They choose me.'

'Veronica Shildon was a patient of yours, too, wasn't she?'

'Yes. But I can say even less about her. She's still alive.'

Judging by how little Ursula Kelly had said about Caroline, Banks knew not to expect very much.

'Was Veronica particularly upset about anything that last session?'

She shook her head. 'Your sergeant asked me that, and the answer is the same. No. It was a perfectly normal session as far as I was concerned.'

'No sudden traumas?'

'None.' She leaned forward and rested her hands on the desk. 'Look, Chief Inspector, you might not think I've been very forthcoming. That is your prerogative. In my business you soon become privy to the innermost fears and secrets of the people you deal with, and you get into the habit of keeping them to yourself. You're looking for facts. I don't have any. Even if I did tell you what happened during my sessions with Caroline and Veronica, it wouldn't help you. I deal with a world of shadows, of dreams and nightmares, signs and symbols. What my patients *feel* is the only reality we have to work with. And I have already told you, in all honesty, that as far as I know neither Caroline nor Veronica was in any way especially disturbed of late. If you need to know more, try talking to Veronica herself.'

'I already have.'

'And?'

'I think she's holding back.'

'Well, that is your problem.'

Banks pushed his chair back and stood up. 'I think you're holding back, too,' he said. 'Believe me, if I find out that you are and that it's relevant to Caroline's murder, I'll make sure you know about it. You'll need twenty years in analysis to rid yourself of the guilt.'

Her jaw muscles clenched and her eyes hardened.

'Should that occur, it will be my burden.'

Banks walked out and slammed the door behind him. He didn't feel good about his anger and his pathetic threat, but people like Ursula Kelly, with her smug generalizations and pompous, self-righteous air, brought out the worst in him. He took a couple of deep breaths and looked at his watch. Five thirty. Time to catch the end of rehearsal.

THREE

Richmond parked his car outside a pub on the main street, got out and sniffed the air. There was no reason, he thought, why it should smell so different up here, but it did have a damper, more acrid quality. Barnard Castle was only twenty or so miles from Eastvale, but it was over the Durham border in Teesdale.

According to his map, the shop should be on his right about halfway down the hill just in front of him. It seemed to be the main tourist street, with an Indian restaurant, coffeehouse, bookshop and antique shop all rubbing shoulders with places that sold souvenirs along with walking and camping gear.

The toy shop was indeed about halfway down the hill. First, Richmond looked in the window at the array of goods. Hardly any of them seemed familiar, nothing at all like the toys he had played with as a child. In fact, mostly he had had to use his imagination and pretend that a stick was a sword. It wasn't that his parents had been exceptionally poor, but they had strict priorities, and toys had come very low on the list.

The bell pinged as he entered and a young woman

behind the counter looked up from behind a ledger. He guessed her to be in her mid-twenties, and she had a fine head of tangled auburn hair that cascaded over her shoulders and framed an attractive, freckled, oval face. She wore a long, loose cardigan, grey with a maroon pattern, and from what Richmond could see of her above the counter, she seemed to have a slim, shapely figure. A pair of glasses dangled on a chain around her neck, but she didn't put them on as he walked towards her.

'What can I do for you, sir?' she said with a lilting, Geordie accent in a slightly husky voice. 'Would it be something for your boy, or your little girl, perhaps?'

Richmond noticed the glint of humour in her eyes. 'I'm not married,' he said, mentally kicking himself even before he had got the words out. 'I mean, I'm not here to buy anything.'

She looked at him steadily, fingering the spectacles chain as she did so.

'CID,' he said, fumbling for his identification. 'I spoke with the manager a couple of days ago, when you were on holiday.'

She raised her eyebrows. 'Ah, yes. Mr Holbrook told me about you. Tell me, do all policemen dress as well as you do?'

Richmond wondered if she were being sarcastic. He took pride in his dress, certainly. He had the kind of tall, trim, athletic body that clothes looked good on, and he always favoured a suit, white shirt and tie, unlike Banks, who went in for the more casual, rumpled look.

'I'll take that as a compliment,' he said finally. 'Look, I'm at a bit of a disadvantage. I'm afraid he didn't tell me your name.'

She smiled. 'It's Rachel, Rachel Pierce. Pleased to meet

you.' She held out her hand. Richmond shook it. He noticed there was no sign of either a wedding ring or an engagement ring.

She seemed to be laughing at him, and it made him feel foolish and disconcerted. How could he question her seriously when she looked at him like that? He remembered his training and aimed for the correct tone.

'Well, Miss Pierce,' he began, 'as you may be aware, we are investigating—'

She burst out laughing. Richmond felt himself flush to the tips of his moustache. 'What the . . .?'

She put her hand to her mouth and quietened down. 'I'm sorry,' she said, seeming more than a little embarrassed herself. 'I don't usually giggle. It's just that you seem so stuffy and formal.'

'Well, I'm sorry if—'

She waved her hand. 'No, no. Don't apologize. It's my fault. I know you have a job to do. It's just that it gets a bit lonely in here after Christmas and I'm afraid that seems to affect my manners. Look,' she went on, 'it would make this a lot easier for me if you'd let me lock up and make you a cup of tea before we talk. It's near enough closing time already and the only customer I've had all day was a young lad wanting to exchange his Christmas present.'

Richmond, encouraged by her friendliness, smiled. 'If you're closing anyway,' he said, 'maybe we could go for a drink and a bit to eat?'

She chewed on her lower lip and looked at him. 'All right,' she said. 'Just give me a minute to make sure everything's secure.'

In ten minutes, they were sitting in a cosy pub, Richmond nursing a pint and Rachel sipping rum and coke.

'I'm ready,' she said, sitting back and folding her arms. 'Grill away, Mr CID.'

Richmond smiled. 'There's not much to ask, really. You know Charles Cooper?'

'Yes. He's the general manager.'

'I understand he's been very busy lately making sure everything was in order for Christmas.'

Rachel nodded.

'Do you remember December the twenty-second?'

She wrinkled her brow and thought, then said, 'Yes. He was here that day sorting out some stock problems. You see, Mr Curtis, the manager, had forgotten to reorder some . . . But you don't want to hear about that, do you?'

Richmond wasn't too sure. He felt like pinching himself to see if he could escape the way just listening to her voice and watching her animated face made him feel. He tried it – just a little nip at the back of his thigh – but it did no good. He took a deep breath. 'How long was he at the shop?' he asked.

'Oh, a couple of hours, perhaps.'

'Between what times?'

'He got here about four, or thereabouts, and left at six.'

'He left at six o'clock?'

'Yes. You sound surprised. Why?'

'It's nothing.' It was, though. Unless he had gone to another branch – and neither Cooper nor his wife had mentioned anything about that – then he had left the shop at six and not got home until eleven. Where the hell had he been, and why had he lied?

'Are you sure he left at six o'clock?' he asked.

'Well, it can't have been much after,' Rachel answered. 'We closed at seven – extra hours for the holiday period – and he was gone a while before then. He said he'd try to shift some stock over from the Skipton shop before Christmas Eve.'

'Did you get the impression he was going to go to Skipton right then?'

'No. They'd be closed, too. Wouldn't be any point, would there?'

'Presumably, if he's the general manager, he's got a key?'

'Yes, but he doesn't go carrying boxes of toys around, does he, if he's the general manager. He gets some dogsbody to do that.'

Richmond fingered his moustache. 'Maybe you're right. What was your impression of him? Do you know him well?'

She shook her head. 'Not well, no. He'd drop in once in a while. We might have a cup of tea and a chat about how things were going.'

'That's all?'

She raised her left eyebrow and squinted her right eye almost shut. 'And just what might you mean by that?'

'I'm not sure, really. He didn't make a pass at you or anything?'

'Mr Cooper? Make a pass?' She laughed. 'You obviously don't know him.'

'So he never did?'

'Never. The thought of it . . .' She laughed again.

'Did he ever talk about things other than business? Personal things.'

'No. He kept himself to himself.'

'Did you ever hear him mention a woman called Caroline Hartley?'

She shook her head.

'Veronica Shildon?'

'No. He hardly ever mentioned his own wife, only when I asked after her. I'd met her once or twice at company do's, you see, so it's only polite to ask after her, isn't it?'

'Was there anything odd about him at all?' Richmond asked. 'Think. Surely you must have felt or noticed something at some time?'

Rachel frowned. 'Look, there *is* something . . . but I don't like to speak out of turn.'

'It's not out of turn,' Richmond said, leaning forward. 'Remember, this is a murder investigation. What is it?'

'Well, I could be wrong. It was just a couple of times, you know.'

'What?'

'I think he's a drinker.'

'In what way? We're drinking right now.'

'I don't know, but not like this. A secret drinker, a problem drinker, whatever you call it.'

'What makes you say that?'

'I could smell alcohol on his breath sometimes, early in the day, when he hadn't bothered to take one of those awful breath mints he usually smelled of. And once I saw him take a little flask out of his pocket in the stockroom when he thought I wasn't looking. I can't be sure what it was, of course, but . . .'

Could there be anything in it? Richmond wondered. Rachel Pierce had certainly given him a new perspective on the Coopers, but whether it would lead him to a murderer, he couldn't tell. So the man drank, so he had lied about his alibi – a silly lie, at that, an easy one to check – but it might not mean anything. One thing was certain, though, Banks would want to visit the Coopers again very soon, and he wouldn't be as gentle as he had been on previous occasions.

Richmond looked over at Rachel. Her glass was nearly empty.

'Another?' he asked.

'I shouldn't.'

He glanced at his watch. 'I think I can say I'm officially off duty now,' he said. 'Come on, it won't do any harm.'

She looked at him a long time. He couldn't fathom the expression on her face. Then she said, 'All right, then. Another one.'

'Wonderful. There's just one thing I have to do first.'

She raised an eyebrow.

'Call my boss,' Richmond said. 'Don't go away. I won't be a minute.'

He glanced back and saw her smiling into her glass as he made for the telephone.

FOUR

> *Disguise, I see thou art a wickedness*
> *Wherein the pregnant enemy does much.*
> *How easy is it for the proper – false*
> *In women's waxen hearts to set their forms!*
> *Alas, our frailty is the cause, not we!*
> *For such as we are made of, such we be.*
> *How will this fadge? My master loves her dearly,*
> *And I, poor monster, fond as much on him;*
> *And she, mistaken, seems to dote on me.*
> *What will become of this? As I am man,*
> *My state is desperate for my master's love.*
> *As I am woman – now alas the day! –*
> *What thriftless sighs shall poor Olivia breathe!*
> *O Time, thou must untangle this, not I;*
> *It is too hard a knot for me t'untie!*

'Better, Faith darling, much better! Perhaps just a bit more introspection – remember, it *is* a soliloquy – but not too serious.' James Conran turned to Banks. 'What did you think?'

'I thought she was very good.'

'Do you know the play?'

'Yes. Not well. But I know it.'

'So you know how it "fadges" then?'

'They all marry the ones they want and live happily ever after.'

Conran stuck a finger in the air. 'Ah, not quite, Chief Inspector. Malvolio, remember, ends by vowing revenge on the lot of them for making a fool of him.'

All that Banks remembered about the end of *Twelfth Night* was the beautiful song the Clown sang alone when everyone else had walked off to their fates. It was on his Deller Consort tape. 'For the rain it raineth every day,' the refrain went. It had always seemed a curiously sombre song to end a comedy with. But nothing was black and white, especially in Shakespeare's world.

'Perhaps you'd care to see us on opening night,' Conran said. 'Complimentary tickets, of course.'

'Yes, I would. Very much.' Accepting free tickets to an amateur production could hardly be called being on the take, Banks thought. 'Will you be much longer here?' he asked. 'I'd like to talk to some of the cast members. Maybe it would be more comfortable over in the Crooked Billet.'

Conran frowned. 'What on earth would you want to talk to them about?'

'Police business.'

Definitely not pleased, Conran looked at his watch and clapped his hands. The actors walked off stage and went for their coats.

After they had dashed down the alley in the chilly evening, the warmth of the Crooked Billet greeted them like a long lost friend. They unbuttoned their coats and hung them by the door, then pulled two tables together near the fire to accommodate the thirsty thespians. Banks tried to keep track of the introductions and the links between actors and roles. Olivia, played by Teresa Pedmore, and Viola, Faith Green, interested him the most. Marcia Cunningham, the costumes and props manager, was there too. It was a casual and unorthodox method of questioning possible suspects, Banks was aware, but he wanted to get as much of a feel of the troupe as he could before he decided where to go from there.

'I still can't imagine why you want to talk to the cast,' Conran complained. 'Surely you can't think one of us had anything to do with poor Caroline's death?'

'Don't be so bloody naive, Mr Conran. There's a chance that anyone who knew her might have done it. Certainly she seemed to know her killer, as there was no sign of forced entry. How long did you stay at the pub the night she died?'

'I don't know. About an hour, I suppose. Maybe a bit longer.'

'Until just after seven?'

'About that, yes.'

'Then you went home?'

'Yes. I told you.'

'There you are, then. You could be lying. You've got no alibi at all.'

Conran reddened and his hand tightened on his glass. 'Now just wait—'

But Banks ignored Conran completely and went to the bar for another drink. The director certainly seemed jumpy. Banks wondered why. Maybe it was just his artistic temperament.

When he got back to the table, his seat had been taken by a distraught Sir Toby Belch, who seemed to think his part could do with some expansion (perhaps to match his stomach) despite the limitations Shakespeare had imposed.

Banks managed to squeeze himself in between Teresa Pedmore and Faith Green, not a bad place to be at all. Teresa was deep in conversation with the man on her right, so Banks turned to Faith and complimented her on her rendering of Viola's soliloquy. She blushed and replied quickly, her breathy voice pitched quite low.

'Thank you. It's very difficult. I have no formal training. I'm a schoolteacher and I do like to get involved with the plays the department puts on, but . . . It's so difficult doing *Twelfth Night*. I have to remember that I'm really a woman dressed as a man talking about a woman who seems to have fallen in love with me. It's all very strange, a bit perverted really.' She put her hand to her mouth and touched Banks's arm. 'Oh God, I shouldn't have said that, should I? Not after poor Caroline . . .'

'I'm sure she'd forgive you,' Banks said. 'Did you have any idea of her sexual inclinations before her death?'

'None at all. None of us did. Not until I read about it in the papers. If you'd asked me, I'd have said she was man-mad.'

'Why?'

Faith waved her hand in the air. 'Oh, just the way she behaved. She knew how to string a man along. A woman knows about these things. At least, I thought I did.'

'But you never actually saw her with a man?'

'Not in the way you mean, no. I'm talking about her

general effect, the way she could turn heads.'

'Did you notice any personality conflicts among the cast? Especially involving Caroline.'

Faith rubbed one of her long, blue tear-drop earrings between her finger and thumb. She was probably in her early twenties, Banks thought, with especially beautiful silvery hair hanging in a fringe and straight down to her shoulders. It looked so vibrant and satiny he wanted to reach out and touch it. He was sure sparks would fly if he did. Her eyes were a little too close together and her lower lip pouted a bit, but the total effect had an interesting kind of unity. As he had noticed on the stage, she was tall and well-formed. It would be difficult, without very good costumes, to conceal the fact that Faith Green was all woman.

She leaned closer to speak to Banks and he smelled her perfume. It was subtle, and probably not cheap. He also smelled the Martini Rossi on her breath.

'I didn't notice anything in particular,' she said, flicking her eyes towards the rubicund Sir Toby and Malvolio, who looked like an undertaker's assistant, 'but some of the men aren't too keen on Mr Conran.'

'Oh? Why's that?'

'I think they're jealous.'

'But the women like him?'

'Most of them, yes. And that's partly why the others are jealous. You'd be surprised what shady motives people have for joining in amateur events like this.' She widened her eyes and Banks noticed that they were smiling. 'S-e-x,' she said. 'But he's not my type. I like my men dark and handsome.' She looked Banks up and down. 'Not necessarily tall, mind you. I don't mind being bigger than my boyfriends.'

Banks noticed the plural. Surely there had never been schoolteachers like this in his time?

'I hear there was something between Mr Conran and Olivia – Teresa, that is.'

'You'll have to ask her about that,' Faith said. 'I'll not tell tales on my friends out of school.' She wrinkled her nose.

'Can you tell me anything more about Caroline?'

Faith shrugged. 'Not really. I mean, I hardly knew her. She was beautiful in a petite, girlish sort of way, but I can't say she made much of an impression on me. As I said before, I thought she was a bit of a flirt, myself, but I don't suppose she could help the way the men flocked to her.'

'Anyone in particular?'

'No, just in general, really. Most of the men seemed to like being with her, including our director.'

'Did he make a pass at her?'

'No, he's too subtle for that. He plays the shy and vulnerable one until women approach him, then he reels them in. At least he did with Teresa.' She clapped a hand to her mouth. 'Look, I *am* telling tales out of school. How do you do it?'

Banks smiled. 'Professional secret. So in your opinion, Caroline Hartley was a flirt, but nothing ever came of it?'

'Yes. I suppose that's how she kept them at bay.' Faith shook her head and her hair sparked like electricity. 'Maybe I was blind, but I'm damned if I could see what she really was.'

'What did you think of her as an actress?'

Faith traced a ring around the top of her glass. 'She was young, inexperienced. She had a long way to go. And it was only a small part, after all. Young Maggie over there's taken it on now.' She nodded towards a serious-looking young woman sitting next to Conran.

'But she was talented?'

'Who am I to say? Perhaps. In time. Look—'

'Did anything odd happen at rehearsal the day Caroline was killed? Does any incident stand out in your mind, however petty it might have seemed at the time?'

'No, not that I remember. Look, will you excuse me for a min? Have to pee.'

'Of course.'

Banks waited a moment or two, then attracted Teresa Pedmore's attention. Her hair was as dark as Faith's was silver. She had the healthy complexion of a young country-woman, and it didn't surprise Banks to discover that she was a milkman's daughter from Mortsett, now working in the main Eastvale Post Office and living in town. But that was where her rusticity ended. The haughty tilt of her head when she spoke and her fierce dark eyes had nothing to do with simple country life. There was an aura of mystery about her; Banks found its source hard to pin down. Something to do with the economy of her body language, perhaps, or the faintly sardonic tone of her voice. And she was ambitious; he could sense that from the start.

'It's about Caroline Hartley, isn't it?' she said before Banks could open his mouth. As she spoke, Banks noticed, she was looking over at James Conran, who was watching her with a frown on his face.

'Yes,' Banks answered. 'Can you tell me anything about her?'

Teresa shook her head. Coal-black hair danced about her shoulders. 'I hardly knew her. Even less so than I thought at the time, according to the papers.'

'I understand you were involved with Mr Conran?'

'Who told you that? Faith?'

Banks shook his head. 'Faith was subtly evasive. Were you?'

'What if I was? We're both single. James is fun once you get to know him. At least he was.'

'And did Caroline Hartley spoil that fun for you?'

'Of course not. How could she?'

'Didn't he switch his attentions from you to her?'

'Look, I don't know who's been telling you all this, but it's rubbish. Or are you just making it up? James and I ended our little fling ages ago.'

'So you weren't jealous of Caroline?'

'Not at all.'

'How did Caroline behave among the other women in the cast?'

Teresa laughed, showing a set of straight white teeth rarely seen outside America. 'I don't know what you're getting at.'

'Was she close to anyone?'

'No. I thought she always seemed aloof. You know, friendly but distant. Casual.'

'So you didn't like her very much.'

'I can't say I cared one way or the other. Not that I'm glad she's . . . you know. This is only the second play the company's done since James took over, but it was Caroline's first. None of us knew her that well.'

'How did she get the part?'

Teresa raised her dark, arched eyebrows. 'Auditioned, I should think. Like everybody else.'

'You didn't notice her form any close attachments to other women in the play?'

'There are only three of us. What are you trying to say, that I'm a lesbian too?'

Banks shifted in his seat. 'No. No, I'd say that was very unlikely, wouldn't you?'

Slowly, she relaxed. 'Well . . .'

'What about Faith?'

Teresa gave her cigarette a short, sharp flick with her thumbnail. 'What did she tell you? I saw you talking to her.'

'She told me nothing. That's why I'm asking you.'

'There was nothing between them, I can assure you of that. Faith's as straight as I am.' She took a breath, sipped some milky Pernod and water, then smiled. 'As far as the others go, I don't think you've got much chance of finding a murderer among them, quite frankly. Malvolio's such a puritan prig he probably even whips himself for taking part in such a sinful hobby as acting. Sir Andrew's thick as pigshit – excuse my French – and Orsino's so wrapped up in himself he wouldn't notice if Samantha Fox waggled her boobs in front of his face.'

Banks looked over at Orsino. He had muscular shoulders – clearly the fruits of regular weight-training – dark, wavy hair, hollow cheeks, bright eyes and an expression set in a permanent sneer, as if all he saw outside a mirror was unworthy of his regard.

'None of them three had much to do with Caroline anyway, as far as I noticed. They had some scenes together, but I never saw them communicate much off-stage. And you can forget the others, too. I know for a fact that Antonio's queer as a three-pound note, Sebastian's very happily married with a mortgage, a dog and two-point-five kids, and the Clown, well . . . he's very quiet actually, and he never seems to socialize with us.'

'Have you ever noticed him talking to Caroline off-stage or between scenes?'

'I've never noticed him talking to anyone. Period. One of the strangest transformations you can imagine. A wonderful Clown, but such a dull, depressing-looking man.'

Banks asked her a few more general questions but found out nothing else. Before long, Teresa was asking him about his most exciting cases and it was time to move on. He chatted briefly with some of the others but got no further. Finally, he went back to James Conran, excused himself from the company and walked out into the cold evening, but not before Faith Green managed to catch him at the door and slip him her telephone number.

Outside, Banks caught his breath at the cold. Bright stars stabbed pinpoints of light in the clear sky. Who, Banks wondered, had believed that the sky was just a kind of black-velvet curtain and the light of heaven beyond showed through the holes in it? The Greeks? Anyway, on nights like this it felt exactly that way.

There had been something wrong about his conversations in the Crooked Billet. He couldn't put his finger on it, but everything had seemed too easy, too chummy. Everyone he spoke to had been nervous, worried about something. He hadn't missed the way Faith excused herself before answering one of his questions, nor the way Teresa played with her cigarette when he asked her questions she didn't like. Those two would merit further talking to, definitely. Surely there must have been minor tiffs or conflicts among the cast of a play? According to the people he had talked to, it had all been happy families – much too squeaky clean for his liking. What were they covering up, and when had they decided to do so?

He put his headphones on. In winter they acted as earmuffs, too. The tape he had in was a collection of jazz pieces by the likes of Milhaud, Gershwin and Stravinsky performed by Simon Rattle and the London Sinfonietta. Tracy had bought it him for Christmas, clearly under instructions from Sandra. When Banks switched on the Walkman the erotic clarinet glissando at the opening of Gershwin's *Rhapsody in Blue* almost bowled him over. He turned down the volume and walked on.

The tree was still lit up outside the church in the market square, but there were no carol singers in evidence this evening. The cobblestones were icy and he had to step carefully. The blue lamp glowed coldly outside the police station. It was seven o'clock. Just time to drop in and see if any new information had turned up before going home for dinner.

He walked into the bustle of the police station and went straight upstairs to his office. Before he could even shut the door, Susan Gay called after him and entered.

Banks sat down and took his headphones off. 'Anything new?'

'I followed up on the record shops,' she said breathlessly. 'Most of them are open now because they're having post Christmas sales. Anyway, I've tracked down two copies of that *Luddite poori* thing sold in the past three weeks.'

'Good work. Where from?'

'One from a small speciality shop in Skipton and another from the Classical Record Shop in Leeds. But there's more, sir,' she went on. 'It seemed a long shot, but I asked for a description of the purchaser in both instances.'

'And?'

'The Leeds shop, sir. Before I'd even started he told me who'd bought it. The salesman recognized him.'

'Claude Ivers?'

'Yes, sir.'

'Well, well, well,' Banks said. 'So he was lying after all. Why aren't I surprised? You've done a great job, Susan. In fact I think you deserve a day at the seaside tomorrow.'

Susan smiled. 'Yes, sir. Oh, and DS Richmond phoned from Barnard Castle with a message about Charles Cooper's alibi. It seems things are getting a bit complicated, doesn't it?'

7

ONE

A sea mist clung to the coastline when Banks and Susan arrived in Redburn at eleven o'clock the next morning. Icy roads over the vale and freezing rain on the moors had made driving difficult all the way, and now, as they came down from the land to the sea, the clash of the two elements had produced a fog that reduced visibility to no more than a few yards.

Susan, Banks could tell, was surprised at being chauffeured by a senior officer. But she would soon learn. He preferred his own car because of the stereo and the generous mileage allowance, and he actually enjoyed driving in Yorkshire, even in poor conditions such as these. On the way, he had been listening to *Metamorphosen*, Richard Strauss's haunting string elegy for the bombing of the Munich Hoftheater, and he hadn't spoken much. He didn't know whether Susan liked the music. She had been as silent as he and had spent most of the journey looking out the window, lost in thought.

He parked the car outside the Lobster Inn again, and they made their way up the path to Ivers's cottage. The mist seemed to permeate everything, and by the time they got to the cottage they were glad of the fire blazing in the hearth.

Again it was Pasty Janowski who answered the door.

This time, when Banks introduced Detective Constable Gay, her big brown eyes clouded with worry and fixed on the door handle. She was wearing tight jeans and a dark-green turtle-neck sweater. Her dark hair, which still fell almost to her eyes in a ragged fringe, was tied back in a ponytail. Her smooth complexion was tinged with the kind of flush that a brisk walk in fresh weather brings.

'He'll be down in a few minutes,' she said. 'Sit down and warm yourselves. I'll make some tea.'

'Shouldn't we go up, sir?' Susan asked when Patsy had left the room. 'It'll give us an edge.'

Banks shook his head. 'He'll be no trouble. Besides, I want to talk to her alone first.' They sat in the creaky wooden chairs near the fire, and Banks rubbed his hands in front of the flames. Although he had been wearing gloves on this trip, the chill seemed to have penetrated right through both leather and flesh. When he felt warm enough, he took off his overcoat and lit a cigarette. Warm air from the fire hooked the smoke and sucked it up the chimney.

Patsy returned with the tea tray and set it down beside them. There was no fresh-made bread this time.

'What is it?' she asked, joining them by the fire. 'Have you found the killer?'

Banks ignored her question and picked up his mug of tea. 'Tell me,' he asked, 'where did you drive to when you left your parking spot behind the Lobster Inn the evening Caroline Hartley was killed?'

Patsy stared at his breast pocket, her eyes wide open and afraid, like a hunted doe's. 'I . . . I . . . You can't expect me to remember a particular night just like that. Days are much the same out here.'

'I can imagine that, but it was the evening before my

last visit. I asked you then, very specifically, where you'd been the night before, and you both told me you'd stayed in. Now I'm asking you again.'

Patsy shrugged. 'If I said I stayed in, I guess that's what I did.'

'But you were seen leaving the car park.'

'It must have been someone else.'

'I don't think so. Unless you're in the habit of lending out your car. Where did you go?'

She stirred a spoonful of sugar into her tea and gazed into the steaming mug as she spoke. 'I don't remember going anywhere, but I might have gone for a drive early on. I sometimes do that. But I wouldn't have been gone long. There are some beautiful vantage points along the coast, but you have to drive out there, then walk a fair distance to find them.'

'Even in this weather?'

'Sure. I'd hardly live here if I minded a bit of rough weather, would I? I like it when the sea gets all churned up.'

She seemed to be regaining her composure, but Banks still didn't believe her story. 'Why didn't you mention this little drive?' he asked.

She smiled at the fireplace. 'It didn't seem important, I guess. I mean, it was nothing to do with what you were asking about.'

'Did you go alone?'

She hesitated, then said, 'Yes.'

'Where was Mr Ivers?'

'Back here, working.'

'Then who was using *his* car?'

Her hand went to her mouth. 'I . . . I don't understand.'

'It's simple, really, Ms Janowski. His car was missing

from its usual spot. If he was here working, who was using it?'

Patsy was saved from having to answer by the creak of the stairs as Ivers came down. He was dressed in much the same kind of baggy jeans and loose jersey as he had been on Banks's first visit, but this time he had combed back his longish grey hair. He ducked underneath the low lintel beam and walked into the room, where his height and gaunt features commanded attention. The room had seemed crowded enough with three people in it, but with four it felt cluttered and claustrophobic.

'What's going on?' he asked, looking over at Patsy, who was squeezing her plump lower lip between her fingers and staring out of the window.

Banks stood up. 'Ah, Mr Ivers. Please join us. Sit down.'

'I hardly need to be invited to sit down in my own house,' Ivers said, but he sat.

Banks lit another cigarette and leaned against the stone mantelpiece. Not a tall man himself, he wanted the advantage of height. Susan remained where she was, her notebook in her lap. Ivers glanced nervously at her, but Banks didn't introduce them.

'We were just talking about memory,' he said. 'How deceptive it can be.'

Ivers frowned. 'I don't understand.'

'Seems to be a lot of that about,' Banks said.

'Mr Ivers,' Susan asked, 'where did you drive to on the evening of December twenty-second?'

He stared at her but didn't appear to see her, then he turned towards Banks and gripped the arms of his chair. He thrust himself forward in as menacing a manner as possible. 'What is this? What are you insinuating?'

Banks flicked a column of ash into the fire. 'We're just asking you a simple question,' he said. 'Where did you go?'

'I told you I didn't go anywhere.'

'I know. But you were lying.'

Ivers half rose. 'Now look—'

Banks stepped forward and gently pushed him back. 'No. You look. Let me save us all a lot of time and effort and tell you what happened.'

Ivers settled back and fumbled for his pipe and tobacco in his trouser pocket. Patsy poured him some tea and passed it over. Her hand was shaking. The corner of his thin mouth twitched for her in what was meant to be a reassuring smile.

'That evening,' Banks began, 'you decided to take Veronica her Christmas present. It was a record you bought for her at the Classical Record Shop in the Merrion Centre in Leeds, Vivaldi's *Laudate pueri*, sung by Magda Kalmár, a singer you knew had impressed her. But when you got to the house, just after seven, say, she was out. Caroline Hartley answered the door and let you in. You were simply going to drop off the present, but something happened, something made you angry. Perhaps she said something about your virility, I don't know, or maybe the rage you felt about her stealing Veronica from you finally boiled over. You fought, hit her, then stabbed her with the kitchen knife you found on the table.'

'Ingenious,' Ivers said. 'But not a word of it is true.'

Banks knew full well that his theory was full of holes – the two female visitors Caroline Hartley had received *after* Ivers had apparently left, for example – but he went on regardless. He wanted to shake Ivers up a bit, at the very least.

'I don't know why you put the record on, but you did. Perhaps you wanted to make it look like the work of a psychopath. That could also have been why you removed her robe after you hit her. Anyway, when it was done, you washed the knife in the sink. I imagine you must have got blood on your gloves and sleeves, but it would have been easy enough to destroy that evidence when you got home.' Banks flicked his cigarette end into the fire. 'Right there.'

Ivers shook his head and clamped his teeth down on his pipe.

'Well?' Banks said.

'No,' he whispered between clenched teeth. 'It didn't happen like that at all. I didn't kill her.'

'Did you know that Caroline Hartley had once had a baby?' Banks asked.

Ivers took his pipe out of his mouth in surprise. 'What? No. All I know is that she was the bitch who corrupted my wife and induced her to leave me.'

'Which gives you a very good motive for wanting to be rid of her,' Susan said, looking up from her notebook.

Again Ivers looked at her but hardly appeared to see her.

'Perhaps so,' he said. 'But I'm not a killer. I create, I don't destroy.'

Patsy leaned forward and took his hand in hers. With his other hand, he held on to his pipe.

'What happened?' Banks asked.

Ivers sighed and stood up. He stroked Patsy's cheek and went to the fireplace where he knocked out his pipe. He seemed more stooped and frail now, somehow, and his cultured voice no longer held its authoritative tone.

'You're right,' he said, 'I did go over to Eastvale that evening. I shouldn't have lied. I should have told you the truth. But when you told me what had happened, I was certain I'd be a suspect, and I was right, wasn't I? I couldn't bear the thought of any serious interruption to my work. But I swear, Chief Inspector, that when I left Caroline Hartley, the little slut was as alive as you and I. Yes, I went to the house. Yes, Veronica was out shopping. Caroline let me in grudgingly, but she let me in because it was cold and snowing and she didn't want to leave the door open. I wasn't in there more than a few minutes. Out of politeness, I asked how she was and asked about Veronica, then I just handed over the present and left. And that's the truth, whether you believe it or not.'

'I'd find it easier to believe if you'd told me the first time I called,' Banks said. 'You've wasted a lot of our time.'

'I've already explained why I couldn't tell you. Good Lord, man, what would you have done in my position?'

Banks always hated it when people asked him that. In ninety-nine per cent of cases he would have done exactly as they had: the wrong thing.

'How could you even imagine that we wouldn't trace the buyer of the record?'

Ivers shrugged. 'I've no idea what you can or can't do. I don't read mystery novels or watch police shows on television. We don't even have a television. Never have had. I knew I hadn't put a gift tag on the record – I remembered I'd forgotten to do that shortly after I left Veronica's – so when you mentioned Vivaldi last time you called I had a good idea you were only guessing it was me. You never asked me outright whether I took her the record or not.'

'When you left,' Banks said, 'was the record still wrapped or had it been opened?'

'Still wrapped, of course. Why should it have been opened?'

'I don't know. But it was. Could Caroline have opened it?'

'She may have done, just to have a laugh at me and my tastes, I suppose. She always said I was an old bore. She once told Veronica she thought my music sounded like the kind of sounds you'd get from a constipated camel.'

If Ivers was telling the truth, Banks wondered, then how had the record come to be unwrapped? Unless either Caroline had opened it out of malicious curiosity – 'Hello darling, look what the boring old fart's bought you for Christmas!' – or Veronica Shildon herself had returned to the house and opened it. But why should she do that with a Christmas present? Surely she would have put it under the tree with the rest and waited until the morning of the twenty-fifth? And she certainly wouldn't have done anything so mundane if she had walked into the room and found Caroline's body.

'Did you tell her what it was?' Banks asked.

'Not in so many words.'

'What did you say?'

'Just that it was something very special for Veronica.'

'How did Caroline react?'

'She didn't. She just glanced at it, and I put it down.'

'Did you argue with her?'

Ivers shook his head. 'Not this time, no. It was cool between us, but civilized. I've told you, I was out again within five minutes.'

'What did you do then?'

'I drove over to the shopping centre – I wanted to buy a few last minute things I couldn't get here in the village – then I came home.'

'What things?'

Ivers frowned. 'Oh, I can't remember. Books, a sweater

Patsy wanted, a case of decent claret . . . that kind of thing.'

'You didn't by any chance see your wife in the shopping centre, did you?'

'No. I'd have mentioned it if I did. It's a fairly large place, you know, and it was very busy.'

'Why did you go to Eastvale that night in particular?'

'Because it was so close to Christmas and Patsy and I . . . well, I always leave things till the last minute, and we just didn't want to have to go anywhere over the next few days. I'm very involved in a complex piece of music right now. It's all to do with the rhythms of the sea, so I don't want to spend more time than necessary away from here. I have no other commitments until after the new year, so I thought I'd get the shopping and Veronica's present out of the way, then my time would be my own.' He returned to the chair and started to refill his pipe. 'Believe me, it's nothing more sinister than that. I haven't killed anyone. I couldn't. Not even someone I hated the way I hated Caroline Hartley. If I'd been stupid enough to believe that killing Caroline would bring back Veronica, I'd have done it two years ago. But I've got a new life now, with Patsy. It's been tough getting here, but I've put Veronica behind me now.'

'Yet you still took her a *special* Christmas present. Rather a sentimental gesture, wouldn't you say?'

'I never claimed to have no feelings for her. After so long, you can't help that. She put me through hell, but that's over.' He took Patsy's hand. 'I'm happier now than I've ever been.'

It was the second time Banks had heard someone refer to having a motive for killing Caroline some years ago but not in the present. Ivers's story rang truer than Gary

Hartley's, though. In the first place, Ivers obviously did have a comfortable life with an attractive younger woman, a cosy cottage by the sea and his music. Gary Hartley had nothing. On the other hand, Ivers could easily have lost his temper and lashed out at something Caroline said. Sometimes, after all the big things have been endured and overcome, some apparently inconsequential matter sets off an explosion. There was no real evidence pointing either way, though the use of a knife so close to hand indicated a spontaneous act. If he charged Claude Ivers with murder now, he wouldn't have had much of a case.

'I'd like you to drop by the Eastvale police station tomorrow morning and sign a statement,' Banks said, gesturing for Susan to close her notebook.

'Must I . . .? My work . . .?'

'Much as I love your music, Mr Ivers,' Banks said, 'I'm afraid you must.' He smiled. 'Look at it this way, it's a hell of a lot better than being charged with murder and sitting in a cell with the drunks on New Year's Eve.'

'You're not charging me?'

'Not yet. But I want you to stay where I can find you. Any unexpected moves on your part will be considered as very suspicious behaviour indeed.'

Ivers nodded. 'I wasn't going anywhere.'

'Good. See you tomorrow then.'

Banks and Susan made their way back down the winding path to the car. On their left, only partially obscured by wraiths of mist, the sea lay quiet and the small waves lapped and hissed on the sands. Banks wondered what Ivers's winter sea music would sound like. Something along the lines of Peter Maxwell Davies's Third Symphony perhaps, or the 'Sea Interludes' from Britten's *Peter Grimes*? There was certainly a lot of potential in the idea.

They had just reached the road when Banks became aware of a figure running after them. It was Patsy Janowksi, and she hadn't even bothered to put an overcoat on. They turned, and she stood facing them, shivering, with her arms wrapped around her chest. 'I need to talk to you,' she said. 'Please. It's really important.'

Banks nodded. 'Go on.'

She looked around. 'Is there somewhere we can go? I'm freezing.'

They were outside the Lobster Inn, and Banks could think of no better place to talk. They went inside and found the lounge almost deserted except for the landlord and a couple of gnarled old men chatting at the bar. The large room was cold and draughty, even by the hearth where they sat. The fire clearly hadn't been lit long and the pub had not yet warmed up.

Banks walked to the bar. The two old men flicked their hooded eyes in his direction and continued talking in low voices, thick with local dialect. The landlord shuffled over and stood in front of Banks drying a glass. He neither spoke nor looked up. Banks found himself marvelling at Jim Hatchley for getting information out of such a taciturn old bugger. One day he'd have to ask Jim how he'd managed it.

He asked for three whiskies and the landlord ambled off without a word. The entire transaction took place in silence. When he got back to the table, Banks found Patsy and Susan Gay huddled around the meagre fire trying to get warm.

'It's not the cold I mind,' Patsy was saying, 'but the goddamn *chill*. It's so damp it gets right in your bones.'

'Where are you from?' Banks asked.

'Huntington Beach, California.'

'Warm there?'

Patsy managed a smile. 'All year round. They even play beach volley ball in winter. Don't get me wrong, though. I love England, even the weather. I'm just not dressed right for outdoors today.'

Banks passed her the whisky. 'Here. This should warm the cockles of your heart, as we say up here.'

'Thank you.' She took a sip and smacked her lips. Her eyes ranged around the pub and settled briefly, like a butterfly, on various objects: a dented ashtray, the range of wine glasses above the bar, an optic, the old fishing print on the far wall.

Banks lit a cigarette and leaned back in his chair. 'What was it you wanted to tell us?'

Patsy frowned. 'I know it must seem too late to you, that we've told so many lies, but Claude was telling the truth just now, honestly he was. We only lied because we knew he'd be the main suspect.'

'You must have known we'd find out the truth sooner or later.'

She shook her head. 'Claude said it's only on television that things like that happen. Not in real life. Despite what he says, he *has* watched television. He said policemen in real life are just thick.' She put her hand to her mouth. 'Oh shit, I'm sorry.'

Banks smiled. 'Where *did* you drive to that night?'

'Well, that's just what I came out to tell you. I know Claude can't have killed Caroline Hartley because I went to see her after he'd left, and I can assure you she was still alive then.'

'What do you mean?'

Patsy rubbed her temple and frowned. 'What I say. Look, I know it's not very nice, but I was . . . well, checking up on him.'

'You suspected he was still involved with Veronica Shildon?'

'Yes. He still loves her, there's no doubt about that. You heard what he said. But I did hope he really had put her behind him . . . and I know he loves me, too. I suppose I'm just jealous, possessive. I've been burned before by people hung up on past relationships.'

'Did you know him when he split up with her?'

'No. We met afterwards. He was in real bad shape.'

'In what way?'

'In every way. Claude is a naturally confident man, used to getting what he wants and having his own way, but after he split with Veronica his self-esteem was at rock-bottom. He felt betrayed and . . . well . . . sexually, too, he felt worthless and unwanted. He told me he never thought another woman would want him as long as he lived.' She smiled and looked into the fire. 'I know it sounds like a come-on, but it wasn't. You have to know him. When we got together I helped him build up his confidence again. There was nothing wrong with him, really. It was all just the psychological mess caused by what that woman did to him.'

'Caroline?'

'No, Veronica. He always blamed Caroline, and I never contradicted him. But if anyone's the bitch, Veronica is, the way she treated him. All of a sudden, she comes along and tells him, 'I'm not really the woman you think I am. In fact, I never have been. It's all been an illusion, an act, just to please you. But I can't do it any more. I've seen the light. I've found someone else – a woman, in fact – and I'm leaving you to go and live with her.' I'm sure you can imagine the impact of something like that on a man better than I can. Especially a man as sensitive and vulnerable as

Claude. The bitch! Anyway, he never saw it that way. He always saw Caroline as the enemy, the wife-stealer, and Veronica as the victim. He thought she'd end up getting hurt, discarded, when Caroline had finished with her. After all, there was ten years between them.' She held up her hand before anyone could say a word. 'All right, I know, I know. I'm nobody to talk. There are nearly thirty years between Claude and me. But that's different.'

Nobody challenged her. Banks had almost finished his whisky. He felt like another one. A single shouldn't put him over the limit for driving. This time Susan offered to go and buy the drinks.

'What are you trying to say, Ms Janowski?' Banks asked, swirling the amber-gold liquid in the bottom of the glass. 'That you were jealous of Claude Ivers's relationship with his wife and that you followed him that night to find out if he was still seeing her secretly?'

'I didn't exactly follow him,' she said. 'You've got to understand how difficult all this has been for Claude and me. We've had one or two rows about his seeing Veronica, usually after he's been for dinner with her and got back late. I don't know . . . as I said, I must be a terribly jealous person, but I couldn't just sit back and accept it. Oh, it's not even as if I thought they were having an affair or anything. Sometimes an emotional attachment to another person can seem like just as much of a threat or betrayal as a sexual one – maybe even more so. Can you understand that?' Banks nodded. Susan came back with the drinks. 'Anyway,' Patsy went on, 'he didn't tell me where he was going that evening, and I figured because of the rows we'd had, he was keeping it from me, you know, that he was going to see *her*. That got me all worried. I just couldn't stay in the house alone, so I decided to call at Veronica's to see if I was right.'

'And what happened?'

'I couldn't see his car anywhere. You can't park in the street, of course, but it wasn't even anywhere in sight on King Street. Then I finally plucked up my courage and went to the house. I knocked on the door and Caroline Hartley answered. I didn't think she'd recognize me because we'd hardly met, but she did. She must be very good with faces. She asked me in, but I didn't want to go. I asked her if Claude was in the house and she laughed. She told me he had called but Veronica was out and he clearly hadn't wanted to spend a minute longer than he had to with her. He'd left his present and gone. I thanked her and went back to the car. Then I drove home. That's all.'

'What time did you arrive at the house?'

'About a quarter after seven, twenty after, maybe. It took about an hour and a quarter to drive from Redburn, then five minutes or so to walk from where I parked the car.'

'Did you see anyone else approaching the house as you left?'

Patsy shook her head. 'No. I don't think so. The street was quiet. I . . . I can't really remember. There were a few people in King Street, shoppers. I'm so confused about it.'

'Think,' Banks said. 'Try to rerun the scene in your mind. Let us know if you remember anything at all. It could be important. Will you try?'

Patsy nodded. 'All right.'

'Was Mr Ivers in when you got home?'

'No. He got back later with the shopping.'

'Didn't you ask where he'd been?'

'Yes. We had a row. A bad one. But we made up.' She blushed and looked into the fireplace.

Banks lit a cigarette and let a few moments pass, then he asked, 'How did Caroline Hartley seem when you saw her?'

Patsy shrugged. 'Fine, I guess. I never really thought about it. She was obviously being sarcastic about Claude, but that was only to be expected.'

'She didn't seem worried or frightened when she answered the door?'

'Not at all.'

'What was she wearing?'

'Some sort of kimono-style bathrobe, as if she'd just come out of the shower or something.'

'Could you hear music playing?'

'No.'

'Can you remember exactly what she said to you?'

Patsy sipped some whisky and frowned. 'Just that he'd been and gone and left some boring classical record for Veronica. That's all.'

'She knew what the present was?'

'Seemed to, yes. She didn't mention the title, the one you talked about the other day, but she did use the words "boring classical record". I remember that because I took it as an insult to Claude.'

'She could have been just guessing,' Susan said. 'After all, Mr Ivers *is* a classical musician, and he knows Veronica's tastes. He'd hardly be likely to bring her the Rolling Stones or something, would he?'

'Possibly not,' Banks said. 'Either that, or she'd opened it to see what was so special that she didn't know about. Anyway, it doesn't matter for now.' He turned back to Patsy. 'What happened next?'

'Nothing. I told you. I left and drove home.'

Banks stubbed out his cigarette and looked closely at

her. She stared back defiantly, lips close together, eyes serious. 'Look,' she said, 'I know what you're thinking. I didn't kill her. Think about it. I'd hardly do that, would I? With her out of the way there was more chance of my losing Claude back to Veronica, wasn't there?'

It made a kind of sense, but Banks knew that murders are rarely so logically committed. Still, he felt inclined to believe her for the moment. For one thing, her story tallied with what the neighbours had seen: one man – Ivers, obviously – and two women. The one who had simply knocked at the door like a salesperson had been Patsy, then, asking after Ivers. And unless she had returned later, she was in the clear.

So if Patsy was the first woman visitor, and she was telling the truth, then who was the next: Faith Green? Teresa Pedmore? Veronica herself? Ruth, the mystery woman from London? Or had someone called even later than the last woman, someone none of the neighbours had seen? A man? It was possible. Gary Hartley? James Conran? Someone else from the dramatic society? The father of Caroline's child? A psychopath? Even Ivers himself could have returned. He hadn't been at home when Patsy got back to Redburn. Banks made a note to question the neighbours again and see if he could get a better description. It was unlikely, especially after so much time had elapsed, but still worth a try. At least someone might be able to tell them whether the woman who had knocked at the door and gone away was dressed the same as the one who did go in later.

Banks finished his drink. 'Thank you, Ms Janowski,' he said. 'I think you'd better come along tomorrow with Mr Ivers and make a statement, all right?'

She nodded. 'Yes, yes, of course.' Then she knocked back the rest of her drink and left.

'What do you think?' Banks asked Susan.

'I don't know. I'd want to keep an eye on them.'

'Maybe I'll ask Jim Hatchley to drop by once or twice over the next few days and make sure they're not up to anything. Any ideas about what did happen that night?'

Susan paused, took a delicate sip of whisky, then said, 'I've been wondering about Veronica Shildon. I know she doesn't seem to have a motive, but I can't help but keep coming back to her. Maybe everything wasn't as wonderful as she made out between her and Caroline Hartley. I mean, what if she was jealous? What if she saw Patsy Janowski leaving the house and thought there was something to it? Maybe there even *was* something to it. Caroline Hartley could have taken her own robe off, and if Veronica had found her naked . . . She could have charged in, had a row with Caroline and killed her. Then she could have changed her clothes, sneaked out and come back later.'

They walked out into the cold and sat in the car while it warmed up. 'It's possible,' Banks said. 'But we checked the entire house for blood-stained clothing and found nothing. There were no pieces of charred cloth in the fire either. I'm not saying she couldn't have found a way, just that I haven't figured it out yet. We seem to have too many suspects. Too many motives and opportunities.' He slammed the wheel with the flat of his hand. 'I still keep coming back to that damn record, though. Why? Why would somebody put a record on and leave it to repeat?'

'Perhaps Caroline herself put it on.'

'She hated classical music. She may have opened it, but I doubt she'd have played it.'

'But if Veronica had come back . . .?'

'If it happened the way you suggest, and she'd seen

Patsy leaving, she'd have been on the warpath. She'd hardly have stopped to listen to her Christmas present first, especially on December twenty-second. No. It doesn't make sense.' He spoke quietly, almost to himself. 'But the music is for the burial of a very small child. Caroline's child could be anything up to nine or ten by now. Maybe if I can track the kid down . . .'

'That's if whoever put the record on knew what it was and knew what it meant.'

'Oh, the killer knew all right, I'm sure of that.'

'Are you sure you're not making too much of it, sir?'

'I might be. But you've got to admit it's a puzzle.'

'Talking about records, sir . . .'

'Yes?'

'Do you think you could play something different on the way back? I don't mean to be rude, sir, but that music you were playing on the way over was so boring it nearly put me to sleep.'

Banks laughed and drove off. 'Your wish is my command.'

TWO

'Well, well, well, if it isn't Mr Banks. It's a rare treat seeing you in here.'

'Sorry, Vicar. There's something about my job that disinclines me to believe in a benevolent deity.'

'You catch your criminals sometimes, don't you?'

'Yes.'

'Well, there you are. The Lord works in mysterious ways.'

The Reverend Piers Catcott's eyes twinkled. He was a

slight man in his late forties, who looked more like an accountant than a minister: spectacles, thinning silver hair, slight stoop and an anaemic, well-scrubbed complexion. He was also, Banks had discovered from their discussions and arguments over pints in the Queen's Arms, an extraordinarily erudite and intelligent man. Pity, Banks thought, about the superstition he deemed fit to embrace.

'Still,' Catcott said, 'I don't think you made the supreme sacrifice of entering this hallowed place just to argue theology, did you?'

Banks smiled. 'That's right, Vicar. We can do that much better in the pub. No, it's just some background information I want. Knowledge, rather. I want to pick your brains.'

'Oh dear, I should think that'll be much more comfortable sitting down. That is if you've no objection to taking a pew. Or we could go into the vestry?'

'A pew'll do fine,' Banks said, 'as long as you don't expect me to kneel.'

The small church was dim and cool. Weak evening sunlight filtered through the stained-glass windows. Banks had seen more of it from the outside than in, though he had been in once or twice to look at the Celtic cross and stone font. The pews creaked as they sat down.

'What's the liturgy?' Banks asked.

'Oh, come on, Mr Banks,' Catcott said with a thin-lipped smile. 'Surely even a heathen like yourself knows that?'

'Humour me.'

Catcott put a pale, slender forefinger to his lips. 'Very well. The liturgy. The word is often used to refer to the *Book of Common Prayer*, of course, but the meaning goes back a long time beyond that, a long time. Essentially, it's simply the order of services in the church. As even you probably know, we have different services at different times of the year – Christmas, Easter, Harvest Festival and the like. And, you might remember from your misspent youth, we sing different hymns and have different lessons according to the nature of the service. Do you follow so far?'

Banks nodded.

'There is a liturgical calendar to cover the year's worship. Advent, the fourth Sunday before Christmas, came first, then Christmas itself, ending with Epiphany, the sixth of January, or twelfth night, to you. Then we have the Pre-Lenten season, followed by Lent, when you're supposed to give up bad habits –' here he paused and cast a narrow-eyed look at Banks – 'and the last three are Eastertide, Pentecost and Trinity. But what on earth do you want to know all this for? Surely you're not thinking of—'

'No, I'm not. And believe me, Vicar, you'd be better off not knowing. I'm particularly interested in the music that goes along with these services.'

'Liturgical music? Well, that's a slightly different matter. It's very complicated. Goes back to Gregorian chants. But basically, each part of the year has its own biblical texts, and early composers set these to music. People still do it, of course – Vaughan Williams, Finzi and Britten did quite a bit – but it's rarely part of a normal church service these days. What you're probably talking about are biblical texts, or parts of texts, set to music. Actually, most of them were abolished in 1563.'

'What kind of music are you talking about?'

'All kinds, right from early polyphonic motets. A composer would take a text, perhaps a psalm, and set it to music. In Latin, of course.'

'Like a *Gloria* or a *Magnificat*?'

'Actually, the *Gloria* is part of the Mass, which has its own liturgy. I told you, it can get quite complicated.'

Banks remembered the section titles from his tapes of masses and requiems: *Kyrie Eleison, Agnus Dei, Credo.* 'I think I'm getting the idea,' he said. 'What about *Laudate pueri*?'

'Ah, yes, "*Laudate pueri, Dominum . . .*" It means "Praise the Lord, ye children." That was a popular liturgical work. Based on Psalm 112, if my memory serves me right.'

'Do you know Vivaldi's settings?'

'Indeed I do. Magnificent.'

'It says in the notes to my tape that the piece may have been used as part of the burial service for a small child. Is that right?'

Catcott rubbed his smooth chin. 'That would make sense, yes.'

'Would that be fairly common knowledge?'

'Well, *you* knew it, didn't you? I'd say any reasonably well-educated person might have a chance of knowing.'

'Would someone like Claude Ivers know?'

'Ivers? Of course. I remember reading an article about him in *Gramophone* and he's extremely knowledgeable about sacred music. Pity he doesn't see fit to write any himself instead of that monotonous stuff he churns out.'

Banks smiled. Catcott had sown the seeds of another Queen's Arms argument, but there was no time to pursue the point now.

'Thank you, Vicar.' Banks stood up and shook hands with Catcott, then headed out. His footsteps echoed on the cold stone. Just before he got to the door he heard the vicar call out from behind him, 'The collection box for the restoration fund is to your right.'

Banks felt in his pocket for a pound, dropped it in the box and left.

THREE

Fortunately, Charles Cooper was at home when Banks and Richmond called just after teatime that day. Mrs Cooper flitted about the kitchen offering coffee, but Banks suggested he and Richmond retire with her husband somewhere private. Mrs Cooper seemed worried by that, but she raised no real objection. They settled for the living room, dominated by a huge television screen, and Richmond took out his notebook.

Cooper, Banks noticed, looked a few years older than his wife. He had a weak chin and a veined nose; his sparse grey hair was combed straight back. He was an odd shape, mostly skin and bone with rounded shoulders, but he had a substantial pot-belly bulging through his grey pullover.

'It's a pleasure to meet you at last,' said Cooper. 'Of course, I've heard all about the business from my wife. Dreadful.'

He seemed nervous and fidgety, Banks thought, though his tone seemed calm and genuine enough.

'What did you do on the evening of December the twenty-second?' Banks asked.

'I worked,' Cooper said with a sigh. 'I seemed to do nothing else around that time.'

'I understand you're general manager of a chain of toy shops?'

'That's right.'

'And on the twenty-second you were dealing with some stock shortages in the Barnard Castle branch?'

185

Cooper nodded.

'What time did you leave?'

He paused. 'Well, let me see . . . I got home about eleven.'

'Yes, but what time did you leave the shop?'

'It's about a half-hour drive, a little slower in the snow. I suppose it'd be about ten fifteen.'

'You left the shop at ten fifteen and came straight home?'

'Why, yes. Look, is—'

'Are you sure, Mr Cooper?'

Cooper looked towards the sideboard and nervously licked his lips. 'I ought to know,' he said.

Richmond glanced up from his notes. 'It's just that the lady who works there told me you left about six, Mr Cooper. Would she have any reason to lie?'

Cooper looked from Richmond to Banks and back. 'I . . . I don't understand.'

Banks leaned forward. 'It's perfectly simple,' he said. 'You left the shop at six o'clock, not at ten fifteen, as you led us to believe. What were you doing all that time?'

Cooper pursed his lips and looked down at the liver spots on the backs of his hands.

'What was your relationship with Caroline Hartley?' Banks asked.

'What do you mean?' he said. 'I didn't have a relationship with her.'

'Were you fond of her?'

'I suppose so. We were just acquaintances.'

'She didn't remind you of your late daughter, Corinne?'

Cooper turned red. 'I don't know who told you that, but it's not true. And you've no right to bring my daughter into it. It's exactly as I said. We were neighbours. Yes, I liked the girl, but that's all.'

'You didn't attempt to start an affair with her?'

'Don't be ridiculous! She was young enough to be my . . . Besides, you know as well as I do she wasn't interested in men.'

'But you did try?'

'I did no such thing.' He grasped the chair arms and started to get up. 'I think you ought to leave now.'

'We'll leave when we're satisfied, Mr Cooper,' Banks said. 'Please sit down.'

Cooper slumped back in his chair and started twisting his hands in his lap.

'Do have a drink if you want,' Banks said. 'That *is* what's on your mind, isn't it?'

'Damn you!' Cooper jumped up with surprising agility, took a bottle of Scotch from the sideboard and poured himself three fingers. He didn't offer any to Banks or Richmond. He sat down again and drank half of it in one gulp.

'We're not satisfied yet, Mr Cooper,' Banks said. 'We're not satisfied at all. You've been lying to us. Now, that's nothing new. In our business, we expect it.' He jerked his thumb towards the wall. 'But a young woman was brutally murdered next door on December the twenty-second, a woman you liked, who reminded you of your daughter. Now I'd think that unless you killed her yourself you'd want to help, you'd want to tell us the truth.'

'I didn't kill her, for God's sake. Why on earth would I do that?'

'You tell me.'

'I told you, I didn't kill her. And whatever I did that night has no bearing whatsoever on what happened next door.'

'Let me be the judge of that.'

Cooper swirled his drink and took another long sip.

'We'll stay until you tell us,' Banks said. 'Unless you'd prefer to get your coat and—'

'All right, all right.' Mr Cooper waved his free hand. 'I did leave the shop at six, but I wasn't anywhere near Eastvale until eleven, I swear it.'

'Where were you?'

'Does it really matter?'

'We have to check.'

Cooper got up and poured himself another drink. He cocked his ear towards the living-room door, then, satisfied by the sound of washing-up water running in the kitchen, spoke quietly.

'I drink, Mr Banks,' he said. 'Simple as that. Ever since Corinne . . . well, you don't need to know about that. But Christine doesn't approve.' He looked at his glass. 'Oh, she's not a teetotaller or anything. She'll allow the occasional glass of Scotch after dinner, but more than one and I can even smell the disapproval. So I drink elsewhere.'

'Where were you drinking that night?' Banks asked.

'Tan Hill,' said Cooper. 'It's an isolated spot. I like it up there.'

'Were you alone?'

'No. There's a group of regulars.'

'Names?'

Cooper gave the names and Richmond wrote them down.

'What time did you leave?'

'About ten thirty. I daren't be *too* late. And I keep some breath mints in the car so Christine can't smell anything.'

'Anything else to tell us?'

Cooper shook his head. 'No, nothing. That's it. Look, I'm sorry, I . . . I didn't mean to cause any problems. It's really nothing to do with poor Caroline's death at all.'

'We'll see,' said Banks, and got up to leave with Richmond.

'There is one small thing,' Cooper said before they got to the door.

Banks turned. 'Yes?'

'The driving. I mean, I'd had a few drinks. I wasn't drunk, honestly. You won't do anything to my licence, will you?'

'I shouldn't worry about that,' Banks said. 'I think the statute of limitations has just about run out.' He made a mental note to find out the licence number of Cooper's car and alert the local police patrols.

'Fancy a trip to Tan Hill?' Banks asked Richmond outside.

'Tonight?'

'Sooner the better, don't you think?'

Richmond looked at his watch and frowned. 'Well, I did have a . . . er—'

'Take her with you,' Banks said. 'It's a routine enquiry. Won't take long.'

Richmond touched his moustache. 'Not a bad idea,' he said. 'Not bad at all.'

'Off you go then. I'll see if I can get anything more out of the people across the street.'

FOUR

It was a cold night – spiky, needle-sharp cold rather than the damp, numbing chill of the sea mist – and the crusts of ice over puddles on the pavements cracked as Banks walked over them, hands deep in his fur-lined car-coat pockets. He decided to call first on Patrick Farlowe, who had originally said he was sure he had noticed two women and a man call at the house on separate occasions between about six and seven thirty on 22 December.

Farlowe was finishing his dinner when Banks arrived, and there was still a little wine left in the bottle. Banks accepted a glass and the invitation to join Farlowe in the den while his wife cleared the table. They certainly lived well in Oakwood Mews, Banks noted: remains of sirloin steaks on the plates, fine cutlery, a cut-glass vase holding two long-stemmed roses. The wine was a decent Crozes-Hermitage.

The den was an upstairs study with two walls of dark bookcases, a deep, leather armchair by a standard lamp and a small teak table beside it for resting cups of coffee, pencils and notepads. The light gleamed on the dark, varnished surfaces of the wood. The Hartley place in Harrogate would have been a larger version of this, Banks thought, before Gary let it fall to ruin.

Farlowe relaxed in his armchair and Banks took the swivel chair in front of the writing desk. One sniff of the clean, leather-scented air tipped him off that this was a non-smoking room.

'We're very grateful for the information you gave us,' Banks began, 'but I was wondering if you remembered anything else about that evening.'

Farlowe, a small, roly-poly man with tufts of grey hair over his ears, still wearing a three-piece suit, pressed his damp lips together and scratched the side of his nose. Finally he shook his head. The roll of pink fat around his neck wobbled. 'Can't say as I do, no.'

'Do you mind if we go over a couple of points?'

'Not at all. Be pleased to.'

Banks sipped some wine and asked about the timing.

Farlowe strained to remember for a moment, then answered. 'I know the first one, the man, called at about seven o'clock because we'd just had supper and I was in the front room turning the Christmas-tree lights on. Then I caught a glimpse of the woman standing on the doorstep when I went to replace a burnt-out bulb a bit later. The door was open and she was talking to the Hartley woman.'

'Did you get a clear look at her?'

'No. She had her back to me. Nicely shaped, though.'

'So there's no doubt it was a woman?'

'None at all.'

'What was she wearing?'

He put a pudgy finger to his lips and whistled while trying to recall the scene. 'Let me see . . . It was a winter jacket of some kind, padded or thickly lined. Waist-length, no longer, because I could see the outline of her hips. That's how I knew it was a woman. A youngish one, I'd say. And she wore tight jeans. Lovely long legs she had.' He winked.

'What about her hair?'

'It was wrapped in a scarf. I really couldn't see it at all. And she was silhouetted by the hall light of the house, of course, so I couldn't make out any detail. It was only a quick glimpse I got. I already told all this to your constable the other night.'

'I know, and I'm sorry to put you through it again, sir. Sometimes, believe it or not, people do remember more when they're given a few days to think about it. What was Caroline Hartley wearing?'

'As far as I could tell, it was some kind of bathrobe. She held it wrapped tight around her while she stood at the door, as if she was feeling the cold. I'm sorry I can't be of any more help. I'd like to see the blighter caught, of course. Don't like the idea of a murderer stalking the neighbourhood.'

'The third visitor,' Banks asked. 'Can you be clearer about the time?'

'I have given the matter some thought,' Farlowe said, reaching for a decanter on the table beside him. 'Port?'

Banks tossed back the rest of his wine and held his glass out. 'Please. And . . .?'

'I'm trying to recollect why I was at the front window again, but it's slipped my mind. Perhaps I'd heard a noise or something . . .' He tapped the side of head. 'That's it! I remember. I heard some music and I went out to see if we had carol singers in the street. Plagued by them we are.' He made them sound like an infestation of rodents. 'I consider I've handed out my fair share this year. Should be restricted to Christmas Eve, if you ask me. Anyway, it was only the wife, putting the radio on.'

'Do you remember the time?'

'No. All I remember, now I come to think about it, is hearing "Away in a Manger" and heading for the window. But there was no one at the door. I noticed a woman going into the house over the street, the house where the woman was murdered.'

'Can you add anything to your earlier description?'

'I'm sorry. It all happened so fast. I have to admit, I was rather angry at the thought of more singers and I just caught the figure out of the corner of my eye.'

'But you're sure it was a woman?'

'Well, this one was wearing a light coat, belted, I think, because it came in at the waist, right down to mid-calves, and she definitely didn't have any trousers on. I thought I could see the bottom of a dress or skirt, too, as if the coat was just a bit too short to cover the dress. And you could see her legs below that.'

'What about height? Any idea?'

'A little taller than the woman who answered the door, Caroline Hartley.'

'Hair?'

He shook his head. 'Again, her head was covered by a scarf of some kind.'

'And this woman definitely entered the house?'

'Oh, yes. She was walking in when I saw her.'

'So you didn't notice Caroline Hartley's reaction to seeing her?'

'No, not at all. I didn't even see Caroline that time, just this other woman silhouetted as she walked in the door.'

'So Caroline might not have let her in?'

'I suppose that's possible. But there didn't seem anything suspicious about it. She didn't seem to be pushing, and I didn't hear any noise of forced entry or anything like that. It all seemed perfectly normal to me. I try to be a responsible neighbour. If I'd thought there was any trouble I would have called the police.'

'Did you see her leave?'

'No. But then I didn't look out the window again. Anybody could have arrived or left between seven thirty and the time when . . . well, you know . . . and I wouldn't have seen them.'

Banks finished his port and stood up. 'Thank you for being so co-operative, Mr Farlowe. Also for the port. It was very good.'

Farlowe smiled. 'Yes, it is, rather, isn't it. The sixty-three vintage, you know.' He struggled to get out of his armchair, floundering like a seal on a beach.

'Please don't bother showing me out,' Banks said. 'I'll find my own way.'

'Oh, very well. Fine, then. Bye.' And Banks saw Mr Farlowe reach for the decanter again as he left the room. A suitable case for gout, that one. A lot of tipplers, it seemed, on Oakwood Mews.

On the way out, he met Mrs Farlowe in the hall. She had seen nothing that night, but she was able to tell him that the radio had been tuned to Radio Three, as always, when she turned it on. No, she couldn't remember what time, but her husband was right. It was a carol service from King's College. 'Away in a Manger' had been playing. Lovely tune, that one, isn't it? Banks agreed and left.

From Mrs Eldridge at number eight Banks got no further information. She had seen the man go in first, then the woman knocking on the door at about seven fifteen. No, she hadn't seen the man leave in the meantime, but the woman in the short coat and tight jeans definitely didn't enter the house. And it wasn't the same woman as the one who called later. This one was a bit taller and dressed differently. Some kind of long dress under her coat instead of jeans. The way it looked, unless Patsy Janowski had dashed off, changed clothes and added a few inches to her height in the interim, the third visitor couldn't possibly have been her.

He needed to know who this third woman was. Unless someone else had come after her, someone nobody had seen arrive, or unless Claude Ivers had been in the house all the time and nobody had seen him leave, then she was the one, almost certainly, who had killed Caroline Hartley. Was it Veronica Shildon, as Susan had suggested? Banks didn't think so – her love and grief seemed genuine – but he needed to talk to her again. There was a lot of ground yet to cover before he could hope to understand the people, and therefore the motives, involved in this case.

There was, however, one small, practical piece of information he carried away with him. Both Mr and Mrs Farlowe had said that the third woman entered the house – bidden or otherwise – when 'Away in a Manger' was being played on Radio Three. It should be possible to find out from the local BBC station what time the programme started, the order of carols in the concert and the length of each one. Given that information, it would be simple to work out at exactly what time the mysterious third woman had entered Caroline Hartley's house and, in all likelihood, stabbed her to death with a kitchen knife.

8

ONE

Banks walked slowly by the river. He wore his fur-lined suede car-coat, collar up, hands thrust deep in his pockets. As he walked, he breathed out plumes of air. The river wasn't entirely frozen over; ducks paddled as usual, apparently oblivious to the cold, in channels between the lumps of grey ice.

As he walked, he thought about the success he had had that morning with the BBC. A keen young researcher in the local studio had taken the trouble to dig out and listen to the 22 December taped carol broadcast, using a stopwatch. The programme had started at seven sharp. 'Away in a Manger' began just over midway through the broadcast – 7.21, to be exact – and finished two minutes, fourteen seconds later. Banks marvelled at the precision. With such a sense of exact measurement, the young woman perhaps had a future working for the Guinness Book of Records or the Olympic Records Committee. Anyway, they now knew that Caroline's likely killer had been let in between 7.21 and 7.24.

They also knew that it wasn't Charles Cooper. Richmond had talked to the regulars at Tan Hill and confirmed his alibi: Cooper had been drinking there between about six thirty and ten thirty on 22 December and on most other evenings leading up to the Christmas period. It would be more difficult for him to explain long absences to his wife at any other time, Banks thought.

Banks started thinking about the victim, Caroline Hartley, again and realized he still didn't know much about her. She had run away from home at sixteen, gone to London, got herself pregnant, picked up a conviction for soliciting, come back up north and shacked up first with Nancy Wood, who was out of the picture now, and then with Veronica Shildon. Attractive to both men and women – but now interested only in the latter – vivacious and enthusiastic, but given to thoughtful, secretive moods, a budding actress, a good mimic. That was about all. It covered ten years of the woman's life, and it didn't add up to a hell of a lot. There had to be more, and the only place to find out – as Caroline's friends and family either wouldn't talk or didn't know – was in London. But where to start?

Banks picked up a flat stone and skimmed it across the water towards the Green. Briefly, he thought of Jenny Fuller, who lived in one of the Georgian semis there. A lecturer in psychology at York, she had helped Banks before. She would be damn useful in this case, too, he thought. But she'd gone away somewhere warm for Christmas. Tough luck.

Up ahead, near the bridge, Banks saw a boy, no older than twelve or thirteen. He had a catapult and was aiming pebbles at the ducks out on the river. Banks approached him. Before saying a word, he took out his identity card and let the boy have a good long look.

The boy read it, then glanced up at Banks and said, 'Are you really a copper or just one of those perverts? My dad's warned me about blokes like you.'

'Lucky for you, sonny, I'm really a copper,' Banks said,

and snatched the metal catapult from the boy's hand.

'Hey! What you doing? That's mine.'

'That's a dangerous weapon is what that is,' Banks said, slipping it in his coat pocket. 'Think yourself lucky I don't take you in. What do you want to go aiming at those ducks for anyway? What harm have they ever done you?'

'Dunno,' the kid said. 'I wasn't meaning to kill them or anything. I just wanted to see if I could hit one. Can I have my catapult back, mister?'

'No.'

'Go on. It cost me a quid, that did. I saved up out of my pocket money.'

'Well don't bother saving up for another,' Banks said, walking away.

'It's bloody daylight robbery,' the kid called after him. 'You're no better than a thief!'

But Banks ignored him, and soon the shouting died down. There was something in what the boy had said that interested him: 'I wasn't meaning to kill them or anything. I just wanted to see if I could hit one.'

Could he really divorce the action from its result as cleanly and innocently as that? And if he could, could a murderer, too? There was no doubt that whoever plunged the knife into Caroline Hartley's body had meant her to be dead, but had that been the killer's original intention? The bruise on the cheek indicated that she had been hit, perhaps stunned, first. How had that come about? Was it the kind of thing a woman would do, punch another woman?

Could it have been some kind of sexual encounter gone out of control, with the original object not so much murder but just a desire to see how far things could go? A sado-masochistic fantasy turned reality, perhaps? After all,

Caroline Hartley had been naked. But that was absurd. Veronica and Caroline were respectable, middle-class, conservative lesbians; they didn't cruise the gay bars or try to lure innocent schoolgirls back to the house for orgies, like the lesbians one read about in lurid tabloids. Still, when lovers fight, no matter what sex, they can easily become violent towards one another. What happened between the punch and the stabbing? What warped sequence of emotions did the killer feel? Caroline must have been unconscious, or at least momentarily stunned, and the killer must have picked up the knife, which lay so conveniently on the table by the cake.

What made her do it? Would she have done it if the knife hadn't been so close to hand? Would she have gone into the kitchen and taken a knife from the drawer and still had the resolve when she got back to the living room? Impossible questions to answer – the kind that Jenny might have been able to help with – but they had to be answered or he would never find the key to his problem. Banks needed to know what happened in the dark area, what it was that pushed someone beyond argument, past reason, past sex, beyond even simple physical assault, to murder.

He turned his back on the river and started walking up the hill by the formal gardens back around the castle to the market square. Back at the station, as soon as he turned from the stairwell to the corridor that led to his upstairs office, he saw Susan Gay come rushing towards him with a sheet of paper flapping in her hand. She looked like the cat that had got the cream. Her eyes gleamed with success.

'Found her,' she announced. 'Ruth. It's a small London publishing company. Sappho Press. I faxed them the photo and they said they had it taken for a dust jacket and for general publicity.'

'Good work,' Banks said. 'Tell me, what made you call that particular press out of the dozens we had listed?'

Susan looked puzzled. 'I got as far as "S" in the alphabet. It took me all morning.'

'Do you know who Sappho was?'

Susan shook her head.

Gristhorpe would have known, Banks thought, but you could hardly demand a degree in classics of everyone who wanted to join the police. On the other hand, perhaps it wouldn't be a bad idea: an elite squad of literary coppers.

'She was an ancient Greek poet from the isle of Lesbos,' he said.

'Is that . . .?' Susan began.

Banks nodded.

She blushed. 'Well I'd like to say I got the literary clue, like in Agatha Christie,' she said, 'but it was down to pure hard slog.'

Banks laughed. 'Well done, anyway. Tell me the details.'

'Her name's Ruth Dunne and apparently she's published a couple of books. Doing very well for herself in the poetry scene. The woman I spoke to said one of the bigger publishers might be after her soon. Faber and Faber perhaps.'

'What kind of stuff does she write?'

'Well, that's another thing. They told me she started by writing the kind of thing the Sappho Press people support. I assumed it was feminist stuff, but now you mention it . . . Anyway, she's moved away from that, they said, and it looks like she's shifting into a broader market, whatever that means.'

'Did you mention Caroline Hartley?'

'Yes. It's a funny thing. The editor recognized the name. She went to check and then told me Ruth Dunne's second book was dedicated to someone called Caroline. I thought it was odd we didn't find a copy among the victim's things, don't you?'

'She liked to travel light,' Banks said. 'Still, it would have made it a lot easier for us if we had. Maybe they just lost touch with one another.'

Susan passed the paper over. 'Anyway, she lives in Kennington. Here's the address. What now?'

'I'm going down there tomorrow. There's a few things I want to talk to Ruth Dunne about. She's the only link we have so far with Caroline Hartley's child and her life down there. I think she might be able to tell us quite a lot.'

TWO

Perhaps I'm pushing too hard, Susan told herself later that evening. She was trying to decide what to wear for her first real date with James Conran, but she couldn't help going over the past two days' events in her mind. Banks had seemed so calm, so sure of himself, with Claude Ivers. Susan, left to her own devices, would have charged into his studio.

She also doubted that she would have left Redburn without bringing both Ivers and the Janowski woman in for a lengthy interrogation at the station. After all, they had both been at the Oakwood Mews house around the time of Caroline Hartley's murder, and both had lied about it. She couldn't understand Banks's obsession with the record and the meaning of the music. In her experience, criminals weren't intelligent enough to leave erudite musical clues behind them. Things like that only happened in the detective stories she had read as a teenager. But the music *had* been playing, she had to admit, and that was very odd indeed.

She decided on the blue cotton blouse and navy mid-length skirt. Neither were so close fitting that they would reveal what she thought of as an unacceptably thick waist. And she mustn't overdress. Mario's was a little up-market, but it wasn't really posh.

The more she thought about the case, the more she thought about Veronica Shildon. Susan had felt intimidated by the woman's reserve and poise; and the mysterious transition from happily married woman to lesbian disturbed her. It just didn't seem possible.

Ivers could be right in blaming Caroline Hartley. Perhaps Veronica knew this too, deep down, and hated herself for allowing herself to fall so low. Then she found Caroline naked after seeing Patsy Janowski leave the house, and she hit out. That seemed as good an explanation as any to her. All they had to do was discover how Veronica had disposed of her bloody clothing. Surely if Banks put his mind to it, instead of dwelling on that damn music, he could come up with something. Gary Hartley, Susan thought, wasn't capable of the crime. He might be bitter, but he was also weak, a captive in his father's cold, decaying mansion.

Banks seemed to suspect everyone except Veronica Shildon – or at least he didn't see her as a serious contender. Perhaps it was to do with his being a man, Susan thought. Men perceived things differently; they were unsuited to spotting subtle nuances. They were basically selfish and saw things only in relation to their own egos, whereas women spun a more general net of consciousness. She knew Banks was astute enough not to get side-tracked by his feelings, at least most of the time, but maybe he was attracted to Veronica Shildon. There was something in that tension between her strait-laced exterior and inner passions that a man might find sexy. And the fact that he couldn't have her would only add to the excitement, make her seem more of a challenge. Didn't men always want unattainable women?

Rubbish, Susan told herself sharply. She was letting her imagination run away with her. Time to apply a bit of lipstick.

When she was ready, she looked again at her small tree and the few trimmings she had hastily put up on Christmas Eve. They made the place look a bit more like a home. As she looked around the room, she couldn't really see what was missing. The wallpaper, red roses on a cream background, was nice enough; the three-piece suite arranged around the gas fireplace looked a little shabby, but nonetheless cosy; and the bookcase added a learned look. There was a beautiful pine table, too, in the corner by the window, where she ate. So what was it?

Looking again at the Christmas trimmings, she realized with a shock what was missing. So simple, really. If she had been on a case looking objectively at a suspect's apartment and had seen one just like this, she would have known immediately. But because it was her own, she hadn't paid it the same attention. The one personal touch, the Christmas decorations, pointed out that there was nothing of *her* there; the room had no personality. The furniture, wallpaper, carpet could all belong to anyone. Where were the knick-knacks that people accumulate over the years? Where were the favourite prints on the walls, the framed photographs of loved ones on the mantelpiece, the ornaments on the windowsill? There were no books, only her textbooks, which she kept in the guest room she used as a study. And where was the music? She had a music centre her parents had bought for her twenty-first birthday, but all she ever listened to was the radio. She had no records or tapes at all.

The doorbell rang. Well, she thought, slipping on her coat, perhaps it's time I started. A nice landscape on the wall, over there, a Constable print or something, a couple of china figurines on the mantelpiece, a few books, and a record of that music Banks played in the car on the way back from Redburn yesterday. She had felt embarrassed and stupid when he had asked what she wanted to listen to, because she had no idea. She heard music on the radio, pop and classical, and enjoyed some of it, but could never remember the names of performers or titles of the pieces.

For some reason she had asked for some vocal music, and he had played a tape of Kiri Te Kanawa singing highlights from *Madama Butterfly*. Even Susan had heard of Kiri Te Kanawa, the soprano from New Zealand who had sung at the wedding of Prince Charles to Lady Di. One song in particular sent shivers all the way up her spine and made the hackles at the back of her neck stand on end. Banks had told her the heroine was imagining the return of her lover in the aria, which translated as 'One Fine Day'. Susan had taken a note of the title, and she would buy it for herself tomorrow, as a start to her collection. Perhaps she would also try to find out what happened in the story: did the lover return, as Butterfly dreamed?

The doorbell rang again. Smiling, Susan went downstairs to the front door to meet James. He told her she looked beautiful. She didn't believe him, but she felt wonderful as they got into his car and drove off into the icy night.

THREE

'Sorry about the mess,' Veronica Shildon said as she let Banks in. He looked around. There was no mess, really. He sat down. Veronica stood by the kitchen door with her arms folded.

'The reason I came,' he said, 'is to tell you that we've tracked down the woman in the picture.'

Veronica shifted her weight from one foot to the other. 'Yes?'

'Her name is Ruth Dunne. She's a poet, as you said, published by a small feminist press, and she lives in London.'

'You have an address?'

'Yes.'

'Thank you for telling me, Chief Inspector. I realize it might have been unethical.'

'Ms Shildon, I never do anything unethical.' His eyes twinkled when he smiled.

'I – I didn't mean . . .'

'It's all right.'

'Would you like some tea? I was just about to make some.'

'Yes, please. It's a bit nippy out there.'

'If you'd like something stronger . . .?'

'No, tea will do fine.'

While Veronica made the tea, Banks looked around the room. It was in a state of flux. In the first place, there was hardly anywhere to sit. The suite was gone, leaving only a couple of hard-backed chairs at the table by the window. Also, the sideboard had been moved, and the Christmas tree, along with all the trimmings, was gone, even though it was only 29 December. Banks wondered if Veronica could have done it all herself.

'Have you talked to her?' Veronica asked, placing the tray on the table and sitting opposite him.

'No, not yet. I'm going down there tomorrow morning. It wouldn't be wise to phone ahead.'

'You don't mean she's a suspect?'

'Until I find out otherwise, she is, and I don't want to give her any reason to run off if she thinks she's sitting pretty.'

'It must be an awful job you do,' Veronica said.

'Sometimes. But not as awful as the things the people we try to catch do.'

'Touché.'

'Anyway, I just thought I'd let you know.'

'And I'm grateful.' Veronica put her cup and saucer down. 'I'd like to see her,' she said. 'Ruth Dunne. If it's not too much of an imposition, may I travel down with you?'

Banks scratched the scar by his right eye, then crossed his legs. He knew he should say no. Officially, Veronica Shildon was a major suspect in her lover's murder. He had told her about Ruth Dunne only partly out of goodwill; mainly he had been interested in her reaction to the news. On the other hand, if he got her out of her normal environment, out of this house and out of Eastvale, he might be able to get her to open up a bit more about Caroline's background. Was that worth the risk of her making a break for it? It would be easy for her to disappear in a city as large as London. But why should she? They had no real evidence against her; they couldn't put her under arrest.

'I'm going by train,' he said. 'I won't be driving down. I never could stand driving in London.'

'Are you trying to put me off? I know it's an unusual

request to make Chief Inspector, but I've heard about Ruth often enough from Caroline, though never more than her first name and what a good friend she was. Somehow, now that Caroline's gone, I just feel I'd like to meet her. There's very little else left.'

Banks sipped at his tea and let a minute pass. 'On two conditions,' he said finally. 'First of all, I can't allow you to be present at the interview, and second, you'll have to wait until I've talked to her before you see her.'

Veronica nodded. 'That sounds fair.'

'I haven't finished yet.'

'But that was two.'

'I'll make it three, then. I reserve the right to stop you seeing her at all if for any reason I feel it necessary.'

'But why on earth . . .?'

'It should be obvious. If Ruth Dunne turns out to be even more of a suspect than she is now, I can't allow the two of you to discuss the case together. Do you agree to the terms?'

Veronica nodded slowly. 'I suppose I'll have to.'

'And you'll also have to return with me.'

'I was thinking of looking up an old friend,' Veronica said. 'Perhaps staying down for New Year . . .'

Banks shook his head. 'I'm already going out on a limb.'

Veronica stood up. 'Very well. I understand.'

'Right,' he said at the door. 'Eight twenty from Eastvale, change at Leeds.'

'I'll be there,' she said, and closed the door behind him.

FOUR

Mario's was a cosy restaurant in a narrow cul-de-sac of gift shops off North Market Street. It had a small bar at one end of the long room, stucco walls and small tables with red and white checked cloths and candles in orange pressed-glass jars. A man with a guitar sat on a stool at the far end quietly crooning Italian love songs.

The place was full when James and Susan got there and they had to sit for ten minutes at the bar. James ordered a half litre of Barolo, which they sipped as they waited.

He looked good, Susan thought. Clearly he had made some sartorial effort, replacing cords and polo-neck with grey slacks, a white shirt and a well-tailored, dark-blue sports jacket. His fair hair, thinning and combed forward flat against his skull, looked newly washed, and he had also shaved, as a couple of nicks under his chin testified. His grey eyes seemed bluer tonight, and they sparkled with life and mischief.

'You'll just love the cannelloni,' he said, putting his fingers to his lips and making a kissing gesture.

Susan laughed. How long was it since an attractive man had made her laugh? She had no idea. But very quickly she seemed to be getting over the idea of James Conran as drama teacher and moving towards . . . Well, she didn't quite know and didn't really want to contemplate just yet. At least not tonight. James chatted easily with the barman in fluent Italian and Susan sipped her wine, reading the labels of the liqueur bottles behind the bar. Soon, a white-jacketed waiter ushered them with a flourish to a table for two. Luckily, Susan thought, it wasn't too close to the singer, now lost in the throes of 'O Sole Mio'.

They examined their menus in silence, and Susan finally decided to take James's advice on the cannelloni. He ordered linguine in a white wine and clam sauce for himself. He had recommended that, too, but she was allergic to shellfish.

'I must say again,' he said, raising his glass in a toast, 'that you look gorgeous tonight.'

'Oh, don't be stupid.' Susan felt herself blush. She had done the best she could with her appearance, accenting her rather too thin lips and playing down the extra fat on her cheekbones with powder. She knew that she wasn't bad looking; her large eyes were a beautiful ultramarine colour and her short, blonde hair, naturally thick and curly, gave her no trouble at all. If she could just lose a couple of inches from her waist and three or four from her hips, she thought, she'd be more inclined to believe compliments and wolf whistles. Still, it was a long time since she'd gone to such lengths for a date. She smiled and clinked glasses with James.

'All you lack is confidence,' he said, as if reading her thoughts. 'You have to believe in yourself more.'

'I do,' Susan answered. 'How do you think I've got where I am?'

'I mean your personality, the image you project. Believe you're lovely and people will see you that way.'

'Is that what you do?'

James winced in mock agony. 'Oh, now you're being cruel.'

'I'm sorry.'

'It's all right. I'll survive.' He leaned forward. 'Tell me, I've always wondered, what did you think of me when you were at school? I mean, what did the girls think of me?'

Susan laughed and put her hand to her mouth. 'They thought you were gay.'

James's face showed no expression, but a sudden chill seemed to emanate from him.

'I'm sorry,' Susan said, feeling flustered. 'I didn't mean anything by it. *I* didn't think so, if that's any consolation. And it was just because you were in the arts.'

'In the arts?'

'Yes, you know how people in the performance arts always seem to be thought of as gay. If it'll make you feel any better, they thought Mr Curlew was that way, too.'

James stared at her, then burst into laughter. 'Peter Curlew? The music teacher?'

Susan nodded.

'Well, that's a good one. I do feel better now. Curly was a happily married man with four kids. Devoted family man.'

Susan laughed with him. 'That just shows you how wrong we were, I suppose. I liked the way he used to conduct to himself whenever he played a record for us. He really got quite worked up, in a world of his own.'

'Of course, you lot were all snickering at him behind your hands, weren't you?'

'Yes. Yes, I'm afraid we were.' Susan felt strangely ashamed to admit it now, though she hadn't thought of Mr Curlew for years.

'He was a very talented pianist, you know. He could have gone a long way, but those years of dreary teaching broke his spirit.'

Susan felt embarrassed. 'How are you getting on without Caroline?' she asked, to change the subject.

James paused for a few seconds, as if deep in thought, before answering. 'Fine, I suppose. It wasn't a difficult part, it was just that, well, Caroline was special, that's all. Are you any closer?'

Susan shook her head. Not that she would have said even if they were closer to finding Caroline's killer. She frowned. 'Do you think anyone in the production could have been involved in her death?'

He cupped his chin in his hand and thought for a moment. 'No,' he said finally. 'No, I can't see it. Nobody knew her that well.'

'Her killer didn't need to know her well. She let him or her in, but he or she could have been merely an acquaintance, someone come to talk to her about something.'

'I still can't see it.'

'There must have been friction with the other women, the leads.'

'Why?'

'Competition.'

'Over what?'

'Anything. Men. Lines. Parts.'

'There wasn't. I'm not saying we were a totally happy family, we had our ups and downs, our off days, but you're grasping at straws. Remember, it's the *amateur* dramatic society. People join for pleasure, not profit. I'd like to think, though, that we're far from amateur in quality.'

Susan smiled. 'I'm sure you are. Tell me, what was Caroline Hartley really like?'

'I'm sorry, Susan, it's still very upsetting for me, such a loss. I just don't want to – ah, look, here's our food.' He rubbed his hands together. 'Delightful. And another half litre of your best Barolo, please, Enzo.'

'Do you think we should?' Susan asked. 'I've still got half a glass left. I'm not certain I can drink any more.'

'Well if you can't, I can. I know I should be drinking white with the linguine, but what the hell, I prefer Barolo. Worry not, not a drop will be wasted. What did you do for Christmas?'

'I – I . . .'

'Well, what? Did you visit your parents?' He gathered a forkful of food and lifted it to his mouth, his eyes probing her face for an answer all the time.

Susan looked down at her plate. 'I . . . not really, no, I didn't. I was busy with the case.'

'You don't get on with them, do you?' he said, still looking directly at her, with just a glint of satisfaction in his eyes. She found his gaze disconcerting and looked down at her plate again to cut off a bit of cannelloni.

'I don't suppose I do,' she admitted when she'd finished chewing. She shrugged. 'It's nothing serious. Just that holidays at home can be awfully depressing.'

'I suppose so,' James said. 'I'm an orphan myself and I always find Christmas terribly gloomy. It brings back memories of those awful orphanage dinners and enforced festivities. But you have a family. You shouldn't neglect them, you know. One day, it'll be too late.'

'Look,' Susan said, reaching for her glass, 'when I want a lecture on a daughter's responsibility, I'll ask for one.'

James stood up. 'I'm sorry, really I am.' He patted her arm. 'Excuse me for a moment.'

Susan held her anger in check and tossed back the last of her wine. The second half litre arrived. She refilled her glass and took a long swig. To hell with caution; she could get as pissed as the next person if she wanted to. Why couldn't she talk about her parents without getting so damned emotional? she asked herself. She picked away at her cannelloni, which was very good, until James came back. Then she took a deep breath and put down her knife and fork.

'I'm the one that should apologise,' she said. 'I didn't mean to blow up like that. It's just that it's *my* problem, all right?'

'Fine,' James said. 'Fine. So what *did* you do?'

She sighed. 'I stayed at home. I had quite a nice day actually. I'd dashed out and bought a small tree and a few decorations the night before, so the place looked quite seasonal. I watched the Queen's message and a variety show and read a book on homicide investigation.'

James laughed, a forkful of pasta halfway to his mouth. 'You read a textbook on homicide on Christmas Day?'

Susan blushed. At that moment the manager walked by. He nodded at James as he passed.

'I don't believe it,' James said. 'You sitting there by the Christmas tree listening to carols, reading about dead bodies and poisons and ballistics.'

'Well it's true,' Susan said, managing a smile. 'Anyway, if my job dis—'

But she had no time to finish. Before she could even get the word out, a man appeared beside her and began singing into her ear. She didn't know the song, but she could make out words like *bella* and *amore*. She wished she could shrink to nothing and disappear down a crack in the floor. James sat opposite, hands folded on his lap, watching with cool amusement in his eyes. When the singer had gone and Susan had grudgingly thanked him, she turned to James with fury in her eyes.

'You set that up, didn't you, when you went to the gents'? You talked to the manager. Go on, admit it.'

'Very well.' James turned his hands palms up. '*Mea culpa.* I just thought you might enjoy it, that's all.'

'I've never been so embarrassed in my life. I've a good mind—' Susan dropped her napkin on the table and pushed back her chair, but James leaned forward and put his hand gently on her arm. She could see the mild amusement in his eyes turn to concern.

'Don't go, Susan. I just meant I thought it might cheer you up, after a Christmas spent alone. Honestly, I didn't mean to embarrass you. I never thought you wouldn't like it. How could I know?'

Looking at his eyes again, she could see he was sincere. Not so much that, but it hadn't even occurred to him that the singer might embarrass her. She eased the chair towards the table again and relaxed.

'All right,' she said, forcing a smile. 'I'll let you off just this once. But don't you ever—'

'I won't,' James said. 'I promise. Scout's honour. Cross my heart and hope to die. Come on, eat your cannelloni and drink your wine. Enjoy.' And he let his hand rest on hers on the checked tablecloth for a long moment before taking it away.

FIVE

Banks switched off Milhaud's 'Creation' as he pulled up outside Faith Green's block of flats. It was a small unit, only three stories high, with six flats on each floor. He looked at his watch: 8.50. Plenty of time for Faith to have come home from the Crooked Billet, if she hadn't gone out on a date.

Luckily, she was in. When he knocked, he heard someone cross the room and saw the tiny peephole in the door darken.

'Inspector Banks!' Faith said as she pulled the door open with a dramatic flourish. 'What a surprise. Do come in. Let me take your coat.' She hung up his coat, then took his arm and led him into the spacious living room. A number of framed posters from old movies hung on the pastel-green walls: Bogart in *Casablanca*, Garbo in *Camille*, John Garfield and Lana Turner in *The Postman Always Rings Twice*. Faith gestured towards the modular sofa that covered almost two walls, and Banks sat down.

'Drink?'

'Maybe just a small Scotch, if you have it.'

'Of course.' Faith opened up a glass-fronted cocktail cabinet and poured them both drinks. Banks's was about two fingers taller than he would have liked.

'To what do I owe this pleasure?' Faith asked in her husky voice. 'If only you'd told me you were coming, I could have at least put my face on. I must look terrible.'

She didn't. With her beautiful eyes and silvery, page-boy hair, it would have been difficult for Faith Green to look terrible. She wore no make-up, but that didn't matter. Her high cheekbones needed no highlights, her full, pink lips no colouring. In skin-tight black slacks and a dark-green silk blouse, her figure, slim at the waist, nicely curved at the hips and well-rounded at the bust, looked terrific. The perfume she wore was the same one Banks remembered from their brief chat at the Crooked Billet – very subtle, with a hint of jasmine.

She settled close to Banks on the sofa and cradled a glass of white wine in her hands. 'You should have phoned first,' she said. 'I gave you my number.'

'Maybe you didn't know I was married.'

She laughed. 'I've never known that to make very much difference to men.' Given the way she was sitting and looking at him, he could well believe her. He fiddled for his cigarettes.

'Oh, you're not going to smoke, are you?' She pouted. 'Please don't. It's not that I'm so anti, but I just can't bear my flat smelling of smoke. Please?'

Banks removed his hand from his jacket pocket and took a long swig of Scotch. He waited until the pleasant burning sensation had subsided, then said, 'Remember the last time we talked? About how things were going between the people in the play?'

'Of course I do.' Her eyes twinkled. 'I told you I liked my men dark and handsome, and not necessarily tall.'

If Banks had been wearing a tie, he would have loosened it at this point. 'Miss Green—'

'Faith, please. It's not such a bad name, is it? There are three of us, sisters, but my parents never were that well up on the Bible. The youngest's called Chastity.'

Banks laughed. 'Faith it is, then. You told me you had no idea that Caroline Hartley was a lesbian. Are you sure you didn't?'

Faith frowned. 'Of course not. What an odd question. She didn't walk around with it written on her forehead. Besides, it's not as obvious in a woman as it sometimes is in a man, is it? I mean, I've known a few homosexuals, and most of them don't mince around and lisp, but you have to admit that some conform to the stereotype. How could you possibly tell with a woman unless she went about dressed like a man or something?'

'Perhaps you would just sense it?'

'Well, I didn't. Not with Caroline. And *she* certainly didn't walk around dressed like a man.'

'So she told no one?'

'Not as far as I know, she didn't. She certainly didn't

tell me. I can't vouch for the others. Another drink?'

Banks looked at his glass, amazed to find it empty so soon. 'No thanks.'

'Oh, come on,' Faith said, and took it from him. She brought it back only slightly fuller than the last time and sat about six inches closer. Banks held his ground.

'There's something missing,' he said. 'Some factor, maybe just a little thing, and I'm trying to find out what it is. I get the feeling that people – you especially – are holding something back, hiding something.'

'Little me? Hiding something? Like what?' She spread her hands and looked down as if to indicate that all she had was on display. She wasn't far from the truth.

'I don't know. Do you think there might be a chance that Caroline Hartley was having an affair with someone other than the woman she was living with, perhaps someone in the theatre company?'

Faith stared at him, then backed away a few inches, burst out laughing and pointed at her chest. 'Me? You think I'm a lesbian?'

Given the situation, her physical closeness and the heady aura of sex that seemed to emanate from her, it did seem rather a silly thing to think.

'Not you specifically,' Banks said. 'Anyone.'

When Faith had stopped laughing, she moved closer again and said, 'Well, I can assure you *I'm* not.' She shifted her legs. The material swished as her thighs brushed together. 'In fact, if you let me, I can even prove to you I'm not.'

Banks held her gaze. 'It's quite possible for a person to be bisexual,' he said. 'Especially if he or she is over-sexed to start with.'

Faith seemed to recede several feet into the distance,

though she hadn't moved at all. 'I ought to be insulted,' she said with a pout, 'but I'm not. Disappointed in you, yes, but not insulted. Do you really think I'm over-sexed?'

Banks put his thumb and forefinger close together and smiled. 'Maybe just a little bit.'

All the seductiveness, the heat and smell of sexuality, had gone from her manner, and what sat next to him was a very attractive young woman, perhaps a little shy, a little vulnerable. Perhaps it had all been an act. Could she turn her sexual power on and off at will? Why did he keep forgetting that there were so many actors on the fringes of Caroline Hartley's death?

'I didn't mean it as an insult,' Banks went on. 'It just seemed the best way to cut the games and get down to business. I really do need information. That's why I'm here.'

Faith nodded, then smiled. 'All right, I'll play fair. But I'm not just all talk, you know.' Just for a moment she upped the voltage again and Banks felt the current.

'Could Caroline have been seeing someone?' he asked quickly.

'She could have been, yes. But I can't help you there. Caroline kept herself to herself. Nobody knew anything about her private life, I'm certain. After a couple of drinks, she'd go off home—'

'By herself?'

'Usually. If it was an especially nasty night James would give her a lift. And before you make too much out of that, he would take Teresa too, and drop her off last.' She paused for effect, then added huskily. 'At his place, sometimes.'

'Teresa told me she didn't care about James's attraction to Caroline. What would you say about that?'

Faith put a slender finger to her lips, then said. 'Well, I wouldn't quite put it that way. I don't like to tell tales out of school, but . . .'

'But what? It could be important.'

'Teresa's very emotional.'

'You mean she fought with Caroline?'

'Not exactly.'

'With James Conran?'

Faith swirled her drink and nodded slowly. 'I heard them talking once or twice,' she said. 'Caroline's name came up.'

'In what way?'

Faith lowered her voice and leaned closer to Banks. 'Usually as that "prick-teasing little bitch." Teresa's a good friend,' she added, settling back, 'but you *did* say it was important.'

So Teresa Pedmore had more of a grudge against Caroline Hartley than she had cared to admit. She could have been the woman who visited Caroline's house after Patsy Janowski. On the other hand, so could Faith Green, who was being much more circumspect about her own involvement in the thespian intrigues, if she had any. Both were a little taller than Caroline Hartley. Banks would have to have a word with Teresa later and see what she, in turn, had to say about her friend.

'You say James seemed attracted enough to Caroline to upset Teresa,' he said. 'How strong would you say his interest was?'

'He flirted with her in the pub. That was all I ever saw.'

'How did she react?'

'She gave as good as she got.'

'Did they sleep together?'

'Not as far as I know.'

'Teresa never referred to them doing that?'

'No, just to the way James fussed about her. It wasn't Caroline who manoeuvred the seating in the pub. If anyone, Teresa should have blamed James, not Caroline.'

'People aren't very logical when it comes to blame,' Banks said, thinking of what Claude Ivers and Patsy Janowski had said about Caroline and Veronica.

'Where did you all go after the rehearsal on the day of Caroline's death?'

'I came home. Honestly. I was tired. I didn't even have a date.'

'Why didn't you all go for a drink as usual?'

Faith shrugged. 'No special reason. Sometimes we just didn't, that's all. People just wandered off home. There's nothing more to it than that. It was close to Christmas. There was shopping to do, family to visit.'

Banks didn't believe her. She fiddled with her pearl necklace as she spoke and looked away from him. She also spoke as if there was nobody listening to her.

'Did something happen at that rehearsal, Faith?' he asked. 'Was there a row between Caroline and Teresa?'

Faith shifted in her seat. She turned her eyes on him again. They gave away nothing. A waft of perfume drifted over.

'Another drink?'

'No. Tell me what happened.'

'Leave me alone. Nothing happened.'

Banks put his glass down on the St Ives coaster and stood up.

Faith scratched the inside of her elbow. 'Are you going now?' she asked. All of a sudden she seemed like a frightened girl whose parents were about to turn the lights out.

'Yes. Thanks very much for the drinks. You've been a great help.'

She touched his arm. 'Nothing happened. Really. Believe me. We just finished our rehearsal and we all went home. Don't you believe me?'

Banks moved towards the door. Faith walked beside him, still holding on. 'You must catch him soon, you know,' she said.

'Him?'

'Whoever killed Caroline. Was it a woman? I suppose it could have been. But you must.'

'Don't worry. We will. With or without your help. Why are you so concerned?'

Faith let go of his arm. 'The rest of us are in danger, aren't we? It stands to reason.'

'What do you mean?'

'Whoever killed Caroline. He might be stalking the cast. A serial killer.'

'A psychopathic killer? It's possible, but I don't think so. You've been reading too many books, Faith.'

'So you really don't think the rest of us are in danger?'

'No. But you might as well keep your door locked anyway. And always look and see who's there.' He paused, half out of the door.

'What is it?' Faith asked.

'Some of you *could* be in danger,' he added slowly, 'if you know more about the crime than you're telling, and if the killer knows you know, or suspects that you do.'

Faith shook her head. 'I know nothing more than I told you.'

'Then you've nothing to worry about, have you?'

Banks smiled and left. He wanted to get Teresa's version of that final night, but she would have to wait. It was going on for ten o'clock, he was tired, and he was going to London early in the morning. If he still needed to talk to her when he got back, he could do it then.

As he walked over the brittle ice listening to the rest of the Milhaud piece, he recalled Faith Green's expression at the door. She had told him that she knew nothing, but had looked distinctly worried when he had hinted she might be in danger. Of course, knowing her, it could have been just another act, but perhaps, he thought, it wouldn't be a bad idea to have Richmond and Susan Gay keep an eye on the thespians while he was in London.

9

ONE

It wasn't until the Intercity train pulled out of Leeds City Station that Veronica Shildon seemed to relax.

Banks had met her at Eastvale Station early that morning and they had paced the platform, shivering and breathing plumes of mist, until the overheated old diesel rattled in and carried them off. Silent but for small talk, they'd watched the shrouded landscape roll by. South of Ripon, the dales and moors to the west gave way to rolling farmland, where patches of frozen brown earth and clumps of bare trees showed through the gauze of snow, and, finally, to the suburbs and industrial estates of the city itself. They had endured a half-hour wait on the cold, grimy platform at Leeds, breathing in the diesel smell of warm engines and listening to the crackly voice over the loudspeaker.

Now, well past the sign at the station's entrance in honour of the local beer magnate – 'Joshua Tetley Welcomes You to Leeds' – Banks looked over his shoulder and watched the city recede into the distance. First it filled the horizon, an urban sprawl under a heavy sky. Tall chimneys and church spires poked through the grey-brown snow; the town hall dome and the white university library tower dominated the distance. Then the city was gone and only bare fields stretched east and west.

Veronica took off her heavy blue winter coat and, folding it carefully, placed it in the luggage rack. Then she smoothed her tweed skirt and sat back down opposite Banks, resting her hands on the table between them.

'I'm sorry,' she said with an embarrassed smile. 'I know I must be a burden, but I didn't like the idea of travelling down by myself. It's a while since I've been anywhere alone.'

'That's all right,' said Banks, who had been uncharitably wishing he could spend the journey with the *Guardian* crossword and some Poulenc chamber music on his Walkman. 'Coffee?'

'Yes, please.'

The buffet car hadn't opened yet, but a British Rail steward was making his way slowly along the corridor with an urn and a selection of biscuits. Banks headed him off, bought two coffees and pushed one over the smooth table to Veronica. Automatically, he reached for his cigarettes, then remembered he was in a non-smoking carriage.

It wasn't Veronica's fault; she would have been happy to sit anywhere with him since he had allowed her to come along. The problem was that there was only one smokers' car on the entire train and, as usual, it was almost full and completely unventilated. Even Banks refused to sit in it. He could do without a cigarette for a couple of hours, easily. It might even do him good. As an alternative, he caught up with the steward and bought a Penguin biscuit.

After Wakefield, they sped along past dreary fields and embankments trying to sip the hot, weak coffee without spilling any. Their carriage was unusually quiet and empty. Perhaps, Banks guessed, this was because they were in that limbo between Christmas and New Year.

Everyone was both broke and in need of a brief hibernation period of recovering between the two festive occasions.

Deep into South Yorkshire, Banks noticed Veronica looking out at the desolate landscape of pit wheels and slag heaps and asked her what she was thinking about.

'It's funny,' she said, 'but I was thinking how I still feel only half there. Do you know what I mean? I can accept that Caroline is gone, that she's dead and I'll never see her again, but I can't believe that my life is whole, or even real, without her.' She nodded towards the window. 'Even the world out there doesn't seem real, somehow. Not any more.'

'That's understandable,' Banks said. 'It takes time. How did you meet her?'

Veronica gave him a long, appraising look and then leaned forward and rested her arms on the table, clasping her slim, freckled hands.

'It must seem very odd to you. Perverted, even. But it's not. There was nothing sordid about it.'

Banks said nothing.

Veronica sighed and went on. 'I first met Caroline at the café where she worked. I used to go for long walks by the river . . . oh, just thinking about my life and how empty it felt . . . somehow, the moving water seemed to help soothe me. We got on speaking terms, then once I saw her in the market square and we went for a coffee. We discovered we were both in therapy. After that . . . well, it didn't happen quickly.'

'What attracted you to her?'

'I didn't even know I *was* attracted to her at first. Could you imagine someone like me admitting I'd fallen in love with a woman? But Caroline was so alive, so childlike in her enthusiasm for life. It was infectious. I'd felt half dead for years. I'd been shutting the world out. It's possible to do that, you know. So many people accept what life dishes out to them. Apart from the occasional daydream, they never imagine it could be any different, any better. Even the half-life I have now is preferable to what my life was like before Caroline. There's no going back. I was living like a zombie, denying everything that counts, until Caroline came along. She showed me how good it was to *feel* again. She made me feel alive for the first time. She got me interested in things because she was so passionate about them herself.'

'Like what?'

'Oh, theatre, books, film. So many things. And music. Claude was always trying to get me interested in music, and it really frustrated him that I didn't seem to care as much as he did, or notice as much about it as he did. I suppose I loved opera most of all, but he never had much time for it. Most seasons I went to Leeds to see Opera North by myself. I liked to listen – I still do like classical music – but I never actually bought records for myself. There always seemed something stuffy about the music we listened to, perhaps because Claude hated anything popular, anything outside the classical field. But with Caroline it was jazz and blues and folk music. Somehow it just seemed more alive. We even went to clubs to see folk groups perform. I'd never done that before. Ever.'

'But your husband's a musician himself. He loves music. Didn't he mean anything to you? Why couldn't you respond to his enthusiasm?'

Veronica lowered her head and scratched the table surface with her thumb nail. The train hit a bumpy stretch of track and rocked.

'I don't know. Somehow I just felt completely stifled by his existence. That's the only way I can put it. Like it didn't matter what I thought or felt or did because he was the one our lives revolved around. I depended on him for everything, even for my tastes in music and books. I was suffocated by his presence. Anything I did would have been insignificant beside what he did. He was the great Claude Ivers, after all, always the teacher, the master. One dismissive comment from him on anything that mattered to me and I was reduced to silence, or tears, so I learned not to let things matter. I was the great man's wife, not a person in my own right.'

She sat up straight, her brow furrowed. 'How can I explain it to you? Claude wasn't cruel, he didn't do any of it on purpose. It's just the way he is, and the way I am, or was. I still have my problems, more than ever now Caroline's gone, I suppose, but when I look back I can't believe I'm the same person I was then. She worked an act of magic – she breathed life into dust. And I know I can carry on somehow, no matter how hard, just because of her, just because I had her in my life, even for such a short time.' She paused and glanced out the window. Banks could read the intense feeling in the set of her jaw, the way the small muscles below her cheekbones seemed drawn tight.

'Do you see?' she went on, turning her clear, grey-green eyes on Banks. 'It wasn't black and white. He wasn't a bad husband. Neglectful, maybe. Certainly the last few years he was far too wrapped up in his work to notice me. And I was dying, drying up inside. If Caroline hadn't come along I don't know what would have become of me.'

'But you started seeing the therapist before you met Caroline,' Banks said. 'What made you do that?'

'Desperation, despair. I'd read an article about Jungian therapy in a women's magazine. It sounded interesting, but not for me. Time passed and I became so miserable I had to do something or I was frightened I would try to kill myself. I suppose I told myself therapy was a sort of intellectual fun, not anything deep and personal. More like going to an evening class – you know, pottery, basket weaving or creative writing. It wasn't like going to the real doctor or to a psychiatrist, and somehow I could handle that. It still took a lot of nerve, more than I believed I ever had. But I was so unhappy. And it helped. It can be a painful process, you know. You keep circling things without ever really zooming in on them, and sometimes you feel it's a waste of time, it's going nowhere. Then you do focus on things and you find you were circling them for good reason. Occasionally you get some kind of insight, and that sustains you for a while. Then I met Caroline.'

'Had you experienced feelings like that before?' Banks asked.

'Towards another woman?'

'Yes.'

Veronica shook her head. 'I hadn't experienced feelings like that for *anyone* before, male or female. Somehow or other, her being a woman just wasn't an issue. Not after a while, anyway. Everything began to feel so natural I didn't even have to think.'

'What about your past, your upbringing?'

Veronica smiled. 'Yes, isn't it tempting to try and put everything down to that? I don't mean to be dismissive, but I don't think it's so. I had no horrible experiences with men in my past. I'd never been abused, raped or beaten.' She paused. 'At least not physically.'

'What was your family background like?'

'Solid, suburban, upper middle class. Very repressed. Utterly cold. We never spoke about feelings and nobody told me about the facts of life. My mother was well bred, very Victorian, and my father was kind and gentle but rather distant, aloof. And he was away a lot. I never had much contact with boys while I was growing up. I went to convent school, and even at university I didn't mix very much. I was in an all-girls residence and I tended to stay at home and study a lot. I was shy. Men frightened me with their deep voices and their aggressive mannerisms. I don't know why. When I met Claude he was a guest lecturer for a music appreciation course. It was the kind of thing genteel young ladies did, appreciate music, so I took the course. I was fascinated by his knowledge and his obvious passion for his subject – the very things I came to hate later. For some reason he noticed me. He was an older man, much safer than the randy boys in the campus pub. I was twenty-one when I married him.'

'So you never had any other boyfriends?'

'Never. I was reclusive, frightened as a mouse. Believe it or not, when Claude seemed to lose interest in sex, that suited me fine. Now, when I look back, I can't remember what I did from day to day. How I got through. I was a housewife. I had no outside job. I suppose I cleaned and cooked and watched daytime television in a kind of trance. Then there was the Valium, of course.'

'How long were you married?'

'We were together for fifteen years. I never complained. I never took an interest in life outside his circle of friends and acquaintances. I had no passions of my own. I don't blame Claude for that. He had his own life, and music was more important to him even than marriage. I think it has to be like that with a great artist, don't you? And I believe

Claude *is* a great artist. But great artists make lousy husbands.'

'Did you ever think of having children?'

'I did. But Claude thought they would interfere with his peace and quiet. He never really liked children. And I suppose I was, am, afraid of childbirth. Terrified, to be honest. Anyway, he just went ahead and had a vasectomy. He never even told me until it was done. What do you think of childless marriages, Mr Banks?'

Banks shrugged. 'I wouldn't know. Never had one.'

'Some people say there's no love in them, but I don't agree. Sometimes I think it would be best if we were all childless. Childless and parentless.' She caught the paradox and smiled. 'Impossible, I realize. There'd be no one here to feel anything. I know I feel alone and it hurts because Caroline isn't here. But at the same time I seem to be saying we'd all be better off without any feelings or any other attachments. I want it both ways, don't I?'

'Don't we all? Look, this philosophy's made me thirsty. I know it's early, but how about a drink?'

Veronica laughed. 'Have I driven you to drink already? All right, I'll have a gin and tonic.'

Banks made his way down to the buffet car, holding on to the tops of seats to keep his balance in the rocking train. Most of the other passengers seemed to be business people with their heads buried deep in the *Financial Times* or briefcases full of papers open in front of them. One man even tapped away at the keys of a laptop computer. After a short queue, Banks got Veronica's drink and a miniature Bell's for himself. Going back one-handed was a little more difficult, but he made it without falling or dropping anything.

Back in his seat, he poured the drinks. They passed a

small town: smoking chimneys; grimy factory yards stacked with pallets; a new red-brick school with hardly any windows; a roundabout; snow-covered playing fields as white as the rugby posts. The train's rhythm was soothing, even if it wasn't the same as the steam-train journeys Banks remembered taking with his father when he was young. The sound was different, and he missed the tangy smell of the smoke, the sight of it curling over trees by a wooded embankment where the track curved and he could see the engine through the window.

Veronica seemed content to sip her drink in silence. There was so much more he wanted to ask her, to understand about her relationship with Caroline Hartley, but he didn't feel he could justify his questions. He thought of what she had said about a childless and parentless life and remembered the Philip Larkin poem, which he had recently reread. It was certainly depressing – the ending as much as the beginning – but he found something in the wit and gusto of Larkin's colloquial style that brought a smile to the lips, too. Perhaps that was the secret of great art, it could engender more than one feeling in the spectator at the same time: tragedy and comedy, laughter and tears, irony and passion, hope and despair.

'What's your wife like?'

The suddenness of the question surprised Banks, and he guessed he must have shown it.

'I'm sorry,' Veronica went on quickly, blushing, 'I hope I'm not being presumptuous.'

'No. I was just thinking about something else, that's all. My wife? Well, she's just an inch or so shorter than I am. She's slim, with an oval face, blonde hair and dark eyebrows, what I'd call a no-nonsense personality and . . . let me think . . .'

Veronica laughed and held up her hand. 'No, no. That'll do. I didn't want a *policeman's* description. I suppose I hadn't thought how difficult it is to answer off the cuff like that. If anyone had asked me to describe Caroline I wouldn't have known where to start.'

'You did well enough earlier.'

'But that was just scratching the surface.'

She drank some more gin and tonic and looked at her reflection in the window, as if she couldn't believe what she was seeing.

'I suppose my wife and I are still together,' Banks said, 'because she has always been determined and independent. She'd hate to be a housewife worrying about meals and threepence-off coupons in the papers. Some people might see that as a fault, but I don't. It's what she is and I wouldn't want to turn her into some sort of chattel or slave. And she wouldn't want to depend on me to entertain her or keep her happy. Oh, we've had some dull patches and a few close shaves on both sides, but I think we do pretty well.'

'And you put it down to her independence?'

'Mostly, yes. More an independent spirit, really. And intelligence. It's very hard being a policeman's wife. It's not so much the worry, though that's there, but the long absences and the unpredictability. I've seen plenty of marriages go down the tubes because the wife hasn't been able to take it any more. But Sandra has always had a mind of her own. And a life of her own – photography, the gallery, friends, books. She doesn't let herself get bored – she loves life too much – so I don't feel I have to be around to entertain her or pay attention to her all the time.'

'That sounds like Caroline and me. Though I suppose I depended on her quite a lot, especially at first. But she helped me become more independent, she and Ursula.'

Banks wondered why on earth he had opened up that way to Veronica. There was something about the woman he couldn't quite put his finger on. A terrible honesty, a visible effort she made to communicate, to be open. She was working at living, not simply coasting through life like so many. She didn't shirk experience, and Banks found it was impossible not to be as frank in return with someone like that. Was he letting his feelings overrun his judgement? After all, this woman *could* be a murderess.

'How long had you known Caroline before you left your husband?' Banks asked.

'Known her? A few months, but mostly just casually.'

'But how did you know how you felt, what you wanted to do?'

'I just knew. Do you mean sexually?'

'Well . . .'

'I don't know,' she went on, cutting through his embarrassment. 'Certainly it wasn't anything I'd experienced or even thought about before. I suppose I must have, but I don't remember. Of course, there were crushes and a little petting at school, but I imagine everyone indulges in that. I don't know. It was awkward. We were at her flat and she just . . . took me. After that, I knew. I knew what had been missing in my life, what I had been repressing, if you like. And I knew I had to change things. I was buoyant with love and I suppose I expected Claude to understand when I told him.'

'But he didn't?'

'It was the closest he ever came to hitting me.'

Banks remembered the ex-husband's anger, his humiliation. 'What happened?'

'Oh, I know what I did wrong now. At least I think I do.'

She laughed at herself. 'I was crazy with joy then. I expected him to feel happy for me. Can you believe that? Anyway, I moved out the next day and went to live with Caroline in her flat. Then he sold the house and left Eastvale. Later we got the little place on Oakwood Mews. The rest you know.'

'And you never looked back.'

'Never. I'd found what I was looking for.'

'And now?'

Veronica's face darkened. 'Now I don't know.'

'But you wouldn't go back to him?'

'To Claude? I couldn't do that. Even if he wanted to.' She shook her head slowly. 'No, whatever the future holds for me, it's certainly not more of my miserable mistake of a past.'

In the silence that followed, Banks glanced out the window and was surprised to find the train was passing Peterborough. The landmarks were so familiar: the tall kiln chimneys of the brick factory growing straight from the ground; the white sign of the Great Northern Hotel against its charcoal-grey stone; the truncated cathedral tower.

'What is it?' Veronica asked. 'You look so engrossed. Have you seen something?'

'My home town,' Banks explained. 'Not much of a place, but mine own.'

Veronica laughed.

'Where do you come from?' Banks asked.

'Crosby. Near Liverpool, but light-years away, really. It's a horribly stuck-up suburb, at least it was then.'

'I'd hardly say Peterborough was stuck-up,' Banks said. 'Doesn't your poet, Larkin, have something to say about childhood places?'

'You've been doing your research, I see. Yes, he does. And he set it on a train journey like this. It's very funny and very sad. It ends, "Nothing, like something, can happen anywhere."'

'Do you read a lot of poetry?'

'Yes. Quite a bit.'

'Do you read any journals?'

'Some. The *Poetry Review* occasionally. Mostly I read old stuff. I prefer rhyme and metre, so I tend to stay away from contemporary work, except Larkin, Seamus Heaney and a couple of others, of course. That's one area Caroline and I disagreed on. She liked free verse and I never could see the point of it. What was it Robert Frost said? Like playing tennis without a net?'

'But you've never noticed Ruth Dunne's name in print, never come across her work?'

Veronica tightened her lips and looked out the window. She seemed irritated that Banks had broken the spell and plunged into what must have felt like an interrogation.

'I don't remember it, no. Why?'

'I just wondered what kind of stuff she writes, and why Caroline didn't tell you about her.'

'Because she tended to be secretive about her past. Sketchy, anyway. I also suspect that maybe she didn't want to make me jealous.'

'Were they still seeing one another?'

'As far as I know, Caroline made no trips to London while we were together, I haven't even been myself for at least three years. No, I mean jealous of a past lover. It can happen, you know – people have even been jealous over *dead* lovers – and I was especially vulnerable, being in such a new and frightening relationship.'

'Frightening?'

'Well, yes. Of course. Especially at first. Do you imagine it was easy for me, with my background and my sheltered existence, to go to bed with a woman, to give up my marriage and live with one?'

'Was there anyone else who might have been jealous enough of Caroline's relationship with you?'

Veronica raised her eyebrows. 'You're never very far away from your job, are you? It makes it hard to trust you, to open up to you. I can never tell what you're thinking from your expression.'

Banks laughed. 'That's because I'm a good poker player. But seriously, despite all evidence to the contrary, I *am* a human being. And I'd be a liar if I didn't admit that the foremost thing on my mind is catching Caroline's killer right now. The work is never far away. That's because somebody took something they had no right to.'

'And do you think catching and punishing the criminal will do any good?'

'I don't know. It becomes too abstract for me at that point. I told you, I like concrete things. Put it this way, I wouldn't like to think that the person who stabbed Caroline is going to be walking around Eastvale, or anywhere else for that matter, whistling "Oh, What a Beautiful Mornin'" for the rest of his or her life. Do you know what I mean?'

'Revenge?'

'Perhaps. But I don't think so. Something more subtle, more *right* than mere revenge.'

'But why do you take it so personally?'

'Somebody has to. Caroline isn't around to take it so personally herself.'

Veronica stared at Banks. Her eyes narrowed, then she shook her head.

'What?' Banks asked.

'Nothing. Just trying to understand, thinking what a strange job you do, what a strange man you are. Do all policemen get as involved in their cases?'

Banks shrugged. 'I don't know. For some it's just a day's work. Like anyone else, they'll skive off as much as they can. Some get very cynical, some are lazy, some are cruel, vicious bastards with brains the size of a pea. Just people.'

'You probably think I don't care about revenge or justice or whatever it is.'

'No. I think you're confused and you're too shaken by Caroline's death to think about whoever did it. You're also probably too civilized to feel the blood lust of revenge.'

'Repressed?'

'Maybe.'

'Then perhaps a little repression is a good thing. I'll have to tell Ursula that before she releases the raging beast inside me.'

Banks smiled. 'I hope we've got the killer safely behind bars long before that.'

The train passed a patch of waste ground scattered with bright yellow oil drums and old tyres, then a factory yard, a housing estate and a graffiti-scarred embankment. Soon, Banks could see Alexandra Palace through the window.

'Better get ready,' he said, standing up and reaching for his camel-hair overcoat. 'We'll be at King's Cross in a few minutes.'

TWO

Half an hour later, Banks looked across the street at the Gothic extravaganza of St Pancras, complete with its chimneys, crocketed towers and crenellated gables. So, here he was, back in London for the first time in almost three years. Black taxis and red double-decker buses clogged the roads and poisoned the streets with exhaust fumes. Horns honked, drivers yelled at one another and pedestrians took their lives into their hands crossing the street.

Veronica had taken a taxi to her friend's house. For Banks, the first priority was lunch, which meant a pint and a sandwich. He walked down Euston Road for a while, taking in the atmosphere, loving it almost as much as he hated it. There didn't appear to have been much snow down here. Apart from occasional lumps of grey slush in the gutters, the streets were mostly clear. The sky was leaden, though, and seemed to promise at least a cold drizzle before the end of the day.

He turned down Tottenham Court Road, found a cosy pub and managed to elbow himself a place at the bar. It was lunchtime, so the place was crowded with hungry and thirsty clerks come to slag the boss and gird up their loins for another session at the grindstone. Banks had forgotten how much he liked London pubs. The Yorkshire people were so proud of their beer and their pubs, it had been easy to forget that a London boozer could be as much fun as any up north. Banks drank a pint of draught Guinness and ate a thick ham and cheese sandwich. As always in London, such gourmet treats cost an arm and a leg; even the pint cost a good deal more than it would in Eastvale.

Luckily, he was on expenses.

The raised voices all around him, with their London accents, brought it all back, the good and the bad. For years he had loved the city's streets, their energy. Even some of the villains he'd nicked had a bit of class, and those that lacked class at least had a sense of humour.

He pushed his plate aside and lit a cigarette. The bottles ranged at the back of the bar were reflected in the gilt-edged mirror. The barmaid had broken into a sweat trying to keep up with the customers – her upper lip and brow were moist with it – but she managed to maintain her smile. Banks ordered another pint.

He couldn't put his finger on when it had all started to go wrong for him in London. It had been a series of events, most likely, over a long period. But somehow it all merged into one big mess when he looked back: Brian getting into fights at school; his own marriage on the rocks; anxiety attacks that had convinced him he was dying.

But the worst thing of all had been the job. Slowly, subtly, it had changed. And Banks had found himself changing with it. He was becoming more like the vicious criminals he dealt with day in, day out, less able to see good in people and hope for the world. He ran on pure anger and cynicism, occasionally thumped suspects in interrogation and trampled over everyone's rights. And the damnedest thing was, it was all getting him good results, gaining him a reputation as a good copper. He sacrificed his humanity for his job, and he grew to hate himself, what he had become. He had been no better than Dirty Dick Burgess, a superintendent from the Met with whom he had recently done battle in Eastvale.

Life had dragged on without joy, without love. He was losing Sandra and he couldn't even talk to her about it. He was living in a sewer crowded with rats fighting for food and space: no air, no light, no escape. The move up north, if he admitted it, had been his way of escape. Put simply, he had run away before it got too late.

And just in time. Whilst everything in Eastvale hadn't been roses, it had been a damn sight better than those last months in London, during which he seemed to do nothing but stand over corpses in stinking, run-down slums: a woman ripped open from pubes to breast bone, intestines spilling on the carpet; the decaying body of a man with his head hacked off and placed between his legs. He had seen those things, dreamed about them, and he knew he could never forget. Even in Eastvale, he sometimes awoke in a cold sweat as the head tried to speak to him.

He finished his pint quickly and walked outside, pulling up his overcoat collar against the chill. So, he was back, but not to stay. Never to stay. So enjoy it. The city seemed noisier, busier and dirtier than ever, but a fresh breeze brought the smell of roast chestnuts from a street vendor on Oxford Street. Banks thought of the good days, the good years: searching for old, leather-bound editions of Dickens on autumn afternoons along Charing Cross Road; Portobello Road market on a crisp, windy spring morning; playing darts with Barney Merritt and his other mates in the Magpie and Stump after a hard day in the witness box; family outings to Epping Forest on Sunday afternoons; drinks in the street on warm summer nights at the back of Leicester Square after going to the pictures with Sandra, the kids safe with a sister. No, it hadn't all been bad. Not even Soho. Even that had its comic moments, its heart. At least it had seemed so before everything went wrong. Still, he felt human again. He was out of the sewer, and a brief visit like this one wasn't going to suck him back into it.

First he made a phone call to Barney Merritt, an old friend from the Yard, to confirm his bed for the night. That done, he caught the Tube to the Oval. As he sat in the small compartment and read the ads above the windows, he remembered the countless other Underground journeys he had made because he always tried to avoid driving in London. He remembered standing in the smoking car, crushed together with a hundred or more other commuters, all hanging on their straps, trying to read the paper and puffing away. It had been awful, but part of the ritual. How he'd managed to breathe, he had no idea. Now you couldn't even smoke on the platforms and escalators, let alone on the trains.

He walked down Kennington Road and found the turn-off, a narrow street of three-storey terrace houses divided into flats, each floor with its own bay window. At number twenty-three, a huge cactus stood in the window of the middle flat, and in the top oriel he could see what looked a stuffed toy animal of some kind. Her name was printed above the top bell: R. Dunne. No first name, to discourage weirdos, but all the weirdos knew that only women left out their first names. There was no intercom. Banks pushed the bell and waited. Would she be in? What did poets do all day? Stare at the sky with their eyes in a 'fine frenzy rolling'?

Just when he was beginning to think she wasn't home, he heard footsteps inside the hall and the door opened on a chain. A face – *the* face – peered round at him.

'Yes?'

Banks showed his identification card and told her the purpose of his visit. She shut the door, slid off the chain and let him in.

Banks followed the slender, boyish figure in turquoise

slacks and baggy orange sweatshirt all the way up the carpeted stairs to the top. The place was clean and brightly decorated, with none of the smells and graffiti he had encountered in such places so often in the past. In fact, he told himself, flats like this must cost a fortune these days. How much did poets make? Surely not that much. It would be rude to ask.

The flat itself was small. The door opened on a narrow corridor, and Banks followed Ruth Dunne to the right into the living room. He hadn't known what to expect, had no preconceived idea of what a poet's dwelling should look like, but whatever he might have imagined, it wasn't this. There was a divan in front of the gas fire covered with a gaudy, crocheted quilt and flanked on both sides by sagging armchairs, similarly draped. He was surprised to find no bookshelves in evidence and assumed her study was elsewhere in the flat, but what was there surprised him as much as what wasn't: several stuffed toys – a green elephant, a pink frog, a magenta giraffe – lay around in alcoves and on the edge by the bay window, and on three of the four walls elaborate cuckoo clocks ticked, all set at different times.

'It must be noisy,' Banks said, nodding at the clocks.

Ruth Dunne smiled. 'You get used to it.'

'Why the different times?'

'I'm not interested in time, just clocks. In fact my friends tell me I'm a chronically late person.'

On the low table between the divan and the fire lay a coffee-table book on watch making, a couple of bills, an ashtray and a pack of unfiltered Gauloises.

'Make yourself comfortable,' Ruth said. 'I've never been interrogated by the police before. At least not by a detective chief inspector. Would you like some coffee?'

'Please.'

'It's instant, I'm afraid.'

'That'll do fine. Black.'

Ruth nodded and left the room. If Banks had expected a hostile welcome, for whatever reason, he was certainly disarmed by Ruth Dunne's charm and hospitality. And by her appearance. Her shiny brown hair, medium length, was combed casually back, parted at one side, and the forelock almost covered her left eye. Her face was unlined and without make-up. Strong-featured, handsome rather than pretty, but with a great deal of character in the eyes. They'd seen a lot, Banks reckoned, those hazel eyes. Felt a lot, too. In life, she looked far more natural and approachable than the arrogant, knowing woman in the photograph, yet there was certainly something regal in her bearing.

'How did you find me?' she asked, bringing back two mugs of steaming black coffee and sitting with her legs curled under her on the divan. She held her mug with both hands and sniffed the aroma. The gas fire hissed quietly in the background. Banks sat in one of the armchairs, the kind that seem to embrace you like an old friend, and lit a cigarette. Then he showed her the photograph, which she laughed at, and told her.

'So easy,' she said when he'd finished.

'A lot of police work is. Easy and boring. Time-consuming, too.'

'I hope that's not a subtle way of hinting I should have come forward earlier?'

'No reason to, had you? Did you know about Caroline's death?'

Ruth reached for the blue paper packet of Gauloises, tapped one out and nodded. 'Read about it in the paper.

Not much of a report, really. Can you tell me what happened?'

Banks wished he could, but knew he couldn't. If he told her, then he'd have no way of checking what she already knew.

She noticed his hesitation and waved her hand. 'All right. I suppose I should think myself lucky to be spared the gory details. Look, I imagine I'm a suspect, if you've come all this way. Can we get that out of the way first? I might have an alibi, you never know, and it'll make for a hell of a more pleasant afternoon if you don't keep thinking of me as a crazed, butch dyke killer.' She finally lit the cigarette she'd been toying with, and the acrid tang of French tobacco infused the air.

Banks asked her where she had been and what she had been doing on 22 December. Ruth sucked on her Gauloise, thought for a moment, then got up and disappeared down the corridor. When she reappeared, she held an open appointment calendar and carried it over to him.

'I was giving a poetry reading in Leamington Spa, of all places,' she said. 'Very supportive of the arts they are up there.'

'What time did it start?'

'About eight.'

'How did you get there?'

'I drove. I've got a Fiesta. It's life in the fast lane all the way for us poets, you know. I was a bit early, too, for a change, so the organizers should remember me.'

'Good audience?'

'Pretty good. Adrian Henri and Wendy Cope were reading there, too, if you want to check with them.'

Banks noted down the details. If Ruth Dunne had indeed been in Leamington Spa at eight o'clock that evening, there was no conceivable way she could have been in Eastvale at seven twenty or later. If she was telling the truth about the reading, which could be easily checked, then she was in the clear.

'One thing puzzles me,' Banks said. 'Caroline had your picture but we couldn't find a copy of your book among her things. Can you think why that might be?'

'Plenty of reasons. She wasn't much of a one for material possessions, wasn't Caroline. She never did seem to hang on to things like the rest of us acquire possessions. I always envied her that. I did give her a copy of the first book, but I've no idea what happened to it. I sent the second one, too, the one I dedicated to her, but I wasn't sure what her address was then. The odds are it went to an old address and got lost in the system.'

Either that or Nancy Wood had run off with both of them, Banks thought, nodding.

'But she hung on to the photograph.'

'Maybe she liked my looks better than my poetry.'

'What kind of poetry do you write, if you don't mind me asking?'

'I don't mind, but it's a hard one to answer.' She tapped the fingers holding the cigarette against her cheek. The short blonde hairs on the back of her hand caught the light. 'Let me see, I don't write confessional lesbian poetry, nor do I go in for feminist diatribes. A little wit, I like to think, a good sense of structure, land-scape, emotion, myth . . . Will that do to be going on with?'

'Do you like Larkin?'

Ruth laughed. 'I shouldn't, but I do. It's hard not to. I never much admired his conservative, middle-class little Englandism, but the bugger certainly had a way with a stanza.' She cocked her head. 'Do we have a literary copper here? Another Adam Dalgliesh?'

Banks smiled. He didn't know who Adam Dalgliesh was. Some television detective, no doubt, who went around quoting Shakespeare.

'Just curious, that's all,' he answered. 'Who's your favourite?'

'H. D. A woman called Hilda Doolittle, friend of Ezra Pound's.'

Banks shook his head. 'Never heard of her.'

'Ah. Clearly *not* a literary copper then. Give her a try.'

'Maybe I will.' Banks took another sip of his coffee and fiddled for a cigarette. 'Back to Caroline. When did you last see her?'

'Let me see . . . It was years ago, five or six at least. I think she was about twenty or twenty-one at the time. Twenty going on sixty.'

'Why do you say that?' Banks remembered Caroline as beautiful and youthful even in death.

'The kind of life she was leading ages a woman fast – especially on the inside.'

'What life?'

'You mean you don't know?'

'Tell me.'

Ruth shifted into the cross-legged position. 'Oh, I get it. You ask the questions, I answer them. Right?'

Banks allowed himself a smile. 'I'm not meaning to be rude,' he said, 'but that's basically how it goes. I need all the information I can get on Caroline. So far I don't have a hell of a lot, especially about the time she spent in London. If it'll make talking easier for you, I can tell you that we already know she had a conviction for soliciting and gave birth to a child. That's all.'

Ruth looked down into her coffee and Banks was surprised to see tears rolling over her cheeks.

'I'm sorry,' she said, putting the mug down and wiping her face with the back of her hand. 'It just sounds so sad, so pathetic. You mustn't think I'm being flippant, the way I talk. I don't get many visitors so I try to enjoy everyone I meet. I was very upset when I read about Caroline, but I hadn't seen her for a long time. I'll tell you anything I can.' A marmalade cat slipped into the room, looked once at Banks, then jumped on the divan next to Ruth and purred. 'Meet T.S. Eliot,' Ruth said. 'He named so many cats, so I thought at least one should be named after him. I call him T.S. for short.'

Banks said hello to T.S., who seemed more interested in nestling into the hollow formed by Ruth's crossed legs. She picked up her coffee again with both hands and blew gently on the surface before drinking.

'Caroline started as a dancer,' she said. 'An exotic dancer, I believe they're called. Well, it's not too much of a leap from that to pleasing the odd, and I do mean *odd*, punter or two for extra pocket money. I'm sure you know much more about vice here than I do, but before long she was doing the lot: dancing, peep shows, turning tricks. She was a beautiful child, and she looked even younger than she was. A lot of men around that scene have a taste for fourteen- or fifteen-year-olds, or even younger, and Caroline could fulfil that fantasy when she was eighteen.'

'Was she on drugs?'

Ruth frowned and shook her head. 'Not as far as I know. Not like some of them. She might have had the odd joint, maybe an upper or a downer now and then – who doesn't? – but nothing really heavy or habitual. She wasn't hooked on anything.'

'What about her pimp?'

'Bloke called Reggie. Charming character. One of his women did for him with a Woolworth's sheath knife shortly before Caroline broke away. You can check your records, I'm sure they'll have all the details. Caroline wasn't involved, but it was a godsend for her in a way.'

'How?'

'Surely it's obvious. She was scared stiff of Reggie. He used to bash her about regularly. With him out of the way, she had a chance to slip between the cracks before the next snake came along.'

'When did she break away?'

Ruth leaned forward and stubbed out her cigarette. 'About a year before she went back up north.'

'And you knew her during that period?'

'We lived together. Here. I got this place before the prices rocketed. You wouldn't believe how cheap it was. I knew her before for a little while, too. I'd like to think I played a small part in getting her out of the life.'

'Who played the biggest part?'

'She did that herself. She was a bright kid and she saw where she was heading. Not many you can say that about. She'd been wanting out for a while, but Reggie wouldn't let go and she didn't know where to run.'

'How did you come to meet her?'

'After a poetry reading. Funny, I can remember it like it was yesterday. Out in Camden Town. All we had in the audience was a prostitute and a drunk who wanted to grab the mike and sing 'Your Cheating Heart'. He did, too, right in the middle of my best poem. Afterwards we drove down to Soho – not the drunk, just me and my fellow readers – to the Pillars of Hercules. Know it?'

Banks nodded. He'd enjoyed many a pint of draught Beck's there.

'We just happened to be jammed in a corner next to Caroline and another girl. We got talking, and one thing led to another. Right from the start Caroline struck me as intelligent and wise, wasted on that scummy life. She knew it too, but she didn't know what else she could do. We soon became close friends. We went to the theatre a lot and she loved it. Cinema, art exhibitions.' She gave a small laugh. 'Anything but classical music or opera. She didn't mind ballet, though. It was all a world she'd never known.'

'Was that all there was to your relationship?'

Ruth paused to light another Gauloise before answering. 'Of course not. We were lovers. But don't look at me as if I was some kind of corrupter of youth. Caroline knew exactly what she was doing.'

'Were you the first woman she'd had such a relationship with?'

'Yes. That was obvious right from the start. She was shy about things at first, but she soon learned.' Ruth inhaled the smoke deeply and blew it out. 'God, did she learn.'

One of the cuckoo clocks went through its motions. They waited until it stopped.

'What do you think turned her into a lesbian?' Banks asked.

Ruth shifted on the sofa and T.S. scampered off. 'It doesn't happen like that. Women don't suddenly, quote, turn into lesbians, unquote. They discover that's what they are, what they always were but were afraid to admit because there was too much working against them – social morality, male domination, you name it.'

'Do you think there are a lot of women in that situation?'

'More than you imagine.'

'What about the men in her life?'

'Work it out for yourself. What do you think it does to a woman to have gross old men sticking their willies in her and meek suburban husbands asking if they can pee in her mouth? You've got the pimp at one end and the perverts at the other. No quarter.'

'So Caroline discovered her lesbianism under your guidance?'

Ruth flicked a column of ash into the tray. 'You could put it like that, yes. I seduced her. It didn't take her long to figure out that she loathed and feared sex with men. The only difficult thing was overcoming the taboos and learning how to respond to a woman's body, a woman's way of making love. And I'm not talking about dildos and vibrators.'

'Why did you split up?'

'Why does anybody split up? I think we'd done what we could for each other. Caroline was restless. She wanted to go back up north. There were no great rows or anything, just a mutual agreement, and off she went.'

'Did you know she had a baby?'

'Yes. Colm's. But that was before I met her. She told me she'd just arrived in London and was lucky enough to meet Colm in a pub. Apparently he was a decent enough bloke, just broke all the time. Some of his mates weren't so decent and that's partly what got Caroline involved in the game to start with. You know, just a temporary dancing job at this club, no harm in it, is there? Bit of extra cash, no questions asked. Creeps. In all fairness, I don't think Colm knew. At least not for a while. Then she had his baby and they put it up for adoption.'

'Do you remember the name of the club?'

'Yes. It was the Hole-in-the-Wall, just off Greek Street. Dingy looking place.'

'This Colm,' Banks asked. 'Do you know his second name?'

'No. It's funny, but come to think of it, Caroline never used last names when she spoke about people.'

'Seen him lately?'

'Me? I've never seen him.'

'How come you know so much about him?'

'Because Caroline told me about him when we were first getting to know each other.'

'Where did he live?'

'Notting Hill somewhere. Or it could have been Muswell Hill. I'm not sure. Honestly, I can't help you on that one. She never was much of a one for details, just the broad gesture.'

'Are you sure Caroline wasn't already pregnant when she arrived in London?'

Ruth frowned and paused, as if she had suddenly remembered something. She turned her eyes away, and when she spoke there was an odd, distant tone to her voice. 'What do you mean?'

'I'm just asking.'

'As far as I know she wasn't. Unless she was lying to me. I suppose Colm will be able to confirm it if you can find him.'

'Why did that question upset you so much?'

She put her hand to her chest. 'I don't know what you're talking about.'

'You're more defensive than you were earlier.'

Ruth shrugged. 'It just reminded me of something, that's all.'

'Reminded you of what?'

Ruth reached for her coffee cup, but it was empty. Banks waited. He noticed her hand was shaking a little.

'Something that was bothering Caroline. It's not important,' Ruth said. 'Probably not even true.'

'Let me decide.'

'Well, it was those dreams she'd been having, and the things she'd been remembering. At least she thought she had. She didn't really know if they were memories or fantasies.'

'What about?'

Ruth looked him in the eye, her cheeks flushed. 'Oh hell,' she said. 'Caroline was beginning to think she'd been molested as a child. She felt she'd repressed the incident, but it was making its way back up from her subconscious, perhaps because of all the weird johns she was servicing.'

'Molested? When? Where? Who by?'

'I've told you, she wasn't sure she believed it herself.'

'Do you know?'

'Shit, yes. When she was a kid. At home. By her father.'

10

ONE

'**You knew, didn't you?**' Banks challenged Veronica Shildon later that evening. They were eating in an Indonesian restaurant in Soho. The view out of the window was hardly romantic – a peep show offering 'NAKED GIRLS IN BED' for 50p – but the food was excellent and the bar served Tiger beer.

Veronica played with her *nasi goreng*, mixing the shrimp in with the rice. 'Knew what?'

'About Caroline's past.'

'No. Not the way you think.'

'You could have saved me a lot of time and effort.'

Veronica shook her head. Her eyes looked watery, on the verge of tears. Banks couldn't be sure whether it was emotion or the hot chili peppers. His own scalp was prickling with the heat and his nose was starting to run. He took another swig of cold Tiger.

'Some things I knew,' she said finally. 'I knew Caroline had been on the streets, but I didn't know any of the names or places involved. When she talked about Ruth she always spoke with affection, but she never mentioned her second name or where they'd lived.'

'You knew they were lovers, though?'

'Yes.'

'But weren't you jealous? Didn't you question Caroline about it?'

Veronica snorted. 'I had little right to be jealous, did I? Remember where I was coming from. Caroline told me there'd been others. She was even living with Nancy Wood when I first met her. And I was with Claude. You must be very naive, Mr Banks, if you think we walked into our relationship like a couple of virgins with no emotional baggage. And, somehow, I don't honestly believe you are naive.'

'No matter what the rules are,' Banks said, 'no matter what people try to convince themselves about what they accept and understand, about how open-minded they are, they still can't stop feeling things like jealousy, hatred and fear. Those are powerful, primitive emotions – instincts, if you like – and you can't convince me that you were both so bloody civilized you calmly decided not to feel anything about one another's pasts.'

Veronica put down her fork and poured some more beer into her half empty glass. 'Quite a speech. And not so long ago you were telling me I was too civilized to feel the need to revenge Caroline's murder.'

'Perhaps you are. But that's another matter. Can you answer my question?'

'Yes. I didn't feel jealous about Ruth Dunne. For one thing, it was years ago, and for another, from what I could gather she'd done Caroline a big favour, perhaps the same kind of favour Caroline later did for me. As I said, I didn't know all the details, but I know the gist. And when I talked to Ruth this afternoon after you'd been to see her, I liked her. I was *glad* to think Caroline had met and loved someone like her. That's my answer. Believe it or not, as you choose. Or do you think people like us are just so perverted that all we do is rip each other's clothes off and jump into bed together?'

Banks said nothing. He ate a mouthful of pork *satay* and washed it down with beer. Attracting the waiter's attention, he then ordered two more Tigers. He did believe Veronica. After all, she had felt secure in her relationship with Caroline, and Ruth Dunne had certainly posed no threat.

'So why didn't you tell me what you did know about Caroline's past?' he asked after the beers had arrived.

'I've already told you. I hardly knew anything.'

'Maybe not, but if you'd told us what you *did* know, it would have made it easier for us to find out the rest.'

Veronica slammed her knife and fork down. Her cheeks flushed and her eyes narrowed to glaring slits. 'All right, damn you! So I'm sorry. What more do you want me to say?'

Some of the other diners looked around and frowned, whispering comments to one another. Veronica held Banks's gaze for a few seconds, then picked up her fork again and speared a spicy shrimp far too violently. A few grains of rice skipped off the edge of her plate onto the napkin on her knee.

'What I want to know,' Banks said, 'is why you didn't tell me what you knew, and whether there's anything else you've been keeping to yourself. See, it's simple really.'

Veronica sighed. 'You're an exasperating man,' she said. 'Do you know that?'

Banks smiled.

'All right. I didn't tell you because I didn't want to . . . to soil Caroline's memory. She wasn't that kind of person any more. I couldn't see how it would do any good to drag all that up and let the newspapers get hold of it. Is that good enough?'

'It's a start. But I'll bet there's more to it than that.'

Veronica said nothing. Her mouth was pressed shut so tight the edges of her lips turned white.

Banks went on. 'You didn't want me or anyone else to think you were the kind of woman to be living with someone with such a lurid past? Am I right?'

'You're a bastard, is what you are,' said Veronica through gritted teeth. 'What you don't understand is that it takes more than a couple of years of therapy to undo a lifetime's damage. Christ, all the time I keep hearing my mother's voice in my mind, calling me dirty, calling me perverted. Maybe you're right and I didn't want that guilt by association. But I still don't see what good knowing that does you.'

'The reason for Caroline's murder could lie in her past. She was running with a pretty rough crowd. I know some of them. I worked the vice squad in Soho for eighteen months, and it's not as glamorous as *Miami Vice*, you can be sure of that. Drugs. Prostitution. Gambling. Big criminal business. Very profitable and very dangerous. If Caroline maintained any kind of involvement with these people it could explain a lot.'

'But she didn't,' Veronica insisted, pressing her hands together and leaning across the table. 'She didn't. I lived with her for two years. In all that time we never went to London and she never mentioned much about her life there. Don't you see? It was the future we wanted, not the past. Both of us had had enough of the past.'

Banks pushed his empty plate aside, asked Veronica's permission to smoke and reached for his cigarettes. When he'd lit one and inhaled, he took a sip of beer. Veronica folded her napkin in a perfect square and laid it on the coral tablecloth beside her plate. A small mound of rice dotted with chunks of garlic, onion and diced pork remained, but the shrimp were all gone.

Banks glanced out the window and watched a punter in a cloth cap and donkey jacket hesitate outside the peep show. He was probably having a hard time making up his mind with so much to choose from: NUDE NAUGHTY AND NASTY down the street, LIVE EROTIC NUDE BED SHOW next door, and now NAKED GIRLS IN BED opposite. Shoving his hands in his pockets, he hunched his shoulders and carried on towards Leicester Square. Either lost his bottle or come to his senses, Banks thought.

Veronica had been watching him, and when Banks turned back to face her she gave him a small smile. 'What were you looking at?'

'Nothing.'

'But you were watching so intently.'

Banks shrugged. 'Coffee? Liqueur?'

'I'd love a Cointreau, if they've got any.'

'They'll have it.' Banks called the waiter. He ordered a Drambuie for himself.

'What did you see out there?' Veronica asked again.

'I told you, it was nothing. Just a man, likely down from the provinces for a soccer match or something. He was checking out Soho. Probably surprised it was so cheap.'

'What do you get for 50p?'

'Brief glance at a naked tart, if you're lucky. It's a loss leader, really,' Banks said. 'Supposed to give you a taste for the real action. You sit in a booth, put your coin in the slot and a shutter slides so you can see the girl. As soon as your meter's up, so to speak, the shutter closes. Of course, Soho's been cleaned up a lot lately, but you can't really keep its spirit down.' Already, Banks noticed, his accent and his patterns of speech had reverted to those of his

London days. He had never lost them in almost three years up north, but they had been modified quite a bit. Now here he was, to all intents and purposes a London copper again.

'Do you approve?' Veronica asked.

'It's not a matter of approval. I don't visit the booths or the clubs myself, if that's what you mean.'

'But would you like to see it all stamped out of existence?'

'It'd just spring up somewhere else, wouldn't it? That's what I mean about the spirit. Every big city has its vice area: the Red Light district in Amsterdam, the Reeperbahn, Times Square, the Tenderloin, the Yonge Street strip in Toronto . . . They're all much the same except for what local laws do and don't allow. Prostitution is legal in Amsterdam, for example, and they even have licensed brothels in part of Nevada. Then there's Las Vegas and Atlantic City for gambling. You can't really stamp it out. For better or for worse, it seems to be part of the human condition. I admire its energy, its vitality, but I despise what it does to people. I recognize its humour, too. In my job, you get to see the funny side from time to time. Maybe it actually makes policing easier, so much vice concentrated in one small area. We can keep closer tabs on it. But we'll never stamp it out.'

'I feel so sheltered,' Veronica said, looking out the window again. 'I never knew any of this existed when I was growing up. Even later, it never seemed to have anything to do with my life. I couldn't even imagine what people did together except for . . . you know.' She shook her head.

'And now you're wordly wise?'

'I don't think so, no. But after Caroline, after she brought me to life, at least I was able to see what all the fuss was about. If that's what it felt like, then no wonder everyone went crazy over it. Do you know that Shakespeare sonnet, the one that starts 'The expense of spirit in a waste of shame'? I never understood it until a couple of years ago.'

'It's about lust, isn't it?' Banks said. ' "Had, having, and in quest to have, extreme." ' Christ, he thought, I'm getting just like that Dalgliesh fellow Ruth Dunne mentioned. Better watch it. He nodded towards the window. 'Suits that lot out there more than it suits you.'

Veronica smiled. 'No, you don't know what I mean. At last I could understand. Even *lust* I could finally understand. Do you see?'

'Yes.' Banks lit another cigarette and Veronica held the glass of Cointreau in her hand. 'About Caroline's child,' he said.

'She never told me.'

'Okay. But did she ever make any references to a person called Colm?'

'No. And I'm sure I'd remember a name like that.'

'She had no contact with anyone you didn't know, no mysterious letters or phone calls?'

'Not that I ever found out about. I'm not saying she couldn't have had. She could be very secretive when she wanted. What are you getting at?'

Banks sighed and swirled his Drambuie in its glass. 'I don't know. I thought she might have kept in touch with the foster parents, adopters, whatever.'

'Surely that would have been too painful for her?'

'Maybe so. Forgive me, I'm grasping at straws.' And he was. The child must be about nine or ten now. Far too young to hunt out his mother and stab her with a kitchen knife for abandoning him, or her. Far too young to see the irony in leaving a requiem for himself on the stereo. 'There is one thing you might be able to help me with, though,' he said.

'Yes?'

'Ruth mentioned that Caroline had begun to suspect she'd been sexually abused as a child. Do you know anything about that?'

Veronica blushed and turned her face to the window. Her profile looked stern against the gaudy neon outside, and the muscle at the corner of her jaw twitched.

'Well?'

'I . . . I can't see what it's got to do with—'

'We've already been through that. Let me be the judge.'

'Poor Caroline.' Veronica looked directly at Banks again and her expression seemed to relax into sadness. Melancholy was a better word, Banks decided, a good romantic word. Veronica looked melancholy as she fingered her glass and tilted her head before she spoke. 'I suppose I didn't tell you for the same reason I didn't tell you anything else about her past. I didn't think it mattered and it would only look bad. Now I feel foolish, but I'm not afraid.'

'Did she talk to you about it?'

'Yes. At first it was like Ruth said. She had dreams, terrible dreams. Do you know what sexual abuse does to a child, Mr Banks?'

Banks nodded. Jenny Fuller, the psychologist who occasionally helped with cases, had explained it to him once.

'Then you know they begin to hate themselves. They lose all self-respect, they get depressed, they feel suicidal, and they often seek reckless, self-destructive ways of life. All those things happened to Caroline. And more.'

'Is that why she left home?'

'Yes. But she'd had to wait a long time to get out. Till she was sixteen.'

'What do you mean? When did this start happening?'

'When she was eight.'

'Eight? Jesus Christ! Go on. I take it this is fact, not fantasy?'

'I can't offer you irrefutable proof, especially now Caroline's dead, but you can take my word for it if you're willing. As I said, at first it was just dreams, fears, suspicions, then when she started working on it with Ursula, more memories began to surface. She'd buried the events, of course, which is perfectly natural under the circumstances. Just imagine a child's confusion when the father she loves starts to do strange and frightening things with her body and tells her she must never tell anybody or terrible things will happen to her. It ties her in knots emotionally. It must be good, because Daddy is doing it. Perhaps she even enjoys the attention. But it doesn't *feel* good, it hurts. And why will she go to hell if she ever tells anyone?'

'What happened?'

'As far as she could piece it together, it occurred first when she was eight. Her mother was having a difficult pregnancy and spent the last two weeks of her term in hospital under close observation. Something to do with her blood pressure and the possibility of toxaemia. Caroline was left alone in the big house with her father, and he started coming to her bedroom at nights, asking her to be a good girl and play with him. Before long he was having intercrural sex with her. It's not very clear how far he went. She remembered pain, but not extreme agony or bleeding. Obviously, he was careful. He didn't want anyone to find out.'

'What does "intercrural" mean?' Banks asked. 'I've never heard the word before.'

Veronica blushed. 'I suppose it is a bit technical. It was Ursula who used it first. It means between the thighs, rather than true penetration.'

Banks nodded. 'What happened when the mother came home?'

'It continued, but with even more caution. It didn't stop until she was twelve and had her first period.'

'He wasn't interested after that?'

'No. She'd become a woman. That terrified him, or so Ursula reckoned.'

Banks drew on his cigarette and looked out at the peep show. Two swaying teenagers in studded leather jackets stood in the foyer now, arguing with the cashier. A girl slipped out past them. She couldn't have been more than seventeen or eighteen from what Banks could see of her pale drawn face in the street light. She clutched a short, black, shiny plastic coat tightly around her skinny frame and held her handbag close to her side. She looked hungry, cold and tired. As far as he could make out, she wasn't wearing stockings or tights – in fact she looked naked but for the coat – which probably meant she was on her way to do the same job in another club nearby, after she'd stopped off somewhere for her fix.

'Gary Hartley told DC Gay that his sister had always hated him,' Banks said, almost to himself. 'He said she even tried to drown him in his bath once when he was a baby. Apparently, she made his life a misery. Her mother's, too. Gary blamed her for sending his mother to an early grave. I've met him myself, and he's a very disturbed young man.'

Veronica said nothing. She had finished her drink and

had only the dregs of her coffee left to distract her. The waiter sidled up with the bill.

'What I'd like to know,' Banks said, picking it up, 'is did Gary know why she'd treated him that way right from the start? Just imagine the psychological effect. There he was, someone new and strange, the root and cause of all her suffering at her father's hands. Her mother had deserted her, and now when she came back she was more interested in this whining, crying little brat than in Caroline herself. My sister was born when I was six and I clearly remember feeling jealous. It must have been countless times worse for Caroline, after what had happened with her father. Of course, Gary couldn't have known at the time, not for years perhaps, but did she ever tell him that her father had abused her sexually?'

Veronica started to speak, then stopped herself. She glanced at Banks's cigarette as if she wanted one. Finally, when she could find nowhere to hide, she breathed, 'Yes.'

'When?'

'As soon as she felt certain it was true.'

'Which was?'

'A couple of weeks before she died.'

TWO

Banks walked Veronica to Charing Cross Road and got her a taxi to Holland Park, where she was staying with her friend. After she'd gone, he paused to breathe the night air and feel the cool needles of rain on his face, then went back down Old Compton Street to clubland. It was Friday night, about ten thirty, and the punters were already deserting the Leicester Square boozers for the lure of more drink and a whiff of sex.

In a seedy alley off Greek Street, notable mostly for the rubbish on its pavements, Banks found the Hole-in-the-Wall. Remarkable. It had been there in his days on the vice squad, and it was still there, looking just the same. Not many places had such staying power – except the old landmarks, almost traditions by now, like the Raymond Revue Bar.

He kicked off a sheet of wet newspaper that had stuck to his sole and walked down the steps. The narrow entrance on the street was ringed with low-watt bulbs, and photos in a glass display case showed healthy, smiling, busty young women, some in leather, some in lacy underwear. The sign promised a topless bar and LIVE GIRLS TOTALLY NUDE.

The place was dim and smoky inside, noisy with customers trying to talk above the blaring music. It took Banks a minute or so to get his bearings. During that time, a greasy-haired lad with a sloth-like manner had relieved him of his admittance fee and indicated in slow-motion that there were any number of seats available. Banks chose to sit at the bar.

He ordered a half of lager and tried not to have a heart attack when he heard the price. The woman who served him had a nice smile and tired blue eyes. Her curly blonde hair framed a pale, moon-shaped face with too much red lipstick and blue eyeshadow. Her breasts stood firmly and proudly to attention, evidence, Banks was sure, of a recent silicone job.

Other waitresses out on the dim floor weaving among the smoky spotlights didn't boast the barmaid's dimensions. Still, they came, like fruit, in all shapes and sizes –

melons, apples, pears, mangoes – and, as is the way of all flesh, some were slack and some were firm. The girls themselves looked blank and only seemed to react if some over-eager punter tweaked a nipple, strictly against house rules. Then they would either scold him and walk off in a huff, call one of the bouncers or make arrangements for tweaking the other nipple in private later.

On the stage, gyrating and chewing gum at the same time to a song that seemed to be called 'I Want Your Sex', was a young black woman dressed only in a white G-string. She looked in good shape: strong thighs, flat, taut stomach and firm breasts. Perhaps she really wanted to be a dancer. Some girls on the circuit did. When she wasn't dancing like this to earn a living, Banks thought, she was probably working out on a Nautilus machine or doing ballet exercises in a pink tutu in a studio in Bloomsbury.

Watching the action and thinking his thoughts in the hot and smoky club, Banks felt a surge of the old excitement, the adrenaline. It was good to be back, to be here, where anything could happen. Most of the time his job was routine, but he had to admit to himself that part of its appeal lay in those rare moments out on the edge, never far from trouble or danger, where you could smell evil getting closer and closer.

The lager tasted like piss. Cat's piss, at that. Banks shoved it aside and lit a cigarette. That helped.

'Can I get you anything more, sir?' the barmaid asked. He was sitting and she was standing, which somehow put her exquisitely manufactured breasts at Banks's eye level. He shifted his gaze from the goosebumps around her chocolate-coloured nipples to her eyes. He felt his cheek burn and, if he cared to admit it, more than just that.

'No,' he said, his mouth dry. 'I haven't finished this one yet.'

She smiled. Her teeth were good. 'I know. But people often don't. They tell me it tastes like cat's piss and ask for a real drink.'

'How much does a real drink cost?'

She told him.

'Forget it. I'm here on business. Tuffy in?'

Her eyes narrowed. 'Who are you? You ain't law, are you?'

Banks shook his head. 'Not down here, no. Just tell him Mr Banks wants to see him, will you, love?'

Banks watched her pick up a phone at the back of the bar. It took no more than a few seconds.

'He said to go through.' She seemed surprised by the instruction and looked at Banks in a new light. Clearly, anyone who got in to see the boss that easily had to be a somebody. 'It's down past the—'

'I know where it is, love.' Banks slid off the bar stool and threaded his way past tables of drooling punters to the fire door at the back of the club. Beyond the door was a brightly lit corridor, and at the end was an office door. In front stood two giants. Banks didn't recognize either of them. Turnover in hired muscle was about as fast as that in young female flesh. Both looked in their late twenties, and both had clearly boxed. Judging by the state of their noses, neither had won many bouts; still, they could make mincemeat of Banks with their hands tied behind their backs, unless his speed and slipperiness gave him an edge. He felt a tremor of fear as he neared them, but nothing happened. They stood back like hotel doormen and opened the door for him. One smiled and showed the empty spaces of his failed vocation.

In the office, with its scratched desk, threadbare carpet, telephone, pin-ups on the wall and institutional green filing cabinets, sat Tuffy Telfer himself. About sixty now, he was fat, bald and rubicund, with a birthmark the shape of a teardrop at one side of his fleshy red nose. His eyes were hooded and wary, lizard-like, and they were the one feature that didn't seem to fit the rest of him. They looked more as if they belonged to some sexy Hollywood star of the forties or fifties – Victor Mature, perhaps, or Leslie Howard – rather than an ugly, ageing gangster.

Tuffy was one of the few remaining old-fashioned British gangsters. He had worked his way up from vandalism and burglary as a juvenile, through fencing, refitting stolen cars and pimping to get to the dizzy heights he occupied today. The only good things Banks knew about him were that he loved his wife, a peroxide ex-stripper called Mirabelle, and that he never had anything to do with drugs. As a pimp, he had been one of the few *not* to get his girls hooked. Still, it was no reason to get sentimental over the bastard. He'd had one of his girls splashed with acid for trying to turn him in, though nobody could prove it, and there were plenty of women old before their time thanks to Tuffy Telfer. Banks had been the bane of his existence for about three months many years ago. The evil old sod hadn't been able to make a move without Banks getting there first. The police had never got enough evidence to arrest Tuffy himself, though Banks had managed to put one or two of his minions away for long stretches.

'Well, well, well,' said Tuffy in the East-End accent he usually put on for the punters. He had actually been raised by a meek middle-class family in Wood Green, but few people other than the police knew that. 'If it ain't Inspector Banks.'

'*Chief* Inspector now, Tuffy.'

'I always thought you'd go far, son. Sit down, sit down. A drink?' The only classy piece of furniture in the entire room was a well-stocked cocktail cabinet.

'A real drink?'

'Wha'? Oh, I get it.' Telfer laughed. 'Been sampling the lager downstairs, eh? Yeah, a real drink.'

'I'll have a Scotch then. Mind if I smoke?'

Telfer laughed again. 'Go ahead. Can't indulge no more myself.' He tapped his chest. 'Quack says it's bad for the ticker. But I'll get enough second-hand smoke running this place to see me to my grave. A bit more won't do any harm.'

Tuffy was hamming it up, as usual. He didn't have to be here to run the Hole-in-the-Wall; he had underlings who could do that for him. Nor was he so poor he had to sit in such a poky office night after night. The club was just a minor outpost of Tuffy's empire, and nobody, not even vice, knew where all its colonies were. He had a house in Belgravia and owned property all over the city. He also mixed with the rich and famous. But every Friday and Saturday night he chose to come and sit here, just like in the old days, to run his club. It was part of his image, part of the sentimentality of organized crime.

'Making ends meet?' Banks asked.

'Just. Times is hard, very hard.' One of the musclemen put Banks's drink – a generous helping – on the desk in front of him. 'But what can I say?' Tuffy went on. 'I get by. What you been up to?'

'Moved up north. Yorkshire.'

Tuffy raised his eyebrows. 'Bit drastic, in'it?'

'I like it fine.'

'Whatever suits.'

'Not having a glass yourself?'

Tuffy sniffed. 'Doctor's orders. I'm a sick man, Mr Banks. Old Tuffy's not long for this world, and there'll not be many to mourn his passing, I can tell you that. Except for the nearest and dearest, bless her heart.'

'How is Mirabelle?'

'She's hale and hearty. Thank you for asking, Mr Banks. Remembers you fondly, does my Mirabelle. Wish I could say the same myself.' There was humour in his voice, but hardness in his hooded eyes. Banks heard one of the bruisers shift from foot to foot behind him and a shiver went up his spine. 'What can I do you for?' Tuffy asked.

'Information.'

Tuffy said nothing, just sat staring. Banks sipped some Scotch and cast around for an ashtray. Suddenly, one appeared from behind his shoulder, as if by magic. He set it in front of him.

'A few years ago you had a dancer working the club, name of Caroline Hartley. Remember her?'

'What if I do?' Telfer's expression betrayed no emotion.

'She's dead. Murdered.'

'What's it got to do with me?'

'You tell me, Tuffy.'

Telfer stared at Banks for a moment, then laughed. 'Know how many girls we get passing through here?' he said.

'A fair number, I'll bet.'

'A fair number indeed. These punters are constantly demanding fresh meat. See the same dancer twice they think they've been had. And you're talking how many years ago?'

'Six or seven.'

Telfer rested his pale, pudgy hands on the blotter. 'Well, you can see my point then, can't you?'

'What about your records?'

'Records? What you talking about?'

Banks nodded towards the filing cabinets. 'You must keep clear and accurate records, Tuffy – cash flow, wages, rent, bar take. For the taxman, remember?'

Telfer cleared his throat. 'Yeah, well, what if I do?'

'You could look her up. Come on, Tuffy, we've been through all this before, years ago. I know you keep a few notes on every girl who passes through here in case you might want to use her again, maybe for a video, a stag party, some special—'

Telfer held up a hand. 'All right, all right, I get your drift. It's all above-board. You know that. Cedric, see if you can find the file, will you?'

One of the bruisers opened a filing cabinet. 'Cedric?' Banks whispered, eyebrows raised.

Telfer shrugged. His chins wobbled. They sat silently, Telfer tapping his short fat fingers on the desk while Cedric rummaged through the files, muttering the alphabet to himself as he did so.

'Ain't here,' Cedric announced finally.

'You sure?' Telfer asked. 'It begins with a 'aitch – Hartley. That comes after "gee" and before "eye".'

Cedric grunted. 'Ain't here. Got a Carrie 'Eart, but no Caroline 'Artley.'

'Let's have a look,' Banks said. 'She might have used a stage name.'

Telfer nodded and Cedric handed over the file. Pinned to the top-left corner was a four by five black and white picture of a younger Caroline Hartley, topless and smiling, her small breasts pushed together by her arms. She could easily have passed for a fourteen-year-old, even a mature twelve-year-old. Below the photo, in Telfer's surprisingly neat and elegant hand, were the meagre details that had interested him about Caroline Hartley. 'Vital statistics: 34–22–34. Colour of hair: jet-black. Eyes: blue. Skin: olive and satiny' (Banks hadn't suspected Tuffy had such a poetic streak). And so it went on. Telfer obviously gave his applicants quite an interview.

The one piece of information that Banks hoped he might find was at the end, an address under her real name: 'Caroline Hartley, c/o Colm Grey.' It was old now, of course, and might no longer be of any use. But if it was Colm Grey's address, and he was poor, he might well have hung on to his flat, unless he'd left the city altogether. Also, now Banks had his last name, Colm Grey would be easier to track down. He recognized the street name. It was somewhere between Notting Hill and Westbourne Park. He had lived not far from there himself twenty years ago.

'Got what you want?' asked Telfer.

'Maybe.' Banks handed the file back to Cedric, who replaced it, then finished his Scotch.

'Well, then,' said Tuffy with a smile. 'Nice of you to drop in. But you mustn't let me keep you.' He stood up and shook hands. His grip was firm but his palm was sweaty. 'Not staying long, are you? Around here, I mean.'

Banks smiled. 'No.'

'Not thinking of coming back to stay?'

'No.'

'Good. Good. Just wanted to be sure. Well, do pop in again the next time you're down, won't you, and we'll have another good old natter.'

'Sure, Tuffy. And give my love to Mirabelle.'

'I will. I will, Mr Banks.'

The bruisers stood aside and Banks walked out of the office and down the corridor unscathed. When he got back to the noisy smoky club, he breathed a sigh of relief. Tuffy obviously remembered what a pain in the arse he'd been, but working on the edge of the law, as he did, he had to play it careful. True, plenty of his operations *were* above-board. It was a game – give and take, live and let live – and both sides knew it. Banks had come close to breaking the rules once or twice, and Tuffy wanted to be sure he wouldn't be around to do that again. Questions that sounded like friendly curiosity were often, in fact, thinly veiled threats.

'Another drink, dear?' the mammarially magnificent barmaid said as Banks passed by.

'No, love. Sorry, have to be off now. Maybe another time.'

'Story of my life,' she said, and her breasts swung as she turned away.

Outside, Banks fastened his overcoat, shoved his hands deep in his pockets and walked along Greek Street towards Tottenham Court Road Tube station. He had thought of taking a taxi, but it was only midnight, and Barney lived a stone's throw from the Central line. At Soho Square he saw a drunk in a tweed overcoat and trilby vomiting in the gutter. A tart, inadequately dressed for the cold, stood behind him and leaned against the wall, arms folded across her chest, looking disgusted.

How did that poem end? Banks wondered. The one Veronica had quoted earlier that evening. Then he remembered. After its haunting summary of the horrors of lust, it finished, 'All this world well knows; yet none knows well / To shun the heaven that leads men to this hell.' Certainly knew his stuff, did old Willie. They didn't call him 'the Bard' for nothing, Banks reflected, as he turned up Sutton Row towards the bright lights of Charing Cross Road.

THREE

The next morning, after a chat with Barney over bacon and eggs, Banks set out to find Colm Grey. He had arranged to have lunch with Veronica, and had asked Barney to check Ruth Dunne's alibi and to see what he could find on the stabbing of Caroline's pimp, Reggie, just to cover all the angles.

The rush-hour crowd had dwindled by the time he got a train, and he was even able to grab a seat and read the *Guardian*, the way he used to.

He got off at Westbourne Park and walked towards Notting Hill until he found the address on St Luke's Road. Five names matched the bells beside the front door, and he was in luck: C. Grey was one of them, flat four.

Banks pushed the bell and stood by the intercom. No response. He tried again and waited a couple of minutes. It looked like Grey was out. The way things stood at the moment, Grey was hardly a prime suspect, but he was a loose end that had to be tied up. He was the only one who knew the full story about Caroline Hartley's child. Just as Banks started to walk away, he thought he heard a movement behind the door. Sure enough, it opened and a young man stood there, hair standing on end, eyes bleary, stuffing a white shirt in the waist of his jeans.

He frowned when he saw Banks. 'Wharrisit? What time is it?'

'Half past nine. Sorry to disturb you.' Banks introduced

himself and showed his identification. 'It's about Caroline Hartley.'

The name didn't register at first, then Grey suddenly gaped and said, 'Bloody hell! You'd better come in.'

Banks followed him upstairs to a two-room flat best described as cosy. The furniture needed re-upholstering and the place needed dusting and a damn good tidying up.

'I was sleeping,' Grey said as he bent to turn on the gas fire. 'Excuse me a minute.' When he came back he had washed his face and combed his hair and he carried a cup of instant coffee. 'Want some?' he asked Banks.

'No. This shouldn't take long. Mind if I smoke?'

'Be my guest.'

Grey sat opposite him, leaning forward as if hunched over his steaming coffee cup. He was lanky with a long pale face pitted from ancient acne or chicken-pox. He needed a shave and a trim, and his slightly protruding eyes were watery blue.

'Is it bad news?' he asked, as if he were used to life being one long round of bad news.

'You mean you don't know?'

'Obviously, or I wouldn't be asking. Well?'

Banks took a deep breath. He had assumed Grey would have read about the murder in the papers. 'Caroline Hartley was murdered in Eastvale on December the twenty-second,' he said finally.

At first, Grey didn't seem to react. He couldn't have been much paler, so losing colour would have been no indication, and his eyes were already watery enough to look like they were on the verge on tears. All he did was sit silent and still for about a minute, completely still, and so silent Banks wondered if he were even breathing. Banks tried to imagine Grey and Caroline Hartley as a couple, but he couldn't.

'Are you all right?' he asked.

'Can I have one?' Grey indicated the cigarettes. 'Supposed to have chucked it in, but . . .'

Banks gave him a cigarette, which he lit and puffed on like a dying man on oxygen. 'I don't suppose this is a social call, either?' he said.

Banks shook his head.

Grey sighed. 'I haven't seen Caroline for about eight years. Ever since she started running with the wrong crowd.'

'Tuffy Telfer?'

'That's the bastard. Just like a father to her, he was, to hear her speak.'

Banks hoped not. 'Did you ever meet him?'

'No. I wouldn't have trusted myself with him for ten seconds. I'd have swung for the bastard.'

Not a chance, Banks thought. Colm Grey couldn't have got within a hundred yards of Tuffy Telfer without getting at least both arms and legs broken. 'What caused you and Caroline to split up?' he asked.

'Just about everything.' Grey flicked some ash onto the hearth by the fire and reached for his coffee again. 'I suppose it really started going downhill when she got pregnant.'

'What happened? Did you try to give her the push?'

Grey stared at Banks. 'Couldn't be further from it. We were in love. I was, anyway. When she got pregnant she just turned crazy. I wanted to have it, the kid, even though we were poor, and she didn't want rid of it at first. At least I don't think she did. Maybe I pushed her too hard, I don't know. Maybe she was just doing it to please me. Anyway, she was miserable all the time she was carrying, but she wouldn't have an abortion either. There was time, if she'd wanted, but she kept putting it off until it was too late. Then she was up and down like a yo-yo, one day wishing she could have a miscarriage, taking risks walking out in icy weather, maybe hoping she'd just slip and fall, the next day feeling guilty and hating herself for being so cruel. Then, as soon as the child was born, she couldn't wait to get shot of the blighter.'

'Where is the child now?'

'No idea. Caroline never even wanted to see it. As soon as it was born it was whisked off to its new parents. She didn't even want to know whether it was a girl or a boy. Then things started getting worse for us, fast. Caroline worked at getting her figure back, like nothing had ever happened. As soon as she got introduced to Telfer's crowd, that was it. She seemed hell-bent on self-destruction, don't ask me why.'

'Who introduced her to Telfer?'

Colm bit his lower lip, then said, 'I blamed myself, after I found out. You know what it's like, a man doesn't always choose his friends well. The crowd we went about with, Caroline and me, it was a pretty mixed bunch. Some of them liked to go up West on a weekend and do the clubs. We went along too a few times. Caroline seemed fascinated by it all. Or horrified, I never could make out which. She was well into the scene before I even found out, and there was nothing I could do to stop her. She was a good-looking kid, a real beauty, and she must have caught someone's eye. I should think they're always on the look out for new talent at those places.

'One night she came home really late. I was beside myself with worry and it came out as anger – you know, like when your mother always yelled at you if you were late. We had a blazing row and I called her all the names under the sun. It was then she told me. In detail. And she rubbed my face in it, laughed at me for not catching on sooner. Where did I think her new clothes were coming from? How did I think we could afford to go out so often? I was humiliated. I should have walked out there and then, but I was a fool. Maybe it was just a wild phase, maybe it would go away. That's what I tried to convince myself. But it didn't go away. The trouble was, I still loved her.' Colm rested his chin in his hand and stared at the floor. 'A couple of months later we split up. She left. Just walked out one evening and never came back. Didn't even take her belongings with her, what little she had.' He smiled sadly. 'Never much of a one for possessions, wasn't Caroline. Said they only tied her down.'

'Had you been fighting all that time?'

'No. There was only the one big row, then everything was sort of cold. I was trying to accept what she was up to, but I couldn't. It just wasn't working with her coming in at all hours – or not at all – and me knowing what she'd been up to, imagining her in bed with fat, greasy punters and dancing naked in front of slobbering businessmen.'

'Where did she go?'

'Dunno. Never saw or heard from her again. She was a great kid and I loved her, but I couldn't stand it. I was heading for a breakdown. She was living life in the fast lane, heading for self-destruct. I tried to stop her but she just laughed at me and told me not to be such a bore.'

'Did she ever tell you anything about her past?'

'Not a lot, no. Didn't get on with her mum and dad so she ran off to the big city. Usual story.'

'Ever mention her brother?'

'No. Didn't know she had one.'

'Did she ever tell you about her dreams?'

'Dreams?' He frowned. 'No, why?'

'It doesn't matter. What about you? What did you do after she'd gone?'

'Me? Well, I didn't exactly join the Foreign Legion, but I did run away and try to forget. I sublet the flat for a year and drifted around Europe. France mostly, grape picking and all that. Came back, got a job as a bicycle courier, and now I'm doing 'the Knowledge'. Nearly there, too. With a bit of luck I'll "Get Out" and have my "Bill and Badge" inside a year.'

'Good luck.' Banks had heard how difficult it was riding around on a moped day after day in the traffic fumes, memorizing over eighteen thousand street names and the numerous permutations of routes between them. But that was what one had to do to qualify as a London taxi driver. 'Did you forget her?' he asked.

'You never do, do you, really? What did she do after she left me? Do you know?'

Banks gave him a potted history of Caroline's life up to her death, and again Grey sat still after he'd finished.

'She always was funny about sex,' he said. 'Not that I'd have guessed, like, that she was a lezzie. I've nothing against them – live and let live, I say – but sex always seemed like some kind of trial or test with her, you know, as if she was trying to find out whether she really liked it or not. I suppose not liking it made it easier for her to live on the game, in a way. It was just a job. She didn't have to like it.'

Banks nodded. It was common knowledge that a lot of prostitutes were lesbians.

There was nothing more to say. He stood up and held out his hand. Grey leaned forward and shook it.

'Were you working on the twenty-second?' Banks asked.

Grey smiled. 'My alibi? Yes, yes I was. You can check. And I've got to get started today, too. When you're doing "the Knowledge" you eat, breathe and sleep it.'

'I know.'

'Besides, I don't even know where Eastvale is.'

On his way out, Banks offered Grey another cigarette, but he declined. 'It didn't taste all that good, and I couldn't justify starting again. Thanks for telling me . . . you know . . . about her life. At least someone seemed to make her happy. She deserved that.' He shook his head. 'She was just one fucked-up kid when I knew her. We never had a chance.'

Outside, Banks turned up his collar and walked through the squares and side streets towards Notting Hill Gate. This area had been his first home in London when he had come as a student. Back then, the tall houses with their white facades had been in poor repair, and small flats were just about affordable. Banks had paid seven pounds a week for an L-shaped room, with free mice, in a house that included one out of work jazz trumpeter, an earnest social worker, a morose and anorexic-looking woman on the second floor who wore beads and a kaftan and never spoke to anyone, and Jimmy, the cheerful and charming bus driver who Banks suspected of selling marijuana on the side.

He passed the house, on Powis Terrace, and felt a twinge of nostalgia. That small room, now with lace curtains in the window, was where he and Sandra had first made love in those carefree days when he had been unhappy with his business studies courses but still hadn't quite known what to do with his life.

Back then, the area had been very much a swinging

sixties enclave with its requisite mixture of musicians, poets, artists, dopers, revolutionaries and general drop-outs. It had suited Banks at the time. He enjoyed the music, the animated discussions and the aura of spontaneity, but he could never wholeheartedly turn on, tune in and drop out. He had wanted to get away from home, from the dull routine of Peterborough, and the Notting Hill flat had been both a cheap and exciting way of finding out what life was all about. Ah, to be eighteen again . . .

He walked up to the main intersection and took the Underground at Notting Hill Gate. He was on the Central line, and he still had some time to kill, so he got off at Tottenham Court Road, in the same general area he'd been in the previous evening. He was feeling vaguely depressed after his talk with Colm Grey, which had reduced a couple of his favourite theories to shreds, and thought a city walk in the bracing air might help blow away the blues.

Soho was another world in the daytime. The clubs and love shops and peep shows were still there, but somehow the glitz and sleaze only managed to look anaemic in daylight. The gaudy lights held no allure; they were washed out, paled by even the grey winter light. In the daytime, the siren-song of sex for hire was muted to a distant, nagging whine; there was no hiding the cheap, shabby reality of the product.

But another kind of vital street life took the ascendant – the world of markets, of business. Banks wandered among the stalls on Berwick Street, which seemed to sell everything from pineapples and melons to cotton panties, cups and saucers, watches, mixed nuts and egg cutters. Under one stall, a big brown dog lay sheltered watching the passers-by with mournful eyes.

Feeling better, he found a phone booth on Great

Marlborough Street and called Barney Merritt at Scotland Yard. As Banks had expected, and hoped, Ruth Dunne's alibi checked out.

The stabbing of Reggie Becker was also as clear cut as could be. The killer, a seventeen-year-old prostitute called Brenda Meers, had stabbed Becker five times in broad daylight on Greek Street. At least two of the wounds had nicked major arteries and he had bled to death before the ambulance got there. Eyewitnesses abounded, though fewer came forward later than were present at the time. When asked why she had done it, Brenda Meers said it was because Reggie was trying to make her go with a man who wanted her to drink his urine and eat his faeces. She had been with him before and didn't think she could stand it again. She had begged Reggie all morning not to make her go, but he wouldn't relent, so she walked into Woolworth's, bought a cheap sheath knife and stabbed him. As far as the police were concerned, Reggie Becker was no great loss, and Brenda would at least get the benefit of psychiatric counselling.

So that was that: the London connection ruled out. But maybe he hadn't wasted his time entirely. He now had a much fuller picture of Caroline Hartley, even if he did have to throw out that neat theory of a connection between the Vivaldi *Laudate pueri* and the child she had given birth to. He still believed the music was important, but he could no longer tell how or where it fit.

He looked at his watch. Just time to buy Sandra and Tracy presents in Liberty's, and maybe something for Brian from Virgin Records on Oxford Street. Then it would be time to meet Veronica for lunch and set off. He wondered what, if any, developments would be waiting for him back in Eastvale.

11

ONE

'You don't think he did it, do you?' Susan Gay asked Banks over coffee and toasted teacakes in the Golden Grill. It was two, largely frustrating days after his return from London.

'Gary Hartley?' Banks shrugged. 'I don't know. I don't suppose it makes much sense. Gary finds out Caroline was abused as a child so he kills her? All I know is that she told him about it a couple of weeks before she was killed. But you're right, we've no real motive at all. On the other hand, she *did* make his life a misery. Then she ran off and left him stuck with the old man. A thing like that can fester into hatred. The timing is interesting, too.'

'Does he know anything about classical music?'

'We'll have to find out. He's certainly well read. Look at all those books around the place, and the way he speaks, his vocabulary. He's way beyond the range of most teenagers. He could easily have come across the information about *Laudate pueri* somewhere, then seen the record at Caroline's.'

'So you're going to see him?'

'Yes. And I'd like you to come along if you can spare the time. Anything happening with the break-ins?'

'Nothing that can't wait.'

'Good. Remember, Gary's lied to us before. I want to see the old man, too. Who knows, we might be able to get something out of him.'

'He was pretty useless last time,' Susan said. 'I'm not convinced he's all there.' She shivered.

'Cold?'

She shook her head. 'Just the thought of that house.'

'I know what you mean. Let Phil know, will you? I want the three of us in on this. I'll be with the super, filling him in.' Banks looked at his watch. 'Say half an hour?'

Susan nodded and left.

Thirty minutes later they sat in an unmarked police Rover with Susan at the wheel and Banks hunched rather glumly in the back, missing his music. Sandra was using the Cortina to buy photographic supplies in York, so they had had to sign a car out of the pool. Susan's driving was assured, though not as good as Richmond's, Banks noted. Sergeant Hatchley had been the worst, he remembered, a bloody maniac on the road.

Despite more snow, road conditions were clear enough. It was, in fact, much brighter in the north, for once, than it had been in London, and a weak winter sun shone on the distant snow-covered fells, spreading a pastel coral glow.

In under an hour they pulled into the familiar Harrogate street and rang Hartley's doorbell. As expected, Gary answered. Giving nothing but a 'you again' look, he wandered back into the front room, leaving them to follow.

The room hadn't been cleaned or tidied since their last visit, and a few more beer cans and tab ends had joined the wreckage on the hearth. The air smelled stale, like a pub after closing time. Banks longed to open the window to let

in some air. Before he could get there, Richmond beat him
to it, yanking back the heavy curtains and raising the
window. Gary squinted at the burst of sunlight but said
nothing.

'We've got a few more questions to ask you,' Banks
said, 'but first I'd like a word with your father.'

'You can't. He's sick, he's resting.' Gary gripped the
chair arm and sat up. He reached for a cigarette and lit it.
'Doctor's orders.'

'I'm sorry, Gary. I already know most of it. I just need
him to fill me in on a few details.'

'What do you know? What are you talking about?'

'Caroline . . . your father.'

Gary sagged back into his chair. 'Oh God,' he
whispered. 'You know?'

'Yes.'

'Then you can hardly imagine he's going to tell you
anything, can you? He's asleep, anyway. Practically in a
bloody coma.'

Banks stood up. 'Stay with him, will you, Phil? Susan,
come with me.'

Susan followed Banks upstairs. They both heard Gary
cry 'No!' as they went.

'This way, sir.' Susan pointed to Mr Hartley's door and
Banks pushed it open.

If only Gary had turned off the electric fire, Banks
thought later, the smell wouldn't have been so bad. As it
was, Susan put her hand over nose and mouth and
staggered back, while Banks reached for a handkerchief.
Neither advanced any further into the room. The old man
lay back on his pillows, emaciated almost beyond recog-
nition. Judging by the reddish discolouration of the veins
in his scrawny neck, Banks guessed he had been dead at

least two days. It would take an expert to fix the time more exactly than that, though, as there were many factors to take into consideration, not least among them his age, the state of his health and the warm temperature of the room.

'Call the local CID,' Banks told Susan, 'and tell them to arrange for a police surgeon and a scene-of-crime team. You know the drill.'

Susan hurried downstairs and went to phone while Banks gently closed the door and returned to the front room. Gary looked at him as he entered. The boy seemed drained of all emotion, tired beyond belief. Banks motioned for Richmond to stand by the window, where Gary couldn't see him, then sat down close to Gary and leaned forward.

'Want to tell me about it, son?' he asked.

'What's to tell?' Gary lit a new cigarette from the stub of his old one. His long fingers were stained yellow with nicotine around the nails.

'You know.' Banks pointed at the ceiling. 'What happened?'

Gary shrugged. 'Is he dead?'

'Yes.'

'I told you he was sick.'

'How did he die, Gary?'

'He had cancer.'

'How long has he been dead?'

'How should I know?'

'Why didn't you call a doctor?'

'No point, was there?'

'When did you last look in on him, take him some food?'

Gary sucked on his cigarette and looked away into the

cold hearth, littered with butts and empty beer cans. Sweat formed on his pale brow.

'When did you last go up and see him, Gary?' Banks asked again.

'I don't know.'

'Yesterday? The day before?'

'I don't know.'

'I'm no expert, Gary, but I'd say you haven't been up there for at least three days, have you?'

'If you say so.'

'Did you kill him?'

'He was sick, getting worse.'

'But did you kill him?'

'I never touched him, if that's what you mean. Never laid a finger on the old bastard. I couldn't bear . . .'

Banks noticed the boy was crying. He had turned his head aside but it was shaking, and strange snuffling sounds came from between the fingers he had placed over his mouth and nose.

'You deserted him. You left him up there to die. Is that what you did?'

Banks couldn't be sure, but he thought Gary was nodding.

'Why? For God's sake why?'

'You know,' he said, wiping his nose with the back of his hand and turning to face Banks angrily. 'You told me. You know all about it. What he did . . .'

'For what he did to Caroline?'

'You know it is.'

'What about Caroline? Did you kill her too?'

'Why should I do that?'

'I'm asking. She tried to kill *you* once. Did you?'

Gary sighed and tossed his half-smoked cigarette into

the grate. 'I suppose so,' he said wearily. 'I don't know. I think *he* did, but maybe we all did. Maybe this miserable bloody family killed her.'

TWO

By mid-afternoon the sun had disappeared behind smoke-coloured clouds and Banks had turned his desk lamp on. They sat in his office – Banks, Gary Hartley and Susan Gay – taking notes and waiting for a pot of coffee before getting started on the interrogation.

Gary, sitting in a hard-backed chair opposite Banks, looked frightened now. He wasn't fidgeting or squirming, but his eyes were filled with a kind of resigned, mournful fear. Banks, still not completely sure what had gone on in that large, cold house, wanted him to relax and talk. Fresh, hot coffee might help.

While he waited, Banks glanced over the brief notes the forensic pathologist had made after his preliminary investigation of the scene. He'd estimated time of death at not less than two days and not more than three. For three days then, perhaps – since shortly after Banks's and Richmond's visit – the poor, frightened kid in front of them had sat in the cold ruin of a room, smoking and drinking, knowing the corpse of his father lay rotting upstairs in the heat of an electric fire. The doctor hadn't called; he had no reason to as long as Mr Hartley had a full prescription of pain killers and someone to take care of his basic needs.

'Rigor mortis disappeared . . . greenish discolouration of the abdomen,' the report read, 'reddish veins in neck, shoulders and thighs . . . no marbling as yet.' The temperature would have speeded the process of decomposition considerably, Banks realized. Also, the air was dry, and some degree of mummification might have occurred if the old man had lain there much longer. Banks suspected that cause of death was starvation – Gary had simply left him to die – but it would be a while before more exact information about cause and time could be known. Older persons decompose more slowly than younger ones, and thin ones more slowly than fat ones. Bodies of diseased persons break down quickly. Stomach contents would have to be examined and inner organs checked for the degree of putrefaction.

All very interesting, Banks thought, but none of it really mattered if Gary Hartley confessed.

Finally, PC Tolliver arrived with the coffee and styrofoam cups. Susan poured Gary a cup and pushed the milk and sugar towards him. He didn't acknowledge her. Banks walked over to the window and glanced out at the grey market square, then sat down to begin. He spoke quietly, intimately almost, to put the boy at ease.

'Earlier, Gary, you seemed confused. You said you supposed that you had killed Caroline, then you told me you think your father killed her. Can you be a bit clearer about that?'

'I'm not sure. I . . . I . . .'

'Why not tell me about it, the night you killed her? Start at the beginning.'

'I don't remember.'

'Try. It's important.'

Gary screwed up his eyes in concentration, but when he opened them, he shook his head. 'It's all dark. All dark inside. And it hurts.'

'Where does it hurt, Gary?'

'My head. My eyes. Everywhere.' He covered his face with his hands and shuddered.

Banks let a few seconds pass, then asked, 'How did you get to Eastvale?'

'What?'

'To Eastvale? Did you go by bus or train? Did you borrow a car?'

Gary shook his head. 'I didn't go to Eastvale. I wasn't in Eastvale.'

'Then how did you kill Caroline?'

'I've told you, I don't know.' He hung his head in his hands. 'I just don't know.'

'What happened to your father, Gary?'

'He's dead.'

'How did he die? Did you kill him?'

'No. I didn't go near him.'

'Did you stop going up to his room? Did you stop feeding him?'

'I couldn't go. Not after Caroline, not after I knew. I thought about it and I carried on for a while, but I couldn't.' He looked at Banks, his eyes pleading. 'You must understand. I couldn't. Not after she was dead.'

'So you stopped tending to him?'

'He killed her.'

'But he couldn't have, Gary. He was an invalid, bed-ridden. He couldn't have gone to Eastvale and killed her.'

Suddenly, Gary banged the metal desk with his fist. Susan moved forward but Banks motioned her back.

'I've told you it wasn't in Eastvale!' Gary yelled. 'How many times do I have to tell you? Caroline didn't die in Eastvale.'

'But she did, Gary. Come on, you know that.'

He shook his head. 'He killed her. And I killed her too.'

Susan looked up from her notes and frowned. 'Tell me how he killed her,' Banks asked.

'I don't know. I wasn't there. But he did it like . . . like . . . Oh Christ, she was just a child . . . just a little child!' And he put his head in his hands and sobbed, shaking all over.

Banks stood up and put a comforting arm over his shoulder. At first, Gary didn't react, but then he yielded and buried his head in Banks's chest. Banks held on to him tightly and stroked his hair, then when Gary's grasp loosened, he extricated himself and returned to his chair. Now he thought he understood why Gary was talking the way he was. Now he knew what had happened. Now he understood the Hartley family. But he still had no idea who had killed Caroline Hartley, and why.

THREE

When Susan Gay got to the Crooked Billet at six o'clock, James Conran wasn't there. Casting around for a suitable place to sit, she caught the eye of Marcia Cunningham, the costumes manager, who beckoned her over. Marcia seemed to be sitting with someone, but a group of drinkers blocked Susan's view.

Susan elbowed her way through the after-work crowd, loosening her overcoat as she went. It was cold outside, and enough snow had fallen to speckle her shoulders, but in the pub it was warm. She took off her green woolly gloves and slipped them in her pocket, then, when she reached Marcia, removed her coat and hung it on a peg by the bar. She noted that the buttons of the pink cardigan

Marcia was wearing were incorrectly fastened, making the thing look askew.

'They've not finished yet,' Marcia said. 'What with it being so close to first night, or should I say *twelfth* night, James thought an extra half hour might be in order. Especially with the new Maria. They didn't need me, so he asked me to pass on his apologies if I saw you. He'll be in a little later.'

'Thank you.' Susan smoothed her skirt and sat down.

'How rude of me,' Marcia said, indicating the woman beside her. 'Susan Gay, this is Sandra Banks.' Then she put her hand to her mouth. 'Silly me, I'm forgetting you probably know each other already.'

Susan certainly recognized Sandra. With her looks, she would be hard to miss – that determined mouth, lively blue eyes, long blonde hair and dark eyebrows. She possessed a natural elegance. Susan had always envied her and felt awkward and dowdy when she was around.

'Yes,' Susan said, 'we've met once or twice. Good evening, Mrs Banks.'

'Please, call me Sandra.'

'Sandra was just finishing up some work in the gallery so I popped in and asked if she'd like a drink.'

Susan noticed that their glasses were empty and offered to get a round. When she came back, there was still no sign of James or the others. She didn't know how she was going to maintain small talk with Sandra Banks for the next twenty minutes or so, especially after the emotional scene she had just witnessed between Banks and Gary Hartley. She felt embarrassed. Strong emotion always made her feel that way, and when Banks had hugged the boy close she had had to avert her gaze. But she had seen her boss's expression over the back of the boy's head. It hadn't given much away, but she had noticed compassion in his eyes and she knew from the set of his lips that he shared the boy's pain.

Luckily, Marcia saved her. In appearance rather like one of those plump, ruddy-cheeked characters one sees in illustrations of Dickens novels, she had an ebullient manner to match.

'Any closer to catching those vandals?' she asked.

Conscious of Sandra watching her, Susan said, 'Not yet, I'm afraid. A couple of kids did some damage to a youth club in the north end and we think it's the same ones. We've got our eye on them.'

'Do you think you'll ever catch them?'

Susan caught Sandra smiling at the question and could hardly keep herself from doing the same. Her discomfort waned slightly. Instead of feeling resentful, under scrutiny, she was beginning to feel more as if she had an ally. Sandra had been through it all, knew what it was like to be police in the public eye. But Susan knew she would still have to be cautious. Sandra was, after all, the detective chief inspector's wife, and if Susan made any blunders they would certainly be passed on to Banks.

'Hard to say,' she replied. 'We've got a couple of leads and several likely candidates. That's about all.'

What she hadn't said was that they had at least found a pattern to the kind of places the kids liked to wreck. Most of them were community centres of some kind, never private establishments like cinemas or pubs. As there was a limited number of such social clubs in Eastvale, extra men had been posted on guard. Their instructions were to lie low, blend in and catch the kids in the act, rather than stand as sentries and scare them off. Soon they might put a stop to the trail of vandalism that had cost the town a fortune over the past few months.

'It was such a mess,' Marcia said, shaking her head. 'All those costumes, ruined. I almost sat down and cried. Anyway, I took them home and now I've a bit of time I'm sorting through the remnants to see if I can't resurrect some. I've put a couple together already. I hate waste.'

'That sounds a hell of a job,' said Sandra. 'I don't think I could face it.'

'Oh, I love sewing, fixing things, making things. It makes me feel useful. And I see what I've done at the end. Job satisfaction, I suppose, though it's a pity there's no pay to match.'

Sandra laughed. 'I'd offer to help but I've got two left thumbs when it comes to sewing. I can't even get the bloody thread through the needle. Poor Alan has to sew his own buttons on.'

Susan tried to imagine Detective Chief Inspector Alan Banks sewing buttons on a shirt, but she couldn't.

'It's all right,' Marcia said. 'Keeps me out of mischief these cold winter evenings. Since Frank's been gone I find I need to do more and more to occupy myself.'

'Marcia's husband died six months ago,' Sandra explained to Susan.

'Aye,' said Marcia. 'Just like that, he went. Good as new one moment, then, bang, curtains. And never had a day's illness in his life. Didn't drink and gave up his pipe years ago. Only sixty, he was.'

Susan shook her head. 'It does seem unfair.'

'Whoever told us life would be fair, love? Nobody did, that's who. Anyway, enough of that. Walking out with Mr Conran are you?'

Susan felt herself blushing. 'Well I . . . I . . .'

'I know,' Marcia went on. 'It's none of my business. Tell me to shut up if you want. I'm just an old busybody, that's all.'

Now Susan couldn't help laughing. 'We've been out to dinner a couple of times, and to the pictures. That's all.'

Marcia nodded. 'I wasn't probing into your sex life, lass, just curious, that's all. What's he like when he's out of his director's hat?'

'He makes me laugh.'

'There's a few in that theatre over there could do with a laugh or two.'

Susan leaned forward. 'Marcia, you know that girl who was killed, Caroline Hartley? Was there really anything between her and James?'

'Not that I know of, love,' Marcia answered. 'Just larked around, that's all. Besides, she was one of *them*, wasn't she? Not that I . . . well, you know what I mean.'

'Yes, but James didn't know that. None of you did.'

'Still,' Marcia insisted, 'nothing to it as far as I could see. Oh, he had his eye on her all right. What man wouldn't? Maybe not your *Playboy* material, but dangerous as dynamite nonetheless.'

'What makes you say that?' Sandra chipped in.

'I don't really know. Maybe it's hindsight. I just get feelings about people sometimes, and I knew from the start that one was trouble. Still, it looks as if she meant trouble for herself mostly, doesn't it?'

'Is James Conran a suspect?' Sandra asked.

'Your husband seems to think so,' Susan said. 'But everyone who had anything to do with Caroline Hartley is a suspect.'

'Aren't you worried about getting involved with him?' Sandra asked.

'A bit, I suppose. I mean, not that I think James is guilty of anything, just that being involved might blur my objectivity. It's an awkward position to be in, that's all. Besides,' she laughed, 'he's my old teacher. It feels strange to be having dinner with him. I like him, but I'm keeping him at arm's length. At least until this business is over.'

'Good for you,' Sandra said.

'Anyway, I don't see as it should matter. The chief inspector went off to London with Veronica Shildon, and I'd say she's a prime suspect.' Susan realized too late what she had implied, and wondered if an attempt to backtrack and make her meaning clear would only make things worse.

All Sandra said was, 'I'm sure Alan knows what he's doing.' And Susan could have sworn she noticed a ghost of a smile on her face.

'I know. I'm sorry. I didn't meant to imply . . . just . . .'

'It's all right,' Sandra said. 'I just wanted to point out that what he's doing isn't the same. I'm not criticizing you.'

'I don't suppose I understand his methods yet.'

'I'm not sure I do, either.' Sandra laughed.

Suddenly, Susan's world turned pitch black. She felt a light pressure on her brow and cheeks and she could no longer see Sandra and Marcia. The bustling pub seemed to fall silent, then a voice whispered in her ear, 'Guess who?'

'James,' she said, and her vision was restored.

FOUR

Banks felt unusually tired when he got home about eight o'clock that evening. The paperwork was done, and Gary

Hartley had been sent back to Harrogate to face whatever charges could be made.

Sandra had just got home herself, and both children were out. Over a dinner of left-over chicken casserole, Sandra told him about her evening with Susan and Marcia. In turn, Banks tried to explain Gary Hartley to her.

'He'd always hated Caroline, all his life. She was the bane of his existence. She used to tease him, torment him, torture him, and he never had any idea why. She even tried to drown him once. To cap it all, she left home and he got lumbered with looking after his invalid father, who made it perfectly clear that he still preferred Caroline. When you look at it like that, it's not a bad motive for murder, wouldn't you say?'

'Did he do it?' Sandra asked.

Banks shook his head. 'No. Not literally. When she told him what had happened when her mother had been in hospital having him, he suddenly realized why she hated him. She wanted to apologize, make up even, if she could. But Gary's sensitive. It's not something you can really work out in your mind. Christ, most people don't even talk about it. And Caroline had blanked out the memory for years. It was always there, though, under the surface, shoving and cracking the crust. Gary just reacted emotionally. He was overwhelmed by what she said, and suddenly his whole world was turned upside-down. All his anger had been pointed in the wrong direction – at her – for so long.'

'He killed his father?'

'He sat in his room downstairs and let the old man starve to death.'

Sandra shivered. 'Good God!'

She was right to be so appalled, Banks thought. It was

an act of utmost cruelty, the kind for which a public ignorant of the facts might demand a return of the noose. But still, he couldn't forget Gary's pain and confusion; he couldn't help but feel pity for the boy, no matter what atrocity he had committed. He gave Sandra the gist of their discussion.

'I can see what he meant when he said her father had killed her,' she said, 'but why implicate himself too? You said he didn't do it.'

'But he blamed himself – for being born, if you like. After all, that's when it started. That's when Caroline was left alone with her father. He couldn't give us any concrete details of the crime because he hadn't done it. But in his mind he was responsible. All he could say was that it was all dark to him. Dark and painful.'

'I don't understand,' Sandra said, frowning.

'I think he was describing being born,' Banks said. 'Dark. Dark and painful.'

'My God. And you said Caroline tried to drown him, too?'

'Yes. He was about four and she was twelve. He can't remember the details clearly, of course, and there's no one else alive to tell what happened, but he thinks his mother left him for a moment to fetch some clean towels. She left the bathroom door open and Caroline walked in. He said he remembers how she pulled his feet and his head went under the water. The next thing he knew, he was up again in his mother's arms gasping for air and Caroline was gone. Nobody ever spoke about it afterwards.'

'He must have been terrified of her.'

'He was. And he didn't know why she was treating him that way. She didn't know, either. He turned in on himself to shut it all out.'

'Is he insane?' Sandra asked.

'Not for me to say. He's in need of help, certainly. Just imagine the hatred of all those years boiling over, finding its true object at last. All the humiliation. His own life ruined, knowing he was only second-best to his sister. The only wonder is he didn't do it sooner. It took Caroline's murder and the truth about her childhood to set him free.'

Banks remembered the slouching figure that had shuffled out of his office after telling everything. He would be under care in Harrogate now, perhaps going through the whole story again at the hands of less sympathetic interrogators. After all, look at what he'd done. But Gary Hartley wouldn't be hanged. He wouldn't even be sent to jail. He would first be bound over for psychiatric evaluation, then he might well spend a good part of his life in mental institutions. Which was better? It was impossible for Banks to decide. Gary's life was blighted, just as his sister's had been, though, unlike Caroline, Gary hadn't even managed to snatch his few moments of happiness.

'Then who *did* kill Caroline Hartley?' Sandra asked.

Banks scratched his head. 'I'm buggered if I know. I'm pretty sure we can rule out Gary now, and her friends in London. When Caroline moved on, she always seemed to burn her bridges.'

'Which leaves?'

'Well, unless we're dealing with a psycho, we're back to the locals. Ivers and his girlfriend aren't home-free yet, whatever they told us. They lied to us at the start, and Patsy Janowski has a good motive for corroborating everything Ivers might claim. She loves the man and wants to hang on to him. And then there's the amateur crowd. I've been intending to have another talk with Teresa Podmore.'

'And Veronica Shildon?' Sandra asked. 'Susan Gay seems to think you've been overlooking her.'

'Susan's prejudiced.'

'Are you sure you're not?'

Banks stared at her. 'Don't you know me better than that?'

'Just asking.'

He shook his head. 'Officially she's a suspect, of course, but Veronica Shildon didn't do it. I must be overlooking something.'

'Any idea what?'

Banks brought his fist up slowly to his temple. 'Damned if I know.' Then he stood up. 'Hell, it's been a rough day. I'm having a stiff Scotch then I'm off to bed.' He poured the drink and went into the hall to his jacket. When he came back he said, 'And I'm having a bloody cigarette as well, house rule or no house rule.'

12

ONE

The wind numbed Banks to the marrow when he got out of his car near the Lobster Inn the following afternoon. It was 3 January – only three days to twelfth night. The sky was a pale eggshell blue, with a few wispy grey clouds twisting over the horizon like strips of gauze. But the sun had no warmth in it. The wind kicked up little white caps as it danced over the ruffled water and slid up the rough sea wall right onto the front. Banks dashed into the pub.

There already, ensconced in front of the meagre fire, sat Detective Sergeant Jim Hatchley, pint in one ham-like hand and a huge, foul-smelling cigar smouldering between two sausage-shaped fingers of the other. Banks thought he had put on weight; his bulk seemed to loom larger than ever. The sergeant shifted in his seat when Banks came over and sat opposite him.

'Miserable old bugger saves all his coal till evening,' he said, by way of greeting, gesturing over at the landlord who sat on a high stool behind the bar reading a tabloid. 'Bigger crowd then, you see.'

Banks nodded. 'How's married life treating you?'

'Can't complain. She's a good lass. I could do without being at the bloody seaside in winter, though. Plays havoc with my rheumatism.'

'Didn't know you had it.'

'Nor did I.'

'Never mind. Just wait till spring. You'll be the envy of us all then. Everyone will want to come and visit you on their weekends off.'

'Aye, maybe. We'll have to see about renting out the spare room for bed and breakfast. Carol's got some fancy ideas about starting a garden, too. Sounds like a lot of back breaking work to me.'

And Banks knew what Hatchley felt about work, the dreaded four-letter word, back breaking or not. 'I'm sorry to lumber you with this, Jim,' he said. 'Especially on your honeymoon.'

'That's all right. Gets me out of the house. We're not spring chickens, you know. Can't expect to be at it all the time.' He winked. 'Besides, a man needs time alone with his pint and his paper.'

Banks noticed a copy of the *Sun* folded in Hatchley's pocket. From the little he could see, it looked to be open at page three. An attractive new wife, and he still ogled the naked page-three girl. Old habits die hard.

The landlord stirred; his newspaper began to rustle with impatience. Clearly it was all very well for him to be rude to customers, but customers were not expected to be rude to him by warming themselves in front of the sparse flames for too long without buying a drink. Banks walked over and the paper rose up again, covering the man's beady eyes.

'Two pints of bitter, please,' Banks said, and slowly the paper came to rest on the bar. With a why-can't-everyone-leave-me-alone sigh, the man pulled the pints and plonked them down in front of Banks, holding his other hand out for the money as soon as he had done so. Banks paid and walked back to Sergeant Hatchley.

'Anything come up?' Banks asked, reaching for a cigarette.

Hatchley pulled a cigar tube from his inside pocket. 'Have one of these. Christmas present from the in-laws. Havana. Nice and mild.'

Banks remembered the last cigar he had smoked, one of Dirty Dick Burgess's Tom Thumbs, and declined. 'Best stick with the devil you know,' he said, lighting the cigarette.

'As you like. Well,' Hatchley said, 'there's nowt been happening around here. I've been up with Carol a couple of evenings, for a drink, like, and noticed that Ivers and his fancy woman in here once or twice. Tall chap in need of a hair cut. Looks a bit like that Irish bloke from *Camelot*, Richard Harris, after a bad night. And that lass of his, young enough to be his granddaughter I'd say. Still, it takes all sorts. Lovely pair of thighs under them tight jeans, and a bum like two peaches in a wet paper bag. Anyroad, they'd come in about nine-ish, nod hello to a few locals, knock back a couple of drinks and leave about ten.'

'Ever talk to them?'

'No. They don't know who I am. They keep themselves to themselves, too. The local constable's a very obliging chap. I've had him keeping an eye open and he says they've done nothing out of the ordinary. Hardly been out of the house. Are they still in the running?'

Banks nodded. 'There's a couple of problems with the timing, but nothing they couldn't have worked out between them.'

'Between them?'

'Yes. If they killed Caroline Hartley, they must have been in it together. It's the only way they could have done it.'

'But you're not sure they did?'

'No. I'm just not satisfied with their stories.'

'What about their motive?'

'That I don't know. The husband had one, clearly enough, but the girl didn't share it. It'd have to be something we don't know about.'

'Money?'

'I don't think so. Caroline Hartley didn't have much. It would have to be something more obscure than that.'

'Perhaps she's the kind who'd do anything for him, just to hang on to him.'

'Maybe.'

'Or they didn't do it?'

'Could be that, too.'

'Or maybe you're over-complicating things as usual?'

Banks grinned. 'Maybe I am.'

'So what now?' Hatchley asked.

'A quick visit, just to let them know we haven't forgotten them.'

'Me too?'

'Yes.'

'But they'll recognize me. They'll know me in future.'

'It won't do them any harm to know we're keeping an eye on them. Come on, sup up.'

Grudgingly, Sergeant Hatchley drained his pint and stubbed out his cigar. 'Still another ten minutes left in that,' he complained.

'Take it with you.'

'Never mind.'

Hatchley followed Banks out into the sharp wind. Thin ice splintered as they made their way up the footpath to Ivers's cottage, from which a welcoming plume of smoke curled and drifted west. Hatchley groaned and panted as they walked. Banks knocked. This time, Ivers himself answered the door.

'Come in. Sit down. Sit down,' he said. Hatchley took the bulky armchair by the mullioned window and Banks lowered himself into a wooden rocker by the fire. 'Have you caught him?' Ivers asked. 'The man who killed Caroline?'

Banks shook his head. 'Afraid not.'

Ivers frowned. 'Oh . . . well. Patsy! Patsy! Some tea, if you've got a minute.'

Patsy Janowski came in from her study, glared at Banks's right shoelace and went into the kitchen.

'How do you think I can help you again?' Ivers asked.

'I'm not sure,' Banks said. 'First, I'd just like to go over one or two details.'

'Shall we wait for Patsy with the tea?'

They waited. Banks passed the time talking music with Ivers, who was excited about the harmonic breakthroughs he had made over the past two days. Hatchley, hands folded in his lap, looked bored.

Finally, Patsy emerged with a tray and put it down on the table in front of the fire. She wore jeans with a plain white shirt, the top two buttons undone. Banks noticed Hatchley take a discreet look down the front as she bent to put the tray down. She didn't seem pleased to see Banks, and if either of them recognized Sergeant Hatchley, they didn't show it. This time, Patsy was surly and evasive and Ivers seemed open and helpful. Luckily, Banks had learned never to take anything at face value. When tea was poured, he began with the questions.

'It's the timing that's important, you see,' he opened. 'Can you be any clearer about what time you delivered the Christmas present, Mr Ivers?'

'I'm sorry, I can't. Sometime around seven, I'm sure of that.'

'And you stayed how long?'

'No more than five minutes.'

'That's rather a long time, isn't it?'

'What do you mean?'

'People have funny ideas about time, about how short or long various periods are. I'd say five minutes was a bit long to spend with someone you didn't like on an errand like that. Why not just hand over the present and leave?'

'Maybe it wasn't that long,' Ivers said. 'I just went in, handed it over, exchanged a few insincere pleasantries and left. Maybe two minutes, I don't know.'

Banks sipped some tea, then lit a cigarette. Patsy, legs curled under her on the rug in front of the fire, passed him an ashtray from the hearth.

'What pleasantries?' he asked. 'What did you say to each other?'

'As I said before, I asked how she was, how Veronica was, made a remark about the weather. And she answered me politely. I handed over the record, told her it was something special for Veronica for Christmas, then I left. We'd at least reached a stage where we could behave in a civilized manner towards one another.'

'You said it was something special?'

'Something like that.'

'How did she react?'

Ivers closed his eyes for a moment and frowned. 'She didn't, really. I mean, she didn't say anything. She looked interested, though. Curious.'

'That may be why she opened it, if she did,' Banks said, almost to himself. 'Did she seem at all strange to you? Did she say anything odd?'

Ivers shook his head. 'No.'

'Did she seem to be expecting someone?'

'How would I know? She certainly didn't say anything if she was.'

'Was she on edge? Did she keep glancing towards the door? Did she give the impression she wanted you out of the way as soon as possible?'

'I'd say yes to the latter,' Ivers answered, 'but no to the others. She seemed perfectly all right to me.'

'What was she doing?'

'Doing?'

'Yes. When you called. You went into the front room, didn't you? Was she listening to music, polishing the silver, watching television, reading?'

'I don't know. Nothing . . . I . . . eating, perhaps. There was some cake on the table. I remember that.'

'What was she wearing?'

'I can't remember.'

'Claude's hopeless about things like that,' Patsy cut in. 'Half the time he doesn't even notice what *I'm* wearing.'

Taking in the stooped, lanky figure of the composer in his usual baggy clothes, Banks was inclined to believe her. Here was the genius so wrapped up in his music that he didn't notice such mundane things as what other people said, did or wore.

On the other hand, Ivers obviously had a taste for attractive women. In different ways, both Veronica and Patsy were evidence enough of that. And what red-blooded male would forget a woman as beautiful as Caroline Hartley answering the door in her bathrobe? Surely a man with a taste for so seductive a woman as Patsy Janowksi couldn't fail to remember, or to react? But then Ivers knew Caroline; he knew she was a lesbian. Perhaps it was all a matter of perspective. Banks pressed on.

'What about you, Ms Janowski? Can you remember what she was wearing?'

'I didn't even go into the house. I only saw her standing in the doorway.'

'Can you remember?'

'It looked like some kind of bathrobe to me, a kimono-style thing. Dark green I think the colour was. She was hugging it tight around her because of the cold.'

'What time did you arrive?'

'After seven. I left here about twenty minutes after Claude.'

'How long after seven?'

'I'm not sure. I told you before. Maybe about a quarter after, twenty past.'

'What were you wearing?'

'Wearing?' Patsy frowned. 'I don't see what that's—'

'Just answer, please.'

She shot his right lapel a baleful glance. 'Jeans, boots and my fur-lined jacket.'

'How long is the jacket?'

'It comes down to my waist,' Patsy said, looking puzzled. 'Look, I don't—'

'Would you say that Caroline was expecting someone else? Someone other than you?'

'I couldn't say, really.'

'Did she react as if she had been expecting someone else when she saw you standing there at the door? Did she show any disappointment?'

'No, not especially.' Patsy thought for a moment. 'She was real nice, given who I am. I'm sorry, but it all happened so quickly and I was too concerned about Claude to pay much attention.'

'Did she seem nervous or surprised to see you, anxious for you to leave quickly?'

'No, not at all. She was surprised to see me, of course, but that's only natural. And she wanted to shut the door because of the cold.'

'Why didn't she ask you in?'

Patsy looked at the hearth. 'She hardly knew me. Besides, all I had to ask her was whether Claude was there.'

'And she said he wasn't.'

'Yes.'

'And you believed her?'

Patsy's tone hardened. She spoke between clenched teeth. 'Of course I did.'

'Are you *sure* he wasn't still in the house?'

Ivers leaned forward. 'Now wait—'

'Let her answer, Mr Ivers,' Sergeant Hatchley said.

'Caroline said he'd gone. She said he'd just left the record and gone. I hadn't any reason to believe she was lying.'

'Was she in a hurry to get rid of you?'

'I've told you, no. Everything was normal as far as I could tell.'

'But she didn't invite you inside. Doesn't that seem odd to you, Ms Janowski? You've already said it was so cold on the doorstep that Caroline Hartley had to hold her robe tight around her. Wouldn't it have made more sense to invite you in, even if just for a few minutes? After all, Mr Ivers here says he only stayed for five minutes.'

'Are you trying to suggest that I *did* go inside?' Patsy exploded. 'Just what's going on in that policeman's mind of yours? Are you accusing me of killing her? Because if you are you'd better damn well arrest me right now and let me call my lawyer!'

'There's no reason to be melodramatic, Ms Janowski,' Banks said. 'I'm not suggesting anything of the kind. I happen to know already that you didn't enter the house.'

Patsy's brow furrowed and some of the angry red colour drained from her cheeks. 'Then I . . . I don't understand.'

'Did you hear music playing?'

'No. I can't remember any.'

'And you didn't ask to go inside, to look around?'

'No. Why should I? I knew he wouldn't still be there if Veronica wasn't home.'

'The point is,' Banks said, 'that Mr Ivers *could* have been in the house, couldn't he? You've just confirmed to me that you didn't go in and look.'

'I've told you, he wouldn't—'

'Could he have been inside?'

She looked at Ivers, then back to Banks. 'That's an unfair question. The goddamn Duke of Edinburgh *could* have been inside for all I know, but I don't think he was.'

'The thing is,' Banks said, 'that nobody saw Mr Ivers leave. Caroline Hartley didn't invite you in, even though it was cold, and you didn't insist on seeing for yourself.'

'That doesn't mean anything,' Ivers burst out, 'and you know it. It was pure bloody luck on your part that anyone noticed me arrive, or Patsy. You can't expect them to be watching for me to leave, too.'

'Maybe not, but it would have made everything a lot tidier.'

'And if you're suggesting that Caroline didn't let Patsy in because *I* was there, have you considered that she might have been hiding someone else? Have you thought about that?'

'Yes, Mr Ivers, I've thought about that. The problem is,

no one else was seen near the house between your visit and Ms Janowski's.' He turned to Patsy. 'When you left, did you notice anyone hanging around the area?'

'I don't think so.'

'Concentrate. It could be important. I've asked you before to try to visualize the scene. Did you see anyone behaving strangely, or anyone who looked furtive, suspicious, out of place?'

Pasty closed her eyes. 'No, I'm sure I didn't . . . Except—'

'What?'

'I'm not very clear. There was a woman.'

'Where?'

'The end of the street. It was dark there . . . snowing. And she was some distance away from me. But I remember thinking there was something odd about her, I don't know what. I'm damned if I can think what it was.'

'Think,' Banks encouraged her. The timing was certainly right. Patsy had called at about twenty past seven, and the killer – if indeed the last observed visitor was the killer – only two or three minutes later. There was a good chance that they had passed in the street.

Patsy opened her eyes. 'It's no good. It was ages ago now and I hardly paid any attention at the time. It's just one of those odd little things, like a déjà vu.'

'Did you think you knew this woman, recognized her?'

'No. It wasn't anything like that. I'd remember that. It was when I got to King Street. She was crossing over, as if she was heading for the mews. We were on opposite sides and I didn't get a very close look. It was something else, just a little thing. I'm sorry, Chief Inspector, really I am. Especially,' she added sharply, 'as any information I might give could get us off the hook. I simply can't remember.'

'If you do remember anything at all about the woman,' Banks said, 'no matter how minor a detail it might seem to you, call me immediately, is that clear?'

Patsy nodded.

'And you're not off the hook yet. Not by a long chalk.'

Banks gestured for Hatchley to get up, a lengthy task that involved quite a bit of heaving and puffing, then they left. Banks almost slipped on the icy pathway, but Hatchley caught his arm and steadied him just in time.

'Well,' said the sergeant, stamping and rubbing his hands outside the Lobster Inn, 'that's that then. I don't mind doing a bit of extra work, you know,' he said, glancing longingly at the pub, 'even when I'm supposed to be on my honeymoon. I know it's not my case, but I wish you'd fill me in on a few more details.'

Banks caught his glance and interpreted the signals. 'Fine,' he said. 'Over a pint?'

Hatchley beamed. 'Well, if you insist . . .'

TWO

'Susan, love, could I have a word?'

'Of course.'

Susan and Marcia were sitting in the Crooked Billet with the entire cast of *Twelfth Night* after rehearsal. It had gone badly, and those who weren't busy arguing were drowning their depression in drink. James didn't seem too concerned, Susan thought, watching him listen patiently to Malvolio's complaints about the final scene. But he was used to it; he'd directed plays before. She shifted along the bench to let Marcia Cunningham sit beside her. 'What is it?'

Marcia looked puzzled. 'I'm not sure. It's nothing really. At least I don't think it is. But it's very odd.'

'Police business?'

'Well, it might have something to do with the break-in. You did say to mention anything that came up.'

'Go on.'

'But that's just it, you see, love. It doesn't make sense.'

'Marcia,' Susan said, 'why don't you just tell me? Get it off your chest.'

Marcia frowned. 'It's hard to explain. You'd probably think I was just being silly if I told you. Can't you pop around and have a look for yourself? I don't live far away.'

'What, now?'

'Whenever you can spare the time, love.' Marcia looked at her watch. 'I'll have to be off in a few minutes, anyway.'

Susan recognized a deadline when she heard one. Now she was with CID she was never really off duty. She wouldn't get anywhere if she put personal pleasure before the job, however fruitless the trek to Marcia's might seem. And the vandalism was *her* case. A success so early in her CID career would look good. What could she do but agree? As Marcia couldn't be induced to say any more, Susan would have to put James off and go with her. It wouldn't take long, Marcia had assured her, so she wouldn't have to cancel their dinner date, just postpone it for half an hour or so. James would understand. He certainly had plenty to occupy himself with in her absence.

'All right,' Susan said. 'I'll come with you.'

'Thanks, love. It might be a waste of time but well, wait till you see.'

Susan told James she had to nip out for a while and would be back in half an hour or so, then she buttoned up her winter coat and left with Marcia. They walked north-east along York Road, past the excavated pre-Roman site, where the little burial mounds and hut foundations looked eerie under their carapace of moonlit ice.

'It's just down here.' Marcia led Susan down a sloping street of pre-war semis opposite the site. Though the house itself was small, it had gardens at both front and back and a fine view of the river and the Green from the kitchen window. The furniture looked dated and worn, and swaths of material lay scattered here and there, along with stacks of patterns and magazines, in the untidy living room. Marcia didn't apologize for the mess. Her sense of disorder, Susan realized, didn't stop at the way she dressed.

On the mantelpiece above the electric fire stood a framed photograph of Marcia's late husband, a handsome man, posing on the seafront at some holiday resort with a pipe in his mouth. Marcia switched on the fire. Susan took off her coat and knelt by the reddening element, rubbing her hands. She could smell dust burning as it heated up.

'Sorry it's so cold,' Marcia said. 'We wanted central heating, but since my Frank died I just haven't been able to afford it.'

'I don't have it either,' Susan said. 'I always do this when I get home.' She stood up and turned. 'What is it you've got to show me?'

Marcia dragged a large box into the centre of the room. 'It's this. Remember I told you yesterday I was patching up some of the damage those hooligans did to the costumes?'

Susan nodded.

'Well, I have. Look.' She held up a long pearl gown with shoulder straps and plunging neckline.

Susan looked closely. 'But surely . . .?'

'Cut to shreds, it was,' Marcia said. 'Look.' She pointed

out the faint lines of stitching. 'Of course, you'd never get away with wearing it for a banquet at the Ritz, but it'll do for a stage performance. Even the nobs in the front row wouldn't be able to see how it had been sewn back together.'

'You're a genius, Marcia,' Susan exclaimed, touching the fabric. 'You should have been a surgeon.'

Marcia shrugged. 'Can't stand the sight of blood. Anyway, it was just like doing a jigsaw puzzle really.' And she showed Susan more dresses and gowns she had resurrected from the box of snipped-up originals. That so untidy a person should be able to bring such order out of chaos astonished Susan.

'You didn't bring me here just to praise you, did you?' she said finally. 'I don't mean to be rude, but I told James I'd be back in half an hour.'

'Sorry, love,' Marcia said. 'Just got carried away, that's all. Forgot how impatient young love is.'

Susan blushed. 'Marcia! The point.'

'Yes, well.' Marcia reached into the box and took out a simple burgundy dress. 'This is the point. I worked on this one all afternoon.' She held it up, and Susan could see that the sleeves had been cut off up to elbow-level and a large patch of the front, around the breasts, was also missing.

'I don't understand,' she said. 'Haven't you finished?'

'I've done all I could, love. That's the point. This is it. All there was.'

'I still don't understand.'

'And you a copper, too. It's simple. I managed to sort out the bits and pieces of the other dresses here and patch them together, as you've seen.'

Susan nodded.

'But when it came to this one, I couldn't find all the pieces. Some of them've plain disappeared.'

'Disappeared?'

'Wake up, lass. Yes, disappeared. I've looked everywhere. Even back at the centre to see if they'd fallen on the floor or something. Not a trace.'

'But it doesn't make any sense,' Susan said slowly. 'Who on earth would want to steal pieces of a ruined dress?'

'My point exactly,' Marcia said. 'That's why I asked you to come here and see it for yourself. Who would do such a thing? And why?'

'There has to be a simple explanation.'

Marcia nodded. 'Yes. But what is it? Your lot didn't take any for analysis or whatever, did they?'

Susan shook her head. 'No. They must have dropped out somewhere. Maybe when you were bringing the box home.'

'I looked everywhere. I'm telling you, love, if there'd been pieces I would've found them.'

Susan couldn't help but feel disappointed. It was hardly an important discovery – certainly not one that would lead to the identity of the vandals – but Marcia was right in that it was mystifying. It was slightly disturbing, too. When Susan picked up the dress and held it in front of her, she shivered as if someone had just walked over her grave. It looked as if the arms had been deliberately cut off rather than torn, and two circles of fabric around the breasts had been snipped out in a similar way. Shaking her head, Susan folded the dress and handed it back to Marcia.

THREE

'Chief Inspector Banks! Have you any news?'

'No news,' Banks said. 'Maybe a few questions.'

'Come in.' Veronica Shildon led him into her front room. It looked larger and colder than it had before, as if even all the heat from the fiercely burning fire in the hearth couldn't penetrate every shadowy corner. Two small, threadbare armchairs stood in front of the fire.

'Christine Cooper let me have them until I get around to buying a new suite,' Veronica said, noticing Banks looking at them. 'She was going to throw them out.'

Banks nodded. After Veronica had taken his coat, he sat in one of the armchairs and warmed himself by the flames. 'It's certainly more comfortable than a hard-backed chair,' he said.

'Can I offer you a drink?' she asked.

'Tea would do nicely.'

Veronica brewed the tea and came to sit in the other armchair, placed so they didn't face each other directly but at an angle that required a slight turning of the head to make eye-contact. The fire danced in the hollows of Veronica's cheeks and reflected like tiny orange candle flames in her eyes.

'I don't feel I thanked you enough for letting me come to London with you,' she said, crossing her legs and sitting back in the chair. 'It can't have been an easy decision for you to make. Anyway, I'm grateful. Somehow, seeing Ruth Dunne gave me more of Caroline than I'd had, if you can understand that.'

Banks, who had more than once spent hours with colleagues extolling the virtues and playfully noting the faults of deceased friends, knew exactly what Veronica meant. Somehow, sharing memories of the dead seemed to make them live larger in one's mind and heart, and Veronica had had nobody in Eastvale to talk to about Caroline because nobody here had really known her.

Banks nodded. 'I don't really know why I *am* here, to tell the truth,' he said finally. 'Nothing I learned in London really helped. Now it's early evening on a cold January day and I'm still no closer to the solution than I was last week. Maybe I'm just the cop who came in from the cold.'

Veronica raised an eyebrow. 'Frustration?'

'Certainly. More than that.'

'Tell me,' she said slowly, 'am I . . . I mean, do you still believe that *I* might have murdered Caroline?'

Banks lit a cigarette and shifted his legs. The fire was burning his shins. 'Ms Shildon,' he said, 'we've no evidence at all to link you to the crime. We never have had. Everything you told us checks out, and we found no traces of blood-stained clothing in the house. Nor did there appear to be any blood on your person. Unless you're an especially clever and cold-blooded killer, which I don't think you are, then I don't see how you could have murdered Caroline. You also appear to lack a motive. At least I haven't been able to find one I'm comfortable with.'

'But surely you don't take things at face value?'

'No, I don't. It's a simple statistic that most murders are committed by people who are close to the victim, often family members or lovers. Given that, you're obviously a prime suspect. There could have been a way, certainly, if you'd been planning the act. There could also be a motive we don't know about. Caroline *could* have been having an affair and you *could* have found out about it.'

'So you still think I might have done it?'

Banks shrugged. 'It's not so much a matter of what I think. It's maybe not probable, but it certainly is possible. Until I find out exactly who did do it, I can't count anybody from Caroline's circle out.'

'Including me?'

'Including you.'

'God, what a terrible job it must be, having to see people that way all the time, as potential criminals. How can you ever get close to anyone?'

'You're exaggerating. It's my job, not my life. Do you think doctors go around all the time seeing everyone as potential patients, for example, or lawyers as potential clients?'

'Of the latter I'm quite certain,' Veronica said with a quiet laugh, 'but as for doctors, the only ones I've known get very irritated when guests ask their advice about aches and pains at cocktail parties.'

'Anyway,' Banks went on, 'people create their own problems.'

'What do you mean?'

'Everyone lies, evades or holds back the full truth. Oh, you all have your own perfectly good reasons for doing it – protecting Caroline's memory, covering up a petty crime, unwillingness to reveal an unattractive aspect of your own personality, inability to face up to things or simply not wanting to get involved. But can't you see where that leaves us? If we're faced with several people all closely connected to the victim, and they all lie to us, one of them could conceivably be lying to cover up murder.'

'But surely you must have instincts? You must trust some people.'

'Yes, I do. My instincts tell me that you didn't kill

Caroline, but I'd be a proper fool if I let my heart rule my head and overlooked an important piece of evidence. That's the trouble, trusting your instincts can sometimes blind you to the obvious. Already I've told you too much.'

'Does your instinct tell you who did kill her?'

Banks shook his head and flicked a column of ash into the fire. 'Unfortunately, no. Gary Hartley confessed, in a way, but . . .' He told her what had happened in Harrogate. Veronica sat forward and clasped her hands on her lap as he spoke.

'The poor boy,' she said when he'd finished. 'Is there anything I can do?'

'I don't think so. He's undergoing psychiatric tests right now. But the point is, whatever he did do, he didn't kill Caroline. If anything, towards the end, when he knew the full story, he felt pity for her. It was his father he turned on, with years of pent-up hatred. I still can't imagine what torture it must have been for both of them. The old man unable to help himself, unable to get out of bed, starving and lying in his own waste; and Gary downstairs getting drunk and listening to the feeble cries and taps growing fainter, knowing he was slowly killing his own father.' Banks shuddered. 'There are some things it doesn't do to dwell on, perhaps. But none of this gets us any closer to Caroline's killer.'

'It's the "why" I can't understand,' Veronica said. 'Who could possibly have had a reason for killing Caroline?'

'That we don't know.' Banks sipped some tea. 'I thought it might have had something to do with her past, but neither Ruth Dunne nor Colm Grey, the father of her child, had anything to do with it. Unless there's a very obscure connection, such as a dissatisfied customer come back to wreak revenge, which hardly seems likely, all we can surmise is that it was someone she knew, and someone who hadn't planned to kill her.'

'How do you know that?'

'There was no sign of forced entry, and the weapon, it just came to hand.'

'But she didn't know many people,' Veronica said. 'Surely that would be a help.'

'It is and it isn't. If she didn't know many people very well, then how could she offend someone so much they'd want to kill her?'

'Why do you say offend? Maybe you're wrong. Perhaps she found out something that someone didn't want known, or she saw something she shouldn't have.'

'But according to what everyone tells me – yourself included – she wasn't acting at all strangely prior to her death. Surely if something along those lines was bothering her she should have been.'

Veronica shook her head. 'I don't know . . . she could have been holding back, pretending . . . for my sake.'

'But you didn't get that impression? Your instinct didn't tell you so?'

'No. Then, I never known whether to trust my instincts or not. I've made mistakes.'

'We all have,' Banks said. 'But you're right to consider other motives. We shouldn't overlook the possibility that someone had a very practical reason for wanting her out of the way. The problem is, it just makes the motive harder to get at, because it's less personal. Let's say, to be absurd, that she saw two spies exchanging documents. In the first place, how would she know they were doing anything illegal, and in the second, how would they know she was a threat?' He shook his head. 'That kind of thing only happens in books. Real murders are much simpler, in a way – at least as far as motive is concerned – but not necessarily easier to solve. Gary Hartley might have had a deep-seated reason to kill his sister, but he didn't do it. Your estranged husband had a motive, too. He blamed Caroline for the separation. But he seems happy enough in his new life with Patsy. Why would he do anything to ruin that? On the other hand, who knows what people really feel?'

'What do you mean?'

'He could have done it, if Patsy Janowski is in it with him or is lying to protect him. He delivered the record, we know that for a fact. As to who put it on the turntable . . .'

Veronica shook her head slowly. 'Claude couldn't murder anyone. Oh, he has his moods and his rages, but he's not a killer. Anyway, do you really think the music is important?'

'It's a clue of some kind, but it didn't mean what I thought it did. I believe Caroline opened it out of curiosity. She wanted to know what Claude thought was so special to you. Beyond that, your guess is as good as mine. Maybe she would even play a little of it, again to satisfy her curiosity, but I can't believe she'd leave the arm up so it would repeat forever.'

Veronica smiled. 'That's just like Caroline,' she said quietly. 'Such curiosity. You know, she always wanted to shake all her Christmas presents. It was well nigh impossible to stop her opening them on Christmas Eve.'

Banks laughed. 'I know, my daughter's the same.'

Veronica shook her head. 'Such a child . . . in some ways.'

Banks leaned forward. 'What did you say?'

'About Caroline. I said she was such a child in so many ways.'

'Yes,' Banks whispered. 'Yes, she was.' He remembered something Ruth Dunne had said to him in London. He tossed his cigarette end into the fire and finished his tea.

'Does it mean something?' Veronica asked.

'It might do.' He stood up. 'If it does, I've been a bit slow on the uptake. Look, I'd better go now. Much as I'd like to stay here and keep warm, I've got work to do. I'm sorry.'

'It's all right. You don't have to apologize. I don't expect you to keep me company. That's not part of your job.'

Banks put the empty teacup on the table. 'It's not a task I despise,' he said. 'But there are a few points I have to review back at the station.'

'When you find out,' Veronica said, twisting the silver ring around her middle finger, 'will you let me know?'

'You'd find out soon enough.'

'No. I don't want to find out from the papers. I want *you* to let me know. As soon as you find out. No matter what the time, day or night. Will you do that for me?'

'Is this some sort of desire for revenge? Do you need an object to hate?'

'No. You once told me I was far too civilized for such feelings. I just want to understand. I want to know why Caroline had to die, what the killer was feeling.'

'We might never know that.'

She put her hand on his sleeve. 'But you will tell me, won't you, when you know? Promise?'

'I'll do my best,' Banks said.

Veronica sighed. 'Good.'

'What about the record?' Banks said at the door. 'Technically, it's yours, you know.'

Veronica leaned against the doorjamb and wrapped her

arms around her to keep warm. 'I can live in this house,' she said, 'especially when I get it redecorated and bring new furniture in. But do you know something? I think that if I ever heard that music again I'd go insane.'

Banks said goodnight and Veronica closed the door. It was a shame, he thought, that such a glorious and transcendent piece of music should be associated with such a bloody deed, but at least he thought he now knew why the record had been left playing, if not who had put it on.

FOUR

Susan systematically picked the strips of glittering silver tinsel from her tiny artificial Christmas tree. Carefully, she replaced each flimsy strand on the card from which it came, to put away for next year. She did the same with the single string of lights and the red and green coloured balls, the only decorations she had bought.

When she had finished with the tree, she stood on a chair and untapped the intricate concertinas of coloured crêpe paper she had draped across the ceiling and folded them together. Apart from the Father Christmas above the mantelpiece, a three-dimensional figure that closed like a book when you folded it in half, that was it.

When she had put all traces of Christmas in the cupboard, Susan stood in the centre of her living room and gazed around. Somehow, even without all the festive decorations she had dashed out and bought at the last moment, the place was beginning to feel a little more like a home. There was still a lot to do – framed prints to buy, perhaps a few ornaments – but she was getting there. Already she had found time to buy three records:

highlights from *Madame Butterfly*, *The Four Seasons* and a recording of traditional folk music, the kind she had heard a few times at university many years ago. The opening chords of 'Autumn' were playing as she walked into the kitchen to make some cocoa.

James hadn't seen the inside of her flat yet. She would have to invite him soon if he was going to keep on taking her to dinner – not that he paid, Susan always insisted on going Dutch – but something held her back. Perhaps it was the same thing that had held her back so far from stopping in at his place for a nightcap. Damn it all, the man had been her teacher at school, and that was a difficult image to throw out. Still, at least she would make sure she had a few more books and records when she did invite him. She wouldn't want him to think she lived in such a cultural vacuum.

She poured out her cup of cocoa and sat down to listen to the music, curling her feet under her in the small armchair. If she was honest with herself, she decided, her resistance to James had little to do with the fact that he had been her teacher, and was only partly related to his involvement in the case. As far as Susan was concerned, Veronica Shildon was guilty, and it was simply a matter of proving it, of finding evidence that she had returned earlier than she said and murdered her lover – such a distasteful word, Susan thought, when applied to a relationship like theirs – out of jealousy, self-disgust or some other powerful, negative emotion. Either that or the estranged husband had done it because Caroline had corrupted and stolen his wife. So, although James and the theatre crowd were officially suspects, Susan couldn't believe that any of them were really guilty. No, it was something else that kept her at arm's length from James.

She had for some reason stayed away from sexual relationships over the past few years. And, again if she was honest, it wasn't only because of her career. That was important to her, yes, but many women could manage both a lover and a career. Some of her colleagues, and, stranger still, a couple of the more charming villains she had nicked, had asked her out, but she had always said no. Somehow they had all been too close to home. She didn't want to be talked about around the station. She had dated occasionally, but had never been able to commit herself to anything. She supposed that, as far as the men were concerned, there always seemed to be a million things she would rather be doing than being with them, and they were right. Because of that, she had spent too many evenings alone in her soulless flat. But also, because of that, she had passed all her examinations and her career was flourishing.

She certainly found James attractive, as well as charming and lively company. He was a great ham, had a fine sense of the dramatic. But there was more to him than that, an intensity and a kind of masculine self-assurance. He would probably make a fine lover. So why was she avoiding the inevitable? Her excuse was the case, but her real reason was fear. Fear of what? she asked herself. He hadn't even tried to touch her yet, though she was sure she had seen the desire in his eyes. Was she afraid of enjoying herself? Of losing control? Of feeling nothing? She didn't know, but if she was to change her life in any way at all, she would have to find out. And that meant confronting it. So, when the case was over . . .

A skin had formed on the top of her cocoa. She had never liked that, ever since childhood. That sweet and sticky skin made her shudder when, inadvertently, she had sipped without looking and it had stuck like a warm spider's web to her lips. Carefully, using her spoon, she pushed it to the edge of the cup, dredged it out and laid it in the saucer.

For some reason, that photo of Marcia Cunningham's handsome husband with his pipe at a rakish angle came into her mind. He reminded her of James just a little. Not his looks, but his expression. She found herself looking at the mantelpiece. Now that the Father Christmas was gone, it seemed so empty. She would like to have a photo or two there, but of whom? Not her family, that was for certain. James? Much too early for that yet. Herself, the graduation picture from police college? It would do, for a start.

Then she remembered the dress Marcia had dragged her all that way to look at. There was a puzzle, to be sure. No doubt the vandals would have an explanation, when and if they were caught. Still, it was a strange thing for someone to do. Maybe they had taken strips of material to fasten around their foreheads as Rambo headbands or something. There was no telling what weird fantasies went on in the adolescent mind these days.

Susan put her cup down. The record had finished, and even though it wasn't late she decided to go to bed and have an early night. There was still that American tome on homicide investigation for bedtime reading. Or should she do a little advance reading of Shakespeare from the cut-price *Complete Works* she had picked up at W. H. Smith's?

In a couple of days it would be twelfth night, the first night of the play. She just hoped that no police business came up to stop her from attending. James seemed so much to want her there, even though her knowledge of Shakespeare left a lot to be desired. And she was looking forward to the evening. She couldn't see how any of the present cases would get in her way. There wasn't much else they could do on the Caroline Hartley murder until they got new evidence, or until Banks took his head out of the sand and gave Veronica Shildon a long, hard, objective interrogation. Besides, Susan was only a helper, a note-taker on that one. And as for the vandals, until they were caught red-handed there wasn't much to be done about them, either. Picking up the heavy *Complete Works* from her bookshelf, she wandered off to bed.

FIVE

'A message for you, sir,' Sergeant Rowe called out as Banks walked into the police station after his visit to Veronica Shildon. He handed over a piece of paper. 'It was a woman called Patty Jarouchki, I think. Sounded American. Anyway, she left her number. Said for you to call her as soon as you can.'

Banks thanked him and hurried upstairs to his office, grabbing a black coffee on the way. The CID offices were quiet, the tapping of a keyboard from Richmond's office the only sign of life. He picked up the phone and dialled the number Sergeant Rowe had given him. Patsy Janowski answered on the third ring.

'You had a message for me?' Banks said.

'Yes. Remember you asked me to try and recall if I'd noticed anything unusual in the area?'

'Yes.'

'Well, it's not really . . . I mean, it's not clear at all, but you know I said there was a woman?'

'The one crossing King Street?'

'Yes.'

'What about her?'

'I didn't get a good look or anything – I'm sure it wasn't anyone I knew – but I do remember she was walking funny.'

'In what way?'

'Just . . . funny.'

'Did she have a limp, a wooden leg?'

'No, no, it was nothing like that. At least I don't think so.'

'A strange kind of walk? Some people have them. Bow-legged? Knock-kneed?'

'Not even that. She was just struggling a bit. There was snow on the ground. Oh, I knew I shouldn't have called you. It's still not clear, and it's probably nothing. I feel stupid.'

Banks could imagine her eyes ranging about the room, resting on the tongs by the fire, the old snuff-box on the mantelpiece. 'You did right,' he assured her.

'But I've told you nothing, really.'

'It might mean something. If you think of anything else, will you stop accusing yourself of idiocy and call me?'

He could almost hear her smile at the other end of the line. 'All right,' she said. 'But I don't think it'll get any clearer.'

Banks said goodnight and broke the connection. For a moment he just sat on the edge of his desk, coffee in hand, staring at the calendar. It showed a wintry scene in Aysgarth, Wensleydale. Finally, he lit a cigarette and went over to the window. Outside, beyond the venetian blinds, the market square was deserted. The Christmas-tree lights still twinkled, but nobody passed to see them. It was that time of year when everyone had spent too much and drunk too much and seen too many people; now most

Eastvalers were holed up in their houses keeping warm and watching repeats on television.

The day's depression was still with him, and the mystery of Caroline Hartley's death was still shrouded in fog. There had to be some way of making sense of it all, Banks told himself. He must have overlooked something. The only solution to his bleak mood was mental activity. As he stood at the window looking down on the forlorn Christmas lights, he tried to recreate the sequence of events in his mind.

First of all, he discounted the arrival of yet another visitor after the mysterious woman at seven twenty. He also accepted that by the time Patsy Janowski had called and talked to Caroline Hartley briefly at her door, Claude Ivers was busy doing his last-minute shopping in the centre and getting ready to head back to Redburn, and Veronica Shildon was shopping too.

A woman, perhaps the same one Patsy said walked strangely, knocked at Caroline's door and was admitted to the house. What had happened inside? Had the woman been an ex-lover or a jilted suitor? Had she called to remonstrate and ended up losing her temper and killing Caroline? Presumably there could have been sex involved. After all, Caroline had been naked, and the kind of sex she was interested in wouldn't oblige by leaving semen traces for the forensic boys to track down.

There was just no way of knowing. Caroline's life had been full of mysteries, a breeding ground for motives. As a working hypothesis, Banks accepted that the crime was spur of the moment rather than a planned murder. The use of the handy knife and the lack of precaution about being seen, or caught by Veronica, who had been likely to arrive home at any moment, seemed to point that way. And unless Caroline had been involved in some unknown criminal activity, the odds were that passion of one kind or another lay at the root of her death.

After the murder came the clearing up. The killer had washed the knife, removed any possible fingerprints she might have left, and either put the Vivaldi record on the turntable or lifted up the arm. Given the savage nature of the wounds, the killer must also have got blood on her own clothing. If she had removed her coat before the deed, she could easily have covered her blood-spattered clothing with it and destroyed all evidence as soon as she got home.

Banks went to refill his coffee mug and returned to his office.

Something in Patsy Janowski's sketchy description of the woman bothered him, but he couldn't think what it was. He walked to the filing cabinet and dug out the reports on interviews with Caroline Hartley's neighbours. Nothing much there helped, either. The details were vague, as the evening had been dark and snowy. Again, he read through the descriptions of the mystery woman: Mr Farlow had said she was wearing a mid-length, light trenchcoat with the belt fastened. He had seen her legs beneath it, and perhaps the bottom of a dress. She had been wearing a headscarf, so he had been able to say nothing about her hair. Mrs Eldridge had little to add, but what she remembered agreed with Farlow's account.

Despite the coffee, Banks was getting tired. It really was time to go home. There was nothing to be gained by pacing the office. He slipped on his camel-hair overcoat and put the Walkman in his pocket. After he'd walked down the stairs and said goodnight to Sergeant Rowe at the front desk, he hesitated outside the station under the blue lamp and looked at the Queen's Arms. A rosy glow shone warmly from its smoky windows. But no, he decided, best go home and spend some time with Sandra. It was a clear, quiet night. He would leave the car in the station car park and walk the mile or so home.

He put the headphones on, pressed the button and the opening of Poulenc's 'Gloria' came on. As he walked on the crisp snow down Market Street, he looked at the patterns frost had made on the shop windows and wished that the odd bits and pieces of knowledge he had about the Hartley case could make similar symmetrical shapes. They didn't. He began to walk faster. Christ, his feet were cold. He should have worn sheepskin-lined boots, or at least galoshes. But he had never really thought about walking home until the impulse struck him. Then something leaped into his mind as he turned into his cul-de-sac and saw the welcome lights of home ahead, something that made him forget his cold feet for the last hundred yards.

Patsy Janowksi had said the woman walked strangely. She couldn't explain it any better than that. But Mr Farlowe said he was sure the visitor was a woman because he had seen her legs below her long coat. If that was the case, then her legs were bare; she either wasn't wearing boots at all, or she was wearing very short ones. It had been snowing quite heavily that evening since about five o'clock, and the snow had been forecast as early as the previous evening, so even a woman going to work that morning would have known to take her boots. Even before the snow, the weather had been grey and cold. Most of December had been lined-boots and overcoat weather.

Now why would a woman be trudging around in the snow without boots at seven twenty that night? Banks wondered. She could have been in a hurry and simply slipped on the first pair of shoes that caught her eye. She could have come from somewhere she hadn't needed boots. But that didn't make sense. In such weather, most people wear boots to work, then change into more comfortable shoes when they get there. When it's time to leave, they slip back into their boots for the journey home.

The woman might have arrived by car and parked close by. The nearest space, where Patsy said she and Ivers parked, was a fair distance to walk in the snow without boots. The woman might have driven to Caroline's, found she couldn't park any closer and ended up having to walk farther than she'd bargained for. Which meant it could have been someone who didn't know the area well.

Given what Patsy had said about the walk, it sounded as if the woman had probably been wearing pumps or high heels – most likely the latter. That would explain her odd walk; trying to make one's way through four or five inches of snow in high heels would be difficult indeed. And wet.

Was it, then, someone who had nipped out of a local function, committed the murder and dashed back before she was missed? There had probably been a lot of parties going on that night, Hatchley's wedding reception among them. It couldn't have been anyone from there, of course, as Banks knew most of the guests. But it was an interesting avenue to explore. If he could find someone who had been at such a function that night, someone who had a connection with Caroline Hartley, then maybe he'd get somewhere. Feeling a little more positive about things, he turned off the tape and went into the house.

13

ONE

Teresa Pedmore rented a two-bedroom house on Nelson Grove, in a pleasant enough area of town south of the castle, close to the river. The houses were old but in good repair, and their inhabitants, though only renting, took pride in adding individual touches to the outside trim. A low blue gate led to Teresa's house, where her matching door was edged in white. Lace curtains hung in the windows.

Teresa professed to be surprised to see Banks, though he was never sure what to believe when dealing with actors. Faith could have told Teresa about the visit Banks had paid her earlier, though he thought it unlikely. That would have meant confessing what she had said about Teresa.

The front door led straight into the living room. Cream and red striped wallpaper covered the walls, where a number of framed prints hung. Banks, who had learned what little he knew about art from Sandra, recognized a Constable landscape, a Stubbs horse and a Lowry. Perhaps the most striking thing about the room, though, was that it was furnished with antiques: a Welsh dresser, a Queen Anne writing desk, Regency table and chairs. The only contemporary items were the tan three-piece suite arranged in a semicircle around the hearth and a small television set. Remembering the importance of the music, Banks looked around for evidence of a stereo but could find none.

Teresa gestured towards one of the armchairs and Banks sat down. He was surprised by her taste and impressed with her farm-girl looks, the blushes of red in her creamy cheeks. Her wavy chestnut hair framed a rather chubby, heart-shaped face with a wide, full mouth, an oddly delicate nose that didn't quite seem to belong and thick brows over large almond eyes. She certainly wasn't good-looking in the overtly sexual way Faith Green was, but the fierce confidence and determination in her simplest movements and gestures more than compensated. She was as tall and well-shaped as Faith, and wore a white silky blouse and knee-length navy skirt.

She picked up an engraved silver box from the low table and offered him a cigarette, lighting it with an old lighter as big as a paperweight. It was years since Banks had been offered a cigarette from a box, and he would certainly never have expected it in a small rented terrace house in Eastvale.

The cigarette was too strong, but he persevered. His lungs soon remembered the old days of Capstan Full Strength and rallied to the task. Almost before he had a chance to say yes or no, Teresa was pouring amber liquid from a cut-glass decanter into a crystal snifter. As she handed Banks the glass, the edges of her wide mouth twitched up in a smile.

'I suppose you're wondering where I get my money from,' she said. 'Policemen are always suspicious about people living above their means, aren't they?' She sat down and crossed her long legs.

Banks swirled the glass in his hand and breathed in the

fumes: cognac. '*Are* you living above your means?' he asked.

She laughed, a low, murmuring sound. 'How clever of you. Not at all. It only looks that way. The furniture isn't original, of course. I just like the designs, the look and feel of it. And one day, believe me, I'll have real antiques. I think the only valuable objects in the room are the decanter and the cigarette box, and they belonged to my grandfather. Family heirlooms. The Lowry is a genuine, too, a present from a distant, wealthy relative. As for the rest, cognac and what have you . . . What can I say? I like to live well. I don't drink a lot, but I drink the best. I make decent money, I don't run a car, I have no children and my rent is reasonable.'

Banks, who wondered why she was telling him all this, nodded as if he were suitably impressed. Perhaps she was trying to paint a picture of herself as someone who had far too much class and refined sensibility to commit so taste-less an act as murder. He sipped the cognac. Courvoisier VSOP, he guessed. Maybe she was right.

'I suppose you think I should have stayed on the farm,' she went on. 'Married a local farmer and started having babies.' She made a dismissive gesture with her cigarette.

For Christ's sake, Banks thought, do I look so old that people immediately assume I'm a fuddy-duddy? Still, Teresa couldn't have been more than twenty-two or twenty-three; there were sixteen or seventeen years between them, which made it technically possible for him to be her father. He just didn't feel that old, and he could certainly understand young people wanting to escape what they felt to be claustrophobic social backgrounds.

'What do you want to do?' he asked.

'Act, of course.'

She reminded Banks of Sally Lumb, another, albeit younger, Dales hopeful he had met during the Steadman case eighteen months ago. The memory made him feel sad. Such dreams often turn to pain. But what are we if we don't dream? Banks asked himself. And at least try to make them come true.

'James is trying to fix things so I get a part in *Weymouth Sands*. He's doing the script for the BBC, you know. He knows all the casting people. It's terribly exciting.' The Dales accent was still there, despite the evidence of elocution lessons, and it made the upper-class phrase 'terribly exciting' sound very funny indeed. 'More cognac?'

Banks noticed his snifter was empty. He shook his head. 'No, no thanks. It's very good, but I'd better not.'

Teresa shrugged. She didn't press him. Fine cognac is, after all, very expensive.

'You're still on good terms with James Conran, then?' Banks asked.

Her eyebrows rose. 'Why shouldn't I be?'

'I heard rumours you'd had a falling out.'

'Who told you that?'

'Are they true?'

'It's that common little tramp, Faith, isn't it?'

'Was James Conran paying too much attention to Caroline Hartley?'

The name stopped Teresa in her tracks. She reached for another cigarette from the box but didn't offer Banks one this time. 'It's easy to exaggerate things,' she continued quietly. 'Everyone argues now and then. I'll bet even you argue with your wife, don't you? But it doesn't mean anything.'

'Did you argue with James Conran over Caroline?'

Her eyes flashed briefly, then she drew on her cigarette,

tilted her head back and blew out a long stream of smoke through narrow nostrils. 'What has Faith been saying about me?' she asked. 'I've got a right to know.'

'Look,' Banks said, 'I haven't told you who passed on the information. Nor am I going to. It's not important. What counts is that you answer my questions. And if you won't do it here, you can come down to the police station and answer them.'

'You can't make me do that.' Teresa leaned forward and flicked off a column of ash. 'Surely?'

'What did you do after the rehearsal on December the twenty-second?'

'What? I . . . I came home.'

'Straight home?'

'No. I did some Christmas shopping first. Look—'

'What time did you get home?'

'What is this? Are you trying to imply I might have had something to do with Caroline Hartley's death?'

'I'm not implying anything, I'm asking questions.' Banks pulled out one of his own Silk Cuts and lit up. 'What time did you get home?'

'I don't know. How can I remember? It was ages ago.'

'Did you go out again?'

'No. I stayed at home and worked on my role.'

'You didn't have a date with Mr Conran?'

'No. We . . . I . . .'

'Were you still seeing him at that time?'

'Of course I was.'

'As a lover?'

'That's none of your damn business.' She mashed her cigarette out and clasped her hands in her lap.

'When did you and Mr Conran stop being lovers?'

'I'm not answering that.'

'But you did stop.'

There was a pause, then she hissed, 'Yes.'

'Before Caroline Hartley's murder?'

'Yes.'

'And did Caroline have anything to do with this parting?'

'No. It was completely amicable on both sides. Things just didn't work out that way. We'd never been very deeply involved, anyway, if you know what I mean.'

'A casual affair?'

'You could call it that, though neither of us is married.'

'And Caroline Hartley came between you?'

Teresa scratched her palm and looked down.

'Am I right?' Banks persisted.

'Look,' Teresa answered, 'what if I say you are? It doesn't mean anything, does it? It doesn't mean I'd kill her. I'm not a fanatically jealous woman, but every woman has her pride. Anyway, it wasn't Caroline I blamed.'

'Was Conran having an affair with Caroline?'

She shook her head. 'I don't think so. We didn't know she was gay, but even so there was something about her, something different. Elusive. She could keep the men at bay while seeming to draw them to her. It's difficult to explain. No, I don't think he even saw her outside rehearsals and the pub.'

That seemed to square with what Veronica Shildon had said.

'But he was attracted to her?'

'A bit smitten, you might say,' said Teresa. 'That was what annoyed me, him chatting her up in public like that when everyone could see, the way he looked at her. That kind of thing. But then James is like that. He goes after anything in a skirt.'

'Am I to take it you don't care for him any longer?'

'Not as a man, no. As a professional, I respect him a great deal.'

'That's a very neat distinction.'

'Surely you sometimes have to work with people you respect but don't like?'

'Did you argue over his attentions to Caroline?'

'I told him to stop drooling over her in public. I found it embarrassing. But that was only a part of it. What I said before was true. It wasn't much of a relationship to begin with. It had run its course.'

'Do you think you'll get this part in *Weymouth Sands*?'

'James still appreciates me as an actress,' she said, 'which is more than he does that gossipy bitch who told you all about my personal life.'

'Who's that?'

'Faith bloody Green, obviously. There's no need to be coy. You know damn well it was her who told you. And I can guess why.'

'Why?'

'Why do you think? Because she couldn't get him herself.'

'Did she try?'

Teresa gave Banks a disdainful look. 'You've met Faith, Chief Inspector. What do you think the answer is?'

'But Conran wasn't interested?'

'It appears not.'

'Any reason?'

'Not that I know of. Not his type, perhaps. Too much woman, too aggressive . . . I don't know. I'm just guessing.'

'What did he think of her? Did they have any arguments?'

'If she's been trying to imply I had a good reason for killing Caroline Hartley, it's probably because she had an even better one.'

Banks sat up. 'Why? Over her interest in Conran?'

Teresa sniffed. 'No. It wasn't that. I think she soon realized that her tastes run to rougher trade than James. It was just that she had to try, like she does with every man. No, it was something else that happened.'

'Tell me.'

Teresa leaned forward and lowered her voice dramatically. 'It was after rehearsal that night, the night Caroline was killed.'

'What happened?'

'Most people left early because it was close to Christmas, but James wanted to spend half an hour or so with Faith and myself, just getting the blocking right. Our parts are large and very important, you see. Anyway, James wanted Faith to stay behind, so I left first. But I forgot my scarf, and it was cold outside, so I came back. I don't think they heard me. I was in the props room, you know, where we leave our coats and bags, and I heard voices out in the auditorium. I'm not a naturally nosy person, but I wondered what was going on. Anyway, to cut a long story short, I walked a little closer and listened. And guess what?'

'What?'

Teresa smiled. 'They were arguing. I bet she didn't tell you about *that*, did she?'

'What were they arguing about?'

'Caroline Hartley. As far as I could gather, James was telling Faith that if she didn't do a better job of learning her lines, he'd give her part to Caroline.'

'What was Faith's reaction?'

'She walked out in a huff. I had to be quick to hide behind a door without being seen.'

'Can you remember their exact words?'

'I can remember what Faith said to James before she left. She said, "You'd do anything to get into that little slut's pants, wouldn't you?" I wish I'd been there to see his face. Of course, he can't have meant it about giving her part away. James would know quite well there wasn't enough time for Caroline to take over Faith's role. He was just trying to get her to try a bit harder.'

'What happened after that?'

'I don't know. As soon as Faith had left, I got out of there pretty quickly. I didn't want to be caught snooping.'

'Where was Conran?'

'Still in the auditorium, as far as I know.'

'Could he have left by the front door?'

Teresa shook her head. 'No, we always use the back during rehearsals. The front's kept locked after the gallery closes, unless there's some sort of an event on.'

'Who has the key to the back door?'

'Only Marcia and James from the dramatic society, as far as I know. Usually one or the other would be last to leave. James, more often than not, as Marcia was always first to arrive, and she tended to disappear to the pub early if she knew she wasn't needed.'

'What time did this argument occur?'

'Six. Maybe a little after.'

'What were you wearing?'

Teresa frowned and sat back in her chair. 'What do you mean?'

'What clothes were you wearing?'

'Me? Jeans, a leather coat, my wool scarf. Same as usual for rehearsals.'

'What about footwear?'

'I had my boots on. It *is* winter, after all. I don't see what—'

'And Faith?'

'I can't remember. I doubt I paid much attention.'

'What did she usually wear? Jeans? Skirt and blouse? Dress?'

'She usually wore a skirt and blouse. She is a teacher, believe it or not. She came straight from school. But I don't know for sure what she was wearing that day.'

'What about her overcoat?'

'What she always wore, I suppose.'

'Which is?'

'A long coat, like a light raincoat with epaulettes, but lined.'

'Belted?'

'Yes.'

'And her footwear?'

'How should I know?'

'Was she wearing boots or shoes?'

'Boots, I should think. Because of the weather.'

'But you can't be sure?'

'No. I can't say I pay Faith's feet much attention.'

'Why didn't you tell me all this earlier?' Banks asked.

Teresa sighed and shifted in her chair. 'I don't know. It didn't seem all that important. And I didn't want any trouble, anything spoiling the play. It was bad enough with Caroline getting murdered. When I heard about her being gay, I was sure her death must have had something to do with her private life, that it didn't involve any of us. I know I sound hard, but this play is important to me, believe it or not. If I do well, the TV people will hear about me . . .'

Banks stood up. 'I see.'

'And as for Faith,' Teresa went on. 'I know I sounded bitchy right now, but it was only because I was annoyed at what she'd said to you. She'd no right to go talking about my personal life. But she's not a killer. Not Faith. And certainly not over a petty incident like that.'

Banks buttoned his overcoat and headed for the door. 'Thanks very much,' he said. 'You've been a great help.' And he left her reaching for another cigarette from the engraved silver box.

Damn them all! he cursed as he walked out into the cold night. Of course Faith could have killed Caroline. Perhaps not over a petty matter, such as the argument Teresa had described, but there could have been another reason. A woman like Caroline Hartley, whether intentionally or not, causes violent emotion in all who come into contact with her. Even Veronica Shildon had admitted to Banks that she'd never understood lust until she met Caroline.

Faith could have simmered for a while after the row – it would certainly have been a blow to her pride – and then, if she had something else against Caroline, too, she could have gone to visit her and remonstrate. Faith certainly worked hard at her Mae West role, but what if it was just an act? What if her true inclination lay elsewhere, or she leaned both ways?

It didn't seem likely that James Conran would kill the goose he hoped would lay a golden egg. He had high hopes for Caroline as an actress and he was sexually attracted to her as a woman. He didn't know she was gay. Given his masculine pride and confidence, he probably assumed that she would come around eventually; it was just a matter of time and persistence. Still, there might have been something else in the relationship that Banks didn't know about.

Caroline had seemed to bring out the worst in both Faith and Teresa. How could he be sure either of them was telling him the truth? Instead of feeling that he had cleverly played one off against the other, he was beginning to feel that he might be the one who had been played. Cursing actors, he pulled up in front of his house feeling nothing but frustration.

TWO

The bell was ringing in the distance. All around lay dark jungle: snakes slithered along branches, phosphorescent insects hummed in the air and squat, furry creatures lurked in the lush foliage. But the bell was ringing in the dark and she had to find her way through the jungle to discover why. There were probably booby traps, too – holes lightly covered with grass matting that would give way under her weight to a thirty-foot drop onto sharpened bamboo shoots. And . . .

She was at least half awake now. The jungle had gone, a figment of the night. The ringing was coming from her telephone, in the living room. Hardly a dangerous journey, after all, though one she was loath to make, being so comfortably snuggled up under the warm blankets.

She looked at the bedside clock. Two twenty-three in the morning. Bloody hell. And she hadn't got to bed until midnight. Slowly, without turning on the light, she made her way through to the living-room by touch. She fumbled the receiver and put it to her ear.

'Susan?'

'Mmm.'

'Sergeant Rowe here. Sorry to disturb you, lass, but it's important. At least it might be.'

'What's happened?'

'We've caught the vandals.'

'How? No, wait. I'm coming in. Give me fifteen minutes.'

'Right you are, lass. They'll still be here.'

Susan replaced the receiver and shook her head to clear the cobwebs. Luckily, she hadn't drunk too much at dinner. She put on the living-room light, squinting in the brightness, then went into the bathroom and splashed cold water on her face. There was no time for make-up and grooming, just a quick wash, a brush through the hair and out into the cold quiet night. With luck, there would be fresh coffee at the station.

Holding her coat around her she shivered as she got into the car. It started on the third try. Driving slowly because of the ice, she took nearly ten minutes to get to the car park behind the station. She nipped in through the back door and walked to the front desk.

'They're upstairs,' Sergeant Rowe said.

'Any background information?'

'Aye. Tolliver and Wilson caught them trying to jemmy their way into the Darby and Joan Club on Heughton Drive. Our lads had enough sense to let them jemmy open the lock and step over the threshold before pouncing. A slight altercation ensue—' Sergeant Rowe stopped and smiled at his use of jargon – 'in which said officers managed to apprehend the suspects. In other words, they put up a bit of a fight but came off worst.'

'Do we know who they are?'

'Rob Chalmers and Billy Morley. Both spent time in remand homes.'

'How old are they?'

'We're in luck. One's eighteen, the other seventeen.'

Susan smiled. 'Not a case for the juvenile court, then. Have they been cautioned?'

'Charged and cautioned. We've jot the jemmy and the gloves they were wearing bagged and ready for testing.'

'And?'

'They're not saying owt. Been watching American cop shows like the rest. Refuse to talk till they've seen their lawyer. Lawyers! I ask you.'

'And I assume said lawyers are on their way?'

Rowe scratched his bulbous nose. 'Bit of trouble tracking them down. I think we might manage it by morning.'

'Good. Where are they?'

'Interview rooms upstairs. Tolliver's with one, Wilson's with the other.'

'Right.'

Susan poured herself a mug of coffee and went upstairs, still feeling the same thrill as she had on her first day in CID. She took a few sips of the strong black liquid, hung her coat up in the office, then took a quick glance in her compact mirror and applied a little make-up. At least now she didn't look as if she had got straight out of bed. Satisfied, she smoothed her skirt, ran her hand through her curls, took a deep breath and walked into the first interview room.

PC Tolliver stood by the door, a bruise by the side of his left eye and a crust of blood under his right nostril. Sitting, or rather slouching, behind the table, legs stretched out, arms behind his head, was a youth with dark, oily, slicked-back hair, as if he had used half a jar of Brylcreem. He was wearing a green parka, open over a torn T-shirt, and faded, grubby jeans. Susan could smell beer on his breath even at the door. When he saw her walk in, he didn't move. She ignored him and looked over at Tolliver.

'All right, Mike?'

'I'll mend.'

'Who've we got?'

'Robert S. Chalmers, age eighteen. Unemployed. Previous form for assault, damage to property, theft – all as a juvenile. A real charmer.' Susan winced in acknowledgement of his joke. Bad puns were a thing with PC Tolliver.

Susan sat down. Tolliver went to the chair by the small window in the corner and took out his notebook.

'Hello, Robert,' she said, forcing a smile.

'Fuck off.'

The animosity that came from him was almost overwhelming. Susan tensed up inside, determined not to react. On the outside she remained calm and cool. He had acted in this hostile way partly because she was a woman, she was sure. A thug like Chalmers would take it as an insult that they sent a small woman rather than a burly man to interrogate him. He would also expect to be able to deal with her easily. To him, women were probably creatures to be used and discarded. There wouldn't be any shortage of them in his life. He was good-looking in a surly, James Dean, early Elvis Presley way, his upper lip permanently curved in a sneer.

'I hear you've been attempting to gain unlawful entry to the Darby and Joan Club,' she said. 'What's the problem, can't you wait till you're sixty-five?'

'Very funny.'

'It's not funny, Robert. It's aggravated burglary. Do you know how much time you can get for that?'

Chalmers glared at her. 'I'm not saying anything till my lawyer gets here.'

'It might help you if you did. Co-operation. We'd mention that in court.'

'I told you, I ain't saying nothing. I know you bastards. You'd fit me up with a verbal.' He moved in his chair and Susan saw him wince slightly with pain.

'What's wrong, Robert?'

'Bastard over there beat me up.' He grinned. 'Don't worry, love, he only bruised a rib or two – he didn't damage my tackle.'

Susan bit her tongue. 'Be sensible, Robert, like your friend William.'

Susan saw a flicker of apprehension in the boy's eyes, but they quickly regained their hard-bitten look and he laughed. 'I'm not stupid, you know, love,' he said. 'Pull the other one.'

Susan stared at him, long and hard, and made her assessment. Was it worth pushing at him? She decided not. He'd been through this kind of thing too many times before to fall for the usual tricks or to scare easily. Maybe his accomplice would be softer.

She stood up. 'Right, I'll just go and have another word with your mate, then. He'll be able to fill in all the details. That should give us enough.'

Though hardly anything perceptible changed in Chalmers's expression, Susan somehow knew that what she had said worried him. Not that the other had talked; he wouldn't fall for that. But that Billy Morley was less tough, more nervous, more likely to crack. Chalmers just shrugged and resumed his slouch, gritting his teeth for a second as he shifted. He put his hands in his pockets and pretended to whistle at the ceiling.

Susan went to the next room, stopping to lean against the wall on the way to take a few deep breaths. No matter how often she came across them, people like Chalmers frightened her. They frightened her more than the people who committed crimes out of passion or greed. She could hear her father's voice going on about the younger generation. In his day, the story went, people were frightened of coppers, they respected the law. Now, though, they didn't give a damn; they'd as soon thump a policeman and run. She had to admit there was a lot of truth in what he said. There had always been gangs, youngsters had always been full of mischief and sometimes gone too far, but they certainly used to run when the police arrived. Now they didn't seem to care. Why had it happened? Was television to blame? Partly, perhaps. But it was more than that. Maybe they had become cynical about those in authority after reading about too many corrupt politicians, perverted judges and bent coppers. Everyone was on the fiddle; nothing really mattered any more. But it wasn't Susan's job to analyse society, just to get the truth out of the bastards. Taking a final deep breath, she walked into the next office to confront Billy Morley.

This lad, guarded by PC Wilson, who sported a small cut over his left eye, seemed a little more nervous than his friend. Skinny to the point of emaciation, he had a spotty, weasly face and dark, beady eyes that darted all over the place. He was sitting straight up in his chair rubbing his upper arm and licking his thin lips.

'You the lawyer?' he said hopefully. 'This bastard here nearly broke my arm. Hit me with his stick.'

'You were resisting arrest,' PC Wilson said.

'I wasn't doing nothing of the kind. I was minding my own business.'

'Aye,' said Wilson. 'You and your jemmy.'

'It's not mine. It's—'

'Well?' asked Wilson.

He folded his arms. 'I'm not saying anything.'

By this time Susan had sat down and arranged herself as comfortably as she could in the stiff, bolted-down chair. First she gave PC Wilson the signal to fade into the background and take notes, then she took a good look at Morley. He didn't frighten her nearly as much as Chalmers. Basically, she thought, he was weak – especially alone. He was also the younger of the two. Chalmers, she suspected, was a true hard case, but Morley was just a follower and probably a coward at heart. Chalmers had known that, and the knowledge had flitted across his face for a moment. Being a woman would put Susan at an advantage with someone like Morley, who probably jumped each time his mother yelled.

'I'm not your solicitor, William,' Susan said. 'I'm a detective constable. I've come to ask you a few questions. It's a serious charge you're facing. Do you understand that?'

'What do you mean?'

'Aggravated burglary. Under section ten of the Theft Act, you could do life. Add to that resisting arrest, assaulting a police officer, and I'm pretty sure any judge would come down hard on you.'

'Bollocks! That's crap! You can't get life.' He shook his head. 'Not just for . . . I don't believe you.'

'It's true, William. You're not a juvenile now, you're an adult. No more fun and games.'

'But—'

'But nothing. I'm telling you, William, it doesn't look good. Do you know what *aggravated* burglary means?'

Morley shook his head.

Susan clasped her hands on the table in front of her. 'It means committing a burglary while carrying an offensive weapon.'

'What offensive weapon?'

'The jemmy.'

Susan was interpreting the law with a certain amount of licence. 'Aggravated burglary' usually involved firearms or explosives.

She shook her head. 'The best we could do for you is drop the charge to going equipped for stealing. That's thirteen years. Then there's malicious damage to property . . . Whichever way it cuts, William, you're in a lot of trouble. You can only help yourself by talking to me.'

Morley pinched his long, sharp nose and sniffed. 'I want my lawyer.'

'What were you after?' Susan asked. 'Did someone tell you there was money there?'

'We weren't after no money. We – I'm not saying anything till my law—'

'Your solicitor may be some time, William. Solicitors like a good night's sleep. They don't enjoy getting up at two thirty in the morning just to help a pathetic little creep like you. It'll be better if you co-operate.'

Morley gaped at her, as if her insulting words, delivered in such a matter of fact, even tone, had pricked him like darts. 'I told you,' he stammered. 'I want—'

Susan rested her hands on the table, palms down, and spoke softly. 'William, be sensible for once in your life. Look at the facts. We already know the two of you broke into the Darby and Joan Club. You used a jemmy. It'll have your fingerprints on it. You must have handled it at some time. It's being tested right now. And there'll be fibres we

can match with the gloves you were wearing, too. We
also have two very reliable witnesses. PC Wilson here and
his colleague caught you red-handed. There's no getting
around that, solicitor or no solicitor. We've followed correct procedure so far. You've been warned and charged.
Right now we're reviewing your options, so to speak.'

'He hit me,' Morley whined. 'He's broke my arm. I need
a doctor.'

For a moment Susan thought that might be true. Morley
was pale and his sharp, narrow brow looked clammy.
Then she realized it was fear.

'Look at his eye, William,' she said. 'Nobody's going to
believe he attacked you for no reason.'

Morley fell silent for a while. Susan could almost hear
him thinking, trying to decide what to do.

'It'll go easier for you if you tell us what you were up
to,' she said gently. 'Perhaps you were only trespassing.'
That would never wash, she knew. Trespassing, in itself,
wasn't an offence except in certain special circumstances,
such as poaching and espionage, and breaking the lock of
a club with a jemmy was a long way from simple trespass.
Still, it wouldn't do Morley any harm to let him look on the
bright side.

He remained silent, chewing at the edge of his thumb.

'What's wrong, William? Are you frightened of Robert?
Is that what it is?' She was about to tell him Chalmers had
already talked, tried to put the blame on him, but realized
just in time that such a ploy could ruin any advantage she
had. He might suspect a trick then, no doubt having seen
such tactics used on television, and her carefully con-
structed house of cards would fall down.

'There's nothing to be afraid of. You'll be helping him
too.'

Ten seconds later, Morley took his thumb from his mouth and said, 'We weren't burgling anything. That wasn't it at all.'

'What were you doing there, then?' Susan asked.

'Just having fun.'

'What do you mean, fun?'

'You know, it was something to do. Smashing things and stuff. It wasn't no aggravated burglary, or whatever you call it. You can't charge us with that.'

'It looks like burglary to us, William. Are you trying to tell me you were going to vandalize the place?'

'We weren't going to take anything or hurt anyone. Nothing like that.'

'Were you going to cause damage?'

'Just a bit of fun.'

'Why?'

'What do you mean, why?'

'Why would you want to do such a thing?'

'I dunno.' Morley squirmed in his chair and grasped his arm again. 'Fucking hurts, that.'

'Will you please not use language like that in front of me, William,' Susan said. 'I find it offensive. Answer my question. Why did you do it?'

'No reason. Do you have to have a fucking reason for everything? I told you, it was just fun, that's all.'

'I've told you once,' Susan said, mustering as much quiet authority as she could. 'I don't like that kind of language. Learn some manners.'

Morley tried hard to glare at her, but he looked more ashamed and defeated than defiant.

'Was it the same kind of fun you had in those other places?' Susan asked.

'What other places?'

'Come on, William. You know what I mean. This isn't the first time, is it?'

Morley remained silent for a while, then said quietly, still rubbing his arm. 'I suppose not.'

'Suppose?'

'All right. No, it's not. But we never hurt anyone or anything.'

Susan could taste success. Her first real case. She was only assisting on the Hartley murder, but this one was all hers. If she could wrap up a four-month problem of vandalism with a neat confession, it would look very good on her record. As she listed the dates and places vandalized over the past few months – mostly youth clubs and recreation centres – Morley nodded glumly at each one, until she mentioned the community centre.

'Come again?' he said.

'Eastvale Community Centre, night of December the twenty-second.'

Morley shook his head. 'You can't do us for that one.'

'What are you saying?'

'I'm saying we didn't do it, that's what.'

'Come on, William. What's the point in denying it? It'll all be taken into account. You're doing yourself no good.'

He leaned forward. Spittle collected at the corners of his mouth. 'Because we didn't f— Because we didn't do it, that's why. I wasn't even in Eastvale that night. I spent Christmas with my mother down in Coventry. I can prove it. Call her. Go on.'

Susan took the number. 'What about Robert?'

'How should I know. But *I* didn't do it. He wouldn't do it by himself, would he? Stands to reason. Rob – now, wait a minute, wait a minute! He was out of town, too. He was down in Bristol with his brother over Christmas. We didn't do it, I'm telling you.'

Susan tapped her pen on the desk and sighed. True, it didn't make sense for the lad to lie at this point, when he had confessed to everything else. Damn! Just when she thought she had got it all wrapped up. That meant there must be two sets of vandals. One down, one to go. She stood up. 'Take his statement, will you, John? I'll go and make out a report for the chief inspector. We'll check the alibis for the community centre job tomorrow morning.' As she passed the room where Robert Chalmers was being held, she almost went in for another try. But there was nothing more to learn. Instead, she carried on down the corridor to her office.

THREE

'Of all the times to come pestering me! It's opening night tonight. Don't you know that? How did you even know I'd be here? Normally I'd be at school at this time.'

'I know,' Banks said. 'I phoned. They told me you'd taken the day off.'

'You did what?' Faith Green was really pacing now, arms folded under her breasts. She wore purple tights and a baggy, hip-length sweater with red and blue hoops around it. Her silver hair and matching hoop earrings flashed in the morning sunlight that shone through her large picture window.

'How dare you?' she went on. 'Do you realize what damage that could do my career? It doesn't matter that I'm guilty of nothing. Just a hint of police around that place and the smell sticks.'

'Why don't you sit down?' Banks perched at the edge of his armchair, faintly amused by Faith's performance. It certainly differed from his last visit. His amusement, however, was overshadowed by irritation.

She stopped and glared at him. 'Am I making you nervous? Good.'

Banks leaned back in the chair and crossed his legs. 'Remember last time I called, I asked if you'd noticed anything odd about the rehearsal on December the twenty-second?'

Faith resumed pacing again, stopped in front of the Greta Garbo poster, as if seeking inspiration, and said, with her back to Banks, 'So?'

'Were you telling me the truth?'

'I'm not in the habit of lying.'

'It'd be easier if you sat down,' Banks said.

'Oh, all right, damn you!' Faith flounced towards the sofa and flung herself on to it. 'There,' she said with a pout. 'Does that suit you?'

'Fine. I must say you're not quite as welcoming as you were last time.'

Faith looked at him for a moment, trying to gauge his meaning. 'That was different,' she said finally. 'I didn't see why we had to have such a boring time just because you were asking silly questions.'

'And this time?'

'I should be rehearsing, going through my lines. I'm tense enough as it is. You're upsetting me.'

'How?'

'Asking questions again.'

Banks sighed. 'All right. How about if I stop asking and start telling?' And he relayed what Teresa had told him about the argument between Faith and James Conran. The further he got, the paler Faith's face turned and the more angry her eyes became.

'Who told you this?' she demanded when he'd finished.

'That doesn't matter.'

'It does to me. It couldn't have been James, surely. The last thing *he'd* do is make himself look bad.' She paused, then slapped the arm of the sofa. 'Of course! How stupid of me. It was Teresa, wasn't it? She must have stayed behind and eavesdropped. I thought she'd been behaving oddly towards me lately. Did you tell her what I told you?'

'Look, it really doesn't—'

'The snooping bitch! She's no right, no right at all. And neither had—'

'Is it true?' Banks asked.

'It's none of her—'

'But is it true?'

'—business to listen to my private—'

'So it *is* true?'

Faith hesitated, looked over to Garbo again and sighed deeply. 'All right, so we had a row. I've got nothing to hide. It's nothing new. Happens all the time in the theatre.'

'It's the timing that interests me most,' Banks said. 'You could conceivably have been angry enough at Caroline Hartley to stew over it for a couple of drinks, then go pay her a visit. You didn't know she lived with anyone.'

Faith's jaw dropped. When she finally spoke, it was in a squeaky, uncontrolled voice, far different from her stage speech.

'Are you suggesting that I killed the damn woman over some stupid argument with the director of a small-town play?'

'You did call her a "little slut". I think that suggests a

bit more than a tiff over a part in an amateur production, don't you?'

'It's just a figure of speech, a . . .'

'Why did you call her a slut, Faith? Was it because Conran fancied her but he didn't fancy you? Is that why you told me about him and Teresa, too? Out of jealous spite?'

For the first time, Faith seemed speechless. But it didn't last long. Finally, red-faced, she stretched out her arm dramatically and pointed at the door.

'Out!' she yelled. 'Out, you wretched, insulting little man! Out!'

'Calm down, Faith,' Banks said. 'I need answers. Is that why?'

Faith let her arm fall slowly and sat in silence for a few moments contemplating the upholstery of the sofa. 'What if I did call her a slut?' she said finally. 'Heat of the moment, that's all. And I'll tell you something, the way I felt at the time, if I'd killed anybody it would have been our bloody philandering director. It's unprofessional, letting your prick rule your judgment like that. It happened with Teresa, it was happening with Caroline . . .'

'But it didn't happen with you?'

'Huh! Do you think I really cared about that? I've no trouble finding a man when I want one. A *real* man, too, not some artsy-fartsy wimp like James Conran.'

'But maybe he hurt your pride? Some people don't handle rejection well. Or perhaps it wasn't Conran that really bothered you. Was it Caroline herself?'

Faith stared at him, then spoke slowly. 'Look, you asked me about that the last time you were here. I told you I'm not a lesbian. I told you I could prove it to you. Do you want me to prove it now?'

She sat up, crossed her arms and reached for the bottom of her sweater.

Banks held his hand up. 'No,' he said, 'I'm not asking you to prove it. And quite honestly, it's not really the kind of thing you *can* prove, is it?'

Faith let her hands drop but remained sitting cross-legged on the sofa. 'You mean you think I'm bi?'

Banks shrugged.

'Well, you can't prove that either, can you?'

'We might be able to, if we talk to the right people.'

Faith laughed. 'My ex-lovers? Well, good luck to you, darling. You'll need it.'

'What did you do after the argument?' Banks asked.

'Came home, like I said.' She put her hand to her brow. 'Quite honestly, I was shagged out, dear.'

Faith seemed to have regained her composure since her outburst, or at least her poise. She pushed her fringe back from her eyes and managed a brief smile as she went on. 'Look, Chief Inspector, I know you have to catch your criminal and all that, but it's not me. And I've got a lot of work to do before curtain tonight. Besides, I need to be calm, relaxed. You're making me all flustered. I'll blow my lines. Be a darling and bugger off. You can come back some other time, if you want.'

Banks smiled. 'I shouldn't worry about being nervous. I've heard a bit of anxiety adds an edge to a performance.'

Faith narrowed her eyes at him for a moment, as if wondering whether she was being had. 'Well . . .' she went on, 'if that's all . . .?'

'Far from it. You argued with James Conran in the auditorium, am I right?'

'Yes.'

'What happened next?'

'I left, of course. I don't put up with that kind of treatment – not from anyone.'

'And you went straight home?'

'I did.'

'Was anyone else in the centre at the time?'

'Well, obviously Teresa bloody Pedmore was, but I didn't see her.'

'Anyone else?'

Faith shook her head.

'Are you sure?'

'I told you, I didn't see anyone. But then I didn't see them all leave, either. There are plenty of cubby-holes behind the stage, as you know quite well. The whole bloody cast could have been hiding there and listening, for all I know.'

'But as far as you know, the only person there was James Conran, and you left him in the auditorium.'

Faith nodded, a puzzled expression on her face. 'And Teresa, I suppose, if she saw me leave.'

'Yes,' Banks said. 'And Teresa. What were you wearing that evening?'

'To rehearsal?'

'Yes.'

Faith shrugged. 'Same as I usually wear, I suppose, when I come from school.'

'Which is?'

'They're very conservative, you know. Blouse, skirt and cardigan is required uniform.'

'How long was the skirt?'

She arched her eyebrows. 'Why, Chief Inspector, I didn't know you cared.' She stood up with exaggerated slowness and put the edge of her hand just below her knee. 'About that long,' she said, then she shifted her weight to her left leg, dropping her right hip in a half-comic, half-seductive pose. 'As I said, they're very conservative.'

'What about your overcoat?'

'What is this?'

'Can you tell me?'

'I can do better if it'll get you out of here quicker.' She walked to the hall cupboard and pulled out a long, heavily lined garbardine. 'It's not quite warm enough for this weather we've been having lately,' she said, 'but it'll do until someone buys me a mink.'

'What about footwear?'

She raised one eyebrow. 'You *are* getting intimate, aren't you? Whatever will it be next, I wonder?'

'Footwear?'

'Boots, of course. What do you think I'd be wearing in that weather? Bloody high heels?' She laughed. 'Tell me, have you a shoe fetish or something?'

Banks smiled and got to his feet. 'No. Sorry to disappoint you. Thank you very much for your time. I'll see myself out.'

But Faith followed him to the door and leaned against the frame, arms loosely folded. 'You know, Chief Inspector,' she said, 'I *am* very disappointed in you. I might be persuaded to change my mind, but it would take a lot of doing. I've never been so insulted and abused by a man as I've been by you. But the funny thing is, I still like you.' She took him by the elbow and steered him out the open door. 'And now you really must go.'

Banks headed down the corridor and turned when he heard Faith calling after him.

'Chief Inspector! Will you be there tonight? Will you be watching the play?'

'I'll be there,' Banks said. 'I wouldn't miss it for anything.' And he went on his way.

14

ONE

The community hall was surprisingly full for the first night of an amateur production, Banks thought. There they all sat, chattering and coughing nervously before the play started: a party of fourth-formers from Eastvale Comprehensive, present under sufferance; friends and relatives of the cast; a group of pensioners; members of the local literary institute. The old boiler groaned away in the cellar, but it didn't seem to be doing much good. There was a chill in the hall and most people kept their scarves on and their coats draped over their shoulders.

Banks sat beside Sandra. Their seats, compliments of James Conran, were front and centre, about ten rows back. Further ahead, Banks could make out Susan's blonde curls. The director himself sat beside her, occasionally leaning over to whisper in her ear. He could also see Marcia talking animatedly to a grey-haired man beside her.

It was almost seven thirty. Banks eyed the moth-eaten curtain for signs of movement. Much as he enjoyed Shakespeare, he hoped the performance would not last too long. He remembered an actor telling him once in London that he didn't like doing *Hamlet* because the pubs had always closed by the time it was over. Banks didn't think *Twelfth Night* was that long, but a bad performance could make it seem so.

Finally, the lights went off abruptly, there being no dimmer switch in the Eastvale Community Centre, and the curtains began to jerk open. Rusted rings creaked on the rail. The audience clapped, then made themselves as comfortable as they could in the moulded-plastic chairs.

> *If music be the food of love, play on,*
> *Give me excess of it, that, surfeiting,*
> *The appetite may sicken, and so die . . .*

So spoke the Duke, and the play was underway. The set was simple, Banks noticed. A few well-placed columns, drapes and portraits gave the impression of a palace. Banks recognized the music, played on a lute, as a Dowland melody, fitting enough for the period.

Though he was no Shakespeare expert, Banks had seen two other performances of *Twelfth Night*, one at school and one in Stratford. He remembered the general plot but not the fine details. This time, he noticed, too many cast members shouted or rushed their lines and mauled the poetry of Shakespeare's language in the process. On the other hand, the groupings and movements on stage constantly held the attention. The way people faced one another or paced about as they talked kept everything in motion. From what little he knew of directing, Banks assumed that Conran himself was responsible for this. Occasionally, a member of the audience would shift in his or her seat, and there were quite a few present suffering from coughs and colds, but on the whole most people were attentive. When an actor or actress hesitated over lines, waiting for a prompt, nobody laughed or walked out.

Faith and Teresa were good. They had the poise and the skill to bring off their roles, even if it was difficult to believe in Faith's masquerade as a man. In their scenes together, though, there was an obvious tension, perhaps because Faith knew who had told Banks about her row with Conran, and Teresa knew who had told him about her jealousy over Caroline Hartley. Ironically, this seemed to give an edge to the performances, especially to Viola's initial rudeness on their first meeting. The ambiguity of their relationship – Viola, dressed as a man, courting Olivia on her brother's behalf – soon absorbed Banks. To hear Faith complimenting Teresa's beauty was an odd thing indeed, but to watch their love blossom was even stranger.

For Banks, this had a dark side, too. He couldn't help but think of Caroline and Veronica, knowing, as the characters themselves did not, that both Viola and Olivia were female. Maria, the role that Caroline would have played, was an added reminder of the recent tragedy.

During the intermission, Banks felt distracted. He left Sandra chatting with some acquaintances and nipped out on to North Market Street for a cigarette in the icy cold. The dim gaslights glinted on the snow and ice, and even as he stood, a gentle snowfall began, flakes drifting down like feathers. He shuddered, flicked his half-smoked cigarette end into a grate and went back inside.

The vague connection between the play and reality was beginning to make Banks feel very uneasy. By the fourth act, his attention began to wander – to thoughts of his recent interviews with Faith and Teresa and the pile of unread paperwork in his in-tray, including a report on the arrest of the vandals that Susan had stayed up half the night to prepare. Then his attention would return to the play in time to hear the Clown and Malvolio chatting about Pythagoras's opinion of wild fowl, or Sebastian in raptures about the pearl Olivia had given him. He couldn't maintain lasting concentration. There was something in his mind, a glimmer of an idea, disparate facts coming together, but he couldn't grasp it, couldn't see the complete picture yet. There was an element still missing.

By the final act, Banks's back and buttocks hurt, and he found it difficult to keep still in the hard chair. Surreptitiously, he glanced at his watch. Almost ten. Surely not long to go. Even before he expected it, true identities were revealed, everybody was married off, except for Malvolio, and the Clown began to sing:

> *When that I was and a little tiny boy,*
> *With hey, ho, the wind and the rain,*
> *A foolish thing was but a toy,*
> *For the rain it raineth every day.*

Then the music ended and the curtains closed. The audience applauded; the cast appeared to take bows. Soon the formalities were all over and everyone shuffled out of the hall, relieved to be leaving the hard seats.

'Time for a drink?' Banks said to Sandra as they fastened their coats on the front steps.

Sandra took his arm. 'Of course. Champagne. It's the only civilized thing to do after an evening at the theatre. Except go for dinner.'

'There aren't any restaurants open this late. Maybe Gibson's Fish and—'

Sandra pulled a face and tugged his arm. 'I'll settle for a lager and lime and a packet of cheese and onion crisps.'

'A cheap date,' Banks said. 'Now I know why I married you.'

They set off down North Market Street to the Queens' Arms, which was much closer to the front exit of the community centre than was the usual cast watering-hole out the back, the Crooked Billet.

It was only twenty past ten when they got there, enough time for a couple of pints at least. The pub was quiet at first, but many of the theatre goers following Banks and Sandra seemed to have the same idea about a drink, and it soon got crowded. By then, Banks and Sandra had a small, dimpled, copper-topped table near the fire-place, where they warmed their hands before drinking.

They discussed the play against a background buzz of conversation, but Banks still felt uneasy and found it hard to concentrate. Instead, he couldn't help but put together what he knew about the Caroline Hartley murder, trying different patterns to see if he could at least discover the shape of the missing piece.

'Alan?'

'What? Oh, sorry.'

'What the hell's up with you? I asked you twice what you thought about Malvolio.'

Banks sipped some beer and shook his head. 'Sorry, love. I feel a bit distracted.'

'There's something bothering you, isn't there?'

'Yes.'

She put her hand on his arm. 'About the case? It's only natural, after seeing the play, isn't it? After all, Caroline Hartley was supposed to be in it.'

'It's not just that.' Banks couldn't put his thoughts into words. All he could think of was the woman who walked strangely in the snow and Vivaldi's burial music for a small child. And there was something about the play that snagged on his mind. Not the production details or any particular line, but something else, something obvious that he just couldn't bring into focus. Faith and Teresa? He didn't know. All he knew was that he felt not only puzzled but tense, too, the kind of edginess one has before a storm breaks. Often, he knew, that feeling signalled that he was close to solving the case, but there was even more this time, a sense of danger, of evil he had overlooked.

Suddenly he became aware of someone tapping him on the shoulder. It was Marcia Cunningham.

'Hello, Mr Banks,' she said. 'Wondered if I'd find you here.'

'I'd have thought you'd be at the Crooked Billet with the rest,' Banks said.

Marcia shook her head. 'It was all right during rehearsals, but I don't know if I can handle the first-night post-mortems. Besides, I'm with a friend.'

She introduced Banks to the trim, middle-aged man standing behind her. Albert. There was one more chair at the table, and Banks offered his as well to the two new-comers. They demurred at first, then sat. Banks leaned against the stone fireplace.

'Last orders!' called Cyril, the landlord. 'Last orders, please!'

In the scramble for the bar, Banks managed to get in another round. When he got back to the table Marcia Cunningham was chatting to Sandra.

'I was just saying to Sandra,' she repeated, 'that I was wondering if you'd solved the little mystery of the dress?'

'Pardon?'

'The dress, the one with the pieces missing.'

'I'm sorry, Marcia,' Banks said, 'I've no idea what you're talking about.'

Marcia frowned. 'But surely young Susan must have told you?'

'Whatever it is, I can assure you she didn't. It was her

case, anyway. I've been far too preoccupied with the Caroline Hartley murder.'

Marcia shrugged and smiled at Albert. 'Well, I don't suppose it's very important, really.'

'Why don't you tell me anyway?' Banks asked, realizing he might have been a little abrupt. He remembered what Veronica Shildon had said about people asking doctors for medical advice at cocktail parties. Sometimes being a policeman was much the same; you were never off duty. 'We've caught the vandals, you know,' he added.

Marcia raised her eyebrows. 'You have? Have they told you why they did it?'

'I haven't had time to read Susan's report yet. But don't expect too much. People like that don't have reasons you and I can fathom.'

'Oh, I know that, Mr Banks. I was just wondering what they did with the pieces, that's all.'

Banks frowned. 'I'm sorry. I don't follow.'

Marcia took a sip of mild and launched into her story. Albert sat beside her, still and silent as a faithful retainer. His thin face showed an intricate pattern of pinkish blood vessels just below the skin. He nodded from time to time, as if in support of what Marcia was saying.

'What do you make of it, then?' Marcia asked when she'd finished.

Banks looked at Sandra, who shook her head.

'It's odd behaviour for vandals, I'll give you that,' he said. 'I can't think of any reason—' Then he suddenly fell silent, and the other images that had been haunting him formed into some kind of order – vague and shadowy as yet, without real substance, but still something resembling a pattern. 'That's if . . .' he went on after a pause. 'Look, Marcia, do you still have it, the dress?'

'Of course. It's at home.'

'Could I see it?'

'Any time you want. There's nothing more I can do with it.'

'How about now?'

'Now? Well, I don't know . . . I . . .' she looked at Albert, who smiled.

'Is it really so important, Alan?' Sandra asked, putting a hand on his arm.

'It might be,' he said. 'I can't explain yet, but it might be.'

'All right,' Marcia said. 'We were going home in a minute anyway. It's not far.'

'My car's parked behind the station. I'll give you a lift,' Banks said. He turned to Sandra. 'I'll see you—'

'No you won't. I'm coming with you. I'm damned if I'm walking home alone.'

'All right.'

They grabbed their coats and made for the door.

TWO

'What did you think of it?' James asked Susan after they had carried their drinks to a table for two in the Crooked Billet. His eyes were shining and he seemed to exude a special kind of energy. Susan thought that if she touched him now, she would feel an electric shock like the ones she sometimes got from static.

'I enjoyed it,' she said. 'I thought the cast did a terrific job.' As soon as she'd spoken she knew she had said the wrong thing, even before James's eyes lost a little of their sparkle. It wasn't that she hadn't mentioned his direction, but that her comment had been hopelessly pedestrian. The trouble was, she knew nothing about Shakespeare beyond what James himself had tried to teach her at school. What a confession! And she had forgotten all that. She hadn't got far reading *Twelfth Night* at home, either; the language was too difficult for her to grasp much of what was going on. Next to James, with all his knowledge and enthusiasm, she felt inadequate.

James patted her arm. 'It could have been better,' he said. 'Especially the pacing of the third act, that scene . . .'

And Susan sat back with relief to listen. He hadn't wanted intelligent comments after all, just someone to sound out his theories on. That she could do, and for the next twenty minutes he asked for it. It wasn't so difficult when he got technical. She found she could easily remember scenes that had seemed dull, awkward or over-long, and James confirmed that there were good reasons for this, things he hoped to put right before the next performance tomorrow night.

Occasionally, she drifted off into thoughts of work: her interviews with Chalmers and Morley, the torn dress she hadn't yet told Banks about, the damn nuisance of having even more vandals to chase. But she put her lack of concentration down to tiredness. After all, she had been up most of the night before, and all day.

At eleven twenty, glasses empty and no prospect of another drink, James asked if Susan fancied a nightcap back at his house. A drink and a talk with a friend . . . what could be wrong with that? She couldn't put him off forever. Besides, she needed to relax. She still felt nervous about being alone with him, but she reached for her coat and followed him out into the night anyway. It was just for a drink, after all; she wasn't going to let him seduce her.

They pulled up in the alley at the back of the house,

where James parked his car, and entered through the back door. Susan made herself comfortable in the armchair by the fire, while James busied himself with drinks in the kitchen. Before he settled, he put a compact disc of Beethoven's 'Pastoral' Symphony on.

'Makes me think of spring,' he said, sitting down. 'Somehow, if I close my curtains and relax, I can almost believe winter's over.'

'It soon will be,' Susan said. She felt herself relaxing, becoming warm and heavy-limbed.

'Perhaps when the good weather comes we could take a ride out into the dale now and then?' James suggested. 'Or even venture a little further afield? A short hike and a pub lunch?'

'Sounds marvellous,' Susan murmured. 'Believe it or not, I've hardly ever made time to take advantage of the countryside.'

'You know what they say, "All work and no play" . . .'

Susan laughed. James sat on the floor by her knees, his shoulder resting against the armchair so he could look at her when they talked. It was closer than she would have liked just yet, but not uncomfortably so.

'How's business, anyway?' he asked. 'Caught any big criminals lately?'

Susan shook her head. Then she told him about the previous evening. 'So we're still hot on the trail of your vandals,' she said, cupping the large glass of brandy in both hands. 'They're a strange lot. Can you imagine why any young yob would snip up a dress and then run away with some of the pieces?'

'What?'

Susan explained what Marcia had told her and what she had seen.

'So Marcia still has the dress, then?' he said.

'What's left of it.'

'What's she going to do with it?'

'I don't know,' Susan answered. She was feeling drowsy and vulnerable from the heat and the brandy. 'I suppose I should take it in for analysis. You never know . . .'

'Never know what?'

'What you might find.' She looked down at the top of his head. 'Why are you so interested, anyway, James?'

'Just curiosity, that's all. I suppose they must have had some reason for doing it. Maybe one of them cut himself and used it as a bandage. Another drink?'

Susan looked at her glass. 'No thanks, I'd better not.' Already she felt that warmth, tiredness and alcohol were making her let her guard down more than she cared to, and she certainly didn't want to lose control.

'Busy day at the nick tomorrow?'

Susan laughed. 'Who knows?'

'Excuse me while I get one.'

'Of course.'

While he was gone, Susan listened to the music. She could have sworn she heard a cuckoo in one section, but doubted that anyone as serious as Beethoven would use such a frivolous gimmick.

'Perhaps one of them was a fetishist,' James suggested, after he had sat down at her feet again.

'And liked to wear only little bits of women's clothes? Don't be silly, James. I don't see why you have to keep harping on about it. It's nothing.'

'You'd be surprised the things people like to dress up in.'

'Like you in that policeman's uniform that day?'

'That's different. That was just a joke.'

'I didn't mean to suggest you were kinky or anything,' Susan said. 'But didn't you tell me you were just a little bit shy of making a direct approach to a woman?'

'Yes, well . . . Acting's in my blood, I suppose. Hamming it up. Maybe there are deep-rooted psychological reasons. I don't really know.' He shrugged.

Susan laughed. 'You're always doing melodramatic things like that. Dressing up, arranging for that singer in Mario's. A real practical joker, aren't you?'

'I told you,' James said, a little irritably. 'I'm just a bit insecure. It helps.'

'Especially with women?'

'Yes.'

As soon as Susan realized what she had said, a tiny shiver went up her spine. She could feel the chill, as palpable as the winter night outside, fall between them. James fell silent and Susan sipped at her brandy, thinking, and not liking what she thought: James's penchant for play-acting and dressing up, the vandals' denial of breaking into the community centre, James's attraction to Caroline, the burgundy dress. No, it couldn't be. Not possibly. It was too absurd. But her thoughts suddenly spanned two cases. It was like hot-wiring a car; the engine jumped to life. Now she could think of at least one good reason why the dress had been cut up the way it had.

Before long, she became aware of a slight tickle up the side of her leg. She looked down and saw that James was touching her, very gently. She shifted in her seat – not too abruptly, she hoped – and he stopped.

The music ended and Susan finished what little she had left in her glass. 'I'd better be going,' she said, sitting forward in her chair.

'Don't go just yet,' James said. 'It's been such a wonderful evening. I don't want it to end.'

Susan laughed. Didn't he feel the same unease she did? Maybe not. Better for her that he didn't. She must act naturally, then investigate her vague fears later from a more secure position. Surely, she would then discover how absurd they were. No doubt the beer and brandy had caused her imagination to run wild. It was most important now, though, that she make an early exit without letting James see that she entertained any suspicions at all.

'Don't be such a romantic.' She laughed. 'There'll be plenty of other evenings.'

She tried to sit up, but he was on his knees, blocking her way.

'James!'

'What's the harm in it?' he said, leaning forward towards her.

He put his hands on her shoulders and she pushed them off. 'If this is what a first night does to you . . .' she said, trying for a light tone. But she couldn't think of a way to end her sentence.

Finally, he moved aside and she managed to get to her feet. She felt as if she were treading on thin ice. Did he know what she was beginning to suspect? How could he? Was it obvious that she was humouring him and trying to get out fast? All she knew was that she had to stay cool and get out of here. Maybe then she would be able to dismiss her fears. But she couldn't stay, not after the frightening images had started in her mind. Crazy or not, she had to talk seriously to Banks about James, no matter how difficult it might be to swallow her pride and her feelings.

'Don't sulk,' she said, tousling his hair. 'It doesn't suit you.'

'Damn you!' he said, jerking away from her touch. Anger flashed in his eyes. 'What's wrong with you? Don't you think I'm man enough for you? You're just like her, aren't you?'

Susan felt as if she had been thrust under a cold shower. Every nerve-end tingled. She edged closer to the door. 'Like who, James?' she asked quietly.

He turned to face her, and she could see that he knew. It was too late. 'You know damn well who I'm talking about, don't you?'

'I don't even know what you're talking about,' Susan lied. Somehow, she thought, if she didn't say the name, there was still a chance.

'Don't lie. You can't fool me. I can tell. I can tell what you're thinking. You've been toying with me, leading me on all this time, trying to get me to confess. It's all been a game, hasn't it?' He moved quickly so that he was standing between Susan and the door.

'Don't be stupid,' she said. 'I don't know what you mean. And move out of the way, please. I want to leave.'

Conran shook his head slowly. 'You're thinking about me and Caroline, aren't you?'

There was no point pretending any longer. Susan looked at him and said, 'You went to her, didn't you? That night.'

'It was an accident,' Conran pleaded. 'It was a ghastly accident.'

'James, you've got to—'

'No! That's where you're wrong. No, I don't. It was all an accident. All that stupid bitch's fault.' And suddenly, he didn't look like the James she knew any longer. Not at all like the James she knew and thought she trusted.

THREE

The four of them stood in Marcia Cunningham's front room and looked at the remains of the dress.

'Who would do something like that?' Sandra asked.

'That's the point,' Banks said. 'No casual vandal would go to such trouble, at least not for any reason we can think of.'

'But it must have happened then,' Marcia said. 'I'd have noticed if it had been done before. And certainly no one from the cast would have done it.'

'I'm not saying it was done before,' Banks said. 'What I'm saying is that it's possible vandals didn't do this.'

'Then who?'

'Look at this.' Banks passed the dress to Sandra, who studied the remains of its front. 'Look at those spots.'

'What are they? Paint?'

'Could be. But I don't think so. They're hard to see because the dress is so dark. And we can't be sure, not without forensic examination, but if I'm right . . .'

'What are you getting, Alan?' Sandra asked. 'You're not making much sense, you know.'

'The last person entering Caroline Hartley's house was a woman, according to all our witnesses. And Patsy Janowski said she saw a woman who walked funny at the end of the street. I thought it was because she might have been wearing high heels.'

'But that's stupid,' Sandra said. 'In that weather?'

'Exactly.'

'Are you suggesting that the killer wore this dress?' Marcia asked. 'I can't believe it.' She pointed at the dress. 'And that's . . . that's blood!'

'The way Caroline Hartley was stabbed,' Banks said, 'there was no way the murderer could have avoided blood stains. If she was wearing the dress, it would have been easy enough to put her raincoat on again and get away from the scene, get time to think. I don't think the murder was planned, not right from the start. But then there was still a blood-stained dress to explain. Why not simply cut off the sleeves and the stained front, then stage a break-in and cut up the other dresses? That would raise much less suspicion than just doing away with the dress altogether. If our killer had done that, Marcia would have missed it and started to wonder what might have happened. But how could the killer know that Marcia would be so diligent as to try and sew them back together again?'

'But that means,' Marcia said slowly, 'that the killer was someone who knew about our costumes, someone who had access to them. It means—'

'Yes,' said Banks. 'And if she was wearing shoes, not boots, what does that suggest?'

'We don't have any boots,' Marcia said. 'Not that I know of. Shoes, yes, but not boots.'

'The killer couldn't find any suitable boots to complete the disguise, so had to make do with women's shoes.'

'I still don't understand,' Marcia said.

'It was the play gave me the idea, that and what Patsy said. All that stuff about a woman walking funny, and a play about confused identity. Couldn't it have been a man dressed as a woman? Would any of the shoes have been big enough?'

'Well . . . yes, of course,' Marcia said. 'We have all kinds of sizes. But why? Why would anybody dress up and do that?'

'We don't know,' Banks said. 'A sick joke? Maybe someone knew Caroline was a lesbian, someone who wanted her badly. Do you have a plastic bag?'

'I think so . . . somewhere.' Marcia gestured vaguely, her brows knit together.

'There's one in the larder, by the newspapers, love,' said Albert, who had remained silent until now. 'I'll go and get it.'

Albert brought the bag and Banks put the dress in it.

'What about the break-in?' Marcia asked.

'It could have been staged later, when the killer discovered what he'd done.' Banks looked at his watch. 'It's after eleven thirty,' he said. 'Let's try the Crooked Billet and see if they're still there.'

'Who?' asked Marcia.

'Susan and Conran,' Banks said. 'I assume they *are* together.' He turned to Marcia. 'When did you tell Susan about this dress?'

'The other day. She couldn't make anything of it.'

'That's hardly surprising. Does James Conran know?'

'I haven't told him,' Marcia said.

'Has Susan?'

'I don't know. I mean, she's seeing him. She might have mentioned it. Why?'

Banks looked at Sandra. 'I don't want to alarm anyone,' he said, 'but if I'm right, we'd better try to find Susan right away. Excuse us, Marcia, Albert.' And he took Sandra by the arm and led her to the door.

'But why?' Sandra asked.

'Because I think James Conran's the killer,' Banks said on their way down the path. 'I think he wanted Caroline Hartley so badly he went over to the house to see her. I don't know why he dressed up, or what happened in there, but he's the only one in the society apart from Marcia who had access to the prop room.'

They got in the car and Banks cursed the ignition until it started on his fourth attempt. 'Don't you see?' he said as he skidded off. 'According to Faith and Teresa, Conran was the last one to leave the centre. And even if he did go to the pub, he had a key. He could have easily gone back there and changed. Why do you think he was paying so much attention to Susan? He wanted to know how the investigation was going, how close we were.'

'My God,' said Sandra. 'Poor Susan.'

FOUR

James blocked Susan's way. 'She asked for it, you know,' he said. 'She was nothing but a prick-teaser, then she . . .'

'Then she what?' Susan felt real fear now, like ice in her spine. Her mind was racing in search of a way out. If only she had told Banks about the dress, then maybe he would have been able to put two and two together before she had. If only she could keep Conran talking. If only . . .

'You know what,' he said. 'It turned out she didn't like men, she was just playing, leading me on, just like you were, playing me for a fool.'

'That's not true.'

'Stop lying. It's too late now. What are you going to do?' James asked.

'What do you think?'

'Turn me in? Can't you let it go?'

'Don't be an idiot.'

'What is it with you, Susan? Just what makes you tick? Professional all the way?'

'Something like that,' Susan muttered, 'but it doesn't really matter any more, does it?'

'You could forget this ever happened,' James said, moving forward and reaching for her hand. She noticed a sheen of sweat on his forehead and upper lip.

She snatched her hand away. 'No, I couldn't. Don't be a bloody fool, James. Let me go. Don't make things worse.' He was still rational, she thought; James was no madman, just troubled. She could talk sense to him, and he might listen. The main problem was that he was highly strung and, at the moment, in a state of near panic. She would have to be very careful how she handled him.

'Where do you want to go?' he asked.

'To the phone,' she said calmly.

Conran stood aside and let her pass. But no sooner had she picked up the receiver than he grabbed it from her and pulled her back into the front room.

'No!' he said. 'I can't let you. I'm not going to jail. Not just because of that perverted slut. Don't you see? It wasn't my fault.'

'Don't be a fool, James. What's the alternative?'

Conran licked his lips and looked around the room like a caged animal. 'I could get out of here. Go away. You'd never have to see me again. Just don't try to stop me.'

'I have to. You know that.'

'I mean it. I don't want to hurt you. Look, we could go together. I've got some money saved up. Wherever you want. We could go somewhere warm.'

'James,' Susan said softly, 'you've got a problem. You don't necessarily have to go to jail. Maybe you can get help. A doctor—'

'What do you mean, problems? I don't have any problems.' Conran pointed at his chest. 'Me? You tell me

I've got problems? She was the one with the problem. Not me. I'm not queer. I'm not a homosexual. I'm normal.'

His face was flushed and sweaty now and he was breathing fast. Susan wasn't sure if she could talk him down and persuade him to give himself up. Not if he didn't want to.

'Nobody says you're not normal,' she said cautiously. 'But you're obviously upset. You need help. Let me help you, James.'

'I'm not going with you,' he said. 'And if you phone, I won't be here when your friends arrive.'

'You're making it worse,' Susan said. 'At least if you come in with me, it'll look good. It's no use running. We'll get you in the end. You know we will.'

'I don't care. I'm not going to jail. You don't understand. I couldn't live in jail. The things they do in there . . . I've heard about them.' He shuddered.

'I told you, James. It might not mean prison. Perhaps you can get help in a hospital.'

'No! There's nothing wrong with me. I'm perfectly normal. I'll not have doctors poking about in my head.'

Susan got up and walked towards the front door. She held her breath as she turned her back on him. Before she even got to the hallway, she felt his hands around her neck. They were strong and she couldn't pry them apart. Because he was standing behind her, all she could do was wriggle, and it didn't help. She flailed back with her hands but met only empty air. She tried to swing her hips back into his groin, but she couldn't reach him. Her throat hurt and she couldn't breathe. She lashed back with one foot, felt it connect and heard him gasp. But his grip never slackened. She felt all the life and sensation going out of her body, like water down the drain. Her knees buckled and he let her sink forward to the floor, his hands still locked tight around her throat. The blackness had seeped in everywhere now. She thought she could hear someone hammering on the door, then she heard nothing at all.

FIVE

'I'll call an ambulance and stay with her,' Sandra said, kneeling over Susan.

Banks nodded and dashed back to the Cortina. He had heard Conran's car start up as they broke in. There was only one way his back lane led, and that was to the main Swainsdale road. Once there, he could turn back towards Eastvale or head out into the dale. As Banks negotiated the turns, he radioed for help from Eastvale and from Helmthorpe, which had one patrol car. If Conran didn't turn off on one of the side roads, at least they could make sure the main road was blocked and he could get no further than the dale's largest village. At the junction, Conran turned left into Swainsdale.

The Cortina skidded on a patch of ice. Banks steadied it. He knew the road like the back of his hand. Narrow for the most part, with drystone walls on either side, it dipped and meandered, treacherous in the icy darkness. He kept Conran's tail-lights in view, about a couple of hundred yards ahead.

When he got closer, he put his foot down. Conran did the same. It was almost like racing through a dark tunnel, or doing a slalom run. Snow was piled almost as high as the walls at the roadsides. Beyond, the fields stretched up the daleside, an endless swath of dull pearl in the moonlight.

Conran screeched through Fortford, almost losing control as he took the bend by the pub. The car's side scraped against the jutting stones in the wall and sent a shower of sparks out into the night. Banks slowed and the Cortina took the turn easily. He knew there was a long stretch of straight road before the next bend.

Conran had gained a hundred yards or so, but once around the corner, Banks put his foot down and set about catching up. The red tail-lights drew closer. Banks glanced ahead for landmarks and saw the drumlin within the six leaning trees silhouetted by the moon about a mile in front of them. Just before that, there would be another kink in the road.

He was right behind Conran's car now, but there was no easy way to stop him. He couldn't pull in front in such conditions on a narrow road. If he tried, Conran would easily be able to nudge him into the wall. All he could do was ride his tail and push, hoping Conran would panic and make a mistake.

A few moments later, it happened. Either through ignorance, or just plain panic, Conran missed the bend. Banks had already slowed enough to take it, but instead he eased on the brake as he watched Conran's car slide up the heaped snow in slow motion, take off the top of the dry-stone wall, spraying sparks again as it went, and land with a loud thud in the field.

Banks turned off his engine. The silence after the accident was so deep he could hear the blood ring in his ears. On a distant hillside, a sheep bleated – an eerie sound on a winter's night.

Banks got out of the car and climbed the wall to see what had happened. There was very little damage as far as he could tell by the moonlight. Conran's car lay on its side, the two free wheels spinning. Conran himself had managed to get the passenger door open and was now struggling up the hillside, thigh-deep in snow. The farther he went, the deeper the snow became, until he could move no more. Banks walked in his wake and found him curled up and shivering in a cot of snow. He looked up as Banks came towards him.

'Please let me go,' he said. 'Please! I don't want to go to jail. I couldn't stand being in jail.'

Banks thought of Caroline Hartley's body, and of Susan Gay laid out on the floor, her face purple. 'Think yourself bloody lucky we don't still have hanging,' he said, and dragged Conran up out of the snow.

15

ONE

Only the sound of thin ice splintering underfoot acco
panied Banks on his way to Oakwood Mews later t
night. Eastvale was asleep, tucked up warm and safe
bed, and not even the faint sound of a distant car distur
its tranquillity. But the town didn't know what had g
on between Caroline Hartley and James Conran in t
cosy, firelit room with the stately music playing. It did
know what folly, irony and pride had finally erupted
blood. Banks did. Sometimes, as he walked, he thou
that his next step would break the crust over a gr
darkness and he would fall. He told himself not to
ridiculous, to keep going.

Apart from the dim, amber light shed by its wid
spaced, black-leaded gas lamps, Oakwood Mews was
dark as the rest of the side street at that time of night. I
one light showed in a window. Easy, Banks thought, fo
murderer to creep in and out unseen now.

For a moment, he stood by the iron gate and looke
number eleven. Should he? It was two thirty in the morni
He was tired, and Veronica Shildon was no doubt fast asle
She wouldn't be able to get back to sleep after what he l
to tell her. Sighing, he opened the gate. He had a promis
keep.

He pressed the bell and heard the chimes ring faintl

the hall. Nothing happened, so he rang again and stood back. A few seconds later a light came on in the front upstairs window. Banks heard the soft footsteps and the turning of the key in the lock. The door opened an inch or two, on its chain. When Veronica saw who it was she immediately took off the chain and let him in.

'I had an idea it was you,' Veronica said. 'Will you give me a few moments?' She pointed him towards the living room and went back upstairs.

Banks turned on a shaded wall light and sat down. Embers glowed in the grate. It was cool in the room, but the memory of heat, at least, remained. Banks unfastened his heavy coat but didn't take it off.

In a few minutes, Veronica returned in a blue and white track suit. She had combed her hair and washed the sleep out of her eyes.

'Sorry,' she said, 'but I can't stand sitting around in a dressing gown. It always makes me think I'm ill. Let me put this on.' And she switched on a small electric heater. Its bar shone bright red in no time. 'Can I offer you a cup of tea or something?'

'Given the night I've had,' Banks said, 'a drop of whisky would be more welcome. That is, if you have any?'

'Of course. Please forgive me if I don't join you. I'd prefer cocoa.'

While Veronica made her cocoa, Banks sipped the Scotch and stared into the embers. It had all been so easy once they had got back to the station: wet clothes drying over the heater in the cramped office; steam rising; Conran spilling his guts in the hope of some consideration at sentencing. Now came the hard part.

Veronica sat in the armchair near the electric fire and folded her legs under her. She cradled the cocoa mug in both hands and blew on the surface. Banks noticed that her hands were shaking.

'I always used to have cocoa before bed when I was young,' she said. 'It's funny, they say it helps you sleep although it's got caffeine in it. Do you understand that?' Suddenly she looked directly at Banks. He could see the pain and fear in her eyes. 'I'm prattling on, aren't I?' she said. 'I assume you've got something important to tell me, or you wouldn't be here at this time.' She looked away.

Banks lit a cigarette and sucked the smoke in deeply. 'Are you sure you want to know?' he asked.

'No, I'm not sure. I'm frightened. I'd rather forget everything that happened. But I never got anywhere by denying things, refusing to face the truth.'

'All right.' Now he was there, he didn't know where to start. The name, just the bald name, seemed inadequate but the *why* was even more meaningless.

Veronica helped him out. 'Will you tell me who first?' she asked. 'Who killed Caroline?'

Banks flicked some ash into the grate. 'It was James Conran.'

Veronica said nothing at first. Only the nerve twitching at the side of her jaw showed that she reacted in any way. 'How did you find out?' she asked finally.

'I was slow,' Banks replied. 'Almost too slow. Given Caroline's life, her past, I was sure there was a complex reason for her death. There were too many puzzles – Gary Hartley, Ruth Dunne, Colm Grey . . .'

'Me.'

Banks shrugged. 'I didn't look close enough to home.'

'Was there a complicated motive?'

Banks shook his head. 'No, I was wrong. Some crimes are just plain . . . I was going to say accidents, but that's not really the case. Stupid, perhaps, certainly pointless and often just sheer bad luck.'

'Go on.'

'As far as the evidence was concerned, we knew that Conran was attracted to Caroline, but there's nothing unusual about that. She was a very beautiful woman. We also found out he tended to prefer her over other actresses in the cast, which gave rise to a certain amount of jealousy. Caroline dealt with normal male attention by doing what she knew best, what she'd learned on the game – teasing, flirting, stringing them along. It was an ideal way for her because it deflected suspicion away from her true sexual inclinations,' he looked at Veronica, who was staring down into the murky cocoa, 'and it kept them at a distance. Many flirts are afraid of real contact. It's just a game.

'But as I said, I was looking for deep, complex motives – something to do with her family, her time in London, her way of life. As it turns out, her death was to do with all those things, but not directly concerned with any of them.'

'Another drink?' Veronica had noticed his glass was empty and went to refill it. Banks didn't object. Embers shifted with a sigh in the fire place. It was much warmer now the electric fire had heated the room. Banks took his coat off.

'What happened?' Veronica asked, handing him the tumbler.

'On December the twenty-second, after rehearsal, everyone went their separate ways. Caroline came straight home, took a shower and made herself comfortable in the living room with a cup of tea and some chocolate cake. Your husband called with the present, which Caroline opened because he had said it was something special and she wanted to know what could be so special to you. I'm sure she intended to rewrap it before you found out. I'm speculating, of course. No one but Caroline was in the house at this time, so we'll never know all the details. But I think I'm right. It couldn't have happened any other way. Anyway, shortly after Claude Ivers left, Patsy Janowski arrived, checking up on him. She thought he was still involved with you.' Veronica sniffed and shifted position. Banks went on. 'She spoke to Caroline briefly at the door – very briefly, because it was cold and Caroline was only wearing her bathrobe – then she left. On her way down the street, she saw a woman who appeared to be walking oddly, heading across King Street, but thought nothing of it. By then it was dark and the air was filled with snow. It was difficult to look up and keep your eyes open without getting them full of cold snow.'

'What about James Conran?' Veronica asked. 'How does he fit in?'

'I was getting to that. It had been a particularly difficult rehearsal. He had insulted Faith Green by telling her that Caroline could play her part better, and Teresa Pedmore was probably still angry at him for being so obvious about his lust for Caroline in public. By this time, he was pretty well besotted with her, and he's one of those types who's like a little boy who breaks things when he doesn't get his own way. Because of the bad atmosphere, everyone went their separate ways, including Caroline. After he locked up, Conran went to the Crooked Billet and drank several double Scotches very quickly. His row with Faith made him want Caroline all the more. After all he thought he was doing for her, he was getting very impatient that she didn't seem to be keeping up her end of what he thought was the bargain.

'Then he had an idea. He was always a bit of a theatrical type, the kind who got dressed up and recited "The Boy Stood on the Burning Deck" at parties when he was a kid, so he thought that, as a joke, he'd dress up as a woman and go and see Caroline. *Twelfth Night*, as you know, is about a woman who passes herself off as a man, and that's where he got the idea. It would make her laugh, he thought, if he passed himself off as a woman, and when you make women laugh you soften them and break down their reserve. Also, he'd had enough drinks to make it seem a good idea and to make him feel brave enough. He knew where she lived, but he didn't know that she lived with anyone.

'He went back to the community centre – only he and Marcia Cunningham from the dramatic society had keys to the back door – chose a dress, a wig, and found some women's shoes that fit him. But it must have been an uncomfortable walk for him. The shoes were a little too tight and pinched his toes, and it's very hard to walk in high heels in the snow, I should imagine. Especially if you're a man. That's what Patsy Janowski noticed, but she didn't realize what it meant.

'He said Caroline seemed to recognize him, laughed and let him in. She had no reason not to. Apparently he'd done things like that in rehearsal – dressed up, played practical jokes, clowned around – so as far as she was concerned it wasn't out of character for him. She may have been puzzled by his visit, even worried that you would come back and wonder what was going on, but as far as she knew, she had no reason to fear him.'

Veronica grimaced and massaged her right calf. Banks took a sip of fiery Scotch. 'Are you sure you want me to go on?' he asked. 'It isn't very pleasant.'

'I didn't expect it to be,' Veronica said. 'I've got a touch of cramp, that's all. It's not what you're saying that's making me grit my teeth. I want to know everything. But I think I've changed my mind about that drink.' She limped to the cocktail cabinet, poured herself a glass of sherry and sat down again carefully. 'Please go on. I'll be fine.'

'Conran was a little drunk and wanting his oats. Caroline must have seemed especially inviting dressed only in her bathrobe. Eventually, it happened. Conran made a pass and Caroline ducked it. According to him, she made some reference to the way he was dressed and told him she preferred real women. She accused him of playing some kind of sick joke. He was stunned. He had no idea. When he started to protest, she laughed at him and told him the clothes suited him, maybe he ought to consider going after some of the men in the cast. Then he hit her. She fell back on the sofa, stunned by the blow, and her robe fell open. He said he couldn't help himself. He wanted her. And if rape was the only way he could get what he wanted, then so be it. He had to have her right there.'

Veronica was gripping the sherry glass tightly, her face pale. Banks paused and asked if she was all right.

'Yes,' she whispered. 'Go on.' She closed her eyes.

'He couldn't do it,' Banks said. 'There she was, a beautiful, naked woman, just what he'd dreamed about ever since he'd met her, and he couldn't function. He says he doesn't remember the next part very well. Everything was red inside his eyes, he said. And then it was done. He saw what had happened. He'd picked up the knife from the table and stabbed Caroline. When the rage passed and the realization dawned, he didn't panic, he started thinking clearly again. He knew he had to find some way of covering his tracks. First he washed the knife and rinsed the blood off his hands. When he went back into the room he was horrified by what he'd done. He said he sat down and just stared at Caroline, crying like a baby. That's when he saw the record she'd opened. He knew the piece because he'd had a lot to do with church choral music ever since he was young. He knew that the *Laudate pueri* was played at the burial services of small children. That's another reason I should have thought of him sooner, but then almost anyone could have known the significance of the music, or someone might simply have thought it sounded right.'

'But I don't understand,' Veronica said. 'Why did he play it?'

'He said he put it on as a genuine gesture, that Caroline had always seemed childlike in her ways and in her enthusiasms, and she seemed to him especially like a child now as she lay there.'

'So the music was for Caroline?' Veronica asked.

'Yes. A kind of requiem. It was right there in front of him. He was hardly going to search through the whole collection for something else, especially as it seemed so fitting.'

Veronica looked down into her sherry glass and said quietly, 'Then maybe I *can* listen to it again. Go on.'

'You have to remember, too, Veronica, that Conran's a theatre director. He has a sense of the dramatic, a feel for arrangement. He told me that when he had stopped crying for what he'd done, he began to see the whole thing as a scene or a tableau of some kind, and the music seemed right. What he'd done wasn't real to him any more, it was a part of a drama, and it needed the appropriate soundtrack.

'Next he made sure he'd tidied everything up, then he left. He noticed the stains on the dress but could do nothing about them. At least his coat would cover him up until he got home and formed a clear plan. He was just about to burn the dress when he had a better idea. He knew it would be missed if he simply destroyed it. Marcia was in charge of costumes and he knew she was careful and diligent. That was when he came up with the idea of a break-in. There's been a lot of vandalism in the area lately, and he saw it would make a perfect cover for getting rid of the evidence. Remember, he had no idea he would end up killing anyone and ruining the dress when he first put it on and went out, but now he had a serious problem. He went back later that night, careful not to be seen this time, broke in, scrawled a little of the usual graffiti and snipped up the dresses. He also replaced the wig and the shoes, which he'd cleaned carefully. When he got home, he snipped his coat into small pieces and burned them in a metal wastebin, a bit at a time; after that, he cut the sleeves and part of the front off the dress he'd worn and burned them too. He missed a few tiny spots, but the dress was a dark burgundy colour so they were very difficult to see. And that was it. All he had to do was try to stay cool when the questions started. That was easy enough for someone with actor's training, especially as he seemed so able most of the time to divorce himself from the reality of what he'd done. It had been an act, a role, like any other. And there was no reason why we should connect the break-in with the murder.'

'How did you catch him?' Veronica asked.

'It was partly the play. At least that started me thinking about the possibility of someone dressing up. And there were a few other clues. That report about the woman visitor wearing high heels on such a snowy night. The vandals denying that they had wrecked the community centre. Marcia being unable to find the missing pieces of that particular dress. Not to mention that I was running out of other suspects.' But he didn't tell Victoria that Susan Gay had known about the cut up dress for two days and hadn't thought it important enough to mention, nor that he hadn't read her report on the vandals until Conran had already been caught. He had been too concerned about Susan to stop in at the station and check, and as it turned out, his instinct had been right.

'How is she?' Veronica asked, when Banks had told her about the scene at Conran's house.

'She'll be all right. Sandra acted quickly and got her breathing. She won't be talking or eating real food for a while.'

'How does she feel?'

'I don't know. Sandra's still with her at the hospital, along with Superintendent Gristhorpe. She's sedated right now, but when she comes round she'll probably be very hard on herself.' He shrugged. 'I don't know how she'll deal with it.'

And he didn't. Susan had made mistakes, yes, but mistakes that could be easily understood. Everyone new to the job made them. After all, why on earth should she link a partially destroyed dress to a murder. But no matter what anyone said, she would go on believing that she should have linked them, should have known. But she should at least have passed on the information, and verbally, too, not only in a routine report that might get stuck at the bottom of the chief inspector's in-tray for days, especially when he was busy on a murder investigation. And Banks should have read the report. In a perfect world, he would have done. But police, perhaps more than anyone else, get notoriously behind in their paperwork. And so mistakes are made. Susan's career hung in the balance, and Banks couldn't guess which way it would go. Certainly he would support her as far as he could, but it would be her own decisions and actions that counted in the long run, her own strength.

'It all seems so . . . pointless,' Veronica said, 'so absolutely bloody senseless.'

'It was,' Banks agreed. 'Murder often is.' He put down his glass and reached for his coat.

'I'm glad you told me,' she said. 'I mean, I'm glad you came right away like you said you would.'

'What are you going to do now?'

'I'll go back to bed. Don't worry about me. I probably won't be able to sleep but . . . your job's over, you don't have to take care of me.'

'I mean in the future. Have you any plans?'

Veronica uncurled her legs and got to her feet, rubbing her calves to restore the circulation. 'I don't know,' she said. 'Maybe a holiday. Or maybe I'll just struggle on with work and life. I'll manage,' she said, attempting a smile. 'I'm a survivor.'

Banks fastened his coat and headed for the door. Veronica held it open for him. 'Once again,' she said, 'thank you for coming.'

On impulse, Banks leaned forward and kissed her cool forehead. She gave him a puzzled look, then smiled. He hesitated on the path and looked back at her. He could think of nothing else to say. If Conran were mad, his actions might have been easier to explain, or to dismiss. Madmen did strange and evil things, and nobody knew why; it just happened that way. But he wasn't mad. He was highly strung, egotistical, with a deep-rooted fear of his own latent homosexuality, but he wasn't mad. He had sat at that desk in Banks's office and spilled his heart out for over an hour before Banks, disgusted with the man's whining self-pity, had left the task for Phil Richmond to finish.

Veronica's face, shadowed by the hall's soft light, looked drawn but determined. She held herself stiffly, arms crossed, yet there seemed a supple strength in her limbs to match the strength in her spirit. Perhaps that was why he liked her: she tried; she wasn't afraid to face things; she made an effort at life.

At the end of Oakwood Mews, Banks remembered the Walkman in his pocket. He needed music, not so much as the food of love but as something to soothe the savage breast. The tape he had in was at the last movement of Messiaen's 'Quartet for the End of Time'. That eerie, fractured and haunting music would do just fine for the walk home. In his other pocket he felt the catapult he had confiscated from the kid on the riverbank and forgotten about.

He walked up to the market square listening to the music. Piano chords sounded like icicles falling and the violin notes stretched so tight they felt as if they would snap any second. As he walked, he thought about Veronica Shildon, who had tried to face some difficult truths and start a new life. He thought about how that life had been shattered, just like the ice under his feet, by a stupid, drunken, pointless act – lust beyond reason – and about how she would go about putting it together again. Veronica was right, she was a survivor. And Shakespeare was right, too; lust often *is* 'murderous, bloody, full of blame,/Savage, extreme, cruel, not to trust.'

Banks passed the police station with hardly a glance. Sometimes, the formality of the job and its cold, calculated procedures just didn't reflect what really happened, the pain people felt, the pain Banks felt. Perhaps the rites and rituals of the job – the forms to be filled in, the legal procedures to be followed – were intended to keep the pain at a distance. If so, they didn't always succeed.

About twenty yards beyond the station, on Market Street, he stopped and turned. That damn blue light was still shining above the door like a beacon proclaiming benign, paternal innocence and simplicity. Almost without thinking, he took the catapult from his pocket, scraped up a couple of fair-sized stones from the icy gutter, put one in the sling and took aim. The stone clattered on the pavement somewhere along North Market Street. He took a deep breath, sighed out a plume of air, then aimed again carefully, trying to recreate his childhood accuracy. This time the lamp disintegrated in a burst of powder-blue glass and Banks took off down a side street, the back way home, feeling afraid and guilty and oddly elated, like a naughty schoolboy.